GOOD AS GONE

GOOD
AS
GONE

AMY GENTRY

Houghton Mifflin Harcourt
Boston   New York
2016

Copyright © 2016 by Amy Gentry

For information about permission to reproduce selections from this book, write to trade.permissions@hmhco.com or to Permissions, Houghton Mifflin Harcourt Publishing Company, 3 Park Avenue, 19th Floor, New York, New York 10016.

www.hmhco.com

Library of Congress Cataloging-in-Publication Data is available.
ISBN 978-0-544-92095-8

Book design by Chloe Foster

Printed in the United States of America
DOC 10 9 8 7 6 5 4 3 2 1

For Curtis, the best living human

GOOD AS GONE

Prologue

Jane woke up and whispered, "Julie?"

The room yawned around her. After two years of sleeping alone in her own bedroom in the new house, Jane no longer dreamed of the ceiling fan dropping onto the bed and chopping her up. The spiders, too, had vanished from the shadows; ten-year-olds don't need to have the corners checked before bedtime. Only occasionally, when something woke her in the middle of the night, the silence around her ached for Julie's soft breathing. In the old house, she used to hoist one foot over the top bunk railing and giggle until Julie said, *Shhh, Janie, go back to sleep.* Now, she shut her eyes tightly before they could drift toward the dark seams where the walls and ceiling met.

The next noise definitely came from Julie's room.

Jane pulled back the covers and slid her bare feet down to the carpet. In the old house, a braided rug slipped over the smooth wooden floor when she got out of bed. Now her feet barely made a sound on thick carpet as she padded to the door and peered down the dark hallway. A faint rectangle of lighter darkness hovered at the end—a closed door.

They rarely slept with doors closed; Janie's room got too hot, Julie's too cold. Mom grumbled about the air circulation in two-story houses, but Mom and Dad's room downstairs on the first floor was always shut at night, because they were adults. Now Julie was too, or wanted to be. Ever since her thirteenth birthday, she seemed to be practicing for adulthood all the time, brushing her hair slowly in front of the bathroom mirror as if rehearsing for some secret play, sitting at her desk to write in her diary instead of flopping on the bed stomach-first, like Jane. And closing her bedroom door.

At the end of the hall, the pale rectangle shuddered, a crack of darkness opening up around one side. Julie's bedroom door receded inward, four large fingers hooked around its edge.

Before she had time to think, Jane ducked into her closet, crouched down, and pulled the door shut behind her. The fingers —they were too high up on the door to belong to Julie, too large to belong to her mother. They didn't belong to her father either, but she didn't know how she knew they didn't, and that was the most unsettling thing of all.

A tiny, sickening click reminded her that the closet door never stayed closed for long. She threw her hands forward, but the door was already floating slowly open.

Jane squeezed her eyes shut as a soft tread started down the hallway.

When she opened them a moment later, the closet door had come to rest three inches from the door frame. The slice of hallway visible from her hiding place almost glowed against the closet's deeper darkness; she could see every fiber in the beige carpet, every ripple in the wall paint, and, hanging on the wall, half of a framed studio portrait in which long-ago Jane sat on long-ago Julie's lap, wearing a baby dress with a sailboat on it. The sailboat shook on its embroidered waves. Everything else was shaking too. The steps continued toward Jane's room.

The noisy floorboard in the middle of the hall moaned. The owner of the hand was now halfway to her room. Could he hear the creak in her ears each time her thundering heart shook the little boat? Jane resisted the urge to shrink back into her clothes on their rattling hangers.

Just then, a skinny foot appeared against the carpet, a patch of pink polish clinging to the big toenail, and Jane let out her breath. It was only Julie. She'd crouched over her toes perfecting the pink for an hour before her birthday party, but by the middle of the summer, most of it had scraped off on the rough white bottom of the backyard pool, leaving only these little triangles around the edges. So Jane had been wrong about the fingers, seeing things again, like the spiders in the shadows. Sure enough, here came Julie, moving into the frame with her ordinary Mickey Mouse nightshirt flapping around her ordinary knees, heading toward the staircase by Jane's room, probably just going down for a midnight snack. Jane's matching Donald Duck nightshirt was in a brown bag waiting to be taken to Goodwill; she'd already outgrown it. Her mom said she'd be taller than Julie someday. Jane hugged her pajama'd knees in relief.

But the fingers were back, this time perched on Julie's shoulder, clutching at the fabric of her nightshirt, her long blond hair trapped between their knobby knuckles. Jane barely had time to notice Julie's stiff, straight posture, like that of a wide-eyed puppet, before she saw the tall man following close behind her. Julie and the strange man moved together in slow motion, as if his long arm and hairy hand were a chain binding them together.

Wake up, wake up, wake up, Jane told herself, but nothing happened. Everything was frozen, including her, like in a dream; only Julie and the man kept moving. Slow, but faster than frozen; slow, but they were almost to her room. Janie opened her mouth to scream.

Then Julie saw her.

Jane's scream slid back down into her stomach as Julie stared straight into her closet hiding place. Jane stared back, begging Julie to tell her what to do next, readying herself to obey, to yell or cry or maybe even laugh if it was all a joke. Surely Julie wouldn't leave her alone in this bad dream. If Julie would just tell her what to do, Jane promised silently, she would listen to her and never complain from now on.

Without moving her head, Julie lifted her eyebrows and glanced meaningfully toward the man behind her, then back to Jane, as if telling her to take a good look, but Jane didn't want to; she kept her eyes trained on Julie instead. Girl and man turned on the landing without pausing at her door, and Jane saw why Julie was walking so stiffly: the man held the tip of a long, sharp knife to her back. Jane felt a nasty sting like a bug bite between her own shoulder blades, and her eyes filled up with tears.

They were poised at the top of the stairs when a loud tick sounded from the attic. Jane knew it was only the house settling, but the man stopped and looked over his shoulder nervously. In the split second before he looked back, Julie, as if freed from a spell, turned her head to Jane, raised her left index finger to her lips, and formed them into a silent *O.*

Shhh.

Jane obeyed. Julie started down the stairs, followed by the man with the knife.

And that, according to the only witness, is the story of how I lost my daughter—both my daughters, everything, everything—in a single night.

1

Julie's been gone for eight years, but she's been dead much longer—centuries—when I step outside into the steaming air on my way to teach my last class of the spring semester. The middle of May is as hot as human breath in Houston. Before I've even locked the door behind me, a damp friction starts up between my skin and clothes; five more paces to the garage, and every hidden place slickens. By the time I get to the car, the crooks of my knuckles are sweating up the plastic sides of the insulated travel cup, and my grip slips as I climb into the SUV, throwing oily beads of black coffee onto the lid. A few on my hand, too, but I let them burn and turn on the air conditioning.

Summer comes a little earlier every year.

I back the car out past the driveway security gate we installed after it was too late, thread through the neighborhood to the feeder road, and then merge onto I-10, where concrete climbs the sky in massive on-ramps like the ribbed tails of dinosaurs. By 8:00

a.m., the clogged-artery-and-triple-bypassed heart of rush hour, I am pushing my way into fourteen lanes of gridlock, a landscape of flashing hoods and red taillights winking feebly in the dingy morning.

I need to see over the cars, so the gas-saving Prius sits in the garage while I drive Tom's hulking black Range Rover—it's not as if he's using it—down three different freeways to the university and back every day. Crawling along at a snail's pace, I can forget about the other commuters and focus on the chipped letters mounted on the concrete awnings of strip malls: BIG BOY DOLLAR STORE, CARTRIDGE WORLD, L-A HAIR. The neon-pink grin of a Mexican restaurant, the yellow-and-blue behemoth of an IKEA rearing up behind the toll road, the jaundiced brick of apartment complexes barely shielded from the freeway by straggling rows of crape myrtles—everything reminds me that the worst has already happened. I need them like my mother needed her rosary. *Hail, Mister Carwash, full of grace, the Lord is with thee. Pray for us, O Qwik-Fast Printing. Our Lady of Self-Storage, to thee do we send up our sighs.*

Even Julie's billboards are gone. There used to be one right here, at the intersection of I-10 and Loop 610, by the senior-living tower wedged between First Baptist and a concrete flyover, but the trustees decided the billboards should come down five years ago. Or has it been longer? I believe it was due to the expense, though I never had any idea how much they were costing—the Julie Fund was Tom's territory. These days, the giant, tooth-whitened smile of a megachurch pastor beams down from the billboard next to the words FAITH EVERY DAY, NOT EVERY-DAY FAITH. I wonder if they papered him right over her face or if they tore her off in strips first. Ridiculous thought; the billboard's advertised a lot of things since then. Dentists, vasectomy reversals.

A line of Wordsworth from today's lesson plan rattles through my head like a bad joke: *Whither is fled the visionary gleam? / Where is it now, the glory and the dream?*

I flip my blinker and merge onto the loop. Despite all the time I've spent reading and studying Wordsworth's poetry—despite the fact that I am going to teach it in a few hours to a class full of impressionable young students and plan to continue teaching it as long as my university allows me to cling to my position without publication, committee work, or any effort besides the not-insubstantial difficulty I have getting out of bed every morning to face a world where the worst thing has already happened and somehow I'm still alive—I don't believe in the glory and the dream. I believe in statistics.

The statistics say that most abducted children are taken by people they know; Julie was taken by a stranger. The statistics say that most child abductors attempt to lure their victims into a vehicle; Julie was taken from her own bedroom at knifepoint in the middle of the night while my other daughter, Jane, watched from a closet. And finally, the statistics say that three-quarters of abducted children who are murdered are dead within the first three hours of being taken. Three hours is just about how long we think Jane sat in her closet, rigid with fear, before rousing Tom and me with panicked crying.

By the time we knew Julie was gone, her fate was sealed.

The inevitability of it has spread like an infection or the smell of gasoline. To make myself know that Julie is dead, I tell myself she always was—before she was born, before I was born. Before Wordsworth was born. Passing the pines of Memorial Park,

I picture her staring upward with sightless eyes under a blanket of reddish-gold needles. Driving by Crestview Apartments, I see her buried in the azalea bed. The strip mall with the SunRay Nail Salon and Spa yields visions of the dumpster behind the SunRay Nail Salon and Spa. That's my visionary gleam.

I used to want the world for Julie. Now I just want something to bury.

My class—the last before summer break—passes in a blur. I could teach Wordsworth in my sleep, and although I'm not sleeping now, I am dreaming. I see the crystal blue of the pool, shining like a plastic gem, surrounded by a freshly sanded deck under the tall, spindly pines. The girls were so excited about the pool, and I remember asking Tom, the accountant, whether we could afford it. The Energy Corridor District, with its surplus of Starbucks and neighborhood country clubs, wasn't really our style—especially not mine. But the girls loved the pool even more than they loved having their own rooms. They didn't seem to notice that we were moving out of shabby university housing to a part of town with two-story houses and two-car garages and green lawns studded with signs supporting high-school football teams. There are several reasons why we did that, but the one you want to hear, of course, is that we thought it would be safer.

"Class dismissed. Don't forget, your final papers are due in my box on the twenty-eighth, no later than five o'clock." By the time I get to "Have a nice summer," most of them are out of the door already.

As I walk down the hall to my office, I feel a light *brr* against my hip. It's a text from Tom.

Can you pick up Jane? IAH 4:05, United 1093.

I put the phone down, turn to my computer, and look up the University of Washington academic calendar. Then I check the university directory and call up a University of Washington administrator I know from grad school. A brief conversation follows.

I text Tom back. *Should I get dinner too?*

A few minutes later: *Nope.* And that's apparently all Tom and I are going to say to each other about Jane coming home early from her freshman year of college.

It's tricky picking Jane out of a crowd these days. You never know what color her hair is going to be. I stand close to baggage carousel 9 and wait until a tall girl with burgundy-black hair emerges from the crowd of passengers, a lock of faded-out green dangling in front of her eyes, having survived yet another dye job intact.

"Hi, Mom," she says.

"Hi, Jane." We hug, her heavy satchel thwacking my hip as she leans over, and then the empty baggage carousel utters a shuddering shriek and we both turn to look at it while I decide how best not to ask about her unexpected arrival.

"You changed your hair again," I observe.

"Yep."

Everything Jane says and does is a variation on the slammed door that first became her calling card in middle school, a couple of years after Julie was taken. In high school, Jane added loud music, hair dye, and random piercings to her repertoire, but the slammed door remained the centerpiece of the performance. Tom used to follow her dutifully up the stairs, where he weathered the sobs and yells I heard only in muffled form. I figured she needed her privacy.

"Did you have a good flight?"

"It was okay."

It was long. I suspect Jane chose the University of Washington because of its distance from Houston. When she was a little girl she used to say she wanted to go to the university where I teach, but the pennants came down around the same time the door slamming began. She might have ended up in Alaska if she hadn't insisted on going to a school that had quarters instead of semesters—every possible difference a crucial one. All typical teenage behavior, no doubt, but with Jane, it made a particular kind of perverse sense—as does the fact that, according to the registrar, she took incompletes in all her spring-quarter classes.

This after she'd stayed in Seattle through the entire school year. I didn't think much about her not coming home for Thanksgiving; it's commonly skipped by students on the quarter system, since the fall quarter starts so late. But when she explained to us over the phone in mid-December that she was just settling in, that one of her professors had invited her to a holiday dinner, that our family never really celebrated Christmas anyway, did we?, and that she felt like it would be good for her sense of independence to stay, I could practically hear Tom's heart breaking over the extension. I covered for his silence by saying the sensible thing, the only possible thing, really: "We'll miss you, of course, but we understand."

Now it seems the whole holiday situation was yet another slammed door to which I'd failed to respond properly.

"So," I say, starting again. "You still enjoying U-Dub?"

"Go Huskies," she says with a limp fist-pump. "Yeah, Mom. Nothing's really changed since last time we talked." The bags start dropping onto the conveyor belt, and we both lean forward.

"Was that coat warm enough for January up there? Winter stuff is on clearance, we could go shopping."

She picks self-consciously at the army jacket she's worn since she was sixteen. "This is fine. I told you guys, it doesn't get that cold."

"Classes going okay?"

"Yeah," she says. "Why?"

"Just making small talk."

"Well, they're going really well," she says. "Actually, they're going so well, my professors are letting me turn in papers in lieu of exams."

In lieu of exams! That sounds official. I wonder how she got them to agree to give her incompletes rather than failing her. My students usually just say "Family emergency" and hope I don't press them for details.

Carefully, I ask, "Is that something they do a lot at U-Dub?"

"Mom," she says. "Just say 'University of Washington.'"

I give her shoulder a quick squeeze. "We're just glad you're home." I lower my arm and we stand there, side by side, staring at the shiny metal chute, until half the passengers on the flight have claimed their bags and wheeled them off, their absence making the juddering of the conveyor belt sound even louder. Finally, Jane's rolling suitcase somersaults down the chute and thunks onto the belt in front of us. It was a graduation present—apple green and already dingy from its maiden voyage to Seattle and back, it almost matches her dyed-green streak. She grabs the suitcase before I can make a move but lets me take her satchel when she stops to peel off her army jacket in the blast of humid air that hits us outside the automatic sliding doors.

"I see we're in swamp mode already."

"No place like home," I reply and am rewarded with a half smile of acknowledgment.

The ride home is rocky, though. I'm shooting blanks on college life despite spending most of my time in a university.

"How are the dorms?"

"Pretty good."

"You still like your roommate?"

"She's fine. We stay out of each other's way."

"Are you going to room with her next year?"

"Probably not."

Finally I resort to a subject I'm sure will get results, although it pains me. "So, tell me about this English professor you ate Christmas dinner with."

"Her name is Caitlyn, and actually she's a professor of semiotics."

Caitlyn. "I didn't know they still taught semiotics in English departments."

"The course is called Intersectionalities. It's an English class, but it's cross-listed with linguistics, gender studies, and anthro. There are supposed to be all these prerequisites, but I went to Caitlyn's office hours on the first day and convinced her to let me in."

I can't help but feel a glow of pride. A true professor's kid, Jane knows all the angles. Moreover, this is the longest string of consecutive words she's spoken to me without Tom around for ages. "Tell me more about it, what did you read?"

"I think I'd rather wait and talk about it with Dad too," she says.

"Of course," I say.

"I don't want to say it all twice."

"Sure, sweetie."

I turn on NPR, and the measured, comforting sound of rush-hour news commentary fills the car as we inch past a firing range and a gym where an Olympian gymnastics coach is probably even now yelling at ponytailed girls in formation. Jane stares out her window. I assume she is wondering why Tom didn't come to pick her up instead of me. I'm wondering too.

A few minutes later we both find out. Pulling into the driveway, the sky just starting to glow with dusk, I spot Tom through the kitchen window, making dinner. As I open the door and walk in, I smell Jane's favorite pasta dish: fettuccine Alfredo tossed with breaded shrimp and grilled asparagus, a ridiculously decadent recipe Tom got off the Food Network and makes only on special occasions. An expiatory salad of fresh greens is in a bowl next to the cutting board, ready to join the bright Fiestaware on the dining-room table.

"Janie!" Tom opens his arms and steps forward, and Jane throws her arms around him, squeezing her eyes shut against his chest. I slip off to the bathroom, then to the bedroom to change out of my teaching outfit into more comfortable jeans, loitering for a few minutes to put away some laundry that's been sitting, folded, in a basket at the foot of the bed. When I return, they are talking animatedly, Tom's back to me as he chops heirloom tomatoes for the salad, Jane resting the tips of her fingers on the butcher block as if playing a piano.

"Dad, you would not believe the names people were throwing around in this class," she says. "Derrida, stuff like that. Everyone was so much smarter than me."

"Hey, she let you in, and she's the MacArthur Genius lady."

"Every time I opened my mouth I sounded like an idiot."

"At least you opened your mouth," he says, resting the knife to the side of the cutting board for a moment while he looks her in the eye. "I bet there were some people who were too scared to talk."

Jane's grateful smile, just visible over Tom's shoulder, curdles me like milk. As if he can sense it, Tom turns around and sees me standing there. He throws a handful of chopped tomatoes onto the pile of greens and picks up the salad bowl.

"Everything's ready!" he says. "Grab the pasta, Jane. Let's sit down and eat our first family dinner in God knows how long."

And that, believe it or not, is when the doorbell rings.

2

The first thing I see is her pale hair, all lit up in the rosy, polluted glow of the Houston sunset.

Then her face—ashen skin stretched thin over wide cheekbones flushed red across the top so that the dark circles stand out under her sunken eyes. The face looks both young and old. She wears worn-out jeans with holes at the knees, a T-shirt. She opens her mouth to speak, and I see that her feet are bare.

There's something familiar about her, but it's like my entire body has become fused with my surroundings, my brain rewired to resemble blind hands fumbling, the sensory data bumping uselessly around in search of something to latch onto: *Hair. Eyes. Young. Bare.*

Her eyes widen, and the color drains from her face.

My hands stretch out in front of me, palms out, fingers spread wide, ready to shield me from the nuclear sunset or as if I'm about to fall down, but it's the girl on the porch who falls, her knees buckling so that she folds up neatly as she collapses onto the mat, blond hair catching lightly in the azalea bushes on her way down. I open my mouth and I think I must be yelling for Tom, although I can't hear it because my brain is still blinded by the sunset glancing off her face. He comes running up behind me, stops, and then thunders through the doorway. When I look again, the girl has all but vanished into his arms, the loops and tangles of her hair crushed between his fingers as he hugs her to his chest, rocking back and forth. "Julie, Julie, Julie," he is sobbing, like the chorus of the nightmares that I now know have never stopped but have been unreeling every night for eight years, and perhaps all day long as well, in a continuous stream I have simply chosen to deny.

The sight of Jane standing stock-still in the hallway flips the light switch back on in my head. "Call 911," I manage to say. "Tell them we need an ambulance." To Tom, who is making strange, animal sounds of grief I have also heard in my dreams, I say, "Bring her in."

And just like that, the worst unhappens. Julie is home.

The first twenty-four hours after Julie's reappearance are oddly similar to the first twenty-four hours after her disappearance, a mirror symmetry that lends extra significance to every detail. There's the humidity of the long, hot summer's beginning, the crape myrtles that were already dropping their flowers when she was taken in early fall just now starting to put out blossoms like crumpled scraps of tissue paper. There are the sirens blaring their way through the neighborhood up to our house, just like last time, but bringing EMS rather than the police and at sunset rather than sunrise, so the neighbors who open their front doors to see what's happening are wearing work clothes rather than bathrobes, holding oven mitts rather than newspapers. Everything is backward, like a photo negative of tragedy.

Only one of us can ride in the ambulance with Julie, and Tom immediately steps forward, so Jane and I climb into the SUV and follow behind. When we pull up to the ED, they are unloading her gurney, now connected to a rolling IV, and she is wheeled inside and installed in a curtained-off room with that excruciating combination of slowness and urgency native to emergency departments.

The next thirty minutes pass like hours under the fluorescent lights. Julie wakes, mumbles, sleeps again. Tom sits by the bedside, holding Julie's hand and murmuring something unintelligible; I pace; Jane leans; nurses come in at odd intervals, never telling us anything but instead asking for details about insurance or Julie's medical history, questions that seem so useless and redundant that I become convinced some of these people just want to see the famous Whitaker girl in the flesh. One nurse comes in to draw blood, and Julie starts awake at the cold wet cotton swab on her inner forearm, keeps her eyes open just long enough to nod vaguely at the nurse's bright questions, then fades as soon as the needle is in. The curtain that separates us from the hall flutters as people rush by and does nothing to block out the cacophony of squeaking wheels, indecipherable PA announcements, and hallway conferences punctuated with loud sighs and occasional laughter.

When the doctor finally comes, she sends everyone out of the room over Tom's and my objections.

"I just need her for two seconds," she says. "You—Mom, Dad —don't go anywhere."

Needless to say, we don't, but Jane takes the opportunity to find a restroom. The doctor emerges from the curtained room after a hushed conversation I strain unsuccessfully to hear, and I glimpse Julie in the background, awake but flushed and disoriented, before she pulls the curtain shut behind her. Julie is dehydrated, the doctor tells us, suffering from exhaustion and exposure, and hasn't eaten for a few days, but there don't seem to be any injuries or illnesses, no substances in her bloodstream. "After the fluids take effect, most likely she'll be right as rain," she finishes, her use of the expression *right as rain* proving she cannot possibly have read the chart, or she has never watched the news, or she is so calloused by her job that she lacks the power to think past a stock phrase indelibly associated in her mind with the word *fluids*. "Just get her to the clinic for a follow-up after a few weeks. They'll schedule her when she's discharged."

As we file back into Julie's room, there's a knock on the wall, and a police detective steps in after us. Fortyish, with dark hair, looking not unlike a police detective from a TV show but far less attractive, he leaves the curtain open a foot and stares at Julie from the improvised doorway.

"Julie Whitaker," he says. "Unbelievable."

Julie doesn't take any notice of him, but on seeing Tom and me again, she collapses back onto the pillow, crying tearlessly. Tom rushes to enfold her in his arms. Noting my expression, the doctor says they'll move Julie to a room with a door as soon as one opens up, and then she hustles out. The cop introduces himself as Detective Overbey and starts asking me questions about the circumstances of Julie's arrival, which I answer as best I can considering that, for all I know, she could have come straight out of the glowing orange sunset or a god's forehead or the side of a man opened up while he was sleeping. The question of how she was delivered to us seems that unimportant.

In the background, I hear Tom repeating the words "You're safe now. It's okay. The doctor says you're going to be okay." He is talking to himself as much as to her, and though the words aren't meant for me, they're so comforting that I let my attention drift toward them and away from Detective Overbey's questions.

He notices. "I'd like to talk to Julie alone for just a few minutes."

"No," Julie says, clutching Tom's arm but looking at me. "Don't go."

"This won't take long."

Tom stands directly in front of Julie's bed. He's a tall, broad man, imposing even with a gut. "Absolutely not. We left her alone once tonight, for the doctor. We're not leaving her again."

Tom and the detective begin to argue back and forth, and the tiny curtained room shrinks. The same words keep coming up, and at first I think Detective Overbey is questioning our mental health or Julie's; he is talking about the *sane*, the *safe*. Finally, he addresses Julie directly, speaking right through Tom. "I know you're not feeling well, ma'am, and I hate to bother you right now," he says. "But I need to ask: Were you sexually assaulted?"

Julie just looks at the detective and nods. Tom sets his jaw, and I find a moment to be glad Jane is still not back from the restroom.

Detective Overbey explains about the forensic exam, and I realize SANE and SAFE are acronyms. "The sexual assault nurse examiner has already been dispatched," he says. "She should be here soon to set up the exam room. The minute you're off the IV, she can get started."

Julie shakes her head no, and Tom steps forward, looking ready for a fistfight.

Detective Overbey, equally imposing, stands his ground. "If there's any evidence of sexual assault, it's best to collect it—"

"Listen," Tom says, pointing his finger at the detective for emphasis. "We've done everything the police told us to since day one and never asked a single question we weren't supposed to. Eight years later, after we've—" He chokes. "Years since we've heard any news, and our missing daughter shows up on our doorstep, no thanks to you. And now you want to keep her up all night asking her questions, treating her like a crime scene?" He snorts. "We'll come in tomorrow."

Detective Overbey starts to answer but a faint noise from Julie's bed stops him.

"The last time was—a long time ago," she says quietly. "At least six months."

Detective Overbey sighs as if the news that our daughter hasn't been raped in six months is disappointing but acceptable. "Okay, then. We still recommend you come back for the exam, but from a forensic perspective there's no rush. Rest up, and we'll get a full statement from you folks at the station tomorrow."

Julie nods weakly. Tom slumps forward, hands on knees.

Jane comes in, a juice box in her hand. She must have gotten it from the nurses' station. When she sees Julie awake, she smiles shyly and says, "Welcome back."

Six hours later, in the middle of the night, Julie is discharged, fully hydrated and wearing hospital scrubs to replace the scruffy T-shirt and jeans the police took for evidence. She leans on Tom's arm while I sweep everything into my purse: prophylactic antibiotics for chlamydia and gonorrhea, a prescription for Valium in case she has trouble sleeping, and a folder stuffed to bursting with pamphlets on sexual assault and Xeroxed phone lists for HPD Victim Services and various women's shelters. It also holds Detective Overbey's card, tucked into four slits in the front of the folder so it won't get lost. I remove it and slip it into the back pocket of my jeans.

Tom drives us home, Julie sleeping in the back seat of the SUV on the disposable pillow they let her keep. Jane, who slept quite a bit in the hospital, now stares at Julie silently. Nobody talks—in part because we don't want to wake Julie, but also because we ourselves do not want to wake up. Or maybe that's just me.

It's 3:00 a.m. when we open the back door and walk into the kitchen through the laundry room. It looks like some other family's house preserved on a perfectly normal day, a museum of ordinariness: over the washing machine, a blouse drips dry; on the cutting board, a heap of glistening red chopped tomatoes lies next to a knife in a puddle of red juice. Through the doorway to the dining room, Jane's elaborate homecoming meal sits forgotten on the dining-room table, the salad wilted, the breading on the fried shrimp gone soggy, the sauce jelled on the cold, gummy pasta. As the others pass through the kitchen into the living room, I head into the dining room and start picking up the dishes full of pasta. It takes only a moment for me to stack the evidence that we were surviving in the kitchen sink.

When I join them in the living room, Jane and Tom are standing awkwardly by the sofa with Julie, like people putting up a distant relative for the night. Tom is shaking his head, red-faced, and when I realize what they are discussing, my efforts in the dining room seem futile.

Tom moved his office into Julie's room seven years ago. He did not discuss it with me first; nor did he let me know he was quitting his accounting job, the job we moved to the Energy Corridor for in the first place, to go into private practice as a tax consultant. One day I passed her room and saw it had been transformed from bedroom to carefully tended shrine, a desk and file cabinet where her bed used to be, posters replaced with framed pictures of Julie. I understood without being told that this new office was to be his command center for the search, that he was turning his longing for her into a full-time job. Only now, with Julie standing in front of us, does it look like an exorcism.

"I don't mind the sofa," Julie is saying.

"She can have my room," Jane says, still hanging back, like she's afraid to stand too close. Clutching her elbow awkwardly, she looks more like her ten-year-old self than I would have thought possible, though I notice with a pang that she's taller than Julie by quite a few inches. Jane stares at Julie, not hungrily, like Tom, who looks as if he'll never let her out of his sight again, but with a wary expression. "I don't mind."

"No, please," Julie says. "I don't want to take anyone's room."

I have a sudden longing to bed her down between Tom and me, like we did when she was a seven-year-old with a fever and couldn't stop shivering. This, however, is not practical, and meanwhile, the living room yawns open like a mouth around us, the windows dark behind the curtains.

"Tom, the air mattress?" I offer. "She could be in her room until we can move your desk out."

"A door that closes would be nice," she says, and it's decided. She has no toiletries or luggage, and no one wants to ask why, so Jane gives her a T-shirt and shorts to sleep in and I scrounge up a spare toothbrush still in its package. After the bustle is over, Julie disappears behind the door of Tom's office like the sun behind a cloud. I wonder if she is comforted or disturbed by all the pictures of her in there.

By the time we have seen Jane to bed as well, with reassurances that she can decide if she wants to come to the station when she wakes up, it's almost dawn. The bedroom door closes and my legs want to buckle under me, but I also feel more awake than I have for years. My mind is racing, or rather somersaulting, tumbling over itself as I go through my bathroom routine.

Tom says, "Anna?" in a way that suggests it is the second or third time. I come out of the bathroom and see him lying on his side of the bed, looking up expectantly.

Instead of finding out what he wants, I surprise myself by saying exactly what I'm thinking: "What are we going to do?"

"She's back," he says. "We don't have to do anything anymore."

I slide out of my jeans, keeping my T-shirt on to sleep in.

"She's back," he repeats, like a stubborn child.

"We don't know what she's been through." I think of the detective's card tucked into the pocket of my jeans as I hang them on the back of the closet door. "We have to be careful."

"We should have been more careful then." His voice breaks a little.

I emerge from the closet. "She may not be—the same."

"None of us are," Tom says. There's a long pause. "You didn't believe she would ever come home."

I sit down on the edge of the bed. I can feel his eyes burrowing into the back of my head, and I close my own, tasting the accusation.

After a moment I turn to face him. "I didn't believe we would *find* her," I say, trusting him to know the difference.

He doesn't answer. But as I lean over to turn off the light on my nightstand, I feel something shift, just a little piece of the night air between us moving aside, like a breeze wafting through a chink in a wall. He turns onto his side, facing away from me, but there's something about this argument that reminds me of the marriage we used to have, the arguments that bubbled up only when we were in bed together. How gamely we entered every fight back then, knowing we'd still wake up next to each other in the morning.

Now, staring at Tom's back, I think, *Julie is home. Anything can happen.*

I see her face again the way I saw it on the front porch, just barely familiar, the flesh melted away from her cheekbones and jaw, leaving a butterfly of bone.

"Good night," I say.

I sleep until noon and wake to the noise of pans clattering downstairs, voices in the kitchen.

I know this dream. It's the one where Julie shows up, and I say, "I've dreamed about you so many times, but this time you're really home." Now I get up and splash water on my face in the bathroom and look at myself in the mirror, waiting for the features to distort, to drift. Everything stays put. This one is real.

A chill runs through me and a faint headache alights in my frontal lobe. I pull on my jeans from last night and head downstairs.

The kitchen table is bathed in light. My radiantly blond daughter sits on the side nearest the window, still wearing Jane's T-shirt, which is too big on her. Tom beams at her from the head of the table as they talk—about nothing, it seems: orange juice, the weather, does anybody want more eggs. For a moment it looks almost normal. Then Jane comes in with a glass in her hand and sits across from Julie, and a shiver walks down my spine as I observe the odd regularity that has returned to our family: a girl for each side of the table, four sides for four people. The words *fearful symmetry* pop into my head.

"Good morning," I say from the doorway.

"You slept forever," Jane says, but Julie is already getting up and in three long strides she has embraced me. It takes me aback. How long has it been since a daughter of mine came rushing into *my* arms from across the room? Just as I am starting to notice the scent of her hair, she pulls back and looks at me, her hands sliding down my arms to grasp my hands. "Hi, Mom," she says, a little awkwardly, and for a moment we are looking straight into each other's eyes.

I have become accustomed to looking at Jane, who shares my distinctive features, my sharp nose and deep-set eyes. As I stare into Julie's woman's face, I realize there are no moles, no bumps or blemishes or wrinkles.

She's *perfect*.

She breaks away, embarrassed, and I realize I have been staring.

"I'm sorry," I say. "I haven't seen your face in so long."

"I know," Tom says.

"Sit down, I'm just getting some coffee," I say. "Did you sleep okay?" There's a big pan on the stove with some scrambled eggs left in it, and I put some on a plate, suddenly ravenous.

"I slept very well," she says, like a polite guest. "The air mattress was comfortable."

"She's only been up for a few minutes," Tom says. "I've been fielding phone calls from the police department all morning. *Come in whenever you want* apparently means 'If you're not here by nine you'll be hearing from us.'" His face darkens. "I suppose it makes sense. They're worried about the press. I'm sure that'll be starting anytime now."

Julie's smile fades. "I guess we should probably go, now that Mom's awake."

Tom puts a hand over hers on the table. "You take as much time as you need."

"The sooner we go, the sooner it'll be over," I say.

Tom's eyes tear up, and I realize he doesn't want to know what she went through. At the same time, it occurs to me that I do.

Julie is studying my face with an almost grateful expression. "Yes," she says. "I want to get it over with." I can tell by the way she's looking at me that Julie needs me there, and no one else. I can't keep Tom away from the police station, but I decide I'm going to persuade him to stay out in the hall, which means Jane will have to come too, to give him someone to look after.

"Come on, Julie," I say. "I'll find you something in my closet to wear." A skirt, I think, looking at her dwindled frame. And I'll need some safety pins.

"He said he would kill me if I struggled. Kill my family."

"You believed him?" says Overbey.

We are sitting in the police station—me, Julie, Overbey, and a younger female detective, Detective Harris—in a private room with frosted-glass windows and a single table. Tom is outside waiting in the lobby with Jane, per Julie's request. Overbey wanted to question Julie alone, but she looked from his face to my face and then back, and he sighed and invited me in. I'm holding but not drinking a cup of black coffee so weak you can see air bubbles clinging to the inside of the Styrofoam, read the imprint of the serial number on the bottom. It was brought to me by Detective Harris—*Typical,* I think—while Overbey asked the questions.

"Of course I believed him," Julie says now. "He had a knife at my throat."

"A kitchen knife," Overbey says, consulting his notes, as if he doesn't already know everything in the case file. "Taken from the household. Any other weapons?"

"She was thirteen," I break in, but Overbey holds up his hand and nods for Julie to go on, and it's true she doesn't seem upset.

"Not that I saw. But I believed him. And if it was happening to me again now, knowing what I know about him, I would still believe him." She takes a breath. "Once we were out of the house, we got on a bus just by the CVS, there on Memorial Drive, and went to the bus station downtown."

"Did anyone see you?"

"The bus driver, maybe, but I was too scared to say anything. At the bus station he bought two tickets. We got off in El Paso." She pauses, and her eyes go dead. "That's where he raped me for the first time."

"Do you remember where you were?"

"Some motel. I don't remember which one."

"Motel Six? Econo Lodge?"

She glares at him icily. "Sorry. We stayed there for only a couple days and then we were gone again. We moved all the time. He stole a car in El Paso"—Overbey makes a subtle gesture without looking at Harris, who writes something down—"and for a while we drove that, but he sold it somehow, I guess. He just came back without it one day."

"He left you alone?"

"Yes. He left me tied up and gagged when he had to go out. We were in Mexico when he sold the car, I think, but I'm not sure because I was blindfolded, and then I was in the back of a van for a long time." The duct-taped-in-a-van dream floats before my eyes. "It took me a while to find out he'd sold me."

"He what?" Overbey looks up sharply.

"He sold me," she says. "Five men, maybe six."

Harris nods and returns to writing.

"Did those men—"

"Oh yes." She gives a cold, brittle smile. "Yes, they did."

My eyes close.

"Mrs. Whitaker, are you all right?" It's Harris's voice. I am sinking, eyes shut, into a cold black vapor that prickles at my extremities. I hear Overbey correct his partner—"Mrs. *Davalos* goes by her maiden name"—and snap my eyes back open, but the black dots take a moment to clear.

"I'm fine," I whisper. I want to reach for Julie's hand, but her arms are folded tightly across her chest.

"Could you identify any of the men?"

"I was blindfolded," she repeats patiently.

"Any accents?"

She thinks. "Some of them spoke Spanish to each other, but none of them talked very much. Anyway, that was a couple of days

—I think? I can't remember it very well. Then they sold me again. To someone important this time."

The detectives look meaningfully at each other. "Who?"

"I never knew his name. The other men called him El Jefe when they were talking about him, *señor* to his face."

"Go on," Overbey says calmly while Harris scribbles furiously. "How did you know he was important?"

"He had a giant house, like a compound, with bodyguards and a household staff and a lot of men with big guns coming to him for orders." She stops and takes a breath. "Please don't ask me where, I don't know. I didn't go outside."

"For how long?"

"For eight years."

Later, I tell Tom as little as I can get away with, enough to explain the pages of thumbnail photos Julie looked through at the station, pictures of Mexican men in their fifties with high foreheads and thick chins. I narrate the various stages of her captivity, but not the cigarette burns she got when she tried to escape; the years of rape, but not the way she spoke of them, as if describing the plot of a not particularly interesting television show. I tell him that her captor tired of her, but not that she was too old for him once out of her teens; I tell him that she was blindfolded and taken in a helicopter to a rooftop in Juárez, but not that the guard was most likely supposed to kill her rather than let her go. I tell him that she hid in the back of a truck to get across the border, but not that she was afraid of the U.S. Border Patrol because she wasn't sure she could still speak English, or anything at all, after so long; that she jumped out of the truck at a stoplight and ran, but not that she dragged herself foot after foot along the I-10 feeder road for miles, invisible from the freeway, like the people you learn not to see stumbling through gas-station parking lots, clutching their possessions in plastic bags.

"My God," he says under his breath. We are at the kitchen table and the girls are upstairs in bed, a peculiar throwback to the quiet discussions we used to have long ago, about topics so trivial I can't imagine why we bothered hiding them. "So she was sold to a human-trafficking ring, then to some drug lord?"

It's strange how hearing him say those phrases out loud makes it into a story more than the jumbled words in the interview room did. "That's what it sounds like, yes."

Tom is leaning forward on his elbows on the kitchen table, holding on to himself, every muscle tensed. "Well, is that what the detectives say?"

"They didn't say much at all, really. They were just taking her statement, asking questions."

"Right. They don't want to say anything that might upset us, like, you know, *human trafficking* or *forced prostitution.* That might imply they know about it and can't do anything to stop it!" Tom's voice breaks on this last exclamation. He's not bothering to lower his voice anymore.

"I think they may know something. Harris mentioned a task force—"

"Yes, there's a statewide task force on human trafficking," Tom surprises me by saying. I am reminded of how much work he has done, how many search organizations he's joined, the support group for parents of missing children, the Facebook pages, and wonder what else he knows that I don't. "They formed it a couple of years ago, after a big report came out. Obviously it came too late to help Julie. But I guess we should be thrilled that she can help them." He sighs heavily. "How was she in there?"

"She seemed—fine," I say. "All things considered. One of the detectives told me she's in shock and needs to see a therapist."

"Of course," Tom says. "I'll find someone. I'll call tonight."

3

To get through the first week, I take her shopping. What else am I going to do with this twenty-one-year-old woman who has shown up to replace my missing thirteen-year-old daughter? Besides, she doesn't have any clothes. The first few days, I lend her things of mine to wear—she's closer to my size than Jane's—but it gives me the strangest feeling to see her draped in one of my severe black tunics, her blond hair swallowed up in its oversize cowl, like a paper doll dressed for a funeral.

"I have some errands to run at Target," I lie. "Want to come? We can get you some clothes."

Julie used to love back-to-school shopping with me, especially picking out all the notebooks and pens and pencils in purple and pink and glittery green. On top of buying her the usual jeans and T-shirts and underwear, I always got her one completely new first-day-of-school outfit, and she would keep it hanging on her doorknob for weeks, counting down the days. I still go to the same Target, which has, of course, barely changed at all in eight years, and I wonder whether the memories it brings back of one of our few mother-daughter activities are as pleasant to her as they are to me.

But once we're there, the red walls seem too aggressive some-how, the fluorescent lights glaring on the white linoleum walkways headache-inducing. Julie follows me obediently around the store as if it's her first time in there, or indeed in any store, and I can't help but wince at the racks of neon bikinis all tangled up on their hangers, the viscose minidresses lying on the floor under the sale rack, the red-and-white bull's-eye logo suspended over bins of brightly colored underwear. If the clothes in my closet seem too dour for a twenty-one-year-old, everything here seems too flimsy and disposable for someone with a face like Julie's. Hurrying us past the clothing department, I grab a cheese grater at random from the kitchen section and we stand, a little absurdly, in the express lane, waiting to check out.

Julie stares fixedly at the rows of candy bars in their bright boxes, and I am struck by how much this is like standing at the baggage carousel with Jane, the silence of two people trying to pretend it's ordinary how little they're talking. Except with Jane, I know she doesn't want to talk, not to me anyway. With Julie—who knows. But whatever conversation I am waiting to have with her, we are not going to have it in the express lane of Target, not even with the extra two minutes gained from the woman in front of us arguing over a sale price. I've heard the story, but who really knows what she's been through or how she feels about it? *Look at her now,* I think, *staring at nothing.*

But she's not. Once we get through the line and out into the car, she says, "I used to love that movie."

"What movie?"

"*A Little Princess.*"

Now I recall seeing it on the display stand near the register. I don't remember much about the movie aside from its exceptionally lurid color palette. It's one of those boarding-school stories, I know, where they're mean to the orphan girl. They keep her up in the attic. I feel a hint of panic.

"You should have said something. We could have bought it."

"It's okay, I don't want it."

"We can go back."

"Mom. I was just remembering."

But I'm almost crying in the silence that follows. She turns her head toward the window and says, "The Indian Gentleman searches everywhere for her so he can pass on her father's fortune, but it turns out she's been next door to him the whole time."

I try to speak, but nothing comes out.

"I used to think about that sometimes," she says shortly, by way of explanation, turning her head back to me. The veil of kindness has dropped back over her eyes. Outside, it starts to rain.

We speed toward Nordstrom, where I buy her heaping armfuls of silk tank tops, designer jeans, cashmere sweaters on ultra-sale, collared shirts and peasant blouses and plain, tissue-thin T-shirts at fifty bucks a pop. I buy her a purse, a wallet, a belt. A pair of brown calfskin loafers and some white sandals and three pairs of flats in different colors, all designer, but with the logo-print fabric tucked away on the inside, so you can't tell how expensive they are. I'll know, though.

Julie will know too, although I do my best to keep the price tags away from her after I catch her checking the tag on a blouse and then trying unobtrusively to hang it back on the rack. "Julie," I say firmly. She nods with a small smile, and I feel a rush of elation, strong, like the first sip of coffee after a good night's rest.

For the next two hours I stand outside the dressing room and hand her sizes and shades and styles of everything: bras, blazers, even swimsuits. While I am pondering which fancy restaurant we will take her out to first, she cracks the door open and holds out her hand for a smaller size of a fitted, knee-length dress in royal blue. Handing it to her, I glimpse, through the gaping sleeve openings of the too-big dress, a coin-size blob on her rib cage in a bluish-greenish shade of black that seems somehow wrong for a bruise. The door closes before I can ask her about it, and the dress doesn't suit her, so we don't end up buying it. We have plenty of other options.

We walk out with four giant shopping bags stuffed to their tops, two bags apiece, like a scene in a movie about rich and powerful women. And I *do* feel powerful, almost if we've gotten away with something, though the four-figure total on the receipt shows otherwise. Julie is smiling too, unabashedly, wearing a knit top and jeans that we ripped the tags off, right at the register, while the long receipt was still whirring its way out of the printer. The sun came out from behind clouds while we were inside and is now steaming away the new puddles in the parking lot, high and bright. Everything sparkles. I think with a sharp thrill of Tom, at his computer, seeing the transaction come up in his linked accounting software. It's more than our monthly house payment.

Only late at night, just as I'm drifting off, does that precise shade of bluish-greenish black on her rib cage evoke the word *tattoo*.

The next day, I drive her to a pebbled-concrete office complex off Memorial Drive, Tom's phone call having yielded a referral to the dark and slightly down-at-heel office of Carol Morse, PsyD. Julie goes in, and in the waiting area, where the ficus trees are mysteriously flourishing in the absence of natural light, I pull out a book on Byron and landscape, then put it down and spend ninety minutes paging through magazines instead. I think about the many appointments in my future, all the waiting rooms in store for me, and hope they update the magazines regularly.

On the way home, Julie asks if she can drive herself to her therapy appointments.

Tom and I argue about it for three days straight.

"She can't drive without a license," he says. "End of story."

"The therapist's office isn't that far away. She won't have to go on the highway —"

"Then we'll get her a bike."

But in a city without sidewalks, a bike feels more dangerous to me than a car. "And have her get honked at, even hit? People get abducted off bikes, Tom. And the bus is just as bad." *Unprotected,* I want to say. I think of Julie walking along the feeder road. "Of course she'll get a license, but it takes months, and there are all those tests and forms and documents. What does she do until then? She'll have to get a vision test —"

"She should! There are reasons for those things," Tom says, but I can tell he's wavering, and so I keep fighting. It's the first thing Julie has really asked me for, and she asked *me,* not Tom. I assume she wants to be alone in the car for the same reason I do: that sheltered, armored feeling of sitting high up behind the tinted windows in the recycled, air-conditioned air, the total privacy. It's something I can give her that's better than clothes.

In the end, we compromise. I sign her up for the midsummer session of driver's ed at the community college near our house, and Tom agrees to take Julie out for driving lessons now so she can get herself to therapy and back, carefully, using the neighborhood roads. The private lessons are what clinches it; his resolve crumbles in the face of her obvious delight at the prospect, and for the next week they wake up conspiratorially early and head off to various parking structures around town for a few hours. When they come back, we eat lunch together, and then Tom goes to work while Julie and I swim in the pool. In the afternoons, I take her out shopping—we buy all her bedroom furniture in one trip to IKEA, as if she's a college student—or to her therapy appointment, when she has one, or, a few times, to an afternoon movie. After a family dinner, we watch TV with Jane curled up nearby, absorbed in her notebook. It's a cozy routine, one where Julie is always accounted for and our time together is comfortably filled with tasks so no one has to reach far for things to talk about that aren't Julie's eight-year absence or find reasons to gently touch her forearm that aren't, at least not obviously, about checking to make sure she's still there.

For the first few weeks, this routine feels like it could last forever, in spite of minor disturbances. Tom answers the phone sharply when he doesn't recognize the caller ID, telling the reporters that we're not interested in talking; "I don't know when," he snaps, "our family needs privacy right now." Eventually he turns the ringer off, and I sink back into the bliss of knowing he is taking care of things, as he did in the days after it happened. In the back of my mind are certain topics I avoid thinking about—my job, Jane's incompletes, the SANE, the SAFE—but then I send my department chair an e-mail telling him my grades will be late and decide that Jane, who has grown quieter in Julie's presence, must be making progress on her late papers. What else could she be writing about in her notebook all the time? And when Julie starts driving after a few weeks of early-morning lessons with Tom, she gets to her appointments and back just fine, as I knew she would. This is our new normal, and it feels like something we are all learning together, as a family.

Tom and I even start having sex again, something that hasn't happened regularly for years. He touches me gingerly, as if he can sense that my skin feels almost raw. Julie has been in the house for a few weeks, and though I'm getting used to it, it still feels like someone has rubbed me all over with a rasp. Every pore seems to be open, every hair a fine filament ready to shoot me full of sensation at the slightest breeze. I have been fighting for so long to stifle sensation. I remember when the grief was so potent I would lie on the sofa with the television on drinking vodka gimlets, one after the other, just waiting to pass out, staying as still as possible, teaching myself the art of numbness. And now it is as if I've been dropped into scalding water and the numbness has peeled away and the skin underneath is affronted by air.

If there is something missing—if I am afraid to love her quite as much as before—it is only because the potential for love feels so big and so intense that I fear I will disappear in the expression of it, that it will blow my skin away like clouds and I will be nothing.

· · ·

I wake up one morning with Jane standing over me, shaking my elbow. For a moment, caught in dreams I can't remember, I think we're doing the whole thing over again.

"Mom," she whispers urgently. "Mom, can you wake up?"

I reach a hand instinctively over to Tom.

"Don't wake Dad. Just come quick, okay?"

I'm naked under the covers, I realize in time to keep from pushing them off me. Jane sees. "I'll wait outside. It's Julie," she adds unnecessarily, since even as I wake up completely I'm still reliving that day.

I skip the bathrobe and pull on jeans and yesterday's shirt in case we need to get right into the car. "Gone?" I ask when I'm out of the bedroom, my skin clamping shut under the air conditioning.

Jane looks at me oddly and shakes her head. "No, nothing like that. I think she's sick."

We're still whispering as she leads me upstairs. Jane peers down the hall at the closed bathroom door.

"It's locked," she says helplessly.

"How long?"

"I don't know," she says. "Since before I got up, half an hour ago. I thought she was taking a bath but then I heard her—moaning, or something. I knocked, but she won't answer." Her voice is quavering.

I walk to the bathroom door, knock softly. "Julie?"

There is no moaning now, only a rhythmic click and shuffle that I associate immediately with a night spent doubled over on the toilet.

"Baby, are you okay in there? Are you hurting?"

Two words sent explosively outward on an expulsion of breath, barely audible.

"What?"

"Go away." Followed by a gasp of pain.

I turn to Jane. "Get a blanket from the hall closet and put it in the car. My keys are on the table. I'll be down in a few minutes." She leaves immediately to follow my orders.

Facing the bathroom door, I say, "Julie. You're going to have to let me in. You're going to unlock the door, okay?"

Nothing but a moan and the rhythm of the clicking toilet seat.

The next thing I know, I am in the bathroom. I don't remember this part, but Tom tells me later that he woke up to pounding (mine) and screaming (Julie's), and that by the time he made it to the hall in his boxers, my arm had already disappeared up to the shoulder in a ragged hole in the bathroom door, and then I was turning the doorknob from the inside, pulling my arm out, and opening the door. Between my bloody fist and the blood on the bathroom floor, there was blood everywhere, and he turned around and around looking for the intruder who had laid waste to the household.

But however I got in, when I see Julie, I know what's happening to her right away. I had one myself, after Jane. It's a painful, bloody thing, though I remember wishing during the worst times that I had lost Julie that way instead of the other.

Tears are streaming down her face, and I wrap a towel around her shoulders and help her to her feet. "I'll call you from the hospital," I tell Tom, who is still shaking as he follows us down the stairs and into the kitchen. The last thing I say to him, as he stands by the island in his boxers, is "I didn't know we even had a gun." More to remind him he's holding it than anything else. He stares down at it in his hand as if he hadn't known either.

"She's okay," I tell Tom over the phone from my chair in the wait-ing area. "Ovarian cysts can be very painful when they rupture. Tell Jane it's okay." He protests. "Yes, they're concerned about the blood too, but they don't think it's anything serious. It was mostly mine, from the door. The ultrasound—"

The ultrasound showed a tiny, irregular smudge, already half disintegrating, washed out in the early morning, tiny bits of tissue in a thick red exodus. When she saw what was on the monitor, she went pale and silent, dropped my hand, and said, "Get out." I got out, but before I did, I saw her face.

She knew.

I end the call with Tom, put the phone back in my purse, and sit. If any of the staff in the emergency department heard me and knew I was lying, they didn't care enough to give me even a glance. I bet they've heard plenty of miscarriages become ovarian cysts on the phone with Dad.

I reach for a magazine and wince at the pain in my bandaged knuckles. Thinking of the clothes I bought her, I grimace. Have the snug jeans become more snug in the past few weeks? Have I failed to notice? I remember the tattoo, remember, above all, what she told the police: "Six months." Now seven. And hate my-self for thinking, *She lied, she lied, she lied.*

But omissions aren't necessarily lies, are they? This is what the therapy is for, telling the horrible details that don't add up but make all the difference. Surely that's what she does in the thera-pist's office for ninety minutes twice a week: talks to a surrogate me—isn't that the theory? A trained professional onto whom she can project a version of me that, unlike the real me, will be able to handle everything, hold everything, make it all make sense?

The therapist, Carol Morse, suddenly seems like the answer. She can't tell me anything confidential, of course, but maybe under the circumstances—a pregnancy, a miscarriage, Julie's health at stake—she'll find a way to give me some insights into what's going on with my daughter. There's so much more to her than I know, but I can handle Julie's truth. I've already had the worst thing happen to me that can ever happen to a parent. And now, in a sense, Julie has too. It's something we share.

When she's finally discharged, we walk to the car. Another late night has turned into early morning during our time in the hospital. The sun is coming up, the freeway still clear, the heat just a soft shimmer that promises more to come. We drive for a few minutes in silence.

"It was the guard," she says. "In the helicopter. I don't know why I didn't want to say. I guess because—" She struggles. "It wasn't really rape."

Pause. I take in this detail, try to make it fit.

"What I mean is, I offered. I thought he'd be less likely to kill me. I—I didn't want to tell you. Because I was ashamed. Anyway I thought—" She gasps a little. "I thought I couldn't get pregnant. My period has never been regular since—" She stops when a tear rolls down my cheek. "Well, ever."

I nod. This woman is older than twenty-one. I am not as old as she is, and I am forty-six, with lines of mourning etched all over my face that will never go away. But she knew. I saw her face when she looked at the ultrasound screen.

"I love you," I say, and it's the truth, the absolute truth. But in this new world, after the miscarriage, it sounds like a lie.

"Mom," she says, despairingly.

"I won't tell your father or Jane. This is between us."

A warm wave of relief radiates from her as she settles back in her seat. This is what she has wanted all along. She looks out the window, and I look at the road ahead, and we are closer in our secret than we have ever been.

Julie

woke up to a fresh round of cramps with a strangled cry.

The television was on, but muted; was it the same movie she fell asleep to or a different one? While she was still half asleep, Tom came running down the stairs from her bedroom, which he was using as an office during the daytime while they figured out where to move his desk. This made her nervous, but she didn't want to say anything about it.

Looking at him now, standing at the bottom of the stairs, she briefly remembered him from last night, holding a gun. She wondered where it was now.

"Did I hear you calling? Are you okay?"

"I'm fine. Just a bad dream." At first she'd dreamed of Cal, but it got bad near the end, when the cramps started rocketing through her body louder and louder. She couldn't remember the worst of it with Tom standing there, just a feeling of dirt all around her mouth and the colors yellow and red—the shades of the afghan, she noted with disgust, throwing it off her. Now that she was awake, the sharp pain in her abdomen was already subsiding to a dull, empty ache.

"Can I make you some tea?"

"I'd like to get out of the house." The air in here was somehow both cold and stifling, and the big windows made her feel like some kind of specimen under glass. Or maybe it was the way they all watched her. "Can I take the car?"

"You mother left a few minutes ago. Jane's got mine," he said swiftly. She could tell the idea of her driving without a license still made him uncomfortable. "Your mom should be back soon. She was just going by her office for some late term papers. Why don't you keep resting for a while? You could watch another movie."

She swiveled her feet to the ground. "It's okay. I'll just take a walk."

He watched her doubtfully as she pushed herself to standing. Her legs felt quivery, as if her feet were still in the stirrups. "I'll be fine, Dad," she forced herself to say. "I just need some head space. Let me go get dressed, okay?"

He nodded. "I'll be in the kitchen."

She went up to her room, opened the closet door, and stared at the rows of brand-new flats and boots, some she hadn't worn yet that were still in their boxes. She could see, down the hall in Jane's room, a pair of beat-up Converse high-top sneakers slouching toe to heel by the side of Jane's bed, where it was her habit to kick them off. On an impulse, she walked down the hall and grabbed them. They gaped a little, so she added a second pair of socks, and, instead of wrapping the laces around the ankles like Jane, she laced them all the way to the top and double-tied the knot.

She wanted something that wouldn't come off if she had to start running.

The thought made her legs feel wobblier than ever. She grabbed a hoodie out of Jane's closet, then thought better of it — Tom might notice — and hung it back up. There was nothing like a hoodie in her own closet, just cardigans and blazers and other things she'd never worn before. They'd excited her in the store for that reason, but now their unfaded pastels looked like candy to her. Too visible. She grabbed the most subdued cardigan, a soft gray one, and put it on. Then she reached under her brand-new and punishingly stiff mattress, slid the phone out from between it and the box spring, and tucked it into her front pocket, hoping the cardigan would mostly cover it.

Downstairs, she breezed past Tom, grabbed her new purse, and yelled, "I'll be back before dinner," over her shoulder as the door swung shut behind her. The outside air hit her face like steam off a bowl of soup; sitting in Tom and Anna's freezing house, you forgot the sweltering heat waiting on the other side of the window. She peeled her cardigan off at the bottom of the driveway and stuffed it into her purse.

At the end of the block, she slipped the phone out of her pocket and turned it on, grateful for her last-minute inspiration to ditch it with her IDs in the front bushes before ringing the doorbell. Losing consciousness had not been part of the plan. Maybe it was the heat and all the walking, but when Jane stepped into the hallway, Julie had thought she was seeing Charlotte's ghost. The hospital had not been part of the plan either, but at least the doctor had shed light on certain particulars.

Particulars that, of course, Anna now knew too.

No wonder she'd felt so weak. This whole time she'd thought it was love she was fighting against, or tearing herself away from, that feeling of warm belonging that threatened to betray her whenever Cal looked at her. Now she knew the betrayal ran deeper, down into her blood, bones, and tissue. No wonder she'd felt violated. No wonder she'd felt possessed.

It was a lucky thing he never found out what was inside her.

Recovering the phone had been tricky, since they watched her so closely those first few days. But on the third day she'd slipped out for the mail and picked it up on the way back in. Thank God the phone had stayed dry under the awning, and the IDs were all still there, rubber-banded to its back. When she'd powered it up, the screen flashed on, and there was Cal, smiling at her with that infuriating expression of faith and love she'd drunk in so deeply and grown so strong on—strong enough to remember who she really was and why he couldn't find out. By the time she saw the article in the library that day—Cal had dropped her off there to study the GED books—she was strong enough to tear herself away.

She'd scrubbed everything else off her phone before she was out of Seattle, but she couldn't quite bring herself to get rid of Cal. She felt as if he were with her still in some indefinable way. When, at the hospital, she'd learned what it was, she'd thought, maybe, somehow, when she was finished here, she could go back.

She knew it was a stupid idea, and her body agreed. It had made the decision for her.

She took one last, long look at the face on the screen, and for a moment she was lying next to him again, her fingers tracing his chest lightly, his fingers twined in her hair, listening as he described his mother's white face, one eye swollen shut, framed in the rear window of his aunt's Volkswagen. Sending one last, blank look in the direction of the small black boy crying at the kitchen window before twisting her blond head away and turning her back on him forever.

She got the point, and it wasn't just that she, too, was a blond. Sometimes people had to leave, she'd thought to herself. She took a deep breath and pressed delete.

Then she noticed the new voicemail message. Not recognizing the number, she pushed play and listened but a moment later jerked the phone away from her ear like it had bitten her. How many times would she have to delete him before he was gone? And how many times would it still hurt? She'd never picked up, and she'd stopped listening to the messages after the first few; they all said the same thing. Now he was trying her from different numbers, hoping to catch her off guard. She glanced once more at the unknown number, and then with a jolt recognized the area code: Portland, Oregon. It might be a coincidence, a cell phone borrowed from a friend. But what if he actually had gone to Portland? It might mean he was trying to find her, following her trail, starting with Will. Of course that's where he would start. He'd always wanted an excuse to confront Will and get her stuff back; he'd said facing the past was important, as if he'd know the first thing about it. He could be finding out, though, right now. And once he started in that direction, how long would it be until he found her?

Looking around at Tom and Anna's neighborhood, she could barely believe she was here, much less picture Cal turning up. Empty of pedestrians in the heat of the afternoon, the neighborhood had high white curbs but no sidewalks, and she walked in the street, stepping around straggling ropes of soft tar. She passed house after house, all of them huge to her after Cal's pinched Seattle apartment, their plush lawns trimmed with fat shrubs and clumps of begonias so perfect and motionless in the dead air, they looked like silk flowers. Some of the porches had columns, like plantation houses.

Following the noise of traffic, she stepped out of the subdivision and started walking along a busy thoroughfare. Cars spat hot breath and gravel at her ankles as they raced by. There was no sidewalk here either, no curb even, just a narrow trail worn in the crabgrass near the greasy roadside before it plunged into runoff ditches padded at the bottom with tangled weeds. She walked past a rambling strip mall: Kroger, Qwik Klean, Jenny's Gifts, the streaky glass box of a Dairy Queen. The only logical destination of this ragged path was the bus stop. She cast a glance toward the kiosk and saw three women waiting for the bus in service uniforms, each with a rolling cart full of bottles. Cleaning ladies. Her back hurt just looking at them.

As she passed a McDonald's, she saw a long blue awning peeking out from the strip center behind it: BOBBY'S POOL HALL, in dingy white block letters. She walked toward it in relief. So there were hiding places here, after all. Although the other stores in the strip center had glass fronts, she noted that Bobby's windows were covered with weather-beaten plywood and wondered if there was any business in the back. Not that she needed any, she hurriedly told herself; she was going to be here only a few weeks. But it wasn't a bad idea to find out what was around. Besides, she had money in her wallet, and maybe what she really wanted was to sit for a few hours away from the roadside, drinking away the pain in her gut.

At this time of the afternoon, there were only a few bar-flies. They sat close to the entrance, talking with a curly-haired woman behind the bar who laughed loudly as she wedged limes on a cutting board. None of them paid any attention to her until she leaned against the bar. Then the bartender stopped laughing abruptly.

"What do you want, honey?" She squinted. "Job? You gotta be eighteen."

"Corona, please."

The woman laughed. "You're going to have to show me some ID, hon."

Julie dug through her new wallet and pulled out one that said she was twenty-four. Even as she handed it over, she felt a moment of panic. It was a California driver's license, a real one, the kind you can get in a lot of trouble for stealing.

The bartender gave it a long, hard look, then glanced at her, then back down at the ID. "Mercedes Rodriguez?" she said, drawing out the syllables like it was an impossible name for anyone to have.

"Mercy," she said automatically. The last time she'd used Mercy, she'd had short brown hair, but it was dark in Bobby's Pool Hall, and the wide-cheekboned face and blue eyes looked close enough. *Mercy, Mercy,* she told her face, *look like Mercy.*

It almost worked. She could feel the woman struggling to care. Then someone called "Bev!" from the end of the bar, and the bartender glanced anxiously over her shoulder, and by the time she looked back at Mercy, she was having none of it. "Sorry, señorita," she said, all the patience draining from her voice. "You don't look twenty-four, and it's an out-of-state ID. I gotta be careful in this neighborhood. For all I know, you wandered over from the high school." Bev threw the ID down on the counter and hustled off.

This goddamn city. She wasn't planning to be here long, but she'd already flashed a fake ID within ten blocks of Tom and Anna's house and been turned down. *Don't shit where you eat* meant something different when she was working at the Black Rose, but it applied here too. She grabbed the ID off the counter and shoved it back into her pocket.

Now the two men at the bar were staring at her. One of them said, "Come on, Bev, have a heart!"

The other chimed in, "She's old enough. I can always tell, like rings on a tree." He guffawed.

Now she really had to get away. On a sudden instinct, she pulled the phone out and dialed one of the numbers Tom and Anna had made her write down on a scrap of paper and keep in her new wallet.

"Hello?" The voice had the doubtful tone of someone picking up an unknown number.

"Hey, Jane," she said. "It's Julie."

"Where are you? What number is this?"

She looked out the window and saw a sign across the street. "I'm at the Starbucks by our house. I borrowed a phone off someone. Listen, I had to get out of there, Mom and Dad were hovering. Can you pick me up?"

"Are you at the Starbucks on Memorial?"

"Yeah. I have to go, this lady needs her phone back."

"Just hang on, I'm at a friend's house. I'll be there in a few minutes." Jane hung up.

She slammed the bar door behind her as hard as she dared, but it bounced on a cushion of air six inches from the frame and she could still hear the voices inside laughing at her as she hurriedly crossed the street.

Fifteen minutes later, Jane pulled into the Starbucks parking lot in Tom's SUV, rolled down the window, and said, "Nice shoes."

"Thanks." Julie looked down and saw Jane's Converse on her feet. "I mean, I'm sorry."

"It's okay." Despite the dark hair and bangs, Jane didn't look much like Charlotte at all. Jane was taller, stronger, Julie told herself.

"Mom got me all these flats," she apologized. "I just wanted something I could walk in." She pulled the heavy passenger-side door open and climbed in.

"I said it was okay." Looking closely at Jane's face, especially when she smiled, Julie could tell she had never been very far from home. College didn't count, even if it was halfway across the country—it was still closer to home than a single bus ride could take you. If you looked past Jane's piercings (two: nose and eyebrow), tattoos (two small ones, one on her shoulder and one on her hip, and Anna didn't know about either), and hair (the bleach-and-green was clearly a home job, but the black dye was from a salon), you saw a girl who'd never had to take the bus all that much.

Julie regretted putting her own hair through this last round of bleach. It had looked smooth enough at first, but now the ends were getting ragged, the part below her shoulders breaking off and poofing out. Worst of all, darker hair was creeping in at her hairline. If she hadn't needed to look the part so desperately, she could probably have gotten away with dirty blond.

But she hadn't wanted to be a dirty blond. She'd wanted to be Julie.

Jane clicked her keys against the wheel impatiently. "So where are we going?"

"I want to chop all this off," Julie said, holding out a handful of split ends.

"Like, right now?"

"Yeah, right now. And dye it, maybe. I figured you'd know a good place for that."

Jane looked impressed. "I can take you to the place I go. It's in Montrose. What color are you going to dye it?" She squinted shrewdly. "Better not be black."

"I don't know, maybe red," she said without thinking. At the Rose, she'd always made bank with red hair. Besides, white-blond Julie was starting to get to her. She'd stared at the pictures of the missing girl and at herself in the mirror beforehand, but when she started playing Julie for Anna and Tom and Jane, something shifted. She saw Julie's innocence in the way all three of them looked at her, and it was unnerving. Anna, in particular, watched her as if she might break.

Jane was already pulling out of the parking lot, her strong jaw set under its sprinkling of covered-up acne, saying, "Cool, let's get out of here." If Julie was worried about Anna, she should have started with Jane in the first place. Shutting Anna out was Jane's superpower.

Tom's Range Rover was a smooth ride, just more ease and luxury so built into Jane's existence she didn't even know it was there. Jane wove in and out of the four-lane traffic on Westheimer as she drove toward the city, the SUV soon dwarfed by hulking black Suburbans with tinted windows, shiny trucks that were all tire and no flatbed, a Hummer that looked like it could transform into a robot. A few lanes away, a silver convertible idled like a half-melted bullet in the sun. The apartments gave way to sparkling-white office buildings set on lots kissed around their edges with manicured shrubs and palm trees. Everything gleamed, even the street signs, which were mounted on giant chrome arcs.

"Can you believe how much the Galleria has changed?"

She caught the small dip in Jane's voice and immediately felt a prickling on the back of her neck, alerting her to a shared memory she was in no position to ignore.

"Yeah, I know," she said.

"Do you remember that time Mom dropped us off at the Galleria to do our Christmas shopping?"

"That's what I was thinking about too."

"I thought we were so cool," Jane went on, her eyes on the taillights ahead of them. The traffic light had changed and they were inching sluggishly forward, but they weren't going to make it past the danger zone on this green. "It felt like we were so grown up. You must have been in, what, sixth or seventh grade? Because —" She broke off. "And I would have been in fourth or fifth. We bought lunch at that one fancy food-court place with the crepes. Do you remember splitting up for an hour to buy each other's presents? That was my favorite part. We, like, synchronized our watches and met at the bakery afterward." She laughed. "I even doubled back and hid which direction I was coming from so you wouldn't guess where I bought your present. I think it was Claire's or something."

Jane's voice tugged at her ear, but Julie was distracted by a boy of around twelve or thirteen in a T-shirt and saggy, wide-legged blue jeans weighed down with a heavy wallet chain who was striding through the still-sidewalk-less guts of the drainage ditch parallel to the road. His tangled hair was long and brown and very deliberately shielding his face as he marched, hands in pockets, visibly sweating. He reached the base of one of the chrome arcs, which proved to be a formidable obstacle at ground level. Trapped between an evergreen shrub and the curved chrome, he hiked up his billowing, half-shredded pants leg with one hand and stepped over it, like a cartoon lady pulling up her skirts to step over a puddle.

"Julie?" Jane's voice came back to her, and she realized she'd missed a question. The music was quieter; Jane must have just turned it down. "Do you remember? What you did that time when we split up?"

"Tried on prom dresses," she said. "Pretended I was a princess."

"Oh," Jane said, and laughed. "Well, that definitely explains why I ended up getting a gift certificate from Waldenbooks that year."

She knew better than to let this moment pass because of some stupid kid. "I thought you loved reading!"

"You could have picked out a book, though." Impossibly, Jane sounded hurt, although she was still laughing. "You know, I don't think I ever used the gift certificate. I mean, after everything happened."

The light changed, and they barely made it through the intersection this time, moving at a snail's pace. She watched the boy swim through the weeds by the side of the road until they gained on him, pulled ahead, and finally passed him. In the rearview mirror he looked almost motionless.

She turned back to Jane. "Look, pull the car over. Do you want

me to get you the newest Baby-Sitters Club book? They're probably on number ten thousand by now."

It worked. Jane laughed and turned the music up.

In Montrose, they parked the car outside a hair salon that had a
tattoo parlor upstairs. They got out, and Jane took a deep breath.
This must be where Jane went to feel like Houston was her city,
not just some place she accidentally wound up because her parents
lived there. The sad part was Jane's pride in her insider knowledge,
as if it were hard-won. As if anyone couldn't walk into any city and
find the artists and gays and addicts and tattoo parlors within half
an hour by bumming a couple of cigarettes and picking up the free
papers on the street corner.

The salon was full of clients, but the woman behind the counter
eyed Julie and said she could get her color started and then cut her
next customer's hair while the dye was processing. Julie eased into
the chair, felt the woman's fingers in her hair, and saw her look
down critically; she said, "Short and red," fast, before the woman
could comment on her roots. The woman met her eyes in the mirror and said, "Okay, hon, let me get the book." She left and came
back with a floppy binder full of inch-long swatches like the silken
manes of tiny horses or trophies of all the girls she'd ever been.
Julie pointed to one, and the woman nodded. "Oh, sure, number
eight, that'll look good on you," and she disappeared into the back
to mix the dye.

Jane stood behind her, looking at her face in the mirror. "Mom'll
freak," she said. "But I think it's going to look amazing."

"What do you want to do while I'm cooking?"

"Look at magazines, I guess." Jane shrugged. Julie could see the realization dawning in Jane's eyes that there was nothing particularly special about this place. Anywhere must seem hip when you're getting your hair dyed to piss off your mom.

That gave Julie an idea. "You could go upstairs," she said. "Get a tattoo while you're waiting."

"Think I'm made of money?"

"Don't you have a credit card?"

"Mom cosigned. It'll show up on her bill."

A wave of generosity, accompanied by the need to get Jane out of the room before it became obvious she had roots, made Julie point at her Anna-bought purse on the floor. "She gave me a couple hundred bucks. Why don't you pay for my hair with your card, and I'll give you the cash? You can spend it upstairs."

Jane hesitated.

"Don't tell me you don't have your next one already picked out." Julie predicted something small and discreet, but visible.

"I was thinking of a little outline of Texas on my left ring finger," Jane admitted.

"So get one!"

"Mom will see," Jane said. "I figured I'd wait—"

"Until what? Until you're thirty? Come on, quit hiding who you really are."

She could tell Jane was eating this up. "You'll be okay down here?" she said, reaching for the purse.

"Yeah. I don't mind magazines." It was true. She used to ogle them in their plastic folders at the library when Cal dropped her off to study for the GED. Once she'd even smuggled a *Better Homes and Gardens* into the restroom and ripped out a picture of a fluffy white cake surrounded by silver and gold Christmas ornaments

—not for the recipe, just the picture. Now the magazine cake was crumpled in a dumpster somewhere in Jersey Village, where the bus had dropped her off, along with her shoes, a cheap gold necklace with a dangling horse charm, and her backpack full of souvenirs. All her earthly possessions. Except—

She lurched forward, but it was too late; Jane was already digging through the floppy bag. Before she could even form the words *Give it to me, I'll find it,* Jane had the wallet in her hand and was fanning the ATM-fresh twenties out of its pocket. Julie sat back quickly, willing Jane not to notice the IDs in the wallet, the phone in the inner pocket of the purse, or her own momentary panic.

But Jane just beamed at the stack of bills. "Thanks!" she said and headed for the stairs.

Just in time. The hairstylist was back in a black apron holding a bowl full of glowing red paste in one hand and a brush in the other. "This is going to be gorgeous," she said, "trust me," and Julie did, she really did. She leaned back and felt the cold goop applied to her part. "We're getting rid of those nasty roots first," the stylist said and continued to chatter, the way good hairdressers do when they can tell you don't want to say much. At one point she said, "My sister and I are like y'all—we look so different, people never believe we're related."

She let the stylist tilt her chin down toward the floor and finally figured out something that had been bothering her since her arrival in Houston. It had been nagging at the corners of her vision everywhere she went, from Target to the therapist to Bobby's Pool Hall to the weathered-brick coffee shop where Jane had insisted on stopping for pastries on the way to the hair place.

Something not quite right, some quality that made the whole city feel like a stage set. Now, surrounded by other clients and with her head pointed floorward, looking under the table with its big mirror, she could see them propped up on footrests on the other side, all in a row: the shoes.

They were pristine. The patent-leather flats so shiny, the soles of the Reebok sneakers fluorescent yellow, the miraculously white leather sandals with gold lions on them framing brightly polished toenails without a single chip. Staring at the floor, she cast her mind back through the past few weeks and saw a parade of flip-flops and leather boots looking as unscuffed as if they'd just come out of the box. She could see, framed by the black plastic smock, her own feet perched on the silver bar in Jane's Converse, which had felt comfortably worn. Now she noticed that the tiny holes in the canvas—one near the right toe, another on the side, another near the heel—were too perfectly placed. She'd worn through shoes before; the canvas should have been frayed under the laces, the holes should have bloomed unattractively along the seam of the heel, not in neat little ovals in the middle of the fabric, and the rubber should have been thin enough under the soles for her to feel every pebble on the sidewalk. These weren't worn; they were distressed.

She imagined a city divided between those like herself and the kid with the oversize pants—people whose shoes endured a constant pounding, scuffing, sweating, straining, and staining with grass and mud and soft, oozing tar—and those who whooshed past them in SUVs, the ones who never walked more than twenty steps outside each day, much less to a bus stop or convenience store, and whose shoes, therefore, *never wore out.*

She wished for a moment she could tell Cal.

Not Jane, though. Jane had never walked anywhere. She would have found ways to rebel against Anna and Tom without ever having to rebel against that.

The hairdresser tilted Julie's head back up, and she glanced at the ceiling, hoping, for Jane's sake, that the needle upstairs wasn't hurting her too much.

4

If Tom suspects the ovarian cyst is not an ovarian cyst, he doesn't say anything about it, and I, in return, say nothing about the gun that appeared in his hand last night. After we settle Julie on the sofa Monday morning with hot tea and the remote control, she turns on a cable movie that's already halfway over, one of those holiday-themed romantic comedies with six different plots so isolated from one another that most of the stars probably never shared a soundstage. I notice *A Little Princess,* which I went back and got her that first week, still lying in its plastic wrapping on top of the Blu-ray player.

I sit next to her with her feet in my lap under the afghan, rubbing them absently. She looks incredibly weary, and within fifteen minutes she has fallen asleep, her night in pain having caught up with her.

I move her bundled feet gently off my lap, slip the remote from under her arm, and mute the television just as some stockbroker in a natty suit looks up, realizes it's five minutes until midnight, and tears out of his office to propose to the actress on the other side of the movie. Tom is in the kitchen, putting the breakfast dishes away before he goes upstairs to work.

The thought of Tom's presence in Julie's room is not the only reason I don't want to go back to bed. The tiredness nags at me, but something else does too.

"I have to pick up some papers from my office," I say. "I hate to leave just now, but she'll sleep for a while." I glance at Julie. "And I need to get it over with so I can start working on grades." Tom doesn't need to know that I've successfully lobbied the chair of my department to let me turn in final grades at the end of the summer. It's amazing how sensitive department heads are to my particular brand of family emergency—the kind that involves knives and young daughters and the national news.

Tom looks at me mutely from the kitchen, and I admit to myself that I'd feel better if I knew how long I've been living in a house with a loaded gun. "Will you be around in case she wakes up?" I ask instead.

"Of course," he says. "Is she—"

"I told you, she's fine," I snap. Then soften. "I just don't want her to wake up all alone."

He nods.

On the phone with Carol Morse in the car, I must sound a little off, although I feel my request to see her is perfectly reasonable. After all, she's invited me to make an appointment with her before. "Do you want to come in with Julie this afternoon?" she asks.

I know Julie won't be coming this afternoon—she'll be sleeping. But I can tell Carol about that when I see her.

"No, I thought this time I would just—I want to see you by myself."

"All right," she says, and then, "I have a cancellation this morning at eleven. Can you make that?"

It's probably her lunch break. Maybe I sound worse than I think I do.

I kill an hour at the paperback bookstore next to her office, thumbing through romances and mysteries. When I walk in, I'm somewhat surprised to find her younger than I remembered, no older than me, and wearing chino capris. For some reason, this bothers me.

"Come in, come in," she says and gestures me over to a sofa with a woven blanket draped over one arm. I notice a box of tissues sitting on the side table by a lamp with an artfully lumpy ceramic base, and I wonder if Julie ever cries here. Carol Morse closes the door and sits opposite me in a low-backed chair.

"Thanks for fitting me in," I say, suddenly nervous. "I hope this is—it's a little strange. It's about Julie."

"How is Julie?" she asks with an appropriate degree of concern.

"Fine. Well, not fine," I say. "She's sick today, so she won't be coming in." Carol just looks at me, but for some reason I don't want to tell her about the hospital. Right now it's the only secret Julie and I share; perhaps I'm afraid to find out Carol already knows. I continue, probing to see whether she'll volunteer the information on her own. "I was sort of hoping you could help me out with Julie a little. I feel like—I feel like she's keeping things from me. And I know you can't talk about what she says to you, but I have some things to tell you that might change your mind on that."

"On patient confidentiality? That's impossible."

"Even for a parent?"

"Especially for a parent." She looks at me levelly. "Anna, are you aware that your daughter hasn't come to her sessions for the past two weeks?"

After a stunned pause, I manage to say, "Carol, how could I be aware of that, since nobody bothered to tell me?" She stays silent for long enough that I become uncomfortably conscious of my hostile tone. "I mean, no, no, I had no idea. She's been saying she's coming here, I just assumed—I mean, wouldn't you think we would want to know that?"

"Julie is an adult," the woman says coolly. "Her appointments are completely confidential." I have a sudden picture of Carol Morse at home with her husband, listening to Fleetwood Mac in the Jacuzzi she surely has on the back deck of the house she purchased by taking strangers' money for reassurances that their lives are okay, that everything will work out.

With difficulty, I control my urge to get up. "She was here for the first two sessions, I know she was," I say. "Can you tell me anything about what she said? Can you tell me—anything at all?" I have to get something out of this woman. "Please. She hasn't told us anything beyond what's in the police report. Which—" I can't bring myself to say that what she told the police isn't true. Not all of it anyway.

While I am searching for the words to tell her about the hospital and the ultrasound, Carol Morse says, "Have you asked Julie?"

Have I asked Julie? Have I—something shorts out in my brain. I want to stand and shriek; I want to knock over the artful ceramic lamp and fling the woven throw to the ground and stomp on it.

Instead I ask, "Do you have children?"

"No, I don't," she says evenly.

"I can tell," I say. I grab my purse, standing up.

"Mrs. Whitaker," she says.

"Dr.," I snap.

"Dr.—"

"Davalos."

"Dr. Dava—"

"Oh, you can call me Anna."

"Anna," she says, refusing to take the bait. She's not even standing, and although I want to storm out, somehow the fact that she is still sitting in her low-backed chair keeps me from doing so for a moment longer. "Anna, Julie has had an incredibly difficult time. I can tell you that much. The trauma of what she's been through is not something most people can imagine."

She wants to talk about trauma.

"Many survivors of sexual abuse feel an overwhelming sense of shame," she says. "Especially when the abuse is prolonged and combined with other trauma. She needs to feel that she's safe talking to you."

"Of course she's safe," I say. Angry tears have started streaming down my face despite my efforts.

"She's not sure how to relate to her family anymore, or to anyone who hasn't been through what she has. She might protect you from the details because she doesn't want to make you sad or upset."

"Just tell me," I beg.

"Your job is to let her know you love her, no matter what happened."

"Please."

"Anna, don't you want to come sit down? We have thirty more

minutes in this appointment. I feel like it would be good for you to talk to someone as well. Don't you think that's true?"

I get out of there and into my car so fast I'm almost halfway home before it occurs to me to swing by the university. Both to substantiate my lie—there might really be student papers, after all—and to sit behind a closed door with a lock on it and think. I don't want to see or talk to anyone right now, not even Julie. When I get to my office, I notice a flashing red light on the phone, indicating that I have messages. It takes me a second to figure out how to retrieve them; hardly anybody calls office phones these days. The first three messages are from reporters, and I delete them without listening past the introduction.

After the fourth beep: "Uh, Dr. Davalos, this is Alex Mercado. I'm a private investigator. I know you aren't talking to the press right now, and I don't need to ask you any questions. Actually, I have some information to share with you—some things I think you'll be interested in knowing. So, uh, give me a call back." He leaves a phone number. "Again, it's Alex Mercado, and I'd like to meet somewhere and talk face to face, if that's okay."

"End of message," says the female voice recording. "To repeat this message, press—"

I copy the number down on the second listening. Then I listen to the message two or three more times before deleting it, just to make sure I'm really hearing someone self-identify as a "private investigator" on my voicemail. I am.

We never hired a PI to find Julie. We had so much faith in the police then—a thought that presses a burst of angry laughter out of me now. I suppose I thought of private eyes as a solution only for people in movies. But then, I wasn't the one in charge of the solutions, or much of anything, for a while. The first thing I do now is turn on my desktop computer and Google *Alex Mercado private investigator*. He comes up right away under a link for AMI Inc., which leads to a website so corny I think, *There's no way this isn't fake.* There's actually a fedora in the logo. What next, a magnifying glass? I open a new tab and start looking around for websites where PIs are registered, searching for credentials.

Back when Julie disappeared, there were crackpots. We didn't want to change our number because we still believed she might try to contact us, and even though the police had a special tip line set aside for Julie, we still got the calls: *I have information you'll want to know,* they always said, or *I saw her, I swear to God it was her, she's in Tucson,* or *She's in Jacksonville,* or *She's in Missouri City.* One or two of them refused to be referred to the police. *It has to be you, and it has to be in person.* Needless to say, the police were listening in on our line, which I assume had as much to do with their suspicion of Tom and me as anything else — God, what a time — and the calls must have all been traced to lonely middle-aged men living with their ailing mothers or teenagers playing games of truth or dare because none of them turned up any leads.

At the time, I found it hard to believe that so many people would want to be a part of such a horrible circumstance, but in the years since, the years of forgotten nightmares and long commutes past her hundreds of imaginary graves, I have almost felt I understood them. It's so easy to forget how terrible the world is. Tragedy reminds us. It is purifying in that way. But when it starts to fade, you have to return to the source, over and over.

When I find a reliable-looking registration site searchable by ZIP code, I'm surprised to find that Alex Mercado Investigations is the second name to come up. On the AMI website, I click the

About Us link and am treated to Alex Mercado's credentials: Almost three years as a police detective in the special victims unit of the Houston Police Department. Six years as a private detective. A few links to news stories about crimes that the agency claims to have helped solve; one of the links mentions his name.

I pick up the phone and dial. A male voice answers after the second ring.

"Alex Mercado Investigations. Is this Anna Davalos?"

"Yes," I say, a bit startled, although of course he would have caller ID. "You left a message earlier."

"Thanks for getting back to me," he says. "Look, I realize this is a little odd, but I would really like to meet with you and talk about some things."

"About Julie?"

"Of course. I don't feel comfortable saying more on the phone. Would you be able to meet me somewhere?"

"Yes, but it has to be today. It has to be now." It's remarkable how easy it is to finish this conversation: I suggest a diner, not the cutesy retro kind you find around my neighborhood, but a Waffle House near the freeway. I feel my pulse racing, but my voice stays absolutely cool and untroubled as I say, "I'll meet you there in half an hour." It's like I set up things like this every day.

Just before I'm about to hang up, he asks one last question, as if he can't resist. "Have you ever heard of Gretchen Farber?"

"No," I say. "Who's that?"

"Don't worry about it," he says. "I'll see you in half an hour."

Gretchen

made one mistake, and the mistake's name was Cal. He was supposed to be another rung on the ladder out of the dark hole she had come from. It was her fault he'd become more.

At the time, she'd been planning her next move for so long it felt inevitable. As soon as the set was over, she smiled, murmured "Thank you" into the mic, and slipped offstage fast. She headed toward the ladies' room but swerved past it fluidly at the last second, slipping out the back door instead and then pounding through the alleyway and around to the front entrance. Then she waited. One minute, two minutes, three minutes, heart throbbing painfully from the sprint and her skin prickling in the chill. Coatless, her black Salvation Army trench still slouched up alibi-style next to her purse backstage. At least it wasn't raining, for once, aside from a little halo of mist around the neon club sign.

And then he was there, pulling his collar up as he emerged onto the sidewalk, the neon light shining pink on his shaved head. She steeled herself to make his dreams come true, trying to look as if she'd been waiting for someone else when he happened to step into her path. "Hey, do you have a cigarette? I'm dying."

He just looked at her, blinked for a moment, then broke into a helpless smile. "I don't smoke," he said. "I'm sorry."

"Don't be. It's a nasty habit. I'm not supposed to be doing it. If my band sees me, they'll kill me." She gestured toward her throat, opened her mouth, pointing into it as if he could see the damage that cigarettes had already done to her vocal cords. Then she remembered Will's hands at her neck, how she'd worn a turtleneck but couldn't sing for two days afterward. Will had told Dave and Len she had laryngitis.

"Are you okay?" he asked suddenly, his smile going out.

She had only thirty more seconds to get this settled, so she let herself come a little unsewn, just enough to throw a natural wobble into her voice. "Rough night," she admitted. "Honestly, I kind of need a break from those guys. Where are you headed?"

"Nowhere," he said. "Home. Do you need a ride?"

"Yeah," she said. "If you're okay swinging by a drugstore or something for smokes." She laughed. "I'm sorry, I feel like a complete weirdo."

"No, it's okay," he said, and she knew it was far more than that. She was still watching the door just behind him out of the corner of her eye. Plenty of people were smoking under the sign, but there was no one out here she didn't want to see—yet. The door flapped open incessantly, burping out a few more plaid-flannel shirts each time. He noticed her noticing and twitched to look over his shoulder, and she willed her eyes to become china plates fixed on his until he stopped.

"I'm Cal," he said, extending a hand. "And it's right around midnight, so you"—he gestured toward the dingy marquee—"must be Gretchen."

She wasn't, but he was so proud of that line she knew immediately he didn't have any others. So she just nodded yes and grasped his warm hand, cracking open a little at the thought of all the things he was taking on faith. When she said, "Thanks, Cal," her voice broke again, not on purpose this time, and she pulled her hand back fast; he took a step forward, like you do when you see something just beginning to topple off a shelf.

She righted herself and said, "So, where are you parked?"

"That way." He pointed, and she let him march past her with just the faintest brush of shoulders, falling in a little behind. Giving him some time without her in his sightline so that he could reflect on his unbelievable good luck. That idea was so sad she almost laughed. She hoped he would forget about the cigarettes, because although she could hold a lungful of pot for a minute and a half before letting it out, cigarettes made her cough and cough.

He didn't forget. The car slowed down five blocks from the club and he prepared to turn into a gas station.

"What I really am is hungry," she said suddenly, like a confession. "Are you hungry?"

"I could eat."

"Do you know anywhere that's open? I've only been to Seattle for gigs, I don't know anything around here."

"Sure, yeah." Cal seemed unfazed by the sudden switch. "Do you have to get back anytime soon?"

"I'm just hungry," she repeated.

She wondered if they'd found her purse sitting under the stool yet, then realized Cal was saying something she'd missed. "I'm sorry, what? I'm—"

"You're tired too," he said. "I was just saying it was a great set. Are you always this worn out after a performance?"

"No," she said, leaning back into the passenger seat as the warm, familiar exhaustion of being borne away washed over her. The feeling of leaving: a perfect feeling, better than any safety in the world.

She was glad when the diner turned out to be fifteen minutes out along a highway between tall traffic barriers and taller trees. It was dark, but she could barely see the Space Needle poking up over a hill; that was how far away downtown was, with the club, and the van, and Will, who would by now be looking around impatiently, maybe sending someone into the ladies' room to check on her.

Cal opened the door for her. The diner had steam on the insides of its windows and smelled wonderful.

"This is perfect," she said as they slid onto the curved benches of wood-grain Formica. She ordered a burger and fries. Cal got a tuna melt with a salad.

"So you come up here for gigs a lot?" Cal asked.

"You should know."

He blushed. *Very pretty,* she thought.

"Yeah, I've seen you a few times," he said carefully. "You guys play a lot in Portland?"

"A couple times a week," she said.

"How long have you been singing?"

She looked for something on the table to play with, found the ridged white saltshaker. "I've been with the band six months."

"Do you like it?"

"I like being good at it," she said.

"That's not really the same," he said. "Do you like the *feeling?*"

"I like the *feeling* of being good at it."

"I mean, do you need to sing to live? Because when I see you up there, you look like you do."

"Well, I don't," she said, annoyed by the idea. "I'm just trying to do a good job."

"Well, that's what you look like. It's amazing to see. It's—like nobody else should see it, you know?"

"Yeah, that's what Will thinks too," she said with a short laugh. "I'm the only reason we're getting booked or he'd lock me up and make me sing just for him."

"I didn't mean that," Cal said.

"I know you didn't. But that's what it's like."

Cal furrowed his brow, obviously trying to think of something to say. She decided to save him the effort.

"He hits me," she said levelly. "I'm running away from him."

"He hits you."

"And I'm running away from him."

He took the saltshaker out of her hands and set it upright in front of her. She could feel him taking in, for the first time, her lack of a coat, her lack of a purse. Now was the moment when he would also surmise, correctly, that he was buying her dinner. She tried not to hold her breath waiting for his next question.

"How can I help?"

She looked into his eyes, which were dark brown with watery blue rings around the irises, and made her voice soft. "You're helping right now. Didn't you know?" She took the shaker back and laid it on its side, spun it around so that a few tiny salt grains flew out onto the table with every whirl. She let the salt lie, knowing instinctively how much he wanted to sweep it away. He didn't.

The food came. She picked up the burger and crammed in a

bite. Out of the corner of her eye, she noticed Cal giving a thank-you nod to the waitress, and only after she walked away did he unroll his fork and knife and spread the paper napkin in his lap. Then he picked up the knife and cut the sandwich in half diagonally.

"Wow," she said.

"What?" He picked up one triangle and bit off the corner.

Her mouth full, she gestured toward his sandwich with the hamburger in her hands.

"I like to eat one half at a time, in case I want to take the rest home," he said. "And I find triangles aesthetically pleasing."

"That's creepy." She laughed. "Like a serial killer."

"How old are you?" he asked.

"What an impolite question!"

"Forget it," he said. "You're obviously not old enough to want to hide your age, so you must be too young."

"Twenty-seven."

"Bullshit," he said.

"How old are you?" She put a French fry in her mouth, left it between her teeth for a moment too long before biting down.

He raised an eyebrow at her. "Too old for you."

"Forty?"

"Thanks." He laughed. "Thirty, actually."

"I'm twenty-five."

"Yeah, I bet," he said. "Christ. Shouldn't you be in college or something?"

"I graduated early," she said. "I'm a fast learner."

"How about that," Cal said.

"You're not, though."

"How do you know?"

She aimed a French fry at his nose and fired. "Because you didn't see that coming."

She hadn't seen it coming either. This flirtatious buoyancy was new to her. She'd never been anything but sultry or sweet with Will, as the situation demanded; with Lina, silent and compliant. She wondered in a detached way how much of this was an act, how much a real response to the warm diner, the food hitting her stomach, her muscles relaxing. The absence of fear, for the first time in months.

Meanwhile, Cal was studying her with a serious expression. "Listen, Gretchen," he said. "I can find you a place to stay for a while."

"Can I stay with you?"

He hesitated. "Do you have anyone else you can call?"

"Do I look like I have anyone else I can call?" she said with a gesture that took in the two of them, alone, and the midnight diner.

"Well . . ." He paused, then sighed. "I guess you can crash at my place tonight."

"You do this often? Offer strangers a bed?"

"I knew someone else who had to leave a bad situation in a hurry once," he said, ignoring her provocation.

She'd stopped listening, though, after the word *tonight*. The rest would come. Once she was inside his house, she knew well enough how to make it stick. She just didn't know it would stick for her too. That was her mistake.

5

Alex Mercado looks about ten years younger than any private investigator I've ever seen in a movie or TV show. He has a round, boyish face, tan and clean-shaven. To my relief, he's not wearing a fedora—I realize now that I've been picturing him in one because of the website, but of course he's dressed unobtrusively, in jeans and an untucked polo shirt. Nevertheless, in a Waffle House sparsely populated with single men drinking coffee alone in booths, I can tell right away which one is looking for me, and he confirms it by standing and leaning over to shake my hand across the booth.

"I'm Alex. Thanks for coming," he says and gestures for me to sit across from him. The brown plastic of the booth squeaks as I slide toward the wall with its frosted-glass partition on top. It's been a long time since I've been in a Waffle House. Looking around, I wonder if this is the type of place where my students hang out when they're hung over. Its smell—cinnamon apples and slightly rancid cooking oil—is strangely pleasant.

"You come here often?" I ask. "I think I've seen you here before."

He looks slightly taken aback, and I think, *That's for the caller ID, buddy.*

"I just wanted somewhere we could talk without being interrupted," he says. His voice is a little raspy, but instead of making him seem older, it makes him sound almost adolescent, like his voice is breaking. He looks around and laughs. "There's only one waitress working the floor right now, and believe me, she's not all that attentive."

"Just so you're aware, my husband knows I'm here."

"Okay," he says. I can tell he doesn't believe me.

"Shoot," I say to get the pleasantries over with.

"I know this is a delicate subject," he says, pronouncing the word *delicate* with more attention to each syllable than is usual. "I know you're probably feeling very—"

"Yes, I am," I say. "So what's this all about?"

"Have you talked to your daughter about what happened?"

"The police report—"

"I know what's in the police report."

"You do?" I have, of course, seen news footage from the press conference the police gave, but without the family there as a central attraction, it went fast, just someone speaking the words *safe and sound* and *human-trafficking task force* and then *safe and sound* one more time amid flashing cameras while Julie's seventh-grade picture floated in one corner and a banner scrolled across the bottom of the screen: KIDNAPPED 13-YEAR-OLD HOME SAFE EIGHT

YEARS LATER. Certainly no details from the police report have been released to the public. "How do you know?"

"I read it," he says.

"How?"

"I'm a PI, I have my ways. But I didn't ask about the report. Have you talked to your daughter about what happened?"

"I was there when she gave her statement."

He just looks at me.

"We don't spend every waking minute talking about it," I say. "If that's what you mean."

"You don't want to know?"

"I don't want to pry."

"Mrs. Davalos."

"*Dr.,*" I say without thinking, but he presses on.

"Have you noticed any inconsistencies in Julie's story?"

Four missed therapy appointments. A tattoo. The look on her face when she saw the ultrasound screen. Her voice: *Get out.*

"Has it ever occurred to you to wonder—" He breaks off and drops his voice, putting on a serious face, not quite apologetic, but concerned. "Look, Mrs.—*Dr.* Davalos. There have been cases of—it's unusual, but frankly, so is a missing child showing up on her own eight years later, out of nowhere. Even after just three days, when no ransom has been set and there's a weapon involved, the likelihood of recovery—"

"I'm aware."

"Now, the cops aren't going to question it. She's home, she's safe, and she's not their problem anymore."

"They're still looking for—"

He cuts me off. "Sure, it would look great for them to pull in the bad guy after all this time, expose a human-trafficking ring. Terrific headline. But I have to tell you, Doc, from what I read, that is one bizarre trafficking ring. You don't kidnap a kid in Texas and drag her across three states if you're trying to get her to Mexico. The border's right there."

"Maybe the kidnapper didn't have a plan," I say.

"Sure," Alex says. "Maybe he's a garden-variety psychopath— I mean, they're not that common, but maybe. And he sees her somewhere, who knows where, and takes her opportunistically, on an impulse, and then he needs to get rid of her fast after— okay. And he happens to bump into this trafficking ring, and she winds up in Mexico with El Jefe the drug lord who lives on a compound right out of a movie." He pauses, shakes his head. "That was a gutsy move, but smart."

"What do you mean, smart?" I say. "What move?"

"Because now the FBI is involved." He's starting to talk more to himself than to me, the concern yielding to an expression I find almost unbearable—one of *interest.* "Then there's the statewide task force, HPD, and the county, all these levels trying to work together. Everything gets complicated, and it gets slow. The investigation could drag on for months and months. And in the meantime, do you think the cops *want* her face in the media, reminding everyone how they dropped the ball for eight years? Why do you think that press conference went by in such a hurry? You think they want to remind everyone that America's kidnapping sweetheart just wandered back on her own?" Alex has been talking rapidly, and now he pauses, so I know I am in for it. "Especially when she was probably right under their noses the whole time, and they didn't do anything to save her?"

"Under their—" *But she's safe,* I think.

He pushes a large manila envelope across the table to me, and although I feel a warning signal going off somewhere in my head —*Don't open it, don't open it*— I pry open the metal fastener and lift the flap. I lay it flat on the table, put two fingers in, and slide out some articles and a photograph. The photograph doesn't make sense to me at first, and then it does, for a brief sickening instant —scraps of rotting fabric, and something worse—and I look away and catch a glimpse of the headlines: *River Oaks. Houston Neighborhood.*

Remains Found.

I push everything back into the envelope and press the flap over the fastener as my stomach heaves into my throat.

"Who hired you?" My voice is shaking.

"I was just starting out on the force when your daughter disappeared," Alex says conversationally, without answering or touching the envelope, as if suddenly we've been lifted out of this nightmarish Waffle House and dropped into the getting-to-know-you phase of an awkward first date. "I hated it. I was out in a couple of years. Believe me, to walk away from those benefits just gets harder, so if you find out it's not for you, you have to leave fast." He laughs once. "My wife evidently thought the same thing."

"Who hired you?" I repeat.

"Nobody—"

"Then what the hell are you trying to do here?"

A waitress walks up with a tall plastic carafe in hand, and, unbelievably, Alex gestures toward his cup and lets her fill it up. He gives her a little nod of thanks and watches as she walks away, then turns back to me. As he opens his mouth, I feel a buzz at my hip. Tom must be wondering where I am. What time is it anyway?

"Anna, I was there. Don't you want to know why they never found your daughter?"

"I assume gross incompetence was an issue." The sound of my first name in his scraping voice makes me so angry I can barely contain myself. It's time to end this farcical conversation. "I have to go," I say, standing up. Distantly, I feel my phone vibrate in my purse a second time.

"You want the truth. So do I. Well, I have reason to believe the truth is . . . worse than we thought. What's in that envelope"—he's talking faster and faster, jabbing his pointer finger at the unspeakable thing burning a yellow rectangle on the bottom of my cornea—"they're not even going to compare it with your daughter's dental records. Julie Whitaker's been removed from the missing-persons database. I checked."

"Because she's home," I whisper. Lying on the sofa under an afghan.

Brr. Another text.

"They think the remains are eight to ten years old, Anna. They think it's a thirteen-year-old girl. But Julie's name won't come up at all—"

"Why should it?"

"—unless you introduce a reasonable doubt that the woman living in your house is not who she says she is."

"The woman living in my house?" I repeat, like an idiot.

"Could you just do me a favor? Could you get me a sample of her DNA? Some hair off a brush, ideally."

Brr. Brr. I pull the phone out of my purse, look down briefly, read Tom's latest text, and feel suddenly dizzy.

But Alex goes on. "I have a friend in the crime lab who'll run a hair sample and see if it's a match. We don't go to anyone, and no one finds out, not even her, until you're—until we have an answer."

"I'm sorry." I push the envelope back across the table, like an entrée I can't finish.

"Put it this way. You're sure it's her? Okay. So this is just confirmation, peace of mind." He looks at me shrewdly.

Brr.

"But you're not sure, are you? Not entirely."

He's still seated with his hands folded in front of him on the table, but it feels like he's looming over me, reaching into the innermost recesses of my mind, putting his fingers all over everything. It's the kind of violation that implicates you through and through, like failing to set the alarm or leaving the door unlocked or simply living in a world where anyone can walk into your kitchen and take your daughter away at knifepoint. A world where that can happen is a world where I can fail at every act of faith and trust, a world where the best thing that ever happened to me is just another mask for the worst thing, and the worst thing that ever happened to me fits inside a manila envelope, fits into two words, really: *Remains Found.*

"I'm sure," I say.

"You have my number," he says. He doesn't offer me the envelope again. "Call me if you want to talk more."

My phone is buzzing continuously now. I have to get home to Tom and face the punishments already raining down on us for my doubts. I start toward the door. It feels like I've been gone forever, impossible to believe I stormed out of Carol Morse's office just a few hours ago. But the thought of the missed therapy appointments suddenly gives me a use for the wrecking ball in the booth behind me. I turn and take a couple of quick steps back toward the table.

"I don't give a damn about *that*," I say, refusing to look at the envelope again. "But if you really want to help me, find out where she goes on Tuesday and Thursday afternoons. She leaves the house at one thirty. Follow her."

"I thought you'd never ask."

"This is not pro bono," I say. "This is for me. I'll pay."

"Okay." He nods. "But you do something for me too, Anna. Search for a band called Gretchen at Midnight. Look for a video on YouTube. Tell me whose face you see. And if it changes your mind, call me."

Vi

woke up at seven in the morning with a stiff jaw and sticky yellow stars behind her eyes. Will was still passed out beside her, snoring and rasping.

For a moment she didn't remember why her jaw hurt. Then she stepped into the bathroom and saw the shower curtain half pulled down and the shampoo bottles arrested mid-roll in the tub, remembered his hands holding her neck against the wall under a rain of water. When he'd released her, she'd grabbed at the curtain blindly to keep from falling, with predictable results. She'd stayed huddled there, listening to the sound the water made hitting the plastic curtain over her head, waiting for him to come back and yell at her for the mess she'd made. He never came.

It was the first time Will had hit her, but not the first time she'd thought he was going to. She was already intimately familiar with the song he'd sing when he woke up after a night like last night. How could he trust her, with her past? Dancing for all those men—women too—more than dancing. That was the first verse. Then came the chorus, in which he avoided last night's sour names, just cried and swore he'd never believe he was enough for her. Second verse, same as the first. Then, best of all, the bridge: Didn't she understand he'd been betrayed before? He was a virgin until he was twenty-two because his college girlfriend said she wasn't ready, but then it turned out she was sleeping with someone else. He'd been a perfect gentleman, and she'd *betrayed* him.

Vi always pretended she was hearing it for the first time. He'd cry and cry and beg for forgiveness, but somehow, it would still be her fault. And his memory of having apologized and groveled and told her the humiliating story once again would only make the next time worse.

She went back to the bedroom and looked at him. Will was beautiful in repose. He had a jaw like a statue's, hard and rounded at the same time, and his bluish whisker shadow made his skin look like marble. She imagined putting her hand on him where his had been on her, just under the jaw, then leaning down and squeezing hard.

His eyelids, almost translucent, fluttered, and she suddenly put a hand to her own tender jaw. The bruises were forming just under the jawline, where they could be swaddled in a scarf or turtleneck. No one would have to see.

Almost as if he knew just where to grab. Almost as if he'd done this before.

The bathroom took only a few minutes to clean up. He would cry, yes, and apologize, but he wouldn't want to see any reminders. He'd want to have sex first thing, when her breasts were still slick with his tears, and she would accommodate him gently, lovingly; there was, even now, a calculating little twitch in her groin at the thought. She lay back down in her underwear and carefully arranged herself in bed next to his still form, draping the sheet over them both, tucking them in. She closed her eyes. She wasn't going to be able to go back to sleep, but that was fine. She used the time behind her eyelids to make a plan.

The plan involved Seattle. Will had been booking gigs there to get her out of town. He was worried she'd fall in with her old crowd again, Lina's crowd, even though none of them would talk to her after the breakup. Most of them she hadn't known well in the first place, so when she was out playing gigs with Will and saw them once in a while, it wasn't strange for them to pretend they didn't recognize her. She did the same.

It didn't happen much, though, because they weren't playing lesbian dive bars anymore. Will had called up two of his old band mates and said, "I have a girl singer." Vi's haunting vocals were laid over electric guitar, and she was singing lead, not backup. The lyrics sounded to her like badly written suicide notes, but you couldn't hear them all that well, so it didn't matter much. Will was right; people liked to see a girl fronting a band. It didn't seem to matter what kind of ripped-up clothes she was wearing; their faces turned up toward her like flowers, like she was an angel of light. And sometimes she really felt like one. The stage lights bleached out her eyeballs under the lids so she felt like she was staring straight up into heaven, and if the lights left dark splotches in her vision after she opened them, it just meant she had to look at the world around her a little less.

The band was called, depressingly, Midnight. But after a while it became clear that people were showing up for Vi, and in a moment of inspiration, Will suggested they change the name of the band to Gretchen at Midnight, after some children's story his mom had read to him when he was little. She was ready to say goodbye to Vi by this time anyway, and, just as she suspected, people started calling her Gretchen. She liked it. Gretchen was a healthier name than Violet, and Gretchen was a healthier girl, not a night bloomer but a bright yellow flower. Her hair grew longer and she started bleaching streaks into it, and the blonder it got, the better it looked with the dark T-shirts and jeans she wore on-stage, and everything was more or less fine.

At least, it was in a holding pattern until she slipped and said something stupid that exposed her, lethally, two different ways at once. Dave and Len were talking about hitting up strip clubs after a gig, and they mentioned the Black Rose. A little high off the crowd that night, she cracked a dumb joke about the dykes who went there for fresh fish, and Will, with his occasional radar for such things, looked at her with a sudden, uncanny flicker of recognition and said, "How do you know?"

She didn't bother denying it; he'd kissed the tiny black rose on her rib cage a hundred times without knowing what it stood for. Now he stared at her and she felt the tattoo burning under her T-shirt, its meaning suddenly unmistakable.

It was over, a fact that she knew right away and he, danger-ously, didn't. From that point on, whenever she stood on the stage glowing like a street sign, he didn't see Vi anymore, he saw Starr dancing under the hot lights, Starr who should have been long gone. After shows, no matter how happy he seemed with the band's share of the door, he said, "Every single person in that room wanted you."

She just shrugged, because wasn't that kind of the point?

At first it turned him on. When they got home, he'd grab her hard, lift her shirt and rub his thumb over the tattoo until the skin under her left breast was bruised and raw, fuck her like he was trying to own her from the inside out. Useless, she could have told him; nobody owned what was in there, not even her. But it wasn't long before disgust eclipsed desire, and then his eyes went black, and fucking her wasn't enough, he had to get in some other way.

The shower rod had broken, and she could feel more breakage on the way. It was time to get out, but her next situation had to be something different. No more Linas, no more Wills. She was done playing a rag doll, whether she got tucked in at night or thrown against the wall.

Anyway, the band was starting to get too popular. At almost every show now, she saw a few glowing rectangles held aloft to record, and she didn't like it. She knew she'd have to plan tight and move fast, because these days Will never let her out of his sight for long. When they were all on the road together, he played her guardian angel, meaning she and Will had a cheap motel room while the rest of the band crashed on sofas. One day soon he'd start making her crack the door open while she peed, and she'd never be alone again, not even in the john.

She started drinking a beer with the band before the show, in the round on the house that took the sting out of dismal pay. Will liked her taking part in this pre-show ritual; he'd warned her enough times, crushing his fifth or sixth empty while she kept herself sharp, not to act any better than she was. The tide would eventually turn, of course, but she thought she knew approximately how much longer she could drink with the guys before that happened. She snuggled up closer to Will to buy herself a little more time, ignoring Dave and Len as much as she could with them all crammed into a booth together, and made sure everyone saw her hit the ladies' room just before they all went onstage together. Will laughed and said it was stage fright, but when the time was right, missing this step would give her an excuse to disappear immediately after the set.

Every time they played Seattle she felt like a kid on a swing, scanning the ground as she whooshed forward, looking for the perfect moment to jump off. She didn't know exactly who she was looking for until she saw him: a man in the audience at the Ploughman she'd seen before, always alone. Just a man, but that night onstage, as the hot red lights lay on her face like a mask she could slip out from under, she sensed him like a wet stain on the front of a blouse, felt him watching her, and when she saw his dark face ringed by lighter faces, a hole in the pale crowd, she knew. She closed her eyes, let her voice hover in the alto register for a few lines, and then reached out for him with her soprano, scaling the stage lights with her voice and bursting upward into the quiet dark at their center like a surfacing diver.

That night in October, with the mantle of drizzle descending again, a curtain that wouldn't lift for the next seven months, she jumped.

6

By the time I get home, I've forgotten all about the video and Gretchen Farber, because she's gone, Julie is gone.

I want to scream at Tom for letting her leave the house. Of course, he doesn't know about the miscarriage, he doesn't know she's supposed to stay off her feet for twenty-four hours. He doesn't know she might be bleeding, she might be hurting. But still—when I get home, she has been gone for five hours with no word, and he is frantic. We drive up and down Memorial, stopping in coffee shops and stores, asking if anyone has seen her. One barista at Starbucks says he thinks he saw her get into an SUV outside.

We aren't so crazed that we don't think of Jane, out somewhere in Tom's SUV. When Jane's phone goes straight to voicemail, the way it does when it's dead, that's when the scenarios begin to spiral out of control. Some men from Mexico have been looking for Julie and have finally found her, perhaps when the girls were together, and they've taken both of them, or it was Jane who picked Julie up, but they were T-boned at an intersection and are now lying comatose in a hospital; catastrophic scenes tantalizing because they're impossible, like lightning striking twice in the same spot. I yell at Tom and Tom yells back and then we hug each other tightly, and Tom calls the police. He's on hold with them when the two girls finally stumble into our kitchen after dark, sopping wet and giggling like mad.

It's the laughter that unhinges me. For the past four hours, since I came home to find both girls gone, I have been sitting at this kitchen table believing with a morbid certainty that this is my fault. That going to Julie's therapist and, worse, meeting with that Mercado person, some crank who got my work number off the faculty website, was a betrayal that meant I was unworthy of having Julie back. As I made my way through the list of Jane's friends —Bella, April, then further, to friends she probably doesn't hang out with anymore but whose parents' numbers we have—and Tom shouted between hold times at Detectives Harris and Overbey and anyone else who would listen, I knew, deep down, that they were gone because of me.

And now they are here, and they are laughing.

"Where have you been?" I ask quietly.

They're still in their sister bubble—Julie and Janie, Janie and Julie, just like old times, though Julie, already detecting something wrong, has started to sober up a little.

"Oh my God, so many places!" Jane puts a hand on Julie's shoulder to steady herself.

"You could start by explaining why you're soaking wet."

"Oh," she says. "Yes. That was mostly an accident." There's something a little hectic in Jane's voice, but I'm in no mood to listen to it. She can see my expression, though. "You tell her, Julie. She likes you." She explodes into nervous titters.

Julie starts to explain. "The traffic was bad on the way home, so we stopped to eat. And then Jane wanted to show me the sculpture garden, but it was already closed—"

"We jumped the wall," Jane says. "I've done it a lot, but this is the first time I've ever been chased off by a security guard!" She's giggling again. "So then we went to that big fountain in the middle of the roundabout in Hermann Park—"

"We wanted to make a wish."

"—and things got a little out of hand. And we went swimming."

"She was taking money out of the fountain!" says Julie, starting to laugh a little again.

"Well, I didn't have any change. I didn't think the wishes would mind being recycled."

They've already forgotten the expression on my face that stopped them in their tracks a moment before. In their minds they're still tumbling together into the broad bowl of the giant fountain, chasing each other through the arcing spray while cars honk all around.

It's too much to bear. I get up from the kitchen table. I don't even know what I'm doing or which one of them I'm moving toward, but Julie sees me coming and melts into the door frame. Without breaking stride, I slap Jane's cheek.

"Anna!" Tom shouts.

"What were you thinking?" I demand. "We must have left two dozen messages. What the hell happened?"

Tom crosses over to where Julie is hugging the door frame and puts one arm around her. He is not standing between Jane and me, but he looks like he is ready to be in an instant.

Jane holds her hand to her face, stunned. "You hit me."

Baby, I'm sorry is what I mean to say, but harsher words come out: "You owe your father and me an apology."

"You hit me," says Jane. "You fucking *bitch*."

"Jane." Tom steps in with a warning tone.

"My phone must have died! Jeez, I'll look if you want." She fumbles through her bag until she finds the phone, pushes the "on" button, and waves it around. "See? Dead!"

"It's your responsibility to keep it charged, always. You know that."

"Since when do you care?" Jane drops the phone back in her purse. "This isn't even about me. I've been five minutes late before and you haven't even noticed."

"You're five hours late, not five minutes," says Tom. "We had no idea where you were."

"I miss dinner all the time," Jane says. "Nobody's ever hit me before. Hell, nothing I do around here raises an eyebrow." She laughs. "Why is it different when she's with me? Is it because you're afraid something will happen to the one who matters?"

"You can take care of yourself," I spit.

"What's that supposed to mean?"

"You let her go once!" I'm yelling now. "You watched her walk out the door!"

Jane's eyes widen. She comes over to me, close enough for me to feel how much taller than me she is. She raises a hand, and for a moment, I think she's going to slap me. Instead, she points to Julie.

"Blame me if you want to, but don't forget, she's standing right over there. You can ask her whatever questions you want."

My eyes follow the pointing finger, and for the first time, I notice Julie's hair, which is wet and plastered to her head like Jane's but starting to dry. I see the short, feathery red cap, fluffed upward at the hairline by a cowlick, and for a moment, I can't even speak.

"I told you she would freak out," Jane says, but nobody pays attention now.

"I'm sorry," Julie whispers.

"Why—" I take a step toward Julie, reach out a hand, and tentatively touch the place over her ears where her long, silvery-pale hair used to be. I ruffle the side hair, pull it forward, check that it's real.

Then I start crying. I can't help it.

"I can't believe this," says Jane. "She's the one who left the house today without telling anyone where she was going. She's the one who disappeared. Not me. Not me!" There's a bandage on Jane's left ring finger that has come loose and is flapping around. When she sees that no one will try to stop her, she doesn't bother stomping, just rushes upstairs and slams the door to her room.

Julie follows, but slowly, one foot in front of the other, wading through my grief like it's a current in a flood, like she might lose her footing and be swept away. She looks as if she has lost more children than I can possibly imagine.

My mother slapped me once.

The summer after fifth grade, Angie Pugh invited me to spend part of my summer vacation with her family in Northeast Harbor. My mother, who had strong ideas about raising girls, reluctantly agreed, but I had outgrown my swimsuit, and shopping for a new one was torture. She stood behind me in the corner of the dressing room, watching with a frown as I tugged each suit over my newly widened hips. The suit we finally picked out had polka dots and a full, ruffled skirt that hung halfway to my knees—I had maxed out my growth spurt the year before and would never be an inch over five feet.

The first day of my vacation with Angie, she made a face at the polka-dotted suit and said, "Here, take one of mine." She opened up a drawer full of bikinis from the juniors' department, bathing suits my mom would never even let me take off the rack. I tried a crocheted bikini with a halter top and beaded hip ties that clicked when I walked. Angie looked at me appraisingly and said, "Now I get what it's *supposed* to look like." She sounded jealous, but only a little; after all, she was the one with the vacation home in Northeast Harbor, and I was the one with the Catholic mother.

For ten days we played tetherball and Ping-Pong, walked to the old-fashioned soda fountain for Coke floats, told each other ghost stories under the covers with a flashlight. At the end of the vacation I gave Angie her suit back, but I hadn't thought about the tan lines. My mother, who did not believe in knocking, came in while I was changing.

As I cried from the sting, she yelled, "Do you know what the men who saw you were thinking? Do you?"

I didn't believe her. To me, it was just a body. But when summer ended I found out that to the boys in my school, the men in the streets, to anyone who looked, it was more than that; it was an open book full of horrible secrets, a dirty magazine anyone could paw through. My mother never hit me again, but I hated her for being right.

My mother died before Julie's hips ever filled out a skirt. She never saw me get my first heart-stop—that moment when you look at your girl in a certain light and see that she'll eventually become a woman, and it reminds you of every boy who put a pencil up your skirt when you walked ahead of him on the stairs, every man who stared at you at the bus stop, every honk on the street, every leering comment. You remember being alone, gloriously alone, reading a book in a sundress, feeling the grass prickling your thighs and the sun on your forearms, and then realizing that you weren't alone at all as a man you were ashamed to feel afraid of walked up and asked if he could put sunscreen on your back. You look at your daughter and it all comes back, every microsecond when you felt that twin surge of shame and fear, but this time it's outside of you, happening to a body that feels like yours but doesn't belong to you, so there's no way to protect it.

It stopped my heart back then. I was scared for her, scared *of* her. I held my breath and thought, *This will be over soon enough. By the time she's a teenager, she'll wise up. Like I did.*

She didn't make it.

"How dare you." Tom is angrier at me than I've ever seen him, leaning down to force eye contact but still looking every inch of the foot taller than me he is. "We do not do that, Anna. We don't do that to our kids."

"You were as scared as I was."

"I don't care how scared you were," he says, his frame growing larger every second. "We agreed: Never in our house. I saw too much of it in mine."

"And how are your sisters doing, Tom?" I say, raising my eyes to his suddenly.

"Scared shitless of their father!" he snaps back. "And probably their husbands too! Is that what you want?"

"*And how many of them were kidnapped and sold to the highest bid-*

der?" I yell. "*And how many of them were raped every day for eight years?*"

"Anna—"

"They were *safe,* Tom! They were *kept* safe!"

He puts his finger right up in my face and bites off every word with a growl. "If you think that's how it felt growing up with my father, you don't know the first goddamn *thing* about safe."

But I'm beyond reason now. The screaming has unleashed something too big to make a sound. I think I am sobbing, but then I realize I am only gasping, again and again, struggling for air. I feel dizzy, and my vision clouds. The next minute I come to, still standing in the same place, crushed against Tom's chest. It is as if he's pushing the air back into my lungs, and the big black thing in me dissolves into ordinary tears.

"Why did she do it," I say, sobbing against him. "Why?"

"You know Jane," he says. "She lost track of time. And Julie, I think she was just feeling cooped up, trapped. You know what she's been through." He shudders and gives a deep sigh. "I was as worried as you—and as angry. But now that we know they're okay, honestly, I think it was probably good for the girls to get some bonding time."

"I meant—her hair."

Tom releases me, takes a step backward, and stares. "You can't be serious."

I know he's kept up with Jane all these years, fighting through the traps she set to keep us away, while I was too happy to believe she didn't want my interference. But Julie—how has he kept up with her too? How does he still have that connection from before? How did he know to move straight to Julie and hold her close when I went straight to Jane and did what I did?

"They're like strangers."

He looks at me with disbelief. "Anna. That's how all mothers of teenage girls feel."

But Julie, as Carol Morse reminded me, is an adult. Tom doesn't know about Carol Morse and the miscarriage, Alex Mercado and the envelope. He doesn't look into those eyes and wonder if they're the right shade of blue and then think to himself, *Would I even know the difference?*

I could tell Tom everything, but I'm the one who let the poison in, and we're already being punished for it. What better proof of my sacrilege than this horrible feeling of not recognizing my own children, kicking them out of the nest for having the wrong scent, striking them when I want to hold them, all because they disappear at odd times of the day and night and I never know what they will look like when they return?

"You're right," I say. "I know you're right."

Tom and I can afford only one fight a night. We are too newly repaired for more. I allow myself to be taken to bed. When he is asleep, I slip into the bathroom with my phone, mute the volume, and search until I find a YouTube video called "Gretchen at Midnight @ Chapel Pub—10/2/14." I push the triangle to play the clip and watch as Julie's face, no bigger than a smudged white thumbprint on the screen, opens its mouth under stage lights and silently sings.

Violet

sang for the first time in Lina's backyard.

Violet never thought of it as *her* backyard, although she'd lived there almost a year, long enough to dye her hair blue and then bleach it and clip it short and start growing it out all over again as a ripe strawberry blond. Short hair was nothing special in this company, of course, but she could tell Lina liked it better show-pony-long, no matter the color.

Lina had friends over, and they'd all been drinking. It had gotten dark and a little chilly, so they lit up the fire pit out back and dragged chairs from the kitchen around it. Lina never smoked pot, so Violet usually avoided it too. It should have been a sign to her that she was ready for a change when, this time, she took the joint that appeared on her left as if by magic, held in Susan's hand. "Vee," said Lina, but she turned and shrugged almost immediately as Violet took a long pull.

Violet relished the small opportunity to remind Lina she was not a knickknack picked up somewhere exotic for a song. Nobody except Lina operated on the assumption that getting Violet off the pole was the same as having bought and paid for her, but it lingered on the air like the smell of fireworks, the scent of a dangerous excitement that was over before anyone else could enjoy it. Expelling a lungful of pot smoke without a sound, Violet handed the joint back to Susan, who grinned handsomely and passed it on.

Once rid of the joint, Susan pulled a guitar from behind her seat.

"Troubadour time already?" said Susan's girlfriend, Beck, from across the circle, where she was wrapped in a woven blanket.

But Susan didn't sing a love song. She began by strumming the guitar with her bare knuckles, and then started up a picking pattern that reminded Violet of running water, dissolving the chords into individual notes. The joint was loosening the knots in Violet's limbs one by one, and the tension of her status as a trophy girlfriend who should be seen and not heard began unfurling like cream in coffee. Susan's fingers on the strings plucked at her arm hairs, her leg hairs, the hairs on the back of her neck.

Then Susan started singing in a throaty alto, a folk song. *She walks these hills in a long, black veil. She visits my grave when the night winds wail.* The song was strangely familiar—or maybe she was just stoned—and Violet's mind raced to grab the tail of each line, never quite catching up. Then the guitar's rounded edge bumped against her bare knee, sending its shiver up her thigh to her cunt, and for the first time, she was attracted to a woman, really attracted. And it wasn't Lina.

Beck was looking over at Susan with an expression in which patience and paranoia mingled—she was high too—but most of the others were still chatting and laughing and clinking beer bottles and wineglasses onto the ground or scraping sandaled feet across the concrete to grab another bottle from inside.

Then Violet started to sing.

At first she sang along with Susan, and then she started to split on the rhyming words — *veil, wail, sees, me* — soaring upward in response to Susan's emphasis, following the bumps of her voice the way she used to follow John David's. And then, finally, she peeled her voice off the back of Susan's, as if she'd been riding along on the back of a bird, and, catching the feeling of flight, spread her own wings. After that it was like dancing. She and Susan breathed in together and spent their breath together, vibrating like two strings on the same instrument.

Outside the pocket of air where they were singing, wineglasses dangled and beer bottles hung in the air, suspended halfway to parted lips.

When the notes knit themselves back into chords, Violet knew it was done, and the high flew out of her just like that, leaving a sleepy vacancy.

The women in the circle clapped and exclaimed over Violet as if she were a precocious child or an animal that could talk. Someone said, "Lina, where have you been hiding this one?" As though she hadn't been to all their poetry readings and dinner parties this summer, not to mention the Black Rose, where she'd watched them get lap dances from her former coworkers.

While Lina lapped up the praise, Susan put a hand on her arm and asked, "Where did you learn to sing like that?"

"Church," she answered truthfully, and because she was still a little high, the word seemed to encompass everything she meant by it, which was John David and the darkness at the center of light and the things both ugly and sweet she would offer anyone if it meant survival. Susan nodded, and Violet thought for a moment she really understood. What could have happened to Susan that she did?

"If you ever want to join me for an open mic sometime," Susan said and patted her arm twice with a wink.

Violet knew by the prickling in her skin, and by Lina's eyes on her, that the circle had become charged with a dangerous energy. She imagined herself transforming into the sputtering, sparkling catherine wheel that would burn down Susan and Beck's life together, forcing them to decide who would keep the condo in Northwest and the restaurant they co-owned and their four-year-old son. She weighed all that against the pot-fueled flickering in her cunt that she could exhaust in a single evening or at most a few weeks.

It was tempting.

She snuffed out the tiny flame. "I don't think I could," she said. Susan was too complicated.

Anyway, saying no to Susan had an upside. Lina was so grateful that when the next chance came around, as Violet had known it would, Lina said yes. And then Violet was singing folk music with trios in little cafés, filling out harmonies here and there with other kinds of bands too, and she felt the satisfaction of belatedly scrubbing away the last of Starr the stripper with the red waterfall of hair down her back, and flipping into her new identity, Violet the singer with the strawberry-blond bob that was growing out, little by little. She drifted from gig to gig, band to band, until she ran into a male drummer.

Will was single, so all she had to break up was a band.

7

When I wake up the next morning, Tom is outside cleaning the pool.

I watch him through the bedroom window as he stands at the pool's pebbled ledge, sweeping the long pole of the vacuum slowly across the bottom like a gondolier. With each measured stroke, last night feels farther away. The tingle in my palm from slapping Jane, Tom's yelling, and, most of all, the face on my cell-phone screen cradled in my palm as I crouched in the bathroom—it's all gone now, washed clean by sleep and early-morning showers. A mistake. A misunderstanding. A blond girl in a blurry video. I grab a pair of fresh jeans out of the laundry basket and pull them on, then feel a lump in the back pocket and find Detective Overbey's card, pulped in the washing machine and fuzzed from the dryer, unreadable. I throw it in the trash.

I take my coffee outside and settle into a deck chair to watch Tom's rhythmic movements. It's one of those rare, sparkling, rain-cooled mornings that occasionally graces Houston in June, a throwback to March, a day you could almost mistake for an ordinary summer day in a more hospitable climate. The shadows of the tall pine trees move on the deck; the breezes that languidly stir their tops back and forth barely reach me. A yellow worm of late-season oak pollen drops into my mug, and I fish it out. We may have our problems, but after all, we are a family again, husband and wife and two beautiful daughters, together at last.

The door opens and Jane comes out, rolling a suitcase behind her.

"Sweetie?" Tom calls as she wheels the suitcase to the car, ignoring us. I hear a car door open, then close again with a thump. As she passes by the deck without her suitcase, Tom says, "Jane?"

"I'm going back. I bought my ticket last night. I'm staying with April tonight, and she's taking me to the airport tomorrow morning."

Tom turns off the vacuum and leans the handle against a tree. "Sweetie—we talked about this. Maybe you need some time to—"

"I want to go back. Now." Tom doesn't ask why. Neither of us do. "Will you take me to April's house?"

"Sure, sure," he says. She disappears back inside. He turns to me.

It's my cue. "I'll apologize," I say. And then, when he looks down at his sandaled feet: "I'm sorry." He doesn't look up as I walk past, but his anger is palpable.

I go upstairs and knock on Jane's door and, when there is no reply, open it an inch at a time, softly saying, "Hey."

Jane is rummaging through her closet. She looks at me over her shoulder and then returns immediately to what she is doing, which is stuffing an open duffle bag full of things she is apparently choosing more or less at random.

Behind me, the shower starts running, and I think of Julie's new hair. I wonder how much of the excess dye will wash down the drain, whether the red will stain the tub. Then I snap back to Jane standing in front of me, back turned.

"I'm so sorry, Jane. There was no excuse for that. We were just —I was so worried."

Jane yanks a sweater off a hanger and throws it into the bag. "Be worried," she says. "You can do it without me around."

I take a step inside the door and close it behind me. She whirls.

"Did I say you could come in?"

"Jane, please."

"Please what? Please stay out of the way so you can be with your other daughter, your real daughter, the one you care about? Please be fine, so you don't have to give me any of your precious time or listen to what I say?"

"Please stay." She looks at me with such longing, her jaw set and quivering, like she used to when she was a child. "Your father needs you."

Her eyes drop to the floor, and when they come up her chin isn't shaking anymore. "I'll go out for breakfast with him on the way to April's. Would that make him happy?"

"I think he would like that, yes."

"I'll miss him. I'll miss both of you—all of you." She wipes her eyes with her flannel shirtsleeve. "I just—can't be here right now. It's making me crazy. She's my sister too, you know. I missed her too. I was frightened too all these years." She looks around at the room, at her closet. "I hate this room. Sleeping here still gives me nightmares."

"We couldn't move," I say. "We—"

"I know, I know, you wanted her to be able to find you. And she did. So that's all that matters. I get it." She goes back to stuffing more things into the bag. "I don't even mind that you've barely asked me about my school situation at all—"

"Jane—"

"Don't. I'll figure it out on my own. I always do." She finishes her job and grabs the bag off the floor, throws it on her bed. "Just don't take it out on me because she found you, not the other way around."

There's a gentle knock at the door, and Jane pushes past me to open it.

Julie is standing in the doorway holding a pair of black high-top tennis shoes in her hands. With her short hair plastered wetly to her skull, she looks older and smaller, almost birdlike.

"You'll need these," she says, holding out the shoes.

"You can keep them," Jane says, her voice roughening around the edges. "I need a new pair anyway."

"Are you sure?" says Julie.

"Yeah," Jane says. "I want you to have them."

"Thanks," says Julie.

"You have my e-mail address, right?" Jane asks. I feel like I should be leaving the girls alone to say goodbye, but they are directly blocking the door, so I just stand, hands in jean pockets, waiting.

"Yeah," Julie says. "Thanks for hanging out. I had a nice time."

"Me too," says Jane. She lunges forward and gives Julie a quick hug. "I love you. I'm glad you're home."

Then she turns to zip up the bag on the bed. She grabs a stack of notebooks from her desk and loops her book bag over one shoulder. By the time she turns back to the door, Julie is gone, the door to her room shut.

I reach out my hand for a bag, but Jane shakes her head, grabs the duffle, and moves out the door. She makes it all the way down the stairs at a brisk march, *thump-thump-thump,* the heavy, purposeful Jane step, as if she's shipping out; I follow in her footsteps more softly and slowly. Tom gets up from the kitchen table when he sees her and steps toward her, reaching out for the bags. She surrenders everything to him, even the notebooks, and he silently carries them out to the car. I keep shadowing her until we reach the back door, where Julie must have hovered long ago, a knife at her back, before taking her last step over the threshold of childhood and into whatever was waiting for her on the other side.

My hands still in my pockets, I want to reach out for Jane's shoulder. I don't, but maybe some invisible part of me does, like a phantom limb, because she turns around anyway.

"Mom," she says, and she buries her head in my shoulder for a second, her arms pinning mine down, almost hurting me.

When she pulls away, I've got tears in my eyes, but I let them stand and subside and pull my hands out of my pockets at last, rest one on her elbow. "I love you," I say.

Her face is serious and a little sad. "Mom," she says. "I think you should know something. Julie has a cell phone. She told me she borrowed one to call me yesterday, but then I saw it in her purse." She reaches into her pocket and pulls out a slip of paper. "I wrote the number down." She gently takes my hand away from her elbow, and the last bit of Jane I feel is her fingers pressing the paper into my palm.

Then she's gone. The car growls down the driveway, and I stand there a bit too long before putting the paper in my pocket, still feeling Jane's touch and wondering absently why she has a white bandage around one of her fingers.

When I turn, Julie is standing by the kitchen island, looking at me. I wonder how long she's been there, what she heard and what she saw.

Starr

learned how to lie at the Black Rose in Portland, Oregon. Not that she'd never lied before — to police officers, to foster parents, to anyone who looked like he or she might use the truth to hurt her. But those were lies she told with words, and anyone who was really paying attention could see through words. At the Black Rose, she learned to lie with her whole body.

She'd washed up in Pioneer Courthouse Square as Mercy with brown, shoulder-length, under-the-radar hair, and walked due east over the river until she was through with walking. She'd passed two other clubs, but the Rose was the first one with a picture on the dingy sign, and the swirls of dark petals surrounded by a spiky halo appealed to her. She didn't even have to take her clothes off to get the job, just show Gary, a tall, skinny guy with a hipster mustache, proof that she was over twenty-one. He explained that she'd be renting her mandatory stage time with watery ten-dollar drinks the customers bought her, ten drinks for one stage dance, twenty for two, and so on. If she didn't make her drink quota, she'd be buying the rest herself at the end of the night, out of the cash she made from lap dances and stage dollars—*after* tipping out the bar, the door, the waitresses, and the security staff. So it would *behoove* her, Gary said, enjoying the use of the word, to hustle as many drinks off her lap dances as she could.

As for rules—well, since deregulation, anything went. No no-touch rule, no three-foot rule, and nothing had to be covered. He gestured over to one of the armchairs that lined the walls, where a dancer was sitting naked in a customer's lap, her legs open, his fingers sunk inside her up to the third joint. The customer's head leaned back against the wall while the dancer rolled on him absently. "Thank you, Oregon Supreme Court," Gary said, with a smile implied but none on his face.

She didn't have to do that stuff, of course. The point was, she could do just about whatever she wanted. She could light her pubes on fire for all he cared. There was just one thing.

"You can't be Mercy. We've got one already."

Starr's first stage dance was on a Thursday afternoon, too early, though you couldn't tell what time it was inside the windowless club, where the fog machine churned day and night. She gyrated awkwardly to the music, slithering out of the makeshift girl-next-door costume she'd cobbled together with a stolen G-string from a mall store, and awaited the exposed and endangered feeling. But the closer she got to peeling the G-string down around her ankles, the more clothed she felt. Naked on the stage save for neon-yellow platform heels, she was unassailable, stripped down to armor that could never be taken off.

When she got down from the stage and walked among her prey, the feeling faded—they were sad daytime customers, and since there was a club on every block, it was nothing they hadn't seen before. The newly eviscerated vice laws meant the strippers could use their bodies to wrest money from wallets with brazen aggression. Some of the girls ended every dance lying on their backs, arms pasted to the floor, waving their legs like strange underwater plants around naked genitals elevated to customer-face level. Their pussies were as dry as mouths left open too long and as impersonal as rubber chickens, but it didn't matter; men stood transfixed, peering into the permanent gooseflesh as if they could will its transformation into warm, wet intimacy. Starr tried the helicopter move at home once, but her abdominal muscles were pathetic. She could barely manage the most basic pole moves, though she was learning from her roommates, most of whom were dancers too.

Gary had pointed her toward the dilapidated Victorian off Hawthorne with half the front steps rotted out and black-taped windows that beaded up and sweated in the never-ending drizzle. She didn't leave anything there; her backpack full of trophies and her slowly growing collection of outfits were safer in a locker at the Rose, and she wore her only jewelry, the gold chain with the little horse charm, around her ankle while she danced.

For all she was addicted to the hot lights on her sweaty skin and the bitter taste of the fog machine in the back of her throat, there was no doubt Starr was a terrible stage dancer. Her lap dances were more successful. She hated being down on the floor amid the stares and gropes and was distant and sullen. But sullen had its own appeal for some, and she had her customers just like the girls who giggled and flirted had theirs. Enthusiasm was not required so long as she got the script right, and the lines were almost painfully easy to memorize; it didn't matter whether or not they believed her, it was all part of the transaction. She learned which customers to tell it was only her first or second time doing this, which to tell that she was saving money for college or some new toys for her kid. With others, she didn't say anything about herself at all, just made a kind of purring noise, as if she felt lucky to be grinding on their crotches.

Still, there were too many strippers and not enough customers. Some of the girls rolled their eyes about the "de-reg" and bitched that a worse thing had never happened. Some nights Starr barely took home anything after tip-out. Plus, there were a million ways you could slip and fall in the newly permissive atmosphere, a million ways you could ruin everything in the split second between a smile and a nod. She had seen girls followed out back on their cigarette breaks by their favorite customers after an offer to make a little extra money and then come back that same night with a black eye or a broken strap, or not at all.

Starr, remembering the Petes, had no interest in these side transactions. But if she said no too many times, she risked losing herself a regular, which meant losing the club a regular, and that wasn't good either. So her job was to say nothing at all, to communicate neither yes nor no but keep looking as if she might say yes someday, as if she were just waiting for the right moment. It was an education in disappearing.

Graduation came when another dancer handed her a plastic tub half full of Manic Panic hair dye in an unmissable shade of red and said, "Trust me. It'll show up under the lights." Advice of this nature didn't come often, so Starr took it and found that being brighter on the outside meant, paradoxically, making an even darker hiding place for herself on the inside.

Over the next eight months she learned it didn't have to be just hair; it could be an accent, or a strange last name, or a fake tattoo on the back of her neck. It could be bright blue eyeliner, a pair of cowboy boots, or something outlandish she made up on the spot when customers asked where she was from: a farm she had grown up on, a famous ballerina she had studied with. When you looked like she did, with wide cheekbones and smooth, white skin and big, blank kewpie-doll eyes, people would accept anything about you but the truth. Whether she told them she'd been a porn star or a prizefighter, they believed her, in a way they'd never believed or cared about her invented baby sister or community college courses. She started making real cash, buying four stage dances a night and entertaining tables of a dozen customers or more who came in just for her. Moreover, they bought drinks for any girls she brought over, and that made the other dancers friendly.

After one particularly full shift, she and a few other girls went down the street and got matching tattoos of the spiky-haloed rose on the club's sign. She didn't know what else she could spend cash on that wouldn't weigh her down.

But the other law of being highly visible was you had to leave while the shine was still on. So when a group of women started frequenting the Black Rose during her shifts, Starr took note.

Lina, short for Carolina, was a fifty-five-year-old El Salvadorian with a short, grizzled mane, a thick neck, and a body that was round and pleasant. Lina came in all the time with her girlfriend, Heidi, who looked a bit like Starr without her makeup. Then one time Lina came in without Heidi, and Starr, who was ready to quit the club and move out of the Hawthorne house, got the message. She left with Lina at the end of her shift.

Lina lived in a huge Victorian in Northeast so high up it was practically on stilts. A beard of ground cover spilled down over a mossy concrete wall that looked barely adequate to keep the front yard from tumbling into the street. A stone staircase studded with clumps of tiny violets pinched shut in the predawn chill led from sidewalk to front door. Starr climbed up first, past gnarled Japanese maples with spidery leaves and bleeding-heart bushes whose hot-pink blossoms looked frozen in the act of ripping themselves open. The rough steps seemed endless after a long shift, but when Starr got to the top, she could see it was going to be worth it. The oval of stained glass in the door was just catching the first rays of sunlight.

Lina opened the door and let Starr in. The floor was made of cool, silky wood, covered with a big, soft rug of yellowish-white fur.

"Alpaca," Lina said, watching Starr's face as she wiggled her toes in the shag. "From home. They're very cheap there. I got that for three hundred bucks."

That didn't sound cheap to Starr, but she just said, "It's nice." The ceiling was vaulted over the living room, and there was a large abstract painting hanging on the wall. It looked like fruit dropped from a great height. "Did you paint that?" she asked.

"As a matter of fact, I did," Lina said. Her voice toughened up and she looked around the room casually. "You like it?"

"It makes me feel a little dizzy," Starr said truthfully. "Can I lie down?"

"Of course," said Lina, and she ushered her out of the vaulted living room and into a side room lined with raw wood where there was a tall bed covered by a shimmering, reddish-orange comforter. The wooden blinds were drawn, and it was blessedly dark. Without hesitation, Starr pulled off her shoes and climbed up on the mattress, which sank under her weight. She slid to the center and flipped over onto her back, exhausted, staring at the motionless ceiling fan of dark wood. She wondered what used to go through Heidi's head when she stared at the ceiling fan. Where had Heidi worked before Lina came along? Had she fallen in love with Lina?

"Why don't you tell me your real name? I don't think it's Starr."

She could feel the tiny beads embroidered on the comforter biting into her spine, like the princess and the pea. "Violet," she said, thinking of the purple flowers outside on the steep lawn. It wasn't the most convincing name she'd ever come up with, but she needed something as good as Heidi—who'd surely made up her name, too, before she'd been extracted as neatly as a tooth so that Starr could occupy her dent in the bed. Wouldn't it be easier if she could just use Heidi's name? She imagined herself saying, *Heidi*, and Lina saying, *What a coincidence*.

But the bed was the softest place she'd been in months, and she accidentally said the second part out loud. Just as Lina said, "What is?" Starr let go of the ceiling fan with her eyes and fell backward into slumber.

8

As the door closes behind her, the superficial layer of animation Jane brings to the house falls away, and the uneasy secrets Julie and I share swell up to fill the kitchen like a scent.

"How are you feeling today?" I ask.

"Okay," she says, placing a hand on her stomach. "Like a bad period."

I nod, remembering my miscarriage. "Did you tell Jane?"

She shakes her head. "No. We were having a nice time. I didn't want to make her feel bad."

"You know, you could have called me to pick you up. If you wanted to get out of the house." She's silent. "We could have gotten lunch or something. Gone shopping."

"More shopping?" she says with a quick laugh. Then she puts on an appreciative face. "I just wanted my sister."

. . . *and now she's gone.* The second half of the statement trails along in its wake like a ghost.

"I'm glad you girls got to spend a little time together. And I'm so sorry for the way I behaved. I just wish we had known where you were." I'm choosing my words carefully, giving her plenty of space, like she's a deer behind a tree instead of a girl behind a butcher block.

"I'm really sorry about that," she says. "I guess I started feeling a little—trapped."

I can't even think about what that word must mean for her. Hearing her say it is different from when Tom said it last night. It makes me feel trapped too, suffocated by grief. Like she's keeping me in a room with all the lights off. I scramble at the evidence of her lies, the paper folded up in the pocket of my jeans, but I am so afraid of confronting her with it that what I end up saying instead is "Julie, I think it's time we get you a cell phone."

She doesn't blink. I let a beat go by before I continue. "For Tom and me, really. So we can reach you, and you can reach us, if you need to."

Should I have waited a moment longer? Was her mouth opening to tell me the truth when I cut her off? *I have one already, it's in my bag, here's a plausible explanation of how I came to have it, along with my very good reasons for not mentioning it.*

At any rate, what she says now is "Thanks, Mom." And I feel a strange relief that I don't yet have to hear the plausible explanation, the very good reasons. She goes on: "Can I ask you something I've been worried about?"

"Of course." *Maybe it is coming, right now, after all.*

"I'm kind of worried about . . . money."

It's so unexpected, so unlike something Jane, for instance, would say, that I just repeat the word blankly. "Money?"

"Well, I know I'll have to get a job at some point."

"Oh, honey, you don't need to think about—"

"But I do need to think about it. I do," she insists. "We haven't talked about what it was like for you guys after it happened, but I know you must have spent a lot of—I mean, I know it's expensive. I've—seen the billboards."

"You have?"

"I looked up some stuff about my case on the Internet," she says.

Has she been on Tom's computer? Or did she use the secret phone?

"I just—I know Dad left his job. And Jane's in college—"

"Your father does fine, and so do I. We're fine, Julie."

"—and now I'm here."

"Which is the best and luckiest and most wonderful thing that could ever have happened to us."

"I know. I know. I just—" She throws up her hands. "I have to figure out what I'm going to do with my life." And then, in a slightly different tone: "I've been applying for jobs, you know."

I'm caught off guard. "What kind of jobs?"

"Oh, anything," she says evasively. "Baristas, cashiers. I even went inside that bar around the corner yesterday—I forget the name—to ask if they needed a dishwasher."

It takes me a moment to realize what bar she's talking about. That squalid, sad little bar in the strip center? Billy's or Bobby's or something? She went in *there?* She's watching my face, hanging on my flickering expressions, so I try to look expectant, like I'm waiting without judgment for her to finish.

"I tried Starbucks too," she goes on quickly, "but I didn't end up applying there. I was too tired. And kind of addled, I guess from the painkillers. That's when I called Jane."

"On a borrowed phone," I add. I can't help it.

"Yeah. I don't know why I didn't call Dad, except I knew Jane had the car and that he would have to walk in the heat to come get me. I didn't want to be too much of a bother. And I was kind of—not thinking too straight."

This whole conversation is a lie.

"Anyway, so I wanted to tell you—I feel really bad about this, but I want you to know where I've been." She takes a breath, steeling herself for the big revelation. "For the past few weeks, I haven't been going to therapy."

I brace myself. She's going to tell me everything. And it will make sense. It will make perfect sense.

"I've just been driving around," she says, and so it's to be another lie after all, I think, and then immediately afterward I'm not sure. "I can't bear to think of all that money it's costing, so I just cancel, and then I drive around trying to figure out what I'm going to do. If I get a job, like as a waitress or something, I can study for my GED at night, and then—maybe I'll go to college too, someday. Like Jane." She looks up on that last phrase with an absurd kind of hope, daring me to disbelieve the emotion underneath those words. It works; the thought of all the opportunities Jane's had, all the opportunities Julie missed out on and that can never be made up, is paralyzing.

My head hurts from trying to separate what's real from what's not. "That's—I'm glad you're thinking about your future," I manage. "I mean, I want those things for you too, if that's what you want. But for now, you have to see a therapist. Someone else, if you don't like her. Money doesn't come into it. We'll be fine, we'll manage."

"You've spent so much on me already," she presses on. "All those clothes, new furniture, and now a phone. And if I ever do catch up enough to get into college—I don't know what college costs, but I doubt there are special scholarships for kidnapped girls."

The word *scholarships* makes me think of something. "The Julie Fund," I say.

"What's that?" she asks.

"The public donation fund in your name. It's how we paid for the billboards and the reward money and—everything else." *We* did? Tom, the accountant, did. He handled everything, while I —who knows what I was doing. I can barely remember the days, weeks, months. "There was a sum put aside for ransom. We were going to use it to set up a scholarship in your name if—" I can't finish.

"Can't we use it now?" she says. "I mean, I'm back."

"It doesn't work like that," I say, groping through hazy memories for the details. "There are restrictions to what public donations can be used for, and somebody who's not in the family has to be in charge of it. Tom and I can't even make a withdrawal without getting in touch with the fund administrator."

Just as I realize I don't know the answer to the next question she's going to ask, she asks it: "Who's the fund administrator?"

"Oh, I'd have to find out from your dad," I reply lamely. "But you're the sole beneficiary."

I look up and realize she's staring at me.

I can almost see the next words forming on her lips, so before she can ask, I say, "Somewhere in the neighborhood of fifty thousand dollars."

She doesn't even try to conceal how much larger the number

is than she was expecting. "Wow," she says. And then tears start wobbling in her blue eyes; her chin shakes. "You must have really wanted to find me."

It's only after she goes upstairs to take a bath, and I hear her sobs coming from the bathroom, that I wonder how she could have read enough to find out about the billboards without coming across anything about the Julie Fund.

The New Girl

was thinking about her next name as she watched Mercedes gather the sheet taut with one hand, lift the mattress corner with the other, flip up a folded white triangle, smooth the crease, and tuck it in. Before she could catch the trick of the fold, Mercedes had already finished and moved over to her side of the bed. It took the more experienced woman fifteen seconds to pull out the new girl's lousy attempt at a hospital corner and refold it.

"It looks like putting on a diaper," the new girl said.

Mercedes paused what she was doing—scooting on one knee from corner to corner as she tucked in the bottom edge of the sheet—and rolled her unusual blue eyes. "Guess you've never done that before either, huh?"

The new girl felt herself flush.

Later, when they were in the supply closet together loading the cart with wrapped rolls of toilet paper, Mercedes said, "Maybe you do have a little one?" The new girl didn't answer right away. "I shouldn't have assumed."

The new girl shrugged and ran the palm of her hand lightly over the spray tops hooked on the cart, feeling for the empties. "Do you have kids?" she asked.

"*Dos,* and that's it for me," Mercedes said, crossing herself with a laugh. "It's all I can handle."

"I couldn't even handle one."

"You're too young," Mercedes said. "Better wait until you're my age."

"How old are you?"

"Twenty-four."

It did seem old to the new girl, enviably so. She'd gotten a nasty shock when she ran out of bus money in Eugene and found out at the first strip club she tried that you had to be twenty-one to work there. Her fake IDs were good enough to get her waved into bars, but she knew they'd never survive close inspection in the back office of a club where alcohol was served. Still, she'd given it one shot with Jessica Morgenstern, her twenty-two-year-old Texas blond-blue, at a second club.

The guy barely glanced at it under the black light before tossing it back to her. "Try across the parking lot," he said. "They hire illegals over there."

She snatched the fake ID back and crossed over to the Budget Village Inn and Suites. Maids made tips, didn't they? She wasn't entirely convinced, but the motel staff was overwhelmed that morning because of some college football game. She hardly had time to think about it, much less drop a fake, before the desk manager, balancing the telephone receiver on one shoulder, shoved a uniform at her across the counter and pointed her toward Mercedes's cart down the hall. "Just do what she tells you, *comprende?*" he said with his hand over the mouthpiece, barely glancing at her.

At the back of the motel, a large storage room full of broken furniture culled from the suites hosted a rotating circle of undocumented workers who didn't have family members in town. The young woman with whom she shared a sprung mattress mumbled in her sleep, but at least it was a bed. The work seemed all right too, at first, and she congratulated herself on her sturdy back and legs, strong from riding horses in Red Bluff.

More troubling to her were the crowds of college-age kids and their parents all decked out in green-and-yellow T-shirts with duck mascots on them, loud and patronizing and always annoyed when they had to cross over to the other side of the hall to accommodate the squealing housekeeping carts. She stared hardest at the blond, ponytailed girls. When she entered their rooms, she touched charm bracelets left carelessly on dressers, expensive-looking bottles of hair conditioner in showers, logoed duffles spilling sandals and pink pajamas onto the floor.

On the third day, searing pains started up in the new girl's shoulders, lower back, neck, and upper arms. She could barely roll out of the storage-room bed, and vacuuming sent shooting pains up through her skull in rhythm with the roar of the machine. That morning, while Mercedes was cleaning a bathroom, the new girl stole a moment to rub her shoulders while the vacuum idled. She spotted a long green-and-yellow ribbon on the dresser, lifted it up, and tied it around her own ponytail, wincing at the burn in her triceps, then stared at herself in the mirror and pursed her lips up in a tight, rosebud smile. When she heard the toilet flush, distant and faint behind the vacuum noise, she yanked the ribbon off. Mercedes emerged from the bathroom holding a dwindled roll of toilet paper and exaggeratedly mouthing the word *Restock*.

After they finished up in the supply closet, Mercedes said, "I know where you've been sleeping, and girl, you're going to kill your back that way. Come home with me tonight. We have an extra bed since my cousin moved out."

The new girl nodded, and Mercedes smiled briefly before wheeling the cart back out to knock on the next door.

Home was a second-story apartment in a red-brick apartment block about an hour away by bus, including fifteen minutes waiting for a transfer in the misty drizzle. The new girl resented having to pick the bus fare out of her meager tips, but when they climbed the stairs after dark she could see from the steam on the kitchen window that a meal was waiting. Mercedes opened the door to the warm sounds of television commercials and a running faucet, and the larger of two small boys lying in front of the TV set looked over his shoulder and said, "Hi, Mom," then turned back as a cartoon started.

From the kitchen, a woman was already talking to Mercedes in Spanish, running through the events of an exhausting day, from the sound of it. Mercedes cut her off, also in Spanish, and gestured toward the new girl, who closed the door behind them and relaxed into the noisy, steamy apartment. The woman who turned from the sink looked about ten years older than Mercedes, but it was hard to tell under her heavy makeup.

"That's my sister Lucia. Sit down," Mercedes commanded, pointing, then she launched into a fresh round of Spanish directed at her sister, gesturing toward the single plate set on the kitchen table. The woman barely glanced at the new girl, not smiling, and shrugged. Wordlessly, she opened the kitchen cabinet, removed a plate, gathered up silverware from a drawer, and set them all on the low counter that separated kitchen from dining area. Then, grabbing the magazine that had been open in front of her on the counter, she walked out of the kitchen, past the children in the TV room, and into the hall.

"Is she okay?" the new girl whispered as Mercedes moved around the counter into the kitchen and started scooping some chicken and rice out of a pot on the stove onto the plate.

"She's fine, she's okay. She watches the kids until I get home, then she has to go to sleep to get up early to open at the department store." But by the time Mercedes had finished serving up her own plate and brought it to the table, another TV had started up in the back bedroom, Spanish voices clearly audible through the thin walls, clashing with the English-language cartoons. "Eat."

The new girl obeyed. The food was good, and she said so.

"It's been a while for home cooking, huh? Lucia's a good cook. She won't let me pick up McDonald's for everyone on the way home; she says the boys have to eat everything fresh." She shuddered over a forkful of chicken. "I couldn't do it with my hours at the motel, but she's going to try to get me hired at the store when she's been there a little while longer."

The new girl felt the warmth of the meal spreading through her. The chicken leg on her plate was so tender, the meat fell off the bone with the gentlest prod of her fork. She thought about what it would be like to have a girlfriend, someone to talk things over with while they waited in the kiosk. She imagined them in their uniforms, side by side on the bus, laughing about—what?

"It's my turn!" "No, *mine!*" The cartoon show's credits were rolling, and the boys were struggling for the remote. When one started wailing, Mercedes snapped her head over her shoulder, the smile dropping from her face like a mask.

"Boys!" she shouted. "It's bedtime! I'll be in your room to tuck you in in five minutes, so start brushing your teeth *now!*" She looked back at the new girl apologetically. "I'll go make sure you've got clean sheets and put the boys to bed. You have more food if you like, watch TV." She gestured vaguely, then got up and walked through the TV room, stopping a few times to pick up toys on the floor before vanishing around the corner.

As closet doors opened and closed somewhere in the apartment and the two boys squabbled over something—"Give it!"—the new girl eyed Mercedes's purse where it lay, unzipped, on the kitchen counter. One half of her brain was still riding the bus into work the next day, and the other half was adding up her tips, subtracting bus fare, calculating if the rest would cover brown hair dye. There was no need to steal money when all that stood between her and real earning potential was a little plastic rectangle saying *Mercedes Rodriguez, California, brown hair, blue eyes, twenty-four years old* lying in an unzipped bag three feet away. If the universe was handing out mercy, she'd take it.

9

Tom doesn't come home after eating breakfast with Jane. He doesn't come home for lunch either.

It occurs to me for the first time that Tom has not so much as mentioned the Julie Fund since our daughter's return. Surely he has thought about what we could or should do with the money —whether we should proceed with the scholarship in Julie's name or if, as Julie hinted, we could convert it into a kind of scholarship for her. Or maybe, now that Julie is twenty-one, it's her money, her decision. "Sole beneficiary." Then what about the trustees, the administrator? Tom has dealt with everyone, even our lawyer, for so long that I find myself completely at a loss as to where to begin.

Tom's desk is in the room where Julie lies sleeping. I gave her a Valium after she got out of the bathtub, and she swallowed it with her skin still steaming, slipped under the covers, bathrobe and all, and closed her swollen eyes immediately.

Now I walk down the hall and, after listening for a moment

to her gentle wheezing from just outside the door, nudge it open. She hasn't moved, not even to roll over; the covers are still where I placed them, her red hair sticking out in strange directions, the way short hair does when you go to bed with it wet. I can just see a faint pinkish shadow seeping out from under her head on the pillow.

I turn my back to her and sit down at Tom's desk, conscious of the magnified squeak of the office chair, the brittle sound of its wheels rolling over the plastic carpet protector. At one point I jerk around, positive I heard Julie stir, but she's still lying motionless, facing away from the desk.

Tom's desk is almost antiseptically organized, writing tools neatly ensconced in sectioned pencil holders, notepads and graph paper slotted away in stacking mesh trays. A tiny, dry-needled cactus perches on the windowsill behind the desk, just catching a sliver of light from a four-inch suspension of the wide-slat blinds. A studio portrait of the four of us sits in the corner of the desk, and in front of it, a shot of Julie—not the one we used for the missing-person picture that was all over the news, but one from the Grand Canyon, the last family vacation we ever took. It's a posed shot. From that trip, there are countless pictures of Jane straddling voids, her feet on two boulders, hands on hips, elbows akimbo. Julie, who had just gone through a growth spurt and seemed unsure how long her limbs were, kept slipping as we climbed the rocks, and stayed well away from the edge. In the photo, she's perched uncertainly on a rock, one foot up in front of her, elbow on knee, chin in hand.

After a moment I move the mouse and am relieved to see the monitor come to life with no password prompt. The desktop photo is a landscape, some generic tropical island at sunset, and the folders are arranged with painstaking neatness. I do a file search, typing in key words one after the other—*Julie, fund, trust, trustees, donation, reward*—thinking there must be a spreadsheet somewhere, a record of incoming donations and search-related expenses, or at the very least a file with the contact information of the trustees. Nothing comes up, and I find myself wondering whether Julie's done this same search recently. If so, she couldn't have had better luck than I'm having. I open the web browser and check the history—nothing. Which, considering she just told me she's been looking up her case on the Internet, makes it look an awful lot like she cleared the browser history herself.

Pushing away this thought, I start pulling out desk drawers but encounter only the expected debris of empty mechanical pencils, rubber bands, and paper clips. A side drawer holds stacks of blank tax forms that make my head spin just to look at them. I slide them all shut as quietly as possible and tug the handle of the file drawer. Locked.

Shit.

Who needs computer passwords if you keep the hard copies under lock and key? These must be client files—highly confidential. Suddenly I feel certain the information on the Julie Fund is in this drawer. I think I've seen a desk key on his key chain before, but keys always come in twos; there must be a spare somewhere. I open the shallow drawer again to make sure there are no diminutive keys jumbled in with the paper clips. In a fit of inspiration I lift up the plastic separator and peek under the molded plastic, where I find some dust, at least, but no key. I open the other shallow drawers so I can rifle through them, but there's nothing to rifle through. How can anyone be expected to find anything in all this not-mess?

This time the noise behind me is real, and I whip around, cringing at the creaking chair. Julie has turned her face toward me, but her eyes are still closed, and after another murmur and a sigh, she goes silent again. I wonder if she's faking it, if she opened her eyes and saw me, closed them when I turned around. After a frozen moment in which my limbs go numb anticipating her slightest movement, I decide it doesn't matter. If she's seen me, it's already too late, and I might as well get what I came for. And maybe she hasn't. Choosing to believe the latter, I rack my brain one more time for the key's hiding place.

I've never been a big snooper. You'd think after Julie's disappearance I would have watched Jane like a hawk, would have flipped through her phone, once she got one, for her contacts and text-message history, read her diary—not that Julie's diary, which the police scoured, contained anything more interesting than track practice and homework and *i*'s dotted with hearts. Still, I used to think that by resisting the urge, I was honoring Jane's privacy. Now I realize the urge was never there; I just didn't want to know. Jane's rebellion was healthy, proportionate—the constantly re-dyed hair, the piercings. What more could I gain by prying? I thought if I let her have her private world, if I let her slam the door and listen to her music, one day she would come out and thank me for giving her the space. Now that she's left the house, the city, the state, I realize she *wanted* me to pry. I remember the stack of notebooks she was carrying as she left the house this morning. Those were journals; she actually left her old journals in the house when she went to college. She left them for me to find. And now that I'm just catching up to her need for me, it's too late.

And then I know where the key is, and that Tom has hidden it not just from the world at large, but specifically from me. He put it in the very last place I would look.

I reach for Julie's picture, turn it around, and find the key tucked under one of the metal clamps that holds in the photo. I pull it out. I open the drawer.

At the back, behind fifteen inches of client files, there's an unmarked folder. I pull it out. Then I rearrange the files to hide the missing one to the best of my ability, lock the drawer, replace the key, and extract myself from the room full of Julie's warm, sleepy breath as quickly and silently as possible, taking the folder with me.

I am expecting, perhaps, something thicker, a dusty file full of newspaper clippings, our correspondence with the parents' group, media, and law enforcement. Instead, I find a few forms clipped together, folded because they're larger than letter size: the bank documents for setting up the trust. I scan the top part, but it's all standard language, dense as a block of wood to me. There are appended documents, and when I unfold them I see the notarized signature at the bottom of the fund-administrator form. *Alma Josefina Ruiz.* I have no idea who that is, but she holds the purse strings to what I now see was an impressive $240,000 of collected donations in 2008. Who knows what's left now, but it might be enough to pay for GED classes, or even a few years of college if she gets into a state school.

I don't remember an Alma. But then I don't remember much of anything from that period. I drank a lot. I slept for days at a time. I took pills so I could sleep at night after having slept all through the day. Above all, I didn't want to know details. I wanted everything to blur, fade, go away forever. I wanted to be left alone.

Now, faced for the first time with everything I blocked out quantified starkly in dollars, I finally feel how alone I have succeeded in making myself.

I check the time and wonder when Tom will be getting home. He used to go to the support group for parents of missing children on Sunday evenings, but does he still, now that Julie is home? Is he allowed? What would it be like to be surrounded by the faces of those whose children are still and always missing after your own prayers have been answered?

Then I remember.

Ask Alma if anybody knows what hers looks like.

It was the billboards. The last night I ever went to the support group with Tom, they turned on us, on me, about the billboards.

"Your girl is everywhere," a woman—Connie, I think her name was—said that final evening. "I see her face every time I run out to the corner store. When was the last time you saw my girl Shawnna's face? Do you even know what she looks like?" She turned from side to side, staring down the people sitting near her. "That's right. I guess you know she's black, that's about it. Fourteen-year-old black girl, probably just ran away, right? Nobody gives a shit. Ask Alma if anybody knows what hers looks like."

In my memory, Alma has downcast eyes, dark lashes, hair in a tight, tucked-under French braid.

The group leader said something about the importance of each focusing on our own feelings, and Connie said, "Pissed off," and a mumble started up around the circle among the parents of kids who had been abducted in more ordinary ways: picked up from school by an ex-husband and whisked across state lines, like Alma's daughter, or talked into driving off in an older boyfriend's truck. Kids who were too poor or too brown, too old or too badly behaved to wind up on the news night after night for weeks and months after they were gone.

Julie's wide-eyed innocence, however, seemed made for TV. She was a character in a comic-book crime: one of America's pink-cheeked, golden-haired daughters, stalked by a psycho and stolen at knifepoint from under her very own roof. That round face with the flat upper lip that made her look childish in precisely the way adult women are supposed to try to look childish; her ice-blue eyes, the limp, pale flag of her hair. I used to look at the stubby eyelashes that were dark near the roots and that vanished toward the tips and think, *When this girl puts on makeup, we will all be doomed*. Of course, we didn't have to wait that long.

One by one, the group members' faces turned toward us with envy, even hatred. As if our worst nightmare had been orchestrated to steal the spotlight from theirs. As if we were lucky to have had our daughter stolen by a true psychopath.

I say *we*, but I'm the mother. They stared at me, and I felt myself turn to stone.

"I'm so glad we're talking about the anger we feel," the group leader said. "I'm so glad we're sharing these feelings."

She's just as dead as all of yours, I wanted to say. But instead I walked out and never came back, leaving Tom behind to give conciliatory speeches. I never asked how he got home at the end of the night.

Suddenly I feel sure it was Alma who gave him a ride.

Karen

's seventeenth birthday party consisted of three people: Karen and Melinda and Bob McGinty.

"Happy birthday," Melinda said, handing her a cardboard box. Melinda's iron-gray cap of hair was as smooth and prim as ever, but she wore earrings that bobbed against her turtleneck, and her large teeth were visible through a stretched-open smile. Even Bob looked pleased.

Karen opened the little box. In it lay a necklace with a horse charm.

The riding thing was how Karen survived public school in Red Bluff, California, a wasteland of baseball-playing thugs dating girls with faces like sour milk. Because she rode, she didn't have to take gym, and she had a social status independent of what she wore. That was fortunate, because dressed in the skirts and tights and sweaters the McGintys bought her—and some of it wasn't even bought but handed down from a niece who'd dropped out of high school fifteen years ago and was roughly her size—Karen looked awkward at best. Melinda and Bob didn't have a daughter of their own, although they'd tried, and their son hadn't been home since he was eighteen. Whatever it was he was off doing in New York, if he was still there, it was nothing he wanted to tell his parents about. They got a postcard every year or so, Melinda told her, adding, "So we know he's still alive," in a matter-of-fact way that suggested a lot of tears had already gone into that phrase.

Karen had heard all this, or some version of it, before. She'd stopped being surprised when foster parents told her the story of why they were fostering. It happened so often she almost always knew exactly for whom she was substituting: a child never born but longed for, begged for, and finally given up on; a dead child; a missing child; an older brother or sister who drove away on a motorcycle forty years ago and never came back. She learned to distrust the big families, where the real siblings presented a united front against her, tolerating her in front of the parents but ignoring her behind their backs. ("Don't worry about learning all our names, you won't be here long.") The parents might act like they had too much love and needed to keep giving it away, but there was, of course, the money. She didn't blame them, but she wouldn't thank them either.

Whatever role Karen was playing for her temporary parents, she was never interested in playing it well. She knew she was just killing time before aging out. Fostering with a family had risks, but it was usually safer than the streets. And when it got unsafe, when a father walked in on her changing and lingered a moment too long before backing out and shutting the door, when a cousin came into her room during the family barbecue—well, she had calibrated the precise moment past which she could no longer measure out her body's worth in string cheese and Snack Packs. At that point, she would run away, taking something small with her.

Nothing valuable; she didn't want to end up in juvie. She aimed for sentiment instead. Things that wouldn't be missed for some time but would spill tears when they were. Two years in foster care had left her with a small collection of these trophies, including a Precious Moments figurine with an onion head and teary eyes clutching a teddy bear whose ear had chipped off in her backpack; a souvenir thimble from Niagara Falls she had found in the drawer of a foster mom's bedside table; a finger painting, yellowed with age, *Deacon, 4 yr.,* in a preschool teacher's handwriting in the corner. She'd hesitated over the last one, remembering the sick little boy, but then she remembered what Deacon's older brother had done to her and the hard smack Deacon's mom had given her when she ratted him out. She kept it folded up in quarters so she wouldn't see the messy swipes of red and blue paint.

But the McGintys were different. They gave her plenty of space, because they themselves liked a lot of space. They were both retired, but Melinda volunteered at the library every morning, as if constant pillow-straightening and counter-wiping were not enough of an outlet for her precision. At first Karen thought she'd been brought in to babysit Bob during Melinda's library shifts. Each morning after Melinda drove off, Karen had waited for his perversion to emerge, but Bob only nursed his coffee for an hour or two before heading out to his woodshop to putter away the day. She'd go upstairs, close her door, and lie on her bed for hours at a time, staring up at the light fixture, gripped with a suffocating feeling she couldn't understand, like a hand wrapped around her throat. It had been a long time since she'd been bored.

Horse camp saved her from certain desperate acts of vandalism she was beginning to contemplate. Melinda signed her up for eight weeks at a ranch run by an old friend of hers just down the road. Karen assumed it was a favor between friends, because although two months of camp sounded expensive, Melinda didn't seem to care whether she went or not. "Bob'll take you if you want to go," she said. "Or you can walk half an hour down the FM 229, that'll get you there. Starts at ten in the morning every weekday." Karen was noncommittal, but when the time came, after Melinda left for the library and Bob folded his paper and wandered off to the woodshop, and she saw they really weren't going to push it, she decided a walk sounded better than another morning alone with the wallpaper. Besides, she had a kind of distant curiosity about horses. As a child, she'd had fantasies of a silvery-white steed invisible to everyone but her who galloped the horizon silently as a cloud, watching her from afar.

When she first entered the stables, the sweaty, rank, shiver-skinned reality of horses made her ashamed of the fairy-tale version she'd envisioned. They frightened her, all twitching muscles and rolling eyes and hooves that hit the earth with a shudder she could feel through her sneakers. But as a rule, Karen showed fear only when it helped minimize damage, and she could tell right away that cringing wouldn't get her anywhere with animals this powerful. Besides, the half a dozen other kids at the camp, many of whom were already accomplished riders, were years younger than her. The youngest was nine. When Karen petted the giant head of a chestnut mare on her first visit to the stables, she made sure the instructor, the nine-year-old, and anyone else watching saw that her hand didn't tremble.

She went back the next day, and the next, and over eight weeks, she got pretty good at being around horses—riding them, taking care of them, cleaning up after them. Not great, but comfortable. At the end of the summer, Melinda left the library early every day to watch her ride, and as much as being on the back of a strong, fast animal meant to Karen, watching Karen seemed to mean even more to Melinda.

It was the horse charm that made Karen understand how much, though. Looking down at the flimsy charm, she thought that nobody had given one like it to Melinda and that she must have wanted one, probably from someone in particular.

"We want to get a real one for you someday," Melinda said. "A horse, I mean. Our finances just aren't in order this year, but it'll happen sometime." The McGintys occasionally referred to a distant, more prosperous past in which they'd owned horses, but this was the first they'd ever mentioned buying one.

"Wow, thanks," Karen said.

"You've made good grades this year," Melinda continued. "We're proud of you." Bob nodded agreement. "Anyway, we'd like to talk about taking the next step. We want to adopt you, Karen."

My name isn't Karen was the first thought that came into her mind. "I love the necklace" is what she said. "Thank you so much." She meant it. The charm on the thin gold chain was cheap, one side flat and the other sculpted to look three-dimensional. But the horse was running.

"You don't have to decide right now," Melinda said. "We just wanted you to know that we consider you our daughter."

What Melinda wasn't saying but Karen heard in her words was the concern over her aging out. Karen had listened to the stories in the group home. She thought of the Petes with a shudder.

She weighed her memories of them against Melinda's long,

strong face, which was more than plain, almost ugly. Strong, bitter lines cut a path from the corners of her mouth to the underside of her chin — that son — but a smile softened her eyes to a watery gray. Karen's future with Melinda and Bob might involve horses, but it would also involve community college, a job in Red Bluff or Redding or even Sacramento. More: A baseball thug of her own, maybe a walk down a church aisle trimmed with ribbons and foldout bells made of tissue paper. And then, one day, this house with the clapboard siding and peaked roof would be hers, and she would sleep in the master suite that faced the wooded mountains and take her own children to the coast once a year. Snug as a fork in a drawer.

"This is the best birthday I've ever had," Karen said. It was close enough to the truth, even if it wasn't really her birthday, just a random date that happened to stick.

The next time she was out riding at the stables, she imagined leaning forward just a little more, urging the powerful creature to a trot, then a gallop, until it looked like the horse charm on her necklace. Leaping over the low wooden fence and cantering through pastures and woods and then up into the mountains. That was sheer fantasy, of course, another version of the silvery-white steed; she didn't know how to jump, would kill herself and maybe the horse too trying. Horses didn't do well in mountains, and neither would she. Anyway, how far could a girl get on a horse these days?

So she started thinking bus routes. It was time to head to Portland, where she'd heard there were more strip clubs per capita than in any other city in the U.S. That sounded like cash waiting to be made with no strings attached. When the time came, after Melinda left for the library and Bob folded his paper and wandered off to the woodshop and Karen set off down her usual path, she was surprised and relieved at how natural it felt to turn in the wrong direction on FM 229 and just walk away. She'd wrapped the necklace chain twice around her ankle, and the little gold charm clicked against her anklebone as she walked. Every eighth step or so, the charm slid into her shoe and got trapped against her skin for a second, then it popped out with a thwack, worked its way around her ankle, and slithered down again. The rhythm was nice, like the tiny horse was galloping away, and she was riding it out of town instead of a Greyhound bus.

10

"You think he's cheating?" Alex Mercado says, casual but interested, like someone discussing odds in a race he's not betting on.

"No. I don't know. I just—" A shadow passes the narrow, frosted window outside my office door, and I shift the phone to my other ear. There's always someone lurking around the department, even on the weekends.

"You want me to find out if he's cheating," he rephrases. "I'm happy to follow him, find out where he goes." *It'll cost you* runs the unspoken part of the sentence.

"Would you just look into something—someone—for me instead?" I say, lowering my voice. "Alma Josefina Ruiz."

"Basic background?" he says. "Or follow her?"

"Background," I say hurriedly. "She's a trustee for our donation fund. The fund administrator, actually."

"Ah," Alex says. "Maybe that's why the name sounds familiar. Shouldn't be hard to find out what's up with her." *And if she's seeing your husband.* "Oh, and do you want me to keep tailing Julie? I found out where she's going." Before I can ask, he says, still in that maddeningly offhand voice, "She goes to church."

"What? What church?"

"The Gate."

I'm speechless. The Gate is the megachurch whose billboard I pass at the 610 flyover on my way to work every day. They meet in the goddamn Astrodome.

"She doesn't go in," he says. "She just sits in her car. Your husband's car," he corrects himself. "In the parking lot."

"What is she doing?"

"I don't know. It's a freaking compound, there's a lot going on in there. Three Bible study groups around that time, a singles bowling league, and something called the Circle of Healing." He sounds amused. "You never went to that church?"

"We never went to church at all," I say. "I mean, Julie went with a friend once in a while after a sleepover. Trying it out, the way kids do." I think of the televangelist's enlarged grin on the billboard. *Faith every day, not everyday faith.* "I just can't imagine Julie wanting to go someplace like *that.*"

He's silent for a moment. "Did you watch the video, Anna?"

"Yes, I watched it. Gretchen Farber. That band in—Portland, was it?"

"And?"

"And—yes, it looks like her. Maybe. But the image is so fuzzy, it's not like you can say for sure." It feels like honesty, because I watched it only once, in the middle of the night, with the sound off. And because I can hardly be sure of anything these days.

"Cell-phone video," he concedes, but I get the uneasy feeling he's humoring me. "Not a great image."

"Exactly," I say. "And Portland—"

"—is not Mexico," he finishes.

There's a pause, so I go on the offensive. "May I ask why you were looking in Portland?"

"I wasn't," he says. "I've been checking police reports filed all over around the time Julie arrived, anything involving a woman her age, hoping something might turn up. There's a missing-persons report out on this Gretchen Farber—not in Portland, actually, but in Seattle. It's from a couple days after Julie showed up—"

"After she came home."

"You have to wait three days to file a missing-persons report for an adult, especially if it's the husband or boyfriend filing—in case it's what they call a lover's quarrel. This was filed by a boyfriend, Calvin something. Anyway, I got lucky"—*Lucky*, I think—"because there's a video of her. Don't worry, I'm looking into it, calling the bars, trying to nail the ID." He pauses, and I can hear papers shuffling. "There's one other possibility I'm exploring."

"You mean for identifying the impostor?" I ask, attempting to sound sarcastic, but Alex doesn't skip a beat.

"Charlotte Willard," he says. "Same age as Julie, ran away from her home in Louisiana shortly after Julie—uh, disappeared. Maybe it's nothing, but there's a Charlotte from seven years ago—going by a different last name, of course—picked up in San Francisco, spends a while in foster care, and then sort of falls off the map. Switched up her name again or something."

"So?"

"So, I'm not sure," he admits. "But I think Charlotte may be Gretchen. And Gretchen may be—well, Julie."

"And why would this Charlotte or Gretchen or whoever she is be posing as my daughter?" I hear my voice climbing to a higher pitch and try to wrangle it back down, unsuccessfully. "What could she possibly want?"

I push the Julie Fund out of my mind, though Alex surely hasn't forgotten why I called him in the first place.

"Honestly, Anna, I don't know yet. I'll let you know when I find something else."

His tact annoys me. "Say what you're thinking. You think it's the money, don't you? The money in the fund?"

"I won't know what to think until you get me that DNA sample."

I hang up without saying goodbye and open the browser on my desktop.

The Gate's website features an elaborate series of Flash animations, which I click through impatiently until I find the Circle of Healing. When I click on the link, an animated drop of water falls into the middle of the words, pushing them out into concentric circles that ripple over the whole screen. When the screen goes smooth again, this description appears:

> *We invite to the Circle of Healing all who feel broken.*
> *When we ask forgiveness in the Circle of Healing,*
> *God will show us that we have already been healed.*

At the bottom of the screen, a series of faces fade in and out, each with a testimonial: an elderly woman blinded by cataracts until the Circle of Healing taught her she could already see. An African American teenager saved from dropping out of school by the Circle of Healing. A man, once homeless, discovered the path to financial security through the Circle of Healing. *God's plan is for abundance,* the quote says. *The Lord makes His Kingdom great!*

I scribble the meeting times on a Post-it note and go back to the search screen, where another listing is a link to a recent magazine profile of Reverend Chuck Maxwell, the man whose face looms over our local urban landscape on billboards at every bottleneck. The article is called "'It Ain't Luck, Chuck': How Rev. Chuck Maxwell Landed the Biggest Pulpit in Texas":

> *Chuck Maxwell is handsomer in person than on the billboards for his Houston megachurch, The Gate. The 42-year-old pastor with the grizzled beard and piercing stare is 6 foot 2 and unexpectedly graceful. It's easy to see how this man has built a spiritual—and financial—empire.*

Oh, it's going to be one of *those* profiles.

> *Maxwell has never been ordained in any denomination, nor does he hold degrees in religion or philosophy; indeed, he never finished college. Yet every week he stands in what was once the Houston Astrodome and delivers a sermon to 30,000 parishioners and up to 10 million remote viewers via his television and Internet ministries.*

I skip down a few paragraphs.

> *After dropping out of Texas Christian University, he snagged a production job for Houston's fire-and-brimstone televangelist Jim Wilton. It was there that Maxwell says he began to have strong ideas for a Christian message he felt uniquely suited to deliver.*
>   *"I wouldn't say I had a falling-out with the Baptist Church,"*

*he says. "But the message was so negative: 'You're messing up! Get
right with God!'" He laughs. "But God doesn't want you to focus
on your sins of the past! God says, make it new!"*

My English-professor eye snags on *make it new*, Ezra Pound's
modernist slogan, and I enjoy a brief moment of imagining the
elitist, anti-Semitic old creep rolling in his grave. I keep skimming,
and Maxwell keeps preaching endless reinvention, spreading the
word that nothing matters but the present moment. Could that
be what Julie's after? The profile goes on for three more pages,
covering Maxwell's massive donations to a nonprofit for missing
children—that, of course, catches my eye—but I can't stomach
reading to the end. The thought of Julie needing Maxwell's message—*Erase the past, live in the now!*—is too repellent to dwell on.
Jane and Tom and I are, after all, Julie's past. Or we're supposed
to be.

Which brings me to my final call.

I get out the piece of paper Jane gave me, still wadded up in
my pocket, and stare at it. The area code looks familiar, but I can't
quite place it until I look it up: Seattle.

Jane must be playing some kind of trick on me. This is the phone
number of a friend of hers, her roommate, somebody she's put up
to this. I feel a hot rush of anger, followed by a guilty twinge. I've
neglected Jane—willfully ignored her, at times—over the past
eight years. Every time I looked at her, all I could see was her failure to scream in the closet that night, the three hours she spent
huddled among her shoes with tears and snot streaming down her
face while Julie—I know it wasn't Jane's fault, but I couldn't help
it. Casting doubts on Julie's identity would be a particularly cruel
way to get back at me, but effective. My hand is shaking.

I dial the number and wait. It rings half a dozen times, as if someone on the other end is staring at the caller ID, deciding whether to pick up. Then someone does.

"Stop this," Julie says.

I'm shocked into silence.

"Well, say something, Cal," she says, her voice weary. "I finally picked up one of your mystery numbers, so say something. I know it's you. Calling from every stop on your grand tour of my life, aren't you?" She pauses. "Well, you found me. You're here. So what is it you want to say?"

I hold my breath.

"What dirty little secret have you found out about me now? I guarantee, no matter what it is, there's something worse about me you still don't know."

I know nothing, absolutely nothing.

On the other end of the connection, Julie says, "Fuck you, Cal. I left. It's over. *Go home.*" The call ends.

Charlotte

sat in a dingy room with the social worker and a bearded man who kept trying to get her to tell him the name of her pimp. Officer Pete used that word too, but she didn't know what it meant, just that there was a thrill of secrets around it, like a curse word. It made her think of pimples, but she wasn't telling the bearded man that.

"I don't have one of those," she said, unable to make herself repeat the word.

"Come on, what did he tell you?" said the bearded man. "He told you you were special, he'd treat you right?"

The only person she could think of who fit that description was John David. Was he a pimp? *Her* pimp? She wasn't sure. There was no way this bearded man could know about John David, was there? But a deep black well hovered just under that thought, waiting for her to slip and fall in. She shook her head.

"He convinced you to start trading it for money, right? Only he gets all the money."

Now she understood, and a wave of heat exploded just under her jaw. "I've only done that a couple times," she mumbled.

"Okay, just once or twice," he said in a too-nice voice. "Just to help him out. So you want to protect him, because he protects you, right? You think he's your friend? Maybe your boyfriend?"

"I don't have a boyfriend," she said, the heat spreading up from her jawline until even her eyeballs felt hot. She pushed all her hate out through her eyes and straight into his bushy brown beard. At least Officer Pete believed her. She drew a breath to say so but realized she didn't know Officer Pete's real name.

"He bought you things at first?" the beard continued to prompt her. "Maybe he got your nails done."

She pulled her hands off the table self-consciously. There were lines of black beneath the ragged nails, and one had a red, puffy bump of skin around the corner where it was torn. She noticed the social worker, a brown-skinned woman with a pair of glasses on a chain around her neck, shake her head and roll her eyes quickly, then look away.

But the bearded guy went on for another five or ten minutes before finally standing up. He flipped a card onto the table in front of her, pressing one finger down on its corner as he said, "If you remember anything, call me at this number. Just remember, he's a predator. You're the victim here." As he lifted his hand away, his sweaty finger tugged the corner of the card just enough to knock it out of its perfect alignment with the fake wood grain on the table. She watched the card settle into its skewed position in front of her, memorizing the angle to keep from reading the name. When she looked up, the man was gone, and the social worker had taken his seat across the table from her with an expression of clear relief.

"I'm Wanda, Charlotte."

She almost jumped. Although it was the name she'd put on the paperwork, the first one that popped into her head, nobody had called her that yet — the cops who'd shuffled her from room to room had said "you" or "young lady" or, when they were talking about her like she wasn't there, "the juvenile." Hearing the name said out loud for the first time, she realized how weak and stupid she had been to use it just because it made her feel brave to claim it as her own. Now it sounded like an accusation.

"Charlotte," Wanda went on, as if determined to damn her as often as possible, "I was told you'd like to be in foster care. We call it out-of-home care these days. Do you have a safe home?"

She tried to think of home, but instead she saw a pair of blank, staring, upside-down eyes. Their un-wet opacity.

"No."

"You don't have a home?" Wanda prodded. "Or you feel it's not safe for you there?"

It sounded like a trick question. This Wanda wasn't like Officer Pete, mouthing off after a long day, or the asshole with the beard, drilling down in hopes of finding something in her he could use. No home, or not safe? She stared at the corners of Wanda's mouth, watching for a flicker to tell her which one the social worker wanted to hear, but Wanda only waited, her face relaxed and expressionless.

"I'm. It's." Where to begin? "Not safe."

It wasn't exactly a lie.

Wanda just nodded, an expression not so much of approval but of completion, a box ticked off. "And Charlotte, are you hoping to be in out-of-home care for just a short time or for a longer while?"

Multiple choice again. She'd been good at tests, once. "I want an emergency placement," she said, remembering what Officer Pete told her to say.

"I'd like that for you too, Charlotte," the social worker said. "Unfortunately we have a shortage of options just at the moment. Child Protective Services will handle all that, I'm just making the referral. But I have to tell you something. If you're entering out-of-home care right now, you're very likely going to have to stay in a group home for a time while they look for a placement for you."

She nodded. Group.

"It'll only be temporary, but I just want to prepare you for that. Are you sure there's not a friend or family member you could stay with? Somewhere you'll be safe? Think."

She thought, hard this time. All the places she could go, she'd need to be a kid, and she wasn't a kid anymore. Kids didn't go to dirty apartments and have babies scraped out of them. Kids didn't do with Petes what she'd done with Petes. Kids didn't do to other kids what she'd done to the girl in the basement.

She didn't know what she was.

"I'll go to group," she said.

As the two of them left the police station, she said, "What about my things?" But even before Wanda opened her mouth to say the words, Charlotte knew the stolen knife was gone forever.

It didn't matter, because in group, only the biggest kids got to have knives. They hid them in their mattresses or taped them to the bottoms of drawers. Nobody stole them and nobody told on the kids. One of the scrawny little boys tried making his own out of a plastic butter knife that he snapped in half. He showed it around, bragging, until one of the big kids took it away in the night and did something to him that didn't show.

Because of obvious rules like that, group was easier than she'd thought it would be. In her mind she called the biggest kids Enforcers. She herself tried to be an Invisible, obviously the safest course of action.

Her roommate Beth was an Eager. Eagers played along with whatever the counselors asked, volunteering in group sessions and earning gold stars and sparkly toothbrushes and puffy stickers for good behavior. The stars and puffy stickers were worse than pointless; too permanent, they left a hard, sticky gum behind that ruined clothes and had to be scrubbed off skin with a scouring pad. The undersides of the chairs and the walls behind the beds were lousy with them.

Toothbrushes were different. She'd lived without one before, and the flimsy plastic stick they handed her when she first arrived was better than nothing, but its thin row of stiff, hard bristles hurt her gums. One day she picked up Beth's toothbrush and flipped it over, looking into the pink translucent depths of the sparkly plastic, letting her eyes slide along the buried bubbles and shimmering threads that caught the light as she turned it from side to side.

"Hey, put that down. That's mine," said Beth from the doorway.

"It's nice," said Charlotte, but she didn't put the toothbrush down. She waited to see what Beth would do. Beth, who was only eleven, wriggled uncomfortably. "It's pretty," Charlotte added encouragingly.

"Thanks," said Beth. After a brief interior struggle, her wide eyes almost filling with tears, she said, "You can have it." Her teeth dragging on every syllable.

Charlotte put it down with a thwack. "That's gross. I don't want your used toothbrush."

But later on, she took it anyway.

11

Monday afternoon, I get in the car and head to the Gate.

Ironic, isn't it? I've been telling Tom for two weeks I'm going to work, and Julie's been telling us she's going to therapy, and now we're both lying to go the same place. I turn into the parking lot, where new construction shields the former Astrodome from the neighboring NRG Stadium, and take note of the aerial walkway between the two buildings. The Gate must get a healthy amount of foot traffic during playoff season. As if on cue, the digital marquee flashes—WITH GOD, ALL THINGS ARE POSSIBLE—and I give an anxious snort of laughter.

There are a hundred or so vehicles clustered around the entrance. It's not Julie's therapy day, so I know she doesn't have a car, but I still feel nervous that I might see her, or she might, at this moment, be seeing me. The parking terrain is vast and includes a five-level garage that looks empty from here. I park and approach the modern, streamlined, steeple-and-stone façade that has been added to the gargantuan inverted bowl in an unsuccessful attempt to bring it down to human scale. I open one giant glass door and enter a lobby as airy and clean as an airport VIP lounge. Screens hang from the ceiling at regular intervals, their resting faces the church's glowing-gate logo. The sea-green carpet is dotted with pristine rugs of white shag across which clean-lined chairs face one another in decorous intimacy. Very soft music is being piped in over invisible speakers, and off in the corner of the vast lobby, a vacuum cleaner drones. Monday must be a slow day.

There's a mounted map of the church just to the right of the entrance, and a brief consultation points me in the direction of a corridor with the word FAITH hanging over it in brushed steel. The room number I'm looking for is 19F, and I find a moment to wonder whether there's a LOVE wing where all the room numbers have *L*s in them. The vacuum cleaner shuts off, and, looking back, I see my tracks, a line of slightly darker sea-green footprints trailing across the sea-green carpet. *That must be where God carried me,* I think. I've always had trouble taking religion seriously, but this place seems like a massive joke.

The heavy wooden door to 19F is closed and windowless, and after only a moment of hesitation, I push the door open on one end of a room the size of a high-school gymnasium. A hundred or so people stand hand in hand in a flattened-out oval that runs the length of the room, eyes closed, heads bowed, some rocking back and forth rhythmically, others stock-still. I enter and close the door softly behind me, and the low murmuring of the circle enfolds me. I had imagined chairs or somewhere to sit and observe, but there is no room for anything in the windowless hall except the humming, breathing circle. Without opening their eyes or looking at me, the two supplicants nearest the door release each other's hands and take a half step outward, opening the circle and extending their arms. My stomach turns over. This feels much more real than I was expecting and at the same time embarrassingly fake. When I step forward and grasp the hands on either side of me—one the dry, rough, thick-jointed hand of an old man, the other the horrifyingly moist and malleable hand of a teenage boy—I am officially an impostor.

At first I can't tell where the murmuring is coming from; amplified around me on all sides and in all keys, it doesn't appear to originate from any one place. I keep my eyes open and run them over as many members of the circle as I can see, but if there's a starting point for the praying, it must be somewhere close to the other end of the oval, the part hidden by its longer side. Looking around, all I see is an endless train of sweatshirted senior citizens, pimpled teenagers, and ponytailed women in yoga pants, all echoing one another's words. I close my eyes, and after a moment one of the voices seems to separate itself from the muddled sea of noise it's been swimming in and rise a few inches above. It's an ordinary man's voice, the vowels pinched by that indefinable Houston accent. Nevertheless, I can hear the words, crystal clear, as if they were being spoken directly into my ear.

"Found." The word drops like a stone into the pool of murmurs. "What was lost has been found. Furthermore, it was never lost."

"Furthermore, it was never lost," echoes the rest of the circle.

"Do you look to your Heavenly Father, who offers you armfuls of blessings, and ask for a single favor? If you are handed a plate of food at a wedding, do you beg the giver for a bite? You have what you need right in front of you. Do the lilies of the field cast their faces down in supplication? Do the sparrows moan to the heavens in despair? No. The lilies raise their faces to the Lord in awe and delight. The sparrows lift their voices in songs of praise. They decorate God's creation with their thanks. Does a grateful daughter clothe herself in rags? No—she shows the world her father loves her. She is thankful for his love. What was lost has been found. It was never lost. What was lost has been found. It was never lost. What was lost has been found. It was never lost."

"What was lost has been found. It was never lost." Some of them continue to chant the phrase while others move on with him, repeating his words just a few seconds after he says them, as clumsily as wet sand on a beach casting itself in the image of the waves that roll over it.

"What you need is already in your life," the speaker goes on. "Christ was wounded forever that we might be whole."

Some of the chanters change their mantra at this. One begins weeping loudly.

"Our Lord has a hole in His side so that we can be whole inside."

At this abjectly dumb wordplay I stifle a snicker, but as the phrase ripples through the circle, taken up by the chorus of voices, the suppressed hiccup undergoes some kind of emotional alchemy in my stomach. Unbelievably, I feel my eyes start to prickle.

"We are whole in every aspect of our lives. Do you want a new job? You're already doing it. A spouse? You're already married, but neither of you know it yet. Relief from a debt? It has been paid, now and forever. A release from pain? There is no pain except in your mind."

A second weeper has begun, this one gasping for air in between sobs. Every sob that rings out is immediately encircled and washed away in the mumbling tide, so that the next one feels entirely new, as if it's from a different planet.

"Rejoice! What was lost has been found. It was never lost. It was you who were lost. The son who was dead is now living again; he who was lost is found. But he was never truly dead; he was never really lost."

I can't take much more of this. I snap my eyes open. Nobody notices. Then I spot someone across the circle from me. An elderly woman sitting in a wheelchair, wearing a Mickey Mouse sweatshirt.

I yank my hands away and grab blindly for the door, my sweaty fingers slipping on the handle as I heave it open and run, run, back across the sea-green carpet, where my tracks have already been vacuumed away.

Back in my office, I dial the number and the phone rings and rings, but Alex Mercado isn't picking up, so I'll have to find what I'm looking for on my own. I type the damning words into the search engine and wait for the most recent news story to come up: BOMB SHELTER REMAINS BELONG TO 13-YEAR-OLD GIRL, EXPERTS SAY.

The lead photo shows a one-story brick bungalow in River Oaks, an old central neighborhood shaded by massive trees and, these days, condos crowded onto too-small plots. The house in the photo was being leveled to make way for one more condo when bulldozers uncovered extra pipelines going to a bomb shelter buried in ten feet of concrete in the backyard. Another photo shows twisted pipes leading to a broken concrete shell. There are no pictures of what they found inside. I keep digging: The house was seized in 2008 from the owner, nursing-home resident Nadine Reynolds, for delinquent property-tax payments. Sold at auction to an out-of-town investor who rented it for years without crossing the threshold, it changed hands several times before being picked up in 2015 by the most recent developer, who decided it would make more money as condos.

But it's the photo that's important, not the house. I wind up on the Texas DPS website, where there's a statewide database of missing persons, over three hundred listings. So many missing; so many unidentified bodies, each one corresponding to a lost daughter or husband or wife or son, like a massive jigsaw puzzle with pieces scattered all over the globe.

I click through the most recent Harris County listings and see the thumbnails of male faces with eyes closed, oddly dignified and brutally sad. Then a head-shaped outline with a question mark. The death date is indeterminate, 2008 or 2009, the approximate time all of our lives fell apart. I hold my breath and click, and the photo that has been haunting me pops up, the horrifying details cropped in order to focus on a single rotted scrap of faded black cloth shaped like two circles connected by a partially eroded isthmus of faded black.

I can see why I didn't recognize it at first. After all, it's been eaten by the air in the bomb shelter for eight years. No one could have recognized it right away, not even someone who's been carrying around the memory of her daughter's nightshirt for eight years. A nightshirt now reduced to a pair of Mickey Mouse ears.

I just want the body, I once said in the support group, before I left forever. *I just want something to bury.* The chorus of police voices and therapist voices and media voices chanting in tandem *—The first three hours, the first three days—*made it hard to conceive of a world in which my daughter was living. Now I feel a strange numbness settle over me at the thought that she hasn't been. That she isn't. I didn't recognize it right away, because I didn't want to. I didn't want Mercado to be right about Julie being dead. I didn't want him to be right about *anything* that had to do with my daughter. I wanted to be the one who knew her better than anyone.

My cell phone is ringing; it's Alex, calling me back. I hit the green icon to pick up, ready to make a full confession. But I never get a chance.

"I have some bad news," Alex says.

Petes

is what she called them, even the ones who bought the pills and weed she'd stolen from the shopping cart under the bridge without even asking her to suck their dicks or let them shove them inside her. She'd learned to spit in her hand and wrap it around fast, so there was a chance they'd forget about putting it inside her if she moved quick enough. And if they remembered, it'd go a little easier, be over a little faster.

By the time she got to San Francisco, she'd lost track of the men who got her there, but at least she remembered their names. Their names were Pete. Two Petes in the bus station. A Pete in the bathroom of a Diamond Shamrock gas station. One Pete on the bus she'd tried to fight off with the knife, but then she'd let it go and took his wallet instead. He sat next to her the whole way to Sacramento with his dirty fingers interlaced with hers, like they were girlfriend and boyfriend. She turned fourteen between Petes, but she wasn't sure when exactly the day passed, and anyway, to

Petes she was sixteen, to police, eighteen. She had the birth year for eighteen memorized, and when asked to move along—*How old are you, young lady, aren't you supposed to be home at this hour? Oh, really, what's your birthday?*—she gave random dates from that year, once accidentally saying that day's date without realizing it. That policeman said, "Happy birthday," and made a face.

The last Pete turned out to be a cop. And when she got into his car and he asked for her date of birth, she'd rattled one off and he just looked at her and shook his head. "You sure you're eighteen?" he said. "You know you could be charged as an adult."

He hit something and a siren went on, and she looked and saw that the doors didn't have locks on the inside, and her door didn't even have a handle.

"January eleventh, 1989," she said immediately. It wasn't the right day or the right year, but it put her two years closer to her real age.

"That's more like it. We're going to get you a social worker and get a case opened up on you before you get into a situation you can't get out of."

I've been in one, she thought. *I got out.*

"I know you think you're tough and all," he said, giving her a quick sidelong glance. "But you were about to get picked up by somebody who would have hurt you pretty bad. Juárez owns this block. That was one of his boys in the beater, just before I pulled up."

The rust-blotched Honda had slowed and the driver had rolled down its window, but then he rolled it up and sped away before she could step off the curb.

"They took off when they saw me. They know I'm a plain-clothes cop," he said. "It's a good thing, too, because you were about to get pounded to within an inch of your life. Then you'd get dumped somewhere conveniently near Juárez's place — that's not his real name, by the way, he just wants everyone to think he was a big shot in Mexico — and he'd talk you into a kind of a deal, like you'd crash at his place and work for him, and he'd make sure nobody hassled you out on the street, make sure nobody ever came after you again. And a week later you'd see the one who raped and beat you sitting in your living room eating a Pop-Tart on your sofa and you'd figure it out, but it would be too late."

She sat silently during this lecture. Officer Pete, as she had begun to think of him, had a weariness to his voice and a tic of flicking his nose. He did it regularly, a little more toward the end of the speech, so quickly his other hand didn't even whiten on the steering wheel.

He cleared his throat. "So, anyway, you're welcome," he muttered. "Now we're going to meet the nice social-worker lady who's going to open a case file on you and get you in a foster home."

She started upright. "I don't need to be in a home. I'm eighteen."

"So you said the first time. What's your birthday again?" He laughed. "I bet you can't remember either one of them."

"I don't need to be in a home."

"I don't want you on the streets getting knifed by some pimp. You haven't been on your own very long, have you?"

She considered the question. Was John David on her own? She didn't know, but she shook her head anyway.

"I thought so. You've been in town for less than a week?"

Two days.

"You don't love this work you're doing, do you? It's not your passion?"

She shook her head again.

"Okay. So you need a place to stay for free. At the very least, you'll go to a group home for a while."

A group home. She'd heard of them. If she didn't know any details, it was only because kids on the street who said "I just ran away from group" weren't saying it to share their life stories. They were saying it to scare the shit out of you.

He saw the expression on her face. "Relax, I'm not driving you straight there," he said. "You'll talk to Wanda, and Wanda will figure out what to do with you. If you're so scared of group, tell her you want emergency placement and then you want to be adopted by a nice family that doesn't beat you or whatever yours did." He flicked his nose again and stole a glance at her that he probably thought was surreptitious. "I'm sorry about whatever it was. I guess it was pretty bad. Still, this is a hell of a dangerous way to survive. You dead set against going home?"

She thought about home for a long moment. It seemed less real than what she had done, not just with the Petes to survive, but the other time. She remembered a wicked little blade and scrambling out of a hole on hands and knees slippery with blood. She thought of who was waiting for her at the hole's mouth. Whose blood was drying on the bunker floor.

"It wasn't—" she said, and tried again: "I just needed to get—"

"To San Francisco. I know." He sighed deeply, and she hated him with every fiber of her being, the stupid Pete. "You didn't invent it," he said.

She knew she didn't. Petes did. Janiece did. John David did.

12

Tom is finishing off some reheated food at the kitchen table when I get home. There's no sign of Julie.

"Where's the money," I say. The words are thick and wavy, as if seen through a streaky window.

He puts his fork down. "Anna," he says, already desperate enough that I know I'm right.

"Where is the money in the Julie Fund," I clarify, "and are you fucking Alma?"

"No."

"Liar." I can't believe it even occurs to me to feel anger at this. I have been lying, Julie has been lying. Jane, too, about school if nothing else. Tom, though—I honestly didn't know there was a part of me left that still needed him to be truthful, to be the good one, but there was. I wanted to have all the bad feelings to myself, cope with Julie's death—*Yes,* I tell myself, *her death*—in the worst,

most self-destructive way possible. And he let me think I was doing just that. This is the ultimate betrayal, then. Not that he was
the liar, the cheater, this whole time but that he let me think *I*
was.

"Anna, listen," he says. "You were drinking so much. And you
wouldn't talk to me, you wouldn't listen. I was so alone. You
wouldn't even come to the support group with me."

I want to yell that I stopped going to the group because it was
killing me. The hope, yes, but also the sight of other people's pain,
the thought of other people's daughters. Only my pain mattered.

"Do not put this on me," I start.

"You left, and I needed someone. I didn't love Julie any less
than you did. I didn't miss her any less than you did."

"You're the one who managed the fund," I say. "You're the one
who kept up the message board, distributed the flyers. You arranged the damn billboards. You talked to the trustees. And you
put *Alma* in charge of the money."

"Yes," he says.

"Where's the money, Tom?"

"I can't talk to you when you're like this."

"Like what? You stole Julie's money and gave it to your whore!"

"Anna!"

"Deny that you gave it to *Alma Ruiz*," I say, spitting out the
name.

He puts his head in his hands. "I gave it to Alma. Yes. Some
lowlifes working for her ex-husband came forward with a ransom
request—maybe the ex's girlfriend ditched him and he figured
out raising a kid alone isn't such a cakewalk, I don't know. I made
her the admin so she could sign off on my emptying the account,

and I gave it to her for ransom money, and she got her daughter back."

"Now deny that you slept with her."

There is a long pause.

"Deny it. Go ahead. I want to hear you."

"Once," he says, miserable. "After that—we went our separate ways."

"I guess you'd served your purpose."

He stands up, suddenly angry. "You don't get to say that."

"I think I get to say whatever I want right now," I say, but he's talking over me.

"You think you're telling me something I don't know? Yeah, maybe it was about the money, and maybe I was so damn lonely and messed up—anyway, we had it and she didn't. I don't blame her, I would have done the same in a heartbeat to get Julie back. If I thought fifty thousand dollars was all it took, I'd have slept with anyone for it. I'd have *killed* for it." He's trembling. "You would have too."

I can't think. I can't let myself. "What if we had needed it for a ransom for Julie?"

"But we didn't." He swallows, looks down, then back up at me. "You want me to admit it? I thought she was dead, Anna. It was easier to believe that than to hope." This breaks him. He bows his head, starts to shudder, dry-eyed, crying without tears. It is gruesome. "Can you forgive me?"

Right here is where I'm supposed to go to him, put my arms around his neck and let him hug my waist, and start crying as I confess that I, too, believed the worst. And follow that with the horrible truth: that I was right, and therefore he was right too.

Right to fuck Alma, right to save Alma's kid instead of holding out hope for our own. That by the time he was giving the money away, Julie was dead. Dead, dead, dead.

But I can't even think about doing any of that because I hate him for not believing in Julie's return. All these years, I doubted it only because I thought he believed. The thought of us side by side, each locked in our private mausoleums, mourning Julie alone, year after year, is depressing and enraging. All these years I've been jealous of his faith. If I'd known he was doubting, I could have been the one to hold out hope. It could have been *me* going to those meetings, *me* keeping the search alive for as long as the money held out. It could have been me.

"Anna, please," he says, looking up.

I walk out of the kitchen without saying a word. I've got to get to the meeting I set up with Alex after he told me about the Julie Fund, but first I need to find something in my nightstand. The IHOP on I-10 is too close to the house, but I want this over with fast, before I change my mind.

The manila envelope has grown fatter, as if it has been eating steadily since the last time I saw it. It no longer closes but gapes open on the sticky table between us, the contents partially obscured by the dog-eared flap. I wonder what Mercado has collected in that envelope about Tom and me, about Alma Ruiz, about Gretchen Farber. My life, in layer upon layer of sedimentary lies, beneath which, at the very bottom, I can see a glossy corner of the truth: the photograph. I hold the flap to the table with one thumb and pry the picture out.

I hold it in my hands and force myself not to look away. The original is so much bigger than the thumbnail, and so much more horrible. Bones bleached a dirty yellow by the flash, skull slumped to one side, a crescent of reflected light cradled in each blank eye pit. Scraps of black clinging to the rib cage in that shape I now recognize as an awful parody of a child's cartoon.

I just want the body.

I try to paint my daughter's face over the skull's awful blankness. I build up the soft cheeks, fill in the eye pits, give her blue eyes and white-blond hair that spills over the ground. But it is too much, and instead I find myself thinking of Julie, of not-Julie, of the woman living in my house who says she is my daughter—for money, for kicks, for some other reason too awful to imagine. Her face intrudes even on this moment. The photograph goes blurry but I keep staring, the tears rolling down my face.

"I'm so sorry, Anna," Alex says softly, and he puts his hand on my forearm, where the muscles that keep my fingers pressed around the photo are jumping. He leaves it there for a long moment, then pulls back.

I set her down on the table as gently as I would lay a baby down in a crib.

"You're sure, now," says Alex, voice still low but with the piercing, restless quality already coming back. "Why?"

I reach into my purse, pull out the photograph, put it on the table, and turn both photos toward Alex.

He immediately sucks in his breath. "The nightshirt," he says. "I don't know why I didn't—"

"I had to see them together to be sure." The photo is from Christmas morning nine months before it happened. She's sitting up on her knees in front of the last Christmas tree we ever had, holding her new diary in one hand and the too-large box we'd purposely wrapped it in to throw her off the trail in the other, smiling with the goofy, groggy happiness of a child still young enough to care about Christmas.

"Why don't the police have this?" Alex mutters, still staring.

"They asked for recent pictures," I explain. "I just didn't think to—I mean, look at her. She's still a little girl." But it was only nine months between when the picture was taken and when Julie disappeared. How could she have changed so much in nine months? It's the smile, of course. This is the last picture of Julie smiling the way kids do, with her mouth all the way open, showing her teeth. Shortly after that, she became a close-lipped teenager. And then she was gone.

"No, no," he says. "I mean, there's not even one photo of her in that nightshirt anywhere in the case files, just a description. I assumed you just didn't have any. That's exactly the kind of carelessness that would never have happened if this had been treated—" He breaks off, shakes his head, looks at the two photos again, and sighs. "Well, this puts that theory to bed anyway."

"What theory?"

"That Julie ran away."

I stare at him.

"Oh, come on, Anna. You had to know that was a possibility. It just didn't look like a kidnapping." He shakes his head. "Why do you think they investigated you and Tom so closely?"

"But Jane saw—"

"Eyewitness testimony from a ten-year-old? At that angle, from a dark closet, in a dark house? Not particularly reliable," he says. "Honestly, Anna, there was always more than a little reason to believe she'd made it all up or was convinced to lie. Or, if she did see something, didn't understand what she was seeing."

"But—" *They gave her a lollipop for sitting so long with the police sketch artist,* I want to say, but the words sound stupid even in my head. "The investigation—"

"Sure, big, high-profile case, leave no stone unturned. With no other leads, they were ready to take her story seriously, in public at least. Behind closed doors, though—believe me, I was there, I know where it was headed. I saw all the signs."

"No," I say. It seems important to keep saying this, because what he is implying is actually worse than my worst nightmare. It's something I have never even repressed. I never had to, because I simply never thought of it. Although now, with the word *runaway* instead of *abduction* ringing in my ears, I suddenly wonder why not.

As if reading my mind, he pries back the index finger of his left hand with the index finger of his right and starts on his list of evidence. "Minimal signs of forced entry. Almost staged, like someone just jiggled a lock pick around for a while, then opened the door with a key. The alarm wasn't even on."

"We sometimes—"

"I know, you didn't set it every night, okay," he says. "Could be. Or could be she disarmed it herself." He moves on to the middle finger. "No weapon."

"The knife—"

"*Your* knife, which he takes from the kitchen after he breaks in. He comes to this house in the middle of the night completely unarmed. And he walks straight up the stairs; he knows exactly which room—"

"We went over all this with the police. They said he must have staked out the house."

"I'm not saying he didn't," Alex reminds me. "I'm saying what the police were saying. I was there, remember? I've seen the file."

I sink, deflated, back into my booth.

"They didn't believe there was any man. And even if there was —she almost had to have known him, Anna."

I struggle to keep from raising my voice, and it comes out strangled. "Look, I don't care if she knew him beforehand or not. She was thirteen. That's child abduction."

"Absolutely. Still a crime. But a very different kind of investigation. Runaways are a lot harder to find, because they don't want to be found." He waits for a second as if weighing whether to speak, then goes ahead. "I don't know how to put this. If she'd been in my neighborhood, there would have been no question that she was a runaway."

"But Julie was only thirteen—"

"So was Stephanie Vargas. She climbed into a car with a friend of the family in 2005. My little sister went to high school with her brother. We didn't lift a damn finger for the Vargas family. She and her brother were staying with an uncle while Mom visited relatives in Mexico." He sighs. "Stephanie was a straight-A student. She played the clarinet. She practiced every day." He looks straight into my eyes. "Her body was found less than a mile from her house. Dumped in a drainage ditch."

I shut my mouth. His face looks older, years older, and I can see the shadow of punches thrown. It fills me with rage. "So you knew," I say. "You knew about this, you knew they weren't really looking for Julie because they didn't really look for this other girl, and instead of coming forward, instead of fighting for all those girls"—*For Julie, Julie, Julie*—"you just fucking quit?"

"I didn't quit. I was kicked off."

"That's not what you told me before."

"I lied."

You and everybody else, I think. "So why didn't you come to us back then?" I ask, relentless. "If you're such a white knight, where were you eight years ago? When it mattered?"

"I can't say for sure, but if I had to guess, I'd say blackout drunk in a public restroom somewhere," he says. "Or in a parking lot, or behind a dumpster. It takes effort and determination to get kicked off the force just for being a drunk. Really fills up your social calendar." He sighs. "Look, to be honest, even after I sobered up, I wasn't too sure of myself." He leans forward. "But I've tried to find her. Please believe me, Anna, I've tried."

"Why do you even care?"

He shrugs uncomfortably. "Some cases you never forget. They just nag at you. You're sure you screwed the pooch, but there's no proof."

We both stare at the photos on the table.

"Until now. We don't need a DNA sample, not with this. I can take it to the police. You lay low; you don't even need to be involved. They'll compare the forensic report on the remains with Julie's records. And we'll find out what we already know." He looks me in the eye. "Just say the word."

But I can't say anything.

"Do I have your permission?"

I look away. I nod.

"I know it's too late, Anna. I know I can never undo what I did, or didn't do, while I was drinking. But this is all I've got." He pauses. "It's all I can do to make amends."

"I don't want your amends."

I want my baby.

Baby

woke up without opening her eyes. Her insides hurt, like her stomach was a fist squeezing itself as hard as it could. Or like falling asleep with a rubber band in wet hair and trying to pull it out in the morning. Like something that wouldn't let go grabbing at something that wasn't there anymore. She doubled up to push the walls of her insides tighter together to fill the hole, but her body moved sluggishly, and when she tried to wrap her arms around her knees, her wrists felt pinned to the ground by powerful magnets. She stayed like that, curled on her side, knees to chin, arms dead.

Her body was slow, but her mind was waking up fast. The absence that hurt her stomach sang in her ears like an alarm bell, ringing louder and louder, shivering up and down her spine. She had won. Esther was bleeding out of her onto a fat strip of towel wedged thick between her legs. Esther was gone at last and, with her, the last of John David.

She tried to conjure up his image, the way she had seen him

once, wearing a wobbling halo of light. But when she saw a halo of light now, it was the glowing globe in the kitchen where she lay hard-backed on the table with her legs spread wide, and the darkness at the center of the light wasn't John David but a man in scrubs with a surgical mask and gloves who gave her a sweet pill to melt her to the table until she sank right through it. Then her spirit went up, up, toward the light fixture, where the outlines of winged insects with burned-out guts lay in a dusty pile. With her last bit of will she flew up into that globe light and let her tissue get burned right out of her. And now she was an outline only she could fill in.

When she woke up again she was in so much more pain that she could hardly stand it. The bed hurt her bones. Where was she?

Because it was dark outside, it took a moment to realize she wasn't on a bed at all. She lay on a slanted, corrugated slab of concrete under a bridge, the smell of gasoline and something sour filling her nostrils. Janiece sat a few feet away, her head and shoulders emerging from a mass of blankets. She stirred, and Janiece turned toward her.

"Hey, Baby, you feeling better?" Janiece asked. She leaned forward and adjusted some of the blankets without leaving her own nest. "You been making some noise there."

She opened her mouth to say *It hurts,* but there was only a gasp of air where her voice should be, just as if the fist in her belly were squeezing her lungs too.

Janiece nodded. "Yeah, you got the cramps," she said. "They're nasty. I had the cramps real bad after mine."

At the thought of Janiece with a baby in her belly, she blinked.

"I got nothing to give you for it, Baby," Janiece continued. "Aw, don't look at me like that. They don't send you home with nothing over at Smith's place. They give you one big double dose to knock you on your ass, but after that it's 'Naw, you gonna sell it' or 'You gonna snort it.' Baby, they don't give you nothing at Doc Smith's. They don't trust you for shit." She was talking more to herself now, but loud, as if she had an audience under the bridge, where the pigeons were wedged up under the shit-streaked concrete like a row of stuffed animals on a shelf.

She opened her mouth to speak again, but her breath kept snagging.

"What is it, Baby?"

"Stop calling me Baby."

Janiece just looked at her, unimpressed. "Well, you ain't Wig Girl anymore. What's your name?"

She thought for a minute. She stayed silent.

"That's right, Baby," Janiece said. "You can be Baby for a little while, it won't kill you." She leaned over again, put out her hand. The fingers touched Baby's hair and Baby couldn't help it, she relaxed. The fingers were warm and heavy against her scalp, and the rough dry skin caught her hair and gave it little pulls, and her own skin tingled around the pulled hairs.

Baby lay on her side all night, but she didn't sleep. Her stomach ached so much she couldn't imagine feeling anything else. "You just need something to eat," Janiece said. "Hang on, we'll get something when Pete comes by."

Baby didn't ask who Pete was; she just nodded.

They waited and waited for Pete. Cars swooshed by at random intervals, sometimes several at a time, sometimes thirty seconds with none and then only one every ten seconds for a while. Baby counted them but she couldn't see what color they were, or what kind. Janiece stared car-ward, immobile as the pigeons.

When Pete finally came, though, Baby knew she, too, had been sitting like a pigeon all this time, because Pete brought so much motion to the concrete ramp that Baby felt self-conscious, even while fresh rounds of cramps made her insides rattle like the wheels of the shopping cart that Pete pushed in front of him. When he got close, he pulled some scraps of blanket from around his wrist and tied them around the shopping cart's wheels so it wouldn't roll down the concrete slope.

"Took you long enough," said Janiece. "I thought we were gonna rot over here. Look, Pete, I gotta get her taken care of so I can go get something to eat. I'm starving. I've been taking care of this baby all day and all night."

"What do you need, J?" Pete asked without looking at Baby even for a second.

"What do you have to take the edge off?" she said. "Opes?"

"You wish," Pete said. "I can get you some later but you have to hook me up, understand?"

"Tylenol?"

"No way. Sorry."

"What the hell are you good for, Pete? Why have we been sitting here all night waiting for your sorry ass?"

"Go down to camp if you want Tylenol."

"Not with this one," she said, looking at Baby again. "She can't fend yet."

"Or the clinic."

"We're not going to any more clinics for a while," Janiece said in a low, gravelly tone.

"Fine," he said. "What I've got's a little weed, that's all I've got for now."

"I knew you weren't useless." She smiled. "Come on, Baby, I

got something for you. It's going to help, trust me." Baby willed her limbs to move, but the bumpy concrete was harder to navigate than she thought. "Come on, do you want it or don't you? It's going to fix those cramps up for you. And then I can go get us something to eat."

Baby pushed herself halfway upright and saw Pete looking at her for the first time. A warm, rank scent filled the air, something like the insides of shoes but also like the steam off a cup of tea, not entirely unpleasant.

"Here, honey," Janiece said, pushing the joint in her face.

Baby had seen a joint before when a boy brought one to school, though some other boys said it was oregano. It was certainly not something she ever would have associated with the smell that hit her in the face when Janiece handed her the twist of brittle paper, warm from the burning breath that had already passed through it.

"You gotta be kidding me," Janiece said, seeing her confusion. "Like this, Baby, see?" She kissed the wrinkled tip of the joint with her cracked and puckered lips, sucked, held the lungful of smoke, and exploded it out with a cough. "You really are a baby." She passed the joint, and Baby took it, tentatively kissed the moist tip, and sucked in. The smoke surprised her, a square feeling in her chest, something with corners and hard edges. She tried to hold it but her lungs convulsed, punching the smoke back out into the air. She started coughing uncontrollably.

"That's fine," Janiece said. "Take another. Don't worry about me, Baby, you finish that yourself. It's all for you. I was just showing you."

"Sure," said Pete. "I don't want any. Never saw you turn down a joint, though, J."

"I was just showing Baby how," she said. Meanwhile, Baby was coughing again, but a thick syrup had dripped down over her so she hardly even felt like she was coughing. Then came a deliciousness in her stomach that was like the easing of the fist, or maybe, when she noticed it, the fist was still there, clenched as tight as ever, but she didn't care anymore because all the muscles had started turning into elastic one by one, or something gummier that could stretch forever, like Silly Putty. Her skin shivered under scores of hair follicles that seemed to have turned into little antennae, and her whole body dissolved into points of light. Or bubbles, like the ones in a soft drink. She felt so happy, so safe. Even the under-freeway had turned into a vault, and she was something precious tucked away inside, hidden where no one could find her.

"You feeling a little better, Baby?" said Janiece, and now she could nod. Her mouth opened up as if on its own, and "Yes, thank you," came out as if from a pull-string dolly.

"So polite! That's good. That's real good. You keep puffing on that. But you're gonna get hungry next. I gotta go get some food from the camp. Here's Pete, he's going to look after you while I'm gone."

Baby shook her head from side to side at the sight of Janiece rising to her feet. Suddenly Janiece looked very skillful standing on her two feet, since the whole world was tilted and she was balancing perfectly on the side of it. Baby twisted her neck to make the world go straight again, but it settled back into a slant and she remembered that it really was slanted, and that struck her as funny, so funny that she started laughing and laughing. Her stomach hurt from laughter, not from cramps, unless they were the same thing. She had forgotten what the cramped feeling was about. There was nothing inside her. She was Nothing.

By now Janiece was gone, and suddenly Baby understood what

was happening with crystal clarity. It was too late for her to move, of course, she was pigeoned against the concrete like a doll on a shelf with huge, glassy eyes that wouldn't stay closed, even when Pete began fumbling at her clothes under her sleeping bag, and the smells of him became overwhelming. *Okay,* she told herself, because the panic was starting to rise in her, thick and warm, and she knew beyond a shadow of a doubt that screaming for Janiece or anyone would do absolutely nothing, because this was just another path she had chosen to walk down, remember? From now on she was choosing everything that filled her, and right now it was Nothing, right now it was Pete, right now it was a thing she had to do to earn the warm syrup of smoke coating her insides with glitter paint.

This slow, syrupy world gave her all the time she needed to understand what to do next. It was like she was in a bubble with the man named Pete and the sleeping bag and the pigeons and the cars, whose headlights never illuminated the place behind the pillar for more than a quarter of a second, but in those flashes she saw that Pete had fists and that there was a knife concealed in his pockets, and why wouldn't there be? It wouldn't be the first wicked blade she had stolen.

Baby lay still, waiting for it to be over. Nothing watched for an angle.

13

I watch her all week long, waiting for something to happen.

Now I am thankful for her short red hair, which both reveals and defamiliarizes her face. I retrace its contours, not with a mother's intimate knowledge but with a stranger's curiosity. I try not to superimpose the real Julie over the false Julie, compare line to line, but rather to learn every curve and dimple anew. Her chin is fine and pointed, but her jaw is sharper and squarer than it looks at first glance, her forehead higher and shadowed with the very first creases that no amount of blank-facing will completely smooth away. I try to determine the degree of the slight angle between the bridge and the tip of her nose, trace the flanges of her nostrils.

I do not look at her eyes if I can avoid it. Too dangerous. She'll feel me looking, and I'll feel something that may or may not be real.

Even so, I'm making her uneasy. She drops a glass in the sink

Wednesday morning and it shatters; Tom has to take her by the shoulders and move her aside so he can clean it up. She runs to her room and closes the door, dramatically but as quietly as if she's performing a role in a silent film. She can get up and down the stairs with hardly a creak or thump. I wonder if she is pacing in her bedroom; if so, we hear nothing of it downstairs.

Tom and I don't talk about it. We haven't spoken since Monday, and he sleeps in Jane's empty room, where he has moved his computer desk. I assume he works in there during the day. Perhaps Julie comes and goes while Tom stares at his screen and tries not to notice.

As for me, I go to work too. Once I'm in my office, door locked against the department secretary, I'm oblivious to faculty and students passing in the halls; nothing can hurt me. I put my cell phone on my desk and lay my head down next to it, waiting for Alex to call, waiting for news about the DNA test. Sometimes I grow impatient and imagine calling the police myself, telling them my doubts about the woman in my house. Things would move much more quickly after that. But I threw Overbey's number away and finding it again would take more willpower than I have at my disposal.

Besides, this way, like Alex said, I don't have to be involved. She'll never know it was me. That's the beauty of ID'ing a corpse rather than a living girl.

And what will happen when they get the results? I imagine the police bursting into the house, ready to cuff her and drag her away. She's sitting on the sofa under the afghan, watching a movie; she turns around at the noise. I try to inoculate myself against the expression on her face as they come for her. Shock? Rage? But I never see it. Instead, I keep seeing her expression illuminated by the ultrasound screen: bottomless grief, hopeless despair.

And what if I'm wrong?

But these are the habits of denial. When I feel myself starting to indulge them, I force myself to think of the photo.

It's a short trip from there to thoughts of Tom's gun. When did Tom take the classes, when did he get a license to own a handgun? Just another thing he was doing on his own, though I know it doesn't take long. I know, because I once planned to buy one. I told myself that's why I went to the firing range: I was practicing to get my license, firing rounds into a piece of paper shaped like a man for entirely pragmatic reasons. If something like that ever happened again, I told myself, I wanted to be ready.

It was a lie. I wanted to pretend, in every possible scenario, that I was killing him. Every time the gun discharged and I felt the jolt go through me, I felt exhilaration at the thought that maybe I had missed the heart, hit a shoulder or a knee or the groin, so I could have the chance to do it again and again. I wanted to kill him forever.

One day when I drove to the firing range, I realized it wasn't really Julie's abductor I wanted to kill. It was someone else, the person who was really to blame for Julie's death—and even if she wasn't to blame, she was the only person I could hold accountable. A firing range is the easiest place in the world to kill yourself; you don't have to own a firearm to shoot one. It was raining hard, one of those summer downpours where the air feels inside out, like a monsoon, and I almost wrecked the car getting there. I was too drunk to write my name on the sign-in sheet that day, and they turned me away.

I never went back. That was the beginning of the end of the drinking, and when I sobered up, I decided not to buy a gun.

But there are laws of inevitability at work in our lives. While I was crying drunkenly in my car, shuddering away from the brink, Tom, somewhere across the city, was making a different decision. And now the gun is in our house, like it was always meant to be.

Now that I've lost her again, I can always use it.

Friday night after dinner, Tom goes up to Jane's room and shuts the door while I sit on the sofa and idly browse the cable channels. Something has to give; something has to break. I believe it will happen tonight.

Halfway into a rerun of *Roseanne,* Julie confirms it by striding quickly past the sofa on her way out. I hear the garage door open, catch a glimpse through the kitchen window of Tom's car backing out. Leaving the television on, I wait a few seconds and follow her in my car.

At night, the freeway is less clogged, and the rosary beads flash past instead of scrolling slowly by. The faded awnings and new construction and apartment buildings look flat and dull at night, irrelevant. I can barely distinguish one from the other. Up ahead, the Range Rover weaves expertly around slower cars, in and out of lanes—*Julie's a good driver for someone who's only just learned,* I think to myself with some sarcasm. Though there are plenty of cars on the road, I can always see her. The SUV sticks out over the other cars, highly visible even to me in my squat little Prius. I know where she's going before she puts on the turn signal.

At night, the Gate is a bald hill wreathed in glowing glass. The surface parking lot is full—there's something going on, one of the nighttime services that are among the church's most heavily attended offerings. I turn into the garage, where suited attendants direct a line of creeping cars farther and farther up, and a steady stream of people flows back down a central staircase from the roof. I go where I'm directed, ascending past thousands of cars to the top level of the garage.

Every time I pass the staircase, I glance at the line of people, and just as I'm turning the corner to the top level, driving toward the open spots in the distance, I finally catch a glimpse of Julie heading downward with the rest of the crowd. She's wearing a long skirt and cardigan I bought her just a few weeks ago, when things were so different.

I park and walk down the staircase with the rest of the stragglers: a lean older couple wearing matching denim shirts and shining belt buckles, the woman carrying a leather purse dangling fat silver charms; a black woman about my age, in jeans and a ruffled blouse, herding two children in front of her; an elderly woman with a cane; a towering Latino man with a potbelly and a bullet-shaped head who pushes past everyone impatiently. All of us emerge together onto the surface lot, then stream down a walkway to the lobby, which is teeming with people. The hanging monitors and clerestory lighting feel different at night, surrounded by the faintest hint of a stadium echo that no amount of plush carpet and soft, shaggy area rugs can dampen. It makes the air feel a little fizzy, so that it's obvious this structure was originally built for excitement.

The escalators that cleave the entryway in half are covered with people, but I don't see Julie anywhere. I hurry past the information desk and step onto the escalator to avoid the enthusiastic greeters, only to be delivered straight into the hands of a thin woman with large, bright-awake eyes behind oversize glasses at the top of the escalator. "Program?"

I take the glossy trifold, still scanning the crowded horizon for Julie, and she spots my hesitation.

"Is this your first time visitin'?" she asks with a heavy Houston accent, flattening the vowels, chewing and pinching off the consonants.

"Um, yes." I nod, and she puts her hand on my forearm.

"Well, listen, honey, here's what you're going to do. You're going right back down this escalator and—you see that desk on your right? Well, now, usually Sheena is up here at the top of the stairs with me, but you can see her down there—"

I start to panic. What if Julie sees me, stopped here at the top of the escalator? "Can I just seat myself?"

"Of course, honey," she says but then calls after me as I'm moving away: "It's just since you're new, we'd rather you got one of the *really good* seats."

For my money, a good seat is one where you can see the lay of the land without attracting attention. I walk around the stadium's curve on the second floor, following the flow of people past a room with a sign saying COMMUNION, more video screens, and an unmanned, recessed information booth that used to be a concession stand or bar when this was a stadium. Then I step into the sanctuary itself.

It is cavernously huge. Cluster lights illuminate dust motes a hundred feet away against the bluish-black vault of what used to be the Astrodome, only the intricate starburst pattern of rectangular skylights on the ceiling hinting at its former identity. Gone is the Astroturf, replaced by acres of beige carpet; the folding seats lining the walls have been tastefully reupholstered in navy. Jumbotron screens flank the stage, and a TV camera on a crane swoops over the red-carpeted dais as if it's limbering up for the show. I find a seat halfway down the top section, close to the aisle, and sit down.

After a few minutes, the lights dim and the stadium, still steadily filling with people, erupts into applause. Audience members stand in waves, shouting, "Jesus lives!" and "Praise Him!" over the band, which has started up a dramatic, throbbing hum. Seven singers emerge from the depths of the altar, dressed in television-friendly stage outfits and holding wireless mics. All at once, the music bursts out, a heavy beat thrumming through the whole stadium, as loud as any rock concert, basketball game, or monster-truck rally. The laser light show begins, brilliant beams of green and blue sweeping the stadium. One moves across my face for a split second and I feel a shot of adrenaline, the chemical response to being bathed, suddenly and forcefully, in a powerful light. My heart feels as if it's actually leaping up, like in the Wordsworth poem; I've always wondered what that would be like.

The music thuds explosively onward. It's a soaring pop anthem, the song you hear near the end of a film about teenagers in love. The Jumbotrons cut between the singers' faces, the band sweatily playing their instruments, and a montage of images: fast-motion sunsets and sunrises, flowers opening in a tenth of a second, young people driving a jeep across dunes, a beautiful blond girl lying on her back beside a campfire, a black baby stumbling forward on chubby legs while a white woman kneels with her hands out, a sailboat speeding across a giant lake in time with the clouds.

After a few minutes of this, the singers part and recede around a lone figure who walks to the front of the stage. The people begin pumping their fists, the cries of "Praise Him!" louder and louder.

"I'm here for you," he says simply. "And so is the Lord."

I recognize the voice from the Circle of Healing, but this is my first glimpse of Chuck Maxwell in person. He looks like a country-pop singer at the Houston Livestock Show and Rodeo or the long-lost father on a soap opera. The Jumbotron gives me a close-up of the kindest, crinkliest pair of blue eyes I have ever seen.

"I'm here to tell you, the Lord has great things in store for you, His children," Maxwell says to screaming and applause. "And you're here for one reason: to listen, to know, and to praise His Holy Name. Because nothing happens by chance in this great universe the Lord has made. He's bigger than your problems. And when He calls your name, they'll be *gone!*"

"A-*men!*" a voice just behind me yells out.

Maxwell pauses and lets them scream for a while, a smile crinkling his beard around his neck. "Listen," he says. Another dramatic pause. The music is swelling and people are shifting from side to side, shaking their heads back and forth. "Tell it, Chuck!" a voice rings out.

"I will tell it! I will!" he yells. "Why are you here today, people? Let me just ask you that, why are you here?" He puts the microphone out and cups his other hand behind his ear as the audience yells in one voice: "It ain't luck, Chuck!"

He puts the mic back by his beard and says, "That's right, y'all. It ain't luck. Nothing is luck in this universe the Lord has made for us. He loves each and every one of us, we are all His very special favorites, and He will bring us something that is beyond our imagining very soon. And whatever it is He has in store for us, y'all"—he pauses again—"it's gonna be *worth* it!"

The screaming and clapping erupts once more, and the singers melt forward to begin a song, obscuring him from view temporarily. The man sitting to my left taps my shoulder and hands over a blue plastic bucket filled with envelopes and cash, a crisp hundred-dollar bill sitting at the top of the pile. I pass the bucket to the usher at the end of the aisle, who smiles beatifically at me although I haven't put anything in.

"Y'all, His blessings are gonna rain down upon us," says Maxwell confidingly as the music subsides. "I know you're worried. I know you've got the day job or the sick kid or the people coming after you about the bills. I know you've got the son-in-law who hasn't come to Jesus yet. You turn on the news, and you think this world is getting darker, turning its face from God. I'm here to tell you some of the best news of all: *Don't worry about it!* Let the Lord look after your neighbor and your kid and your landlord and your boss. What you're waiting for is coming, and the only reason it hasn't come yet is your faith ain't *strong* enough yet!"

The music starts up again, but this time slower, more hymn-like. "Now, this next song, I and my team of prayer leaders will descend down off this stage, and anyone who wants to can come on up here and pray with us. Just go on up to the head of your section, and a prayer leader will listen to you and pray with you, pray you get the wisdom to see what the Lord is already giving you. And the rest of you can take your seats and just listen to these inspired singers tell you about God's love."

As the crowd rises as one and surges toward the dais, I begin to understand what the "*really good* seats" are good for. Lines form, filling the stadium floor and trailing up the aisles, while Maxwell and a handful of other elders begin quietly conferring with the first few who make it to the stage. I sweep my eyes back and forth, searching for a redhead in the crowd, but the stadium floor is rapidly becoming an undifferentiated mass of people milling forward for their personalized prayers.

Just as I'm deciding this is an impossible task, there she is, on the prayer-cam, the features I've been studying so minutely blown up and hanging overhead on a Jumbotron screen. I watch, transfixed, as Maxwell appears next to her, his face tilted down toward hers, his eyebrows bent into a serious, compassionate expression, one hand resting on her shoulder. The redhead turns her face up toward his, stands on tiptoe until she's almost his height, and draws so close it looks like she's about to kiss him. She puts her lips to his ear and whispers something. Maxwell's expression changes dramatically. His eyes go suddenly wide, his eyebrows shoot upward, and his mouth opens in a gasp, like he's been kneed in the groin.

The camera cuts to someone else.

I drag my gaze from the screen down to the stadium floor, desperate to find her before the moment is over. There she is, one hand steadying herself on Maxwell's padded jacket shoulder so she can stay on tiptoe, the other pointing a finger at his chest. He jerks backward as she sinks down to her heels and turns to walk away. Two men in suits who have been standing nearby emerge from the crowd and start moving toward her, but Maxwell gets there first. He lunges, grabs her forearm, and leans in close, his whole body tensed toward her, enfolding her in a terrible intimacy. He gives her arm a single shake, and she tears out of his grasp and pushes off to the side, losing the two bodyguards, and my gaze, in the crowd.

When I look back at Maxwell, he's already talking to the next woman in line, their foreheads so close they're almost touching, and yet even I can tell his mind isn't with the woman he's absolving. It's with Julie, and Julie is gone.

I start up out of my seat to follow her but then stop myself and sink back down again. She's on the ground floor, and I'm upstairs; by the time I get out of the Gate, she'll be halfway to Tom's car, and I'm parked farther away than she is. Anyway, I have no idea what I've just seen and thus no idea what I'd say if I caught up to her now. Only one thing is clear: Judging from Maxwell's alarmed expression and the ferocious intimacy of his body language on the stadium floor, they know each other. What did she whisper in his ear? A threat? What could Julie possibly have on Maxwell?

Not Julie, I remind myself.

As the service comes to a close, the music swells and thunders, the screens flash and go black again, the slices of red dawn outline the Gate logo, and, in the grand finale, it opens. When the praise band finally decrescendos, the people around me look happily exhausted by the barrage of positivity. I stumble out, feeling emptied. Out in the night air, I check my phone; there's a new voicemail from twenty minutes ago. The signal must be spotty inside the concrete stadium, because I never felt it buzz. Then I see the number and hurriedly put the phone to my ear to listen to the message.

"Hi, Cal. It's Gretchen."

It's the same voice that cried, "Mom, Dad," when she hugged us in the emergency room, the same voice that whispered, "You must have really wanted to find me," before breaking into tears. And now this voice confesses out loud that she, the woman living in my house, is not my daughter. After everything I know, it shouldn't surprise me. But this is more damning than a fuzzy You-Tube video, more damning even than a crime scene photo. Only now do I realize I've been holding on to some last, slender thread of hope. These words—*It's Gretchen*—are the sound of it snapping.

The message continues. "I need your help, Cal. I'm scared." She starts crying. "If you're still at this number, you're in Houston. And if you found me here, maybe you already know everything about me. Maybe you know the worst." She sobs thickly. "If you come for me after finding out the worst, I'll know you still love me. I'm going to the Water Wall to confront the man who did this to me. He'll be there at midnight. Please come. I don't want to go alone."

On the voicemail, there's the sound of a horn honking, followed by a clatter, as if she's dropped the phone. Then: "Cal, I don't know if this makes any difference, but for a few weeks, I was—we were—I think it was a girl."

The voicemail beeps. "Press seven to repeat this message. Press eight to delete this message. Press nine to save—"

I press 9. When I confront her, I want to have her own voice in my pocket as proof. By the time I reach my car, it's 11:35, and I know I have to find her now, tonight, before I lose my nerve, and demand to know what she's doing here, why she's tormenting my family.

Now that I know Julie is only Gretchen after all, a blurry face on a YouTube video, a second-rate performer, an impostor, a fake, I have no choice. It's been Gretchen this whole time. And soon it will be midnight.

She

didn't feel the blow but she felt the black. It was like water she was sinking into, or that was sinking into her. There was a redness at the top of it, and the closer she got to the red the more it hurt. Whereas the black was as soft and lustrous blue-black as clouds of birds taking flight. The black was as soft and lustrous green-black as the ocean floor. The black was as soft as the black velvet pillow that swallows the diamond ring. The black was as black as her sleeping self.

She swam toward the red, she fought red-ward even though the black was trying to swallow her like a diamond, it was wrapping eyeless tendrils around her ankles and dragging her gently down, it was surrounding her with silent caws and carrying her into a blue-black sky. But every time she rested into its softness, she heard Charlotte screaming. Then there was a blow and the screaming stopped.

Then another noise, a mewling, that didn't sound like Charlotte or like anyone. Was it her? Her tongue was dead in her mouth, a dead bird with blue-black wings. The noise went on, a gurgling and then another thud that she felt inside her eyelids.

If she concentrated every red particle of energy to her fingertips, she could just feel the ground. It was slick and hot and red; she could feel the red stinging her fingertips. Or maybe it wasn't a feeling but a smell, a pointed smell that was both clean and dirty at the same time. It was the smell of losing a tooth, which was also a taste, warm electrified metallic.

She tried to pull her fingers back but the birds had all been clubbed out of the air one by one and she must be made of them from head to toe. So her dead-bird fingers rested in the electric red pool that smelled like teeth.

There were words being said, a litany, a prayer. They were being said in a voice she knew well, John David's voice, but they were angry. Maybe they were God's words, and it was God who was angry.

"You little shit. Goddamn little shit" were the words said over and over again.

The bird in her mouth twitched and she knew it was alive after all. It wanted to scream. She clamped down hard.

"What am I going to do. What am I going do. What am I going to do."

Thumping, retreating, ascending, and fading. He ascended into heaven. He had rolled the stone away and now He was climbing the basement stairs into the sky.

She opened her eyes.

Charlotte lay crumpled before her, upside down, four feet away, staring at her through eyes filled with blood.

She stared into Charlotte's upside-down eyes. They seemed full of wisdom.

Charlotte was trying to tell her something. Charlotte was the brave one, Charlotte was the smart one. She had even stolen the wicked little blade from John David's trash can to saw through the duct tape.

No, that was Julie who had stolen the blade.

Charlotte wasn't looking into her eyes after all. She was looking at Julie's right hand, curled an inch from her face. She was staring at something Julie could feel lying under the back of her hand, digging into one knuckle with a sharp corner. A wicked little corner.

When she moved her hand, the blade scraped the floor underneath and then there it was, a cold slice of air a few inches from her face, doubled and blurred but unmistakable. Her left hand slid toward it, fingertips dragging electric trails through the red liquid that was even now less hot than it had been, even now just barely warmer than the air itself. Her bloody fingers closed around one side of the blade.

Feet appeared on the stairs and, next to them, the head of an ax.

For just a moment, she squinted her eyes shut again. Just to remember what life was like when she didn't know that Charlotte was dead, and she was next.

An unexpected noise of retching came from the corner. She opened her eyes and John David was on his knees, facing away from her and Charlotte. He was not praying. A puddle of vomit snaked away past John David's knees toward the place where the blood was, where she was.

Before the puddle reached her, she was up on her feet. She hardly knew how she got there; her head was like a cinder block, but she stacked it on top of her body and stacked her body on top of her legs and then she was standing, towering over the broken doll that was Charlotte and the hunched figure of John David groaning in the corner. He spat, groaned again, and gasped for breath. A wave of dizziness swept over her suddenly, the red coming back to cloud her vision with blue-black dots swimming around the edges, threatening to rise up again like smoke. She put a bare foot out to steady herself, and the noise made the emptied-out John David whirl around on his knees, one hand still on the ax handle, one foot already making contact with the floor to push himself to standing. But as he pulled the other foot up, the heel of his boot came down in the snaky trail of vomit and his boot shot out from under him like a Russian dancer's, and he landed hard on the hand still holding the ax, so hard that his full weight crushed his fingers between the ax handle and the floor and he yelped in pain.

She stood, holding the razor blade out in front of her, but as he scrambled for purchase on the floor that was slippery with so much blood and vomit, she gave a cry and ran up the narrow stairs, not quite on all fours because she was still clutching the razor in her left hand but almost, using her arms like in dreams of running on all fours, some kind of throwback, maybe, to a time when hands were useful for something more than holding a feebly small razor blade that, although wicked, was nothing in comparison to the vast, smiling cruelty of an ax. Her knees, her everything, was slippery with blood.

"Esther! Esther!" The voice was behind her, beneath her, but how far? "Esther, come back! I won't hurt you!"

She was at the top of the stairs, and he was at the bottom. She looked at him there, so tiny, and saw the beginnings of a bald spot coming out at the very top of his head. She had never been taller than him before.

"Esther!" he cried again, but his hand was still on the ax, choked up now near the head. His voice grew wheedling. "I never meant to hurt you, Esther. Charlotte was the bad one. I only knocked you out so you wouldn't have to see."

"My name's not Esther," she shouted, but it came out in a whisper.

"No," he agreed.

She was shocked.

"It's Ruth. For you have seen much."

She stood stock-still.

"Ruth," he said, "you have passed the test. You have made a blood sacrifice."

His tone had lost its frantic edge and grown soothing, honeyed. "You did the right thing, Ruth. She tried to run away, and you stopped her. Now we can be a happy family again, just you and me."

"I—"

"You called for help. She overpowered you, and you called for help. And I came."

Although her head was swimming she knew that was not what had happened at all.

She shook her head to clear the cobwebs. "My name is Julie." That was the only thing that made sense, but it made his hands tighten around the ax handle. She turned and ran just as he sprang up the stairs after her.

His legs were longer than hers, but she darted around the cor-

ner just as he reached out to grab her ankle, the ax handle clattering clumsily against the stairs. She got around to the other side
of the kitchen table as he appeared at the top of the stairs, but
then realized she had pinned herself against the wall. He held the
ax with both hands, shifting its weight from one to the other as
if he enjoyed the feel of it in his palms. "Don't make me kill you,
Esther," he said.

"I thought my name was Ruth now," she said, this time forcing
the words to come out loud and strong.

"Whoever you are!" he yelled. "Don't make me kill you, because I will if I have to, but God does not want you dead."

"God is shit," Julie said.

"God is love, and *you* are shit," he returned. "Never forget that."
He slammed the ax blade into the middle of the table, and the
Formica cracked down the center with the blade stuck in it. She
grabbed the table from her side and shoved as hard as she could,
just hard enough to make John David fall on his ass, the ax still in
the table, and she almost laughed at how funny this was, but now
John David was scrambling along the floor after her, grabbing for
her ankles with his bare hands, knocking aside the chair she threw
back at him until finally she was at the door.

She managed to get one foot onto the concrete step before a
hand grabbed the pitiful bedsheet that was still tangled around
her like a robe. She tried to slam the screen door behind her, but it
bounced on his arm. She leaned back as hard as she could, hurling
her entire weight against the door. His hand jolted loose for an
instant, but then the fingers gripped her upper arm and squeezed
hard.

"I've got you," he said, panting, and his hot breath warmed
her cheek through the screen door. "I've got you." He leaned

hard on his side of the door, and she could feel his weight through the mesh, curiously soft and intimate against her own, and what a time to remember his bulk on her, what a time to remember those nightmare communions, what a time to suddenly feel more his than ever, in this moment of almost-freedom, of failed freedom.

"What happened here is your fault," he breathed through the mesh. "You aren't Ruth. You aren't Esther. You're *nothing.*"

But in her bloody hands, something wicked still remained.

She slashed blindly with the blade at his fingers, and when they opened, she ran.

Nothing nothing nothing
  Nothing nothing nothing nothing
  Nothing
She ran to the rhythm of what she was.

There was something, though, curled right up in her core, and every pounding, naked footfall sent shock waves through her legs to say hello to it.

Goodbye, she told it.

I don't care, she told it.

You're nothing, she told it. But she knew she was wrong.

She remembered a distant promise of help—peaches in syrup, canned corn—and ran hopelessly toward it. Every ounce of effort went into not tripping on the uneven sidewalks or getting smacked in the face with low-hanging branches or tangling herself up in her sheet, which was trailing. She could not take the time to look back and see if he was ten steps behind, twenty, or none; one fall, and his hands could close around her throat, bloody hands she'd slashed open herself with the wicked little blade, the same blade she'd used to commit the sin that could never be erased. Oh, Charlotte. Poor, poor Charlotte.

She ran through the old Houston neighborhood of hunched brick houses concealing God knows how many pulped skulls and ruined little girls, houses with who knew how many buried secrets in the backyard, zigzagging crazily around corners. The quaint old fairy-tale curves of the houses with their thick climbing vines nauseated her, and she ran past them in search of the larger streets that would signify civilization, and possibly help. But the streets were eerily bare—was it too early, even, for morning walks?

She emerged from the stifling neighborhood onto a corner with a stoplight and paused to catch her breath. A small park lay on her right next to a long, rectangular building with a covered walkway running its whole length. She recognized the sculpture on the lawn, a canal of rusty metal sunk into the grass in a random, nonsensical pattern like a dropped ribbon, and vaguely remembered visiting this museum on a long-ago field trip.

Looking around, she realized that it wasn't morning after all; though the light was at half strength and she felt that she'd lived through a long night, the colors weren't right for sunrise. The sky was a dingy, opaque white that made her feel as if she were still indoors, just in a bigger room. The trees loomed large, so dense and saturated with green, the color seemed to bleed off the edges of the leaves. That and the fact that the trees were absolutely motionless in the dead air made them look like fake trees on a stage set, or in a dream. She ran into the empty street and, craning her neck to the right, saw a freeway.

Then she saw it, towering above her, taller than the trees, taller than the lampposts. *Missing:* A girl, blond, beautiful, and pink-cheeked.

It wasn't her. Nothing like. She looked at the billboard and then down at herself, barefoot, filthy after months in the dark with him and the things he'd done to her. And now she had the something that wasn't nothing curled up in her gut to remind her of those things. To remind her, too, of what she'd done to Charlotte. The girl on the billboard knew nothing about that. She was perfect.

The next moment, as if someone had ripped a Band-Aid off the sky, a wall of rain fell down. In a few seconds it made a river that flowed past her bare feet and hid the billboard almost completely. She started running again.

By the time she got to the food pantry, the rain had slackened to a drizzle like laundry being squeezed out, and the sun was poking out from behind wet-flannel clouds, making the last drops sparkle in midair. The ground was already starting to steam, but she shivered in front of the thin plywood stall. It was padlocked shut.

"If you need anything," the woman with the peaches had said. She needed lots of things. Her stomach swam with the sickness that could attack her at any time of day, especially when she hadn't eaten. The only thing that kept her from vomiting was the thought of being found on her knees on the concrete, alone, in front of the pantry stall. She circled around behind it.

A figure leaned against the back of the pantry stall, sheltered behind it on the concrete slab, smoking a cigarette. The woman heard her and swiveled her head slowly in her direction, as if she anticipated being bored by the sight. She took her in from head to toe with a long look, exhaled, and waited with the cigarette held between two fingers down by her knees. She seemed like she was used to waiting.

Suddenly the woman snapped to attention and took another,

quicker drag off her cigarette. Then she leveled it out in front of her, pointing. "Wig Girl!" she said. "I know you. You're that wig girl. Where's your wig at?"

The girl opened her mouth to say something, but just then the cigarette smoke from the woman's outstretched hand caught the breeze and drifted toward her. The rush of nausea it induced sent her to her knees in the mud, and she puked into the long, wet grass behind the wooden stall, but there was nothing to puke, just acid that burned her throat. Afterward she couldn't see anything but green and yellow flecks for a while, and then there was a moment of blackness before she felt a warm hand on the back of her neck.

"Wig Girl, you don't look so good," the woman said as she helped her to a sitting position on the concrete. The flecks cleared, and she saw the woman's face more clearly. The weave was gone, and the woman's short black hair shot back away from her face in stiff little flames. "My name's Janiece. And your name's about to be Mama, if I'm any judge."

The girl breathed in and out, taking long gulps of the now smoke-free air. "I ran away," she said, and then paused. She couldn't think of the words for what had happened. She'd lied. She'd killed. She'd tried to be good. She'd failed.

"Yeah, I got that," Janiece said. "You got people you can go to?"

She shook her head.

"You need some clothes? A place to stay?"

She nodded.

"You need to get rid of that?" Janiece pointed.

For a moment she was confused.

"Whose baby you having, honey?" the woman asked a little more softly.

The retching came from so deep within her this time that she thought she would be torn to pieces. Except that wasn't even a possibility. To have pieces, you have to be *something.*

Janiece watched her as she came up wiping her mouth with the back of her hand. "Okay, then, never mind about that. You need some food in you either way."

She looked mutely toward the food pantry behind them.

"Oh, hell no," said Janiece. "Rhonda's a nice lady, but one look at that four-months-gone belly and she ain't letting you out of her sight. They got a room for you."

"A—room?"

"Look at that, it talks! Yeah, they got a special room with a special movie. They're *Catholics,* understand? You don't want to mess with Catholics in your condition, shit."

"She said—if I needed—"

"If what you need is a lecture on keeping your legs closed. And I ain't saying you don't."

"I need—" Every word felt pulled from a bottomless well. Sometimes the bucket hit water, and sometimes it went down and down and dangled in space.

"I know what you need, and I can tell you right now, you can't get it—not without a bunch of papers signed by your folks back home. Hell, it's probably someone there did it to you in the first place."

Home.

You're nothing.

"Come on. You're coming with me." Janiece helped her up and sighed. "Whoever did that to you, I hope he rots in hell, because getting it out is going to be a whole lot of trouble. Money too." A sideways glance. "But we'll talk about that part later."

She thought about hell. She thought about heaven. She thought about what was inside her, the life, the heartbeat. Then she thought about John David, his weight on top of her again and again. She hadn't crawled out of the hole after all. It was inside her. Its name was Esther.

14

In 2002, a rock climber named Ryan Hartley scaled the Transco Tower using a small pick. When he reached the thirtieth floor —almost halfway up—he jumped.

On his broken body they found a note protesting the war in Iraq. Presumably he chose the Transco Tower because it was a symbol of Houston's oil boom: sixty-four stories of silver-black glass thrusting heavenward, alone in the middle of a retail and residential area, the tallest skyscraper ever built outside of a central business district. Pure energy shooting out of the center of the earth, as if a geyser of oil could be caught, purified, and transformed into a prism of light. As if anything could be that pure.

Opposite the tower, across a rectangle of grass, stands the Water Wall fountain, a horseshoe-shaped artificial waterfall exactly sixty-four feet tall, each foot representing one floor of the Transco Tower. Once, we took the girls there after Christmas shopping at the Galleria. Jane, three at the time, pulled away from my hand

and ran up to the edge of the water, and Tom took off running to catch up with her. Adventurous Jane stopped right at the bottom of the steps and looked straight up at the curved wall. Then, dizzied by the rushing water, she took a step forward. Her legs buckled under her. She sat down and let out a wail.

Julie, five, lay on the concrete, her head tipped back to see the giant arc of rushing water from a safe distance. While Tom gathered Jane up in his arms, I lay down next to Julie so that I could see what she saw. I remember her warm head nestled into my temple, her wispy hair blowing against my cheek. Together we listened to the sounds of Tom comforting Jane, barely audible over the noise from the waterfall. The water slammed down the wall so fast that it hardly looked like it was moving at all.

When Julie spoke, her words went right into my ear. "Mommy," she said. "Is the sky falling down?"

I made a mental note to repeat it to Tom later that night, after the girls went to bed, and said in a loud voice that the water noise turned into a whisper, "Don't worry, honey, it can't get us here."

I felt rather than saw her brave little smile.

Seen from a distance, silhouetted against the lit-up Water Wall and framed by a stone archway, they could be a couple taking engagement photos: Gretchen and Maxwell, their hands clasped together, Gretchen leaning backward in a graceful bow shape against his weight. Then he jerks her forward like a dancer and clasps his arms around her, and they become one dark figure, waltzing back and forth in front of the illuminated wall of water. But as I hurry toward them over wet grass that gets muddier closer to the fountain, I see her elbows angling out as she tries to push him away, his arms pinning them back down again. They are both fighting to get at her purse, which looks as if it has been wrapped around her neck in the struggle. I break into a run.

I always forget how loud the Water Wall is up close, a pounding roar that changes pitch and intensity with my every step, fading one moment into the background in the manner of white noise, then throbbing with renewed intensity. A mist fills the round concrete plaza in front of the curved wall of the fountain, making the ground treacherously slippery, and at night the light is a yellowish, jaundiced glow emanating from the underwater fountain lights. Just as I cross under the archway onto the plaza, the conjoined silhouettes tilt alarmingly and skid on their fulcrum. Gretchen stumbles backward over something lying on the ground and then she's down, her head bouncing at the impact, Maxwell collapsing on top of her. He continues to flail for a moment like some deep-sea creature washed up on the shore, then pulls back, separating their bodies. A sliver of light outlines his beard and briefly illuminates a panicked snarl of animal rage on his face before he leans into the darkness, reaching for the purse that is now lying halfway under Gretchen's limp body on the wet concrete.

The man who did this to me. That's what she called Maxwell on the recording. I don't know what he did or who she is, but seeing his hand reach toward her motionless form, I know I have to stop what he's going to do next.

I propel myself forward as hard as I can, and then my shoes are sliding on the wet concrete, just as Gretchen's did a moment before, and my feet slip out from under me. I manage to get my hand out in front of me and drop to one shin, but my teeth close on a millimeter of tongue when I hit the ground, and a flower of heat spreads through my mouth. Maxwell sees me and springs to his feet, still straddling Gretchen's limp body. When he opens his mouth and speaks, his deep voice carries over the rushing of the water behind him, just as it carried over the sea of voices at the Circle of Healing.

"I know what this looks like," he says, panting. "But you don't know what this girl is capable of. She's dangerously disturbed. She lies. She's a killer."

"I don't believe you," I say, but I can't hear my own words, and I know that the lying part is true.

"She's been stalking me, making threats. She tried to blackmail me. She wants my money." He gestures toward a duffle bag lying slumped on the wet ground a few feet away. "She forced me to come here, threatened me. And then she attacked me." I look down at the unmoving body on the concrete. "I swear, I was defending myself! She's got a gun in her purse!"

But it's a mistake, because now I will never let him get that purse in his hands. "If all she wants is your money, why would she attack you?"

He licks his lips. "Like I said, she's disturbed. I'm successful, I help people." His voice rises petulantly, his beard bulging over his Adam's apple. "Girls like that can't stand a—"

"Girls like what?"

He looks at me with a faint air of surprise. "Whores."

I suck in my breath through clenched teeth. "You don't talk about my daughter that way," I say. And even though it isn't her, it suddenly is.

He lunges for the purse but I get to him first and push him into the trough at the base of the fountain with so much explosive force that the next thing I know I'm kneeling in six inches of water on top of his chest. Behind me, his legs flail and jerk in the water, kicking toward my back, my head, but I am mostly in the air and he is mostly underwater, which makes me heavier, tempo-rarily. My knees are on his shoulders, and I can feel his hand grab-bing for my hair, and *Good luck, motherfucker,* I think; I cut it short when Julie was born, I gave it to motherhood, along with dan-gly earrings and peace of mind and the ability to *not! give! a! fuck! about! anyone! And! dreams! of! my! own! And! a! heart! in! my! body!* With my fingers snarled in his tangled hair, I slam his head on the bottom of the fountain as hard as I can, like punching through the bathroom door when I thought Julie was hurt on the other side, but the water puts up too much resistance and what I get instead of a smack is a splash and a host of crazy shadows leaping up and careening away to the rhythm of my rage.

Behind me a voice cuts through the thundering water. "John David." There's a click I recognize from my fantasies. In the split second that my grip relaxes, he is scrabbling backward, kicking me away, until he's up against the water-covered slope. And then I see a look on Maxwell's face that says he wishes he hadn't kicked me away so quickly, and when I turn, I know why.

Gretchen is standing, holding the gun.

The pounding of the falling water is like a blank piece of paper, and the gun is the point of a pencil hovering a millimeter above it, sketching the three of us invisibly on the air before committing us to the page.

Our bodies hold the corners of a triangle open: The man with his hands up in front of him, back pressed against the slope, water pouring over his shoulders and pummeling his neck so that his head shakes with the effort of steadiness. Me on one knee in the water, frozen in the act of rising. Gretchen, standing with the gun.

"Esther," says Maxwell. "Please."

She ignores him, addresses me instead. "He's right, you know. I've had sex for money, more times than I can count. That makes me a whore. I've done a lot worse things too. Lied and stolen from the people who loved me. Used them. Left them."

"Julie," I say, forgetting.

She snaps toward me, and the gun flickers my way. When I flinch, the gun moves to Maxwell again. "Don't call me that. I'm done with Julie."

Something breaks off inside. It feels like a piece of my lungs, or like the water in the fountain is boiling and the skin is falling off my foot from the ankle down. That is all an exaggeration. What I should say is that it feels like all the parts of my body are going their separate ways. It feels like I am being abandoned by everything that has ever felt like a part of me. Maybe once you've been left by the most important person in your life, you can never be unleft again. Maybe you're destined to be abandoned even by your own guts, maybe your foot walks off with your thighbone, why not, stranger things have happened.

Like, for example, right at this instant, Gretchen, or Esther, or whoever she is, is pointing the gun at Maxwell and saying words that make no sense.

"I went back to our old place, John David. It took me forever to figure out where it was. I couldn't remember what the house looked like from the outside, but it doesn't matter, because it's not there anymore. Just an empty lot, except for the police tape, and a cross, and a bunch of flowers and teddy bears." She pauses. "I guess after you convinced me I killed Charlotte, you just bricked up the bunker and started over. God knows I've tried to do the same." Her face is already too wet from the spray in the air for me to see tears, but I can hear her gasping. "But other people care about that dead girl in there. You should see all the candles. Nobody knows who she is, but they don't just smooth it over and move on." She takes a step forward. "Neither do I. I didn't kill anyone. I'm not thirteen anymore, and you can't tell me it's my fault." She takes another step forward and levels the gun. "I won't let you."

"Help me, Anna, please help me," Maxwell says, a couple of yards to my left.

As unobtrusively as possible, I steady my foot on the bottom of the fountain.

"Stay back!" she yells.

"Okay," I say. It feels like there's a wall between us, seething with metric tons of water that I have to push through. "Gretchen."

That gets her attention. Her head jerks toward me.

"I know who you are. And I know about Cal." I'm rising slowly to my feet. "I know it was his. Maybe you love him."

She says, "Don't."

"I just want you to think about what you're doing. Think before you pull the trigger."

"I've had plenty of time to think."

"Me too," I say. I'm standing now, still in the water. I begin to slowly inch one foot forward. "I don't think you're a killer."

"I'm nothing."

But she's not nothing to me. For the past month, I've fed and clothed this girl. I've held her sobbing body on the bathroom floor. I've sat in waiting rooms praying for her to be okay, and I don't pray. I can't take my eyes off her now or the gun will go off. One foot is almost to the lip of the fountain. Every step I take toward her, her face looks younger and younger. I am fighting the wall, dragging my feet through her resistance as if it's a river running fast. "You're my daughter."

I am close enough to put a hand across her wrists. They are stone, untrembling.

"Julie."

She shakes her head at me. "Anna," she whispers with frightened eyes.

"*Mom.*" I gently wrap my fingers around the muzzle of the gun, expecting any moment to feel a searing, scalding heat.

"I'm not who you think I am," she says, and I'm barely close enough to hear it.

"Whoever you are, I love you," I say. And then I have the gun in my hands, and I'm feeling for the safety, slowly and carefully, as I keep my eyes glued to hers. "And whatever he did, it's not worth ruining your life over."

"He kidnapped Julie." Her eyes are wide and blue. "Mom. It's him."

The words slow everything down, expanding the waterfall's roar around an eye of silence. At my feet, the duffle bag has burst open, and shiny stacks of paper are sliding out, dampening and unfolding in the mist. As the breeze flip-flops one of them over the concrete, I see that it's a church bulletin.

Somewhere inside the eye of silence, Maxwell is screaming: "She's a liar, Anna!"

But something she said a moment ago is ringing in my ears. The bunker. The police tape. *Our old place.*

"I see you know my name," I say to him, and pull the trigger.

Esther

*was a virgin, an orphan girl living with her uncle Mordecai. But Esther
was made for great things.*

*One day the King of Light called her to his palace, for he needed a new
wife, and she was the most beautiful virgin in all the land. Esther was
scared. She was only a girl, and she did not want to shame herself in the
King of Light's palace in her dirty clothes. But she recognized the voice of
God in the King of Light's call, and she knew that when the Lord calls, He
must be obeyed. So she went to the king. He saw her and loved her immediately, but he refused to touch her. "Your garments are dirty," he said. "You
must not defile my bed."*

What happened then?

Esther wept for shame.

*Esther wept for shame. But the King of Light said, "Don't cry, my
child. Have faith in the Lord, and one day you will be cleaner and more
beautiful than you have ever imagined." And what did she think?*

She thought he must be mistaken.

Because?

Because she was unworthy.

But?

She did not question the King of Light.

Why?

Because he spoke with the Lord's voice.

"What must I do?" Esther asked.

"You must live in the palace with my concubines for a year," he said.

Esther heard the Lord's voice in the commands of the king, and she knew that the Lord must be obeyed. So she bowed her head and went to live with the concubines.

The concubines bathed and perfumed her and braided her hair. For a year they did not clothe her, so that she would learn humility. They taught her ways of pleasing the King of Light. They beat her when she spoke, but never left a scar. She never thought of running away, for she was willing to endure all for love of the King of Light, who was chosen of the Lord.

How did she feel?

She felt so alone. She felt like she was dead.

But?

But she knew that her clay was being shaped for the spirit.

So?

So she endured.

Other maidens were sent to the house of the concubines, and she saw them weep and complain, and some of them fled. But in the whole year, Esther never wept a single tear, and though other maidens were sent to the King of Light's bed, Esther knew they had not pleased him, for they returned to the house of concubines afterward and became the king's slaves.

One day, a year after she had first seen the King of Light, he called her to his bed. He was so pleased with her that he chose her to be his queen, the Queen of Light. And from that day forward she has been God's chosen.

What does she do?

She follows the Lord's commandments.

How?

She listens to her king.

Who is her king?

The King of Light.

Who is she?

The Queen of Light.

Is she happy?

This was the part she got wrong at first. Too many times. She had a round, red spot on the inside of her upper arm from the first time, purple and faded. The new ones were on the insides of her thighs.

But not today.

Is she happy?

No.

Why isn't she happy?

The Lord does not want her to be happy.

What does He want?

He wants her to be good.

And?

He wants her to be clean.

And?

He wants her to be beautiful.

She is, Esther. She is.

And then she closed her eyes. The part that always came next didn't hurt at all anymore.

During the day, he preached, and she, his first disciple, held the basket. She wore a sheet wrapped around her, all the way up and over her head at first, like a hood, until he spied a wig in a trash can out in an alleyway behind a building. From then on she wore the wig. It was a black, curly wig with a plasticky halo of frizz at the crown, and half of it was longer than the other, like something you would get at a Halloween store in a plastic bag. The underneath part of it was stiff and scratchy from being crumpled in one position for too long. It poked into her head. It smelled like garbage.

John David said it was to cover her hair, which had grown almost down to her waist and darkened from white-blond to gold. Her hair, he said, was a powerful blessing. God had wreathed her in light. She covered it when they were outdoors so that others wouldn't make her unclean by looking at it.

With the wig, she no longer had to wrap the sheet over her head. She got her peripheral vision back, and this meant she had to relearn to ignore the way people looked at them. She kept her face down most of the time anyway. She barely heard the words that John David yelled at passersby, although she could see their feet as they hurried past them. In his hands, a cardboard sign; at her feet, a basket. If she stared down at the feet hard enough, if she willed them to, sometimes a pair would stop in front of her and throw money into the basket. When this happened, John David never faltered in his harangue, but she could feel how pleased he was with her.

On the best days, they sang.

He would take the money out of the house, away from her, and come home late, smelling sweet and sour, and collapse into his bed without visiting her in the little room. This was the thing she liked most in the world: when he was pleased with her and fell asleep without touching her.

She wanted to be alone with herself, sometimes. She wanted to meditate on her sins. They were legion.

Once they went to the soup kitchen, but the soup kitchen was filled with men who looked, to her, like wild beasts in their dank overcoats and stained sweatshirts. Most of the men left her alone, but a few didn't. A man she sat next to at the long cafeteria table grinned and put his hand between her thighs. She froze. John David was gone for only a moment, and when he came back and saw the leering, stubbly face, he knew what was happening. The man knew too, and he jerked his hand away like it had been burned and picked up his tray and skittered off.

Esther was filled with shame. Later she was punished.

The food pantry, by contrast, was frequented by women with shopping carts and squalling babies who lined up outside until it opened. The food pantry was just a shed in the parking lot of a church, and it wasn't heated, and the people who ran the food pantry were as cold as the cans of peas and corn they passed over the counter. Some days it was all soggy green beans, and when they opened the cans at home and ate the beans, John David made her drink the olive-green salty water with its floating bits of bean skin afterward, because her wrists looked alarming poking out of her robes. Other times they got refried beans, her favorite, and small cans of peaches and pears in syrup. She saved the curled-up aluminum lids, tabs still attached, under her bunk, where they were—not hidden, exactly, but hers. She had no secrets from John David, and he could see everything anyway. He knew the lids were there but benevolently let her have a dark place to hide. While the bed creaked beneath them, she meditated on the accumulation of silver curves, imagined herself ice-skating along their dramatic slopes, hopping from one to the other, or even sailing in them like little boats, and then the boats turned to flower petals bobbing in a pond, and then for one horrible moment they were metal again, scratching and screeching against one another. And then all was silent and he was gone.

One morning, John David didn't come downstairs for her.

Esther waited anxiously in bed. She was not allowed to leave the bed until he bade her to every morning. She was afraid that if she got out of bed now, he would come back and beat her. Or, worse, that he would never come back at all. It might be a test.

Perhaps there was some reason he wouldn't let her out of bed. Perhaps the floor would kill her.

She thought about the lids under the bed. They would not let the floor kill her.

She listened. She waited.

Later, when she had woken and slept innumerable times, her stomach began growling too loudly for her to ignore. It was like a vacuum inside her. She got up, put her feet down without thinking, realized that the floor had not electrocuted her, thanked the lids, and went upstairs. There was only one can of creamed corn on the counter. She opened it and ate it. The sweet starchiness went straight into her bloodstream; for an instant, her brain felt oxygenated and fizzy.

"Where are you?" she dared to ask out loud, partly because she knew he wasn't there and wouldn't answer. She reached for the feeling of his omnipotence, but it shrank back, and she felt that he was not only gone, but also no longer looking at her. The thought made her cold, and she shivered.

On the third day, Esther went to the food pantry alone. It was the bravest thing she'd ever done, but she knew the way. She kept her head down as much as possible and wore a scarf tied around her wig—*A babushka*, she thought, the word surfacing from another plane of existence, as words sometimes did these days. She stood in line.

The women standing in line stared at her. One elderly woman with a babushka like hers leaned forward over a grocery cart she had pushed across the bumpy parking lot. A very tall woman with a short, tight skirt and a long blond wig snuck glances. A junkie, a twitchy woman of indeterminate age with long, greasy brown hair, stared openly for a moment, then looked abruptly away.

A woman with a weave turned away from the counter and walked down the line, humming and swinging a plastic grocery bag clanking with cans. A box of animal crackers rattled on the top of the pile. Esther could feel her approach, could feel everyone else feeling her approach. She needed food.

"Sugar, where your friend at today?" the woman asked.

Esther kept her head down.

"I said, where your friend at?" the woman repeated. "He is your friend, isn't he?"

The others pretended to mind their own business, but the twitchy woman in front of her, angry red marks glaring through the open cuffs of her oversize shirt, was the only one who seemed truly unconcerned with the conversation. Esther could feel the tension mounting. Another woman came shuffling away from the counter, cradling her cans in a windbreaker with its sleeves tied together. There was only one woman ahead of her in line now. She held her breath.

"Sugar, I'm talking to you. Who's that man used to come here with you?"

She had to say something. "He's my dad," she whispered, keeping her head down.

"Mm-hmm. Where'd he run off to?" the woman asked immediately, as if this question were on the tip of her tongue.

Another word floated up through Esther's brain and came out of her mouth in a whisper: "Laundromat." She pointed to her right, as if indicating something around the corner, just a few blocks away at most.

"Huh." The woman looked her up and down, taking in her dirty white sheet and sneakers, which were separating from their soles at the toes, and lingering on the wig. "Your mama know where you at?" the woman demanded.

Esther didn't hesitate. "She's dead," she said, eyes on the ground.

"Uhh-huh." The woman appraised her skeptically.

"Leave her alone, Janiece," said the tall blond with the teetering heels in a low, guttural voice. "It's some custody shit."

The woman named Janiece snapped back. "Mothers gotta be with their daughters. Especially when the father is *unfit*." She drew out the last word with a big pause between the syllables and looked pointedly at the blond woman's heels and ropy, exposed legs.

"Fuck you, J," said the blond, then sighed. "Besides, for all you know, her mama could be worse. I know mine was."

The argument continued, but by this time the junkie was

shuffling away from the front of the line, her baggy jeans and the pocket of her flannel shirt weighed down with cans, and Esther stepped up hurriedly. All the cans of franks were gone, but there was a can of chickpeas and another of refried beans, so she pointed to them wordlessly. The pantry worker was an older woman who was there often. With an expressionless face, she pushed an extra can of peaches across the counter. "Here," she said, "I've been saving these for you. If you ever need anything, let me know."

Esther couldn't bring herself to nod in case he was watching from somewhere close by, testing her. But she made eye contact with the woman for just a moment and tried to thank her for the peaches with a half smile. The woman named Janiece was gone when she turned back, and the tall blond woman had folded her arms and was muttering to herself. The junkie was weaving back and forth down the sidewalk. Suddenly she put her hands up toward heaven and crowed toward the sky.

Esther hurried home, tennis shoes tripping over the tangled sheet. She wondered if John David would know she'd gone out of the house, and if so, what her punishment would be. If this had been a test, she had failed. Esther thought about Abraham in the Bible tying up his son, Isaac, the raised knife flashing in the early-morning sun, like John David told her. God, too, had sacrificed His Son, Jesus. Always sons, never daughters. Were daughters too important? Or was it the opposite?

She walked into the kitchen, ate, went down the stairs at the back of the pantry, and lay down in her bed to await further instructions.

From her bed she heard the back door creak open, and two pairs of feet started moving through the kitchen upstairs. She almost didn't recognize John David's voice at first; it was pitched higher and reminded her of someone she had known a long time ago, a man with a guitar. He was talking with a second voice, and though she couldn't hear the words, the tone was friendly.

The second voice belonged to a girl with heavy footsteps. A chair screeched across the floor, accompanied by a squeal of pain and a burst of laughter. Whoever she was, she was clumsy.

"Esther!" he yelled into the pantry. "Esther, come up here!"

She glanced at the wig, the sheet draped over the foot of the bed. As if he could see her, he yelled, "We're not going outside, don't worry about your shoes and stuff. Just come up and meet someone."

Meet someone. She walked warily up the stairs in her nightshirt. A young girl, maybe a little younger than Esther, stood in the kitchen next to John David. She was short, with dyed-black hair pulled into scraggly pigtails. She wore a black T-shirt and a short black skirt that poofed out above her knees, exposing smudged white legs over faded rainbow socks.

"Esther, this is Charlotte," John David said.

She saw with a shock that he had shaved his beard. A memory fizzed through her brain of a guitar with an embroidered strap, a room with posters on the walls. His skin that had been hidden under the beard looked pinkish and bumpy, like chicken skin; his mouth looked small and thin-lipped; there was a tiny cut above his Adam's apple.

Charlotte rhymes with *harlot*. Esther kept her eyes on the floor, but she was aware that Charlotte was staring at her and became suddenly self-conscious about her appearance: ratty nightshirt over jeans he'd stolen from a dumpster, dirty, naked feet sticking out from the frayed cuffs. She wondered if the nightshirt smelled bad. It had never been washed.

"Charlotte, Esther's my niece. She's been crashing here for a little while." There was that voice again, the new-old John David who reminded her of when she was someone else, a long time ago. He turned and addressed himself to Esther in that kind, friendly voice and it made her want to cover her ears and sing until she couldn't hear it anymore. But she knew better. "Esther, can Charlotte use your computer to check her e-mail? She's a long way from home, and I know she would really appreciate it."

Esther didn't have a computer. She knew what was required of her, though. She nodded without looking up.

"Great. I'll just take her down and get her set up in your room. Do you mind hanging out up here for a few minutes?"

Esther nodded acquiescence and stepped away from the door. As they passed her, Charlotte said, "Thanks." Esther looked up at her quickly, caught a glimpse of brown eyes with a shimmer of green or gold in their depths. She put a hand out to grab Charlotte's arm.

But Charlotte had seen the narrow door in the back of the pantry by then. "Whoa, is this like a secret passage or something?" she said.

"Bomb shelter," John David said, hovering behind her shoulder.

"No way!"

"This house belonged to my grandparents," he said. "My grandfather was a fighter pilot in the Pacific. He was scouted for NASA in '61. They could have moved out to a big house in Clear Lake. But my grandmother believed the Cold War would end in a nuclear holocaust. She believed Jesus would scourge the earth." His voice sounded far away. "She convinced him to build an underground bunker here."

"That is trippy," Charlotte said appreciatively.

It was trippy. Esther had never heard any of it. Thinking about John David's grandparents made him seem suddenly very ordinary.

"You can't have a basement at sea level, but with about ten tons of concrete, you can have a fallout shelter."

The words tumbled through her head, a history lesson, casually delivered, as if the man speaking weren't outside of history, weren't divine. As if he were just a man living in a house.

"Your niece is so lucky. This is the coolest bedroom ever." Charlotte's voice receded down the staircase with her footsteps. As the two of them vanished into blackness, Esther understood for the first time what was going to happen.

She understood for the first time that it had happened to her.

She curled up on the sofa and put her hands over her ears, but she still heard it. No words, just Charlotte's voice getting higher and shriller, and then a thump and another thump, something dropped on the concrete basement floor with a clatter, muffled yells, the sound of shoes sliding against the floor as if scrambling for purchase. A short silence. Something heavy being dragged. And then a sort of stuttering bark she recognized, after a moment, as the sound of duct tape being ripped off a roll.

John David appeared at the top of the stairs, looking weary, and dropped a bundle of clothes on the pantry floor. He filled a plastic bucket with water at the kitchen sink and handed it to Esther. "Bathe her," he said.

The concubines bathed and perfumed her and braided her hair.

The sponge was a new blue kitchen sponge, soft on one side and scratchy on the other. The bucket was unexpectedly heavy and swung a little as she took it, splashing a bit of water over the edge onto his shoes.

He walked to the sofa to lie down. The exercise had exhausted him, drained him of the emotional electricity that usually seemed to vibrate off him in waves. Lying with his eyes closed, he looked smaller. She took a step toward him, but he drew his elbow up over his eyes and turned toward the sofa back. In a moment he was snoring.

She wondered what he was doing up here all those times while she trembled in her room downstairs. Napping on the sofa? Fixing himself a sandwich? These thoughts filled her with dread. She turned away and walked to the pantry door. She stepped over the pile of clothes, pulled this way and that like a cast-aside doll. The black T-shirt lay on top, inside out and twisted double, so that the picture on the front was only a blocky outline puckering the fabric, the letters on the back backward and illegible. She started down the stairs.

Before she could see Charlotte, she smelled her; she'd peed herself. Then her eyes adjusted, and gradually a glimmer of whiteness grew and spread into the shape of a torso. Charlotte lay naked on the floor. Her hands were duct-taped behind her back, her shins duct-taped solidly together in a silver column, so that in the dim light it looked as if her legs had been cut off below the knees, her white feet lying nearby like a pair of sneakers. A piece of duct tape was pressed over the bottom half of her small round face, a little bump showing where the lip ring was. Her eyes were closed.

The concubines bathed and perfumed her and braided her hair.

Esther knelt down, her knees making cold contact with the concrete. She put the bucket and the sponge on the floor beside her and waited.

This was too much. She would go back upstairs, tell John David she couldn't do it.

Esther inched toward the body on her knees, trying not to look, feeling hot tears coming to her eyes. She put out a hand, moving closer and closer to where angry pink circles blotched the soft white belly in clusters of four, like fingertips, over her ribs, then pulling back. She took up the sponge and dipped it in the water, which had started out lukewarm but was nearly cool by now. Careful to keep the rough side of the sponge facing away from Charlotte, she very gently applied one wet, soft corner to the bruises that stained the white expanse of stomach, as if the water could wash them away.

The girl's eyes flew open.

Esther started backward with a shriek.

Charlotte, unable to scream, moaned into the tape and raised her head only to shake it wildly back and forth, strands of her too-black hair coming out of her pigtails and floating in front of eyes that were all white. She rolled onto one shoulder and jackknifed her bound legs back and forth until she managed to kick Esther hard on the side of her knee.

Esther gasped and put a hand to her leg. But the impact of the kick overbalanced Charlotte and she fell back and hit her head on the concrete. Then she lay still.

Esther picked up the sponge, which had landed close to her feet in the scuffle. "I'm just going to give you a bath," she reassured Charlotte. "It won't hurt."

The concubines bathed and perfumed her and braided her hair.

"I have to bathe you," she said. "You have to be made clean."

The girl began moving her legs again, but slowly this time, as if tired out by her initial fury, bracing her feet against the floor to push herself around, leaving her head limp. Still flat on the ground, she rotated clockwise by inches, like a fat white goldfish in a koi pond. Every minute or two, she would stop and lie still for a moment. Then she would start again. When she was facing away from Esther, she stopped and lay completely still.

Esther got up and walked around to Charlotte's other side so she could see her face, wondering if Charlotte would begin inching around to escape her again. But Charlotte appeared to be looking at something.

Esther got down on her knees and put her head close to where Charlotte's head was and looked. And she saw them. The lids, curled up on the floor like they were hiding under the bed.

No, like trash.

They smelled like trash. The whole room did. It reeked with a faint sickly-sweetness that Esther had never noticed before. She'd been sleeping on a bed of garbage. Her stomach turned. She looked around at the tiny, windowless room. Not a basement. You can't have basements at sea level. A prison. A torture chamber. The bed covered with its tattered blanket. Her whole world, so small.

When she looked back at Charlotte again, she knew that Charlotte didn't belong here. She'd never submit to this atmosphere. She would disrupt everything, had disrupted everything already. She had twisted the room inside out, changed it somehow, like the inside-out T-shirt. Esther could almost read a message coming through the thin fabric of her reality, but the letters were backward and didn't make sense. She had to straighten everything out.

She had to get rid of Charlotte, and she knew how. It would be a sin, but then, John David had told her often enough she was a sinner.

Esther crept up the stairs. John David lay on the sofa, unmoving, and she was struck by how peaceful he looked. With his newly shaven face and without his towering height above her, he looked more like a boy than a man. There, as she'd remembered, was the tiny red bump on his Adam's apple where he'd cut himself shaving.

He'd *cut* himself.

There was a razor in the house.

The most logical place to look was the bathroom attached to John David's bedroom, but she had never gone in there. All of the bedrooms were off-limits, so that even stepping into the dark, doglegged hallway gave her a shiver of discomfort. She had seen only the kitchen and the bunker, though she was allowed to use the half-bathroom up here instead of the tiny metal toilet in the bunker, which required buckets of water to operate. When she peered into the bedrooms at the end of the hall, she understood for the first time that it was an ordinary house, even comfortable. The beds were covered with bedspreads and sheets. There were lamps, teal carpets, and wallpaper — one room covered in flowers, one pebbled with gold. On the nightstand in the unused bedroom stood a bronze deer and a box of tissues with a knit cozy over it and a dust ruffle sewed to the bottom. The upper reaches of the single white tissue were coated with dust, and a few severed threads of cobweb floated in the still air.

John David's bedroom looked much the same. She had pictured him on a pallet of some kind, but he slept on a king-size bed under a painting of a landscape, somewhere dry with mountains, as different from Houston as she could imagine.

The bathroom cabinets still held grandparent clutter: Nearly empty bottles with varying degrees of stickiness settled around their bottom edges. Small, beaked vials of eardrops and eyedrops. Silver cards bubbled with fading pills. Plastic pill cases marked with the days of the week. Nothing useful.

As she turned to go, she spotted one more thing: a trash can behind the door. She could just see, under a wad of tissues and curled-up dental floss, a wicked glint.

She looked down at Charlotte, whose eyes wobbled with tears, her penciled eyebrows tilting upward at the middle, chin dimpled beneath the duct tape. Esther put a finger to her lips. "Shhh," she warned.

Then she ripped off the duct tape.

They stared at each other. Charlotte's eyes were so big that for a moment, the rest of her face disappeared, and Esther felt like she was looking into a mirror, staring into her own eyes, and the rest of her became disconnected. Esther took a bundle of used Kleenex out of her pocket and began unwrapping it cautiously until she felt the razor blade in her hands: a small, wicked thing. A sin.

She showed Charlotte the blade and said, "Hold still." The duct tape around Charlotte's wrists was accordioned into thick, sweat-stiffened pleats. Sawing at the tape, she felt all the girl's resistance—to John David, to the hole they were in, even to her. The tension was hot in Charlotte's wrists. Charlotte had fought John David. She would fight anyone, and she'd never stop fighting.

Julie, that worthless whore, had lain down without a struggle.

The names popping into Esther's head were tumbling over one another, confusing her. Every tug of the blade through the duct tape freed her a little more—freed whom, though? Charlotte? Esther? Or the other girl? She kept cutting, hearing the soft protesting squeak of the tape against the absurdly small blade as she worked it patiently back and forth, the heavy tape grabbing and twisting at the tiny blade so that she had to stop and unstick it from time to time with a small smacking noise. After an eternity, the last fibers on one side of the thick sleeve of duct tape gave. Charlotte wrenched away from her, twisting her arms apart so that the skin stretched white and red until one of them pried itself free. Her arms were surprisingly strong for being so short and thin, but Esther knew they must be sore from being taped behind her back.

Charlotte was the bravest, strongest girl she had ever seen. Tears came to Esther's eyes, and she started wriggling out of her nightshirt, keeping it right-side out as she shrugged it off over her head.

"Here," she said.

Charlotte took the warm shirt right away and slipped into it without so much as glancing at Esther. Then she held out her hand for the razor and started hacking at the tape on her shins. Esther grabbed the sheet off the foot of the bed and wrapped it around her torso and shoulders, tucked it under her arms. She'd worn a sheet many times before.

"Give me a hand, would you? Get this off," Charlotte said, and Esther started peeling the damp swaths of slashed tape away from her calves while Charlotte kept working on the tape with the razor. "Okay," she said. "I'm getting the fuck out of here. You're going to help me, or I'll cut you with this." She held up the razor blade. "Got it?"

Esther nodded with a smile. She knew Charlotte wouldn't really hurt her.

"What's your name?" Charlotte asked.

"Esther."

"Is that your real name?"

Esther thought about that, but Charlotte was already back to working on her knees. "That guy is a sick fuck," Charlotte said. "Come on, tell me your real name."

"My name is Esther."

"Like hell it is," Charlotte said, and with a snap, she jerked the blade through the last strand of duct tape. As she clawed the tape away from her legs and stood up, the blade dropped to the floor. The barest nudge from Charlotte's foot sent it skittering away as lightly as a leaf. It stopped and spun in place on an uneven bit of concrete for a moment before coming to rest. "Come on. Look, you helped me. You have guts. We're going to get out of here. Now, what's your name?"

Julie started to speak, but Charlotte wasn't looking at her anymore. She was looking at something right behind her and opening her mouth.

15

The visitation room at the Harris County Jail is a hellish, echoing cacophony; there are no handsets to use to communicate through the Plexiglas windows, and the speakers embedded in them barely work, so dozens of visitors, many with children in tow, are reduced to screaming through the glass. After Tom's first visit, I tell him not to come back, and please, for the love of God, not to let Julie come either.

Instead, I call Jane. Once a day, in the morning, I dial her cell phone using an insanely expensive third-party account and listen to her talk until my fifteen minutes is up and the call auto-terminates. She sounds remarkably normal—tells me about her summer makeup classes, complains about finishing her papers, contemplates joining a kickball league. It's like my transgression has opened a floodgate in her, and Jane is bubbling over with the details she'd wanted me to work so hard for before. They are details of a life that turns out to be gloriously mundane, only superficially rebellious, on the level of hair dye. Having to define herself in relation to someone who wasn't there and who was therefore always perfect was existentially confusing for Jane. Now, with an actual person to compare herself to, she doesn't seem to need the big gestures anymore. From what I can tell, she is flourishing.

It's a little exhausting to listen to, but she repays my years of neglect by not asking me any questions about myself, not even a *How are you?,* which I appreciate. She doesn't ask about Julie either, but Tom says she and Julie e-mail regularly.

("Of course I knew it was her," Jane said when I finally got up the courage to ask, speaking in a tone that suggested I was not a bad mother, just stupid. When I reminded her she was the one who told me Julie was lying about the cell phone, she said, "I don't see what difference that makes. I lie all the time, but it's still me.")

A tiny, lonely part of me is angry that Jane hasn't offered to come home, but long days of contemplation have convinced me that she's waiting for me to ask, and until I stop being afraid she'll say no, we're at an impasse.

In the meantime, I can't say I don't enjoy living vicariously through Jane, a little bit. How exciting to believe in your own ability to defy the world's expectations of you even as you fulfill them, one cliché after another. I have spent my own life looking to my left and right and finding only the well-worn tracks of my own thoughts and behavior hemming me in. Maybe it's a side effect of studying the Romantics, those fetishists of originality who unwittingly invented two centuries' worth of platitudes; maybe that's why I can't seem to respond normally to those who love me and whom I love. But I try, with Jane. I listen, I imagine the thwack of a wet kickball against a shoe on the quad, and at the end of every phone call, I feel the dingy, fluorescent-lit jail cell settle a little heavier on my shoulders.

There were witnesses—a teenage couple trudging up the lawn to make out by the glowing waterfall that night. The young man has a criminal record that will keep him off the stand, but the young woman will testify that, although she couldn't see Julie and me from where she was, the victim was clearly visible in the fountain lights, holding up his hands and pleading for his life. She heard a shot and saw him sink into the water, but she didn't make the 911 call.

I did that.

As luck would have it, the judge assigned to our high-profile case is a former district attorney, notorious for following her cases up the chain of appeals, attaching herself to the prosecution, and even submitting testimony condemning defendants she's already ruled against. She's also vocal about her relationship with Christ, and, if I had to guess, I'd say Chuck Maxwell donated to her campaign. The thought of a godless academic rotting away in the county jail, a facility well known for abuses, perhaps getting softened up for a plea bargain at the hands of her cellmates, must appeal to Judge Crofford as much as it does to the prosecution, who file motion after motion to delay my bond hearing, using every excuse from the live-stream footage of Julie whispering in Maxwell's ear to the inflamed public sentiment over this appalling attack on a pillar of the community.

It's true that jail is dirty, overcrowded, humiliating, and excruciatingly boring—you can't get phone calls, incoming letters are limited in length and heavily censored, and the official process for getting a single book approved and ordered from the publisher can take months. I'd pay a lot of money for something to read to take my mind off my dismal surroundings. But if Crofford expects the inmates to harass me, she's wrong. The women leave me alone. Word must have spread pretty quickly among them that I shot the man who kidnapped and raped my daughter.

That's the rumor they've heard anyway. Proving that's what happened is much harder, of course, and my self-defense claim rests on it. At the police station I begged them to check his DNA against the bunker-house crime scene in River Oaks, and I used my one phone call to leave a message for Alex Mercado. I have to admit that although I can see the resemblance in the shape of Maxwell's low brows and hooded blue eyes, the bearded, square-jawed billboard minister doesn't otherwise bear much resemblance to ten-year-old Jane's police-artist sketch of a skinny, ponytailed guy in a hoodie.

And then there's what Maxwell is saying: that Julie and I were blackmailing him together.

Yes, Maxwell is very much alive. Not for lack of my trying. My shot hit him low on the shoulder, and he went down on his back into the shallow water before I saw the bullet wouldn't kill him. That's for the best, because if I had seen right away, I would no doubt have kept on shooting until there were no bullets left. I'm glad I didn't, and it's not because I feel Maxwell's death would have been such a great loss to the world; it's not even that I prefer to see him humiliated and exposed and put away for life rather than dead. It's just that if he'd died as a result of my shooting him, prosecutors might be pushing for a capital murder charge right now—in Texas, even an accidental death that occurs during the commission of a felony can be punished with the death penalty, and blackmail is a felony. When I pulled the trigger, the preservation of my own life was not high on my priority list.

But everything's different now, because I have my daughter back.

I wish I could say it happened in a flash, that standing there at the Water Wall with a gun pointed at Chuck Maxwell, I could suddenly see thirteen-year-old Julie in twenty-one-year-old Julie's face, like a Magic Eye poster you've been staring at for weeks that suddenly leaps into focus. But that wouldn't be right, because I always saw her there, from the very beginning, from the moment she appeared on our doorstep. I knew; I just didn't *believe*. Her lies and evasions made doubting easier, gave me something concrete to focus on. My new version of Julie was like the optical illusion of the candlestick-shaped negative space between two profiles. Imagine two faces—Julie then and Julie now—staring at each other in profile across a gash of grief. All this time I've been seeing only the ugly shape of what's between them. The negative space of trauma.

I haven't talked to Julie since I was arrested, so I still don't know what's in that black hole, but I'm ready to accept what's on either side of it. Julie, before; Julie, after.

In the pretrial hearing, the prosecutors ask to have the trial date pushed back. At first I think it's more intimidation—keep me stewing longer—but then I hear the words "River Oaks murder victim," and I know Alex Mercado must have gotten my phone message. The lead attorney on my case asks again for bail while the police investigate a link between Maxwell, Julie, and Charlotte Willard, a thirteen-year-old girl who disappeared from her home just across the Louisiana border in Beauregard Parish about six months after Julie did. It's Charlotte Willard whose DNA they eventually matched to the remains in the bomb shelter, and it was Maxwell's grandmother who originally owned the house; I imagine Alex has left me messages to that effect on my phone, but I'll have to wait to check them. I remember what Julie called the house: *our old place.* Alex was wrong about Julie being dead, but he wasn't wrong about everything. He just had the girls mixed up— who'd escaped and who was dead. It could have gone either way, really. I think of the awful photograph again, and the horror that befell this girl who is not my daughter suffocates me. I cry for her mother and wish once more my shot had killed him.

The judge denies bail again, but my attorney looks hopeful. In the hallway, she tells me of an anonymous blog post whose writer claims to have been sexually molested by Maxwell at the Gate, her mother allegedly ejected from church membership for bringing a complaint. A former member of Springshire Methodist, this one named, alleges that Maxwell was fired from a briefly held leadership position in the youth group nine years ago after abusing her daughter. Both women were immediately served with cease-and-desist orders from the Gate's attorneys.

But by this time, other people's daughters have started coming forward.

As an inmate at Harris County Jail, I can't receive phone calls, uncensored letters, or unapproved books, but I have unlimited access to legal documents related to my upcoming trial. At our next meeting, my attorney hands me a fat folder. "A transcript from the deposition," she says. "I think you should read this, Anna."

Any distraction is welcome, and I tell her so.

She sighs. "What's in there—I want to warn you, it's not an easy read."

Thumbing through what look to be hundreds of pages in Q-and-A format, I see one name after another highlighted in yellow. I feel a surge of horror. "Are these all Maxwell's victims?"

"No," she says. "Just one."

Julie

still feels like someone else.

She's me. I'm her. I don't mean to say I don't know that.

Maybe I'm just embarrassed. Julie seems like such an idiot to me now. She used to have an imaginary friend when she was very young. It was a horse from a book, I don't even remember which one. A white horse with a silver mane. When she rode the bus in elementary school, she used to look out the window and imagine the horse galloping alongside the bus. She'd make little motions under her backpack like she was feeding him sugar. It was more than a fantasy; she could almost see him.

I could almost see him. It was me. I have to tell Julie's story as if it were my own. For her sake, I'm going to try.

I must have been about five when I asked my mom who God was. It's one of Julie's earliest memories. *My* earliest memories.

She laughed and said, "Just some guy." When I asked where he lived, she said, "Probably San Diego." Then she told me to go ask Dad.

I did, but I don't remember what he said. I liked the idea of God living in San Diego. That's where Grandma and Grandpa retired to—which I guess was the joke, how much better it was than Houston. At the time, I knew there was a joke somewhere in her answer, but I didn't understand where. I knew she was laughing, but I thought she was laughing at me.

Anyway, that summer—or maybe this happened before, I'm not really sure—we actually went to San Diego to visit Grandma and Grandpa. They had these special buckets shaped like sand castles, so if you packed them with wet sand and turned them over, they looked like towers, with tooth-shaped ridges around the top and dents on the sides for windows. I remember I got sand stuck in my eye trying to look in through the pretend windows, and it hurt really bad. Dad helped me rinse the grit out, and after I was done crying, he said, "It's more fun anyway to just imagine what's inside." So I did. By the time Jane put her fist in one of the towers and the whole castle crumbled to the beach, I didn't mind. I had already built a new one in my mind, and it was better, because nobody could destroy it.

I'm not saying that these things had anything to do with what happened later on. I'm just bringing them up to say Julie had a history of belief. She wanted to believe there was an inside to the castle, even though she'd packed it full of wet sand herself. She wanted to believe God was a beautiful man who lived with her beautiful grandparents on a beautiful beach, and maybe someday they could all live together inside that beautiful imaginary castle.

On the same trip, Dad told me glass was made out of melted sand. How was God any harder to believe than that?

I keep trying to find the *before*. But once something like that happens to you, there is no *before* anymore. It takes the before away. And if there's no before, then there's no order I can tell it in that makes any sense, and no reason to choose one particular place over any other.

I'd start with the shame, but everything gets there eventually. So, no hurry, I guess.

I met Charlie in Sunday school the summer after the seventh grade, when I went to church with Candyce.

I don't know if my parents would even remember Candyce. She always wore these big bows in her hair that her mom made with a hot-glue gun to match her outfits. Julie was a little jealous of them. I was jealous, I mean. I can't imagine caring about that, but Julie did. Candyce's mom bought her pretty clothes and made pretty bows to go with them. My mom just sort of looked at me when I wore pretty clothes, her lips pressed together. She's very serious; she's a professor.

Anyway, I went to Sunday school for the first time with Candyce, and there he was—not Chuck Maxwell from the article I found all those years later, not even John David yet, just Charlie, a skinny guy with a guitar leading the class in a half hour of songs. I liked school fine, but this was different. There was one kid at school who was, I don't know what you're supposed to call it, but in seventh grade they said "retarded" and threw French fries at him in the cafeteria. His name was Jason. In Sunday school Jason sat with the cool kids in the front row, and nobody bothered him, not even the boys. He looked so happy, singing along and doing the arm motions that went with the songs. It was almost like he had friends. Charlie made everyone feel that way.

The rest of church was confusing to me. The hallways were hung with felt banners showing scenes from the Bible: women putting babies in baskets and floating them down the river, women carrying water jugs on their heads, women washing Jesus's feet with their hair. But the sermons were always about traffic or primetime television or an article in *Newsweek,* which didn't seem to have anything to do with the banners and the hymns and the Bible readings. Candyce and I would tune out and write each other notes on the church bulletins using the golf pencils in the backs of the pews, make little cartoons with speech bubbles. Her parents didn't care as long as we stayed quiet.

After the service, Candyce and I would link arms and walk down to the Sunday school room, which had sofas and a big-screen TV and posters on the wall that looked like graffiti but with Bible verses. There was no sermon in Sunday school, just goofy songs, and then what Charlie called "real talk," where we sat on the floor in a circle.

Sometimes it would start with a Bible verse, but pretty soon kids would begin talking about their problems. A lot of the problems were about girls: what they wore, who they danced with, whether they were godly and how godly were they and how much did it matter. One week they spent the whole time debating if it was okay for a girl to lie and say she liked her friend's outfit if she actually hated it. I remember one guy in the eighth grade wanted to ask a Jewish girl out, and they talked for an hour about whether or not Jews were going to hell and, if they were, whether it was their responsibility to share Jesus's message with them. Some kids were concerned about the silver James Avery crosses that were popular, whether girls should be wearing them if they were wearing them only for looks.

I watched from the sidelines. In our house, my mom was all-knowing, and my dad could answer any question in a way I understood. But it turned out there were questions I didn't even know needed asking, a whole world happening in another dimension, and my parents didn't seem to know anything about it. It turned out there were battles being fought all around me, that every word and action had a deeper meaning, and even the jewelry that a person wore could be related to something called salvation.

Charlie didn't egg them on; he just sat on the floor and listened, nodding when the arguments got more heated. Then, toward the end of the hour, he'd finally start talking, and everybody would shut up. He'd explain that God was watching us, and that He loved us more than we could possibly love ourselves, and that all we had to do was try to be worthy of that love. Jesus, he said, had become a man so He could understand what it was like. He understood how hard it was not to sin, and He paid the ultimate price so we wouldn't have to. Class dismissed.

In other words, Charlie didn't give us any answers at all.

Candyce was happy to supply the answers that Charlie wouldn't. "No offense," she said one day while we were walking down the hall after service, "but the Bible says your parents are going to hell."

That was the day I cried in Sunday school. I was so embarrassed I couldn't even speak when Charlie asked if I wanted to stay afterward and talk. But I nodded: *Yes*.

• • •

There's no before anymore. Everything in my memory is colored by what happened, like one of those old photographs where the tints are all weird. His offer to drive me home after Candyce rolled her eyes and said her parents were waiting in the breezeway, so could I please hurry up? His smile when he said Candyce and I shouldn't tell our parents or anyone else he was driving me home, because there was a lot of insurance paperwork he'd have to fill out first. His assurance, when Candyce left the room, that he was willing to risk it — because I was special.

I mean, he didn't come out and say that, but he implied it. I was special. Me, Julie, unchurched child of unchurched parents. Not even Easter-and-Christmas parents but never-ever parents.

When Charlie and I sat together in his office with the door cracked open, and I asked how God could damn my parents and Jane to hell, he told me that only God could judge, and anyone who said anyone else was going to hell was trying to do God's job. And that wasn't right.

"But not believing in God isn't right either," I said. "The Bible says you have to believe in Jesus."

"The Bible also says it's easier for a camel to get through the eye of a needle than for a rich man to go to heaven," he said with a smirk. I wasn't sure whether we were rich or not, but I knew for certain Candyce was; I'd slept over at her house enough times.

Then he said the important thing wasn't whether anyone else was damned but whether you yourself were saved. He said I was very brave to come to church on my own. He said I had the soul of a seeker.

My whole life, ever since I could remember, I'd always hated the thought that no one could ever know what anyone else was feeling or thinking. The fact that no one could ever be inside my head with me seemed like the loneliest thing in the world. I wanted so bad for there to be something that could make those boundaries just disappear. Something so big it was like air, a magic flowing across the planet, connecting everyone and everything.

When Charlie spoke to me, I saw the boundaries disappearing. Now I see a careful distance narrowing.

Charlie drove me home from church three times. Each time he dropped me off in the parking lot at the CVS at Kirkwood, and I'd buy something cheap—candy or a magazine—so that when I walked the four blocks home, I'd have an explanation for why Candyce's parents had dropped me off there. I had the answer all worked out, but my mom never asked. It was spring, and she was usually doing something in the yard when I got home with my plastic CVS bag. I guess she never thought about how uncomfortable it was to walk four blocks in church flats.

In the parking lot of the CVS, my conversations with Charlie went deeper than the ones we had in his little cubby in the church office, where the church secretary kept barging in to use the copier. In the CVS parking lot, Charlie told me that he wasn't sure he even believed in hell. He told me everybody wants a rule book, that people want an instruction manual to life. They want to be told exactly what to do. But Jesus came to destroy all that. Jesus came to erase the laws that were written on the stone tablets and write them on our hearts instead. He told me Jesus wants us to *feel* what's right, inside, when we pray to Him. "God sent Jesus as a man," he said. "To teach us how to be men."

His hand rested on the back of my seat, and I could smell that he used some kind of prickly aftershave and see that he had blue eyes and that his blond eyelashes were longer than I'd thought.

"Never forget this," he told me, and I haven't. "People will always let you down. Candyce will let you down. Your parents will let you down. *I* will let you down. Only God will always be there for you."

I nodded, staring into his eyes. His thumb was touching my shoulder, just a little. He took his hand off the seat back, letting out his breath.

I'd been holding mine too.

Back in my bedroom, I changed out of church clothes, but instead of going downstairs, I crept into bed and pulled the covers over my head.

God sent Jesus as a man to teach us how to be men.

Who had God sent to teach me how to be a woman? Was it Charlie?

When I went back to Sunday school the next week, he was gone.

One of the church elders, a woman in her fifties, ran the Sunday school class. She told us that for personal reasons, Charlie had had to resign. It was unlikely he'd be able to return to the position, she said. They were already beginning the search for a new youth pastor, and in the meantime, fellowship would be suspended and Sunday school would be taught by members of the Christian Education committee.

"Can we say goodbye?" someone asked.

"I'll get a card," Candyce said. "We can all sign it."

"That would be very nice," the elder said. "Now, get out your Bibles and turn to First Corinthians, chapter thirteen."

Even I knew that verse. It was printed on the church bulletins and embroidered on some of the tapestries in the halls. But this time, the words seemed to be pointed straight at me: *If I have a faith that can move mountains, but have not love, I am nothing.*

Charlie had said he would let me down. And he was right.

With Charlie gone, church got very boring, and I stopped sleeping over at Candyce's house. At school, I went out for the track team and made it. I was not a good speed runner, but I could run distances, and I could propel myself into the air and sail over the hurdles with my legs in front of me. Looking around at the girls I'd be training with over the summer, all of us standing on the dusty track, our skinny legs sticking out of nylon shorts, I knew I didn't need Candyce or church or Charlie anymore. In eighth grade, I would have friends, real girlfriends who would show me how to brush my hair, put on makeup, and talk to boys. The girls on the track team had sleepovers and away meets; they painted racing stripes and Nike swooshes on one another's faces, finished each other's sentences. They were a tribe. When I was in eighth grade, my life would finally begin.

A few months later, I got the chat invitation.

His name was John David. There was no picture, just an outline of a head with a question mark inside it. According to his Facebook page, he was sixteen, and he had zero friends on his profile.

I tried to think of all the people I knew who went to high school. My friend Angela had an older brother named John; I'd had a crush on him once. Or maybe John David was somebody I knew from school who was just lying about his age, or some mean girls playing a trick on me. Maybe I was going to get reeled in with some phony "secret admirer" plot, and then they would take screenshots and post them for the whole school to see. Something like that had happened to a girl I barely knew, Rebecca. There were other things that had happened to Rebecca too. I unfriended her on Facebook so I didn't have to see them.

I refreshed the screen, half expecting to see the profile's friends shoot up to the hundreds, so that I'd know he was fake, a bot, an empty outline. Nothing happened, except the question mark took a little longer to load the second time. He couldn't contact me until I had accepted his offer, so I clicked on the question mark and a chat box popped up.

Hi. Who are you? I typed. I always spelled out words and added punctuation and capitals, even in chats with friends. I was reading *The Diary of Anne Frank* and couldn't stand how ugly most of my and my friends' writing looked in comparison with those sentences from a girl our age.

The chat box was blank for a few minutes. Then it started blinking as the person on the other end typed. The other person was not into spelling things correctly or capitalizing.

i don't want to give my real name

Do I know you? I wrote back.

There was a long delay while he typed, long enough to make me think he was typing from a phone.

we had amazing conversations together

I started to type another question, and then the chat box blinked again:

soul of a seeker

A wave of heat went up my body, starting from my toes and rushing up to my face until it was burning.

I typed, *Charlie?* but stopped myself from pressing the Enter key just in time and deleted it.

julie? u there?

I let out my breath slowly and typed: *I think I know who you are. You gave me a ride home a few times.* That sounded like I could be talking to a sixteen-year-old. I wondered how old he really was.

yes

Where are you now? You left without saying goodbye.

i had my reasons. u dont know my side of things

Side? I frowned and typed again: *Where are you now?*

i can't see you right now or tell u where i am. i have reasons. u were always smarter than the others. wanted to get back in touch.

It's nice to hear from you, I said, because I didn't know what else to say.

There was another pause.

god is with u all the time. i can see HIM all around u like a halo

My scalp prickled and I could feel his eyes on me suddenly, almost like I'd felt them on our last car ride home together. I wondered how far away he was.

Why did you leave? You left without saying goodbye.

i promise ill tell u the whole story soon but please for now just talk to me. i'm lonely

I tried to picture him in front of a computer screen or hunched over a phone somewhere, but I couldn't. I typed out the words *I miss you,* but then I backed the cursor up over them until they were gone and typed *Everyone misses you* instead.

He responded, *i miss u too,* just as if he could hear the real sentence in my head. *Something really important has happened to me since we talked. i'm going to tell u everything. god has a plan for me and for u too*

This time he didn't have to tell me not to tell my parents. He knew I wouldn't, and I knew he knew, and although the word *God* sent the old thrill spiking through me, it was Charlie's faith in me and the greatness of his need that caught the lightning-flash and amplified it, expanded it, made my entire body warm.

Go on, I wrote.

I saw the face of god, julie. he wants something from me. From you too.

From me? I could only retype the words.

from all of us, he wrote, after a long time.

The Plan felt like a special project we were working on together, or a game. Whenever I was chatting with Charlie — or John David, as I began to think of him — I existed in another dimension. In the beginning, I guarded the screen — my desktop monitor was visible from the doorway, and I jumped every time the floorboards creaked in the hall outside. But then I began to feel comfortable existing in both worlds at once: the ordinary world, which consisted of me eating dinner and finishing my homework and going to track meets after school, and the world of the Plan.

In the ordinary world, I was Julie, maker of As, runner of hurdle races. My grades stayed high, and I didn't drop my after-school activities. That was part of the Plan: No dramatic behavior changes. I worked hard to keep my weight from dropping too, but the pounds seemed to be falling off no matter how much of my dad's lasagna I ate. My mom blamed track and gave me extra helpings at every meal, but I knew it was the Plan working in me, preparing me for something John David called "privations to come."

In the ordinary world, I was ordinary Julie, but in the Plan, I was radiant. He told me that my loveliness was like a bruise in the exact center of a blinding light, like a sunspot. The fire of God shone around me. Even though we never met in person, never video-chatted—too dangerous, he said—I knew he could see me. He said he saw me when he closed his eyes and prayed; he said he saw me standing in front of the sun with it shining all around me. And there were things he seemed to know about me that he could not possibly have gotten from the Internet. He knew, for instance, when I started shaving my legs. I had to, for track; even though my leg hair was barely there, just a glimmer in the sunlight, really, the other girls would have thought I was strange if I didn't shave. He didn't like the thought of me taking a blade to my legs. He told me that afterward, I wouldn't need to do things like that. Things to appease the world.

I didn't know if he was close enough to be literally watching me or whether he was finding out some other way. I didn't want to know. Instead, I started pretending he could see me all the time so I could wear his gaze like a secret under my clothes, against my skin. It made Ordinary Julie a more exciting role, somehow. I performed my ordinariness for him: putting on lip gloss in the bathroom, giggling with other girls, reading *To Kill a Mockingbird* with my feet propped up on the ottoman, helping Mom with the dishes after supper, brushing my hair, writing in my diary—all for him. I even made up some diary entries that were totally ordinary, just listing what I did during the day, things Ordinary Julie did. I pretended to have a crush on this guy at school, Aaron. I felt sure Charlie knew how well I was performing my role, and I began to slip in little hints and references that only he would understand. I drew sheep on my binder and imagined him laughing at the joke. At the pep rally I got a sun painted on my cheek so he'd see it and understand the message. No matter how much I looked like a teenage girl to the others, he was out there somewhere, and as long as he was watching, I was divine.

The only time the two worlds touched each other was under the covers at night. Then I would try to whisper "Jesus," and "John David" would come out instead. Once I dreamed I was falling, flying apart, breaking into a million pieces, becoming the darkness at the center of the light. I clenched my teeth and waited for it to be over. When I opened my eyes, there were red stars.

That's when I realized I'd been in love with Charlie. A wave of shame rushed over me. It was stupid, the whole thing; a crush too embarrassing even to think about on someone who could never think of me that way, because I was a stupid little kid.

Or at least, that's how it had been—then. But I wasn't a kid anymore. The image of Charlie, faded now, seemed smaller than it had before. It had been months since I'd even seen his face. I did not have a schoolgirl crush any longer, because I wasn't a schoolgirl; that was Ordinary Julie. I was divine.

In our chats, the outline of a head and shoulders in the profile window reminded me of a blue shadow cast on the sidewalk by someone you can't see. The shadow was John David, and the everyday, ordinary Charlie who cast the shadow was no more important than the ordinary, everyday Julie. The embarrassing feelings were all for Charlie. John David was different. He was part of the light, surrounded by light. Not a shadow, but a real person standing directly in front of the sun, a person whose shape you can barely make out when you squint, hidden in blinding brightness. Tears came to my eyes, and there was a warmth in my chest, burning in my heart. I closed my eyes and saw the form of John David shining, haloed, a bruise in the center of brightness. He had already changed me. Walking toward him on the road made by his shining, I melted into him, and our darkness became pure light.

. . .

The Plan was an anti-plan, really. It was going to be a total surrender to God. That was all I knew. John David promised we would
surrender ourselves to the source of the light together and sink
into the sea of His love, and we'd never have to make a plan of any
kind ever again.

One night I typed out the verse about the lilies of the field. He
corrected me.

we won't be lilies, he wrote. *we'll be nothing. we'll be nothing at all.*

On the last night before the Plan, Jane looked at me while we
were brushing our teeth and said, "I know something about you."

I was silent. I was counting to a hundred, like I always did
when brushing. I could feel Jane's eyes on me in the bathroom
mirror but pretended I was alone so my face wouldn't move.

"You think nobody notices," Jane said, trying again. Foamy
toothpaste dribbled out of her mouth and she spat it into the
sink. "You think you're so cool."

I did not think I was cool. My parents thought I was cool.
My friends thought I was cool, and some of them were even cool
themselves. But I wasn't. I only looked that way because of my
friends, who were always calling me on the weekends to go to
the mall, where somebody's older sibling would drop us off so we
could try on halter tops at Wet Seal and smell all the perfumes
at Sephora. There were slumber parties at Kristian's house with
the whole team, and late-night chats with Lauren or Maya, some
of which had begun to revolve around Aaron. I wondered if this
was what Jane thought she knew. The made-up crush on Aaron
had begun to take on such a life of its own that sometimes, in a
moment of confusion, I thought it was real.

I refocused on the mirror and noticed that Jane was still staring, but this time her face was flushed and there were tears wobbling in her eyes. "How come you don't like me anymore?"

I reached a hundred just as the subject changed. It was not a coincidence, I knew by now. Nothing was. I leaned over and carefully spat into the sink, then straightened up and rubbed my mouth with the towel. "Why do you think I don't like you?" I asked.

"You could have just said 'I do like you.'" Jane sniffed.

"I do like you!"

"No, you don't," Jane went on. By this time the tears were squeezing out of the corners of her eyes and tracking down her reddened cheeks. Jane cried all the time now. Mom said she was hitting puberty earlier than I had, and at least it was all going to be over sooner that way. In her old-man pajamas, as I called them, the button-down flannel top and drawstring bottoms hanging off her, Jane looked bigger than me, even if she wasn't quite as tall yet. She didn't have boobs either, but there was something about her that looked like the beginning of something. Mom said she might even be taller than me soon.

I won't know, I thought with a pang.

"You're my sister," I explained, "I don't like you, I love you." I had meant it to sound funny, but as I said it, I knew that it was true. We had played and fought and done everything together throughout our childhood, Jane throwing toys when I turned my back and ignored her, me running to Mom when Jane wouldn't obey the rules of a board game or when she quit because she wasn't winning. Tears started tickling my eyes and I wondered, automatically and dispassionately, if I should let them fall, if doing so would benefit the Plan.

"How come you never want to hang out with me, then? You're

always hanging out with your new friends, and I have to stay home and watch TV by myself. You haven't even watched *Beauty and the Beast* with me once all summer."

"That movie is kind of dumb, Jane," I said. "It's a kids' movie."

"It's not dumb! I like the songs." Jane's favorite song was the one in the tavern. Whenever no one was paying attention to her, she'd start singing it, and if you didn't stop and do some of the voices with her, she would continue singing it, louder and louder. Jane was never afraid to be annoying, never afraid to take up space.

"I'm not a little kid anymore, Jane. I don't like princesses and cartoons and stuff."

"I miss you," Jane said.

Now the first tear came out, all of a sudden, after I'd thought the danger was over. *I'm right here,* I started to say, but the words stuck in my throat. "I'll watch it with you this weekend," I said instead, "I promise," and the lie somehow made me stronger, straightened me up.

Ordinary Julie would be there Saturday morning to keep her promise, I told myself. Ordinary Julie would stay behind to see what happened with Jane, watch over her, help her with her homework, tell her not to wear something that would make the kids tease her at school.

"Really?" Jane said.

"Yeah, sure." I looked back at the mirror. "What was the thing you were saying? What do you know about me?"

Jane's tears were gone now. She didn't smile, but she managed to look as if she wanted to. "I know you don't really like track," she said. "I know you're only pretending to like it so you can fit in."

I paused. I had never really thought about whether I liked track or not. It seemed so obvious that if you *could* play a sport, you should, whether or not you enjoyed it, because with a swarm of friends around you, any lie could become the truth. Suddenly I pitied Jane with her awkward face, every emotion going straight from her insides to her outside.

Jane would never be good at sports, I thought. She wouldn't be popular in eighth grade like I was.

"Good night," I said, and I wrapped my arms around her for a moment, long enough to remind us both how much fun we used to have together. When I was ready to pull away, I counted to three first. Ordinary Julie wasn't enough for Jane. She always wanted a little more.

That night I woke up to a rough hand over my mouth. I tried to gasp but couldn't, and, still half asleep, for a moment I thought I was drowning.

When I opened my eyes, there was a bearded man leaning over me. He nodded, and after a moment of paralysis, I nodded back, and he slowly, slowly removed his hand—keeping it near enough to clasp over my mouth again should I scream.

It was Charlie, but also not. His dark blond hair was straggly and long, long enough for a ponytail. His beard was darker than his hair, and a mustache covered his mouth with shadows. He smelled sweet and sour at the same time, like the smell that came out of the recycling bin when I emptied it after school.

That was my first impression of John David, and I immediately wanted to scream.

But I was Plan Julie, and so I repeated over and over in my head: *It's not really kidnapping. It's not real. I'm running away to meet my destiny. This is what I was born for. I am being chosen. He is choosing me.*

I smiled at John David, trying to show him I remembered, I knew. If he smiled back, I couldn't see it under his beard. His hand trembled as he pulled the blankets off me and reached out to help me out of bed, but when I put out my hand, he wrapped his around my wrist instead and pulled me to my feet slowly but forcefully.

We moved deliberately, playing the mirror game, flowing together across the floor, me anticipating his movements so that he wouldn't feel even a hint of resistance. I was so desperate to please him. My eyes did not leave his for a moment, as if we were dancing, his hand wrapped around my wrist, and the rest was all electrical current moving my feet silently across the floor. Then I saw what was in his other hand.

Although the word *knife* had been part of the Plan, I had never actually associated it with the knives hanging in the kitchen; I had never looked at any one of them and thought *Knife* and pictured it in his hand. It drifted up slowly, almost lazily, until it was level with my chest, and I thought, *He doesn't want to scare me* and tried even harder not to be scared. He circled around behind me and clamped his hand down on my shoulder. I felt the tip of the knife press into my back, not hard enough to cut, but hard enough so its cold metal tip separated the fibers of my nightshirt.

Now there was the relief of knowing exactly what to do, because there wasn't a choice.

I thought I'd given up control when we'd started discussing the Plan, but I hadn't—it had all been a game. But now, with him standing invisibly behind me, an unseen presence marching me forward with the pressure of a hand on my shoulder and the sharpness of a knife just to the right of my spine, I knew that the time to decide against the Plan had passed. Thoughts floated through my mind that did not sit comfortably next to one another; for instance, I did not know where he was taking me, and where was Jane? *Oh, safe in bed,* Jane was safe in bed. She'd stay there forever, tucked into a life that would never change.

Then Jane's face suddenly appeared.

I caught sight of her as we approached the open door to her room—we usually slept with the doors open. I could barely see her hiding in her cracked-open closet, down low by the floor, looking at me with eyes that were not closed and warm with sleep but wide and red-rimmed with terror. John David and I stood on the landing. Jane's face peered out at me from behind the closet door, desperately asking me what to do next.

I motioned with my eyes toward John David and willed Jane to sink back into the closet's darkness before he saw her. If she screamed once, it would all be over. He would get her too. And no matter where he was taking me, no matter what he was going to do to me, I would not let him do it to Jane.

Just before John David marched me down the stairs, there was a noise from the attic. I felt the knife's point lessen its tension for just a moment, the hand on my shoulder twist ever so slightly, and knew John David was looking away. As quickly as I could, I raised my hand and put a finger to my lips, *Shhh,* pushing the soft imaginary breath across the room to freeze Jane in place, *shhh,* and goodbye, *shhh,* and goodbye.

And that is how I lost my family, my home, my life, and my self —everything, everything—in one night.

16

One afternoon when I was pregnant with Jane, and Tom was off in an accounting class and we still lived in the little house near my university, Julie sat on the wood floor of the living room in a patch of sunlight. Her baby feet stuck out in front of her, and her wisps of hair were lit up white by the sun. She was concentrating on moving a blue crayon over a newspaper in front of her. When she accidentally squeezed the crayon too hard and it skittered away, she didn't cry, and she didn't get another crayon, even though there were dozens lying all around her. She screwed her face up, made her fingers into clumsy pincers, scooted herself toward the rolling blue crayon, and recovered it. Then she resumed coloring until the whole cycle started over again.

I watched her for maybe half an hour before it hit me: *She likes the color blue.*

It was the first time I understood that there was a whole world in there I would never see, a world so distant from me, and so distinct, that to say that Julie was made from me, that she was my daughter and I was her mother, seemed meaningless. I think I loved her more profoundly in that moment than I have ever loved anyone.

But that's memory for you. At first, I wanted the world for Julie, like all mothers do. Then, for a long time, I only wanted a body to bury.

Now, I just wish I could go back in time and hand her the god-damn blue crayon.

Reading through the transcript, devouring it, in fact, I learn the shape of her trauma, I study the names of all the girls she had to be to survive: Charlotte, Karen, Mercy, Starr, Violet, Gretchen. In her testimony, they struggle, they fight, they fail, but above all, they survive. Even as I choke back tears thinking of all she's been through, I hold each one dear, each of these girls, because each is a layer of my daughter, the one waiting at home with Tom.

But the girl whose story hurts me most is Julie. She's the one I thought I knew but didn't. Worse still, she's the one who knew *me*. Her words give me a picture of myself I don't recognize. I try to remember each moment she describes of her unfolding adoles-cence, to remember and possibly justify the role I played in it, but that feeling of otherness is monumental. I recognize the outlines of the situations, Jane and Tom and me reduced to characters in her story, but it's like seeing them, seeing us all, on an alien planet through an alien atmosphere.

I try to remember Julie asking me about God, but I can't. Who was I, what was I doing that I can't remember? I was finishing up a postdoc, then interviewing for jobs. *I knew she was laughing, but I thought she was laughing at me.*

My mom just sort of looked at me when I wore pretty clothes, her lips pressed together. I don't need a mirror to know what that expression looks like. I saw it on my mother's face over and over again. I didn't know it was on mine.

I had the answer all worked out, but my mom never asked.

I'd believed the girls were benefiting from my example, if not my undivided attention.

I guess she never thought about how uncomfortable it was to walk four blocks in church flats.

I read somewhere that Puritans would sometimes explain the death of a particularly beloved child as the parents' punishment for having loved the child too much. They blamed not the awful winters or the malarial swamps or the lack of good food or clean water, but a jealous God.

I never loved Julie more than Jane, I can say that with confidence. At the same time, there was always something about her. She seemed so complete in herself, so serene. Somewhere deep down, I thought Julie was perfect. Now I wonder: Was I so afraid of finding out she wasn't perfect that I almost killed her?

When they unlock the cell door, they don't tell me where they are taking me. It's strange how little anyone tells prisoners outside of directing them to put their hands out to be cuffed and pointing them down hallways. I guess nobody wants to be responsible for sharing privileged information.

I assume I am being taken to see my lawyer, because that's what has happened every other time I've been brought down this particular corridor. But this time, we take a right instead of a left at the end and go through a door with a wired window in it. And then suddenly, I am standing by the front desk as my cuffs are being removed.

Tom stands there too, awkwardly, his hand fiddling nervously with his keys in his pants pocket.

The guard says, "The charges have been dropped. Your things will be at the front desk in just a minute, you'll need to go over them and sign a paper saying everything's there." My eyes meet hers for only a moment before she looks away. Maybe it's hard for them to make eye contact with us after we're free.

She disappears behind the door again, leaving us alone in the cramped waiting room, the woman who works the front desk presumably off rummaging for the box containing my clothes, my shoes, my purse with the book on Byron and landscape, still half read, tucked inside it. I'm suddenly overwhelmed with a craving to finish it.

"Maxwell confessed," Tom says. "Apparently he was on psych meds—for schizoaffective something or other. But they didn't know that at the hospital, so he didn't get any there, and before they could figure out what was wrong, he started talking to God about his—sins."

"Bet Judge Crofford didn't know about the meds."

"No one did. Not even his top advisers. The drugs kept the worst symptoms under control, but—" He looks down. "Seven more victims have come forward."

Seven. And those are just the ones willing to talk to the police.

"Thanks for coming," I say.

"There wasn't time to schedule a call," he says. "I guess once

the charges are dropped, they're eager to get you off the taxpay-
ers' dime."

"That makes sense."

We stand in silence under the fluorescent lights.

"Anna," he says.

"It's okay," I say.

"I'm sorry."

"It's not your fault," I say. "I wasn't there. I checked out."

"I shouldn't have let you," he says.

"You're a good man," I say, too weary for this. "You always have
to be helping someone. I didn't want your help, so you gave it to
someone else."

"If I could take it back—"

"Don't say that," I interrupt. "Someone got her daughter back
because of you. You wouldn't change that, so don't say you would
because you think it'll please me. It won't."

He looks stricken, and I soften despite myself. "Honestly,
Tom?" I say. "It's a relief to know that you're not an angel. It's a
standard I could never live up to."

I don't tell him how much it hurts to see him tumble from
his pedestal. This is why people need God—because people
are awful, even the good ones. I've always prided myself on being so rational, so unafflicted by spiritual yearnings, not realizing
my personal gods were Tom and Julie, the good people. But nobody ever gets to be good except on the terms the world hands
them.

Finally, the front-desk matron emerges with a plastic bag holding my clothes and purse. I poke through the bag and sign the
papers. Then I take everything into a visitors' restroom, change

back into my street clothes, fold the blue prison scrubs neatly in a pile. I reemerge looking something like myself again.

Tom smiles.

As I set the stack of prison pajamas on the front desk, I wonder if this is it for Tom and me. If he can smile this easily at the sight of me looking like I did before, before all this happened, if he can so quickly forget the image of me as a prisoner, then he is always going to misunderstand who I am and what I am.

We exit into the bright sunlight. The sun is beating down on the Commerce Street port, and the air is scalding hot.

"Do you think Janie will come home?" I ask, thinking of her first date with the guy on the kickball team. I haven't heard how it went. I resisted telling her to meet at a public place, to let a friend know where they were going.

Tom looks uncomfortable. "She's staying up there for a while longer, Anna. She really wants to get back on track, finish all those incompletes and show her professors she can tough it out." He sighs. "I'm sorry. You know Janie."

I do know Janie. The incompletes were nothing more than a cry for attention, but she has terrible timing. Jane functions well under duress, gravitates toward drama, and can be generous as long as no one expects her to be. Then, when the waters still and her dramatics would be entertaining, she's back to her own world. I think of all the journals. "Wait for it. She'll switch her major to creative writing before the year is out."

"Why do you say that?"

"She'll want to start working on her memoirs."

Tom laughs, still a little uneasy, as we get into the SUV. We make our way to I-10, the churning of the air conditioner at full blast filling the silence. It's a little past six, and the rush from downtown has mostly cleared, but when we hit Loop 610, the backup begins. The lowering sun, undaunted by our visors, beats down through the windshield, and the tinting in the back windows only seems to trap the heat. As we slow almost to a standstill somewhere around the Voss exit, the air conditioner, losing velocity from the incoming wind, thumps down a notch in intensity and gives a faint rattle. I wonder if this is going to be the summer the A/C gives out on us. This is the stretch of road where that type of thing always happens.

Suddenly, I say, "Pull the car over."

"We're getting off at the next exit."

"Pull over now!"

He puts on his blinker. Traffic is sluggish, but he cuts across three lanes, nosing over and waving his hand like a flag in front of the rearview mirror. As soon as the tires thunk onto the shoulder, I open the door and Tom slams on the brakes as I stumble out. My stomach heaves up into my mouth and out onto the pavement.

There's not a lot in there, I've barely been eating, but I heave and heave. My vision goes red in the heat, and then black, and then Tom is there, on his knees behind me, with his big arms around me, supporting me. Waves of heat that reek of gasoline and vomit are coming up off the pavement, each one bringing a fresh wave of spasms with it, but his hands on me are warmer still. After a moment, I sink back into him like an armchair, and he settles down under my weight, and we sit together on the gravel at the side of the freeway.

"She left us, Tom," I say, but my voice disappears in the roadside symphony of honking horns and Doppler effects. He continues to smooth my hair back over my sweating temple, but now, despite the heat, I am shivering, cold and hot at the same time. I pull away from him, turn toward his face. I say it louder, but he shakes his head, still not hearing. Finally, I lean toward him and force my mouth to open wide and I yell at the top of my lungs, *"Julie left!"*

This time he understands, but shakes his head back and forth in response. "Come on!" he shouts, and starts to make his way to standing, holding out one hand to me and gesturing toward the car with the other.

But yelling has freed something in me that was pressed into the dingy little cage of a jail cell for the past week. Julie's deposition is still banging around inside me, and if I don't let it out, it will punch holes in my lungs, and I'll drown. *"Tom!"* I yell. "She *left!"*

"I know!" he shouts back.

"How can you be so calm?" I demand.

"Come on, Anna, get in the car!"

But it's easier to scream out here, and this is something I want to scream. "What kind of mother am I, Tom? I didn't know her at all!"

"What do you want me to do about it?" he yells back. "I didn't either!"

"But I'm the *mother!"*

"Yes, you're the mother!" he yells. "You're the mother, and she needs you right now. So let's get in the car, for God's sake, and go home and yell it at *her!"*

The adrenaline drains out of me, and I follow him to the Range

Rover and get in, feeling the car shudder as the traffic going past starts to pick up. The quiet when we shut the doors feels profound.

"You read the deposition?" I say in a voice that is only slightly hoarse.

"I didn't need to read it. I was there to hear most of it."

"How could I have been so blind? How could I have missed all that? It's like I didn't know her at all." I can't let the tears prickle up one more time today, so I press them down. "I know I've been broken since it happened. I know I've been awful with Jane. But I thought — before that, I mean — I thought everything was good. I thought I was a good mother."

There's a long silence. Then he says, "I think it would have been good enough, Anna. But we'll never know now. None of us know who we would have been. He took that away from us."

Tom starts the engine, puts on his blinker, and forces the car out into the Houston traffic. He's a wonderfully aggressive driver.

When we're moving again, he says, "Can I confess something?" I wait. "I wish it had been me who shot Maxwell."

I picture Tom the night Julie had her miscarriage, standing with the gun in his hand as I punched my fist through the bathroom door to get to my daughter. Then I lean over and take his hand.

There's a car parked outside our house, and when we walk in the door, Julie is sitting at the kitchen table with an African American man in a T-shirt and jeans. As soon as we walk in the door, he stands up.

"Mom, Dad, this is Cal," Julie says.

"Mr. Whitaker." Cal extends a hand to Tom, who takes it, though he looks a bit bewildered. Cal is almost a head shorter than Tom, but he doesn't seem as if he's craning his neck up to meet Tom's gaze. "Glad to meet you," says Tom, and I can see Cal scoping me out from the corner of his eye before turning to me.

"Dr. Davalos," he says. Julie must have schooled him in how to address me.

"I understand you helped Julie out of a tough situation," I say to Cal.

"You did too," he says, simply and warmly.

I wonder, *Is this the rest of my life? Are all of Julie's men going to have to live up to me? And do any of them know she was poised with her gun, ready to kill? Do they know what I really saved her from?*

People have a lack of imagination about women like Julie and what they're capable of. I was guilty of it myself once. I know better now, of course. But I would never disabuse the men in her life, the Toms and Cals, of the notion that Julie needs protecting. Fostering that illusion is part of how she's survived this long. To take away that coping mechanism before it has outlived its usefulness would be cruel.

Cal looks to be older than her, though it's hard to tell how much since his skin is unwrinkled everywhere but around his eyes when he smiles. I wonder if he will be with her on the day she outgrows the useful illusion of her frailty and how he will react if he's still around. It might be a long time before that happens, a lifetime, even. I may not live to see it myself.

Meanwhile, it'll be our secret.

"It's very nice to meet you, Cal. Now, would you and Tom mind if I talked to Julie for a few minutes?" I ask. "Alone."

Tom says, "I was just going to run up to the grocery store and get some stuff for dinner. Why don't you come along, Cal. We can get to know each other."

"Sure," Cal says after a backward glance at Julie, who nods. The two men walk out of the kitchen.

When they have been gone for a full thirty seconds, I look at my daughter. I don't know what I'm expecting. A revelation? To find out what color her eyes are, once and for all? I see the same woman I've been looking at for the past month, as much of a mystery to me as ever.

"Why didn't you come back?" I ask. "After you escaped from Maxwell. Why didn't you come home?"

There's a long pause. "I wanted to. I was going to. But it seemed like once he—did that to me, nothing went the way it was supposed to. Things kept happening."

I know some of the things she is talking about, and I don't want her to have to repeat them. At the same time, I don't want to shut her down, ever again. So I wait patiently, and after a moment, she goes on, giving me a strange look that I can't really interpret. "Besides, I didn't know whether you'd want me back."

I choke on my next words. "How can you say that?"

"I thought you'd be mad," she says with a weird smile. "I hated Julie. She was stupid and gullible. And she left you."

"You were only a child. He took you."

"He took me," she agrees. "But to me, it felt like I was leaving on my own."

"That's what he wanted you to think."

"And there was Charlotte. She was dead, and I was scared it was my fault."

"He wanted you to think that too."

"Well, he was good at it. Or I was good at believing it." She shrugs, giving up. "Anyway, I'm not sure it makes me feel any better if I didn't have a choice. If that's true, if I was just a random victim, then my life was ruined for no reason at all."

That, of course, is what I have always believed. I don't say it, but she can see me thinking it.

"You've never believed in God. I don't think Jane does either. Maybe Dad doesn't care either way. But it was different for me; I wanted to find something out there. I still do, I just don't know the word for it."

"Transcendence?" I say. "There's no such thing."

"But maybe there is," she says. "I don't know. Think of all those people at the Gate."

"I'd rather not."

"But you have to," she says. "You have to. What are they looking for? Why are they so happy there? Where else could they find that kind of happiness?"

"Poetry," I say. "Music. Art."

"That's not enough for everyone. It wasn't enough for me."

Her face looks sad and eager at the same time, and I suddenly recognize a glimmer of an expression I remember from her childhood. I never knew what it was before. It reminds me of something.

"'Not in entire forgetfulness, / And not in utter nakedness, / But trailing clouds of glory do we come.'" I almost stop there, but for Julie's sake, I finish: "'From God, who is our home.' Wordsworth."

"Why do you have to put quotation marks around it to understand it?"

"All I have is other people's words, Julie."

They are, at present, failing me. After another long moment

of silence, it occurs to me to that I have nothing to lose by just asking. "You came back for Maxwell, because you saw that magazine profile, okay. But you didn't have to come back as Julie. If you were worried about being blamed for what happened with Charlotte, why didn't you just leave an anonymous tip for the police and let them take care of it? Why did you come back to us after so long when you knew you would have to lie?" I take a deep breath. "Was it the money? It's okay if it was."

She looks up, startled, with china-blue eyes. "I missed you," she says.

The worst doesn't unhappen, but just like that, I am home.

Acknowledgments

The love and support of friends and family made this book possible. I'd like to extend special thanks to the members of my extraordinarily talented and committed writing group, Alissa Zachary, Linden Kueck, Victoria Rossi, Dan Solomon, and Paul Stinson; to Martin Kohout and his late wife, Heather Kohout, for the time I spent working on this novel at Madroño Ranch in Medina, Texas; to my agent, Sharon Pelletier at Dystel & Goderich Literary Management, for her infectious enthusiasm for this project; to Lauren Abramo at DGLM for tirelessly representing me overseas; and to Tim Mudie, my editor at Houghton Mifflin Harcourt, for guiding me patiently and insightfully through the exciting process of turning my words into a book. We did it! Biggest and best thanks are reserved for my husband, Curtis Luciani, for encouraging me to write a novel in the first place, believing in me when I didn't think I could do it, and always making sure I had coffee in the morning and a room of my own.

Faith Fox

By the same author

Fiction

A Long Way from Verona
The Summer after the Funeral
Bilgewater
Black Faces, White Faces
God on the Rocks
The Sidmouth Letters
The Pangs of Love and Other Stories
Crusoe's Daughter
Showing the Flag
The Queen of the Tambourine
Going into a Dark House

For Children

Bridget and William
The Hollow Land
A Few Fair Days

Non-fiction

The Iron Coast

Faith Fox

JANE GARDAM

CARROLL & GRAF PUBLISHERS
NEW YORK

Faith Fox

Carroll & Graf Publishers
An Imprint of Avalon Publishing Group Inc.
245 West 17th Street
New York, NY 10011

First Carroll & Graf edition 2003

Library of Congress Cataloging-in-Publication Data is available.

ISBN: 0-7867-1221-X

Printed in the United States of America
Distributed by Publishers Group West

For Penelope Hoare

And who would rock the cradle
Wherein this infant lies
Must rock with easy motion
And watch with humble eyes.

Austrian carol, 1649

– Part One –

It was terrible when Holly Fox died. Terrible. Just awful.
Pammie Jefford heard first, at the hospital, doing her voluntary
work. At the sluice. In came a nun and hurtled by and out of the
other door. Then after a minute another volunteer came in,
looking white. It was a wonderful hospital. It had not lost a
mother for years and years. Holly was only the third since the
foundation of the place before the war, and the other two had
been foreigners with queer blood groups. Holly Fox. Oh no, no
– not *Holly Fox*! Oh God.

Pammie wouldn't dream of ringing anyone from the
hospital and of course she couldn't stay on there today. 'You
mean you *know* her?' they asked, not yet able to say *knew*; and
Sister Mark said, 'God rest her. God rest her. Yes, away you
go, dear,' and Pammie left, almost forgetting to take off her
apron.

Outside in the drive she stood for minutes together beside
her fast little Peugeot GTI, stood in the sunshine, not able to get
in.

Holly Fox, *Holly Fox*!

Soon all round Surrey the telephones were ringing. Women
were putting down receivers, covering their faces, putting fists
to mouths, going out into gardens and calling people in.
Ringing up yet other people. Holly Fox's own generation
mostly heard later because they were all at work. But these,
Pammie's lot, friends of Holly's mother, were the women who
had all lived at one time, thirty years ago, in the world of one
another's children. Oh – *Holly Fox*!

'A blood clot. It could have happened at any time, apparently. Just a coincidence it was while she was in labour, though I don't suppose that helped. No, an easy time. A very *easy* time. No fuss. Just laughing and joking and deep breathing – well, you know how she was.'

'Was he there? Whatsisname? I never remember the husband's name. Pammie, Pammie – he was a *doctor*. And people don't die in childbirth now.'

'I don't know. It was early. Quite two weeks early. Maybe he was over in his own hospital. There was no sign of him at the nuns'. Well, there was no sign even of . . .'

Now they approached it.

'Even Thomasina wasn't there.'

'Whatever will happen? Oh, poor Thomasina.'

'Poor Thomasina.'

The news spread from Surrey into Hampshire and Sussex.

At a nice house in Liss four friends of Thomasina stopped their Bridge for nearly half an hour and picked up the cards again quite abstractedly. Somebody else near Petersfield was watching the six o'clock news, where a procession of skeletons straggled across a desert. Children's mouths in close-up were patrolled by flies. Starving madonnas, with lakes instead of eyes, rib-cages almost exposed through parchment skin, gazed uninterested at the cameras. 'Hello? No – perfectly good moment. Just the news. Ghastly – but what can one do? I'm waiting for the weather forecast: it's the Ladies' Cup tomorrow. What? *What*? Oh my God, no! Not Holly *Fox*? Oh, poor darling Thomasina! Who told her? Where is she? Where's her husband? Have you rung? I said *rung*? The house, of course. Oh, *course* go round there. Of course you must. If not, I'll go from over here. I'll get in the car now. Don't be *silly*, "butting in". She's somewhere, and the son-in-law's no earthly good. All his family live in Wigan or somewhere. Don't be so *wet*, Pammie. It's not like you. Go round.'

Others, nearer, had already gone round, but Thomasina's house in its large garden stood locked and silent. Florists' bunches were already gathering on the step. Pammie tramped round to the back. All was still and silent. Bulbs had been planted in hundreds under trees. Thomasina's gardening gloves lay together in prayer in the conservatory, beside a sheaf of carefully divided irises.

On the way home Pammie called on another woman, who answered the door, brick-red in the face with shock, glaring in outrage. 'She's at that health farm, Thomasina. That's where she is this week. To "get herself together for being a grandmother", she said, "in good time". It wasn't due, you know. "The first one's never early", she said. She said it here. This Thursday. Standing there where you are now. "May as well have a last fling de luxe", she said, "before my time stops being my own." She was going to be such a grandmother.'

'I know. We said, "She'll outclass Holly." '

'Not that she could have done. Holly was unimprovable. It was all talk with Thomasina. "Taking over"! It wouldn't have happened. She's too erratic. But the help she would have been at first . . . ! Adored it, patronising Holly and saying, "How hopeless," and yet proud as hell that she was such a marvellous mother. Oh God – *would* have been such a marvellous mother. I don't believe it. *I do not believe it.* Holly. That bursting, bursting health.'

'I suppose that's what it was,' said Pammie. 'Yes, please, I'll have another.' She held up her glass. 'Yes, don't stop. It was *bursting* health and she burst.'

'What a foul thing to say.'

'Well, something burst. Gone. Bang. And things will go bang in Thomasina now. You'll see. At last.'

Jinny of the brick-red face whose house it was and who did not have to drive home and whose dinner was already in the Neff awaiting the husband's reliable seven-thirty return had a third whisky and soon began to weep.

'I must go,' said Pammie; 'I've a madrigal group.'

Jinny at the door, sniffing, said, 'Matter of fact, what we were talking about: "*would* have been" a good grandmother? . . . She *is* a grandmother.'

Pammie looked blank and then remembered. 'I never thought,' she said. 'Oh God! Is the child all right? They never said. Have you heard? What was it?'

'I don't know.'

'A boy, I think. Yes, I think now they were saying . . . Yes. A lovely child. Though it may be a girl. I don't know. I can't believe I never asked. One or the other, I suppose.'

Which is how Faith Braithwaite was heralded into the world.

– 2 –

Holly Fox had remained Holly Fox after marriage to Andrew Braithwaite not because of the least breath of feminism in her but because she had always been such a vivid creature that nobody could think of her with any other name.

She really was an extraordinarily nice girl. Well, not nice so much as passionately loving and infectiously happy. She adored people. She adored places. She adored artefacts. At school she had adored games and been wonderfully good at them. She hadn't adored intellectual activities all that much and had often been in tears over her work; but after the tears, great big shiny ones, she had always recovered quickly and was soon laughing. She laughed beautifully – and she had always scraped through her examinations somehow. Holly Fox got by.

She was rather a noisy girl and you could pick out her laughing voice a long way off, but then a lot of girls are noisy, and at least she was tunefully noisy, never strident. She was adored, doted upon by the little girls at school, and to some of the big girls and several members of staff she was the cause of pangs. Her breeziness seemed to feed Sapphic passions which she never reciprocated nor seemed to comprehend, for she sent off shameless little presents quite publicly to all and sundry and jolly birthday cards covered in kisses to home addresses.

Holly Fox was effective. She was never late for anything. She was clean and even in the hideous school uniform of the day she managed to look as if she knew how to wear clothes. She always carried an extra pair of tights about with her in case of ladders and at any time of any day she would have been confident enough to meet the Queen, never without handkerchief, comb, toothbrush, tampon, book of stamps.

She shone with health. Her teeth gleamed. Her strong clean nails were filed into nice white ovals. Her hair sprang up shinily from the scalp on either side of a quarter-inch-deep parting. She never looked weather-beaten or awry but always, even in deep November, bronzy and smooth. She tramped about in wellies and loved a rainy day. Such *fun*!

Her self-confidence was daunting and would have been loathsome had it not been obvious that it sprang from neither conceit nor self-awareness. She was so outgoing, so enthusiastic about her life, her friends, her family, her tennis, her Christianity (she ran astonishingly successful sponsored charities from the age of fourteen: 'Well, we just *know* so many *people* and they're all so *generous*'), that you could not really say that it sprang from self-absorption either.

It probably did spring from self-absorption, of course, for Holly Fox was not altogether a good listener. But how could you mind when the self she presented was so delightful? She never missed a birthday of the most long-ago family cleaning lady, or au pair from earliest childhood, or teacher in her first primary school, or her mother's old, old friends, especially the hairy, warty ones. Her big joy, almost her passion, was the putting of people in touch with other people who were vaguely connected with one another by distant threads of blood, by godchildren of second and third cousins, by half-remembered funerals, the wedding parties of long-lost enemies and old and sometimes desperate-to-be-forgotten passions. Her bulky address book at the age of twenty or so was already like the Almanac de Gotha. Once inscribed in it you were hers for ever. Holly Fox never, never, dropped you.

And men? Sex? No great trouble there either. She *adored* men, and said so. Often. She had adored men since she was born, she said, calling out the information across rooms full of them, laughing not archly but, it has to be said, deliciously.

7

Sometimes chin in hand, eyes large, she said it lovingly, longingly, introspectively, confidently, like an experienced old courtesan who had much that she might tell; or as if she were preparing for a maturity and old age when it would be said that Holly Fox in her prime had been a *femme fatale*, a raving beauty.

And this was untrue. Holly Fox was not beautiful at all, but behaved with a shining openness and an innocent heart so that when she looked at you with big clear eyes she seeemed to expose a classic face. In fact it was broad, freckly, and the chin colossal.

At the time of her death at twenty-eight in the 1990s Holly Fox had settled deeply into the mores of an almost lost generation, her mother's. She wore pearls and good suits and a hat for lunch in London. Do you believe this? Well, it is true. I promise you that Holly Fox at twenty-eight in the early Nineties would wear a hat for lunch in Fortnum & Mason, usually as the guest of older women, and sit there among the antiseptic Americans – who thought, mistakenly, how amazingly English she was – and all the old scrags with their painted faces and tortured voices that floated together, piercingly clear, high up among the pretty lights on the ceiling. So sweet, the old-fashioned voice, the little diamond brooch in the lapel (she loved a diamond). She smiled up at the deadpan waitresses who said to each other, 'Isn't she like *Brief Encounter*, and yet she can't be more than, say, thirty-five?' 'Or *Mrs Miniver*,' they said.

They knew their stuff, these old creaking Fortnum warriors, for Holly Fox was no better educated, no more politically, sociologically or sexually advanced, than either of these wartime film stars of nearly half a century before. Holly Fox was a throwback, a coelacanth. She aimed at being a thoroughly nice girl.

A fool and an idiot, then? A leech upon society? Not at all. Holly Fox before her marriage had been a nurse, a staff nurse in a great London hospital, and though she had had such trouble with her school examinations there was not a thing she balked at or mismanaged or mistook in her medical ones. She

8

won distinctions. Before an examination she was still adept in fanning herself into the proper hysteria – 'I'll never do it, *never*' – but then she would pass out top.

'But I *meant* it!' she would cry. 'I thought I'd made a terrible *mess* of it! I swear. I can't believe it.'

Her nursing gifts, which unfolded naturally, were very thrilling to her. Her father had been a doctor, and his father before him, and instinctively she seemed to know the form, the jargon, the medical mythology. She seemed to comprehend the Hippocratic world so well that she even dared sometimes to send it up. As a first-year nurse she attended the hospital Christmas party dressed as a kissagram and embraced the Dean while ogresses in higher power stood dumbfounded. Sharp-faced, pock-marked authoritarians gaped, bewildered. The nerve of her with her pink glowing face – was it make-up or wasn't it? (It wasn't, it was health) – and her lah-di-dah vowels. 'What sort of example, Nurse Fox?' and so on.

But there was a certain steely authority about Holly Fox. Her credentials were impeccable. Her grandfather and father (and the man soon to be her husband) each had his name painted gold upon mahogany on the honours boards of the hospital Rugby XVs.

Cleverer girls than Holly Fox sometimes said that her confidence beneath the unrelenting sweetness made them sick. Ugly ones said she was over the top, snobbish, no beauty and a pain. But nobody could help liking her genuine good nature and her loving ways and lack of self-consciousness, and the fact that she was exactly the same with everybody, which, incidentally, is only nice if you are nice and not poisonous. Tamburlaine the Great was the same with everybody and so were Napoleon and Mussolini and Ivan the Terrible and Queen Elizabeth the First. But Holly Fox was not like them.

And she was not snobbish. No.

Or was she snobbish?

Oh, God, yes. Holly Fox actually, when you came down to it, was snobbish. Any political party not blue as the summer sky was in unthinkable shadow and she had never once been out with a man who hadn't been to an English public school, though she would have been *thrilled* with Harvard maybe, or Gordonstoun, which was OK because of the royal family.

During her nursing training, when Holly Fox met and worked with proles for the first time (and found them all perfectly sweet), she didn't know them socially. She would have been lost anywhere that her own language was not spoken, both metaphorically and actually, and before meeting her future husband she had never travelled north of the home counties of England except once by air to St Andrews for her mother's golf, and to Dublin for a ball given by a girl at school. She muddled up Westmorland and Wolverhampton.

But look – she was lovely. You could tick off a thousand shortcomings in Holly Fox, failures of imagination, limitations of everyday understanding, and you might not choose to go on holiday with her especially if you were of rather low vitality or cared for guidebooks or for reading on an empty beach in silence. You might not waste a ticket on her for a concert. You might get fed up that every theatre performance she ever went to was pronounced 'absolutely marvellous' and was the more marvellous the less she understood it. And you might not be inclined to tell her any secrets, because although they would be perfectly safe with her (she forgot them) you had to watch them bounce and slide like dandelion clocks off her hands, scarcely touching her consciousness.

All the same, Holly Fox wept with the bereaved, held the hands of the dying, and she was wonderful with patients in pain. Yet the knife-twist of failure or loss somehow you felt never came near her and 'tragedy', a word she used often, was never applied to anything large. She believed effortlessly in God, effortlessly in Christ, hazily in the Holy Spirit. She confused Bethlehem and the Gaza Strip and never thought which language Christ spoke in since what He said had always sounded so English. Eternal life presented no difficulties to Holly Fox for she knew that it must be so, and heaven somewhere or other, or why should such awful things happen to us here? There must be more to us than bodies that rotted and stank and broke apart and grew things both inside and out and looked worse as they aged and loathsome at the last.

Children's bodies, too. All that she had had to see and face head-on in hospital, the facts that so often persuade better-educated, subtler people than Holly Fox against the existence of God, were for her simply proof that there must be something else to come or why should God have bothered? She had a point.

I tell you, everyone looked for the crumbled feet of clay on this shining girl and nobody found them. Certainly men never found them. Holly Fox was physically, uninhibitedly warm-blooded and determined on a lot of sexual love – in time. Not yet. What's more – and this was important to the medical students she usually went about with – she was pretty well-off and well-connected to the top medical mafia. Quite a few were stirred by the heart that beat so strongly beneath the starch that her hospital still insisted upon.

Oh Holly Fox, Holly Fox – she knew in her genes, as many don't, that what the sleazy, exhausted, nearly gutted soul of the young male hospital doctor wants is not femininity and softness, and someone who won't bleat when he's never at home, so much as self-confidence; an effective, fearless sort of woman, preferably a wielder of some sort of power in the profession, who keeps cool, smiles at him when he comes home, ticks him off, keeps her (and his) love affairs to herself, is silent as the grave about gossip, doesn't get drunk at parties and has the makings of a stupendous medically political hostess of the future.

Holly Fox, by the way, had not the least intention of going on with any work after marriage, even if she were to choose a penniless houseman. Her mother and grandmother had never worked; why should she? The penniless housemen in her life did not actually know this yet but, even if they had, it would have made little difference, for the choice – just look at that jaw, those blue eyes perhaps a little cold within the sparkle – the choice was going to be entirely hers. When Holly Fox fell matrimonially in love it was going to be with utter success, a full-scale operation.

'Andrew Braithwaite,' said Thomasina, her mother, to Pammie and Jinny and everyone. 'Poor lamb, she's begun to gaze at him. He hasn't a chance.'

He hadn't.

She got him.

– 3 –

Thomasina, Holly's mother, had been a widow for years and years without the slightest intention of remarriage. Her husband, a general surgeon in the home counties, had dropped down dead in the middle of an operation on a heart that was somehow kept beating while old Herbert's refused every sort of jump-start in the book. He had been dying for a cigarette at the time, and indeed did so. A good marriage really, very devoted, although there had always been a look, a world-weary, wary look, in Thomasina's eye that said she always steered clear of devotion.

Maybe she was a woman who did not really need a man all that much? Maybe a generation on she would have been a lesbian? Herbert and she had got out of the way of discussing their feelings, if they had ever done so, which is improbable. Herbert had been pretty bluff from the nursery, and not often at home in the evenings. Overworked, of course, and no hobbies except smoking. His adoring hospital entourage (he liked girls for suggestive, sexy conversations, no more) had made him as arrogant as the next man in a sycophantic profession, and in his social life at home he postured about, too proud to talk about his work to laymen, afraid at parties that someone would come and ask for free advice. He was a crashing social snob, very keen on his dead relations. His talkativeness at work and his amiability were the same as his daughter's and his laugh was famous. He went caroling through life, probably doing more good than harm.

Thomasina never let on about what had drawn her to him. She had the Surrey way of talking endlessly and objectively about her nearest without the least hint of them being also dear. First meeting, young love, marriage bed and the early years of Thomasina and Herbert Fox were unknown to all, and 'all' now included themselves. The world was kept in darkness. There were no photographs on display except for an unyielding bridal study on Thomasina's dressing table, Herbert blotchy with (perhaps) emotion and in RAMC uniform and Thomasina, twenty-five, looking elderly in a family wedding veil that hung down, all round as if there were lead weights in the hem, like a lace tablecloth at a Mrs Beeton dinner.

Poor Thomasina. You could see the awful honeymoon ahead. You could see the screwed-up damp handkerchiefs at Victoria Station. You could hear the sad boom of the guns, imagine the bomb-torn plain, the mountainous bandages, the terrible and wonderful heroism and patriotism. At home there would be Thomasina in a ghastly white hat and apron with a big red cross stitched on it, making field dressings, running tea stalls, being brave beneath the zeppelins.

Wrong. Wrong. Wrong war. Thomasina in that war was not even a child. It was the second war. Herbert only made RAMC officer because he was doing some national service and Thomasina only looked like Edith Cavell because she had absorbed, as her daughter was to do later, so much of her mother's generation that she looked a generation older than she was. There was a very powerful gene in the female members of this family that held its generations in a vice.

But Thomasina, unlike Holly Fox, who was not given the opportunity, grew younger. If there had been later photographs of her you would have seen her grow clear of the lace and lilies and honeymoon tweeds of the times. In the coming years, with Herbert so often from home, her voice was to become deeper and more confident. Her golf began to be respectable and her tennis even better. The dark face of Thomasina glaring through the racket strings before a particularly devilish smash showed a depth of aggression you'd never have expected in her at a drinks party in her chintzy sitting room or her garden which overflowed with old-fashioned roses all tangled up with shrubs, sweet-smelling herbs, narcissi, dahlias in season, clouds of bluebells in spring, difficult trilliums and lilies and 'anything I feel like sticking in'. Green fingers? Not at all. 'I just buy and pray.'

But that was not altogether true, for in the garden – in dungarees, then tight pants, then jeans, then floppy trousers as the years rolled – Thomasina heaved and dug and slashed about by the hour, the day, the week, the season, clearing, sweeping, replenishing soil, feeding with rich black compost, adding most violent tonics ('chicken shit for choice'), plumping, slapping and puddling everything back in again. She opened for the National Gardens twice a year. It was an almost killing, numbing discipline; introverting, silencing, and bringing great comforts. Thomasina's garden rewarded her with richness: every leaf looked polished or silken, every rose was spotless, thripless, waiting to be photographed, waiting to be admired.

Oh, what was really going on inside Thomasina Fox?

As the marriage waned to a brother-and-sisterishness – except for occasional exercisings in the dark, which were forgotten by morning, never commented upon – brother-and-sisterish tracts of private territory were established. Thomasina became capable of cutting her losses as resolutely as she cut down her sweet peas. Her figure improved. The roundedness beneath the lace tablecloth that had threatened haunches turned to slimness and then to leanness and then to a lanky Sackville-Western ranginess that happened to be fashionable at the time. She flattened out above, which was also timely, for it was now the 1960s, when female beauty became anorexic and young girls yearned sometimes until teenage death for a breastless, stomachless torso. Other women of Thomasina's age responded rebelliously at this time with gathered, bunchy skirts, scooped necklines and beehive hair. Thomasina flaunted her independence by wearing short skirts even in the evening and cutting her hair to near baldness.

She never discussed it. Never said why, and Herbert never noticed. Her friends said things like, 'Oh my! Thomasina!' but she only smiled. To one another they said, 'She looks rather male. Can't say I like it,' or 'She's really far too thin. I hope she's not *got* something,' and, 'It's a bit repulsive really, those hipbones sticking out at the front, like those awful dying cows in the East.' Men liked it, though. During the Sixties and Seventies Englishmen were learning rather guiltily to like women who could look like boys, who grew thinner and thinner, taller and taller, fiercer and fiercer. Their heels became four inches high, puncturing the wooden floors of Europe, the châteaux of the Loire, the assembly rooms at Bath, the little Surrey hospital where Holly Fox was born and where, twenty-eight years later, she was to die.

Thomasina became 'that woman with the marvellous figure' and even when one day it was noticed that her waistline was rather less defined and then a baggish thing emerged between the coat-hanger hip bones, and word went round, 'Good gracious – Thomasina, at last!', she still looked good. Through all the nine months she looked good, indeed wonderful, and felt it. Herbert was delighted and everyone most envious, after Holly was born on Christmas Day, to find Thomasina restored to her flatness and ranginess within days, as if the child had been lifted lightly out from inside some expensively invisible zip-fastener. The nuns all thought her a splendid woman and Herbert was so excited he nearly amputated somebody's good leg. Or said he did. They were being awfully funny and bright and not altogether truthful about this time, the Foxes. They joked and laughed at everything. Even when Herbert died a year or so later Thomasina kept her careful, mocking face in order magnificently. Extraordinary woman. Very brave. Scarcely spoke of him.

But oh, the difference in her.

The difference that followed. The difference centred itself in the intensity of her love for Holly.

From her daughter's birth Thomasina had been ahead of her time, skipping the feminism and going straight into the backlash. She had been an avid non-smoking, non-drinking breast-feeder. Now she became the impassioned mother, she and the baby inseparable. For years she gave up everything: childless friends (except Pammie), Bridge, golf, tennis. She spent her days at tots' dancing classes, music lessons, play-groups, junior-school swimming baths, nursery tea parties. She refused to consider employing a nanny or au pair. She refused drinks parties, fork suppers beloved of the region, men, offers of marriage. She never went on holiday. She and Holly lived intensely together in the black-and-white Thirties-Tudor house in its glossy-mag garden, now rather overgrown. On the telephone (when she couldn't avoid it: it was before answer-phones) she kept up an occasional contact, in a pleasant, shrieking old lingo, with friends – she had no relations to speak of – and she had people to the house only if they had babies. Babies for Holly. Holly must have her friends from the beginning, this only child. Thomasina read Dr Spock, Jung, John Bowlby, Fairbairn.

Yet beneath the ordered, almost ordained, rich, upper-class life of the day, for which everyone about her had fought and which they believed to be a true and gallant way of continuing the country's old validity (not for the money only – this was pre-Thatcher), Thomasina swam in a deep sea of love for her child, a gobbling love, an inordinate affection that blotted out all else and terrified her whenever she had to come up for a gasp of air. She never put into words, not even to herself, what the gasps of air disclosed: that Holly was her passion, her lover, her life. If 'anything should happen' to Holly, Thomasina knew that she would die.

It was inexplicable. It was not what anyone was used to in Edgecombe Park, least of all Thomasina. For years, after all, the Foxes had made no secret of the fact that they didn't want children and with Thomasina growing so masculine and skinny and poor Herbert so glandular and fat – and silly – it had often been said that you only had to look at them to see that the poor things couldn't do it. Some said they never had, that Herbert was all bombast and smut and schoolboy jokes about sex and all his talk about it in the hospital was just talk. But there it was. Holly Fox arrived into Thomasina's world and Thomasina wrapped her now celibate elegant frame in ecstasy.

As Holly's childhood passed, Thomasina began to cope

rather better with this secret life. A perfect mother was not obsessive, must learn to let her child go in order to develop her own relationships, have schoolgirl secrets, go off on school trips. The first of these, no further than the Kensington Science Museum when Holly was eight, marked a vital stage in Thomasina's journey. She spent the hours alone at home hallucinating the upturned coach, little bodies spilled about the road, the Irish bomb, the false step off the pavement. 'We're just going to buy a—' Screech! The ambulance siren, the police cars. The ring at the bell. The funeral procession.

Nobody, *nobody*, knew the immensity of these things, and Holly was greeted on her return by her mother's cool face and nice food waiting in the fridge. Holly overheard girls at school say, 'Holly's mother's *terrific*-looking but she's a bit hard somehow. D'you think she's horrible to Holly?' But how could she be, with Holly such an open, happy girl?

And still open and happy at nine, hugging and hugging her mother goodbye when she went off to boarding school in Kent, excited at all that was to come. Thomasina amazed the school staff that climactic day by her light-hearted adieux. Other mothers sniffled. This one hugged and kissed the child with the greatest good sense and looked understanding and amused as Holly vanished up some stairs, one sock higher than the other, arms full of teddies and a tin of home-made shortbread.

Thomasina left briskly, but as she turned out of the school gates she began to shake. Later she stopped the car in a lay-by on the Hog's Back. She did not weep there, but sat, and the landscape eventually became the landscape again and not the narrow beastly bed on which her daughter would at this minute be arranging her toys and photographs; or flinging herself down, sucking a handkerchief end, tears spilling. Holly was actually signing herself up for various clubs and had made an inseparable friend called Grizelda who the next day turned into another one called Persephone and then another called Emma.

That day it took an hour before Thomasina could restart the car and, driving carefully and slowly, somewhere on the road between Guildford and Liss, was able to take the decision that she would now change. She would never shake again, not even in private. *At this moment,* she thought, *Holly is probably signing herself up for various clubs and forming inseparable friendships.*

'Hello?' she cried on the telephone to Pammie – the car still warm outside in the drive, she still in her coat. 'Hello? Yes. She's *gone!* Oh ghastly, thanks. Ridiculous. I feel quite awful. She's at the South Pole at least. Can't go upstairs yet and pass the bedroom door. Yes, I'd love to. Six o'clock?'

She had declared herself, realigned herself. She would be welcomed back.

And I told the truth, she proudly thought. *I told the truth to them. I do feel awful. I don't want to look in the bedroom. I do think I'm being ridiculous. I'm being very wise and affection-ate to them all to be sharing things with them again.*

But she knew that she hadn't shared them, had not even touched on the depth of her mania, the almost religious fervour of her devotion, the passionate pride in Holly – the Holly, Holly, Holly, that went on in her mind like a love affair that is incurable, that must take its course.

Sometimes, exhausted by the single train of her thought, the drum-beat rhythm of her love, Thomasina nearly screamed or wept. She knew that she ought 'to see someone about it', yet she hardly knew what this meant. Some psychiatrist, perhaps? But you had to be recommended to one by a GP and her GP was an old friend she and Herbert used to have to dinner and talk hospital politics. They'd even been on holidays with him. You couldn't possibly *talk* to him.

And I don't scream, she thought. *I am always only just on the point of screaming. I certainly never actually weep. I am in full control and I'm probably no different from thousands of others. Rich, idle, no job, one child, no husband. And everyone says that Holly is special. I can't be all that wrong, or dotty.*

I wish I could get interested in men again, she thought. *I'm too old now to stand love. Thank God that sort of pain's over. Golf and Bridge and the old gang are the answer. And Surrey's a lovely county to live in. Crazy not to be happy.*

By the time Holly married, Thomasina had become a very differently behaved woman. She seemed most genuinely to welcome Holly's marriage and believed that Andrew Braithwaite was 'perfectly all right'. She laughed publicly and amusingly at Holly's adoration of him and Holly laughed with her. 'Ma, he's *wonderful*. I knew the very first minute . . .'

'I can't say', Thomasina had said to Pammie and Co. over the cards, 'that he exactly causes one to fall back in *wonder*. I mean, of all the ones I've caught a glimpse of this one has the least hair. He's twenty-five, looks forty-three. They say he looked forty-three even at school. Of course, bald men are said to be the sexiest. Bald-*headed* of course. A lot of bald men are like hearth mats underneath.'

'Is Andrew?'

'My *dear*, however should I know? I've not seen him on a beach. It's winter. They only met six weeks ago. He has a good figure, I'll say that for him. He wears his clothes well. Nice long legs, so he can't be Jewish. The stoop will be useful at the bedside. He qualifies this summer.'

'GP?'

'No, no, he'll be a hospital doctor. He doesn't say much about it to me, though he could. I'd like it if he did. He knows I'm used to the vocab. I don't think he even talks about work to Holly much, though I suppose that's not surprising, she's not exactly Alexander Fleming, bless her.' Thomasina had learned the language of Edgecombe Park and led the field now in sardonic depreciation of all that meant most to her. 'This *bloody* dog,' she would cry (she'd been given a dog by Holly for her birthday). 'Look at the parquet! I'll hang you. I'll string you up!' To Holly she would say, 'Your hair is like old hay today. I *loathe* you, darling.'

Andrew and Holly came to Spindleberries to announce their engagement and Thomasina made joyful noises and brought forth the champagne she had been putting in and taking out of the fridge for a month. She excelled herself with the wedding arrangements, looking younger and much more chic (apple-green silk) than the bride, and waved them off from the reception with a smiling face; off for a whole year, to

California, where Andrew had been awarded a research fellowship. 'So *good* for them,' she thought. 'Nobody to tell them what to do or watch how things are going. And away from the dominating old mum.' Andrew's family were in the North; his parents, peculiarly old, had not come to the wedding. 'He won't have to be running up and down there to see them,' she said, 'thank goodness. Northern families can be very demanding. And he has a brother living near them, so he needn't worry. Rather ghastly distance for me, of course. California for a whole year. Boo hoo.'

She embarked on a full year for herself, captaining the Ladies' Golf team, taking herself off in a group organised by Abercrombie & Kent to India, where she stayed in palaces, shuddered at the beggars, suffered with the food and made a couple of thoroughly nice friends. Thanks to Herbert's nifty talent with investments the money was holding up well.

And the year passed and then some more years back in the South of England, with Holly within reach again, and Thomasina's life went on. When at length, after rather a worryingly long time – some years – Holly became pregnant, Thomasina was to the world blasé yet conformingly ecstatic: a mixture of 'And about time too' and 'We don't know what she'll be like with a child, I'm afraid. It'll *wreck* her tennis.'

Away she went, Thomasina, to Challoners Health Farm for a week to prepare herself for the delights of grandmotherhood, full of good nature, good sense and sociability. She had won through. The obsession remained only in her memory of a long-gone shadowy time, a mad time that she could scarcely credit. Now she had at last filled the skin of the part she had played to rid her of it.

She had become the Thomasina that the world had always thought she was. She had been to Challoners before, and loved it. The weather was glorious, her room luxurious, the food – for she wasn't one of those who went there to be dieted – fresh and delicious, and everybody most amusing. At tea on the first day she overheard what she thought of as an 'old army voice' at another table saying, 'Just arrived. Anybody here famous this time? Apart from you and me, of course,' and thought,

What a very nice laugh. When she turned from her silver tea pot to see who owned it, she thought, *And very nice teeth*.

He was all of seventy, long as a lamp post, moustached, blue-eyed and wearing corded clothes of ancient and superb design. They made the other men in the room, who were mostly young and beautiful and wearing dressing gowns and examining their fingernails, look like advertisements for something.

'But of course,' the general called across to her (he looked one, he was one), 'you must be famous. Let me think. Well, you're not a film star. I hear Joan Collins was here last week and she was a network of lines. So they tell me. I don't know who Joan Collins is but I suppose she's a film star because everyone was so surprised.' *No lines on you*, said his eyes; *you're an outdoor woman*.

She thought, *He's very attractive. He still likes women. It's not just that he knows what to say*.

Later they sat cross-legged side by side at an exercise class.

'To the left . . . *bend*. Now to the right . . . *bend*,' and the circle of the self-indulgent, the alcoholic, the arthritic, the over-tired, the lonely, the sad, and people on the run from things, leaned first one way and then the other. 'Stretch *up*. Good. Now *forward*.'

The general creaked to his feet. 'Sorry,' he said, 'no go. Too late. All over. Packing it in for now.'

Thomasina, still lithe as a tendril after the years of golf and gardening, smiled up at his cheerful and admiring face.

The class over, she went for a walk in the woods. In the evening there was Bridge. He played very well, rather noisily, wittily, like a young man, calling out, 'Well played,' to others. At bedtime they found that their doors were opposite each other on the main, the most expensive, corridor; and Thomasina, lying in her bed watching television – she seldom read and neither, he had said, did the general, except for the odd military biography – wondered insanely if she should have locked her door.

All *of seventy*, she thought, and considered what his naked body would look like. Thin, anyway, and he'd at least wear clothes over it. Silk pye-jams probably, not those awful boxer-shorts things and certainly not sweaty and nude – like in television plays – with great tufts sprouting about. She thought that the general would have some tufts but they'd be clean and in the right places. He would smell of coal-tar soap, she thought, and brush his teeth with that lovely toothpaste you can get in the Burlington Arcade. She fell asleep smiling, wondering if she could bear it if the general's tufts turned out to be grey.

The general rose early next morning for a quick swim and a go on the exercise bikes in the gym. Thomasina was not at breakfast. He had his sauna and then his massage. He looked out for her over his mug of Bovril at twelve o'clock. He, too, had not been put on a diet but he had elected himself to one. Liked to feel he could still put himself through things a bit. Hard commons, early rising, never did anybody any harm. He realised after a few minutes that lean and slender Thomasina would not, of course, be on the diet either and would be eating in the dining room, so he swallowed the last of the Bovril and went to his room to change. No appearing in dressing gowns in dining rooms for him.

But she was not there.

He walked to the after-lunch meditation class and she was not there either. He stayed for it, meditating on her, began to float, fell asleep.

Laughing at the end – 'I suppose I was snoring? Yes? Oh God, I *do* apologise' – he groaned to his feet and went in search of her again, finally deciding to knock on her door, though it was not the sort of thing he approved of. Not the way things should be done. God, she might be in her nightdress, resting.

But there was no answer.

The general made his way to the reception hall and front desk, where the big glass doors of the hydro stood open to the sunny park, and the professionally sunny receptionist in white starched overall told him that Mrs Fox had had to leave. She had been unexpectedly called away.

Turning, the general saw through the doorway a humped

old woman being shepherded into a car in the drive by a bald young man. The car drove off very fast.

– 4 –

How wet in the heather. But Jack did not notice. He sat up by the Saxon cross. It was morning. Holly Fox had been dead twenty-four hours.

He had heard the phone ring as he was leaving his private chapel but had not hurried particularly across the courtyard. It had been ringing on and on. His brother's voice, so like his own. They had not spoken since last Christmas.

Andrew sounded unhurried too. Very, very slow, with long pauses. Would Jack please tell their parents?

Jack said at last, 'It's for you to do.'

'No. Better from you. I can't.'

'There's a neighbour,' said Jack. 'She's very good. I'll get the vicar to tell them, and then the neighbour – Middleditch – can go round, just to sit with them.'

'Can't you get there?'

'Yes. I'll go now. Directly.'

'Don't ring anybody up. Just go.'

Jack paused for so long Andrew thought he had hung up. Then Jack said, 'I'll see what's best. You can ring them yourself later – say, after midday. I'll stay with them, but . . .'

'What?'

He could not say the seed potatoes were critical. He said, 'I'll stay with them all afternoon. The child . . . ?'

'She's fine. Fine. Called Faith. I have to go. I'll ring them. Fuck you, Jack, I'll ring them.'

'That's all right. I'll see to it.'

'Is it so much to ask?' Andrew slammed down the phone.

Jack then had taken a piece of bread and gone, gnawing it as he

23

walked from the house. He left by the doors of the Great Solar and crossed his courtyard of hollowed stones, went up through the tilting gravestones to the track, and climbed for a mile here until he reached the ridge road and could see the tides of the moors mounting, mounting on each other's backs, flowing always westward like the Vikings, the prows of crags probing up through the mists. Mounting and mounting, folding and folding. Even in the whitest, thickest, early mist, curlews were crying. Wobbling, liquid, long, long cries ripping the skin of the white lakes.

To Jack's left – he sat on a sopping lump of turf, his back resting against the stone cross – the three golf balls of the early warning system floated on smoke. To his right were the loops of the highest road westward. In front and below were the swooping valleys, the heather giving way to rough stone walls whose pattern thickened towards the valley bottoms. The sun came through with a flourish, lit the miles, lifted the mist, glittered on the waterfalls of ragged bracken and outcrops of stone.

A van came along the ridge, roaring out music like a circus. It stopped beside Jack and a window was wound down, making the circus wild. A package was handed out. The postman said, 'You'll get right wet sitting there, Jack, on that bank.'

'Good morning, Post. Thank you. No – quite all right.'

'Saving me a journey down, then?'

'Saving you a journey down.'

'Yer look peaked, Jack. On a grand morning.'

Jack stood up, skinny as a monk, and watched the sun across the next valley-but-two switch on like a light across a pale, heaving ocean. 'Would you reckon rain, Jimmie?'

'I'd not think so. Not today.'

'Well. Beginning to come through again, the sun?'

'Aye. I'll be on my way, then. You don't want a lift back down?'

'No, thank you. God bless you.'

Before he turned down the track again, Jack felt in the little dip that lay high up above him on the top of the upright of the stone cross. Only your fingertips could tell if there was money there. If there was, you kept it. If there wasn't, you left some. There was a hazard in it. It was bad luck to find no money when you had no money on you, and Jack in his worn-out shirt and tattered trousers never had any money in his pockets – or anywhere else.

But superstition is not Christian. It is for the invaders, the ones of the high prows, and horned helmets, the tin eyes, the old beekeeping sea-rovers who despised Christ and roughed up his dwelling places. Louts from Teesside now did the same, but they were ugly and resentful: nothing splendid about them. Jack smiled, thinking of the sweet dead warrior Holly Fox, and felt high up in the stone, where he found a single gold pound coin. 'Well, well. American tourists.'

Down the track he went again. First he would pray for the child, then ask someone to help him start the car. Yes, he might ring his parents' vicar and that neighbour person if he could find the number, just in case Andrew did ring up when the two old people were alone. Of course, he'd go down himself. If he could. To his ma and pa. Faith's grandparents. His old saints. Yes.

The pound shall be for the child, he thought. *She shall have it when she arrives.*

– 5 –

'We should get ourselves down there,' old Braithwaite shouted, 'that's what we should do. What's the good of us up here? Get me my clothes.'

'What?'

'Get me my clothes. I'm getting up.'

Dolly Braithwaite came padding down the stairs and looked in the dining room, where her husband now slept with a night table beside him bearing reading lamp, urine bottle, gold watch, four pencils, a book of geometrical exercises and seven bottles of pills. The reading lamp was switched on. Old Braithwaite was lying looking at the ceiling. It was three o'clock in the morning.

'Get my clothes.'

'Don't be so silly.' She sat down beside the dead fire in the grate and leaned forward to switch on an electric heater standing near it. She wore floppy flat slippers with matted furry edging, and an old coat. 'Don't be so silly. You're an old man.'

'Haven't you a decent dressing gown?' He had not looked at her, but he knew. This was automatic conversation, a duet between long-mated and now-moulting birds.

'Of course I've a decent dressing gown. I just picked up the first thing I found. You frightened me, bellowing like that. I thought something was wrong.'

'We ought to be down there. Down South.'

'However could we get there? We've never been there. Where would we stay?'

'Well, with Andrew. He's not too grand to give us a bed, is he? He'll have a spare room.'

'He'll be looking after her mother. He rang from her mother's. I wouldn't go and stay there.'

'I'd stay wherever. What's so wrong with her?'

'I don't know. We shouldn't judge. She's probably a nice enough woman, poor soul. But she couldn't take people like us dropping on her now. You couldn't expect it.'

'People like us. We're not "people like us", we're us. Just because she was got up in apple green.'

'Well, at her age.'

'She's a lot less than your age. She might just be in her fifties. She might be your age, mind you, though you'd never guess. It's being South.'

'Well, she's not had to put up with what I've had,' said Andrew's mother, 'and she's always had plenty of money.'

'Well, we've plenty of money. For what we want. And with the social services. They're marvellous. And you've got a better dressing gown than you make out. From Newhouses.'

'For goodness' sake, will you shut up about dressing gowns.

You've a widowed son, and there's this baby . . .' Tears fell.

Soon Toots Braithwaite wept too. The tears wandered down his face to his neck and the pearl button that fastened the top of the Chilprufe vest he wore under his raspberry-striped winceyette pyjamas.

'I'll get a cup of tea,' she said. 'Give me your bottle to empty,' and she went along the passage holding the brimming plastic urine conch and began to drop things on the kitchen floor, looking for matches.

'Take care what you're doing.'

'What?'

'You'll set us alight.'

'Of course I'm all right.'

She came back to the dining room. 'D'you want your wireless on? There's the World Service. You'll go back to sleep after your tea.'

'I'm not ill. For God's sake – I'm lame, that's all, and I'd not be lame if I could get out for a walk. I never get taken out, so I get no practice. That's all it is. Down to that ruddy seat by the churchyard and back again, waddling behind that frame.'

'Here's your tea.'

'Like a dying grasshopper.'

'You should be thankful for the frame. You were worse before you had it. You were impossible.'

'Saw a whole row of them the other day.'

'What, grasshoppers?'

'Old crocks like me. Going along in a row one behind the other off a bus. Ye gods! Like a centipede. A hiccupping centipede.'

'They couldn't all have come off a bus. How could they have got a busload of walking frames on a bus same time as a busload of people?'

'It was an outing. It'd be a special bus. A disabled bus. Built for it,' he said.

'Maybe we should go on outings.'

'We're not poor. Outings are for the poor. "Underprivileged", they call them now. And we're not old enough. What we should have is a taxi now and then to Scarborough. You see some things going on in Scarborough. We're not ninety. We've got money.'

Dolly sat, knees apart to the cold fireplace, the electric fire turned away from her towards Toots's bed, her head bowed.

'Now, there's no use,' he said. 'Don't upset yourself.'

'Oh, Toots. There's nothing to be done.'

'Stop crying. Stop saying there's nothing to be done. What time is it?

'Four o'clock. It's getting light. The birds are started . . . Oh the poor thing. The poor things. That baby . . .'

'What they calling her, you say?' he asked, into a silence.

'Faith.'

'It's a plain sort of name. I'm not altogether taken with it.'

'It's some sort of joke business, apparently. They were all saying, "Holly had faith", "At least she had her faith" – that sort of business. So they called her Faith.'

'I'm not sure that's good taste. At a time like this. Puns.'

'Well, it's true. Holly was a good Christian girl and you don't expect that from down there somehow.'

'Aye. Mind, she let you know it,' said Toots.

'You shouldn't say that, Tom. And she didn't. She was a lovely . . . Oh Lord.'

'Hush, now. Hush, lassie. This what's-this – "Faith"? Did he say?'

'Of course he didn't say. It was all he could do to talk to us at all. Clipped like he is. Like a sneer when words did come out. Not crying. I'm glad Mrs Middleditch had told us first. She broke the back of it a bit. I think . . . It did . . . When it . . .'

'It didn't make it easier,' he said. 'Nothing makes it easier. And that woman – Middleditch. Where's she got it from? Who'd told her? I suppose the whole place knew it before us. She comes round here with that bowl of soup. *Middleditch*.'

'It was all kindness.'

'Kindness! All she fills her time with is kindness and ferreting things out. And that mouth of hers. Like a hen's bottom.'

'She can't help her appearance. And she's been a very good friend to us. Gets us our pensions and she ran the ruby wedding. Ran it single-handed.'

'Holly would have done that. Holly said she would have come all the way up here to run it if she'd only known. And she'd have given us a proper do, too, not tea and whisky and those sandwiches. We'd have had sherries and tartlets and guests of our own class and education.'

'Mrs Middleditch has had education. A lot of education. She was highly trained in a college.'

'Trained what in? College dinners, likely, judging from the look of that soup. Why have we got in with these kinds of people? We're sitting ducks for them, that's why. Told our own news like geriatrics. This ought to have been our affair. Private and personal. Sent in a letter as it was in times past, and we should have been allowed to keep it to ourselves for a bit. Half the parish arriving.'

'The vicar was very good,' she said. 'I'll think better of the vicar after this. I expect he let it out to Mrs Middleditch by accident and she got round here first, living just round the corner.'

'I'd guess it was she told him. She's ahead of the field of knowledge in that church. She'll be a woman priest next. She'll be handing us the cup. What's the matter? You're saying nothing.'

Dolly was getting slowly to her feet. She padded around the large pretty room overcrowded now with invalid furniture, the old family dining table, flaps down, under the window, a mighty sideboard laden with clean clothes, library books, unguents, ointments and sewing things that had wandered in among the decanters and candlesticks and fruit bowls that were still kept bravely about. She started drawing back curtains. She watched the black and white dawn garden, the wet grass. A bird or two hopped along the flower bed. One of them, a fat starling, watched her insolently between pecks at yesterday's dinner-time crumbs. There were no supper crumbs, for there had been no supper. The Middleditch soup still stood on the kitchen draining board. The bird marched up and down, not yet letting go of the night.

'I'd better get myself back to bed,' Dolly said, 'before the day starts up and they all come round again. Jack'll be down first thing.'

'Don't count on it. It's harvest time. And he's got the new intake.'

'I don't. I never count on Jack. He has his life to live.'

'Aye, and his wife and child,' said Toots. 'He's lucky.'

'They never got on, Andrew and Jack.'

'But he'll take the child, you know. You'll see.'

'What – *Jack*? *Jack* take the child? Don't be silly, it's its father's child,' said Dolly.

'And how does a hospital doctor working all hours God gave look after a new-born child?' said Toots. 'Unless they get a nanny. Or Mrs Fox could take over.'

'Over my dead body, she will,' said Dolly, rolling her eyes and looking as once she had done: effective, bellicose and certain.

'It's not up to you and it's not up to me what happens to this child. It's Andrew's and the other grandma's. It's a South-country child. You said yourself at the start, when you knew it was coming, not to get excited, because we'd never see it.'

'Andrew's not out of touch,' said Dolly. 'He still comes up here. He can't be out of touch, it's where he was born and grew up. He'll never get right out of touch from his home.'

'D'you see that Apple Green letting that baby be brought up here? "Talking North"? They think we all say ee bah goom and sit on doorsteps.'

'They know about the Duchess of Kent. She was brought up no distance off. She doesn't sit on doorsteps,' said Dolly.

'They think we either sit on doorsteps or we're the Duchess of Kent, that's the trouble. They don't know there's anything in between, and I'm not surprised if they go by the telly and the papers. "Up North", they call it.'

'Andrew knows,' said Dolly.

'No. No, I don't think Andrew does know any more. He's gone now, Andrew. He's forgotten it here. His home. He'll go right back into his shell again now, like he did at sixteen. He's got a whole world down there we've not a notion of. Go back to bed, Dolly. Go back to bed.'

– 6 –

Faith arrived at Ellerby Priors in a cocoon of shawls and pressed into a travel-cot wedged along the back seat of her father's Toyota. It was autumn and miles of stubble linseed shone dark gold. Well-kept metal field gates looked polished in the sun. Everywhere stood mountains of silage in black plastic rolls.

'Like liquorice,' said Pammie. 'Great fat black beetles. Aren't they horrible? What are they?' She sounded pleased to see some expected ugliness.

'It's a good system,' said Andrew. 'It's the harvest.'

'*Harvest*? In plastic bags?'

'Did you think it was haycocks and gleaning?'

'I don't believe I ever thought – I didn't know there were still any hedges, either. I thought they'd all been dug up and ruined our heritage. I read about it in *Country Life* every time I pick it up.'

'We've kept a few,' said Andrew. He was driving now between two long high ones, weaving across the plain. They delivered him out upon a village with a lawn-like green, duck pond, white posts, sheep wandering.

'It's really very pretty,' she said. 'It's as pretty as the Cotswolds without the coaches, though of course you don't get the wonderful golden stone.'

'You don't?'

'It's rough-looking somehow, isn't it, the stone up here? Very picturesque, though. Lovely churches and houses. They look occupied – I mean in one ownership. Oh, *this* is pretty! Is that a castle? Right in the village. That would be National Trust in Sussex. You'd have to pay to go over it. Where are we?'

Andrew didn't quite know and for the past half-hour had

31

been wondering and wishing for a map. He had been born and bred not thirty miles off and for years before he married had come home for Christmas to his parents' house in Cleveland not more than an hour away. They lived by the sea on the estuary in the shadow of the chemical works. He had always taken the train and then a taxi from Darlington ('Must have cost him all of five pounds,' said Toots) and then another taxi on Boxing Day over to his brother's on the moors, where they were going now on side roads from the motorway. He knew every field and lane and tree round here, or so he had thought, and you only had to look around to see how unchanged these lanes must be. But he hadn't been concentrating, the past hour. Since they had swept off the A1 he had been trying not to hear Pammie's endless patronage of the terrain.

'Not far now,' he said.

'I'm fairly ravenous, Andrew dear. Shall we stop somewhere for lunch? She's being awfully good. We could leave her in the car.'

He set his face. It was a set face by nature. Now he clamped it. 'We are almost there,' he said. 'I think there'd be umbrage taken if we stopped off for lunch. There'll have been preparations. Anyway, there are no restaurants.'

'What – nowhere? Well, a pub, then.'

'I'm sorry, Pammie, I don't think we can leave her outside a pub.'

Pammie thought, *Since he's about to leave her for ever* – and began to seethe.

She had been seething for three months now over the arrangements for the child, Faith Fox: first at Andrew's careless handing over of her to a nanny he had found from somewhere or other, a girl who lumped her about all over Surrey, taking her along to her own friends, and God knows who *they* were. One had turned out to be a prison warder and some others a covey of homosexuals. Once she had disappeared with the baby overnight leaving no message and Andrew, telephoning home and getting no answer, had rung Pammie thinking she would know what had happened.

32

Pammie had suggested the police. Andrew, on duty all night after working all day on the wards, had said it would probably be all right. The girl had good references and had most likely taken the baby to her mother's in Streatham.

'In *Streatham*!'

What's more he'd been right, and nanny and child had come drifting back about eleven o'clock the next morning, the nanny with a hangover and the baby stinking of cigarette smoke.

She'd had to go of course. Pammie had seen to that and Andrew had said yes, she was probably right, and with Pammie's help had engaged someone else, very highly qualified, from Oslo, beautiful and calm and an excellent safe driver. The baby's clothes were washed as white as snow by this paragon and she believed in regular bottles, an eventless day and no brand foods. For such a glowing, clean-looking girl, however, she left very dirty-looking knickers about the bathroom floor and wound herself daily for several hours around the telephone cord. Pammie saw her in this condition, her eyes dreaming, in the window of the front room of Andrew's house whenever she called in, and always talking in Norwegian. On making enquiries, naturally with Andrew's permission, Pammie had discovered that the nanny was ringing Oslo twice a day, the bill already touching three hundred pounds.

Also, she had broken down in the car one morning, flagged down another and asked the driver to take her and the baby to the supermarket, where she had left Faith with him in the car park while she shopped and then got him to drive them both home.

'But he was a *good* man,' she cried as Pammie drove her and her belongings relentlessly to Guildford station.

Pammie had then taken Faith home with her and had cancelled many appointments.

Exhausted Andrew, working a seventy-two-hour week in the hospital with sometimes three hours sleep a night, earning less money than many a nanny, living almost entirely on the wards or in his prison cell of a bedroom, widowed, wretched, had said, 'They must do their best. Whole gang of women with nothing else to do. Let them sort it out.'

From the beginning he had displayed not a suspicion of interest in Faith. The death of life-giving Holly had not so much frozen as embalmed him. For the first weeks he had walked in a dignified trance, inclining as usual graciously from his great height towards all his patients, who thought him a consultant at least. At the funeral he had taken the same stance outside the church door, exasperating, infuriating, the friends of his late wife's mother when they went back to the house afterwards for the wake. The house was (of course) Pammie's. All had talked of Andrew's stateliness and charm and all had said that no man should be able to behave like that, equally to all comers, at his young wife's funeral.

At least the baby hadn't been there. Pammie had seen to that. It would have been embarrassingly heart-rending. Faith had been taken that morning (by Pammie) back to the nuns for the day, though Andrew had not seen why nor appeared to be interested when told.

That had been the really terrible thing, said Pammie, and made you realise just how hard a doctor had to be.

'It is a front,' said Jinny, 'a con. It's against the invasion of privacy. It's called a bedside manner. They're disciplined. They have to be, doctors.'

'Doctors suffer underneath,' said Elaine (or Myra). 'Well, look how half of them are alcoholics.'

'And suicides,' said Viv.

It was Pammie and the nuns together who took Andrew in hand at last. Mother Clare asked to see him in the office when he was visiting the maternity hospital professionally, Faith under two months old. ('And how could he bear to do *that*?' asked Jilly, or Jinny. 'The very *premises*. He's a monster.') Mother Clare had Pammie in at the same time. Together they confronted Andrew with Faith's future.

A brother? Andrew had a brother? Had Andrew thought – ? The North-East was certainly a long way from the child's roots but blood is thicker than – etc. Were his family in the North not concerned? Surely somebody up there must be feeling they

34

should help? Wasn't this family solidarity notable in the North?

Andrew said that he was of very old parents and his father bedridden.

'And the brother?' Mother Clare was not intimidated by young doctors.

Andrew had sat magisterially and made non-committal clearings of the throat.

'The *brother*, Dr Braithwaite?'

'He's nearly twenty years older than I am.'

When he had gone Mother Clare had said, 'God help that child,' and Pammie had exploded.

Yet somehow or other here was the Toyota winding its way across the Plain of York, and Faith lying large-eyed and composed on the back seat, watching the berries fly past her in the hedges.

– 7 –

And where was Thomasina, Thomasina last seen leaving the health farm, broken and finished? Nobody but the general, and Andrew who had not noticed, had seen the blinded old woman feeling out for the handle of the car door. When her friends had met her again later they had seen a new representation of her that had chilled their hearts. A terrible, terrifying, gruesome, sardonic Thomasina, talkative, blank-eyed, trilling with laughter. 'Oh, isn't it a *bore*?' She even said, '*Poor* Holly,' and, 'Funny little scrap. No, not a bit like her Ma. We're calling her *Faith* – awful name, isn't it? Vicar's idea, or the nuns' – Andrew doesn't seem to mind. Oh yes, dear little thing really. Very broad face. Square hands. Yeoman Yorkshire, darling, I'm afraid. Hope she doesn't come with a built-in accent.'

She missed the funeral. Yes – Thomasina missed the funeral. Everyone understood of course, as they looked for her about the crowded church. It would have been too much – too much for Thomasina. All those queer years when she and Holly had opted out together. Someone (Susan) had heard that morning that she had broken down. Someone else thought she had been taken to the Surrey Clinic and was under sedation. Pammie had moved heaven and earth to reach her and even Andrew had looked grave. But Thomasina was nowhere to be found. All that Andrew had said to Pammie about it, which was when he left to go back to the hospital for duty that same evening of the funeral, was that Thomasina's not having taken to the baby was a 'bit of a blow'.

For what everybody had assumed, of course, had scarcely needed to discuss, was that Thomasina would be scooping up Faith to rear her as her own. Thomasina so fit and young for her years. Thomasina so lovely and bereft. Thomasina had separated herself so extraordinarily from her own world for Holly, had dedicated herself utterly, utterly (and what a terrific job she had made of it), she would slip naturally (and therapeutically for all concerned), tenderly, into the new motherhood of Holly's child. They had all so much assumed it that they were already talking about how marvellous it was that it was so, and congratulating the ghost of Holly on the ready-made union. How *wonderful*, if this pointless disaster had had to occur, if fate had had to decide to remove from the world such a golden person, that here was Thomasina with her crooked smile continuing to fly her brave pennant. Well, she didn't.

She wouldn't.

She abandoned them all, the lot of them, Pammie and Jilly and Jinny and Susan and Elaine and the golf club and the NSPCC and her son-in-law Andrew with the great purple sleepless circles under his eyes. Faith Fox she did not look at when she went to say goodbye to Pammie and leave the dog with her – Pammie supervising the sterilisation of bottles, a washing machine nearby whirling with baby clothes. 'Not looked towards the cot, not *once*!'

Thomasina had laughed and kissed Pammie and said that she was off to Egypt. She was wearing a fuchsia-pink trouser suit and big jewellery and there was a man in a splendid old car at the gate who looked like a colonel. '*Very* nice-looking. Very nice car. This is *true*, Elaine.'

The fury of Surrey rang out round its Bridge tables, patios, clubs. Thomasina was now seen as traitor, as Quisling in their midst, for nearly thirty years ungenerous, secretive, across invisible tracts of uncharted snow. Her icy introversion, her uncaring selfishness? How they foamed, and spat, how they snarled, how they thundered. The defection of Thomasina filled their lives up to the end of the second month of Faith's life and died only to flare again more fiercely when picture postcards of the Sphinx began to arrive. These were objects calculated to dumbfound, condemned as in most evil taste.

'If she comes back – *if* she comes back – ' they said (even Pammie), 'I'm afraid I can't know her any more.'

Only an Englishwoman, of course, would have behaved like Thomasina, and I mean English. A Scot might have suffered silently, would have most pointedly not removed herself. A Welshwoman would have wept and chattered but carried on. An Irishwoman would have brooded or keened, explained, referred the matter to higher authority and the world would have slowly healed a little. But an Englishwoman from either of the two main tribes, South and North, above and below the line from the Wash to the Severn, the language-line that is still not quite broken to this day, would act the part of the unconquerable, camouflaging herself, her grief, her fear, behind a mask that can do nothing, is meant to do nothing, but antagonise. It is a mask slapped on out of consideration, out of a wish not to increase concern and also out of a genetic belief that our deepest feelings are diminished when we show them. The fearless, comic, incorruptible battle-axe Englishwoman is now almost gone. There don't seem to be many of the young shaping up in that mould.

And maybe good riddance but maybe more's the pity, for she'll be missed here and there and especially in fiction. But in great grief her ghost walks still, and very mysterious and insulting it seems to those who aren't of her cast of mind and who love her and wish to be near her. But those of her ilk comprehend and talk of her behind her back. They would mostly act the same way themselves.

So Thomasina went off with the general and Faith watched the red berries in the unknown lanes.

– 8 –

The day, then, that Pammie accompanied Andrew Braithwaite to Yorkshire to deposit his daughter Faith Fox (as everybody seemed to be calling her) with his brother Jack, her mind was executing something like a triple fugue. There was first the theme of the north, the foreign country and culture into which the little scrap was to be translated, 'The North' as Pammie imagined it. Then there was the factual 'north' as it was unfolded to her between London and their destination. Then there was the account of both norths that Pammie's mind was automatically preparing to take back to Surrey again. Pammie, whose life consisted of emotional thunderstorms and the describing of them, was as intensely involved in the rumblings and crashes and lightning flashes of this one, the Fox Saga, as an actress who has landed a plum role. Learning the book of all her adventures was as important to Pammie as experiencing them.

And so, when they reached after an hour or so the easeful George Inn at Stamford, she had been trying to square its style with the miners' roadside caffs she had expected and hearing her voice saying back home to Jilly *et al.*, 'I'll say one thing: Andrew didn't stint. It wasn't a Happy Eater or a Little Chef, it was *perfectly* decent,' and wondering like a novelist whether to substitute 'civilised' or even 'marvellous' for 'decent'. And then wondering if Eileen and Nina and Josie and Lizzie perhaps knew this already. She had always rather prided herself on being narrow, and not a traveller. Maybe there were things about The North that were after all *known*?

They had left Surrey at six in the morning. At Stamford, pale stone sleeping in yellow sunshine, they were to stay an hour. In the coffee room of the George Inn the baby slept beside them on a sofa near the bedroom-sized fireplace and transparent sunshiny coal fire. The coffee was brought by a waitress, who set it between them and brought croissants and marmalade and a morning paper. All about the old coaching inn and then from all the town churches the clocks struck ten melodiously. Outside, down the cobbled yard, hanging baskets of autumn flowers glowed. Creepers were a polished dripping crimson over pale walls. The linings to bedroom curtains looked as rich as silk and the menus on the reception desk were expensive and delicious.

'D'you know, Andrew,' said Pammie, 'one could stay here.'

'If one had money.'

'Amazing. A hundred or so miles north of London. I thought this sort of thing didn't happen again until Scotland. I wouldn't at all say no to a weekend here. I'll tell Hugo.'

They were to arrive at Faith's new home at about one o'clock, Pammie imagined for a late lunch, if farmers had lunches. She tried to imagine a farmer's lunch and settled for something between wedges of bread and cheese eaten under a hawthorn bush and roast beef in a pine kitchen with vets rushing in and out to examine diseased livestock outside in a barnyard. Or maybe it would be a gentleman farmer who strolled about his land every other weekend and gave the rest of life to his investments. There would be dry sherry and then a vast dining room with windows looking at a park. Cold meat and mashed potatoes, rice pudding and stewed plums and everybody pretending to like it, because it was like school. Flagged floors and dogs. '*Ice* cold, my dear, and nobody speaking. Heathcliff not in it.' Faith safely deposited, Pammie saw herself in tears as she said goodbye. There would be a wooden cradle on rockers, cobwebs, a family Bible and then the drive with perhaps a taciturn serf to Harrogate for the London train.

39

Andrew was to stay on at his brother's for a couple of days to see the poor child in, to see to the beginning of her life. (A little waif suddenly made its appearance to Pammie; aged eight or nine, she had strings of rain-sodden hair and was dashing across moorland.) Pammie had of course been invited to stay on at the farm too, for as long as she liked, but, 'No, no,' she had cried in Guildford, 'I have commitments. October is a frightful month for me. I couldn't possibly give the time.'

'It is very good of you to do this at all,' Andrew had said.

'Nonsense. As if I could do anything else.'

Thomasina's presence hung in the air.

But to the Bridge mob Pammie had said, 'I must say it does seem rather odd that the one to take her has to be a friend of her *grandmother*. You'd have thought there'd be some friend of his own. I know Thomasina said Andrew was an odd fish and seemed to have no friends, though God knows if that was true, the things we now know about Thomasina. But you would think, wouldn't you, that he could have found some friend of Holly, or another doctor? A woman, of course; babies prefer the smell of a woman. But then I suppose he wouldn't want to turn up at his brother's a few weeks after his wife died with a young woman in the car.'

She didn't say, because she didn't have to as it was what everyone had been thinking since about five minutes after the disaster, that the sooner Andrew remarried, the better. Pammie had sung this little tune once, quietly, the day after the funeral when she had seen signs of June and Desiree and Philippa and Meg getting maudlin. She was a self-protecting woman, Pammie, and speaking out the cold-blooded thought had given her a pretty *frisson*. The 'Oh Pammie, shut up, don't *say* it' always produced the nourishment needed for her essential diet of self-love.

But how unfair. Pammie was a good woman. A healer. When she shocked or mocked, sinews were stiffened. Everyone knew that Pammie had true and deep affections. Pammie often said so herself and discussed them. And she had a huge sense of duty (likewise). She was a woman who had longed for children and they had been denied her and although she took great interest in the children of friends – a thing rare now in childless women – she had been left with a lot of passion going waste. Many love affairs and two engagements in youth had broken down on account of the emotionally exhausted withdrawal from the field of the nervous men involved, and Pammie had been left, for years and years now, with a shadowy old husband who had once been something high up in the Coal Board and sat reading *The Times* all day in a pretty house on Coombe Hill. It had cedar trees and a triple garage.

She deserved much more. She deserved a position of power, did old Pammie. Because of a particularly strained childhood and girlhood – she was always abandoning things from flashy principles, for she had been much admired by indulgent over-serious parents – she had had no real career and had developed no real character. A hundred years before she would have run a household, written papers on women's shameful banishment from great causes. Even in her own time she might have risen high in the Civil Service if she had been more patient and less histrionic, less romantic. She had been too old to be part of the young feminism of the Sixties and Seventies, which she affected to despise as being *déjà vu*.

She was still, for her age, deeply romantic, seriously so. She had once been in love with a patrician who had known the Queen, which gave her a dreamy and knowing look whenever anyone got talking about the monarchy. A 'my lips are sealed' look. It was her one sweet memory, as if she and the Queen had hobnobbed together on dark afternoons at Balmoral over a dying fire.

Pammie was a fearful snob, keen on good taste, and the awful triple garage was the only sop she allowed her husband in this direction. She allowed it and the big Bentley and the other vehicles inside because he was a good man who had worked hard and it is nice to be rich and she felt he should be rewarded for it. The man who had been pally with the Queen had been poor.

'Your father's a schoolmaster, isn't he, Andrew?'
'Was. He retired long ago. He's old. And sick. He's disabled.

41

MS.'

'Oh, I'm so sorry. How dreadful. Shall I meet him?'

'No, they live about fifteen miles away on the coast. I'll be going down to them tomorrow.'

'Oh, I'm so looking forward to seeing the farm,' she said, watching the motorway flip past. 'D'you know, I've never seen a farm. Just slow down and let me undo the strap a moment. I want to have a look at her. She's so quiet.'

'All right?'

'Yes. Adorable. Fast asleep. Is it an *arable* farm?'

'Pammie, I don't believe you've never seen a farm.'

'It's true. How could I?'

'Well, by looking out of the train windows on the way to London.'

'Don't be silly, all you see is motorway between me and Waterloo. Exactly like this. They're all the same. There's no view you can catch. I go by car anyway.'

'More fool you, Pammie. You sound like old Queen Mary who'd never seen a field of hay.'

'Ah, now Queen Mary . . .'

The motorway hours passed, then the hours eastward along the lanes. The Vale of York began. Andrew grew sleepy, grew bored, grew cantankerous with Pammie's pleasantness, then with her critical nothings; became lost in the lanes. Pammie went on discussing lunch.

She thought how good the baby was and how the baby's father did not know it. She talked more about lunch.

She abandoned all hope of lunch.

Faith slept on.

And Andrew cheered up because he had found a small crossroads that led to a side road to a village that led up a steep and swerving hill and shot out on a high and spectacular moor. The moor arrived suddenly and stretched to all horizons. The horizons were broad blue-black ink lines and between them and the car was a world of stormy purple heather. Sheep stood in the heather and other sheep wandered about the road. A few were seated on the road with folded arms, moving their jaws about. They rose resentfully on black feet and ambled to one

42

side. Pammie said, 'They're very skinny, Andrew. More like goats.' ('Dear God, Jinny, it's pretty enough, but that *baby*! What *is* she in for?')

A mile or two along a road stretching along a high ridge, Andrew stopped the car and got out, leaving the door open and a clean wind blowing in on Pammie. He strode away over the grass at the roadside, jumped a ditch and was away into the heather. There he stood, with his back to the car. The sky was high and clear, autumnal light about him. For miles sun shone on heather and granite.

'Andrew? Andrew? Are you all right? What is it?' *How most peculiar.* He began to stride further away from her. *We can't be there yet,* she thought, *there's nothing to see.* 'Hello?' she called. 'Andrew?' He wandered further still. *He must want a pee,* she thought; *I know I do.*

He turned and began to walk, lunging and jumping, slowly back.

'Pammie. I was thinking. I'm not sure that we're not being silly going on to The Priors just now. I think what we might do instead is just drive on down to the coast, to my parents, and drop her off there for the night. They're dying to see her. I'm sorry.'

'But you say it's fifteen miles off.'

'Yes. But Jack goes down to see them a lot. He could come and get Faith from them tomorrow and I'd stay with her of course. I could actually drop you off at Harrogate during this afternoon. I could leave her with the grandparents for an hour or so. I'd ring The Priors from my parents' to say what we're doing, what has happened.'

'*Happened*? But what *has* happened? Harrogate's miles away south. And your father's ill and they're not expecting us. How could they cope all night with a baby with just you and them – you can't even make up a feed?'

'My mother—'

'She's old. You said so. She'll have quite forgotten. Don't be so silly. And you say there'll have been preparations made at the farm.'

'Well, not big preparations. They're not great on prepara-

43

tions.' He stood frowning, pondering the pattern of sheep droppings on the road.

'What you mean is,' said Pammie, 'you don't want me to see your brother. For some reason. Or is it that you don't want your brother to see me? For some reason? I see. And who are the Priors? I thought your brother was called Jack Braithwaite.'

'It's the name of the place, The Priors.'

'I thought it was Ellerby Farm.'

'It's Ellerby Priors. It was a monastery till the sixteenth century. There's farmland with it.'

Pammie's heart lifted. Andrew, it turned out, must be someone.

'It's mostly ruined now,' Andrew said. 'Jack built some of it up and added a lot of sheds and so on. They farm the land and run a God-slot.'

'God-slot?'

'Yes. He's very religious. They're God-botherers. Sort of community. Retreats and hacking mangelwurzels. Not my style. Jack's by way of being a Rev. Maybe a saint. And he's old – much older than me. I was a menopausal surprise.'

'So you don't think I'm fit to be introduced to him? It's not very bright of you, Andrew, I must say. If we – and what about Mother Clare? She'd have been so thrilled if we'd known all about this in Guildford, we'd have been much happier about Faith. Well, really! I've done hassocks for Guildford Cathedral. Get in and come on and don't be so stupid.'

Still he hung in the road.

'Now that you've told me,' she said, 'let me tell you something. I am a religious woman too and all the way here I've been wanting to ask you if you couldn't stop for a moment before we get there to say some prayers.'

'About what?'

'Oh yes I have, so don't look so blank. About Faith, if you really want to know. You and I together, Andrew. But knowing doctors . . . Well, doctors get put off, I can see that. I should have followed my instinct. Andrew, pick up this baby and hand her over to me now. I want to see to the cot, and yes –

I think I'll change her so that she's as she should be when she arrives. I'm very good at it. Oh – *pretty* girl. There. Angel-bird, lamb-child.'

When Faith was back in the cot, squirming a bit, making talking noises and snuffling, giving the occasional squawk and hoot, Pammie said, 'Get in, Andrew. I'm going to say a prayer now and be damned to you. And then let's get on to your brother's.'

'A prayer?' said Andrew. 'What for?'

'Well, for Faith. For her life.'

'Bit over the top, isn't it? I'm not into it, Pammie. And she'll be getting plenty of it soon. And for ever.'

He hurled himself into the car, started it up, roared away in it, peering all the time across the partridge figure of Pammie, smart in her red-brown wool suit, until there appeared at the side of the lonely road, rising black and high, a stone cross. A track led off from it down a steep hill and out of sight.

'What's this?' Pammie was bright with excitement and words were pouring into a rehearsed narration for Coombe Hill. 'An old *cross* – how fascinating! I'd no idea you were so erratic, Andrew. We all thought you were so very set and conventional. I'd no idea you were even from the far North, you know – I thought maybe somewhere like Leicester – until just before dear Holly . . . Do what you like, I shall pray by myself now as we go along. I feel I have Holly with me now, in the car beside me. I feel I can mention her name now in a Christian, *croyant* way, now that I know your brother's a parson. Oh my goodness, I do feel better.

'Dear Holly – so *good*. Didn't your brother adore her? I feel nothing can go wrong now for little Faith. I feel it. "Ellerby Priors". I knew it. What a good man, your brother. I must have met him at the . . . Did he take the service? No, of course he didn't, it was the vicar, and not at his best if I may say so, but I don't remember another dog collar. Oh, he doesn't? Well, so few of them do now. Which one was he? I suppose he's unmarried. The really splendid holy ones seldom are, you know, even now. I hope he has some good women there, though, for Faith. Well, you *said* so. Will there be deaconesses?

45

I hope he's not against WPs. Is it Catholic or Anglo? Andrew, you might have told us, you know. Is he ascetic? Or is it one of these love-and-kisses places? I can't care for that, I have to say. It takes me all my time to face The Peace in church, this newfangled stuff they have, and what's more I know that absolutely everyone feels the same as I do. You can see the whole congregation getting fidgety when it's announced, even the parsons. I mean, in *public*! You should see the poor old souls at St Saviour's. All their lives they've believed in keeping themselves to themselves and now they have to turn round and grin at each other and nod their heads and shake hands. And they see each other nearly every day anyhow and half of them don't altogether get on. Sometimes, you know, there's kissing and *caressing*! No one can really take that, you know, unless it's black people. Is it going to be that sort of place, Andrew?' She tried to imagine – she saw – negroes in a monastic ambience, *in flagrante delicto*, rolling in the heather. She began to edit delightedly for Coombe.

'You should have told me, dear Andrew. All these hours on the road and we've been keeping to trivialities and worldly things, though I did like The George at Stamford. Anyway, too late now and I'm going to pray for the baby. How is she? Can you look in the—? Yes. Oh, angel darling! I'm going to pray now quietly to myself, so just shut up.'

'Too late,' he said. 'We're here. We have to undo this gate.'

'I'll undo it, my dear. My shoes don't matter.'

'No, you pray if you want to.'

'Did you?' he asked as he climbed in after shutting the gate behind them.

He drove down the last of the track, which turned through a medieval and broken-down gatehouse and became a large, paved, unweeded court. Surrounding the court were the remains of ecclesiastical buildings, some of them with agricultural machinery bundled into them. A line of prefabricated huts had been built in the courtyard and a small block of Portacabin water closets nearby. The huts had coloured mantras stuck to the windows and different-coloured front doors. Some of the Portacabins had holy-looking posters

46

gummed to them, too. There was a line of heavy shoes outside one of them. Drab chickens ran about and there was rather a lot of rubbish – not serious rubbish but bits of nylon rope, cardboard, blown-about paper, and metal stands for some sort of leisure equipment, and several unlikely canoes.

'You can't pray properly in sixty seconds, Andrew,' she said, affectionately now. 'Just look at that lovely architecture. What a wonderful east window that must have been. All empty to the air now. But how lovely.'

From one of the huts four or five bulky Eskimo-ish people were emerging. They wandered off towards the Portacabins seeming to give promise by their incurious, in fact rather disgruntled, expressions that Ellerby Priors was not going to be a kissing-and-caressing sort of place.

'By the way,' said Andrew as a bell began to clank somewhere and another sound joined it for a brief moment, a sound as if someone were revving up some mournful trumpet. 'By the way, Jack is married. He married not long after I did. And there's a child, a boy. And here is his wife.'

– 9 –

'Jocasta,' said Andrew, 'this is Pammie. And here is Faith.'

He lifted out the cot and Jocasta held out very small brown hands for it.

He said, 'No. Heavy. She's a whopping great baby. She was nineteen inches long at birth. I'll take her in,' and they all walked across the courtyard and through a decrepit studded door marked 'Office' in runny painted writing, Jocasta saying not a word and Pammie looking around for signs of lunch.

'We're a bit late,' said Andrew. 'I'm sorry. It's been a big day.'

Jocasta said that Jack would be here in a moment.

Nothing happened.

'Is he well?'

'Perfectly,' said Jocasta.

'Well, here's Faith.'

Jocasta looked quickly in the direction of the cot that had been put upon a table and was tipped up somewhat because of the clutter. She looked away. Faith regarded her with solemnity.

'She's been an angel,' said Pammie to keep things going. *Most peculiar,* she thought. *Utterly silent woman, rather oriental-looking and snooty. Not what you'd expect.* 'She's been an angel since the day she was born. I've had her all to myself for the past weeks, so I know. Not a sign of trouble. I've had no broken nights, not personally. I don't know why these young mothers complain about being tired. I've had no children of my own, but with decent daytime help – and I did have a night nurse and a first-rate health visitor and our own GP, who is private but I always think that's money well spent – she's been no trouble at all. And the social services are absolutely *marvellous,* of course – I hope you have them up here. There's just a trace of a sticky eye. Well, I've really *adored* doing it. I shall miss her frightfully.'

Jocasta looked at her. She said, vaguely, 'Yes.'

'You see, I knew Holly.' Pammie looked at Andrew and the look said: She *shall* be mentioned. It is the best way for you. 'I knew Holly. Holly was the light of many people's lives. I know it's perhaps too soon to mention all this in general conversation, Andrew, but you and I have got to know each other on this journey, haven't we? Soon I'll be gone. I'm really Thomasina's friend, Mrs Braithwaite, or I was. I'm afraid she's disappointed us. But . . .' she looked again at Andrew, '. . . there's not one of us who wouldn't have done anything in the world for Holly.'

'He's here,' said Jocasta.

The baby suddenly went stiff all over, red of face, tremulous of lip, for some cataclysmic event seemed to be taking place in the passage outside, as if many heavy things had suddenly collapsed. It was a surprise that such a gentle man came in, and smiled shyly. He went straight to Faith and opened his eyes

48

wide at her, and she grinned.

'My goodness. I believe she smiled,' said Pammie. 'That was an *amused* smile.'

Jack went over to Andrew and put his arms round him and rocked him, turned to Pammie and said, 'Forgive me.'

'Forgive you, Jack? Why?' said Andrew.

'Late, late, *late*, I suppose, Andrew. How do you do? Pammie?' He looked at her with intense and admiring interest. '*Pammie!*'

'She's famished, Jack. We had a croissant in Stamford.'

'It's full of history,' said Jack; 'very beautiful, a sort of miniature Oxford. It was spared by Cromwell.'

'*Food*, Jack. And offices of the house for Pammie. Me, too, in a moment.'

'I'll show you where,' said Jack to Pammie, still staring most lovingly. Jocasta made no move. 'And then we'll go to the refectory.'

He put his curly head back round the door after he'd left with Pammie to say, 'You'll follow, Andrew?'

The office died into silence. The baby had fallen suddenly asleep and through the slit of mullioned window in the stone wall a light fell across the mess surrounding her on the desk: papers, files, posters, telephones, some of them broken, word processors, dull screens, printers, tangled wires, and a pile of yellow T-shirts stamped EP. Metal chairs in a dusty corner sat in one another's laps, curving forwards in a toppling pile. In a niche stood a crucifix with cobwebs. On the walls were pegboards with curling old notices. They were to do with services, walks, activities, discussion groups, mealtimes and weekly terms preposterously cheap and out of date. Beneath the cross stood a vase of last year's dried-up heather.

From Faith's cot came snuffles as sunshine fell across her, too, and Andrew moved over to the narrow window and leaned down to look out through it, his back to the room, his head resting on an arm above the mullion, blocking the light.

Jocasta walked to the cot, looked briefly at the baby, and moved away to the door.

'I'll go now,' she said.

He leaned to the thick grubby glass and drew a line down it with his finger. Looking out over the courtyard, he said, 'I want you in my arms. I want you in my bed. I want my tongue in your mouth. I want—'

Jack came in again and said, 'I've persuaded The Missus to give us a bit of something as well as the soup. Bit of fish. No – leave her, she'll be fine. I'll send someone along. Jocasta has to do the school run but there's plenty of help. What a very nice woman, your Pammie. I must just round up the Tibetans for Evensong.'

When the two brothers had left the room Jocasta waited a moment and then she, too, left it, without looking towards the cot again.

– 10 –

Jack Braithwaite had lately been having trouble with Ellerby Priors, an experimental community that was his passion. He had founded it uncertainly years ago, when ruins were cheap, with the intention of gathering up a clientele from the slums of the North-East, though 'slums' was a word not in fashion then, like the word 'poor'. Both had been swept away with Beveridge in the Fifties, returning in the Eighties translated as 'deprived areas' and 'underprivileged', and they were what Jack cared about. He especially wanted to help the orphaned and children at risk or in care but in fact never turned away anyone the social services sent him. When the underprivileged were in short supply, for the children seemed to come in waves and in smaller waves came the goverment money to support them, Jack struggled on with what was left of his own funds and what he could earn off the farm, which, because of the soil and the climate, was not much. The menus shrank.

At first he had worked on a monthly basis, but lately had taken to offering weekly terms and even weekends for tired housewives, who often fell in love with him and rolled up their sleeves to help. He looked deeply at them in Christian love. He wasn't averse, either, to the terminally but not dangerously ill, though these had been dropping off lately, probably because of the menus. Many were ready to starve in the scruffiness of Ellerby Priors, to shiver in its dusty, freezing dormitories, to be near Jack, but the authorities and sometimes husbands felt otherwise.

Jack, with a great surge of the spirit not unknown to him, had lately decided to launch out among the homeless and the exiled. His last batch of the deprived had been very depressing. Classified Tyneside/Aggressives, they had proved a failure. Most unresponsive. The perfectly adequate medieval accommodation they had pronounced worse than home, the sparse but healthy meals, country air and counselling opportunities had not satisfied and there had been some embarrassing escapes, one whole batch walking out before Vespers, hitching a lift across the moor road after pushing over the Saxon cross and spending a gaudy night breaking up the Whitby promenade. The newspapers had reported this as a 'break-out of abused children held at an isolated moorland detention centre' and a correspondence had begun in the press about public safety. Jack had received questions from the Home Office.

It was a wonderful relief that in the midst of it all Jack, trying to dissuade the county council against the need for electric fences and guard dogs, received notification of a consignment of Tibetans for whom he had been angling for years. Great files of letters, and then faxes even, had passed between Ellerby Priors and Darjeeling, where a Tibetan Centre valiantly but rather glumly soldiered on. Jack and Jocasta had visited it on their honeymoon.

Jack, scholar of Balliol without a string to pull in the world before he arrived there, had turned into the sort of man who had connections. His general air of abstraction and loving kindness caused him, without even trying, to be endlessly invited to high tables and the well-heeled abodes of antique men of letters. Presents came to him which he at once gave to the poor. Cheques went to the upkeep of Ellerby Priors. He fascinated women of all kinds and ages, and people worked for him for nothing – though they often fled at last in tears. Jack was incorruptible.

After the marriage to Jocasta much of Jack's social life had ceased, but Cambridge had invited him to meet the Dalai Lama on his exiled visit there, an occasion Jack remembered precisely though he often forgot his own telephone number. He and the Dalai Lama had discussed the Classics and the concept of divinity and the future of violence and the standard of the King's College breakfast. Jack prayed for the Dalai Lama every day and it seemed to him at once that these miserable prayers had been rewarded when a notification was delivered from the post van, roaring out heavy-metal down the moorland track, to announce that between seven and nine exiled Tibetans would be arriving the coming Wednesday. It was the Monday morning after the inflammatory Saturday of the Tyneside Aggressives, and this gave the resident staff of Jocasta, one woman and two lads (The Smikes) just time to clean up the beer cans, put together the broken furniture, and stick up the cracked windowpanes with cut-out mantras that Jocasta and her son Philip spent all day Sunday painting in bright colours. Jack had been sent down to Whitby to the launderette with all the blankets.

Jack was exalted by the arrival of the Tibetans who came toppling out of a battered grey bus from Liverpool in the dawn, not many days before Andrew's Toyota. The Tibetans had quite put Faith in shadow. Family, as is stated in the Christian gospels, you don't have to get on with; in fact, it's unlikely that you will and often you even have to ditch them. Exiles and refugees and people who have been politically duffed up, on the other hand, must be cherished, put in your own conveyance, taken to some resting place and the bill paid in advance. Up to now the exiles Jack had taken in had been random and proud, outspoken about the Yorkshire weather and often surly about the one stipulation Jack made: that in return for a home at The Priors they must attend for an hour each day one short religious service in the chapel.

This he insisted upon even to the death of his venture, and he looked with his customary shining welcome but also a little anxiously as the Tibetans gathered up their belongings from the bus and walked across the cloister courtyard to their sheds.

– II –

'They'll be there now.'

'Who'll be where?'

'Well, Andrew and the baby. You know quite well what I mean, so don't pretend.'

'I'm not thinking about them.'

'Well, I am.'

'If they can't ring up or drop a line . . . It's not much to ask. Never consulted. We're vegetables now to him. Vegetables. That's what we are. I'm not happy, Dolly.'

'You never are happy, Toots. You never were.'

'I'm not happy about the baby, in with all the loonies. I feel like writing to the authorities – well, the authorities'll be round there. They'll see soon enough. I won't go near the place. The farming side, yes, but what's he want with the loonies? Jack gets no better with age. They'd all be a lot better off in their own homes. He's as daft as he was at school.'

'They don't have homes. The ones he has at present, they certainly don't have homes. They're from Tibet.'

'Tibet! They should have stayed there.'

'You know perfectly well what's happened in Tibet. I don't know, you never stop watching the news and yet you've got no idea of what's going on when it links up with here. You can't imagine being thrown out of your own home. I know I can. You never stirred even when you could have done, got a better job at a better school. You never left this parish. Tibetans are very well-thought-of people. It'd do you no harm to practise a bit of peace and quiet like they do. Meditation's what you want. I'd like to have the chance.'

'They sound a lazy lot to me. No fight in them. And I don't care – that Dalai Lama looks a funny fellow. We had a master at the school like that in 1932.'

'Be careful what you say, now. Don't be blasphemous. It's a serious religion.'

'Hairless blighter. Knew all the answers, yet he never spoke. Like that Greek chap – my memory's going – sits watching you on the sidelines and only drinking water. To think a grand-daughter of ours . . .'

'She's not likely to turn into the Dalai Lama, Toots. Why don't you have a walk up to the seat? I'll listen for the phone.'

'Phone. They'll never phone. I'm not to be told what's happening. I'm not to be told if there's been a crash on the motorway. *I'll* be the last one to hear. I'd have thought that flesh and blood might have been given consideration.'

'I must say,' said Dolly, burrowing about in the wardrobe that had been inserted into the old dining room to take Toots's clothes, 'I hope Andrew knows how to look after her in a car. It's a tremendous way they're coming. They'll need nappies, and how do they manage the feeds? Heating up bottles in a car. She'll be four-hourly still – that's a feed and a half – a tiny little thing like that. They'd have done better on a train, like we always did. Oh, I do want to see her.'

'Well, so do I want to see her. That's what I'm telling you. You can forget Andrew. Forget him. Hard as nails. Son or no son, we're nothing to him now. But her I do want to see, and it's our right. They could have brought her down here first: it's almost on his way. He never thought tuppence of Jack.'

Dolly, who had made a cake and looked out old cot-sized blankets, Andrew's old crib, several teddies, a monumental feeding bottle made of glass with a teat on each end, and a tin of baby milk bought secretly from the chemist and hidden somehow from Mrs Middleditch, said, 'Much better get her there and the journey over and done with. Ellerby's to be her home. She'd best get there and settle. They'll be cuddling her to bits. It's just tonight I'm worried about. Where's she to sleep in that cold place? I hope Jocasta's made everything ready.'

'That'll be the day.'

'Now don't start, Toots. Let's keep off that subject. Here's your scarf and I'll get your frame for you and we'll walk to the seat in the sun. I'll leave you there and come back for you in half an hour.' *Somehow*, she thought, *God give me strength. Why can't they phone? Why can't it just ring* now? *And when they do bring her he'll just give Andrew hell and pretend not to look at her.*

Batting about among the coats in the passage looking for his hat she addressed her God. 'Wherever's Holly gone? Why Holly? Who's to look to the child, us so old and useless and all of them so foolish? (Yes, I'm *coming*.) Why couldn't You have made Jack a good old-fashioned parson instead of all this hobnobbing with Buddhists and the EEC and everything? And Andrew marrying south. Who's to see to this child? I ask You – who's to see to her?'

She followed Toots down the garden path as he proceeded behind the walking frame, slowly, looking left and right with dignity, like a king making a public appearance before his subjects.

'Time that parsley was thrown out, it's rubbish. Great Scot, that onion bed! Get that lot up before anyone sees it. They're a disgrace.'

'If you think I'm starting on onion beds . . . That's Philip's job. Haven't I enough – ?'

'Well, and then you talk about bringing up a baby.'

'We'll never see the baby,' she said, suddenly sighing, holding the front gate open for him to sidle through. 'I begin to think it's all talk, this baby.'

Her mind made one of the leaps it had been taking lately. The baby had not been born. Holly was not dead. This afternoon she would write to Holly and ask her what she wanted for Christmas. She might even ring Holly and ask her if the baby had reached Ellerby safely. She shivered and tried to get back to some idea of the present but at the same time wondered whatever Holly's phone number was now. She used to ring Holly sometimes from the upstairs extension when

Toots was at his worst, just to hear her cheerful voice.

'No, we won't be seeing the baby,' she said to Toots.

'Now then,' he said, 'that's my line. Forget it. Don't upset yourself. There's a handkerchief in my pocket if you can reach. Leave me to do the moaning. We'll have a sherry later. Oh, strike a light – here's Ghent to Aix.'

Mrs Middleditch was waving and flapping down the street.

'They've arrived, they're fine. I came right round to tell you. Put you out of your suspense. Very good journey, not a hitch.'

'We've just stepped out of the house,' said Dolly. 'Well, isn't that – just the *minute* we step out of the house. They couldn't reach us, so they had to ring you. Oh, I do hope it wasn't a nuisance.'

'No, I rang *them*,' said Mrs Middleditch. 'Just thought you'd like to be out of your miseries.'

Toots turned from her and began to pace doggedly towards the seat.

'Go back in, Dolly,' said Mrs Middleditch. 'I'll sit with him a bit. I understand him. I don't mind if he creates. Then I'll bring you both a bit of liver.'

– 12 –

Jocasta had opened her eyes on Andrew for the first time six years ago in a hospital bed and seen a serious tall man in a very clean white coat frowning at a clipboard. A stethoscope hung round his neck correctly. He looked large, Olympian, remote. She thought, *A doctor*, and sank back into shadow.

Andrew had seen a tiny brown woman who opened the moist eyes of a chimpanzee. A sexy mouth. The round eyes stirred him and to forget such a surprise he removed the sheet from her and examined the long wound across her body, jagged across the base of her abdomen above the shaven mound of hair, the lovely thighs. He examined the clips and the bruises and said to someone, 'This might be cleaned up.' A pause. 'Oh yes,' he said, 'and the catheter . . . I think there's not enough going through. Keep her on it for the time being.' With almost disdain he took Jocasta's hand and said in the voice they use to pierce oblivion, 'Everything's fine. You're going to be fine.'

'Was that the surgeon,' she asked much later, 'that doctor?'

'It wouldn't be the surgeon. You'll not be seeing him, dear.'

'But it was somebody. Somebody who looked important.'

'Oh, that'd be Andrew. He's hardly qualified. He looks the part, dear, and he does very well.'

Jocasta floated away, returning later to Andrew's face. She noticed his clean nails. He was still gripping a clipboard and she saw that he was younger than she was.

When he saw her eyes open he said, 'Hello there, Jocasta. What a nice name. How are you now?'

'Did you take the lot?'

'No.'

'What have you left me?'

'An ovary.'

'No womb? Was it cancer?'

'No. We did take the womb but you have had a child, so that's not so bad, is it?'

'I've had *one* child!'

'But there are plenty of women with none. Perhaps I might have a word with your husband.'

'I have no husband.'

Late that night they came to rearrange the catheter and set it up again. Dr Braithwaite had telephoned to say to keep it going.

'Is he worried?'

'Dr Braithwaite is always worried, dear. We're not worried.'

'Where is he?'

'At his home for once. He's usually here night and day.'

'Night and day,' she said.

'Shall I tell you something? Last night while you were asleep he came in and drew the screens round and stood looking at

57

you. He does this sometimes. He stands thinking. But this time it was for half an hour. Don't say I said so. Dr Braithwaite is our favourite. We don't want to embarrass him.'

'What sort of a *doctor* is he?' she said. 'I don't care about your favourites.'

'He's very caring, dear.'

The next time he came to see her they drew the screens round and he sat beside the bed. He said, 'I see you're thirty. It's early for a hysterectomy. I'm so sorry.'

'I buggered myself up,' she said. 'Oh, don't look like that. I say these things to most people. I forget. What I mean is I've been living a messy sort of life.'

'I see.'

'Don't look so stunned. Haven't you met *anyone*? Just bodies, I suppose.'

'I meet people every day who say they have buggered themselves up but they don't look or seem like you.'

'I'm sorry.'

'Will you tell me what happened?'

'Nothing happened. I grew up and had a child. Then the framework packed in.'

'It doesn't happen like that. Were you promiscuous? On drugs? Undernourished? You look so very small. You look a *good* woman.'

'I buggered out off to India and played music. Beads and sandals and smoke. Had the child there. It was after RADA. I failed RADA.'

'A hippie?'

'A bit old for that. I'd got in a mess here. I couldn't get a job. I was trying to find myself.'

'You sound like a schoolgirl.'

'What was I like inside? Have I a disease?'

'You have some dis-ease,' he said. 'Physically you will be all right now, but watch out for depression. It hits people a week or so after this business.'

'I shall watch. And what shall I do when I see this depression coming into sight? Have you any medicine against the dark?'

He got off the bed and patted her hand. 'I'll look in tomorrow.'

Soon he knew that Jocasta had nowhere to go, that her child was being cared for by a friend in a bedsit, that she had long since broken all her ties with England and that she was still searching for the meaning of life. She told him all this in a restaurant a month later after he had taken her to a fleapit cinema to see *La Strada*: the mute waif and the tramp on the eternal road to nowhere, sleeping on heaped rags, the retarded girl shining with love and joy.

'I want to be her,' Jocasta said. 'No luggage.'

'No purpose,' he said. 'Where do you come from, so dead against purpose?'

'Child of the time,' she said.

'Don't be arrogant. You were born twenty years too late. The times now are full of purpose. Money and graft. What's your politics? What's your religion? You're not of the time, you're antique.'

'I'm an animist. I put bunches of flowers round the boles of trees and say prayers to Creation.'

'And skulk round Richmond Park looking for magic mushrooms and eat nothing but brown rice and wear trailing skirts and don't wash. Stop lying.'

'I did all that. I wash now.'

He thought she looked neat and composed. She moved her fingers about fastidiously on the tablecloth. She wore one blue ring. Before she left to go back to her little boy he said, 'You ought to be seeing my brother not me. He's the unworldly one in the family. You're his sort.'

'What sort are your sort?'

'Women? I've never had time for them.'

'You must have had women,' she said. She had a cool clear voice that carried across the restaurant and he looked about him. The restaurant was round the corner from the hospital. Other men's girls said this sort of thing but Andrew was considered senatorial. He gave off an air that great standards were expected of him. Many of his colleagues found him a drag.

'I think,' she said leaning forward and taking both his white hands, 'I think you're really a bit of a joke, you know. You're pompous.'

He read the bill carefully and counted out the money to the nearest penny on the inside lid of an auntie purse. He wore a grey cardigan and collar and tie.

'But,' she said, getting hold of his wrists and sliding her hands up inside the cardigan sleeves, 'I could teach you so much. I adore you.'

A week later he took her to Ellerby, stopping off at Stamford for the night on the way. He had bought her some clothes and signed in for both of them as a married couple. He lay watching her unpack, run herself a bath, wrap herself in the big white towelling robe from the back of the bathroom door. She ordered drinks in the room and sat looking at hers in the window seat far away.

'Come back to bed.'

'Not yet. I'm thinking.'

'You seem very much at home, thinking in a luxury hotel.'

'I am. I'm thinking of Philip. I'll have to do something fast for Philip. Annabel's patience is on the wane.'

'He'll be fine at Ellerby. I promise. You can begin a life there.'

'Will *I* be fine?'

He nearly said, 'Have you any choice?' and thought, *I'm a shit.* 'We can but see,' he said.

She unravelled herself and curled beside him on the bed. 'Oh Andrew, Andrew, you are so good. How can I live so far away from you?'

'I can't marry you. No question of that at all. You know that. I earn twelve thousand a year and I'll be living in the hospital for a year and a half more at least. It's no life for a wife. We'd last six weeks.'

'But afterwards. There would be a life to follow.'

'It would be a long wait.'

'I've learned to wait.'

*

At breakfast next morning at one of the small tables in the hall she ate two croissants. She looked well. She said, 'And where is this depression that was going to strike?' He said, 'I love you,' and she said, 'I would wait, you know.'

A week later he saw her off with Philip for Ellerby Priors, this time on the train, and was struck again by her composure, her knack of fitting her surroundings. In the hotel she had been the experienced guest; at Ellerby, the Art and Drama teacher designate, born for the job; here on the train she was the woman always on a train, waving as it drew away, expert at saying goodbye, never losing tickets, money, baggage, the professional departer, causing no trouble. Philip, five, glared and pulled maniacal faces from his window as she waved a cool hand and turned to find her seat.

Andrew ached when the train was gone. That evening, when he managed to phone Jack and heard that Jocasta was safe there and already sorting dormitory linen and tomorrow was going for Art supplies and to see to Philip's new school, he felt worse. 'Get her away from work tonight, you bloody man,' he shouted. 'She'll be exhausted. Tell her I want to talk to her. She's still not strong.'

'She won't come to the phone, Andrew.'

'I don't believe you. Where's the boy?'

'Off somewhere. They both seem perfectly happy.'

London was a desert. The few hours' sleep he had in the hospital were troubled by dreams of her. Her face kept appearing to him during the day. Not a patient with a scar across her body failed to raise the image of Jocasta's lithe slight frame, her brown-silk skin. He had grown to love the scar, caress it, kiss it, apologise to her for it as she lay looking at the ceiling. Her lovemaking shattered him. Her past she never mentioned. The father of her son seemed not to have existed. Once he asked her and she said, 'He was nothing. I can't remember.'

'Where was Philip born?'

'I can't remember.'

'You forget everything.'

'I don't forget you,' she said. 'Not for a single minute of the day or of the night. Not for a moment do I forget you.'

In the face of fury from the powers above he got leave to go to Ellerby less than a fortnight later, reaching it at night with snow blowing against the windscreen and heaping up against the snow posts along the ridge road. Near the Saxon Cross the car began to slide and he gave up, wrapped himself round with everything he possessed, staggered down to The Priors, once falling up to his shoulders in snow. He banged on the door. It was at last opened by Jack, who thought he beheld a vision.

Jocasta had been sitting in the solar beside an old oil-stove cutting out coloured paper-chains for Christmas. Her hair was done up in a braid and she wore a long brown dress and the expression of acceptance of a dreary Gwen John. She had achieved the poverty-stricken aspect of the surroundings and scarcely looked at him. He went off alone to find a drying room for his clothes and it was Jack who brought him soap and towels and sweaters and trousers.

When finally they were alone, he said, 'You know I love you,' and she replied with the maddening slowness he had once so adored, 'I love you, Andrew, you know,' but she continued to cut out the paper. When he came near to touch her she said, 'I must keep to my own bed here, Andrew. Unless you will marry me.'

It was not the ultimatum that had shocked him, not the bargaining; it was the way she had continued carefully cutting out the paper.

'I am cold,' she said and wrapped a bald coat of Jack's around her. It made her look ugly and old.

He thought of the nights they had had and couldn't believe in them. They seemed months ago, not days. He thought of a party he'd had to go to the week before, all pub glitter and dirty rugger songs and falling beer glasses and young girls with bright lipstick, nurses worn to shreds with work and still managing to dance. Holly Fox had been there. He'd heard of Holly Fox. She had been wearing prickly bunches of holly over

62

each ear and expensive high heels and a silk shirt and she came over to him, laughing, to introduce herself. They had made jokes about medical horrors. She had poured out self-confidence and hope. 'She's after you,' someone said, 'and she gets what she wants, Holly Fox.'

In the wild snowy night at Ellerby Andrew found Jocasta's room and she was crying in her iron bed. She was cold, she was lonely. Philip was being troublesome and she couldn't take all the religion. She wanted to come home.

Making love to her, she came alive again and he knew there was none other.

But in the morning she had disappeared and he found her, wrapped up in old jerseys of Jack's, writing intensely in a notebook by an icy window niche. She covered the writing with her hand.

He found he could not ask her anything, could not tell her anything. He knew that her love for him would drown him, that he could not live with such a passion, with the sense of being always emotionally outclassed. 'I would destroy you, I suppose,' she said. He said, 'Don't worry, I'm leaving. I'm going back right away. I see it's over,' and knew that she knew he was pretending she had been the one to tire.

Jack and some of the others – little Philip was there – walked up the track with him and pushed and shoved to get the car started, towed it along behind a tractor, gave him a shovel to put in the back in case he got stuck further on. He was back on the motorway in an hour, in London as night fell.

An hour later he was on duty. Happy Holly Fox came clattering down the ward on chic black legs. Her unassailable assumption of conquest. He smiled at her.

– 13 –

In the car now, going to fetch her son Philip from school, Jocasta sat silent beside Andrew with her eyes closed. He drove very fast along the moor roads until she said, 'We're not late, you know. Can't you slow down?'

'I'll stop if you like,' he said.

'No, just slow down.'

'I'd forgotten. You're afraid of driving. Even now?'

'I do plenty of it now. I get Philip back and forth every day. But I still hate going fast.'

'I'm sorry. I should have given you this car to go for him by yourself but it's only insured for me. Or I could have come by myself and saved you the journey altogether.'

'It wouldn't have done. I don't let him get into cars with strange men, or men he hasn't seen for six years – which amounts to the same thing if you're eleven.'

'I should have been the one to take Pammie to her train,' he said. 'I hadn't reckoned on Jack wanting to take her. I'm sorry. I've muddled it.'

'Jack seems smitten,' she said. 'Surprise, surprise. He puts us all on pedestals. He loves women.'

They drove along the ridge, where steep clefts either side ran down from the rim of heather to brilliant steep green fields. On the horizon stood the three huge golf balls of the early warning system.

'They still frighten me,' he said, 'even though they're obsolete now, aren't they? Do people still do sit-ins around them? When I was at school there were "observers" coming from all over the place. Americans. Russians. Now they sit there like kids' balloons.'

She had shrunk down in her seat in the Toyota, her ankles demurely crossed like an old woman's. Dressed in black pants and sweater and her hair pulled back in a knob, she looked like a resting ballet dancer. Her hands were clasped so tight there were white marks on the knuckles. Staring at the three domes, her black eyes welled up with tears. She said, 'Oh how could you? How could you have married?'

He gave the cough he reserved for bedsides before imparting bad news. 'It – well, it was taken out of my hands, Jocasta, that's all I can say. She was – very forceful. You met her.'

'I met a hockey-playing extrovert who never stopped laughing. A gymnastic outdoor Betjeman girl. A woman of no subtlety, a bossy, tiny-minded bourgeois. I'm sorry. I know she's dead. I shouldn't say it. You must be suffering, I suppose. In your way. But I can't help being honest.'

'Nor could Holly. She was as honest as you. I think that's why—'

'Oh, don't give me that crap.'

'No, I mean I think that's why I thought I'd be able to manage.'

'*Manage!*'

'Without you.'

'But *why* manage without me? I was there. I was yours. Why?'

'You soon found Jack. Every woman wants Jack and you're the only one—'

'Yes,' she said, looking for a handkerchief, 'I soon found Jack.'

'It looked like pure malice. The timing of it.'

'No,' she said, 'not malice. It was a way of still being near you.'

'And now look what's happened. If you were free now . . . Jocasta, I'm trying to tell you that I'm a man who's made very few mistakes in his life but not marrying you was one of them.'

'And do you honestly believe,' she said, 'truly in your heart, that I would ever consider marrying you now even if I were free as the wind? Do you have any idea how much you've hurt me? And how much better the man I've married? And how much happier I am than I could ever have been with you? And how much *loved* I am now?'

They sat and the wind blew all around the car as if it might knock it over and roll it away. Long minutes passed. One car went by and dwindled away down the ridge and over the moor until it was a speck, and then was gone.

'You kept your secrets,' he said. 'What about Philip? You turned up in London with a five-year-old son and never a word about him.'

'Why ever should I?'

'You know everything about me. I told you everything. I told you long before we were lovers.'

'You never asked.'

'You were so beautiful, Jocasta. Like nobody else. You were like a brown nut. You were skintight like a Red Indian. You were still as a stone. You look no older now. You look untouched by Jack, or anyone.'

'Yes, I'm untouched by everyone. You look older. That great bald head. And your mouth is smaller. And mingier. And it sneers.'

She looked at him to see if she had gone in deep. She had. Bloody good. His transparent London pallor was flushed and his head tilted back in apparent disdain. He turned on the engine and said, 'We'd better get on.'

She put a brown claw on his arm then. Still looking ahead of him, he switched the engine off again. 'Let's get out,' she said.

They walked, a few feet apart, until they came to a long narrow dip in the heather, a swath of green turf scattered with dry black sheep droppings. When they lay down here the heather rose up around them, encircling them, so that they could not be seen by anything but a bird. They had melted into the moor. At the edge of this grass there were bilberries and the sharp arousing mineral smell of them mixed with the sweet smell of warmed grass. She undid each button of his shirt tidily and slowly, one by one. He pulled her sweater over her head and they held each other, she remembering every knob of his spine, he tracing the pattern of ears and jaw and neck, remembering how to undo the pile of black hair to let it fall round her shoulders like a shawl. He put both arms round her, his face in her neck, amazed that she could be so small. 'I think you've shrunk,' he said, and she said, 'No. You have forgotten.' They lay still, folded in to each other, heart upon heart, breath mixed with breath, until they grew warm in the October day, glowing, melded together. 'Now or later?' he said, but she did not answer.

Finding her mouth, he said, 'Now or later?' and she said, 'Now.'

'Right. Finish. Bell. You can all go, and good riddance. Philip Braithwaite, stay behind.'

Philip looked up in mild surprise. He had been drawing passionate lines against his ruler across a piece of graph paper. It was a French lesson. He ambled up in friendly fashion to the master's desk as the others scattered for buses home.

'Hi,' he said. 'Something up?'

'Shut up and wait. Straighten yourself up. Stop being insolent.'

'I only said . . .' Philip helplessly spread his hands. 'I never said . . .'

'You're to go to the Head.'

'What, *now*? I can't.'

'You're to see the Head now. He's waiting for you.'

'I'm sorry. It's not possible. I have to meet my sister. I'm not exactly mad about going to the Head anyway.'

The French master closed his eyes. He clenched his jaw. 'Philip, you haven't a sister. Will you kindly, most graciously, most accommodatingly, get the hell out of this room and go to the Head.'

'OK. Don't hit the ceiling. I'll go, but I've only a minute. They're bringing my sister when they come to collect me. She's only a baby. She can't be kept hanging about.'

He went and burst into the headmaster's office, forgetting to knock. The headmaster, who was standing looking out of the window, told him to go out again and come in properly.

'Sorry, wasn't thinking,' said Philip and retired.

There was silence. The Head opened the door and saw Philip wandering off down the corridor and about to turn the corner. 'What the hell d'you think you're doing, Braithwaite? Come back at once.'

Philip turned, smiled and gave a sketchy wave. 'Oh lord – sorry. Wasn't thinking.'

'I should like to beat you,' said the Head. 'I should like to flay you. I should like to hang you from the light cord. I should like to fling you from this window on to the cement of the school yard and see you founder.'

Philip looked interested and then very sad. 'I'm glad my stepfather can't hear you . . .'

'*Philip Braithwaite*, I have asked you here in order to find out if something is wrong. Something more than ordinarily wrong. We know you have your troubles. We know you live in a lunatic asylum on the moors. We know you are but a simple child in an adult world. We know that your family is beset with God and that God hides His Face, probably exhausted by you all. But we also know that you are a very intelligent, perfectly sane boy with potential to do anything on this earth you set yourself to do. Why, then, will you tell me, do you refuse to attempt to do any work, freak out at every games period, get lost at dinner time and cause general havoc wherever you go? I know I've asked you all this before, several times a week, but today is the end of the road. The end of the *road*, boy.'

Philip looked innocently bewildered. 'It's been all right today. Quite a pleasant day,' he said. 'Sir,' he added, as the Head's face darkened. 'I just had to go down into Whitby to buy a present for my sister.'

'You know perfectly well you're not any of you allowed into Whitby in school hours.'

'There seemed no one to ask.'

'But it is not *allowed*.'

Philip looked pained. 'I told you. I had to get a present . . .'

The Head sat down at the desk and pointed at a chair on the other side of it. Philip sat. The Head covered his eyes with his fingers and then uncovered them to grab Philip's wrists as he stretched forward to pick up an ornament on the desk. 'You bloody little twerp, put that down.'

'It's ormolu. *Sir*. Very nice. Lovely. We've got some Tibetans—'

'Philip, I've had enough. The school has had enough. You lie like an Arab. Look, we're going to have to expel you.'

Philip brightened.

'I should be a happy man, a fulfilled man, if I could only expel you and see the back of you for the last time marching out of that door. Unfortunately, I can't. I tried. I can't.'

'You mean when you got the assessors in? When you wanted me to go to the Dyslexic Centre?'

'I do. And when you spelled "Here" H I Y, I thought we'd got rid of you. But you overdid it. Overacted. As you do.'

'Well, I got interested in the Maths.'

'Unfortunately.'

'And they made a mistake.'

'So you told them.'

'They did. I wasn't exactly mad about telling them but—'

'That will *do*, Philip. The point today is where has all the Art paper gone? That's all I ask. You were working alone in the Art Room last week and all the paper is now missing. Four large rolls of it.'

'Why should it have been me?'

'Was it you?'

'Well, yes. You see—'

'*Philip*!'

'I wanted it for the Tibetans' mantras. We'd run out. Jocasta had something or other on her mind. I brought some back. I'll replace it, honestly. My mother's been awfully busy getting ready for the baby.'

'Baby?'

'My sister. She's just been born.'

'But I saw Jocasta last week . . . You mean there's a *baby*?'

'Just come. I'll be seeing her for the first time this afternoon. They're probably waiting outside for me now.'

The Head looked nervously over his shoulder out of the window and saw a Toyota he did not know approaching the school. Jocasta, light as a leaf, got out of it, her hair floating down her back.

'I'm afraid I shall have to speak to Jocasta and your stepfather again,' he said wearily. 'Philip, Philip, what are we to do with you? Not today, though. I'll make an appointment. Can you give me some satisfaction about the Art paper?'

'Oh yes. I'll get it back,' he said as he stood up. 'I'm sorry,' he added at the door, a smile of delirious enchantment breaking across his face. 'I'd better go. You've been very understanding, sir. Actually, "lie like an Arab" – isn't it a bit racist?'

The Head roared.

A moment later he watched the boy trot across the school yard towards the Toyota. Jocasta, on seeing her son, got back in her seat and sat looking at herself in a little glass and applying lipstick. A man not Philip's stepfather was at the wheel and as far as the Head could see there was not a trace of a baby.

– 14 –

'I believe that car was Andrew's. It looked like Andrew's. My son-in-law.'

The nice old Jaguar swooped down from the high ridge road into a village with soft grass growing down its middle on either side of a stream. There were sheep wandering about and ducks sailing and waddling. A village shop.

'Oh this is so charming,' said Thomasina. 'So lovely to be here after horrible Scotland.'

'Horrible Egypt,' said the general, who had been enjoying Scotland until yesterday and was bemused that Thomasina had elected to leave it. He had been bemused by many things about Thomasina, to whom he was not married but on behalf of whom he had been signing his name in hotel registers for several weeks. The events of the recent past, the months since Holly Fox's death, were proving startling to the general, whose life had gone steadily along since he left the army nearly twenty years before and even more steadily when two years ago he entered a calmly accepted widowhood in Berkshire, near his old garrison. He had been enormously enjoying his disciplined life and finding it very entertaining until his visit to Challoners Health Farm for his joints, and the first sight of Thomasina.

It was not at all that he had fallen for her lustfully, as old men so sadly do. The general's love for Thomasina involved not a jot of desperation. It was seeing her there and recognising a dying breed, his breed, the breed of woman he had always been easy with, a woman untouched by the shabby, messy world that now surrounded him, belaboured him on the television, on public transport, from advertisement hoardings, even in the theatre, the world where everything hangs out. The last time he had been to the opera he had seen somebody in the audience in a vest.

Abroad was not so bad, or at least the abroad he had known so well. India was still recognisable, the beggars more prolific and even more demanding, but there were still hotels there where, on a good package, you could find people wearing the right clothes and speaking in the right voices. Shepheard's Hotel in Cairo was virtually gone – the Shepheard's Hotel that had twisted his heartstrings once – but there were still gentle and spacious havens. There were still, for example, punkahs against the heat in Singapore, though nowadays the fans were worked by electricity and not the toe of a boy. You could still meet an old friend in the Cricket Club and the Straits Chinese were very efficient people. You had to respect them. They had the Club on a good financial footing.

But on the whole he stayed at home. He rarely looked at travel brochures now. The attempted afterglow of the Empire there he found embarrassing, as he did the Royal Family, whom he had abhorred since they had gone public and made love in front of the camera. There were one or two of the Royal Family who were all right. The Queen, of course, and Princess Alexandra. About Princess Alexandra he even had very faint (and very secret) fantasies on the edge of sleep. He rode with her in Abyssinia and Tanganyika in the old days – narrow beautiful jodhpurs – or he fished with her in Scottish burns.

The first view of Thomasina across the salon at Challoners behind her silver teapot had given him an excited lurch, for she

71

had Princess Alexandra's legs and narrow skirt, and when she turned, as he called across to ask her if she were famous, Princess Alexandra's crooked smile.

After Thomasina's tragic departure he had worked vigorously to find her again. He had not been able to extract her address from the place but they had promised to forward a letter. There had been silence. He had at last discovered the reason through a mutual acquaintance run to earth at a party given by a Surrey GP. 'Used to be married to old Herbert Fox. Quite something. Nice woman. Didn't remarry. Very wrapped up in her daughter, who's just died, I understand. Yes – only about a month ago.'

The general tracked down Thomasina and found not Princess Alexandra but the creature now anathema to all her friends. Thomasina encased in glass, untouchable. He also saw her bravery. He saw it in her clothes and careful make-up and flawless social manner, and he still felt, beneath it all, her charm. In the intensity of those first days it is just possible that the general caught a glimpse of Thomasina herself.

He felt a great warmth for her, a wish to be near her, to touch her elbow, enwrap her, take her to leisurely expensive places in his immaculate old car. He wanted to take her to meet the remnants of his own old background, where he knew she would appear deeply, effortlessly at home. She looked so unselfconsciously well-heeled, too. *I could comfort her*, he thought. *If I were younger I'd say I was in love.*

This thought gave him delicious amusement as he went swooping about in the Jaguar. *Seventy-two*, he thought with pride as, approaching Kensington High Street, he cut in on a little Renault driven by a man like Tony Blair and pressed the button that let down the Jaguar's roof. He took to keeping the roof down in all weathers: to wearing a tweed cap. He began to notice girls' legs in the autumn sunshine. He found in Hyde Park one day that he was thoroughly, positively happy.

Not that he'd ever been an unhappy man. Very lucky. Keeping going. Usually possible to find something pleasant to think about. Good health the secret. No bees in the bonnet. No love troubles.

Love troubles, he thought. *Ridiculous. Couldn't do it now.*

He began, though – as he made his toast and porridge for breakfast in the shiny kitchen in his house on the edge of the garrison, calendar on the wall marked off with perhaps a dwindling number of things to look forward to, telephone these days ringing rather less frequently and the dear old dog dead – he began to remember love.

They were hazy creatures, like somebody else's, girls from a pre-war book, girls whose names . . . There came a warm zephyr of a memory, something to do with Egypt, a weekend with a girl at Karnak in the Summer Palace during the war. He had been – what? Under thirty. He remembered a summer frock and a string of little pearls and sunset over the Valley of the Kings. Madeleine. She had been very shy. He'd met his wife Hilda soon afterwards at a noisy tennis party in Hong Kong and loved the way she smashed the ball about and looked so big and sensible and believed in the Empire. *Madeleine*, he thought. *What became of her?* And saw, amazingly, the line of her dress on the terrace of the Summer Palace half a century ago, her fingers tangling in the pearls. He saw that he had suppressed all this – good God, where was it all coming from? Blonde, blonde hair. He saw her longing eyes.

I missed something, he thought. *Bloody fool.*

Continuing the essential ritual of his day, after dinner on the kitchen work-top he poured himself a double Scotch and switched on the ten o'clock news. He switched off when it was over and found that he had not registered one word, but that the Egyptian sunset was still about. He picked up the telephone and fancied that Thomasina's voice was as Madeleine's would be now.

When he took Thomasina to dinner the next evening at his London club he cleared his throat, examined the moulding on the ceiling and suggested that what would do her good would be a package tour to Egypt. 'For me, too,' he said. 'I should like to see Egypt again. Buck us both up. What do you say?'

But Egypt with Thomasina was not to be the gentle time with Madeleine. They began in Cairo with a non-luxury hotel.

There had been no tour available so they had simply bought a couple of airline tickets and made reservations for themselves in something that sounded quiet and where there would be no Americans. The hotel had turned out to be far from the Nile, down a maze of dirty streets and looking over an empty sports stadium, and the general spent the first morning trying to change the reservations, with no success. They had a bad lunch in a restaurant smelling of hamburgers and then trailed about the Museum of Antiquities. Tutankhamun's head was out on loan and round every grubby sarcophagus a dirty fellow with a beckoning finger tried to lure them off to see secret horrors in dark corners denied, they were assured, to the general public. 'Dead babies covered with hair,' one demon promised them.

The general led her away towards the Bazaar but something had happened to the sky. It had turned the colour of uncleaned copper and sand was uneasily snaking the streets. They took a reluctant taxi, in which the driver had been curled up on the floor, to visit friends of the general's dead wife. Valerie had married romantically on leaving Cambridge an Egyptian economist. The apartment was in Stygian darkness owing to a power cut and the darkening sky. 'But we always need the lights on in here, anyway,' said Valerie. Dusty sand lay deep on shelves and tables, in folds of the curtains, along the top of the sunny but fading photograph of Girton girls in caps and gowns, in 1938. The husband sat slumped in a broken chair, his long yellow hands hanging towards the floor. There were little cakes that tasted of sand. The apartment was on a lower floor of an old six-storey block and at intervals loads of rubbish were chucked from above and fell past the window to land with a thud in the street below. The hostess moved with dazed dignity, carrying milk jugs, paper napkins. Sandwiches garnished with parsley the husband turned from with disgust. Suddenly he asked about this year's Boat Race and they all tried to remember it. Valerie mentioned the general's dead wife, Hilda, and then burst into tears.

That night the sandstorm closed the airport and for two days Thomasina and the general stayed in the hideous hotel watching the cars in the streets below being coated with sand

74

as thick as a deep snowfall. The snow was solid and dark and did not melt. The city was silenced. Somehow they forced a cab to take them to the airport to see if they could get out to Karnak on the second evening, and found themselves marooned there, alone except for a party of giant Texans in T-shirts, stetsons and boots. No Egyptians were to be seen except for those bundles of rags blurred into mummified shapes all over the lounges, the duty-free, perhaps even the runways, sleeping till the sand had settled and drifted away, God knew when.

Utter silence covered Cairo. They joined up with the Texans, who were drinking Glenfiddich – which improved things no end – and at last accompanied them to their suite in the Mena House Hotel beside the Pyramid, a fee like the national lottery jackpot being demanded by and paid to a doleful cab driver who implied this would be his last drive on earth. In the Texans' suite Thomasina and the general drank more whisky, ate smoked salmon, talked about racing, entered a violent argument about American politics, were found somehow a single room in the hotel, into which the two of them crammed, became lovers and awoke the next morning to a curiously muffled but sunshiny world.

Thomasina glittered as they caught the plane to Karnak next morning, the general held his head high and the security man in the airport pinched Thomasina's bottom as she stepped through the gate. The general smiled so lovingly at a steward-ess that she blushed and brought them a half bottle of champagne.

At the Winter Palace, where crowds of tourists sat on suitcases weeping at the total failure of all bookings, their air of Olympian confidence, the general's marvellous trousers and Thomasina's tall relaxed figure unfussed among the life-size palms on the grubby marble somehow produced a key a foot long and a room with doors so high they would have admitted giraffes. The bed in this room, which was Farouk Dynasty, was covered in old brown satin. A basin and ewer stood at a tilt on a stalk of twisted metal and from a shadowy dressing room an old gentleman was evicted wearing a long pale-pink robe. He said that he had been expecting to spend the night with them in order to clean their shoes.

Laughing like school children, they ordered dreadful sandwiches and even more dreadful wine and slept together for the second time. In the morning they opened shutters upon the Valley of the Kings, gold and rosy in the dawn, and watched matchstick people with boot-black faces and pastel-coloured robes prancing and jolly on either bank of the Nile. And the Nile ran fast and green, busy with feluccas sharp-winged as ancient birds on a frieze.

Thomasina and the general did not refer to the events of the night, though they both knew they were more precisely and deliciously remembered than even those of the night before, wreathed in sandstorm and whisky; but on the terrace at breakfast they often caught each other's glance and smiled, and the general tenderly asked her if she'd like more coffee. When they crossed by felucca to the tombs, he said, 'I hope you're as happy as I am, Thomasina,' and she smiled and took his arm.

There was a change, though. As they stood in one of the patterned walled tombs of a young queen, there was a little bundle in a corner, the dust of a child. No one knew, said the guide, if it were a miscarried child or a child dead just after birth, but it must have been a child greatly loved or desired to have been buried with such honour. Thomasina said nothing, but afterwards the general remembered the moment. Thomasina's coolness, which had left her at the Mena House for an almost languid glow, returned, and at the dinner table that night she began to work out the expenses of the trip, insisting she pay half. When he protested, she said that times had moved on since his day and she was nobody's mistress.

In bed later he lay in silence and she moved towards him and caressed and cajoled but didn't apologise.

It was a different sort of lovemaking, Thomasina almost ferocious, and the at first reluctant general very surprised.

On the plane home she read a book about the royal houses of the Ptolemaean dynasty and the general thought that he had never seen her more beautiful. He was now as much in love with her as a dizzy boy. He dropped his money about, mislaid his passport, longed for the night. He would even have agreed to staying in Cairo again, even at the hotel overlooking the stadium as they had planned first, but when she said No, home, he agreed. He would have agreed to anything. He wondered when she would tell him that she would marry him. Pale England in the autumn light, the smooth broad road from Heathrow, the luxurious taxicab, the traditional talkative driver, made him feel as if life were just beginning again – real English life as it had once been. He was exalted.

It was only after they were in the taxi and the general leaning forward to tell the driver where in London they should go that it became clear to them both that neither knew where that was.

Thomasina was leaning back, looking reflective.

'My club?' he said.

'Very well.'

'Covent Garden,' he said. 'We can have dinner there.' *But not sleep there*, he thought: *I can't take her to bed there.*

It was a huge distance. On his own the general would have taken the tube or a couple of buses to Berkshire. And the general, Thomasina thought, had not seen her mock-Tudor house near Edgecombe. They sat silently considering these facts.

Thomasina said as the taxi with thirty pounds on the clock reached central London, 'I think we'll make it Waterloo, if you don't mind, Giles. I think I'd like to go home.'

'Right,' he said. 'I shall come with you.'

'Absolutely no.'

'You are being ridiculous,' he said, wondering how he had displeased her.

But she was first out of the taxi and had paid the fare before he had even begun to negotiate the suitcases. She seemed not to notice his annoyance.

He strode off and bought first-class tickets for the train and was ahead of her at Guildford station, finding another taxi fast, helping her aboard; but again lost face because he didn't know the address. He looked stonily at the large house, the overgrown garden. Apples had splattered down among the trees on the front lawn; rambler roses over the trellises needed cutting back. It was a garden he'd like to get his hands on. They waded through the papers and letters behind the door and stood on the parquet and Persian rugs in the hall as she read some of the postcards.

'Shall I open a window or two?'

She frowned, looked at him, read a postcard over again.

'Do you really live all alone here? Is it safe? Great garden all around and right off the road. Bit of a temptation to people, isn't it?'

To his amazement (it was three o'clock in the afternoon, for God's sake), he found himself longing to take her to bed again. *And seventy-two!*

'I'll get some coffee,' and he turned to where he thought there might be a kitchen.

'No,' she said. 'Don't. Stay here.' She went over to him and stroked his cheek. 'I'm sorry. So sorry, Giles. Could you just stay in the hall? I'm going upstairs to change and wash and . . .'

'Very well.'

When she came back he was sitting on an antique oak stool much too small for him, fist on either knee, and her heart melted for a moment. She said, 'It's just it's this house. Spindleberries. Where we lived. I can't come back just yet. I thought I could. I find I can't.'

'I understand.'

Not once had she mentioned Holly's name since they had met. He waited.

'I think I'd like to go to Scotland now,' she said.

'Now? Scotland?'

'Yes, I think I'd like to go to Scotland. We might get sleepers.'

'Out of the question.'

She seemed to brighten up. 'I'll make some tea,' she said, 'Sit down somewhere. You're overdone.'

Later he found on the phone that there were no sleepers for weeks and at her disappointed face said that they might perhaps drive there tomorrow or the next day. Do the old car good, he said. But not straight off. Bit of a rest first. Plenty of friends there – places to stay, and good bed-and-breakfasts. Cousin in Caithness. Lovely in the Highlands just now.

She looked bewildered and then relieved, kissed his forehead as she passed his chair, watched him pick up the suitcases and led him upstairs. In her bedroom she said, 'If you went to get the car now and picked me up here in the morning . . .' but he said, 'No, I'm not going to do that. I'm staying here tonight.'

'You can't sleep with me. Not here.' She was looking over his shoulder.

'I'll sleep in another room. I'm going into London for the car now, and I'll be back here about ten.'

'Can you get dinner somewhere?'

'Of course.' He looked stern. 'You have something in the fridge, I dare say?'

She looked at him scornfully and let him out of the front door, from where he had to walk a mile to the station.

All evening she paced about the house, agonising that he wouldn't come back.

At ten there was no sign of him, nor at half past. She had made up a bed for him and turned up the central heating, picked a few flowers, put together a tray of drinks and taken bread out of the freezer for morning. The house felt frighteningly still and she was wide awake. *Jet lag*, she thought. *I'd better not drink. Yet I never get jet lag and all I've had is horrible aeroplane champagne.*

She couldn't remember if she'd eaten anything since and went to the kitchen, where she found a crumby plate from her supper and some pants and stockings drying on the Aga rail. Upstairs her dresses had been hung up, her sponge bag emptied. She must have been quite busy. She rang Pammie for the third time but there was still no answer. At last she went into Holly's old room. Baby clothes lay in soft neat clumps. Teddies and old dolls were in a box. There was a crib and baby blankets. She sat on the bed.

This is a big step. I am here. Tomorrow I'll start thinking. He will not come back and I shall write to him and finish it off.

79

Good clean break. He was a nice man. It was mad, really. I'm amazed I could remember how to do it.

The lights of the Jaguar swung across the garden, then across the bedroom, and in a moment he was at the door with another suitcase for Scotland and wearing a tweed suit. He smelled of very good soap and walked in as if she were his wife of years. But he made no more enquiries about sleeping quarters and no comment when she said, 'No – not there,' as he made for Holly's room. She opened another door.

'D'you want the landing light left on?' he asked. 'I'll leave my door open.'

She heard him moving about his room, the click as he put down his watch on the bedside table, the little rattle as his cuff links were dropped on the dressing table. She heard him brushing his teeth, drawing back curtains, opening the window a little. The creak as he lowered himself into bed.

Good God, men, she thought. *They're bloody awful. Where have I brought myself? What do I want? Why can't I let myself go? Or get rid of him?*

'It was Andrew's car,' she said, 'and Andrew in it. My son-in-law.'

The general swivelled a tired eye. Thomasina was looking lovelier than ever, he thought, her skin clear from fresh Scottish air, a couple of days' fishing and some splendid rain. He could not look at her without delight. And yet . . .

'Your *son-in-law*? There was nothing up there at all, Thomasina, just the moor.'

'No. There was a car by the roadside. It was Andrew's Toyota. Holly used to drive it.'

He thought, *I must be very careful now, and very kind.*

Before she could have time to wait for his reaction to Holly's name being mentioned at last, he said, 'Oh, I'm sure there are plenty of Toyotas around here, you know.'

'He was with a woman. A very small dark woman. They were sitting talking. Miles from anywhere.'

'No, Thomasina. It would be an extraordinary coincidence, wouldn't it? Wasn't your – wasn't Holly married to a London doctor?'

'There was no sign of the baby in the car, I think,' said Thomasina.

He said carefully, 'Ah. A baby. I think I heard there was a baby.'

'Faith,' she said. 'Ghastly name, isn't it? Better than Hope or Charity, I suppose. Well, it wasn't anything to do with me.'

'I'm afraid I had no children. We didn't have this problem.'

'Perhaps you were lucky.'

Then she saw his face.

'Come,' he said. 'We can get tea here,' and in the teashop, looking at the stream and the white wooden bridges outside over the stream, he said, 'If you would like to talk about . . .'

'Oh,' she said, 'not a bit. Terrible shock, you know, and I keep thinking, "Holly darling, how dare you? Just going off like that and leaving poor old Andrew." But you know, she wasn't one who would want us to *mope*. She was very sensible and positive. Awful bore it happened, but it does happen, doesn't it? Nothing to be done.' Her light voice was the voice he had first heard across the health farm drawing room. He thought, *And it's the voice of the lost.*

'And the – baby? Faith?' he asked.

'Oh. Well, I think she's not really my department. There are the other grandparents, you know, and a brother. They live up here. Just about here. Big Northern family all rallying round. Marvellous people, of course, Yorkshire people.'

'Will you mind her being a North Country granddaughter?'

'Oh, you mean her accent? Well, of course not. That would be too bourgeois. And it can be very homely and nice. I'd have preferred a Scot, of course, but there. Andrew hasn't a trace of Yorkshire in him even though he's from a local school, I believe. Stuffy old stick-in-the-mud, but I have to say you could take him anywhere.'

'He must be very cut up.'

'Yes,' she said. 'Oh, do look at that sheep. Yes, it was strange seeing him just now with that woman. D'you know, it was the first time,' she said with an open and completely empty smile,

81

'that I realised old Holls had gone. Let's get on and find the hotel. Priors Meadow. It can't be far. Actually, it's quite near some of Andrew's family, I think. Next village.'

The general said carefully, 'So it could have been Andrew?'

'Oh yes,' she said. 'It was.'

Pammie at the same moment was settling herself in a first-class carriage as the King's Cross train drew out of York station and laying out for herself on the little shelf beside her the equipment for mixing up a knockout gin and tonic – brittle plastic beaker, three miniature bottles and a plastic swizzle stick. She was alone in the carriage. She kicked off her shoes, took a quick shuftie at the Minster in its cream-and-gold glory behind the scaffolding, wondered about a cigarette, lit a cigarette, lay back, closed her eyes and translated herself to Surrey.

You won't believe this. I'm not sure that I believe it. It was a riot. *Tibetans*, dear. Holy men. Yes, I am talking about Faith Fox and Andrew. She is to live in *ruins* on the North Yorkshire moors. The very strangest people you ever saw in your life and Andrew, let me tell you, quite a different person. D'you know, he got out of the car in this great wilderness, every bit as wild as Dartmoor and not even the cafés and coaches, and he went striding off into the heather leaving me all alone? Well, cold feet, I suppose. His brother, well, you would never, never, dream they were related. Much older. He looks a different generation from Andrew, but masses of curly hair and not grey. He's a sort of evangelist, I suppose, and his wife's tiny and black. No, I don't mean *black* black, I mean sort of dark. All over. Sort of heart of darkness. Gaunt and tiny and intense. Not my sort at all, I'm afraid. You can see she'll be very attractive to men. Great eyes in a little head. No trace of the North about her. I don't know where he can have found her. Rather plummy voice, actually. Overdone Oxford sort of voice, quite old-fashioned. But young, she's young, and she's not a Sloane. Arty. There was a child about somewhere, quite an old one, I think, but I didn't see it. You couldn't think anyone so tiny could have produced a child. She just stands about, looking at you.

Most frightful lunch they gave me. Some sort of salt fish. I expect it must have been got in for the Tibetans, though it would have been a mistake, Tibet being so far from the sea. They probably never touch it. No common sense about. Yes, I saw some Tibetans. They were lumping about in some sheds. They looked fairly doubtful to me.

Cells, my dear, to sleep in. Workshops full of looms. They must have cost a bomb, yet there was no central heating and not a carpet or a curtain. Jack – the brother – showed me around. And, d'you know, Andrew never said goodbye. He went off somewhere with Heart-of-Darkness and it was brother who took me to the train. Thought we'd never get here, he's a frightful driver, and we were in some sort of smelly pick-up full of beer cans. They'd had a batch of hooligans staying from Teesside. They take in the unloved. Our darling Faith! He kept wanting to stop and show me churches and bits of ruins and I had to be quite firm. As it was, I missed the train I'd booked a seat on and I had to jump for the next. I just managed to run into the buffet and grab a drink and leap into the train as the doors banged, dragging my luggage in off the platform. I hadn't *taken* luggage but this Jack had made me bring home a plastic bag full of potatoes. There was no sign of him but, just as we pulled away, here he is, wandering down the platform with his arms full of newspapers for me. The kindest man – but, you know, impossible. He dropped all the papers trying to wave goodbye. Very lovable man. He's asked me to go back, by the way, for a retreat. I retreated all right, straight back south.

She took a swig of gin and looked out eastward over the plain to low hills of hanging woods. A plump and amateurish white horse was picked out in the chalk and above it ran the line of the moor. She felt a surprising pleasure. Finishing the gin, she thought of Thomasina and could not see her anywhere near such a place. *I don't think he'd have asked* her *back*, she thought. *I think I rather hit it off with the evangelist. But by God, I couldn't have taken much more.*

What a day! she thought. *I'm getting too old for this. There and back to North Yorkshire by bedtime. That drive!* She had a frightening moment of being quite unable to remember why she had come and this was followed by something even more unpleasant. It was like pain. It was guilty sorrow. She couldn't place it.

She fell heavily asleep, waking just north of London with enough time to do her face and look at her hair and wriggle herself tidy inside her silk-and-wool suit with the black binding (Harvey Nicks). She patted a black silk scarf, thinking, *Black. Oh dear, Holly's funeral. Oh, poor Holly Fox.*

Back home old Hugo wandered across to her with whisky. 'Child safe?' he asked. 'Settled in?' and Pammie stared, placing the anguish.

She had forgotten to look at Faith before she left or to say goodbye.

The two Smikes were waiting for the go-ahead to set off on their night out when the Toyota arrived in the courtyard on its journey from Philip's school. Philip got out and came over to them. 'Yer goin' down Middlesber?' he enquired in a voice that would have been unrecognisable in his classroom.

'Come back,' Jocasta called. 'Philip, come back and say thank you to Andrew for getting you from school.'

'Thanks, Andrew,' said Philip in Jocasta-speak, then, 'I said, yer goin' down Middlesber? Can ah coom wid yer?'

The Smikes continued to drink out of Coke cans. Jack's pick-up could be heard approaching the gatehouse from its trip to York and Jack climbed down from it and went over to Philip, smiling.

'Now then, Philip, what's this?'

' 'E wantster coom Middlesber,' said Smike One (Ernie). 'We's goin' down Retcer ont bikes.'

'That's a matter for Jocasta,' said Jack and looked across to the Toyota. His brother now seemed to be there alone.

'She's gone to look at Faith, I think,' said Andrew. 'Pammie get off OK?'

'Perfectly. Now, what about Evensong? I thought there should be a little welcoming ceremony for Faith. I thought maybe somebody might carry her up to the altar and I could bless her.'

Andrew looked uneasy.

'Perhaps Philip?' said Jack.

Philip aimed a sudden kick at Smike Two (Nick), who had just lit up a joint and aimed the match in Philip's direction. Then he went into The Priors, looking for food. Andrew thought, *Nasty little prick.*

The journey from school had not been agreeable. Philip had come, almost bustling, to the car in the school yard, climbed in the back and said, 'Hi, Andrew' (after six years). 'Where is she?'

Andrew, dazed from the journey out, warmed and sleepy by the delight of Jocasta's silky thigh beside the handbrake, the smell of her hair and skin, said, 'Where's who?'

Philip didn't answer. As they started for home Philip realised there must have been some mistake. He'd thought – he had *known* – that they were bringing his sister. He knew it was true. He'd heard them all talking and stuff being brought in and so on. Baby. Faith. He'd liked Holly. 'Holly's Faith' they'd all been saying. He wasn't mad about the idea of Holly being dead.

Faith. Coming to live up here. His sister. Like most dyslexics he had a hazy grasp of relationships. Nephews and nieces, cousins and aunts, they were more complicated for him than the construction of computer programmes that would have puzzled Aristotle and came to him like breathing. At eleven, grandparents he could just about understand, maybe because Dolly and Toots were woven into his life. They were Jack's parents and Andrew's parents. He knew this. Jack he had been told was his stepfather only, but he'd never enquired into that. He remembered a time in somewhere vile when there had been no Jack. Some house full of dirty rooms in screaming streets. Bright red buses. Police sirens. Vaguely once a place called Earls Court where there had been acrobats. Jocasta had been there with some people – but no Jack, nobody he knew now.

'Well, but you are my grandparents, though?' he'd asked Dolly and Toots, and Dolly had said, 'Well . . .' and stopped.

Toots had said, 'That's right, boy. Twice over.'

The first and only thing Philip had ever made with Jocasta in one of her craft classes had been a wooden box that stood askew and was narrow at the bottom so that dirt got in the corners and everyone had laughed at it, but when he gave it to Dolly and Toots at Christmas they had been in raptures. 'Put that right there by my bed,' Toots had said. 'Now, that's not to be moved. That's for my papers,' and Dolly had shown it to everyone, especially Mrs Middleditch, who had said that her Bingham couldn't have made it at eleven and he was now a mechanical engineer. These were grandparently events, he sensed. Philip was rather mad about his grandparents.

'You got heather on your back, Jocasta,' he said, 'and bits in your hair.' She said nothing. 'Where's the baby?' he tried again. 'I thought you had brought the baby.'

'She'd had enough driving,' said Andrew. 'She's being looked after at The Priors. You'll see her when we get there.'

'Oh, I don't care about seeing her,' said Philip. 'I just wondered if you could have forgotten her.'

'Don't be a fool, Philip,' said his mother.

'I thought that Philip might carry up Faith this evening,' said Jack at tea, 'bring her up from the body of the chapel to the altar and then I could carry her down again and show her about to the congregation – the visitors and all the staff and everyone. The two youngest ones together.'

'You might do better to get one of the visitors. One of the oldest,' said Alice Banks, The Missus, the housekeeper. 'The one that looks as old as Shangri-La.'

'She's looking after Faith at the moment,' said Jack. 'Well, I think so. I hope so. Have you been to see her, Jocasta? You took her over there, Alice, didn't you, after you'd seen to Andrew's bedroom?'

The Missus said yes, but it had hardly been a question of handing over, the Tibetan lady had carried Faith off in her bosom.

Everyone laughed except Philip.

'Can I go with The Smikes?' he asked.

'Not again,' said The Missus. 'Not again. You can't.'

'Who are The Smikes?' asked Andrew.

'Our saviours,' said Jack. His smile was a light unto his feet. 'Can't do without them. They hold us all together.'

The Missus looked darkly at her plate.

'They're ex-remand boys,' said Jack. 'We've had them a while now. They decided to stay on after they'd done their community service. They were burglars. It's a great tribute to us. But no, Philip, you're not to go with them again.'

'Why not?'

'Because,' said The Missus, 'they're older than you are. They get you in trouble. The trouble they make is their own affair, so I'm told, since they're over eighteen. Now it's all girls and drink, and it's way too soon for you.'

'It's quite right for The Smikes,' said Jack. 'We lead them now, we don't command. We only can suggest right values.'

'Couldn't one of them carry up the baby?' said Philip. 'I'd just drop her or something.' He awaited contradiction.

'Well, if you think you would,' said Jack, and Jocasta said, 'He would. He's not to do it. Her father shall carry her, if anyone.'

'Actually, I don't see why anyone should,' said Andrew. 'She'll be having a christening some time, won't she? She's been jumped round enough for one day. Surrey ladies and Tibetans.'

'So, could I go with The Smikes? I could stay the night, if you like, with Dolly and Toots.'

'No, I don't like the way Nick drives,' said The Missus.

'Oh, come on,' said Jocasta, changing sides.

'They're wonderful drivers,' said Jack. 'People go on about young drivers today but they're better than we are. Wonderful reflexes. I wish mine were anything like them.'

'Oh, I dare say Philip will be safer with them than you,' said his brother.

Looking Philip over, Andrew felt a pang of remorse. He'd not addressed a word to the child in the car, his thoughts being far from step-nephews, his hands trembling, his whole dishevelled being reliving the glory of the journey out. *What a day!* he

87

thought. *Pammie and The George and all that prattle and getting lost and theology and losing courage and nearly going home to Mum and then arriving – and there she was. Oh God. And within two hours, naked in the heather. And now evensong.*

Andrew disliked boys. He disliked children altogether, really. He found them selfish, wrapped up in themselves, expecting attention and interest to be taken. He still couldn't quite believe in Faith. He hadn't been able to take her in at all. But there was something rather arresting about Philip now. Very honest. Yet complex. Well, he was Jocasta's, wasn't he? God knows who the father had been. Good old Jack, taking him on. The boy must have a queer sort of life.

'I'll be going down tomorrow to see Dolly and Toots,' he said. 'I could bring you back, Philip, if these Smikes drop you off there tonight.'

'Only if The Smikes promise to drop you off on their way *in*. We don't want you joining up with them in whatever their goings-on are,' said The Missus. Jocasta moved her fork about. Jack smiled. *Whose the hell's am I?* thought Philip.

'And you must be strapped in that bike this time,' said The Missus, 'and ring up the minute you get there.'

'I must write my few words for the service now,' said Jack. 'What do you say about Philip going, then, Jocasta?'

'Fine,' she said. 'Friday night. No school tomorrow.'

'Then we'll all go to evensong in ten minutes,' said Jack. 'The visitors will be in the chapel already. Shall we gather up Faith and begin?'

'What about this carrying-up thing I have to do?' asked Philip.

'We'll leave it. We'll say some prayers for her, but perhaps we'll leave the presentation until some time like the christening when Dolly and Toots . . . And we might invite that good woman to come back. Jocasta – darling, what's the matter?'

'Tired,' she said. 'I'm going to lie down. I'll miss this.'

During the service the old Tibetan woman, who must have heard some rumour of a ceremony, took matters and Faith into her own hands. In the middle of a hymn in which the Tibetans

88

did not join she suddenly arose with the cot and dumped it on the altar and went back to her place.

'Cheek,' said The Missus.

From the front pew, Philip observed Faith. Strapped on the slanting tray of the cot, she was looking down the tin church this way and that, alertly at the candles on either side of her, wonderingly at the sunlight dying through the metal windows. She began to drum her feet against the tray and opened wide her arms. Squirming rather angrily, she made a sound that might have been either laughter or tears.

– 15 –

'Are yer goin' ont sans?' yelled Philip over the racket of the motorbike. He was in a sidecar hitched to the bike's side with ramshackle hooks and twine. It bobbed up and down like a cockleshell boat. The Smikes, one behind the other, kept their faces forward. 'Don't drop me off at me gran's, Nick. Gi's a break, Nick.' The machine was slowing down at the end of Dolly and Toots's road. Usually Philip was tipped out near old Toots's seat beside the church and walked the rest of the way, but the slowing-down process was being a tricky one tonight and Nick, swearing, decided to pack it in for the time being and drive on. They went over the top of a low sandy roundabout with the sound of a cohort of cavalry, plunged on over a short dead-end of unmade road that led into the sand dunes, and bike and sidecar then performed a ballet in the gloaming across golf bunkers and low grassy hills and swooped down upon the seashore beyond.

It was dark. The sands were hard and wide and appeared to be empty. 'Let yer frottle art,' shouted Ernie to Nick. 'Let 'er go.'

'Yes, let yer frottle art, yer booger,' shouted Philip along-side, bouncing.

89

Nick obliged and the machine with a noise like a steelworks when they open up furnaces took off along the shore, weaving among half-submerged rocks and piles of seaweed and springing like a thoroughbred over a massive rusty sewer pipe. The waves drew back as they passed by.

The bike roared in a crescendo and then faded and stopped at last in a profound silence. Some faint cries reached them from the promenade. Ernie, the quieter Smike, let out a long halloo like a fox yapping and Nick began a paean of demon laughter. Bouncing slowly like an airliner after landing, the hooks of the sidecar suddenly broke and it went careering, with Philip inside it, out into the ocean.

When they'd dragged him out again and failed to re-harness sidecar to bike, they pushed them, with some difficulty – especially for Philip, who was in sole charge of the sidecar – up the deep grubby sand. When Philip reached the promenade both Smikes were leaning against a fishing boat, in conversation with friends. Trying to haul his charger up the steps, Philip called, 'Yer gotter 'elp me, Nick. It's 'eavy.'

'Poor little booger. Poor little soft booger, 'elp yerselluf.'

It was Ernie who came over in the end and got behind Philip to drag and heave the thing, though he looked the less strong of the two. Emaciated, tattooed and earringed, he seemed as he rose up the steps from the strand like someone rescued after weeks in an open boat. This was deeply misleading. Ernie's gentle appearance had stood him in good stead for years, particularly with women of the maternal variety, and had been to his great advantage as a burglar.

The bike and sidecar were brought together among the boats with the intermittent help of new Smike cronies, who had detached themselves from the open doors of the amusement arcade opposite and from the yards and wynds that joined the straggling, clapped-out ex-fishing town to the shore. There followed a big struggle to get the bike and sidecar re-attached and padlocked to the railings of a statue of a bewhiskered Victorian benefactor of the town staring out to sea above their heads.

The amusement palaces behind him wailed and blinked

their lights. 'See yer, Philip,' said Nick making for the pub. 'Git off to yer gran's or we'll cop it.'

'Can I coom wid yer? 'Alf an 'ower?'

'Yer not old enough. Yer eleven.'

'I look more,' said Philip. 'Can I coom wid yer to t' video games, then, Ernie?'

Ernie, who had joined another gang, one of whom had an arm round Ernie's waist, said, 'Garn, Philip, git lost.'

'Oh, garn, Ernie.'

' 'Ow mooch money yer got?'

'Four pound.'

'OK then. Cost yer three.'

Philip handed over three pound coins and accompanied Ernie and his consorts into the arcade. Nick had already disappeared.

At first he let himself drown in the glory of the place, the glitter, the pulse and blood glare of the lights, the filthy floor, the robotic seducers bleeping and flashing, the tremendous satisfaction of the tin music, the shouts and laughs of the clientele. He drifted about, wondering which machine he should honour with his pound. Out of sight, he heard Ernie's gang manning the video games and went to find them. Ernie was in thrall to a naked woman with bared teeth who was surging towards him down a mountain side, whirling a whip. He seemed enchanted, and when the screen went blank said, ' 'ere, Phil, gi's yer pound.'

'I can't,' said Philip. 'I need it.'

'Yer'll just wairst un. Gi's 'ere.'

'Nope,' said Philip, 'I'm not mad 'bout video games,' and he slid off down an aisle to the fruit machines where some of Ernie's mates were trading in Es. A small white pill changed hands for fifteen pounds.

'D'yer want one?'

'What's it do?'

'Yer'll never 'ave lived, mate.'

'If you've any magic mushrooms, I'd like a go at them.'

'I can't 'elp yer but I know a man as can. Seven pound. Mind, they make t'sky bleed.'

'Yuck.'

' 'S great, a great bleedin' sky.'

'I'm putting me last pound int fruit machine, so belt up.'

'Silly fool,' said Ernie coming up. 'That un's a dood. I'd 'ave tellt thee.'

'No, it certainly is not,' said Philip, in excitement turning back to his native tongue. Concentrating, he willed the machine to be his slave. *I'll bloody well, bloody well . . .* he thought. *I'll will the best thing there is on this earth. I'll spend all the cash on it.* In his trouser pocket – which was still his school trouser pocket, as Jocasta had gone to bed with a headache and forgotten to make him change – he felt the present he'd bought for Faith in Whitby in the lunch hour. It was a photograph frame. He'd thought she could put a picture of Holly in it for later on when all the people who'd known Holly were dead. It would be important. He'd have liked a picture of his own father, but Jocasta you couldn't ask. He must be dead. A lot of people seemed to die before Philip had had the chance of . . . He wasn't mad on people dying.

Fastening the fingers of one hand round the edge of the frame, he thought intensely of the child on the altar with its arms spread out and swung down the lever on the machine with force.

Ernie was still saying, 'Well, there goes a fuckin' pound if ever,' when, with a gaping metallic vomiting, money began to shower from the machine all over the floor.

The Ernie brigade were there like pups round a dish of meat and Philip in the middle of them, kicking and punching. A fight began, at first rather merrily, then with just a suggestion in the satanic dark of an intermittent flash of something in someone's hand that clicked open. It came closer, but then Philip felt himself taken by the shoulder. He was pulled away and outside, on to the promenade.

It was a kindly-looking man in a tweed jacket and rather unusual shiny black trousers and trainers. Having hauled Philip away, he at once let go of him, most politely. 'Bad types in there, lad,' he said. 'You don't want anything in those places. Where's your parents?'

'They're somewhere about.'

'You weren't alone in there, then?'

Philip thought of dastardly Ernie. He and his lot had got most of the money and were still fighting.

'That wasn't your brother, was it? With the gold earring and no hair?'

'They're all gold earring and no hair,' said Philip in standard English to match the man's. 'That's Ernie's gang. Nick's lot, not so often, but he's in the pub somewhere.'

'You have two very poor sorts of brother,' said the man.

'They're not my brothers,' said Philip. 'They are *not* my brothers. I have no brothers. I have one sister. Ern and Nick work for my stepfather. They're just looking after me until I go to my gran. I'd better get on there now, by myself. I don't need them at all.'

'Fish and chips?' said the man. 'There's a good chippie down Nelson Street.'

'OK. I can pay,' said Philip. 'I got quite a bit of that off the floor.'

'Wouldn't dream of it,' said the man. 'My invitation. Come on now, and then I'll walk you to the grandparents.'

It was a caff, not just a take-away, and the tables were a cheerful red. The sauce bottles were warm brown with gunge round the tops and the salt cellars were made to look like tomatoes. There were ceramic vases with imitation pink chrysanthemums in them and good loud music. The crackle and swish of the hot fat rose and fell excitingly as the chef, who was unclothed from the waist up and had a towel round his neck like a boxer, swirled about in the vats with a long ladle. A huge plate of golden fish and chips was slapped down in front of Philip.

'Aren't you having some?'

'I have already dined,' said the man.

Philip thought that 'dined' was the sort of thing Jack might say. Or dear old Holly. Must be OK.

'Eat up,' said the man, leaning easily back. 'Then I can take you home or they'll be worrying. Where do the grandparents live?'

Philip was airing fish on the end of his fork. 'It's too hot. I can't eat it any faster.'

The man stared intently.

'They live – oh, quite near.' He couldn't for the life of him remember.

'How near?' The man was leaning forward now. 'Take your time,' he said, watching Philip. 'Your glasses are getting steamed up. You ought to take them off. I'll look after them for you if you like.' He seemed to be trying to find a pocket. Philip removed his glasses but put them in his own pocket, where they rattled against the photograph frame. It seemed to have got broken, he thought, either in the amusement palace or in the sea. As he took his hand away from the shambles within, still airing fish on his fork with the other one, he felt it taken in a vice-like grip under the table and directed towards the shiny stuff of the man's trousers. There it was pressed against something hard and slippery and hot.

Philip dropped his fork, picked up the plate of fish and chips one-handed and slapped it unerringly and equally hard in the man's face. The man's scream was still going on as Philip reached the street outside.

He fled down the back street beside the fish shop and on to the high street where there were plenty of people about. He tore through the pedestrian precinct full of well-lit shops all selling refrigerators. As he approached a police station he thought he'd maybe better slow down; then, as the street became shabbier and darker, he began to run again. He felt wet on his leg and thought he would be sick, but coming to a halt under a street light he found that it was only blood. The clinking in his pocket must be broken glass, either the frame or the specs. He tried to drag some of the tangle out and found a smashed frame and a severed leg of the specs and a cracked lens. He thought, *Now I've done it, I can't see. I haven't a clue where I'm at, as they say*, and fancied he heard the man's padding feet behind him.

He began to race on, turning about here and there, on and on over the cobbles of the old side streets, and at the end of one of them saw a stretch of the doleful dark promenade again. He turned and turned again, and ran on. When he found himself this time on the top of a slope leading to the sea he felt very tired.

If I could bloody well read, he thought. *If I could see the street signs. You'd think I'd remember the address. I'd remember if I heard it or could read it. I'd better go in a pub or something and ask. Braithwaite's not all that common a name.* He found, however, that he was frightened of this idea. 'I'm not exactly mad about asking,' he said, aloud.

Two people came stepping in a dignified way out of a building on a corner of the seafront beside him. They had such a look of respectability that Philip, remembering the man, melted in shadow, but one of them, the woman, called out sharply, 'Hello? Hello there?'

He kept quiet, but, miraculously, she then said, 'Philip? I know who that is – it's Philip. Philip Braithwaite, whatever are you doing out by yourself at this time of night? It's nearly nine o'clock. Does Granny know?'

'Not actually,' said Philip.

'I knew you the minute I saw you,' she said. 'I said to Mr Middleditch, "It's Dolly's Philip." I knew you even without your glasses, you don't fool me. Where are your glasses? Good gracious, you're bleeding. And you're wet. Wet through.'

The Middleditches marched him between them through the streets.

'Just leaving the Chamber of Commerce Ladies Night,' shouted Mrs Middleditch through Dolly's letter box. '*Mercifully*. Now open the door, Dolly. We've found Philip and he's pouring with blood.'

– 16 –

Dolly was answering the telephone in the passage as Mrs Middleditch began her assault through the letter box. From the room near the front door where Toots lay, there rose his howls and roars. 'That bloody woman again. Middle of the night. Bring out your dead! Christ, can't she leave us in peace.'

'Just a minute, Jack,' said Dolly on the phone, 'there's someone at the door. Who is it?'

'Could you let us in, Dolly? Now?'

'Yes, I'll just find the key. I'm on the telephone. Yes. Hello, Jack? Yes, Philip's here.'

'I forgot to ring earlier. Just checking.'

'Yes, they've brought him. When shall we be seeing you?'

'Tomorrow. I'll be down in the morning to fetch Philip back.'

'And you'll bring—?'

'Tell you tomorrow. Something about a gummy eye.'

Dolly unlocked the front door, saying, 'Just Jack to see you'd arrived safely, dear. He'd never said you were coming. Oh dear, oh dear.'

'We'll say nothing tonight,' said Mrs Middleditch. 'It's too late tonight. No need for the police, though who knows? If it hadn't been the Chamber of Commerce and I had not been coming out at that particular— Oh, good heavens!'

Toots had put up the volume of his bedside radio so that the News boomed out as it might have been across Las Vegas.

Philip slid past his grandmother and out of sight.

'I'll have to go. Mrs Middleditch. Is Mr Middleditch . . . ? I'd like to give you both a cup of tea but Toots isn't too well. Thank you so very much.'

'I'll be back first thing in the morning. There are some questions. See to the bleeding.'

They departed.

'Bleeding? Oh Lord – whatever –?' Dolly went into Toots's room and tried to make herself heard above the latest stock-market prices, which were reverberating off the walls. Toots lay as in rigor mortis and Philip stood by the fireplace picking bits of glass out of his pocket.

'Philip, dear, oh dear. How *late*! They shouldn't do it. Those awful boys dropping you off this time of night. Whatever's Jack thinking of? No idea . . .'

'And nor has your mother,' said Toots from his catafalque. 'Nor the whole damn lot of them. Down on that bike in the dark. Had you a helmet? No. Eleven years old. Have you done your homework? No. What's the matter with this country? Tell me. What?'

'No discipline,' said Philip.

'No discipline. And skate-boarding.'

'Skate-boarding's over years ago, Toots.'

'Whatever it is now, then. Drugs. Filth. They're selling the stuff open now to anyone, all ages, twenty pounds a time.'

'Fifteen,' said Philip.

'*What*?'

'Don't be so silly, Toots. Philip doesn't know anything about drugs. He's at a private school and he knows we all love him.'

'What's that blood?' asked Toots, eyes still apparently shut, nose raised to the ceiling.

'It's a photo frame. It broke in my pocket. I've sort of twisted my glasses, too. I guess I can't see till they're mended. Just as well I can't read or I'd be getting held back.'

Dolly came to him with TCP and hot water in a pudding basin and some bandages from a Red Cross box they'd kept since the war.

'Funny thing to keep in a pocket,' said Toots, 'a picture frame.'

'It's just a present.'

'Lot of shoplifting going on at the moment,' said Toots.

'Toots! Will you be quiet! Don't listen to him, Philip. He's a silly old man. He wasn't like this once, you know. He was different when I first married him.'

'I didn't nick it, Toots. I bought it for Faith to put Holly in. Have you got one of Holly?'

'Beg your pardon,' said Toots. 'Apologies. But you smell of fish and chips. That could be something of a private matter.'

'Whatever has fish and chips to do with shoplifting? I tell you, Philip, your grandad's not quite right in the head.'

'It could have a bearing,' said Toots. 'Telling the truth. There's no fish-and-chip shop between here and Ellerby Priors. And no picture-frame shops, either.'

'I bought the frame in Whitby at dinner time. And I got a blasting for it at school. There was going to be some sort of welcome ceremony for her – for my sister – they said. Something in church. I thought there'd be presents. Jack was giving her a pound, he'd found.'

'A welcome? Well, bless me, they never said one word to us. You'd think we'd be invited. D'you know, we've never seen her, Philip. Not even a photograph.'

'Oh well, it all fell through in the end. First yes, then no. I just got this idea there might be. They'd said something about me carrying her up and then Jack would take her and show her round the church, but it didn't come off.'

'No bloody discipline. Where did you get the money?'

'For the frame? Oh, I had some. I've been making a bit lately.'

'Now, Philip.' She had bathed the leg, taken away the water, returned with tea and chocolate cake and a hot-water bottle and sat him in an armchair. 'Now, do just be careful what you say. You don't have to pretend with us.'

'No, it's true. I have made a bit. On an investment. Just simple stuff. I invested a pound. Made about fifty. I'm lucky. I lost a bit of it again, well, most of it, but I've a good scheme. It's concentration. Toots, I could tell you how: you just will something very hard, *really* try.'

'Like you do with your reading.' Toots opened an eye and Philip looked into it. They both laughed. Only Toots could refer to the peculiar nature of Philip's dyslexia. Only Toots could say that not one boy in his day, in all his teaching years, had ever had it except for the obvious loonies. 'Maybe I'm a loonie,' Philip usually said. 'You make a good case for yourself,' usually said Toots; 'd'you want to play chess?'

'D'you want to play chess?' he said now.

'No, not tonight,' said Dolly. 'At this time of night Toots is meant to be asleep. You're not playing chess. Philip's had a big day.'

'I wouldn't say that,' said Philip. 'This and that happened. Faith coming and that.'

'Now then,' said Dolly, knees apart. She picked up a sock of Toots's she had been darning. 'Now then, tell us all about her.'

'Truth, mind,' said Toots. Philip glowered at him.

'She's pretty beautiful,' he said, finishing a third piece of cake. 'Very beautiful. She has thick black curls and dark-green eyes. Lovely ears. And she smiles all the time. Her hands cling on to you. When she yawns she's got a pink tongue. Her nose is very pretty, like a lion cub's, soft and flat, and she smells of roses.'

'Roses,' said Dolly. 'I wish they'd called her Rose. Is Andrew very fond of her? However can he bear to leave her?'

'Yes, he seems very keen on her. He's mad about her, I suppose. I expect he's settled a lot of money on her.'

'And is she going to be happy up there, d'you think?'

'Well, she's awfully fond of me.'

'She is?'

'Yes. Actually, I took her out. She was brought to meet me from school. Jocasta and Andrew brought her.'

'Yes,' said Dolly. 'I thought they would bring her. That was nice.'

'And on the way home she cried and Jocasta couldn't cope and Andrew just said, "Pick her up, Philip," so I did and she stopped crying at once. She just looked me straight in the face and smiled at me. She's got lovely teeth.'

'Teeth?' said Dolly. 'But she's not three months yet.'

'She's advanced,' said Philip. 'They say she'll be walking any day. She looks as if she could talk if she set her mind to it. Actually, Andrew said when we got back and I carried her in for tea, he said, "You can see that baby idolises Philip. She has

99

both arms round his neck." '

'Philip . . .' Dolly was grave. But Toots said, 'That'll do, Dolly. Let him be.'

Soon Philip said he might as well go to bed and wandered off to the room they now called his. Dolly went off in her slippers to get him another hot-water bottle and creaked up the steep stairs with it. He lay in his clothes, fast asleep on top of the covers, and Dolly took off his shoes and lifted his legs up and covered them and tucked the hot-water bottle wrapped in an old petticoat of her own well down near his feet. She managed to drag off his zip jacket without waking him, wondering a little about the coins that kept dropping out of it. She noticed that his face was filthy and longed to get a flannel. 'I'm getting hopeless,' she said. 'I see nothing these days.'

'Tomorrow will do,' she said, and sat on the bed beside him for a time, looking at the sharp little face, the red mark of his specs on the bridge of his nose. Still not much more than the face of a baby himself. What a queer idea he had had about the face of a baby! His clothes seemed very damp and there was a breath of salt water about him. And Toots was right. There was a very definite smell of fish and chips.

– 17 –

Pammie woke next morning in her bedroom of chintz and bits of dressing-table silver to the familiar sight of dear old Hugo standing at the window in his schoolboy dressing gown. She was sitting bolt upright in bed staring at him and wondered why. It must have happened before she noticed him and so could not be simple surprise. There flooded in then the dream of – how long? – a second ago, the terrible dream. A dream of the baby, Faith Fox.

'Good Lord, Hugo, you frightened me. What's wrong?'

'Nothing. Beautiful morning. Glad you're awake. It's seven

o'clock.'

'*Seven*? Well, I don't know— Is she crying? The nurse is there. Oh!'

'Grass needs a last cut. I'll tell Sears. Sopping wet. Heavy dew. The baby's gone, Pammie. Back to her own folk. You're not awake.'

'No,' she said. 'Hugo – awful dream. About the baby. I can't remember it.'

'You're done in,' he said. 'I'll get some tea.'

She waited in the sunny room, listening to the comforting sound of cars going down Coombe Hill towards London, Hugo letting Thomasina's dog out on the lawn, the postman's voice admiring the pompon dahlias. It was warm and still. *Home*, she thought. *I am home too. Yesterday. What a day! That baby.*

'Will you be able to make it?' Hugo put the tray of tea down on a table, trembled some into a rosy china cup and tottered across to the bed with it.

'Make what? Lovely tea, Hugo. Make what?'

'The wedding.'

'*Wedding?*'

'The Seton-Fairley wedding. Farnham.'

'My God, no! Not *today*. It can't be. How can I? I've nothing ready, have I? Oh yes, it's back from the cleaners. Oh, *not* today. I *can't*. It's halfway back to where I was.'

'Hardly say that, dear. Under an hour. Car's coming for us at eleven; then we can have a bite somewhere.'

'Oh, I can't go. Out of the question. We'll write later and say it was a bug. I've sent the present – that's all that matters. We hardly planned this.'

'I've had my tails cleaned,' said Hugo, making a noise drinking his tea. 'I like old Seton-Fairley. Must be ninety. Shan't see him again.'

'That's morbid. Oh, great heaven, *Farnham*. Is the water hot?'

In the bath she thought again of Faith Fox, tried to see her face, her strong, stout little body. She had hardly held her. On the journey, giving her the bottle of milk as the nurse had shown her, she had been delighted with herself, delighted with the waving arm that sought and patted her face. The child so good, so quiet. The nurse had said, 'A paragon.' Well, one almost wondered . . . But no. One could see from her eyes there was nothing funny about her. Nothing retarded or queer there. Dear little soul. Just through and through good.

Let's leave it at that, she thought, finding new tights, getting down to her nails among the silver scent bottles. 'Dear little soul. You know I had her for nearly two months just after she was born? *No trouble.*' She was attending Faith Fox's wedding now, Faith Fox the image of Holly but quieter, more perceptive, gentler. Here came Pammie, twenty years on, chatting and edging along towards the reception line-up, towards the white, white lilies of little Faith's bridal bouquet, bridegroom tall, impeccable, his face a haze, but Faith a star, bending down to Pammie. *'Pammie,'* she cries. 'Oh, darling Pammie. She saved my life, you know, when I was born. Just about brought me up.' There stands Thomasina with her smile. Nobody near her.

Old. We'll all be so old by then. Thomasina's boyfriend will be dead and gone and so will Hugo. Wonder what the rest of us will look like. Much the same, I suppose. We've all beaten the flab now. We've all kept our dogs to walk, and our golf. We do our exercises. I don't see myself changing or getting ill. I'll wear the blue thing today. Not my favourite, but I've overdone the yellow lately. I'd have liked yellow somehow for October but the only decent hat is—

The phone rang during breakfast and she thought. *Thomasina. Very thick with the Seton-Fairleys – oh!*

For where was Thomasina? She'd have to be there, old S-F and Herbert being such buddies long ago. Somebody or other godmother to Holly and all that.

So, she thought, *I'll be seeing Thomasina today, will I? Very interesting. I'll stare her out. Stare her down. I can't talk to her. Yes, someone said she was back from Egypt.*

'Any word of Thomasina, Hugo?' she asked as he came from the phone.

'No, it was some nutty fellow talking about potatoes. Had you got the potatoes and he hopes they weren't a trouble.'

'Oh. Oh yes. That's Jack. Andrew's brother.'

'What, ringing from up there?'

'Yes.'

'Bit extravagant this time in the morning, isn't it? Are you all right? I said you were getting ready to go to a wedding, so he rang off. I thought I heard the child crying somewhere, but he didn't seem to be noticing.'

Pammie said, 'I shall have to ring. Not him. Andrew. To see if the baby's all right.'

'Dammit,' said Hugo. 'Damn and blast it, Pammie, it's for Andrew to ring you, all you've done for him. Glad it's all over and this place back to what it was.'

'Yes,' she said.

'Not that I didn't like it,' he said. 'I rather liked the smell.'

'Smell of the baby?'

'Yes. Don't they say it's like new bread, a baby in a house? Pretty woman, the nurse.'

'A lot of clutter,' said Pammie. 'I'm glad it's over.'

'Not picking up Thomasina, are we?' he asked in the car. 'Easy to do.'

'Hugo – I've just asked you if you know where she is. Nobody's seen her since she went off to Egypt with that man.'

'Oh, jolly good,' said Hugo. 'I remember now there was a card from her yesterday, from the North somewhere. Northumberland. "Coming home by stages", or something.'

'It's probably a week old. She'll be home by now and we'll see her today. I hope you'll ignore her, Hugo. Don't let me down by behaving as if nothing's happened. We've all had Thomasina up to here and if she's been in the North and "coming down by stages" you'd think she'd have looked in on her one and only grandchild on the way. I saw a woman just like Thomasina yesterday – as a matter of fact, now I think of it, in a Jaguar – when I was being taken back to the train and I thought for one moment, "It's Thomasina – come to herself again and off to see the baby," but of course it couldn't have been.'

'Why not?' Hugo liked Thomasina. He hadn't been able to keep up with tales of her rampages of bad behaviour and didn't much care about them. He was one of the few people who had found Holly the lesser woman, both manipulative and rather thick.

'Rather thick girl, Holly,' he said now.

'Pull yourself together, Hugo. Holly's dead. You know she is, so don't pretend you're senile.'

'That little Faith,' he said, 'looked like a better bet. Smiling away.'

'Hardly, at two months,' said Pammie, who had been reading a child-development book or two since the summer. 'They don't smile for a long time. It's parental fantasy.'

'Yes, she did,' said Hugo. 'Got hold of your finger like a vice. Tried to eat it. Put it right in her mouth and chewed. Grinned.'

'Hope it wasn't all nicotine, then. When was all this going on? I'm sure I hadn't time to be tootling at the baby. What I'd like is a real rest now. Abroad. About three weeks in Cyprus.'

'We might go to the North for a weekend maybe,' he said, 'when you're not on the Bench. See the set-up there and how the child goes on. I'd rather like it.'

Pammie found then that she only wanted to go north again by herself. She couldn't see Jack and Hugo getting on. There was absolutely nothing religious about Hugo and he'd be hostile to the Tibetans. *Why ever do I want to go back, anyway?* 'I want to be shot of the lot of them and concentrate on the Ladies' Cup,' said Pammie. 'Anyway, if that was Thomasina I saw, she won't be there today. She couldn't possibly get to Farnham by two o'clock.'

– 18 –

A substantial part of Surrey had been put on hold for the Seton-Fairley wedding, to which seven hundred people had been invited. The police had been augmented by special constables, cones had been seconded from several motorways and parking-meter attendants moved in little coveys about the main street, directing cars to the excellently organised car-parking facilities behind the church in the grounds of some organisation that the Seton-Fairleys nationally organised. Strings of penguined middle-class males threaded their way about the churchyard or stood in knots or hurtled wildly through the tombs looking busy and blasé at the same time. Most were pretty mellow after a luncheon laid on at the local, where some of the girls were still running about and squeaking in the queue for the Ladies. Dozens more were making their way to the church in the extraordinary overdressed condition that the occasion demanded – vast hats, tiny miniskirts, long floating velvets, leather, art-deco jewellery, odd waddly shoes with sequins or teetering Sunset Boulevard heels. Others, making quite another statement, had gone for sloppy silk sweaters and skirts and shoulder bags and greasy hair and were ex-girlfriends of the bridegroom. Their purpose in acceptance of the feast was to show him, and the bride, what the hell.

The bride's family was still a quarter of a mile away, in a gleaming house and weedless garden, fortifying themselves with dry sherry and egg sandwiches. The marquee on the lawn for last night's party was empty now, greenish light within, smelling of grass with only yesterday's embattled flower arrangements standing on the last of the trestle tables and folded cloths. The bride was pretending to be bored, the bridesmaids being frisky or cool as the mood took them, the father feeling confident and not half bad-looking, pulling down the points of his silver-grey waistcoat before the mirror. The mother was being anonymous and unruffled. The grandfather in a wheelchair had closed his eyes and a step-grandmother, Madeleine, was walking in the garden.

Cars arrived and took people away. The bride's car waited, beribboned. A little rain fell and everyone groaned. The sun came out and was greeted like the Holy Ghost. Everyone looked gorgeous. *Gorgeous.* From the front door you could hear the bells of the church coming in fits and starts on the breeze across the meadows.

On the bridegroom's side hunting was the big motif, the pages being dressed in hunting pink and awful gobbling hallooing noises issuing from his guests arriving at the church, stepping out of cars, acknowledging one another among the gravestones. Talk was of cubbing. The bridegroom and best man, well known in hunting circles, which now of course included the saboteurs, were nearly struck by eggs as they walked up the church path and there was an exciting rumour that a demo had been planned for the middle of the service. The bride's grandmother, seeing some saboteurs standing rather apart at the church gates, went across to them to make herself pleasant, thinking they were servants or village people. Some of them pressed pamphlets into her hand, which she clutched along with her service sheet.

As tall Fiona in taut cream satin, her colossal backside hidden by her great-grandmother's veil, walked up the aisle, Madeleine found herself, during the first hymn, examining photographs of the bleeding gobbets of dead foxes in the mouths of hounds. She waited anxiously for her stepson to return to the pew after the handing over of the bride so that she could ask him to explain.

But her son was in his own world, smiling in the obligatory way at his wife as he stepped in beside her to the pew, the wife keeping her eyes forward, steady as the Queen. When his stepmother began to flap the fox photographs at him, he ignored her.

She turned then to the row behind and saw through the mass of hats and heads Thomasina and a tall man being hustled in late to a pew with some cousins, the last two seats in the church. 'My dear, *do* look,' she called, flapping the pamphlet. 'Whatever can they be?' A grandson on her right said, 'It's OK, Gran. Forget it,' and tried to turn her round. 'Oh dear, I hope I can,' said Madeleine, quite loudly for such a gentle woman. She looked again at the photographs. 'Quite awful. I hope you'll come and have tea with me soon, my dear.'

People were either ignoring Madeleine or smiling kindly at her. One or two were saying, out of the corner of the mouth, 'The grandmother. A bit gone.'

Thomasina managed but a glacial smile. Thomasina's escort, who looked flushed and stern and not at all at his ease, gave Madeleine a piercing blue stare.

'Good afternoon, Giles,' said Madeleine. 'How lovely, darling. Do you remember Egypt?'

The great concourse rose at this moment like a surging sea to sing O *Worship the King*, and close family were ushered from the front pews towards the vestry to sign the book, Madeleine now sitting beatifically still until someone came to fetch her and lead her off too. She stopped a couple of times on the way to shake hands with the choir and seemed uncertain what to do when she reached the altar, stopping again to smell some flowers.

'Who is that beautiful woman? How does she know my name?' asked the general.

'Some sort of grandmother,' said Thomasina. 'Madeleine. Early Alzheimer's. Or so they say. She's been like it for years. They think she puts it on. Men still go mad for her.'

'I only know the groom's lot.'

'But what did she mean about Egypt?'

'I've no idea.' He cleared his throat and stood yet straighter. Madeleine. The arthritis was no joke today.

'Are you all right?' she whispered in a wife-like voice which enraged him so that he could not reply but turned towards the happy couple, who were now swimming up the aisle with their train of relations behind them. He was relieved to see Goofo, the father of the groom, who gave him a quick and military nod as he passed.

Of the grandmother there was now no sign and he thought that she must have been kept back in the vestry, by some minder perhaps, or taken out by a back door. He did not know whether to be thankful or not.

But looking down he found Madeleine at his side in the pew, carrying a rose she had removed from the arrangement on the font and sliding a grey silk glove under his elbow.

'I'll come out with you, darling,' she said. 'You don't mind, do you, Thomasina? Where are Herbert and beloved Holly? Oh – and isn't there a dear babe?'

The sternness on the face of the general had established itself long before his arrival at the church. On reaching the porch and hearing the first hymn, he had said they should not go in but wait outside and mingle unobtrusively with the rest of the congregation afterwards during the photographs. Thomasina had paid no attention, but swept in. It was two-twenty. She had said they would be late and they were late and she was satisfied. He, who was never late, could not believe that it was he, Giles, who was tiptoeing so prominently down the aisle behind her. Nor could he believe that he had driven three hundred and seventy miles since breakfast after making love to this woman last night.

They had retired to their bedroom at The Priors Meadow Hotel after their long drive from Northumberland and the momentous conversation at the village teashop about Holly and her child. Thomasina, lovely in her country clothes, her hair wound on top of her head in a coil, hair left to begin to grow nonchalantly grey, which only a few women can get away with as an added attraction ('Why should I care? I'm beautiful. I don't need to attract men, for goodness' sake'), was being the perfect companion. Giles knew they were being noticed at The Priors Meadow Hotel that evening as people who were probably somebody, and certainly from the South. He made himself especially courteous to the waitresses though they were not allowing themselves to be generous with their charms. Most of the other guests had already eaten fast and silently and gone off to their bedrooms to remove their shoes and watch their television set. It was a moorland hotel well known for its away-breaks for the middle-aged: dinner at seven, five enormous courses, and all over by ten to eight. The general and Thomasina, eating slowly, found the lights being put out in other parts of the dining-room until their own table held the one remaining lamp. A sturdy waitress, grim of aspect, stood by them with the cheese as they finished their pudding.

'Are we slow?' asked Thomasina. 'I'm so sorry.'

'You're all right.' She insinuated the cheese between them on the cloth. 'But we like to get cleared up. We've a way to go, all of us, to get home. It's five miles over the top.'

'We'll hurry.'

'Tek yer time. Put the cheese you don't eat under the glass bell. It can stay till morning.' She left them, turning off switches around the bar outside. 'I'll leave you the one to see your way,' she shouted through.

'It is ten minutes past eight,' said Giles. 'By God, I know what they mean about another country. I couldn't put up with this. Do you know, when I was stationed at Catterick I went to a village hop and asked a girl to dance and she said, "Take my friend, I'm sweating." '

'There are bad manners everywhere,' said Thomasina. 'Andrew's are perfect. They're quite nice people up here, really, when you get to know them.'

'We are, are we?' said the waitress stamping by again in a gigantic turquoise padded coat. 'Now, don't forget your room key or you'll be in trouble. There's no one on at night but there's a doctor's phone number by the bed that you have to have by law and most folks coming here are old. I'm not bringing you any coffee; it'll only keep you awake.'

'My God,' said Giles, beginning to undress in the anonymous flower-sprigged bedroom. 'I'm beginning to feel like London again. I wish we could get off right after breakfast.'

'I should be going to London tomorrow,' she said. 'Well, Farnham. It's the Seton-Whatsits' wedding. I accepted three months ago.'

He had slid beside her into the bed, had caught her hand, had hauled up his bony old frame on top of her and let it fall bonily down. His other hand was beginning to do daring things, and Thomasina, after the Scottish and Northumbrian nights when she had been inattentive or sleepy and very different from the way she'd been in the Valley of the Kings, was giving promise of renewed interest.

Tired, he thought. *Well, she's no chicken either. It's a long time since she had any of this – utterly good woman that way, I'd think. Golf and so on. Until we met. Made for each other. Beautiful woman, still* – 'Oh God, Thomasina, you smell wonderful.'

'Couldn't get my hair done in time, anyway.'

'What?' he said, falling back exhausted a while later, extremely happy. 'Hair? Hair's perfect.'

'For the wedding. In Farnham. Seton-Fairley.'

On the edge of sleep, his head on her neat breasts, his chin on her rib-cage, his moustache making the rough patch on her skin of which he was becoming rather proud, he sat up.

'Seton-Fairley?'

'School friend's daughter. Herbert's school friend's daughter. Mad on hunting. Farnham. Must get up and wash.'

When she came back to the bedroom – she had put on the trousers of her silk pyjamas and seemed to have tidied her hair – 'Good God,' he said, '*I'm* going!'

'Where?'

'To the Seton-Doings's wedding. I think. She's marrying my ADC's boy.'

'I can't remember who she's . . . But it's Farnham Castle, two o'clock.'

'I'm invited. I accepted. We'll have to go.'

'Darling – *Farnham.* We're on the Yorkshire moors. Have you sent a present?'

'Yes, of course. Tea knives.'

'Well, that's all right. They'll never notice. I have too.'

'What, tea knives?'

'No. A wok.'

'That's not the point. I'm afraid, Thomasina, we'll have to go. Perfectly possible. Five or six hours and we can leave here by eight o'clock.'

'What about clothes?'

'Ah, clothes. Have you something?'

'Well, I haven't a hat.'

'Tell you what, we'll leave at seven and go round by the garrison and I can get my gear and we'll find you a hat of Hilda's.'

'Hilda?'

'My Hilda. My wife.'

Thomasina looked extremely thoughtful. 'You mean,' she said, 'your wife's clothes . . . ?'

He looked ashamed and said, 'Difficult business, disposing. Never know what to do. Would welcome a bit of help on that, actually.'

He got out of bed and put on dressing gown and slippers.

'Giles?'

'Going down to see about the bill.'

'There's no one there. You know there isn't. The lights were all put out.'

He took off the dressing gown and sat on the edge of the bed and thought. 'I'll get it first thing in the morning. Ask for it at seven. We can't leave without breakfast. Now, don't worry. We'll make it. I can't miss it. I was at Alamein with Goofo.'

'Goofo,' she said, and was silent for a long time.

Then as he was beginning to breathe in what sounded like sweet sleep she said, 'Yes, of course we must go. It decides everything. You can't just ignore a wedding you've accepted for. I know people do. The young, mostly. It's a fashion. But we're not . . . And I'll be able to see Faith some other time. Any time. I could get the Teesside shuttle any day of the week; it's a half hour flight.'

He woke at six and padded to the loo, pleased with himself that he could go through nowadays, though he was only just in time this morning. He stretched himself before the bedroom window on his way back. Glorious morning. Heather magnificent. Miles of it. Wonderful dawn. Mist in the valleys.

A smell of heaven floated in, gold October light, sharp clean air. As heady as spring, really. The baby could hardly suffer, being brought up here instead of Surrey. What was it she'd said?

'Thomasina?'

She was asleep.

'Did you . . . last night . . . were you saying something or did I dream it? Are you wanting to see the baby?'

'What?'

'If you are, my dear . . . My dear, if you are – you are wanting to see the baby – no question, we'll see the baby and Holly's husband's people, of course we will. The wedding's nothing.'

'Why ever should I want to . . . ?' She turned from him, eyes shut.

'You said so. Last night. As you were falling asleep.'

'No. I said it settled it. I needn't go. Great excuse, darling, really. It'll be a nice wedding.'

He saw that her face had lost its quiet mask of sleep and now wore another: one of amused weariness.

'I'm afraid we are not going,' he said; 'we are going to see this child.' Then he asked what he had not dared before. 'Thomasina, *why* not? Why are you such a coward?'

Twenty minutes later, swooping out of the bathroom, she called out, 'Giles, I think you'd better hurry up and get the bill if we're to get off before eight. We're never going to do it by two if we have to go round by your house.'

'We don't. We're not going, not to the garrison nor to the wedding. You want to go to Faith. I know you do. Why can't you just *go*? Thomasina, I know what I'm doing. If you don't face what's happened to Holly, if you don't face the fact that Faith is part of Holly—'

'You have no idea what you're talking about,' she said. Her face looked old, her mouth a trap. 'You and your childless wife.'

'A last chance,' he said in the car. 'North or south? This place where Faith has gone is ten minutes away. I've looked it up.'

'I must go to the wedding.'

On the grind south neither of them said much more. Cars and

lorries roared and spun along, nose to tail, three columns. Past road works, accidents, and police cars sitting in side roads waiting to pounce, they drove, jerking and manoeuvring through the costive approaches to London, round London, out of London.

The general's red-brick box of a house seemed to hold no interest for Thomasina. As he dressed for the wedding upstairs she sat downstairs doing her fingernails on the edge of a businesslike oak desk, not looking out of the window where there were playing fields and skin-head soldiers running. The general, immaculate, came down the stairs, holding several hats made of felt and feathers and a plaited and limp pink turban with a gilded brooch. 'I'm afraid Hilda wasn't great on hats,' he said.

Thomasina had walked away to the hall mirror then, taking a silk scarf from round her neck. She wound it round her head and pinned it with her own brooch, whereupon it became a delicate if slightly precarious hat. 'We must go,' she said.

The house was bleak about them. She saw lists pinned up, memos, framed mementoes of a directed life, many photographs of the regiment and a decoration mounted behind glass in a frame in the hall. The Queen's signature. The place she felt suddenly as a trap, an airlock. Who was he – the man she had clung to naked for three weeks of loving nights, three weeks of days when she had delighted in looking so perfect with him, perfect for him? So safe, so adored. But whoever was he?

'Do you love me?' she asked.

It could not have been a worse moment. The general in his morning coat was checking his watch. 'We'll just about make it. Come along. Sorry about poor Hilda's hats.'

She thought, *And how can he possibly know me if he can offer me her hats?*

Better end it, she thought as they tiptoed agonisingly late into the church, she first, smiling her lovely apologetic smile at faces here and there ('Thomasina's here,' whispered old Hugo to Pammie. 'Man she's with looks a bad-tempered cuss.' 'Don't look,' said Pammie) and Giles behind her, chin out like the rock of ages.

Giles stood to attention through the remainder of the service, trying to breathe steadily and become unnoticeable inside the kaleidoscope of colour, the stained glass of the windows, the pink of the bridesmaids and pages, the creamy, foamy mass of the large, smiling bride, the emerald and silver of the vestments, the flowers everywhere – late roses, phloxes, michaelmas daisies, country things – the young men out in force in their gladrags, the urgent, painted girls, clever and silly, self-interested and yet yearning. Long, long lives ahead. He thought of love and youth. Could he really love Thomasina? He hardly knew the woman. *Better end it.*

The old woman in front of them turned round to him – beautiful woman, old as time, quite bats, obviously rather fun though – she turned to him and said, 'Hello, Giles darling. Do you remember Egypt?'

– 19 –

As Thomasina and the general were sitting down at their moorland hotel for their gigantic breakfast at seven o'clock before their long journey of discord to Surrey, ten miles away across the heather Jack was walking in the wet mist of his fields, conversing with God.

At The Priors the view shone and glittered. The heather was rosy, swimming in miles of light like a coating of pink bluebells. Wet sheep stood in its wooden stalks, silvery on the dark deserted moor roads. Larks were plucked up from it like fish on a line, fluttering and spluttering with enthusiasm for the sunlight. Below them the clefts in the moorland were filled up with mist so that the heather seemed broken with white water. These lakes were just beginning to smoke, drawn up like the larks towards the sun.

As the mists drifted upwards, sometimes masking the road

and the sheep and the heather on the ridges for several minutes and leaving things wetter than ever so that the sheep steamed too and the hard patches of road shimmered with mirage, as it all drifted upwards, the valleys emerged brilliantly green. Little round knolls with trees on top cast miles of shadow over farmland and fields. The ragged ruin of The Priory arch stood over Jack's sheds like an elephant above chickens. It held itself nobly, the sun streaming through the stonework to settle on the prefab jumble of shanties Jack had somehow been allowed to build in the cloister. A number of tombstones had been moved to stand near the gatehouse in a cluster, tipping a bit, their shadows behind them.

Jack went in to his tin-can church now and lay face down, arms outstretched, prostrate in the sunlight, thanking God for the wonder of His grace.

Then he went out and unlatched the door of the chicken houses, determinedly not looking towards the Tibetans' quarters. It saddened him to think that Himalayan people could like to stay in bed in the morning. He had hoped his folded moors might have enlivened them. They were after all mountain folk who would probably never see their own land again. He was having difficulty, more each day, in getting the Tibetans to work in the fields and hoe the late vegetables, which tasks had been part of the deal of their coming. The weather was so warm compared with Lhasa's, the air so easy, and the conditions of life he considered so close to God they ought to bring healing. Jack was the last person to make anyone work any harder. Jocasta in the handicraft and artistic department of The Priors had much more success with the women at the looms. Slowly cloth was beginning to be dyed as they had seen it in Darjeeling on their honeymoon visit to the Tibetan Centre there. Jack tried not to be jealous of Jocasta and was pleased that the newest tenants at The Priors seemed contented enough. He loved to hear the drone of meditation and music coming from the sheds and found that it more than made up for the amount the Tibetans ate and their passion for confectionery. Seven pounds of Cadbury's chocolate fingers and three of chocolate wheatmeal had been consumed in a month. But the perpetual political discussion and rowdy quarrels among the younger ones, all conducted in Liverpool accents, rather disappointed him and the late leek crop went unplanted. He was glad when the two Tibetan men suddenly packed off.

But about the Tibetans' attendance once a day for worship in The Priory he was adamant. He did not care if they conducted their own meditations but he insisted that an hour of worship in the interpretation of God's name must be undertaken. He had assumed that this would come easily to Buddhists and left them to it and they did turn up more or less every day. But in the matter of weeding they needed instruction and they did not present themselves for that. The Smikes, who had been undergoing intermittent instruction for three years, were still not distinguished hoers and the rest of the staff at The Priors were all overworked already with cooking and laundry and teaching and keeping the shabby place going.

Oh, thought Jack, *if Andrew could only stay here a while, it would not only help The Priors but calm him, the poor guy.* He would have liked to work beside Andrew in the fields, two brothers hoeing together in a biblical sort of way. He hardly knew Andrew now, but it was Andrew who had brought him Jocasta, his dark jewel, his strange princess. And, of course, Philip. Thinking of Philip, Jack paused in the shed where he was trying to find a sickle in an unholy clutter of tools. He was unable to get anywhere near Philip, and Jocasta wouldn't speak of him.

I ought to be able to imagine, he thought. *I ought to be able to feel close to Philip. I ought not to expect him at eleven years old to be helpful in the fields, with his school work to do. They say he's very clever, though I must say his handwriting doesn't suggest it. We don't know what sort of life he's had. Jocasta will never say. Pretty rough, I dare say. No spiritual guidance. Jocasta keeps her counsel about Belief. It was God directed Andrew here. Andrew is a good man – fine doctor. To try to help Jocasta he brought her here to me. She was only one patient among many. A routine operation, he said. I never heard exactly what.*

And now Jocasta was his. His own, his one love, his great love before God. It was wonderful of her that she never let him say so.

And her celibacy. So magnificent. He began to hoe, edging cruelly and expertly round the carrots, destroying weeds, worms, creatures of all kinds – and that must be the reason for the Buddhists refusing to work, now he came to think of it. The celibacy was hard on him, he had to say. He felt deprived, though he prayed nightly for patience. He would love to have a child. God had not yet answered him.

At eight o'clock he left the fields and returned to The Priors, where nobody much was about except hens. He found that the eggs had not yet been gathered, filled his pockets with them and cradled the rest in his hands. In the kitchen The Missus was standing over a pan of porridge. He filled a kettle (she was in one of her remote moods) and made coffee for himself. He said, 'Maybe Philip would like an egg.'

'Philip,' she said, 'as I'd have expected you to remember, is not here. He's down Teesside with his grandparents, so-called. Oh yes, and The Smikes didn't come home.'

'I'd forgotten,' said Jack, smiling at something through the window. 'And where is the baby?'

'The Tibetans came for her early. They're good with her. She seems to love them.'

'I'll walk across,' he said. 'Andrew's taking her down to see Toots and my mother today. Exciting moment. I wish I had time to be there with them.'

The Missus said, 'She's not looking her best. Her eye's inflamed. Her granny won't think a lot of that.'

But Jack was not listening. He had seen Jocasta walking across the scruffy cloister wrapped in a purple shawl, and forgot all else. He went out to her and brought her in.

− 20 −

'Dolly,' bellowed Toots. 'Dolly? Where are you? Can't you hear me, Dolly?'

Bumps from the bedroom above. Complaints and sighs. 'I'm coming. Whatever is it?'

'Door bell.'

'Door bell? Whatever—? Half past six in the morning? You're dreaming.'

'Door *bell*.' (It rang piercingly.)

'You'll wake Philip. For heaven's sake, be quiet. On and on.'

She was downstairs and peering from his bedsit window without her teeth in, her hair long and grey, the ghastly old coat again in play. 'I shan't answer it. This time in the morning you never know. It might be burglars. Oh, good gracious me, it's The Smikes. Now what in the world . . . ?'

Ernie and Nick trailed in and were summoned by Toots to stand before him, side by side at the bottom of his bed. 'Great Scot,' said Toots. 'Strike a light. The riffraff of England.'

'I'll make some tea,' said Dolly. 'You both look worn out.'

'Not with any work they've been doing. Give me back twenty years and a good leg, I'd have the pair of you up on that farm knocking weeds down a penny-piece a row *and* cleaning up that filthy yard. Days off all the time. Eating your heads off like you were still in prison. It's the hard world now, boys. They ought to bring back hanging.'

All four began to drink from teacups, Dolly giving no countenance to mugs. For a while she was coming and going with half slices of buttered toast.

'I'm sorry there's no marmalade. At least there is, but it's only Silver Shred. Mrs Middleditch got it for us but it'll have to go back. If either of you two is going past the supermarket you might change it for me. I'll wrap it up. I like a dark marmalade

118

but not that awful stuff with whisky in it.'

'Dolly, will you shut up about marmalade. Just sit down and look at this filth. Come on. Let's hear why you're here.'

The Smikes stood pale and dirty in slept-in clothes.

'Come on. Where did you spend the night? Truth, now.'

'In a boat ont prom. Under t'covers.'

'Why aren't you at Jack's? There's acres of experimental courgettes—'

'Night off,' said Ernie.

'Bike wouldn't start back,' said Nick. 'Full of sea water.'

'Sea water? Great Scot. My godfathers!'

'Sidecar coom off. Philip was bashin' it. It ran into t' sea.'

'Philip never said a thing about it.'

They looked more alert. 'Hast seen 'im?'

'Well, he's in bed upstairs, dead to the world. Arrived here about nine o'clock.'

'Nine twenty-one,' said Toots. 'So he was with you, then? I thought as much. Stinking of grease and chips.'

Nick and Ernie appeared to relax. Ernie sat down on the bed and Nick switched on the electric fire and began to rub the bit of his back between the shoulder blades against the mantelpiece.

'OK, then, was 'e?'

'We don't know what he is until he's awake. Mrs Middleditch found him wandering and brought him here and he's asleep. He was off soon as look at you, in all his clothes. I couldn't get him into night clothes. Why ever didn't you drop him off, Nick, on your way down? If Jack finds out . . .'

This thought seemed to hold no terror for The Smikes. Ernie asked Toots for a fag. Toots said no, pointed to two upright chairs beside a clothes airer Dolly was setting up, and glared. 'Sit,' he commanded. 'The pair of you. You're no better than dogs.'

'I taught you,' he said. 'In my time. In my C stream. My boys. Gallows fodder. It's looking at the likes of you breaks my heart, lying here. Whatever good did I do? Forty years a teacher. Gold earrings, long hair, skinheads. What's going to win the 2.30 at Doncaster, then?'

'Gold Flake,' said Ernie.

'Heart o' Day,' said Nick.

'Get away with the pair of you,' said Toots. 'Nicholas Nickleby. Dead cert. Put me a fiver on it.'

'Toots?' said Dolly.

'Gi's the fiver, Toots,' said Nick, who was undoing his jeans to reveal a wallet stuffed with notes.

'You'll get no cut on this,' said Toots. 'You didn't look after Philip. We know he's no joke to look after but it's no excuse. You've been lads on your own yourselves. Philip's a lad alone. I've no use for you.'

'Get on,' said Nick. 'Philip's got 'undreds round 'im.'

'And would you have been suited brought up up there, then? Sermons and Tibetans?'

'It's good for a laugh,' said Ernie.

'Oh, 'e'll be OK,' said Nick. 'We stick it out, don't we?'

'We've given Jack every loyalty,' said Ernie suddenly lapsing into radio-speak, quite emotionally. 'We support Jack all the way. Jack 'as nowt to complain of in us. 'E's a nutter but 'e's OK. 'E'll do. I reckon 'e needs us to keep in touch with everyday life. I'm a Nationalist meself and I don't see what we need with foreign 'omeless. We're pretty near 'omeless, us two, ant we? Nick and me? It's us 'e ought to be putting first. But we're all like 'is children, Jack. 'E's OK.'

'He has a child now,' said Dolly. 'The baby. Is she nice? I've done you both a bit of bacon. Tell me about little Faith. We haven't seen her yet.'

'She's OK,' said Nick.

'Now, Nick, I asked what is she like.'

The Smikes pondered and looked into their hearts. Nick saw the buggy tray, a bundle strapped across it. Ernie saw a hump in the folds of the Tibetan woman's anorak, the Tibetan woman glaring as she marched away with the hump towards her own domain. 'She's great,' said Ernie. 'Comfortable.'

'Comfortable is not what you call a baby you've never seen before. Who's she like? Not like Toots, I hope.'

'She's more like thee, Dolly,' said Nick, surprisingly. He wiped off his plate with bread and tossed the plate empty on

Toots's bed. 'She's bonny.'

'Blue eyes, I suppose?'

'Oh aye, blue eyes. One of them's all gummed up, they were saying. They were saying they'd have to take her to 'ospital.'

'No! Oh dear. Well, it does happen. Mind, it never happened to either of mine. It's all in the washing powder and the cotton wool you use. And clean hands.'

'The Tibetans is looking after 'er.'

'Smear themselves in rancid butter?' asked Toots.

'Be careful, Toots; that's racial,' said Dolly. 'I've just seen Mrs Middleditch coming.'

'We'll be off, then.' Ernie and Nick rose as one man.

'Don't you want to see Philip?'

'Naah,' said The Smikes together. 'Tell 'im: see yer,' said Nick.

They melted from the room, down the passage, out at the back door and across the cement yard. They knew their way around this house as they knew their way round a number of houses in various parts of the Tees estuary, and perfectly well in the dark. From Toots and Dolly's house, though, they had never lifted a thing, and nor would they, ever.

− 21 −

Suppose yourself a gargoyle or perhaps a bird, or a very small photographer hanging in the basket of a very small balloon up in the vaulted shadows of the roof of the great hall of Farnham Castle on the occasion of the reception for the Seton-Fairley wedding. You will find yourself looking down on a carpet of constantly blowing flowers planted tight from wall to wall. Floating up to you there will be echoing, yapping waves of celebration growing louder and shriller as time goes by. More flowers are constantly cramming themselves through the great doorway of the hall, weaving into the throng like a stream merging into the sea, disappearing at last into the general movement of the tide. There is a serpentine pattern among the flower-heads of coloured chiffon and straw and velvet. They press forward towards a border of alternate black and coloured flowers standing in a row on an underplanting of red carpet. The stream of purples and pinks and greens and yellows and black-and-whites and heliotropes sways up to this little line of the knot garden. Each flower-head bends towards another along the line and then withdraws as in a dance. The little shrieks and exclamations that arise from the line are more perilous and fragile than elsewhere. The glitter of glass, the popping noises like pistols in the corn here and there about the hall, make the flower heads nod and toss a little faster. The feeling now grows gayer. The flowers grow dense as cloth, a tapestry of tight stitches. The music begins.

Stay up there in the rafters for comfort, for Farnham Castle is not one of the great castles of the world and seven hundred flower-heads is its capacity. More than its capacity. Or, if you must – swoop down. Down you go, down and down, and you are standing close, so close up against the backs and fronts and heads and hats, angling your own head so that the domed fronts of men and the brims and chins of women don't get in your eye or sweep your drink from your hand.

And watch out for your feet or they will be trodden to bits by the unseen army of shoes below. Close your eyes against the cigarette lit up beside your left eyeball, tilt your head back against the teeth of mouths laughing. To survive, light a fag yourself, swig down some champagne (it isn't sparkling wine) and start making little screams and signals of your own to anyone, anywhere. 'Aren't you ———?' 'I'm ———' (whoever you are). 'But I'm *sure* you are.' 'Wherever was it we –?' '*Years* ago.' 'How lovely!' 'And how is Deirdre, Angela, Sydonia, Humphrey, dear old Miles?' 'Dead – oh, I'm so sorry.' 'So sorry, darling.' And so on.

There were two considerations at the Seton-Fairley wedding that were of prime importance to both families: one, that the reception should be held in the Castle to show that each side could feel they had rank and, two, that there should be the utter maximum number of guests, three hundred and fifty a side, and all of them closely interwoven to prove level pegging in the social register.

With seven hundred, it is possible that you will not get anywhere near a soul you know. In the depths of the seething flowery streams it occurred even to Pammie (who knows most of the world) that she and Hugo might attend and leave the reception never having seen a familiar face except for the bridal line-up, assuming they should ever reach the bridal line-up. Hugo hoped at most to get a word up there with old Puffy, though even that depended on whether old Puffy could still stand up. He'd been a bit shaky at his retirement and that was twenty years ago.

And Hugo himself wasn't looking too good, thought Pammie. How was she to get him somewhere to sit down? A drink? A canapé? (No food to speak of at this do; who but Christ could feed seven hundred cheek to cheek?)

'Hugo, my love,' said Pammie, 'keep round the edges. There's a thin place here. Stand in it. Don't move until I get someone to find you a chair,' and she stood him beside some silent and unintroduced people all wondering what to say to one another, waiting for alcohol, smiling tightly. She turned away and battled out of sight, the crowd closing behind her.

But Hugo had his stick and leaned on it, and smiled and waited and soon found himself taken up in some undertow and drawn with the silent companions towards the happy couple standing on the red carpet. As he was moved nearer the line he found he couldn't remember who the hell any of them were at this awful bloody wedding, and to get over the fright of this he concentrated on someone in the line who was delivering a top-speed rundown into the ear of the woman on his right, describing all who approached.

'Very old friend of family, second cousin or so over from Singapore, Daisy's aunt, old family retainer, Rosie very nice, not sure of the one on the stick, Thomasina Fox coming next but three, old Herbert's widow, lost her daughter, bit of a mystery about a baby, didn't expect her . . .'

Hugo nodded and mumbled his way along the line, nobody

knowing who he was, which rather pleased him, until he came to Puffy in a wheelchair at the end.

Puffy was looking broad and remote with bloodshot blue eyes and white moustache. He was leaning back, abstracted, like a Viking plotting murder and pillage.

'Great day, Puffy,' said Hugo.

'Got a drink, Hugo?'

'All in good time.'

'Ha!'

Hugo passed along, content, and then stood about waiting for Thomasina. As she fell away from the line he put out both his arms, stick or no, in an attempt to embrace her. But she seemed distracted. For a moment she didn't even seem to recognise him. *She looks haunted*, he thought. *Bags under the eyes. And whatever has she got on her head? Looks like a rag, and it's coming undone.*

'My Thomas*ina*!'

She looked at him, the famous smile forgotten, and he thought, *By God, she's in a mess*, and he took her lean arm and tried to lead her away. She said nothing when they had to stop in the crush, only glared at him. Hugo remembered something of Pammie's about not speaking to her. He hadn't the faintest idea what to do next and the glare began to put him off balance. He prodded his stick into the ancient slabs of the floor, grabbed two drinks from a passing tray, passed one to Thomasina and looked desperately round. There was an old silk shoulder nearby so he grabbed it and turned it towards him. 'Hello. Hello – Hugo Jefford. You remember me? I wonder if you know my friend Thomasina Fox? Er?' and Madeleine, turning round, smiled at Thomasina and held out her hand.

Standing like a quiet queen, Madeleine said, 'My dear, I think we might escape from here, don't you? I was thinking of baked beans. I had no lunch but egg sandwiches. We could find a café somewhere?'

Old Hugo, roaring with bewildered laughter, backed away and disappeared with relief into the mêlée and Thomasina

124

tried to do the same.

'No, no, but I mean it,' said Madeleine. 'It is so important. I've been trying to keep you in view since the church. To tell you about *Giles*. So important.'

She smiled once to left and once to right, touched an arm or two, and took Thomasina's hand. She then led her graciously away, a passage opening up for them. Somebody bossy, some sort of grandchild, tried to suggest otherwise, but Madeleine ruffled its hair with her free hand and passed on.

Thomasina, following, looked back to see if Giles's head was in sight. It usually stood above other heads like a king palm tree, but it was not there. She thought, *He's gone, then. He's left me. I thought so.*

Madeleine was disappearing into a Rolls-Royce and Thomasina followed. The car swooped off in the direction of the town centre.

'A side street,' said Madeleine to the chauffeur, 'we want a side street, and a snack bar will do nicely. Though we're really after baked beans. We're famished.'

The chauffeur looked in his mirror and then away and the car slid down various alleys and stopped outside something called The Sulawesi Johnnie. 'How delightful,' said Madeleine. 'Sauce bottles on all the tables. Now away you go back and thank you so much. I hope you haven't long to wait for whoever's chauffeur you are, but I expect you will have. I suppose you wouldn't care to join us? No – well, I'm not surprised at that either, two old bats like us. Come along, Thomasina.'

– 22 –

Jack was out again with the hoe, his shadow still behind him, the ground still white with dew that looked like snow, and it was all of half an hour after dawn. With every shove of the blade he said, *Jocasta*. He had stopped praying. *Jocasta, Jocasta*, said his mind's voice. For she had come across the cloister and into the kitchen and her purple shawl had fallen round her feet and she had put her arms around him. She reached nowhere near his shoulder and her head was sideways against his heart. She had said nothing but had held him and held him, and he had said, 'Jocasta, Jocasta.'

The Missus at the porridge pot had pursed up her mouth and said, after a wonderfully long moment, 'Well, it's ready. If you're coming for it, that is.' She hadn't liked looking at them standing together as he had buried his face in Jocasta's hair and said, 'Jocasta, Jocasta.' The Missus hadn't known where to look. 'Shameless. And they don't sleep together. You know that, don't you? No, they don't. Him soon as not kipping down anywhere, in the church all night sometimes. Off his rocker, poor old Jack. So funny, Andrew every inch the proper doctor. Never think they were brothers.' The Missus had been a mill girl in Lancashire. Her life now was Jack. She had accompanied him on the last disastrous venture, of which nobody spoke. She was old, vain, plain, and knew it, but The Priors revolved around her because of her unique talent for creating a feeling of guilt in anybody who crossed her path. 'I am old and weak and my life is done but I have run a spotless course. See thou doest likewise,' said every pore and nerve-ending of The Missus. To see Jack and Jocasta standing as one being a few feet from her, Jack breathing deep into Jocasta's hair – it was unknown. It was indecent. Jocasta was doing it to disgust. Jack was of course oblivious.

Jocasta released her husband and went away and Jack sat and ate The Missus's porridge, his face alight with contentment. He smiled at The Missus when she said there'd be no bacon for anyone else if the Tibetans were to have any. The kitchen, the courtyard, the chickens scratching in the tombstones, the throb of music and some shouting from the Tibetan quarters in the early winter sunshine – it was like the first morning of the world. Jack was sure now, unequivocally, that The Priors was the guiding light that God had instructed him to build in a heathen and poisonous world.

Andrew came in and sat down to wait for his bacon and eggs and Jack saw in him a man of sorrows. No wife would come over to him and wordlessly take him in her arms, trustingly, not caring who saw, not needing even to speak any endearment because they were one, one person. Oh poor Jack, poor bright Holly. How could he bear being without her? Much less than half the purpose of his life must remain to him. Holly so strong and vivid and indestructible. And not a sign of self-pity in Andrew. Not a flicker.

'Andrew,' he said, 'I think we should say a prayer.'

'What *now*?'

'Now. A prayer for Holly.'

'I'm off to see if there's more bacon,' said The Missus and Andrew said, 'Sorry, Jack, I'm off to Toots and Dolly.'

'But it's not eight o'clock in the morning. They'll hardly be up.'

'I have to drop in at the hospital in Middlesbrough with Faith. Someone ought to see to her eye.' But he put a hand on Jack's shoulder as he passed him to pour himself tea.

'I said that about her eye two days ago,' said The Missus, slapping down burnt bacon on the table before Jack, who looked at it vaguely. 'Nobody deigns to listen to me.'

'I did. I am,' said Andrew.

'I was one of a large family,' said The Missus.

'And I'm a doctor. There's a test they can do on the eye. Sometimes it's just a blocked tear duct but sometimes not. She would be kept in overnight and back by Monday.'

'Not round here, she wouldn't,' said The Missus. 'There won't be a bed for six months and by then the eye will have cleared itself.'

'I'll get her in,' said Andrew.

'You won't. That doesn't do up here. You're not in your own place south now. Say you're a doctor and you're back of the queue. Not that that's so dreadful. I never found doctors so wonderful. I helped with me mam. Could do the lot – break the waters, untie the cord round the neck. Minute it gets tricky it's "Shall I leave it to the nurse?" That was doctors. Not that I'd speak against the profession publicly. I know my place. Oh yes. But I could massage that eye right with my thumb in ten minutes.'

'And damage the nerve and give her a squint for life. No thanks. I'm taking her down there and then I'll go on and pick up Philip from Toots and Dolly. I'll take Jocasta with me, OK, Jack? Might take her along the beach a bit. Leave the baby for Toots and Dolly to google over for a bit.'

'She's somewhere near,' said Jack, 'she's just left. Take her by all means. Jocasta gets little enough time away. She needs a change.'

Eating toast fast, not looking at Jack, Andrew said, 'Great. We'll be back by lunchtime, then.'

So Jack went back into the field, moving slowly, step by step, down the courgettes. He stopped once or twice to reflect. Once, he picked the pale-primrose trumpet of a flower. He ate it slowly to the last stamen and looked up at the sky. His life was together at last. New year, perhaps a child?

– 23 –

When The Smikes had left and Mrs Middleditch had also departed, carrying an armful of Toots's washing up the street and leaving an atmosphere behind her, Dolly began preparations for the visit of her widowed son and grandchild by draping Toots's best clothes over various pieces of furniture and switching on a second bar of the electric fire to make sure all would be properly aired. Long woollen leggings which he called his knickers and a long-sleeved woollen shirt that would go over the long-sleeved woollen vest he wore in bed and changed on Saturdays were spread across the armchair. Clean socks were put side by side on his bed table and his suit and braces laid across the sideboard with a clothes brush beside them. A new red tie hung round the clock on the mantelpiece. Dolly then came hobbling from the kitchen with beautifully polished black shoes, one of them with a built-up heel. She moved the bed table away from the bed, turned back the bedclothes and brought the walking frame up beside him.

She watched him heave himself over and out and his pyjama trousers fall down round his ankles as they did every morning. She walked behind him down the passage, holding them up. He said, as he did every morning as he led this procession of two, 'Give over. Let them drop. I'll step out of them,' and she said, 'There are some standards you don't let go,' and why couldn't he take the time to fasten the cord? And he said, 'Not worth it just for down the passage.' It was their morning refrain, their matins.

In the invalid bathroom built out on the draughty extension to the kitchen where there had once been a maid and a charwoman under Dolly's eye, she opened the door of the plastic bath as he stepped from the trousers. She helped him out of the pyjama jacket and vest and steadied his shrivelled body on its thin shanks through the little door. She held him as he lowered his thin old bottom on to the bath seat. She ran the water carefully, the cold with the hot, squeezed it warmly over him and soaped all down his back, remembering it when it was young, its muscles like ropes. He'd had hardness and glow to him then. He sat hunched forward now, munching on nothing, staring at nothing, hating the feel of her hands on him. 'It's work for a nurse, this,' he said, the daily introit, and she said, 'Don't be so silly. You'd do it for me.'

He knew he wouldn't. He could never wash an old woman. He knew too that she knew he didn't dislike every aspect of this bathing and soaping. The once irascible, fierce, invincible Toots had discovered that he liked to accept care, as babies accept.

'Well,' he said, 'they'll be on their way.'

She rinsed him with an old sponge they'd long ago brought from Greece. 'Give me that flannel,' he said. 'You're not doing down there.'

'They may well be,' she said. 'There's a lot to do, so get out. You've to shave yet.' She dried him, helped him into his dressing gown with protecting arms and sat him on a cork

129

stool before a mirror that came out like a fake boxing glove on a metal spring, but he couldn't see to shave himself.

'Put your glasses on,' said Dolly.

'I can't get the enthusiasm,' he said, 'when I see the problem. Looks a lot better blurred.'

'Blurred, it looks like an old tramp,' she said. 'Like this designer stubble. Like that Nick.'

'Give us the razor here, then. That's a good point you made.'

There was the ritual drying of the face, the combing of long-gone hair, the procession back to the bedroom, the slow sacrament of dressing. He heaved himself into the Windsor chair with a table in front of him as she toiled about making the bed, hauling at a heavy cover that was meant to make it look like a divan. She came and went with the night bottle and then hid it in a drawer. She knelt before him to ease on the shining shoes. She tied their laces. 'I could do with my coffee,' he said, and she said, 'Well, you can wait till I've dusted and hoovered round.'

'The brasses could do with a rub.'

'They were done yesterday.'

'There's no fruit in that bowl.'

'I'm opening a window before I'm fussing with fruit. The smell in here's disgusting. That's what comes of sleeping where you live all day. We should be out of this house and in care.'

'Living up at Jack's, you mean?' said Toots. They gave each other a glance of understanding and agreement. 'That Jocasta having us sit making cut-outs,' said Toots. 'Like a snake she sits.'

'I don't see what snakes have to do with it.'

'Where you going to set down this baby when they get themselves here?' he asked her. 'Clear a space now some-where.'

'We'll put her on the end of the bed.'

'Well, mind you sit yourself in the upright chair for him to pass her over to you. That other one's far too low and you'll drop her.'

'He's a doctor, Toots: he knows.'

'I'm not going to hold her, mind. I'm not strong enough. I'm 'not well up in babies anyway. I'll be standing back today.'

'You know you'll hold her, given the chance. You know you've always loved babies.'

'Can't stand them,' he said. 'Is that the gate?'

'They can't be here yet,' said Dolly. 'I'll get your coffee and your pills. I might just put the dinner on. He may stay.'

'By God, I should hope he does stay. Not seen him in a year and him widowed and a father and you say will he be staying for his dinner. By God, I'd not be suited if he didn't stay on till after his tea. There's no question about it. I'd take it very badly if he didn't stay.'

'Well, she may not settle, Toots. She may cry. She's unlikely to be settled up here yet and there's this gummy eye. He may want to get her home.'

'What, to yon rural slum? She'd be better off here for cleanliness. Have you looked at Philip?'

Dolly pulled herself once more up the narrow staircase with the scarlet and blue turkey carpet and the polished brass stair rods and examined all she could see of Philip, which was a tuft of hair and a bundle of clothes. She had something for gummy eyes somewhere and began to rustle about in cupboards. She gathered up some glass baby bottles she had put out already and came step by step downstairs again with them. She submerged the bottles and ancient teats in boiling water for a good long sterilisation, then creaked upstairs again for the baby clothes she'd been gathering up from church bazaars for a year, ever since she'd heard that Holly was pregnant. They were in layers of tissue paper on top of her own lavender-smelling underwear. Very pretty. She came awkwardly down the stairs again clutching them with some old toys of Andrew's; a plaster angel to hang over a bed, a mug painted with 1950s sprites, a bone teething ring with a bell on it and a stringy bit of blue ribbon old as the child's father.

'What's that ket?' asked Toots. 'Hello, there's the front door. They're here.'

'Never. I didn't hear the gate. It can't be.'

Nor was it. Only Jocasta came sliding into the room. They hadn't even heard her enter the house. She said, 'Hello, Toots –

Dolly,' and sat sweetly down on the bed with her hands folded, her feet not touching the floor. 'You both look very smart. You must have got up early.'

'Well!' said Dolly. '*Now* then. How lovely!' She always sounded pleased to see people, even if she disliked them. When she saw them in her house she forgot whether or not she disliked them. It was unconscious caution. The gods of hospitality were always on the watch. They could avenge, and Dolly was frightened by her old age. Judgement loomed. Across the room Toots sat on his throne looking ahead into the electric fire, moving his bad ankle up and down against the bar of his walking frame so that it squeaked rhythmically. He waited for Jocasta to wince.

'Can't I go and help him in with her?' said Dolly. 'With the carry-cot? I'll go down to the gate.'

'He couldn't come,' said Jocasta. 'I'm on my own. He's halfway. I left him at the hospital. She has this gummy eye. He sent me on to say he's so sorry but she ought to be looked at straight away. I dropped them both there and I'll pick him up on the way home.'

'She'd to go to *hospital*? With a gummy *eye*?' Dolly's eyes were round.

'They may not take her in. She's had so much excitement, though, the last two days, Andrew thinks she shouldn't be shown around yet.'

After twenty minutes, she left them as quietly as she had arrived and without going up to see Philip. 'I'll leave him for you, Dolly, may I? He loves it here.'

'Well,' said Toots, 'that's something anyway,' and he took off the red silk tie and undid the collar stud.

– 24 –

They sat for some time waiting for the baked beans and a pot of tea, Madeleine touching the forks on the plastic table top, smiling at the salts and peppers. She looked around her once and bowed to someone with severe acne and dressed from head to foot in leathers at the next table. He had a huge hairless head. The open leather jacket showed a gold ring through one of his nipples. He pretended not to see her.

'So sad,' said Madeleine. 'Chemotherapy. It's not necessary to lose your hair now, you know, so long as you see to it that you have the right surgeon.' Turning back to Thomasina she leaned over to her and tucked in a corner of her scarf-hat. 'There,' she said. 'Just the tiniest bit astray.'

Thomasina's hands flew to her head. She said, 'Oh God, I know. It's all I had. Giles and I were on holiday in Yorkshire this morning and we'd quite forgotten the wedding. I'd a dress that would do but no hat.'

'It's charming,' said Madeleine. 'But what about him? Had he the gear?'

The lad in leathers gave her a look and she said, '*Gear*, dear, yes. I'm not an antique.' He rose and left the café.

'We went to get it. To his house. In Berkshire. It's been a long day. Actually . . .'

'Yes?' Madeleine leaned forward with love.

'Actually, when we got there he offered me a hat of his dead wife.'

'Hilda's! Oh my dear, I'm so sorry!'

'It had a pheasant's feather in it.'

'Yes, it would. Oh my darling girl! So it's over, then?'

Thomasina unwound the scarf and shook her hair. She said, 'I'm sorry. I really can't – I can't remember you. I *am* sorry. Maybe we should have had some champagne and then I . . .'

'I wonder if it's licensed here.' Madeleine looked luminously at the girl behind the counter, who said, 'You what?'

'I don't suppose you're licensed? My friend needs a little brandy.' The girl stared. 'No – I'm afraid, quite hopeless,' said Madeleine. 'My dear, you are Thomasina Fox. I don't know you *really* but I know *of* you. Through Pammie Jefford. Now, I have a hopeless memory these days but I'm sure she never told me you'd married dear old Giles.'

'I haven't.'

'Dear child – well, I'm old enough to call you child – *dear* child, I'm so glad. I can talk more freely.'

But she stopped and looked gently round the restaurant, as forlorn a little place on a Saturday afternoon as you could find; the hard bread rolls, the gluey slabs of chrome-yellow flan behind glass, the bag-woman in the corner rustling through newspapers, the two girls all paintwork and thighs leaning their heads towards each other, talking in whispers, the sad young man with a book by the window. 'I always think that Sarajevo must have been like this.'

The baked beans arrived. They looked quite good. The teapot followed. It had strings hanging out of it round the lid, each with a label saying there was a teabag on the other end. Madeleine asked for some real milk instead of the liquid in the little plastic pots but the girl didn't hear. Then Madeleine said, 'But you were *holidaying* with Giles. Would you mind if I asked – is there anything now in the way of lovemaking?'

When Thomasina attacked the baked beans without a word Madeleine continued to sit serene. In a few moments she poured more tea for them both, dribbling it a bit into the thick saucers. She began to spear the orange beans singly and daintily with her fork.

At last Thomasina said, 'I'm sorry. I don't talk about my private life.'

'Oh, that's such a mistake,' said Madeleine. 'Oh, I so wish that I had had someone to tell me what a mistake that is. You have to have *someone*. But there – I expect you have Giles.'

'I hardly know Giles.'

'Yet you make love with him. You didn't say no. I wonder

what he's like. I yearned to know once. I'd guess now he'd be pretty brisk, but that would be better than he was when he was young. He was absolutely terrified then of the whole idea. Not only of sex, but of love. And of course I was terrified too, and so well brought-up. I went to Karnak with him, you know, if you know where that is. It was wartime and I was a Fany (yes, isn't it lewd?) and he asked me to go to the Winter Palace for the weekend. I was in such a *fit*, dear, about contraceptives. I had no idea what to expect. All I knew was from school. One of the big girls had told me that the Ancient Greeks used to use butter and of course you couldn't get butter in the war and it would have seemed a frightful waste. So I just went and hoped for the best. But dear Giles, there was nothing like that at all. He kissed my hand on the Saturday night and we both went to our separate rooms. You wouldn't believe it, would you, all the books you read, but that was quite usual then. Oh I *burned*, dear, in my bed. I left my room unlocked and a huge Egyptian man came in during the night in a long pink thing and asked to clean my shoes and there was no telephone and I said that I should have to scream and then the man went away. I think I was probably very lucky, although the Egyptians are very pleasant, polite people and it may have been no more than affection. I told Giles in the morning and he created a frightful fuss. Well, you know, I expect they all thought my room would be empty, though it would have been more flattering if they had thought *Giles's* room would be empty and he'd be in with me. He was tremendously apologetic. I think he knew that he'd behaved very badly. Very tamely. But, you see, neither of us knew the rules. They were in a state of flux in the Forties. Well, they probably always are. But oh my dear, so shy. That's why he needed Hilda.'

'What was Hilda like?'

'She was like a gun, dear. She went boom. Boom, bang, smash. Tennis nets fainted at the sight of her.' Madeleine leaned sideways in her chair. 'Boom and smash,' she repeated to the two whispering girls, nodding her head. 'Boom, smash.' The girls looked insulted and then hostile. Soon they, too, left the café.

'Oh, Thomasina, Thomasina, do be careful. He's probably more positive now but at heart he hasn't changed at all. Even in appearance. I knew him. Recognised him after fifty years. That's rare – even rarer in a woman, of course. But he has that wooden army face, you know, like the Duke of Wellington. The narrow army face not the plump one. Giles never drank. Just the same jaw as the Iron D – and, of course, I knew each plane of Giles's face, each nostril, darling – thank God youth passes – and each finger and nail on his nice hands. His hands have changed, by the way – has he arthritis? Poor Giles. But it is such a good face, you know. Such a beautiful face that I'm afraid it may have made a barrier between you. We all of us, you know, want a man sometimes whom we don't have to know too well and if he's handsome it's used as a substitute.'

'My husband was like that,' said Thomasina. 'He was a surgeon.'

'Oh yes, of course he was, poor man. But I expect you were a great help to him.'

'I've nothing to do with Medicine.'

'No – I mean in calming him down. From all the excitement. A surgeon's job must be so overheating. It makes them feverish – or sometimes ice-cold.'

'I'm afraid,' said Thomasina, 'I don't think I thought of that. I lived in a bit of a world of my own. It seemed to be what he wanted.'

'He probably admired you no end,' said Madeleine. 'What work did you do?'

'Oh – nothing. I was a very keen gardener.'

'Ah, that's what they say in *Who's Who* if they don't do anything at all.'

Thomasina blazed scarlet. 'I am a very good and serious gardener.' She closed her teeth over a forkful of beans, dragged the fork out empty and slammed it on her plate.

'Darling – I'm so sorry. Children?'

'What the hell d'you mean?'

'You had some children, didn't you? It's more than I did. I've only steps. Barren as the fig.'

'So was Giles,' said Thomasina.

'The poor fellow.' Madeleine sat with an expression of true and profound grief. 'I expect that was Mildred. They don't have many, tennis players. I suppose the wires get twisted. Giles needed children.'

'So what about you?' asked angry Thomasina.

Madeleine only leaned across and touched her hand. 'What about your daughter?' she asked very clearly. 'What about your daughter, Holly?' She let her hand become a handcuff round Thomasina's wrist. 'Your daughter died the other day, I hear, and there is a baby. And I understand you will not see the baby. Why not?'

'This is utterly none of your business.'

'Yes it is. I see a shuttered woman turning to a clammed-up man to save her from the rest of her life and I know that she is laying up for herself nothing but another coat of varnish, like those unhappy quiches on the counter. Oh yes, my dear girl. You'll both look your parts convincingly until you die. You'll take each other down the last years like two beautiful illustrations out of the old England we all love and mourn. And you'll go nowhere. *Nowhere.* Even the lovemaking will be dignified till it peters out altogether, which will be about three weeks after the wedding. It's a bit dignified now, isn't it? You haven't said a thing about it. Is it not the sort of thing you could do to a comfortable de Souza march? Tum-te-tum? Tell me I'm wrong – that it's between two who love each other and long to know each other and love each other more. You can't. You know it is a barrier, the sex between you. Isn't it?'

'It is not,' cried Thomasina, red in the face, almost weeping. 'It's pretty good. Very nice. Sleeping with Giles is the most exciting thing I've done in years. I don't say so. Neither does he. D'you think we're French or something? But we *will* do. We're good at it. The first time was in a sandstorm.'

The café had fallen still. Even the bag-woman had stopped rustling. The young man by the window had laid down his book and taken off his reading glasses and the girl behind the counter had let the microwave ping unheeded.

'And the granddaughter?' Madeleine was in with a thrust as Thomasina began to cry. 'This granddaughter?'

'I've had enough,' wept Thomasina. 'I've had enough of motherhood. What the hell can *you* tell me about its pain! Do you not know, woman' – she stood up – '*my daughter is dead.*'

The general and a boy and a girl, all in wedding clothes, stood in the doorway and the general was at Thomasina's side as she turned to fling herself in his arms. Then she flung herself out of them again, making for the open door, and he went after her and held her from behind by the shoulders, looking round the assembled company with a mixture of terror at being found in such a place in such a way and valour in his determination that nothing would make him retreat from it.

The boy and girl slid down on either side of their seated step-grandmother and the girl looked over at Thomasina and said, 'You mustn't mind, Mrs Fox. Honestly, she's dreadful but it's not her fault. She's, you know, Alzheimer's or something. It's terribly sad. She says terrible things. But then she forgets them.'

The great car that Thomasina and Madeleine had arrived in stood at the café door again with the chauffeur picking his teeth inside it. He'd done a lot of weddings. They'd been saying a thousand bottles of champagne had gone into this one.

'I'll walk,' wailed Thomasina. 'Giles, let's get away.'

'Of course,' he said. 'We'll go straight home.'

'We'll take her back to Puffy,' said the girl. 'Not that he's much better. Come on, Gran darling.'

Madeleine looked around her, bowing separately to each customer, favouring the young man with the book with a caress on the cheek. 'An intellectual,' she said, and in the street, 'Darlings, I've just been telling Mrs Fox that this little place reminds me of Sarajevo. I don't mean the awful Bosnian business, I mean the outbreak of war – The Great War, before even my time. The breaking of nations. The old world disappearing overnight throughout Europe when the silly driver of the emperor's carriage got stuck in a back alley and there was the gunman who'd missed the first shot in the main street having a cup of coffee. Bang! Everything changed. The flower of all our countries gone.' She paused. 'But then, you know,' she said, 'not quite, for here are you, and here am I and there is the general and that nice woman Thomasina Woolf. She wrote *The Waves*, you know. And there have been other turning points. There are. All the time. *All the time.* Thank God.'

'You got her?' asked the grandson.

'Yep,' said his sister.

'Come on, Gran darling. Home we go.'

– Part Two –

— 25 —

At the beginning of December Jocasta sat in the workshops with the Tibetan women cutting paper and half-listening to them talk. The Tibetan men had disappeared. No one spoke of them. Under the coarse, hairy coat of the oldest woman, Pema, Faith lay sleeping. She seemed seldom to be in her cot. A little hammock had been rigged up for her in the visitors' quarters and there she slept now at night. She was with them in the daytime, too, except when a health visitor announced a routine visit and then somehow she was always to be found in the main buildings with The Missus or Jocasta about. But she often became fretful there and was returned to Pema quickly. With Pema she never seemed to cry, passing her days in a sling under Pema's bristly coat, almost hidden, like a chicken under the wings of a hen.

The art class was busy this morning with a huge collage planned for a Nativity tableau on Christmas Eve. The Tibetans were not excited by it. One of them, a girl with good A levels at Liverpool, was wild to get into the Slade. The Priors was only her temporary billet while she waited for interviews. She was building a portfolio in a rather absent-minded way when she wasn't spending time on the telephone sharing long silences with a busking boyfriend in London.

The girl was dismissive of mysterious Jocasta, who had been out of touch with what was going on in Art colleges for over twenty years. The girl sulked and lolled, looking Jocasta up and down, disagreeing with all her theory and practice and scratching her hands through her raspberry-red hair. Only her eyes were Tibetan; her clothes and accent aggressively scouse.

Silly bitch, this girl thought as Jocasta's fingers cut and pasted, *with her posh voice*. Jocasta was talking today about negative space. 'Negative space, for Chrissake,' said the Tibetan girl to herself.

Negative space, thought Jocasta, snipping at shredded silk, daubing it orange for sunrise, *is where I live*.
> *Oh what to me the little room*
> *That was brimmed up with prayer and rest . . .*

She had stopped sleeping with Jack long ago, long before Andrew had returned with the baby. Jack had understood. He had understood perfectly, he said, the urge for celibacy in a woman no longer young and particularly in Jocasta, who had been on an unearthly spiritual plane in India. They had met so late, he said, looking at her with love. Everyone, The Missus, The Smikes, the hangers-on around The Priors, thought Jack was a fool to love Jocasta, who was a cold fish. Jack never complained, seemed to have no conception of infidelity or treachery in anyone. His trust was ridiculous, childlike. He looked, he loved.

But he does want me in his bed, she thought, *and otherwise brimmed up with prayer and rest. And Andrew did let me go. He ditched me. He made a political marriage. And look where it got him.*

But yet there's something good in Andrew. Something fearless, unchanging. Look what happened. Within an hour. He could have held me for ever. He still could hold me for ever. He shall hold me for ever.
> *He bade me out into the gloom*, she thought,
> *And my breast lies upon his breast.*

'D'you never think of going home?' she asked the sulky girl, the Tibetan bohemian. 'Isn't it a bit easier now? Couldn't you get back somehow, at least to Nepal? It's your continent, your culture.'

'I'm not goin' back to that sort o' painting, thanks very much. It's only boys do it anyway and it's all copying old Buddhist stuff. Might as well work for Disney. Coom on, Jocasta, let's get to it. Let's hear this negative space.'

'It's what we're doing here,' she said, and smiled over at

144

unsmiling Pema. 'Move over a bit, could you, Pema, while I open the screen up. Shouldn't you put her down in her cot for a while?'

Pema didn't speak. Knitting without dropping the hump across her chest that was Faith, she waddled to another part of the workshop and sat with her back to everybody. Laying down her needles, she adjusted the baby and began to heat up milk.

'So,' said Jocasta, 'we do this. We block in roughly and then in detail, first sketching, then drawing, then the layers of colours and textures. Cloth – oh, all the substances we want. Grit, glitter, granite chips, bits of heather, coal-dust, beads, baubles, ribbons, glass, net, everything. These are to surround the subject only. The suburbs of the city. The city, we leave bare. We almost reject it. We ignore it. We have no feeling for it, no plans. We do not allow ourselves the concept of a subject. We let it materialise. It emerges by our creation of the material around. Its clothing, if you like. The material is in part its creator: the material is the cause. If we do this faithfully we find in the end that the subject of the work shines out the clearer, apparently of its own accord. Life of its own. It's a way of arriving there by standing back, letting the Creator create so we sometimes get a big surprise. Well, here of course we know what the centre of the thing is going to be because it's for the Christmas do in the chapel. It has to be the Nativity in the centre, obviously. But the idea is that perhaps the central object will be revealed more dramatically, more clearly, if we don't overwork it. Don't work at it exclusively or even at all. Sometimes the subject can only be found if it's crept up on like this. The central point of the picture can turn out to be more than we can bear to reveal directly. Sort of wearing dark glasses. Perpetual light is, after all, unbearable. Well, for mortals.'

'Is it religious, then?' the second Tibetan woman asked. 'Christian. Obey the doctrine and the faith looks after itself?'

'Or Buddhist?' said a third.

'God, let's hope it's not Buddhist,' said the A-level Liverpudlian.

'It's Methodist,' said someone. ' "The trivial round, the common task, would furnish all we ought to ask." Be good like that, keep your eyes down, and you'll get God as a prize at the end. Right at the heart of it all.'

'If you like,' said Jocasta, who kept off God, 'or it is peace, truth, karma, a goal.'

'Keeping your eyes down,' said the other older woman of the group. She held up the thing she was stitching. It was like a little rectangular kit of framework sticks crossed at the corners, the fabric bound round and filled with a pattern of wools in three colours: a black circular pupil, bronze iris against the oval white, a dense, small tapestry about four inches by four. The third eye, held aloft, its last strands not yet all woven in, overlooked the little group. Jocasta shuddered.

'It's not a very adventurous idea,' said the Slade-girl-to-be.

'I think it is, quite,' said Jocasta; 'it is quite brave. And it's a patient way of working with sometimes a great result. I've been surprised almost every time by what comes out at the end. If you push all your ordinary tricks and gimmicks and – persiflages – out of the way. Stop thinking of faith.'

Oh what to me my mother's care, she thought,
The house where I was safe and warm,
The shadowy blossom of my hair
Will hide us from the bitter storm.
Oh Andrew, Andrew, Andrew . . . but how can I leave him? Jack is my mother and my father and he keeps me safe and warm. Or he would if I would let him. But Andrew, oh come in under the blossom of my hair, oh damnation, oh sex. Oh my love.

Pema came across to them again, walking calmly, and sat. She began to feed Faith Fox her bottle of milk and the child's round pink hand like a starfish stretched up and traced a pattern in the air, then patted and stroked the old woman's cheek.

Outside the wind blew. The time was most certainly winter now and becoming cold. Most of Ellerby Priors had been closed down until the spring came. No more groups would be coming, no public events or days of meditation or farm visits.

The curling lists on the notice boards could all be taken down now if somebody remembered. When the Tibetans left in the spring the guest sheds would be closed. The refectory had already been cleared and shuttered, the main priory dormitory stripped, and such heating as there was drained down. The skeleton staff of The Missus, The Smikes, Jack, Jocasta and Philip drew in each night round the stove of the old kitchen. Snow could sometimes begin in December and the steep road off the ridge was regularly blocked during January. The deep-freezes had been filled by The Missus with bread and chunks of long-dead Whitby cod and the barn was full of Jack's potatoes and swedes. There was discussion about the economics of buying half a frozen cow; about how maybe this year it would make sense for Philip to be a full boarder at the school rather than Jocasta having to walk to the cross and coax the car alive and brave the moor road four times a day.

Oh when, oh when, shall I see Andrew? thought Jocasta. *And when he does come back, whatever shall I do? How shall I behave? Surely he'll come at Christmas. He'll want to look at the child. I want him to take me back with him. Yes, I do. And I should. It is right and normal that I should. It's healthy. And I want to do something for Philip. There's nothing here for him. He's not like a child. He's not like any of them up here anyway. They're North, that's all there is about it. They're as intelligent as us. Doctors' and solicitors' children. A private school I said I'd never countenance. They learn French in a fashion. But they're different. It's not the voices, it's the glowering looks they have, and they're so rude and they're North. My God, I hate it here.*

And he spends all his free time with The Smikes and the old funnies at the seaside, so-called grandparents. Oh, but I have no money. I've left all my own life behind me. I'm going nowhere. Teaching Negative Space to Tibetans. I'm lost. Oh, how I want him. Andrew.

– 26 –

Hugo Jefford had been prophetic when he said that the Seton-Fairley wedding would be the last chance for him to see his old friend Puffy, husband of drifting Madeleine. It was Puffy, however, who survived the winter and Hugo who that warm autumn left the world. He left it suddenly, without any goodbyes.

And on such a lovely morning. The dew was on the Coombe Hill lawn and the marks of his bedroom slippers on their last journey suggested some passing giant or summer snowman marching from the house towards the three great garages. He had brought Pammie early tea that morning, a habit that had somehow established itself since her uncharacteristic over-sleeping the day after her return from the North with the bag of potatoes. Hugo appeared to enjoy this new duty. He had stood drinking his own tea at the window, looking over his garden, as Pammie sat up straight against her pillows, sipping and glaring ahead of her.

They said little and pretty well the same things each morning. 'Busy today?' and 'Remarkable weather. Extraordinary autumn, this,' and 'They say it's cold in the North.' 'Yes. Odd. It's like spring here.'

Hugo had stood hunched with his broad old back to her, his ears sticking out. The rising sun shone through them and turned them rosy. 'You ought to get your hair cut,' Pammie had said. Looking hard at his back she felt impatient. She felt young. She felt undervalued.

'Hardly there to cut,' he said; 'not like this wretched lawn. He'll have to go over it again.'

'So you keep saying.'

'So he keeps having to. Makes a fearful hash of it. I'd like to have a go myself.'

'Well, do, if you want a stroke.'

'Stroke, my foot.'

'I don't want to stroke your foot. And I don't want to be landed with someone like poor old Puffy. It's probably Puffy who sent poor Madeleine off her marbles. I mean right off her marbles.'

'Or vice versa,' said Hugo. 'We're very lucky, Pammie, you and I. We're so fit.'

'Well, I'm hardly Madeleine's age, if you don't mind my saying so. You used to be always telling people I could almost be your daughter. Almost.'

'Almost,' he said. 'I told the nurse you could, you know. Just to stop her getting ideas. Then she said, "Well, I could be your granddaughter."' ('And I don't care,' she had also said but Hugo didn't say so now.)

'You liked her, didn't you?' Pammie all of a sudden found that she too liked Hugo and as much as ever. 'Bring me some more tea. You're an old reprobate.' She pulled his head towards her by one of the rosy ears and kissed him.

'That feller's in the garden now,' he said; 'I can hear him. I'll just nip down and catch him. Tell him to get the big mower out, not the Flymo. When it's dried up a bit he could get a cut today.'

'You'll catch cold.'

'No. Lovely morning. Fresh. Like spring.'

Pammie never saw the dark footsteps in the unruly grass because, by the time she discovered Hugo dead beside the Bentley, round which he had been manoeuvring the mower, they had disappeared. Hugo had been mistaken about the gardener. It had been the postman he had heard. He had taken the letters from him and then walked to the garage. He bade the postman a courteous goodbye, took the garage key from its compartment behind a loose brick, wheeled out the mower and leaned to the self-starter.

His death flattened Pammie as nothing in her life had done. It put into proportion deaths of the children of friends and all attendant emotional shocks and sorrows. The weeping for

Holly Fox over tumblers of whisky, Holly's angry funeral, everyone seething at the behaviour of others, the distaste of the whole bazaar for the superficiality of Thomasina, the righteous disgust for her love affair, even the comfortable pride Pammie had begun to develop for the baby: all were revealed as things of a slight order. Most of them she now identified as boredom or self-indulgence, self-importance with almost a whiff of prurience. And most of all Pammie was revolted by her hearty behaviour at The Priors, that madhouse full of cranks. Whatever had she been doing there? Not one's own sort at all. Religious fanatics. She had behaved like a schoolgirl rushing up there with the baby. She had been wanting to show up Thomasina. Now she was ashamed of herself. Seedy eccentricity was not the world of Coombe and it was only a seedy eccentric with a very nice face who had been gushing all over her up there, not someone you could know. You couldn't possibly ask him to dinner. Nor, if it came to that, the laconic brother either. Secretive Andrew, running off in the heather. Not her generation and certainly not her friend. He was no more than the son-in-law of an ex-friend, and she should not have pushed into other people's lives. Riffraff lives. Not worthy behaviour for the wife of Hugo. Hugo the good.

Childless and alone in the huge house except for Hugo's sorrowful old dog, Pammie surprised all her friends by her heaviness and inanition. Hugo had after all for years been no more than a benign shadow seated with glass and newspaper under a standard lamp, Pammie a stocky seraph flying past him at intervals, eyes fixed on her own ploys.

But Pammie the great organiser of Surrey rituals now could not even give orders for the funeral or the wake. Pammie the paradigm of common sense and courage in the face of disaster, so decisive and practical, now allowed letters of condolence to pile up unanswered, gave up her magistrate's duties and her golf and her singing. Bridge she just about managed, 'for her mind's sake', she said, 'and as long as nobody says anything', but she was withdrawn and looked disagreeable and her partner grew fidgety and then sniffy. There was a vulgar, old-persons' sort of row and that was that. Pammie stayed home.

But the worst of the loss of Hugo was how it attacked like a killing virus the very gut of Pammie, her sure, religious life. Froze it. Set it in aspic. God melted under its strobe light. And this hard cold light seemed to Pammie to be some sort of poisoned present Hugo had sent her posthumously from wherever it was he had gone when he fell, face forward, across the mower as the late autumn roses sparkled at him through the open garage doors. Hugo's going pierced that layer of Pammie that she had confidently labelled Christian and out of it spilled only a ragbag of old rubbish.

She examined this ragbag as soon as the stately funeral was over. It had been a rustling, whispering, concerned but not very upsetting funeral. There had been much good fellowship, several rows of stout old gentlemen in long dark overcoats ('Was old Hugo *Jewish*?'), massive wreaths, and several unknown pale new partners from his old city firm. The nurse they'd had for Faith had been there with a white handkerchief to her face, and two or three rather nice-looking women Pammie could not place. There had been white moustachios in cricketing ties. Old Puffy had been there, leaning back in his wheelchair examining the vaulting of the church roof as if in search of angels. He had been attended by a young man in pinstripes with a bowler hat beside him on the pew. Someone said it was a butler. He had wheeled Puffy past Pammie at the church door and bowed. Puffy had said only, 'Bad news, old girl, bad news.'

Madeleine had been absent but Thomasina had been there (without the general) and so had Andrew Braithwaite, with a little dark woman Pammie felt she knew. She wondered if it was a girlfriend and thought, *Oh how splendid*, before all the petty Holly Fox business slid out of her head again. She could not even remember, as they all roared out the last hymn, *Fight the Good Fight*, she could not remember the name of Holly Fox's little baby, who had lived with her and with Hugo under their rose-tiled roof. She could not conceive what she had ever had to do with the child.

But then she saw before her Hugo's face again, the face she had so terrifyingly been unable to recall since the day he died, and his voice saying, 'Gets your finger in a vice. Smiles at you,' and there at last, before the final verse, she began to cry.

It was Thomasina who looked after her. After the funeral she saw to the guests back at the house, ran round after the caterers had gone, tidied up, gathered the service sheets, the tickets from the wreaths, put them on Pammie's desk, said she would deal with them. She had brought whisky and little sandwiches for the evening, for both of them, as if there had been no rift, no death of Holly, no general, no Egypt, no Faith. A little warmth began to ease its way into Pammie again.

Thomasina was now the image of her old self in her gold jewellery and smart shoes and she guided along a conversation almost macabrely ordinary. She suggested that Pammie should come back and stay with her at Spindleberries at least for the next week or so. Later they could talk about holiday plans. Hadn't Pammie been thinking of Cyprus? They discussed Apex fares, then the appeal of going soft and travelling at least Club Class. They discussed dates, fitting them in around various summer appointments: the Chelsea Flower Show, the Cheltenham Festival, and so on. They might go at Easter . . . Or what about Christmas? The cadences of the sentences suggested the old way of things again, that after a stone sinks the water does eventually stop rippling. Their two voices worked for the future, towards a long-term forecast and, damn it all, a pleasant one.

However, the old way of things for Pammie had included her habitual and lengthy conversations with God, which had filled up much of the time when she was not attending to her almost perpetual interior monologues addressed to friends and acquaintance. These monologues now had ceased. Pammie had discovered that they were no longer important, that the unconscious recipients of the monologues were no longer important. She had, she found out, only addressed them anyway to the unimportant. To the Jinnies and Vinnies and Daffies and Janes. Hugo had never been addressed as he had never intruded on any of her dreams, sleeping or waking.

And now that he was gone all that she wanted to do in the

world was to talk to him, and not in her heart or her interior monologue but in her everyday easy voice. And likewise with prayer. Prayer was an intrusion. It was not God she wanted, it was Hugo.

And, when it came right down to it, what had all this 'communion with God' really meant? Why 'God'? Why should there be 'a God'? She had never of course believed in a physical sort of God with arms and legs and private parts and so on, she was a bit better educated than that. She had read her A. N. Wilson. But she had believed in the God of the Apocalypse, in the great formalised throngs of the heavenly host, in precious stones and the horsemen prancing, the halo round the Light of Lights, the great eye that beholds.

She had believed that inside the eye of light there dwelt the essence of love, of love for her, Pammie (and Hugo), whatever she did or said so long as she attended to her worship and said the General Confession in church every Sunday and behaved through the week with a weather eye on doing what is right. But then Holly Fox had died.

A random nonsense.

And now Hugo had died. Wordlessly. One minute drinking tea at the window, the next a sad lump over the mower. Gone. And where? To the hosts of the Apocalypse? To eternal rest? He'd had eternal rest ever since he retired and quite a supply of it before that. What had he ever known about himself? What had she ever really known about him? Why had he wanted to marry her? If she had ever thought to ask him, would he have been able to remember? What had he seen in her as the years went by? A woman tearing about. Church on Sunday, leaving the house in her car at seven forty-five sharp. She had always prayed for him but had of course never said so. Back to breakfast she had zoomed, boiled eggs, *The Sunday Telegraph*, drinks before lunch, snooze, Bridge or the garden, a few friends round, easy telly, supper on knees, bed. What on earth had it all been about? The day God gaveth. 'A good Christian life,' the vicar had said, but what on earth was Christian about it? Christ had said sell up, go out and preach. He had said He brought not peace but a sword. She thought of Hugo happily eating crumpets every day at four o'clock in the centrally heated lounge.

Pammie considered Christ. She walked all round Him. She began to talk to Him, questioning Him keenly as if He were one of her old clients at the Citizens' Advice Bureau. What evidence had He for his doctrine of love? Why should God love her? Ridiculous, when you thought about it.

And what about the texts? 'In the beginning was the Word' – and yet Christ left behind words that now appear to be phoney or mistranslated or mischievous. It appears that we can't understand a word of the Gospels now unless we know both Greek and Hebrew. Mary is no Virgin, just a 'young woman' loosely related to the goddess Diana. As for the Resurrection ... Pammie had never had the least difficulty with the Resurrection until the bishops got on to it. And some of them were homosexuals. And some people say that Christ was one. And that Judas was only misguided and Pilate a tragic hero. 'Do we all have to go out, then, and get ourselves a theological degree?' she enquired of Jesus. 'And where will that leave our good works, the fruits by which we are supposed to be known?'

'I'm afraid I'm having to cut down on my voluntary work,' Pammie wrote round. 'Since the death of my husband I am having a great deal to do with his financial affairs.' This was not true. Hugo had left things magnificently trim. She wrote a great number of these letters. To the vicar she made a telephone call, not wanting to make her resignation from the flower rota too formal and wondering if he might suggest when he heard her voice that he come and talk to her. But the vicar took the news bravely and rang off.

'What cock!' was the next stage, 'what absolute cock it all is!' and, as she said so, something like a heavy old mackintosh she had never much liked fell away from her shoulders. 'I don't really believe a bloody thing,' she said aloud and listened to herself. She prickled with excitement. She eyed the face of Jesus. (Because there's no doubt that He had a face. She didn't doubt the historical figure. She wasn't saying some consortium of magic had made Him up. Oh no.) She eyed Jesus, the middle-class carpenter of Galilee, and said, 'I can't begin to see why we're all so conditioned by You, a Middle-East cult figure with a three-year work span, dead two thousand years. Look where it's got us. Inquisitions, Northern Ireland, Bosnia, the Crusades. Look at this country. Packed once with saints. Holy Ireland. My eye! Rivers of blood, rioting, louts, thugs, football hooligans, mugging, all the churches dropping down. North–South divide. The whole world is a north–south divide. Fighting over religion everywhere. From the beginning. Absolutely all the time. All of us supposed to be united by the Cross. There's only the Catholics now that bother with the Cross and even the nuns didn't send more than a note after all my years of Wednesdays.'

And all this Muslim business.

At this point the face of the Christ began to get hazy, much like the face in the coloured aquatint in Pammie's Confirmation Bible where the hair hung down the shoulders in ripples and The Saviour of the World sat in a white nightgown beside a well, with flowers growing in and out of His toes in the grass.

Well, you could see why Hugo had never bothered with any of it. Just sat rattling the newspaper. Oh, how she wished she had known how stupid she was being. He must have thought it. But he had known – how clearly she saw it now – he had known that her religion then, her church life, was all emptiness. He had never said so, never teased her, but he had known it was all show. Entertainment. Play. Oh, Hugo had been so wise. So clever. All the money he had made and without seeming to try. Tears came as she thought of Hugo sitting wisely, and saying nothing. The only man who had simply listened to her. Had loved her – well, had adored her. Look at all the things he had heaped upon her. She could go shopping and buy anything she wanted, anything in the world, and she still could, for the rest of her life. All she had to do was walk along to the bank. The bank was a limitless pot full of money. Or she assumed it was; she'd never been a spender. No time. *Oh, beloved sweet Hugo, when you think of some men. When you think of the deep certain order of my life with him here, and then of those shipwrecked people in the North, that mad place.* She meditated on the face of Hugo until it was surrounded by a great crater of light, Hugo swirling about somewhere in the depths or heights of it, and the trumpets sounding all about. *Well,* she thought, *I suppose it'll take time to get rid of the imagery. To reach full atheistical purity of thought. But I am on course now for a clean break.*

And when she next went to see friends for drinks it was Advent Sunday and someone was going on about Advent calendars for children. 'Will Thomasina send one to the baby, I wonder?' asked Jilly. Everyone else had rather laid things to do with Thomasina aside by now but Jilly took things slowly and rather hung on to them, and not too many of them since the gin had taken a stronger hold. 'Don't be silly,' said Nicky, 'it's only a baby. Poor brat, I feel like sending her a Christmas thing myself.'

'Maybe *you* will, Pammie?' said Didi.

Pammie examined her nails and said, 'Oh, I've given up all that rubbish. Christmas and so forth. I've forgotten all that Thomasina business. We can suffer far too much for other people.'

An anti-Christmas, anti-Christian gesture she felt must now be made. It must cut right into the heart of her life to show the change in her. Good sense. An appropriate good time. The heart of her life, the place that reflected all she now stood for, all that dear Hugo had stood for, was her house with its silk chairs and matching footstools, its fat curtains, gold wallpaper. She would transform it now into the sort of place she was convinced that Hugo had always wanted. Something to proclaim his wider-than-suburban success.

She would transform the house, beginning with this room. She would fling out the mahogany, sell the upholstered suite, give away the Victorian watercolours on the walls, replaster to remove all traces of the individual picture lights above each canvas, and she would throw away the huge portrait of herself that Hugo had never really liked, had said looked as if she was dying to consult her watch. Yes. And she'd scrap the fitted carpets and have instead a room that Hugo's young successors in the firm might envy, a young room that she should have made for him long ago. The floor would be black tweed; the walls, one coral and the rest white. Enormous floor cushions to sit on and in one corner an arrangement of Japanese lanterns, all hanging at different lengths, some almost touching the floor. She'd have oriental scrolls on pins and a tray of sand sculpture and a few big rocks on a glass table. She would get down to measuring it all out at once.

Pammie walked over to the garage where Hugo had kept tools and plumb lines and measuring rods. It was the first time she had stepped inside since his death.

The mower, of course, had been put away and all was tidy, but looking around for metal rods and measures she saw on a high shelf, almost out of sight behind the oil cans, the mail that Hugo had received the morning of his death.

It was mostly nothing. A few charity things. Some junk mail. The telephone bill she was pleased to see because she had thought it lost. There was also a rather grubby-looking letter stuck over with a Save the Trees label. The address was written in copperplate handwriting and the postmark was Whitby, North Yorkshire.

– 27 –

The Missus had gone. One morning, a Monday, she was not at the stove of the Ellerby Priors kitchen crashing with pans. As everyone appeared for breakfast, one by one, a bitch of a wet day, rain trailing across the courtyard in curtains, swirling down off the moor and quite cold at last, there was no fire lit, no table laid. Philip and (surprisingly) The Smikes arrived first. Philip had to be got to school. They stood about and after some time in came Jocasta, who sent Philip up to The Missus's room to see if she were ill. He came back to say that the room was empty and all her things gone, her car not under the gatehouse and how was he getting to school and it was maths.

Jack came in from the chapel.

This was unthinkable. The Missus had been about for many years, ever since she'd heard Jack preach in Rochdale the year he was ordained.

The Missus, Alice Banks, a sharp little woman, fierce and silent. Her family had been in the mills. She was registered as a Card, was The Missus. She hated joy. Joy got to her. Her *bête noire* was Gracie Fields, the world-famous Lancashire lass of her youth whose nightingale voice had drawn the crowds around her like shawls in their mutual birthplace. A golden creature, all laughter. 'I wouldn't cross t' street for 'er,' had said Alice Banks, The Missus. 'Loud clart. She were comin' back round t' mills that day and they give a holiday to stand int streets for 'er, yellin' and carryin' on. "Are yer not comin', then, Alice?" they said and I said, "I'd not cross t' road till 'er." I went ower t' church instead.'

She didn't say that Jack had been preaching that Friday, a young man like an angel, for she never discussed emotion or devotion. She had stayed behind after the service – the screams for Gracie loud in the street – and taken tea and buns with Jack and the slender congregation. Jack had asked her job and she'd said, 'I don't have un. They've closed t' prints,' and glared at him. 'I can cook,' she'd said, she never knew why. 'That I *can* do,' glaring harder, fit to kill. He had left with the impression that he had met a little bit of rough black jet that could cut you to bits but would never crumble.

He remembered Alice Banks when he went to his first parish and a vicarage the size of a college, a kitchen floor glazed with damp, silverfish flitting between the loose wet tiles, and he had set about finding her. She was there within the week, mouth like a cut, unsmiling eyes, hair of a witch. She looked round the ghastly place and got out her apron and a bucket. And never left him.

She never took a holiday ('Where would I go?') and seldom spoke directly to Jack, although she had made up her mind that he was now her life. She muttered as she worked, was unpopular in every parish, treated all-comers as honoured peasants lucky to be allowed audience, sent them all (including, once, a bishop) round to the back door, and returned meat to the butcher with covering notes saying, 'This won't do for his reverence.' She had been seen in the henhouse haranguing the hens, urging them to point-of-lay. 'Git yersens movin', 'e 'as two eggs to 'is supper.'

The Missus had few possessions and, it appeared, no family. At Christmas there arrived only a very few shabby-looking cards, to which she paid scant attention and often didn't open. She was almost always silent, though if you did want any life to flow from her you had only to mention Gracie Fields.

She loved Jack. Of course she did. She was not in love with him, although she thought about him most of the time, for she saw him as beyond desire; but she was obsessed, nevertheless; by his gentleness, his innocence and his loving looks. They had been the first she had known. The day when, some weeks after her arrival at the first grisly vicarage, she took it upon herself to attend to his laundry was as much a stage in her spiritual life as a novitiate's first vows. Thereafter she rubbed away each week at his socks and underpants and shirts as at a sacrament, always washing by hand, hanging everything out ritually in neat even loops along the clothesline. She ironed and light-starched the oldest of his frayed handkerchiefs with the care of a wardrobe mistress for a star.

She began to knit for him, polish his shoes, restore his chaotic shirts, change his sheets and pillowcases, buy his shaving soap, toilet paper, toothbrushes, which he never acknowledged or noticed and seldom paid for.

Her cooking was dreadful, but Jack didn't seem to notice this either. She spent hours at it, boiling potatoes and cabbages to pulp, turning chops to cinders. She stood over him watching it all go down, stamping in with the second course, puddings like stone, custards covered with mackintosh which she slopped all over the plate from a height. Her expression was at these moments at its least terrifying, its nearest to fulfilment; the Creator surveying Her handiwork and finding it good.

Jack throve. Had it not been for The Missus everyone agreed that he would long ago have left the world, for he never ate unless food was set before him, and his appearance if left entirely to him would have been John the Baptist between locusts and unlikely to impress either the diocese or the Arts Council.

He paid her whatever she asked, which was very little, and had no idea of her needs. She was never ill, never elsewhere. In none of his ministries or ventures had he ever entered the room where she slept. At one place it had been a mattress on the floor of a cellar, but she did not tell him. As evangelical adventure after adventure came to grief under Jack's shining innocence and carelessness, she moved along with him to the next. She even went with him to Oxford, where he was housed for a time in a college, and found herself a job as a bedmaker and sat it out silently. Her conversation, when it came, when it was sometimes forced from her over cups of tea, harked back always to the same subject: Jack, the difficulty of working for him yet his obvious superiority to everyone else in the world. She had feared Oxford. She imagined that plans might be afoot there to trap him and tame him: Oxford, where Jack might forget the open air and where collars were not clean. When he went off with the gift of a disciple's money to set up a centre for Christian farmers in the Yorkshire Dales, where agricultural suicides in the winter months are not uncommon, and when the centre turned out to be a roofless stone shed on the open moor, she set about finding The Priors. Some said helped him buy it. Some said bought it for him outright.

She was growing old now, the cooking worse than ever, the cleaning long in abeyance, for her eyes were fading; but she was still there, still Jack's angry-looking champion, and whatever curiosities appeared in his professional behaviour, whatever hours he kept, when he lay prone on the moor or said the Offices of his faith all night long in the chapel alone, she accepted it with respectful silence. This was the form. This was Jack. He was hers. The marriage had not shaken her. She had detested Jocasta on sight but saw in her a woman without an inkling of how to put herself out for anyone, and therefore, she reasoned, Jack would need his housekeeper all the more.

Far and near, the marriage had been an amazement. It had

enthralled all those who had ever known Jack. Celibate, saintly Jack – and pushing fifty! However had it come about? What sort of proposal had there been? How had it ever been accepted by this smouldering, resentful-looking intellectual gypsy, a woman who never aimed to please, sat apart, never seemed to do more than tolerate even her own son? Jocasta, it was said, would mark the end of Jack's greatest asset in life, The Missus.

But Alice Banks had no concept of physical jealousy. The lusts of the flesh had never come her way. Vaguely she knew that marriage is brought on by passion as pneumonia is preceded by fever. Passion she called daftness. Children resulted from it, but the process by which children were attained sounded to her as unpleasant as hospital treatment, ridiculous as morris dancing or Gracie Fields. She could not see how it could be practised for delight.

Poor, poor Alice Banks, how she hated happiness. Nothing so clamped her jaw as people appearing before her and expressing exuberant pleasure. When Holly Fox had paid a visit, prancing over the kitchen flagstones exclaiming and shrieking and lifting the lids off saucepans in a girlish, mischievous way, it had been a grim moment for The Missus. Holly's sunny smile had got her nowhere. When she had reeled back with a startled but kind smile from a pan full of pink mince, saying faintly, 'How delicious,' The Missus had very nearly slapped her hand with a spoon. 'Delicious, we'll see. It's what his reverence has Mondays, that's all. There's a table to be laid, young lady. It's twelve o'clock.'

When Toots and Dolly had asked The Missus how she had liked Andrew's wife she had said only that she was the music-hall type.

That first shrivelling winter when Jocasta had arrived, inert and beautiful in the corner of the kitchen, she had ignored The Missus. The Missus in turn had ignored her. *Sour little rabbit. Even that pale scrag of a little lad she's got has more life in him.* The Missus hated children but Philip she noticed, and at length found herself disarmed. His eccentricity and honesty and good looks were what had drawn her to Jack; and so with Philip, but, unlike Jack, Philip had attached himself to The Missus like a rather delightful flea. She began by snapping at him, then giving him orders, screaming at him to clean himself up, he wasn't in India now. She seized his shoes in exasperation and polished them, seized his hair and cut it with the kitchen scissors; in time she started playing cards with him. He called her Alice, as only Jack did, and she began to call him Phil, as only Jocasta did. The Smikes, who had known The Missus for years, would watch the quick-witted card games between the boy and the fierce old woman with wonder.

The Missus saw to Philip's school uniform as the years went by, had food ready for him when he got home, helped with his writing with an intense and astonishing patience, sometimes placing her claw of a hand over his and guiding it round the loops. Sometimes she thought, *I dunno. He might be Jack's own. 'E's not slow, 'e's original, that's what 'e is. 'E's 'imself.* 'Jocasta,' she'd shout. 'It's four o'clock. Get off for that boy, you'll be late.'

The fact that Jack and Jocasta did not sleep together did not interest The Missus at all. But once, this winter, after six years, Jocasta had come floating through the kitchen and put her arms round Jack in her presence, and they had stood close – close, close, close – for so long that she had been disgusted. And a little afraid. *What a show! Trying to tell me something. Nasty.*

She had stuck it out. She had gone on stirring at the porridge and her kitchen had survived undefiled. It had been Jocasta who had disentangled herself from Jack's long arms and left the room. And The Missus had reigned on.

Yet, three weeks later, The Missus, Alice Banks, was gone. After more than twenty years, gone. No note. No word. And why? And where?

'There'll be an explanation,' Jack said, looking desperately round. He was frightened that perhaps he had been told and forgotten. Some visit. Some break.

But The Missus never left the place, or just into Whitby or down into Teesside to see Dolly.

'She'll have gone to her family in Rochdale. There must be

some trouble. We'll get a letter. I must have been told. I must think what she said.'

'She'd have said goodbye. *Has* she a family?'

'She doesn't say goodbye,' said Jack. 'I don't think so. I expect there's some family about somewhere. She'll be back.'

But then, her belongings? Her clothes? All were gone from the room over the gatehouse below the guest room in the hospitium. Alice Banks had been no jackdaw but Philip – who had often visited her room to tell her stories as she knitted and listened to Radio Two turned up full blast and said, 'Very well, then, stop romancing. Let's have a spot of truth' – Philip said there had been quite a lot of boxes and newspapers and shoes in rows. All gone now.

Then Jimmie, the postman, stopped off and said that she'd passed him in her car down the ridge, going towards Teesside estuary, the Middlesbrough road. 'She weren't lookin' herself,' he said, 'in a felt hat.'

Andrew said that he and Jocasta would follow The Missus – go down to Toots and Dolly and find out if anything had been seen of her. It was afternoon by now. Philip, who had been taken to school by Andrew, would have to be brought back either by one of The Smikes, who said it was their day off again, or, heaven preserve the child, by Jack. Jack drove sketchily and often turned up at the wrong place, thinking it was a different day and a different mission. Jocasta said no. Not Jack. '*Right?*' She had blazed up like a fire. Everyone stared. 'Jack's not to go for Philip. I'll go. He's not safe.'

'But we have to talk,' said Andrew, following her out to the car. 'You must come with me to Dolly's. It's the only chance we'll get.'

'I can't risk Philip. Jack's driving's lethal. I've risked everything else. I've risked everything for you, Andrew, from the minute I met you. Right up to last night. That's it.'

'Last night can be explained. If we can find her, we can tell her.'

'Nobody explains to that woman. She knows everything, judges everything, forgives nothing. Always Jack, Jack – she's obsessed by him. Oh you fool, fool, fool, Andrew! You knew her long before I did. Jack's her reason for being. She'd die for him. To keep him from hurt is what she thinks she's born for. You and I are nowhere. She'd cut our throats.'

'Then how could she leave him?'

'I don't know. Shock. I think I'll go for Philip.'

'OK, then. I'll go down to Toots. I'll take the baby. They still haven't seen her.'

'Do what you like. I've had enough,' she said.

'So why did you come to me last night?'

She drove off, Andrew watching as the car passed under the gatehouse arch and out of sight. Then he turned and went into the kitchen, where his brother was standing about wondering whether to make tea.

'I suppose we might tell the police,' Jack said, looking childish, with hanging hands, his face quite old. 'Do you suppose . . .' there was a great pause '. . . that I have neglected Alice? I've never sat down with her to talk, you know, not for years. It's possible that it has suddenly come to her that' – he looked up like a penitent – 'I am a very selfish man.'

Andrew took the drooping teapot from his brother's paw and made tea. He did not look at Jack.

They sat and faced each other across the great oak table. A sense of The Missus, black with contempt, hung about the room.

Andrew thought, *I shall tell him now. There will never be a right time. We are alone, for once. It must be done.*

Yet he ought to ask Jocasta first. Jack ought to be told by them both together. He could not bear Jack to hear it from somewhere else and there would probably be a letter from the bloody Missus woman tomorrow, telling all. No, he must tell Jack now.

If of course The Missus could bear to hurt Jack, by letter or in any way. Her flight surely meant that she could not. Her flight was the most abstruse hint that she could give. She would never be able to keep the great hurt that was being done to Jack to herself, to live with it, to watch it happen again and again

164

whenever Andrew came up from London, to watch the unspeakable foulness of it grow familiar. To see Andrew grow easy, smug, sated; to see Jocasta's lazy joy.

The surprise was that The Missus, the night before, hadn't charged him with the enormity of it there and then, head-on in the doorway of his bedroom as she stood there with her pathetic torch. A pointing finger, a loud Lancashire voice shouting, rage and disgust. But she had vanished. At one moment holding the door open wide, her black hair in ridges of metal clips, her midget body swathed in an old brown coat of Jack's trailing on the floor over her nightie, wellingtons on her feet, torch shining on the bed – and he had turned in the bed and seen it all, over his bare shoulder. He had been covering Jocasta, yet she might – must – have seen Jocasta's face, sideways on the pillow, her hair loose, her eyes dreaming. Then the doorway empty and The Missus gone.

And Jocasta had said, 'Don't worry. Stay with me.'

Andrew had climbed out of bed and dressed. 'Stay with me,' she had kept saying. His horror had not been because of being found out or because of what he had done, but because Jocasta had said, 'Stay with me.'

Then fear had come flooding in. He had felt Alice Banks's terrible unblinking eyes.

'Stay with me, Andrew.'

And he had said no and run for it.

Left her alone, not even shutting his door behind him. He had gone across the courtyard to Jocasta's room and sat in it for the rest of the night, taking pleasure in growing colder and colder until dawn came sluggishly and he heard sounds about the place. Over in the dormitories the visitors were stirring and he thought he heard his daughter crying.

The thought – more than the thought: the bright imprinted image – of Holly was suddenly there with him. She seemed to be waving from somewhere or other in a blue dress.

They were in California, picnicking on a jaunt through the gold-rush towns on the way to the Big Trees. Rolls of airy cottonwood floated and scratched about the road ahead of them. Lean men with walnut-creased faces sold walnuts from roadside sacks. A hot fog had come down over the plain, then lifted and left blue air. They sat beside the road together with a thermos flask and sandwiches in the sun – Holly had never taken to American food though she never let on. She would ask scrawny, health-mad LA women to tea and give them little egg-and-cress sandwiches and butterfly cakes, little boat-shaped bridge rolls spread with the Gentleman's Relish sent out by Thomasina from Piccadilly.

'Darling – look!' Far away to the east a snowy fluted blue-white feather lay across the sky.

'What is it?'

'D'you know,' he said, 'it's the High Chaparral – we are actually looking at the High Chaparral.'

She licked Gentleman's Relish off a roll in the sharp autumn air and they laughed like kids. They behaved as though they'd been granted a vision. '*High Chaparral,*' they shouted.

'Oh, I'm halfway to heaven, Andrew. All I want's a baby to make one out of the two of us. We'll call it High Chaparral.'

'Or Klondyke Kate,' he said, 'or Cottonwood, or Redwood, or Gentleman's Relish. You are the Gentleman's Relish.'

The air so clean and gold, the road so white. It stretched so straight and empty over the plain.

Why ever did we come back? he thought. *This bloody, shabby, threadbare, worn-out country. Grubby and poor as a Balkan republic. Medicine in chaos, hospitals closing, no bloody money, tiny, racist, divided North and South, living on its past.*

As he shivered in the crumbling medieval ruin that in the South or in Scotland, even in Ireland, might have had a spot of limewash to brighten it – on the Continent it would have been restored with plaster or pulled down – Andrew saw The Priors in its soggy hollow of the moors as a trashy place, a sentimental notion, cranky, quaint, nostalgic, a half-baked idea of a revival of early Christian asceticism.

'Taking in the poor' – and who are they? Liverpool Tibetans, whatever that means. How could Tibetans get here?

166

Phoneys. Frauds. The whole set-up run by a lunatic, and the lunatic my brother at that.

As it grew light Andrew went looking for a bath but found someone ahead of him in the vaulted bathroom, the geyser roaring angrily. Instead he pulled on some clothes and went out into the first frost of the year, over the courtyard to the sheds. He thought he'd take a look at Faith and found her being dressed, lying on a mat in the steamy dormitory.

Behind her on a shelf there were little lamps flickering. The air was scented with sweet oils. One of the women was praying over the lamps one by one. There were only four Tibetans now, and there were five lamps. Pema, who was bending over his child, looked up at Andrew and then away. Faith lay naked, arms and legs kicking in ecstatic jerks, eyes watching the flickering line of the lamps. She arched her back and complained about being fastened into the nappy, then flopped down again and raised her legs in the air. Far above were her pink feet. She examined her toes. She conversed with them. Her eyes reflected the lamplight. She looked as far back as she could over her head at the ceiling.

'May I take her?'

'No. She has her bottle now.'

'Later?'

'Oh yes. If you like. Come, come; come, pretty,' said Pema.

'She's mine, you know.'

'She's her own girl, right?' said the A-level girl.

'She has good eyes,' he said. 'That right one's cleared up well. Hospital didn't do much good. Just needed time.'

'She sees fine,' said Pema, who had used a salve out of an old cough-sweet tin she kept about her. She'd smeared it over the eyelids every day for a fortnight. 'She sees far away over the mountains.'

And she's mine, thought Andrew, walking fast up towards the ridge. *I must remember.*

His total lack of feeling for the baby, Holly's baby, frightened and shocked him. He tramped off piste into the frosted heather half hoping he could get lost in it.

Oh my God, my God, the child is mine. No one can take her

without my permission. I must get her away from here. Learn to like her. Have to, now. All over here now. Shall go today. End the thing with Jocasta. End this vile mess. Oh God, how terrible. But he could not say 'End this sin'. It was a great sin. To lie with a brother's wife. He could not say it, only feel it deep, deep, far out of words.

He saw The Smikes shambling about below him as he turned and set off bleakly back again. Philip, shoelaces trailing, school tie in a noose, crossed the yard. Then, not wanting to, trying not to, Andrew watched Jocasta and Jack walking side by side to breakfast together, Jocasta composed and neat, Jack tall above her, smiling down. Jocasta was walking calmly towards the kitchen, where reigned The Missus, who had confronted her in the night.

I'll leave now, Andrew thought. *Just go. Send for the child later. Pammie Jefford might come for her. I could even . . .* and, though he knew no reason for it, his eyes all at once brimmed with tears . . . *I could even go to Thomasina. I could beg her.*

With a surge of longing, for some sort of absolution, for the chance of letting in a corner of light on the chasm left by the death of Holly not filled but deepened by the obsession for Jocasta, Andrew thought, *I might tell Thomasina everything.*

He had seen her at the funeral of Pammie Jefford's husband, which he'd gone to out of gratitude and respect for Pammie and hoping ridiculously that Jocasta might be there. And Jocasta had been there. And without Jack, who was tied by the farm, as ever. Afterwards he had spent the night with Jocasta in a hotel room and he had thought there had never been such abandon and happiness and anguish. As he had put her on the train back to The Priors, they had both been dazed, drained, drenched by the night.

Now, the terror of The Missus with her gorgon head of steel, her terrifying passion for Jack, the voice of Jocasta saying, 'Stay with me,' and the sight of her walking unconcernedly beside Jack towards the kitchen for breakfast prepared and presided over by The Missus. And the memory of the child he could not love who stretched up confident arms to things he

168

did not understand, had her eyes fixed on invisible things – all this, and physical exhaustion, too, gathered inside him a well of shame, a glut of shame, a need for cleansing.

It was Thomasina's face at the funeral of Pammie's old man, the face he had known as cynical and witty over the betrothal champagne, bright and competent at her daughter's wedding, unbearable to contemplate in the antiseptic gleam of the health farm, absent at Holly's funeral, blank and lost as she passed him in the Jaguar on the ridge with the ancient boyfriend; the face that he had seen last at Jefford's funeral was a face grown old. Thomasina an old woman. Yet alive now in some sense and perhaps ready now freely to receive, freely to give.

I'll go to Thomasina, now, he thought. *She will take Faith now, I know she will. She will take me. We could live together near London, out of all this, the three of us.*

So right, so beautiful, so inevitable did this solution seem that the night hours, the knowledge of sin and chaos, went into the shadows, thinned, evaporated. He started walking down towards The Priors again as one shriven, even as one blessed.

And he found a cold room, no fire in the stove, no table laid, no food to be seen, everyone gathered helpless and unbelieving.

'Gone?' he said. 'She can't have gone.'

Jocasta turned away and began to cut bread, which she passed round. Philip found some butter and jam and began to eat. Ernie Smike filled a kettle with cold water and slapped it on the coke stove, which had gone out. Nick Smike said there was an electric kettle somewhere, maybe over with the Tibetan lot, but did nothing to find out. Philip opened a can of Coke and swigged it from a hole in the top and said, 'So, who's getting me to school?'

When Jocasta's car had disappeared with Philip, Andrew had stood in the courtyard watching it away, thinking that he had seen Jocasta for the last time. For the last time.

But he could not just go. This morning. Just leave the place and the baby – now. It would look suspiciously wild. He must speak to Thomasina first. Or to Pammie at any rate. He must see Jocasta again and discuss what to tell Jack. He must tell Jocasta, tell her that now that he and the baby and Thomasina would be living together in the south he would not be coming back up here again. Ever. Over. Except of course now and then to see his parents. They were getting old. He'd neglected them for a long time. But he could visit them without coming up to The Priors. No one need ever know of any rift between the brothers.

And, come to that, was there, realistically, any need to tell Jack? Tell him everything? Or – well, anything at all? Jack's shining soul, God help him, would never for an instant suspect. Never suspect his brother's sin. There. He'd said it. Christ! Sin. Not much talk of sin these days. We don't live in classical times. Oedipus. Phaedra. Jocasta. Vengeance of the gods – all unknown now.

We're all trivial now, thought Andrew, *hardly Titans falling from heaven, lost gods lying blinded along a darkened plain. No one believes in heaven. Religion's an affected joke, patchwork, ridiculous, easy to forget. 'Love' is talked about all the time, 'adoration' even, but not in relation to God. No eagles now. All sparrows.*

He thought of silly Holly, sexy and laughing and obvious, of her child in the lamplight, of Jack's narrow sweet face. A wonderful face. His fortune. Women loved it. Always had. Even old Pammie in her pearl studs and her million-pound house.

And Jocasta?

There had been a sensual, submissive quiet about Jocasta walking this morning beside Jack after the tempestuous night. Jack's hand had touched the back of Jocasta's neck for a moment as they had passed through the door to the kitchen and she had not shrunk away. Jack had looked down at her with love.

A great wave of longing for Jocasta filled Andrew now. Jocasta, my Jocasta, his heart called.

Her voice calling after him, 'Stay with me.' Was it, maybe, after all, not unforgivable?

– 28 –

When Pammie saw the letter on the high shelf in the garage above the spot where poor Hugo had laid down his head for the last time, she stood for a moment looking at it. She took it in her hands. The junk mail and the phone bill she put in her pocket. She examined the old-fashioned handwriting on the Yorkshire envelope.

She wondered why she felt so still. Then she realised that she wasn't talking to anyone. The relentless, exhausting inner voice that accompanied her everywhere, even in dreams, was quiet. She had no desire to share this curious event. And at the same time she had the mad notion that the letter must be from Hugo. That he had got it to her from wherever he had gone. And then she thought, *I'm going mad. It must be a letter of condolence*, and walked into the house.

Standing once more in the rosy drawing room about to be demolished in favour of Japan, she thought, *But it couldn't be. He wasn't dead then.*

She considered a letter of condolence for one's own death being put into one's hands ahead of time by the postman. The Black Spot. Enough to give you a heart attack.

But it hadn't been opened. Maybe – stretching up to the shelf and then stooping down to the mower – it had been Hugo's Black Spot. She saw it happen. Yet, even so, the voice of the full-time whispering raconteur, the entertainer of unsuspecting Jinny and Laura and Didi and Wendy and Thomasina, kept silence. For more important than the telling of this macabre little happening, Pammie found, was the happening itself.

And after all, here it was: it was a letter of condolence before death – a letter written two days before Hugo's departure to greener lawns.

'My dear Mrs Jefford,' it said, 'I was so sorry . . .'

It must be from some seer.

But it went on. 'I was so sorry not to have been able to see you properly on to the London train the other day and now I wish so much that I had not burdened you with the potatoes. I very much blame myself after your incredibly tiring day for insisting that we stop to see the church of St Ethelswitha and St Eadburga (who was, of course, King Alfred's mother) and the lovely market town of Stokesley. I very seldom drive these days on account of absent-mindedness and I misjudged the time it would take to get to York. The full glory of the day was upon me, the mixture of sorrow and joy. Our Holly's death and the arrival of Faith at The Priors have rather disoriented me. I don't believe any of us has ever thanked you for the valiant rescue of my niece, but I promise you it will never be forgotten by her family. You and your husband are welcome here not only to see the child but whenever you wish to come for a holiday, to stay as long as possible. We have, as you saw, plenty of room! I should like to say that your bracing presence and common sense – and, if I may say so, your lovely face – steadied us all on a very emotional day and you are remembered in our prayers.

'There is much I want to show you. Our Tibetans. Jocasta, whom you did not really meet. Faith's grandparents, who are very keen to meet and thank you. God bless you. Until your next visit,

'Jack Braithwaite.'

One would have expected this from Andrew, she thought, sitting on a velvet humpty, gazing at the doomed mock-Adam fireplace with its twirl of heather in the grate like *Country Life*. She had found the heather pushed into the top of the bag of potatoes.

The whirlwind day in Yorkshire returned to her. She had forgotten most of it. It seemed distant. Mixed with guilt. The guilt of having left Hugo alone when he had had such a short time to go. That in turn had led to the guilt of having neglected him during the time when they had housed the baby.

Not that she had ever hung over the baby. Like all childless women, Pammie did not believe in hanging over babies.

'Babies need letting alone and if they cry they cry,' thought and declared Pammie, who had never been kept awake by anything in her life. Her dogs as puppies had been banished to an outhouse with a nice rug and a ticking clock for company. They had been very well-behaved dogs; you hardly knew they were there. That is how, she had told the night nurse, she should treat Faith.

Hugo had done more hanging about over Faith than she. The baby had never gripped her finger and smiled. Pammie had a secret notion that it hadn't gripped Hugo's finger either. He'd been so dotty. It was probably the nurse's finger he'd caught hold of.

No. That wouldn't do. Hugo had been faithful. Always. Proud of her and her busy life. Found it commendable. Funny. Liked the way she biffed about. Made jokes about it. She'd liked the jokes and overdid the biffing to have more of them, pinning up lists of future events and phone numbers all over the kitchen, getting Christmas finished before anyone else. All the presents bought and wrapped by December the first. Dear old Hugo.

'*Your lovely face.*'

Well.

She reread the letter, wondering why exactly she liked it so much. *There wouldn't be much bought and wrapped at The Priors by December the first. Or the twenty-first. The state of that office place. And that boy's hair. Looked cut with the kitchen scissors. And the old witch stirring over the stove. And the grease in that refectory!*

She began to consider what she knew of Christmases in religious institutions. Her Christmas cards had often pictured such scenes. *Rollicking tonsures. One couldn't imagine a Christmas card depicting The Priors, not unless it was an appeal for the Third World. But such lovely country. It must be looking beautiful now, probably under snow. Thomasina suggested Cyprus for Christmas but they hadn't done anything about it yet. Not one word from the dreaded Andrew. Good of him to come to the funeral, of course. The little dark woman with him must have been the terrifying Jocasta. How good of*

Jack to send her to stand in for him, especially as she was obviously his wife only in a very bohemian sort of way. She didn't look the type you ordered around. Maybe she was one of those romantics – those Arthurian romantics, playing at courtly love, that you hear about still. Though not likely. She must have wanted to come. I wonder who had the baby overnight. Not a word in this letter about how the baby is doing. Probably hasn't noticed. Unworldly. Not exactly the family man. A bit crazy.

'Lovely face', he says, 'if I may say so.'

And thinking of Hugo's old noddle wagging up and down over the baby's cot Pammie remembered it was Hugo, the morning he died, who had suggested they go north to visit The Priors, together for a nice weekend, and she rose from the humpty, crossed the room and dialled the number.

As the phone rang far away in the cold old ruin she hung on and on, looking out at her garden through the magnificent potted azaleas on the windowsill to the odd rogue rose still dancing and springing about untidily, brilliantly, eight feet high above the box parterre, the odd gold leaf, the odd still-juicy branch of singed and shrivelled buddleia. A desultory blue pyre rose from the last hedge-clippings over on the bonfire place behind and in front of the mirrored trellis and drifting leaves lay all over the grass. *Whatever would Hugo say?*

The phone rang on and on in the office of The Priors, for so long that the Tibetan girl came over at last from the sheds, Faith hanging fore and aft under her arm. But by the time she reached it Pammie had rung off.

'Yes? Hello?' Jocasta, getting out of the car from the school run, saw the girl coming from the office into the courtyard. 'D'you want something? What's under your arm?'

The girl put the roll of padded matting up on her shoulder. A face looked out, like an owl in a hollow tree.

'Oh, Faith. Well, she's warm enough anyway. What do you want?'

'The phone was ringing.'

Jack came from the direction of the chapel, carrying a

174

bucket. '*Yes?* The Missus? Where is she?'

'I missed it. Rang off as I picked it up. Been ringing on and on. Driving you crazy. I went over to try to stop it.'

'Why was no one there?' asked Jocasta.

'I had chickens to feed.' Jack lowered his eyes before her.

'Where's Andrew, then?'

'He's gone down to Toots. In case Alice is there. Or in case they've heard something from her.'

'I thought he wasn't going down there again unless the baby was with him. They're very upset they haven't seen her.'

'I know. He felt he couldn't. She wasn't ready.'

'Pema says 'er eye's gone wrong agen,' said the girl. 'And there's a message from Pema. She says there's more food needed in the sheds. We're out of everythin'.'

'The Missus isn't here today, I'm afraid.' Jack looked helplessly at Jocasta. 'Somebody else will have to take over.'

'I don't cook,' said Jocasta.

'Well, you can eat with us lot if yer like,' said the girl. 'Just get us in some stuff, like. Or I can go down Whitby. I could get some takeaways.'

'Well, I've a class now,' said Jocasta, 'if you're all ready?'

She walked with the baby and the girl to the studio shed while Jack went alone to the office and wondered what to do. Sitting in all the dust, he moved his hands over the mess of papers. The hands were dirtied by the chicken mash and he remembered there'd been no soap in the bathroom this morning. There was a button off his shirt cuff and he pressed the edges together hopefully, wishing they would stick. He thought of Jocasta's neat clothes. *They don't do things for men any more*, he thought, and drooped. He had a facility for this, almost sensuous, a wilting of the frame, head bowed in humility. God watching.

He thought of his mother waddling up and down that passage in the house on the estuary over fifty years. Ten and thirty times a day with offerings for Toots. Paddle, paddle. Carrying Toots's beautifully polished shoes with the pressed laces.

The telephone rang.

175

'Hello? Hello? Missus? Alice?'

'I'm sorry, no. Is that Jack Braithwaite? This is Pammie Jefford.'

He couldn't imagine who that was.

'I've just seen your letter.'

'My letter?'

'Written just before my husband died.'

'Oh. Yes. I do hope that it was helpful.' Then he remembered her. 'Oh, I'm so sorry. I didn't write about that. I purposely sent Jocasta instead to the funeral. The farm . . . I felt that prayers for you would be more valuable. I do hope so. Letters of condolence only have to be answered. I didn't forget you, my dear.'

'Thank you.' *He sounds ninety.* 'No, this was a letter you wrote me earlier. About the day I spent with you. When I brought Faith. I've just found it. It had been – mislaid.'

There was a pause, growing long. Pammie in Coombe felt herself grow shy. When she realised that Jack had forgotten about the letter and the affection in it, she found to her great surprise that she was crying.

'I brought you the baby.'

The pause continued. She had been cut off?

Then Jack said slowly, 'I don't suppose you could possibly . . .'

The wallpapery room swam, the pot plants trembled. Pammie found her handkerchief. She said – and it came out aggressively – 'What?'

'. . . come here again? We're in a bit of trouble. My old housekeeper has, well, actually disappeared. I don't like to ask. I hear you're very high-powered. Justice of the Peace. On committees and so on. Can't pretend it's comfortable here.'

'I'll let you know,' she said and rang off as the room came back into focus.

She tossed the letter into the flower-painted wastepaper basket, chucked the measuring rod for the home improvements on to a chair, went into the kitchen and made coffee. She poured the coffee into an ornate green and gold cup, placed a silver teaspoon in the saucer, carried the coffee to Hugo's old study and sat in his polished swivel chair. She sat. *Bloody cheek*, she thought. Then she swivelled round in it, full circle. Once. She dialled Thomasina.

'My dear! Now, whatever do you think about this? What do you think I should do? Yes – *now*! So I gather. Great crisis. *Oh*, yes. Some sort of walkout by staff. Yes, I gather that too: storms in teacups – they're never without them up there. Not enough to do. They're all a bit mad. Hysterical. Life full of nothing but incidents you and I could fix in five minutes. It's the North. These people talk about them afterwards for years. Oh no – my dear, I am *not* smitten. Yes, I know he's charismatic or whatever they call it. He's years younger than me and he's married. In a sort of way.

'Imposition? Well, I don't know. *Is* it, Thomasina? You? No, you shouldn't be the one to go. Don't let me mess you about, suggesting that. You know how we all felt about Egypt, but that's your affair. You don't have to grovel. Yes – OK, then. I'll leave it. I won't say another word. You've been very good to me since then. Nobody could have been kinder.

'Andrew? Haven't you heard from him? He's *dropped* you! How could he, you're Holly's mother. It just isn't done and even if he's from the back of beyond he's a gent. Yes, I know he's worked off his feet. He looked awful in Yorkshire. His brother's twenty years older, different generation, but he looked the better horse, I must say. Quite young, really. Jack Braithwaite's the sort that doesn't age. It's all that curly hair and the Thomas Hardy look – though, mind you, Thomas Hardy wouldn't have lasted up there ten minutes. No golden harvests and lands of the great dairies up there, Thomasina dear. No cider apples and greenwood trees. A frightful barren place. How he does it with only two village idiots – well, you've been there. I'll give you some of his potatoes.

'Thomasina? Thomasina – are you there? Yes, I'm better, of course I'm better, I started to feel better this morning. Hugo wouldn't have wanted . . . I had a letter from him this morning. No, of course not. From Jack. Written just before dear Hugo set sail. Very nice. Lovely letter. It's what I rang for.

'Yes, it would mean no Cyprus for Christmas . . . I did just wonder, well, it's occurring to me now, actually, I suppose you wouldn't feel like spending Christmas at – well, northwards?'

'I'll ring back,' said Thomasina.

A crash from the kitchen had signalled a crisis from the general, who was making wine on the end of the kitchen table.

'Trouble with the bungs,' he said.

'Pammie,' she said carefully, as she swept up the green splinters into a long-handled dustpan with a long-handled nylon broom – her fingernails so pretty, not a crack in the lacquer – 'Pammie on the phone. She's thinking of going up to see the baby again.'

'It's far too far to go up and back in one day.'

'She *indicated*,' Thomasina handed him the dustpan of debris to carry across the kitchen to the litter bin with its white plastic lining, 'that she might be going to live there.'

'My God!'

'And also she wondered if I'd like to go too. Join her there for Christmas.'

'Alone?' he asked, not looking at her, showering out the broken bits of glass.

'She didn't say. She hasn't actually agreed to go herself yet. She's had some sort of loving letter from Jack. She doesn't know it yet but it's the letter he writes to everyone.'

'But isn't he married?'

'He married a hanger-on of Andrew. To comfort her.'

'Who told you that?'

'Well – Holly, actually.'

'And Holly?' He went over and put his arms round her. '*Holly*? Go on then, Thoms.'

'Well, Holly was rather naughty really. It wasn't a bit like her. She just said once that Andrew had told Jack to have pity on one of his troublesome ex-patients and take her off his hands.'

'Jack was *obliging* Andrew? How very odd.'

She started laughing and the general joined in with a few snorts.

'I mean,' he said, 'dear Jack doesn't sound exactly Heath-cliff.'

'I don't know,' she said. 'Some women go mad for skin and bones. I do rather.'

'And you can't call Pammie Catherine Earnshaw,' said the general.

'I didn't know you were an intellectual, darling.'

'No fear. I saw it on a telly ad. I say – it's rather good to be laughing, Thomasina.'

She was frying (in butter) tiny pieces of liver with sage, dropping them deftly into the pan.

After lunch they were going to Bentalls of Kingston to see after a new eiderdown for Thomasina's bed, getting rid of the vulgar duvet. Then home in time to walk the new dog in the lanes.

At six, over sherry, the general said, 'Happy, Thoms? Not hankering after the blasted heath?'

She said, 'Shall we watch *Blind Date*? It's so awful. I adore it.' She eased off her shoes.

'What thinking?' he asked at bedtime before he set off for home, kissing her cheek.

'Nothing.'

'Tell me.'

Both knew that it had nothing to do with the fact that he was going home.

She closed her eyes and he took her by the shoulders.

'Say it, woman!'

'Wondering,' she said, 'what to buy the wretched baby for Christmas.'

'Why not say "Faith"?'

– 29 –

Toots gave a bellow from his bed at teatime and Dolly came running, to find him pointing a furious finger at the dark winter window. 'She's out there.'

'Who? What are you on about?'

'Her. Middleditch. Standing out on the grass, looking in.'

'Don't be so soft. When did she ever not walk straight in through the door? It's what you can't stand, the way she comes in. It's years since there was by your leave.'

'I tell you, she's out on that grass, looking puzzled.'

'It's too dark to see anyone looking puzzled. It's too dark to see if you're rambling,' said Dolly, 'but just in case you're not . . .' She tapped on the glass and called, 'Mrs Middleditch? Hello? Don't stand in the cold.'

No reply came from the frosty garden but some scuffling sounds were going on in the direction of the front door, a kind of stamping.

'It'll be the boot scraper,' said Dolly. 'She's been in the flower bed. She's gone off her head. What we have to put up with, being old, the sort of people we have to know, and all in the name of charity. It's the worst thing she's ever done, walking in from the flower bed.'

'She'll have buggered up the bulbs. I've a mind to tell the police.'

'Maybe it isn't her at all. It might be muggers.'

But in burst Mrs Middleditch in her broderie anglaise and good cardigan and zip jacket and mackintosh and muffler. She erupted before them.

Curiously she seemed to have nothing to say.

'A cup of tea, Mrs Middleditch?' asked Dolly.

'Oh, no, thank you. I have to be getting back. Actually, I've been thinking . . .'

'Oh yes?'

'I wondered if you'd both like to come round to me for a cuppa?'

'Dolly can go,' said Toots at once. 'It's after dark. I don't stir after dark.' His zimmer frame was by the bed, his calliper alongside on the blankets like a sword on a tomb. A thriller lay across his chest and a bottle of whisky which could be reached at top speed was in the cupboard. 'Do her good. Never goes out.'

'Is it a birthday?' Dolly warily asked.

'No, no. Not at all. But . . .'

They had never seen her hesitant. Nonplussed.

Toots thought, *He's left her. About time.*

'*But*,' said Mrs Middleditch, 'we have a visitor and we don't know what to do with her. I think one of you should come to her since she won't stir. It's that Alice Banks.'

'At your house? The Missus?'

'Yes. She's landed.'

'Now you must have asked her, Beryl,' said Dolly, using the given name on account of the seriousness of the moment.

'Asked her? Never. I hardly know the woman.'

'She must be confused. She's confusing you with us. She's never been very normal.'

'No. I don't think so. She calls me by my name. Arnold would be more *au fait* with what to do about her. Tonight he has to be out, of course, with his work for the Boys' Brigade. She's settled in and her car's locked up in the road. For the night, it looks. Packed with stuff.'

'She's not been in that car – I don't know when I remember her off in that car,' said Dolly. 'What if it snows? She'll never get back.'

'Packed full,' said Beryl Middleditch, flushing, 'to the gunnels. Packed up with shoes and boxes and heaps of rags. There's an electric kettle and a whole pack of grapefruits. I'd think she's left Jack.'

'Dolly, get your hat on,' said Toots. 'And wrap up: it's a cold night. Go after her and bring her round here. I'll settle this.'

'Oh, I'm sure there's no need for that.' Mrs Middleditch was

181

bewildered by another's taking command. She hadn't known Toots at the height of his authoritarian powers. This was part of the trouble. She treated him as an old chap. 'It's just that I find her rather confused,' she said.

'Talking about Gracie Fields, I dare say?'

'Well, as a matter of fact she is.'

'Yes, she does.'

Dolly departed with Middleditch. Toots shot out of bed and, ignoring the hardware around him, made for the cupboard on flat but confident feet. Sitting on the bed end, he took a good swig and filled up the bottle to its previous level from a bottle of ginger ale kept for the purpose. The whisky tasted filthy because of this process having been followed many times before, more ale now than grog. But still, there was something left to cheer the heart. The telephone rang and, being made amiable by the noggin, Toots eased himself down the passage to the hall chair and picked up the phone.

'*Toots!*' said Thomasina. '*Dear* Toots! You have a phone by your bed.'

'Who? Thomasina? Well, my godfathers! Thomasina. I don't believe it. How are you? By Gad, we think of you. Dolly's out. There's a mad woman sitting in somebody's house. How's our granddaughter?'

'Thank you, dear Toots, for your lovely letter,' she said. 'I'm sorry. I couldn't answer. I went to Egypt.'

'Very nice.' He thought, *I mustn't forget to ask after Holly*, and then remembered. He was doing that sort of thing nowadays. 'By Gad,' he said instead, several times, 'Thomasina!'

'I was thinking of coming up.'

'Then you'll stay here,' he said at once. 'We've three spare rooms now that I'm downstairs. And bring that sexy green dress.'

She laughed and said he was a disgraceful old man and who was the mad woman down the street? He listened carefully, on his better ear, to her southern voice. Her face came back to him.

'It's very nice of you to ring here,' he said. 'We can't be very interesting to you.'

'You were always riveting, Toots. The things that went on.'

'I remember you coming visiting here once,' he said. 'I remember you sitting on the piano stool. The first time they came back from California, the three of you together. You've lovely legs.'

'Yes. I remember.'

'I said "You have lovely legs".'

'Now then, Toots. Toots –' she said '– I was just ringing. Wanted to hear you.'

'You're a brave woman, Thomasina.'

'Oh no. I ran to Egypt.'

'Well, who wouldn't run? If we'd lost Jack or Andrew, I don't know how far we'd run. If we had the money. That was our advantage. By, but we pitied you, Thomasina, how we pitied you. We wept for you, and for all of us.'

'Don't, Toots.'

'Baby lovely, I hear.'

'Yes. Well, I expect you know more about that. You'll have seen her often.'

'Well, now then, as a matter of fact – they're very busy up there, you know. And there's the weather. There's always something going on. We'll be going up there for Christmas, unless it snows.'

'That's what I was going to say. Christmas. If I could come up for Christmas – no, we'd stay in a hotel, I wouldn't land the two of us on you. I have a friend. There's a hotel up on the moors near The Priors. But we would see you both, Toots, wouldn't we?'

'We'll be there,' he said. 'Unless it snows. They're putting on a Christmas show up there – three kings and so on, and Faith's to be christened. Nativity thing.'

'And we would see *you*?'

'You would. I'll make sure of it. There's sixes and sevens up there at present with this mad woman. Barmy about Jack for twenty years and she's made off with a car full of shoes. Left him. Housekeeper.'

'Not The Missus! Well! If she wants another job, tell her there's one down here for her. A dotty old lady and a man called Puffy. We – my friends and I – are desperate for them.'

'Oh, everyone's desperate about old folk,' said Toots, 'I can't think why. Everyone's desperate about us two. "Where will it end?" – they hang about the gate saying it to each other – "Where will it end for the pair of them?" That sort of thing. You know, life's very comfortable. It's laughable if you don't read the papers. There's some terrible fools about. But it makes entertainment.'

Ringing off, she thought, *I like those people so.*

Ringing off, he thought, *Well, how about that, then? Thomasina! Lovely woman. Beautiful voice. Like Holly's.*

Dolly, having tottered home and into the overheated house, found him prone upon the bed with his braces loose, and smiling.

'It's The Missus all right,' she said. 'Just sitting there. She doesn't say what she's up to but she can't stop talking and I've had to say she can come here if she wants. I don't think she does. She's laid back on that peach settee with her shoes off. And – Toots – she does smell of fry.'

'What's the matter?' She looked sharply at silent Toots. 'What's this grin about? Have you been in the cupboard?'

'I've been having a conversation,' he informed the light fitting, 'with Apple Green.'

'You rang her? You're drunk.'

'She rang here. Just for a chat. What about that, then? Nice as pie. Voice like the Queen.'

'Thomasina Fox rang *us*?'

'Aye. She's coming to stay,' he said, 'Christmas time. Never a dull minute. She's coming and The Missus is coming. By the way, I've fixed The Missus up with another job.'

− 30 −

Jack scarcely ever visited his parents, though probably he had not realised it. When The Missus flew to them, however, or virtually to them, for the alighting on Mrs Middleditch was only a preliminary settling, it was obvious even to him that he must be the one to fetch her home again.

Jack was not one to seek explanations. Others came to him with their troubles, at which he never seemed surprised. Other people's troubles were his workload. They poured them at his feet like offerings and were comforted by his loving face, or at any rate a face that had set into practised loving lines. His face was a strange face. It sometimes looked quite wooden. It always looked innocent, with candid eyes you never surprised or found assessing.

What lay behind the eyes was a mysterious area for Toots.

But then, Jack had always been a puzzle to Toots. If he'd been anyone else's son he'd have said he was plain dippy, a cartoon loony, but, since he was his own and Toots had his pride, he kept quiet. 'Wonderful boy,' they'd all said when Jack was at school, the school where Toots taught. Toots had watched him effortlessly collecting honours. At the university Jack had won a cricketing blue and a First in Physics before becoming entangled with God. Then followed certain spells in the wilderness, ordination, and more spells in the wilderness. For some years Jack had been cut off from his parents and the North, descending upon them only once or twice from nowhere, sitting smiling in their kitchen, thin as a skeleton, looking at the food Dolly put before him with historical interest, faint reminder of old pleasures. Cricket talk with Toots had been the only thing to raise a flicker of interest.

Toots had grown silent, too, with disappointment. He and Dolly did not discuss Jack together then. Only after the arrival of The Missus and the subsequent more or less straight course of Jack the parish priest did they begin to drop his name into general conversation again. They began to wonder sometimes if after all Jack might reach the high office everyone knew – of course – he deserved. Such ludicrous bishops about, not half as clever as Jack. Dolly always believed he was in with a chance, until he fetched up one day almost on his own home pad, The Missus in attendance like a snappish Sancho Panza, and began his crazy venture on the Yorkshire moors.

By Gad, he's been a funny fellow, the now bedridden Toots thought. *Whatever was it we did wrong?*

He had never once discussed Jack's career with him, never once said that he had been saddened by the fading of the golden years. Now he just brooded on the whole thing from the bed and, when the various Middleditches of the town enquired not quite innocently about Jack, Toots was taciturn but never judgemental. There were private explosions sometimes, though, and as he grew old some weeping sometimes in the night that Dolly knew about. The recent arrival of the Tibetans was the worst thing yet, in Toots's mind, after the bizarre marriage to Jocasta. 'The Snake', Toots called her. Jocasta had represented the depths of Toots's mystification and sadness about his son.

For Dolly, Jack had never done wrong. He could never disappoint. He was unique, her first-born, her star. Andrew, born so long after, walked his steady road uphill towards the London hospital, got clear of his old home, and his parents' friends informed them of how proud they must be, overdoing it rather to try to blot out the embarrassment of Jack. Dolly would have none of it, cutting in on Andrew's praises with anecdotes about her first-born. 'It was Jack had the brains,' she would say. '*Oh*, yes. Andrew was just run-of-the-mill. He was the one who had to work. It all just came to Jack.'

The small bedroom that had once been Jack's Andrew had moved into when his brother went to university, as it was a few feet bigger than his own, but when Andrew left home it became 'Jack's room' again. Dolly carried all Jack's things back into it and moved Andrew's out. She kept it clean and tidy, the old school books dusted on the shelves. She secretly wished she could reconstruct Jack's chaos again, the rubbish she had not been allowed to touch, the greasy plates shoved under the bed and forgotten, the dangling icons, the furniture eased into the middle of the room and surrounded by newspaper screens.

'But *why ever*, Jack?' (His wonderful young face.)

'It's too big. I don't need all this space.'

'Why do you sleep on the floor?'

Jack had grinned and looked away and Toots had said, 'You're a fool, boy. You do no work, just lying there. You'll fail.'

But inside the paper screens something must have been going on, for Jack always passed out top.

'Well, I'm sure – I don't know,' Dolly had said proudly.

Sometimes even now she sat alone in the narrow room. She said to friends that it was a way of getting a break from Toots, the stairs now being far too steep for him. She sat in the three-cornered art-nouveau chair beside the iron bedstead and looked out at the church spire across the allotments, the steelworks behind blossoming scarlet and gold. A solemn church bell. She thought of little Jack hearing the dreary thing all those years (she forgot Andrew) and wondered if that was what had been wrong. *If we'd put him looking over the street or towards the sandbanks*, she thought, *there might have been less religion. But he was a lovely boy.* She sat dreaming of his gaiety. Now when Jack came down very occasionally to see them she had to adjust to the fact that this gaunt, hesitant man had been the quicksilver larky boy who had never once given any hint that what he wanted to do was try to live like Christ.

'Very funny boy, your Jack,' Mrs Middleditch had said after Toots had been insulting her more than usual. 'I remember him, just. He used to like sleeping under his bed. I never thought it was quite nice.'

Yet even Mrs Middleditch was balked by the Jack of today. He met her torrents of instruction to the world with a sweetness – and silence – that threw her off course. She would have liked to tell him a thing or two like you ought to be able to tell a parson, but then she'd known him as a boy and that was always difficult. She'd like to have told him about Toots's drinking and betting with Nick Smike, and the trouble Dolly had bathing him, and his poisonous rudeness to people – quite respectable people – and Dolly's breathlessness going upstairs. But the disturbingly loving face of Jack had her beaten.

She pursed her lips as one who might say much, but 'please yourself, if you don't want to ask'. She scratched the backs of her hands, shuffled on her bottom hoity-toity, wondering how she could get across to Toots and Dolly that Jack was not the Lord God. Now and then she hinted he might do more for them and described the wonderful sense of duty in her own son, Bingham, who lived at home at forty-three and saw to all their shopping.

When Jack at last arrived in quest of The Missus it was with Philip.

It was a cold and nasty day well into December – he hadn't hurried. He was wet, with no coat over his cassock, and Philip not much better in an anorak that had a broken zip and was much too small for him. Jack sat down in the Windsor chair and stared gently at the electric fire. In and out of his mind floated the conviction that God must be with him since Mrs Middleditch hadn't spotted his car at the door and was not yet present. Toots lay staring at the ceiling. Dolly looked down at Jack's wet shoes. One of them had a string for a lace. Philip had disappeared upstairs to wash his hands. 'Is he still washing them?' she said. 'He was at that last time. Every half-hour. I wonder if his bladder's wrong.'

'Is that possible at eleven?' Jack still examined the electric element. 'We'd better get Andrew to look at him.'

'Is Andrew still up there?'

'No, no. I mean next time.' He felt Dolly's eyes shift to his soil-begrimed hands and put them out of sight.

Toots said, 'So you and Philip are down here on your own, then?'

'I'm sorry,' said Jack. 'You'll think I'm making excuses, but they wouldn't let me bring her. I was driving. No one would hear of it.'

'They're ready to risk Philip, then?'

'Well, he's quite a help. He warns me of the traffic lights.'

There was silence between the three of them, all apart yet all aware of what the others thought.

Jack said, 'You're both coming, then, on Christmas Eve? To the christening? And Jocasta's putting on a tableau. That's all fixed if Mrs Middleditch can only bring you and take you back. Faith will be just three months old, I'm to tell you. I'm told it is a lovely age. The eyes have cleared up – they come and go rather. Pema has been going on to Jocasta, saying that a baby looks its brightest and best at three months and all the crumpled red look gone.'

'Pema,' said Dolly. 'I hope we shall be meeting Pema. Whoever she is.'

'Oh, she's been magnificent with Faith,' he said. 'Or, at least, so we all thought.'

'It's funny,' said Dolly. 'Nobody ever tells you about a new baby without saying it hasn't got that crumpled red look. What is it? I've never seen it. Mine were lovely babies from the start. You looked like a curly little gold cherub, Jack.'

Jack's bony Savonarola face lengthened the more.

He had had terrible days since the flight of The Missus. Andrew had announced that he had to be on duty, the first Jack had heard of it, and Jocasta had said she must be on call for meeting Pammie Jefford, to which Jack had agreed. He had been overcome with shyness at the thought of meeting Pammie himself. The Smikes were useless, forever alleging it was their day off or they were too busy in the fields. Then, an hour or so ago, just as he and Philip were setting off, the A-level girl had come wandering by to say that all the Tibetans would be leaving The Priors at Christmas.

'Ah,' he had said, looking away from her.

'Sorry, Jack.'

'But the looms? It was all done for you. It's a charitable trust. Registered. Charity money. You were to stay into next year.'

'There'll be plenty want them. We could get them sold for you if you like. There's someone in Liverpool.'

'Ah. Liverpool.'

'Yeah. We're ever so sorry, Jack, but we don't like it here.'

'You mean with Alice gone? The food?'

'God, no, we like our own. No, it's just it doesn't work here, see. Someone has to tell you. It's different worlds. It's all daft stuff after Liverpool. It's not the teaching we expected.'

'Jocasta? You'll not find anyone better qualified. And all totally free, if you don't mind my saying so.'

The girl gave him a look.

'Well, don't you agree?'

'I guess,' she said. 'But she's old, Jocasta, see. We're sick of this negative-space stuff. It's as long gone as Picasso. Out of date, like. We want to get into New Art and that.'

'I'll let her know,' he said, standing like a pinnacle, staring towards the moor lane. 'We've spent, the charity has spent, a great deal of money.'

'I guess. But you'll get someone else. You might get intellectuals or writers' groups. They're cheaper.'

'Not through the winter. Oh, I might just say that there is a new housekeeper coming. Mrs Jefford, who brought us Faith. Would that make a difference? I think she will be a very dependable woman.'

'I saw her. Christ, Jack, you haven't a hope. Lipstick and lady-dresses. She'll never last here. Oh, and we've told Jocasta already. We told her last week. And the lads.'

'The Smikes know? Jocasta knows?'

'Yeah. Actually, Jack, Nick's comin' wid us.'

'Nick? To Liverpool?'

'Don't go for me! I'm not bothered. "Suit yourself," I said. "Come if you want." But I tellt 'im it wouldn't do 'im no permanent good wid me.'

'You and Nick?'

'He thinks so. I don't. Not permanent. I'm getting to art school next year, the Slade if I can, and I will.'

'Nick is leaving Ernie?'

'I guess.'

What Jack was looking at then in his parents' house was not

the red bar of the fire but these revelations, particularly the bombshell about The Smikes, who had been in the Braithwaite family for years. They were not brothers. The name was a literary joke they both understood but pretended not to. They denied any education. They were not lovers either, Nick sturdy, short-legged, scowling, watchful-eyed, level-headed, Ernie away in a world of his own. They were mates, that was all they had told Jack when he took them on. Neither paid attention to the other's partners and behaved as if they didn't exist. Ernie expected Nick's girlfriends to be slags and never addressed them. Nick, 'on principle', whatever that meant, did not speak of the gay community of the esplanade fun palaces and considered them boring. He worried, though, about Ernie and Aids and occasionally lectured him on the subject, buying him packets of coloured condoms as if they were sugar candy. He urged him to go for his check-ups. They were like unidentical twins. Some bond forged before their times in prison held them, probably Toots, who alone in their school-days had reached the small but deep areas of their unprepossessing souls. After prison, it had been useful to get some work out of Toots's dotty son and it had been Toots's fierce eyes not Jack's holiness that had made them behave on the whole very well as hirelings at the crazy Priors.

Nick and Ernie had moved about the landscape of Cleveland since then as a pair, always together. You couldn't conceive of one Smike without the other.

'Might I ask' – Jack looked hard at the girl – 'what is to happen to Ernie?'

'Well, 'e'll 'ave ter fettle, won't 'e?'

So that Jack had been more than usually distracted on the journey down, what with the flux of The Missus, Nick and the Tibetans, the imminent arrival of the scarce-known southern matron Pammie – she might already be on the train, unstoppable now even if Alice Banks decided to come back after all. The withdrawal of the Tibetans would mean the withdrawal of funds. The Arts Council allowance that was all that saved the place from total collapse. *And the baby?* he eventually thought. *The baby without the Tibetans?* Would Pammie take her on again? As well as the housekeeping? Obviously not. Jocasta, then? But he knew that Jocasta would not.

'Who's going to look after Faith, then?' Philip had asked in the car.

They were groaning along in low gear through sleet that fell on the miles of simmering chemical works. A caravan park lay in their foothills along the main road, old flaking grey vans sunk down in frozen mud. Some were boarded up, but on the step of another a child in nothing but a T-shirt stood braying at a door to get in. Piles of rubbish lay around in long shallow puddles of rain. It was inconceivable that whole lives were being passed in these tin cans, but from one the white old face of a woman looked out, chewing and ruminating like a beast.

'A terrible place,' said Jack and prayed for all who dwelt in it, closing his eyes to do so and narrowly missing a bus.

Philip yelled.

'You'd better get yourself round there now, lad,' said Toots (the boy looked tired), 'before that woman brings her round here and sits listening in to it all with us.'

'She'll sit listening in round there,' said Dolly.

'No,' said Jack. 'I'll speak to Alice alone.'

'She'll be ear to the door. Can you not take Philip with you to stave her off? He's Alice's friend, aren't you, Philip?'

Jack rang the Middleditch bell pull, Philip beside him on the step, and they found The Missus seated on a shell-pink armchair like a sack of coal against a sunrise.

Jack sat down on the apricot settee and Philip stayed outside in the passage examining the brass medallions on the walls and triumphal certificates of the Boys' Brigade. Mrs Middleditch looked him over unenthusiastically before moving into her lounge to preside. She had dressed seriously for the interview in bottle green, with court shoes and earrings. She moved to the piano stool and cleared her throat.

Jack said, 'I wonder if you'd be very good and get poor Toots a hot drink?'

'We ought to get this settled first.'

'It will be. I'm sure. Could I ask if Philip might go with you?'

'I'm fine here,' said Philip from where he was easing out the metal floor of the hall-stand with scientific interest.

'Stop that at once,' said The Missus and Mrs Middleditch together, and somehow Philip and Mrs Middleditch were side by side in the street and heading along the terrace for the other establishment, Mrs Middleditch coatless and insulated only by her wrath.

Silence fell between Jack and The Missus, Jack basking for a moment, thankful that his professional pastoral manner had not quite left him and that he'd got rid of the opposition. Then the silence grew, and the deeper it struck, the shyer he and The Missus became.

'Have you been comfortable?' he asked in the end.

'It's been satisfactory.'

'It is very good of Mrs Middleditch.'

'No. It's what she lives to do. Get in on other people's messes. And I'd no option. I'll send her a present.'

'Send? So you are coming home, Alice?'

She looked over his head at the plastic head of an Airedale that was attached to the wall with its tongue out.

'This is a right tasteless place,' she said. 'Keeps showing me all over it and it's scarcely two up, two down. She's had her downstairs WC done up low-level glaze. Avocado. Joined tank, and a lavvy brush got up like an owl. Taps gold-plate, dead common.'

'But, Alice, she's not even a friend of yours. You landed on her. Don't you see how good—?'

'Bed that soft you can't get out of it of a morning and running about with cups of Ovaltine half the night. You can hear them on and on talking about Toots and Dolly – and you. And how Philip's being neglected and fourpence in the shilling and that Bingham! Stinks of scent. You have to open the bathroom window so's to let in the filth from the works – it's disgusting, but it's better. That Bingham's far too fat. He eats rubbish. They all do. Over the telly. She puts a sheet down.

And he's forty-two.'

'Alice—'

'Little pasties all half-cooked. Never a decent meal. She's got a negligée. This Arnold's supposed to be the great man for running the church but it's all desk work. Never speaks. Not person-to-person.'

'There is absolutely no reason, Alice, why he should.'

'And she took me clothes and put them through her washer. Said you can't be too careful, coming from farms. I ask you! Left me a great dressing gown to get into, all appliqué reveres. Far too long. Sitting in that box of a kitchen you couldn't get past me, watching all me clothes going round as if it was typhoid. The thing began to scream. That was the drier, if you please, all in one, like the WC. They come out bone hard, past ironing – not that she does any, just smoothes them over them Aga domes. Ridiculous in this hen coop, Aga's just showing off, half the size of the house, boils the place out. Not a decent bite for breakfast, mush, skim-milk and hard apples. I'll get 'er some bacon before I go.'

'So – you will be leaving?'

'Oh aye, Jack. I'll have to go. I can't stay 'ere with satin reveres, I'm not Gracie Fields.'

Again there was silence.

'Alice, could you perhaps tell me . . . ? After all you've been to me, all you've done for me – I know I'm not aware of things sometimes, but what have I done in particular to make you leave me?'

'Nothing.'

'Nothing? Then—?'

'It's the rest of them. It's not right.'

'Has someone insulted you?'

'Not me. Nobody insults me. Not even this Middleditch. I'm going to give her me auntie's gold brooch while she's still deriding me round half Cleveland. That'll shame 'er. No. It's not me. It's you they humiliate, Jack. And I won't have it.'

She sat glaring.

'Well,' he said, 'but, Alice, it doesn't happen, you know. I don't notice, and so it doesn't happen.'

'You can be humiliated unawares,' she said darkly.

'I can take it.' He moved across to her to take her hand. It looked unnaturally clean, softer, older, very small. He kissed it.

'You can leave off that rubbish, I'm no film star. I know me limitations and I'm old as your mother just about. But I won't sit by to see you humiliated, Jack, and so I've got to go.'

Looking into Jack's candid eyes the enormity of what had happened at The Priors swept over Alice Banks again, the horror of the scene in the gatehouse, the shattering of the whole structure of the Christian presence which she had thought Jack had created, the shock of watching the anonymity of sexual desire. Andrew's vacant face turned to her. His sweaty back, Jocasta lying there, her legs wide, her skin shiny.

'Where shall you go?'

'There's a job south. Someone of Holly's.'

'Alice! A job south?'

'I've not even been to London,' she said proudly. 'I've never been drawn. I've met plenty of them, God knows, and I'm not impressed. I keep myself apart and I shall do. But I'll go south now if I have to. I'll go anywhere. Don't ask me no more, Jack.'

'Very well,' he said. 'It's a mystery.'

'Oh, please stop,' for tears were coursing. Her warrior's small head seemed to be vibrating as if it were balanced on a shuddering volcano. Her hands gripped the great black handbag on her knee. 'If you could see to my stuff I could go tomorrow. Toots knows all about where. It's convenient. I'll go.'

'I'll see to things.' He knew he couldn't but maybe Jocasta might. Or Pammie?

'Pammie Jefford is coming.'

'So. I'm replaced. It didn't tek long. Very good. Very good.' But the tears still flowed.

'I'm going to take you out to lunch now. Just you and I and Philip.'

'I couldn't eat.'

'There's a very good fish-and-chip shop.'

The tears lessened.

*

In the chip shop she and Jack sat together to heaped plates; Philip had refused to budge from the car. The Missus after a time began to pick about, then to apply herself. She asked for more vinegar and said the plastic tomato cruets needed a scrub. She spoke of the insanitary aspect of the chip-maker's naked torso above his swimming bath of boiling fat. ' 'Is very sweat'll drop in it,' she said, 'and look at them disgusting tattoos.'

— 31 —

Madeleine and Puffy were not native to Farnham. They did not live at the house of the bride in whose garden Madeleine had been drifting on the morning of the Seton-Fairley wedding. That had been her husband's family territory.

Puffy travelled only to important weddings and funerals nowadays and even these were having to be rationed. He lived with Madeleine in East Kent, on the coast, but with no view of the sea. This did not worry Madeleine as she forgot the sea until she saw it again, but it troubled Puffy. He thought of the sea a great deal, tipped back in his orthopaedic chair.

The tiny room he sat in was furnished in Madeleine's aristocratic lack of taste – frills and rosy covers and dozens of photographs in tarnished silver frames of people with dressed hair, a swirl even of a royal signature (Edward VIII), everyone a little sepia. Limoges and Dresden were dotted about and a small television set was hidden in the Adam-style fireplace behind gold-and-white cupboard doors. Madeleine found herself these days spending more and more time away from this low-ceilinged sitting room where Puffy floated like a giant balloon. She had plenty of help, which she took for granted. She had always been an employer of staff. There was a skinny cleaner and a young man called Henry Jones who would do anything, even feed Puffy little bits of food into his mouth like a mother blackbird. Henry Jones cooked a midday meal and always looked in at night to see that the old pair were all right. Henry was what Madeleine called a pansy and Puffy might have called a woofter if he had been able to address the subject. Henry was very fond of old ladies and of Madeleine's swimmy green eyes.

'But I've simply no one for the *nights*,' complained Madeleine. 'Our only difficulty is the nights. Well, that was always the way with marriage, wasn't it? If the nights are all right, then . . . How very outspoken I am! Poor old Puffy.'

Agonised by her beached-whale straining to hear the sound of the sea that was becoming only a memory on the horizon to him, Madeleine had lately taken to calling for a taxi to get her to the London train, and then, wondering at about Ashford whether she had told Puffy she was going, getting off, ringing him up, missing the next train, getting into conversation with people on the platform, sometimes joining their train and finding herself home again.

Or not home again, which was worse. Once she had taken off with an Indian student who said he was a horticulturalist and ended up with him in the Chelsea Physic Garden and writing him a cheque for fifty pounds. She took him out to tea and found she hadn't a penny in her purse to pay for it. When she rang Puffy to ask him where she had been going in the first place, he panicked and struck the alarm signal on his breast, but that did no good at all because when the police arrived he had forgotten the reason for summoning them. Henry Jones wrung his hands over the Chelsea Physic Garden and said that the student might have been a serial killer. Something was obviously going to have to be done.

But Madeleine would not hear of moving to a Home – or even two Homes – and had become convinced that all would be resolved if she could only get a little break on her own. Just a tiny one. No, not with Puffy. 'Beloved Puffy,' she said, 'but I can't get near him in that chair or near anything else. He's swelling like a watermelon. He's a bull in a china shop. He's tethered but he's still a bull. I must get away with darling Giles and that woman. Henrietta. Very nice woman, but nervy. I could probably help her. So hard on Giles. Let's see . . . three months. He'll just be beginning to think of extricating himself. I don't believe in health farms. You form attachments that would be unthinkable if you were in your clothes. Massage makes you careless.'

A little of this she hinted to Giles, whose telephone number she had procured and was making use of several times a day, leaving many messages when he was out.

'I'm afraid Thomasina and I are going to Yorkshire for Christmas,' he told her. 'We're not sure how long we shall stay. I'm sure you wouldn't want to leave Puffy over Christmas.'

'He never knows when it's Christmas,' she said. 'I shall just tell them not to put up any decorations and hide the cards.'

'That seems harsh.'

'Don't be sentimental, Giles. We can pretend it's Christmas when I get back. Then I shall have two.'

'Won't he hear about it on television?'

'No. He hates television. Well, he used to like it but he hardly sees anything now. He can't read the newspaper either. It's the angle of his head.'

'I'm sure the social services—'

'Oh, no need at all. He has all sorts of people coming in to see him. They read to him and bath him and dress him. I'll just tell them to keep off the newspapers and not to let him switch on the wireless.'

'You are a ruthless woman, Madeleine.'

'No, Giles, I am a pragmatic woman, unashamed. I've lived far too close to Puffy for years. In foreign parts, you know – so much more space.'

'I never thought there was a lot of space in Hong Kong.'

'There are different kinds of space. Space for little separations. We were so wonderfully looked-after. *Such* fun.'

'Madeleine, if you're going to talk maids-before-the-war like a ghastly old dowager, goodbye. It's suburban of you. You are a woman who has had everything she ever wanted.'

'Ah,' she said, 'but not for the nights.'

She won of course. A conversation with Thomasina, whom she had also run to earth, led to Thomasina's conversation with

Toots in the draughty passage of the house on Teesside, and then to the journey of The Missus south to pass her Christmas in a foreign land.

'But you can't mean that you've arranged for Madeleine to come *with* us?' Giles had such a look of horror that it was almost a smile. 'My good girl, it'll snow and she'll wander out and get pneumonia and die. Wherever could she stay?'

'Wherever shall *we* stay, come to that?' Thomasina looked very thin today. Rather lost. 'I'm sorry, I've decided I can't take that place on the moors with the whiplash waitress and I'm not staying at The Priors.'

'It would be insulting not to, wouldn't it?'

'No. It's not fit for anybody. I've done it. With Holly and Andrew. It is vile.'

'But – Faith – lives there. Your grandchild. Isn't that the reason we're going?'

'Oh, Giles,' she said, 'stop being a fool. Actually, Pammie Jefford will be there.'

'Pammie *Jefford*?'

'Yes. She's going as housekeeper. I told you she's rather keen on Jack. She's religious. Andrew will be there, too, I imagine. And there's Jocasta, Jack's wife, and her little boy and some serf people who work there. Oh yes, and some Tibetan refugees.'

'It does sound rather full. Yes.'

'Doesn't Madeleine know anybody up there? Someone with a decent house where we could all go?'

'It's rather short notice for Christmas, isn't it? Less than a fortnight now.' However, he rang Madeleine.

As usual, all his exasperation faded at the charm of her voice. The face he saw in the air was at once graced with the young shining hair of a girl; the body was slight and wore a silk dress. It sat on the terrace at Karnak. Its green eyes watched the Nile.

'Hello, Maddie. We were just wondering if you'd thought of anywhere to stay up there. We're not really fixed up yet. Not too comfortable, I hear, Thomasina's grandchild's place. Had you planned something?'

'I'll see to it,' she said. 'But, do you know, your wonderful Thomasina has actually *found* me someone. A housekeeper. She's coming down on the coach and I was just going to ring and see if you'd meet her at Victoria and take her across to Waterloo to catch the Dover train. Henry and I will meet her there of course.'

'Well . . .'

'I'll ask Pammie Jefford,' hissed Thomasina.

'We'll ask Pammie Jefford,' said Giles. 'She's a—'

'Oh, I know who Pammie *Jefford* is.' Madeleine had acquired Pammie's number, too, and the number of The Priors. 'She's up there already, I think, or soon will be. She's the new housekeeper and they're sending the old one down to me. That's to say, to Puffy. *Such* nice people. Rather a strange man answered the phone. Beautiful voice but not worldly, I'd think. Seven-thirty?'

'Seven-thirty?'

'At the coach station tomorrow? Seven thirty *a.m.* of course. She's travelling down overnight.'

'She must be mad.'

'Oh, nonsense, Giles. It's only nine hours. I thought we might all travel up that way, as a matter of fact. It costs twenty pounds instead of hundreds and they have a video and hot drinks and a WC and Big Macs. It's not Dickens now, you know. Not post-horns and outside seats. It's a bit tight round the knees – wouldn't do for Puffy – but we're all slender. Goodbye, darling, I must get Henry to see to the new person's room.'

'We are to meet this woman,' said Giles, 'at the Victoria Coach Station at seven-thirty a.m. We are then to cart her across London and put her on the train to East Kent. Why? Why us? Why at all? Is she infirm? Who fixed this ridiculous transportation of labour? It is inane.'

'We?' said Thomasina. 'Not you, Giles, I'll go. It's my affair. I did it. On the phone in a silly moment. Why should you?'

'Because I can stay overnight at my London club and you can't. Leave it all to me. I'm responsible for Madeleine. We should never have gone to that wedding.'

'You are very good. This is really my affair.'

'It takes two to make an affair,' he said.

'About such things,' she said, 'Giles . . .'

'Not just now.'

'You are looking shifty.'

He was hurt. 'I have never been shifty. That I have not been. I'm going now. What do you want from London? I can walk over from Waterloo to Soho and get some pasta.'

'Oh, lovely.' (She thought, *Better! How easy we are together again. How married we seem.*) She said, 'Thanks. See you for supper, then, tomorrow?'

'Oh, long before that. Tea. At the latest.'

That evening she turned out the rest of Holly's school things from her bedroom drawers and packed them up for Oxfam, even her school reports and her bears. *In the morning I'll nip in and get some figs for supper. Nice after pasta. Figs and cream. Or with fresh oranges. Funny old thing. Getting to be part of the fabric. And maybe a cake for tea.*

All through the night the coach thundered south bearing Alice Banks away from all she stood for, the rectitude of the unswerving North.

Jack had brought her to the coach. They had been driven by Mrs Middleditch with Philip sitting in the back. Mrs Middleditch had not left the car. The Missus had said goodbye and thank you to her then, but had not been able to say a word to Philip, who sat glumly not looking at her, unravelling a thread in the upholstery. Jack and she together carried her three cardboard suitcases and watched them being stowed in the coach's hold. As she climbed aboard, laden with plastic bags and packages, Jack panicked. The sight of her back going away from him, her head not turning, was unknown.

'*Alice!*'

She did turn then. There were people behind her wanting to get on and Jack was in everyone's way. In his old cassock and scarf and ragged duffle coat and a weird yellow semi-balaclava

The Missus had once knitted for him he looked an unlikely divine, too intensely concerned with his passenger. Love and distress were in the air.

'Alice, there's no need for you to go. It's not too late.'

'It is too late.'

'But what have we done to you?'

'Move along, git on,' said the driver, trying to get to his perch. Everyone was aboard now. 'Git off, missus, if you're not comin'.'

She glowered down at Jack.

'All these years, Alice.'

'It's more than I can tell you. You'll find out and you'll understand me then. But it isn't my place to say.'

'Could you write? Write about it? When you get there?'

'I'll see.'

Her intense love for him she disguised with a thrust of her pointed chin, a turning away, a dropping of parcels, and she disappeared down the centre aisle of the coach as he stepped back and trotted down the side of it to see where she settled. But alas, the windows were dark with tinted glass.

'It's to make it go faster,' someone said. 'There's no waving off any more. Same on the trains. You don't get much seeing-off at all now, it's all self-help.'

Jack stood feebly waving at the bus's shadowed flank and then its vanishing backside, before taking the midnight road back to his parents' house. He was not being trusted with the moor road home at night.

And Alice sat in the bus regarding the back of the seat in front of her hardly twelve inches from her nose. Beside her reclined a blond gorilla, who began to snore at Boroughbridge, kept snoring through Wetherby, over the Leeds roundabout, along the Doncaster bypass, through Sherwood Forest, Stamford, Peterborough and the A1 interchange. At first to her left were the Cleveland Hills, invisible. To her right, beyond the gorilla, was the darkened plain that lifted itself far away into the Pennines and the Lake District and subsided again south towards her own Lancashire. Through the night the coach vibrated with the snorts and farts and coughs and moans of people's dreams. Lads swilled lagers in the back and at one time there was some shouting and a clattering of cans and tuneless singing. Shadows blundered up and down the aisle to the WC. The drinks bar alongside it clonked and fizzed. The atmosphere grew fetid and foul. By Worksop quite a few people were smoking. In Northamptonshire, somewhere beyond the Oundle turn-off, Cambridge to the east, The Missus realised that she had not moved a muscle since she stepped aboard.

She reflected objectively on this, presupposed the pains in her joints and decided they could be postponed if she didn't disturb them. She risked uncrossing her feet and recrossing them the other way, winced, and shut her eyes. She did not turn to the packet of sandwiches on her knee. She forgot the thermos of tea Dolly and Toots had insisted upon, Toots even ringing Mrs Middleditch about it and Mrs Middleditch saying what sort of woman did they think she was, she knew her duty.

In the dawn The Missus saw London for the first time, grey and windy and strung with millions of lights like lighted barbed wire in grey air. Hendon came and went and it could have been anywhere. Stockton-on-Tees, say. Swiss Cottage was nothing of the sort. St John's Wood just blocks of flats. Lord's Cricket Ground was a stretch of wall. As they reached Baker Street, Oxford Street, Marble Arch, where she might have seen the big shops, at last she slept, leaning sideways on the gorilla's elbow like a small dead tree. Buckingham Palace with its tumbril spikes was left behind unnoticed, and in the bleached dawn the coach surged into Victoria Station.

Alice found that she could scarcely move. She was longing to pee but never, never, would she use the upright coffin provided at the back of the bus and certainly not now when the coach was stationary. Maybe there would be somewhere else? As she stood waiting for her luggage she was nearly knocked over several times.

'OK, missus?' asked the driver and the familiar title made her small green face soften.

'D'you have toilets down here?'

'Over there, missus.'

'What happens to me luggage?'

'Is someone here for you? OK then, I'll watch it.'

But she was not sure of this and began to gather the luggage and her packages together in a heap against the coach-station wall, making trips back and forth. She hid the smaller bundles behind the bigger ones. But still she disliked the idea of leaving them all, and there were notices saying you mustn't. *That would be bombs*, she thought. She looked about her and saw that David Niven stood nearby, observing her from lamp-post height. 'Miss Banks?' If he was a mugger or a kidnapper or a rapist it was odd that he knew her name. He was springing about now like a grasshopper, calling up a taxi. All of seventy. Whoever was he?

'Hop in. I'll take you somewhere for breakfast.'

'I need the WC.'

'Oh yes, of course. I shouldn't think they're very nice here.'

'I can see the sign. I'll not be long.'

Looking back doubtfully at the luggage and the man presiding over it, she thought, *Or maybe the Anthony Eden type*.

She made off and once inside the ladies room didn't want to leave it. She felt a little weak and sick and was not at all sure she wasn't dreaming. *All them buses*, she thought, threading her way back among them. They were multiplying as she watched, nosing in like great salmon returning to their birthplace. There was Edinburgh, and over there Exeter, and lined up ready for off, just spawned, was Liverpool. And Glasgow. The board beside Liverpool had Preston written underneath in smaller letters. It'd be stopping there. Not far from Oldham and Wigan and Bury and Bolton and Rochdale. Home.

She was almost swept away by the desire for the Rochdale bus. What would they all say, eh, when she walked in the door, her mam at the fireside with her knees apart making toast on the brass fork with the Medusa head on it, and her dad supping his tea? 'Saucering it', he called it, and no shame. *And that cat. It'll be that pleased to see me. They all died in the war, though.*

'Miss Banks? Hello there. Are you all right?'

*

The general armed her to the taxi and they drove up Victoria Street and over the river, which glimmered in the winter morning but Earth had many things to show more fair than the buildings that looked down upon it.

'We'll have some breakfast on the platform,' he was saying. 'There's a good snack bar. There's rather a long time to wait, I'm afraid.' (*Over an hour. I suppose I must stay with her. Good God, what to talk about?*) 'Never here before? Good gracious me. That was the River Thames – so sorry it's dark. And there's the Shell Building. In the distance you can see the National Theatre. Concrete but dressed with a pattern of planks.'

Alice remained unmoved. They left the taxi and on Waterloo's great staircase she spoke at last. 'What's this, then? Backstreet India? Why don't they move them all on? 'Umans in cardboard boxes is a disgrace.'

At the ticket office she insisted on paying her own fare, insisted so ferociously that people turned to look. She returned the stares. 'I've seen this ticket queue on the telly,' she said. 'It was on the news. Someone got murdered in it once for not being quick enough.

'I'm from the North,' she told the man behind the glass. 'I can't think what I'm doing down 'ere.'

'Nobody can,' he said.

The general wondered, too. He wondered very much. There was no porter, no trolley to get the luggage up the escalator, which Alice wouldn't use anyway though she'd been on the ones in Middlesbrough Binns. They had to make several journeys up and down the stairs alongside. Then they trundled it all by slow degrees along passageways and down a stairway to the platform for the Dover train, and then halfway along this to the snack bar, which was shut up and in darkness.

Rain was falling silver and cold on the lines, spitting and hissing against the roof. Now and then a blustering wind flung drops in handfuls across their legs and feet. The overhead signal boards that predicted coming trains creaked. They were all blank.

'Ha,' said the general. 'Well.'

'No trains,' said Alice Banks. 'It's no better here than anywhere else.'

'My dear, none whatever,' said a sweet voice. Seated on a bench, wrapped round with rugs, a fur hat on her head and the *Financial Times* on her knee, sat Madeleine.

— 32 —

Philip, after refusing to go into the chip shop with Jack and Alice, had decided that he couldn't even accept the glossy newspaper parcel of cod and chips Jack had come out waving at him through the car window. Jack had gone back inside and stood looking helpless, whereupon The Missus had said, 'Give us 'ere,' and risen to her feet.

'Just you eat it,' she'd shouted through the glass to Philip. 'Open that window. What's wrong with you?'

'I want to wash my hands. I don't like this chippie.'

'You've just washed your 'ands at your granny's and you can go and wash them there again in 'alf an hour if you want.' She had rattled at the car until he opened his window for her to drop the package in.

Jack's face had brightened when he saw her coming back into the chippie without it. The Missus had not quite disintegrated after all.

After he'd left her at Mrs Middleditch's and arranged about the journey south for the following night, he and Philip had set off back to The Priors, and at the caravan park Jack stopped the car without warning and gazed at the site. It was the bleakest of days, worse than this morning. It was four-thirty and workers were going home. The narrow old trunk road had now for an hour or so become a teeming motorway. A car behind missed bashing into them by two inches and faces from following traffic blazed at them sideways as they passed.

Jack had stopped in the fast lane.

'You'll have us dead, Jack.'

Jack stared tenderly at the mobile homes.

'What's up, Jack?'

'I was thinking. Philip – when the Tibetans go at Christmas, there are people here we might approach.'

'These aren't homeless. They're *in* their homes. They may like them. They'd think you were after rehousing them.'

'I feel I should make contact. I don't think this is accidental. I think we may have been directed here today. I think I should call.'

'Oh please, Jack, no. I want to get back. I've got my homework and I'm going over to the sheds to see my sister.'

'Five minutes.' Jack manoeuvred the car on to the hard shoulder and went walking about the caravans, but nobody seemed to be answering his knock. 'Oh, stuff it,' said Philip. 'Stuffation and grot.' A man had come to the door of the fourth caravan and Jack leaned down to him ceremoniously. Then disappeared inside with him. Not long afterwards he reappeared with the man and walked with him towards the car. Philip, his face squashed against the glass, was looking down and saw dirty trainers in the mud and above them shining black trousers. It was hardly a glance upwards, but eyes met.

The man in his elbow-patched jacket turned and made off back to the caravan.

'Well, most interesting,' said Jack, 'most interesting fellow. I've left our address. He seemed quite enthusiastic. I don't know why he made off like that. Very well-spoken, educated man. An intellectual. This car is a brute to start.'

'For God's sake, get on with it. Quick, get on with it.'

'Not like you to be rude, Philip.'

'I want to see my sister. Get me home. He was horrible.'

Jack brooded. 'Little Faith,' he said, 'dear little Faith.' He imagined a stout and homely soul following on from Pema. Perhaps a fine old gypsy woman. Or a Traveller. The woman gazing from the caravan window, eating a pie? He saw the blotchy face soften, grow gentle, self-respecting, as the child was rocked and serenaded. Maybe the wife of the intellectual man?

And if not her arms, whose? he wondered. *Jocasta's? Oh let it happen. Slowly, slowly. Let her take to Faith. One day a child of our own.*

'I believe you really do think of Faith as your sister, Philip. I wish Jocasta felt more for her.'

'Yes, it's funny. She always wanted a girl.'

After an age – they were climbing now up Sutton Bank, spluttering and groaning, leaving the sprawl of the works below – Jack had said, 'Ah.'

Then later, 'I didn't know that, Philip. I hope it doesn't upset you? Make you feel unwanted in any way? I'm surprised she told you.'

'Oh, Jocasta tells me everything. She told me when she was beginning to think of marrying you. She actually asked my advice. I was quite young, too.'

'Ah.'

'I said – d'you want to know what I said, Jack?'

'Well, I suppose I do really want to know.'

'I said, "Jack's OK, but I don't think we'll like living up there for ever. It's going to be lonely." '

Jack said nothing until, at length, 'And you, Philip? I expect you must be rather lonely. As you expected?'

'No, I'm not now. I like it OK. I wasn't exactly mad about it till Faith came, but now I'm not an only child any more it's fine.'

'You'd like real brothers and sisters, I expect?'

'Faith's real.'

'You are extremely fond of her, aren't you?'

'Well, she's the only one I'll ever have.'

'You never know. You never know, Philip.' He looked beatific again. Light perpetual. Hope perpetual.

'Yes I do. Jocasta's had all the parts you need for childbirth taken out. Didn't you know? I'd have thought you'd know. She's got this great scar across her tum. You must have seen it, Jack, don't be daft. Andrew did it. He helped the surgeon when he was young. What's wrong with this car now? We nearly went over the edge. Shall I drive? I could. I drive the tractor for Nick.'

'I believe,' said Jack twenty minutes later as they reached the cross, 'you may be a bit wrong there, Philip. Wasn't that just something like an appendix or a peritonitis business?'

'D'you mean you've never even *asked* her? Jack, you're crazy. I mean, *I* asked her and I was little. She said that I'd have had to know anyway because it was only fair to me.'

'Only fair,' said Jack. 'I see that.'

The only person he had told of his longing for a child was The Missus. He had not told Jocasta. He had assumed she must know. Any wife would. Naturally. Now he thought that somehow The Missus must have discovered about Jocasta's barrenness and that she had never told him of it. Maybe Andrew or Philip had somehow let it out – Philip playing cards with The Missus in the gatehouse. The Missus couldn't cope with treachery. She smelled it a mile off. Her ferocious face belied her capacity to be deeply shocked and when shocked she fell silent. She collapsed and ran. Out of pity for him The Missus would have sunk deep into herself, glaring, crashing the saucepans, become remote, ready to kill Jocasta for embracing him in the kitchen with her open eyes full of love. Alice was a woman awkward when it came to imparting bad news. Or any news. A difficult, heavy little woman. *I don't know why I kept her so long*, Jack thought, and shocked himself.

But truly The Missus had reacted ridiculously. The trouble was that she deeply hated Jocasta and had done from the beginning. She had simply been waiting for the final coffin nail. He should not have allowed such hatred to fester at The Priors. He must put things right. The first thing he would do when he reached home was tell Jocasta that he loved her and put things right.

He went straight to her room, knocked politely, waited for permission to go in, and found her with her hair loose and an open book face down on the bedcover, staring at the door. She looked as if she had been lying like this for ever, staring ahead.

'Jocasta.' He sat down at the end of the bed. 'In bed early?'

'I was cold.'

'Tell me, do you – did you hate poor Alice Banks?'

She said at once, 'So you know.'

He was surprised that she leaned forward then and picked up one of his hands. She stroked it and laid it against her cheek, 'You know.'

'You're crying.'

'No,' she said.

'Your eyes are enormous. You're so beautiful, Jocasta.'

'I love your eyes, too,' she said. 'I love it when you look like that. All raggety-baggety. You're a loving old Don Quixote. I want to have you in my arms.'

'Then why – why ever? Why won't you ever . . . ?'

'Well, it's not like that.'

'Like what?'

'Sex. I've told you so often. I can't. I just can't. Darling, how could I?'

'You shouldn't have married me without telling me. You must have known then that there was no chance. How could you not have told me? I'm Andrew's brother, for God's sake.'

'But then I couldn't have married you, could I? I wanted to. And you would not have married me. Well, you *shouldn't* have been able to marry me. I should hope not, anyway. I'm the sinner.'

'Of course I would have married you,' he said.

'What? Even knowing . . . ? No, Jack. No!'

'It was Andrew brought you to me. It wasn't his fault you were his patient. You talk as if he'd violated you. He had no choice but to bring you here to me. Yes, he should have told me and you should have told me, that's all I mind about. I could have coped. It's all so sad. But it wouldn't have changed my mind. You know – I am so hopeless I'm beginning to wonder now if you did tell me and I somehow simply forgot.'

'*Forgot!*'

'Well, maybe Andrew thought I knew. In some way. That he'd told me sometime at the very beginning. We've never been close, you know. We never had conversations – he's a different generation. And of course he has no time for religion.'

'Well, heavens. It's hardly a thing he would have dropped into a conversation. It's nothing to do with religion.'

'I truly promise you . . . Of course I'm not, well, happy. Of course it changes the future – our future together. It can't be the same now. But "blame you"? No. I can't. I couldn't. After all, how could you help it, my poor love?'

She stared in disbelief. She dropped his hand. The eyes that had been full of affection and loving tears changed. He saw a younger, harder Jocasta, the one Philip's unknown young father must have met. The Jocasta who had lived by her wits in India after school, the pot-smoking, seriously trendy, guru-seeking, guru-rejecting Jocasta, a King's Road and Carnaby Street Jocasta, a brown-rice, barefoot, Streatham Common Jocasta. The eyes said, What sort of dope is he? You can carry forgiveness too far. He makes me sick.

'You've no anger in you, have you?' she said. 'No passions? You're not even going to throw him out. You'll have him back for Christmas. You won't even hit him.'

'*Hit* him? Hit *Andrew*? Of course not. Why ever should I hit him? He liked you, grew to know you. It wasn't unethical. You'd ceased to be his patient. He was sorry for you and brought you up here to me for a home. I fell in love with you and we were married. He has done nothing *wrong*, then, before or since.'

'Jack,' she leaned forward and took both his hands, 'Andrew and I have both done wrong and doubly wrong not telling you. I am very, very, very sorry. I have never felt this before. I suppose it was The Missus told you. That's why she went off. She couldn't bear it. She has a strain of purest vitriol inside her. She'd kill for you. She discovered it and went. It's a wonder she didn't stay for breakfast and poison Andrew and me together.'

'Oh my dear – come on.'

'Oh, my love, I'm sorry.'

'It's not that serious,' he said. 'I don't think she'd have stayed, as a matter of fact, if we'd *had* a baby. She likes Philip but that's because he's not childish. She's never paid the least attention to Faith.'

Very slowly she said then, 'Do you mean that it's just because you won't be begetting any children by me that it matters? That that's what it's all about? Yourself?'

'Well, partly. Naturally. The other part is your not telling me it was a hysterectomy.'

'And otherwise you don't care?'

'Not at all. Not in the very least.'

'But, Jack, Andrew and I have betrayed you. Philip and I will have to leave you. Andrew and I knew that when we saw The Missus standing staring at us in the doorway.'

'My dear. My dear sweet girl, you are being theatrical. You and I are *married*. We love each other. Whatever does the gynaecological stuff matter? I mean, it's not as if you and Andrew had been having an *affair*, is it? Poor Andrew – just look at his face. He'll mourn poor Holly, I'm afraid, for the rest of his life.'

– 33 –

Every few minutes trains were running into Waterloo East station to tip out their contents. Hundreds of people surged forward, wave upon wave, at a stiff jog-trot towards their daily bread. The trio waiting on the down-line platform was jostled about several times and Alice Banks's suitcases were at continuous risk. No sooner had one train left than in came another. The crowds were being sucked towards London for their execution.

Alice watched and could not see one contented face. *Poor stock*, she thought, *most of them half-breeds. Black and curly, greenish-grey, blotchy brown, some white – well, pink. All of them glazed over like they've got New Forest disease and need their ointment. No shepherds. No dogs to guide them. They all* seemed to know the way, though. Off they went up the slope in a huddle, butting away at each other, left wheel and out of sight. Not one of them turning to run for it. Nobody coming back. *Like death really*, thought The Missus. *So much for London.*

She thought that she'd like to tell Jack of it. It might be a thing for a sermon. Then she thought not, for there was nobody anywhere near Ellerby Priors the least bit interested in the London rush hour. *Fancy*, she thought, *Philip must have seen this. It was his home once.* She thought of him, a sharp-faced baby in a pushchair.

And that Jocasta. There's plenty places she knows about, and us with no idea. You wonder how Philip's grown up natural at all. He's had a break away from all this anyway. He'll be stuck back in it soon, though, mark my words. They'll all be tipped back down here, that Andrew, that Jocasta, Philip. They'll never get heard of more. You'll see.

And me down here, she thought, *whatever am I down here for with this fond pair? Not one of us knows why. The balance of my mind must be disturbed, like in the papers. I've always got the balance of it back talking to Philip in the past, but here's something you can't talk about with Philip, nor yet with Toots and Dolly. You can't tell the best people things like this. That Smike pair, they'd take it. A fancy-boy and a common criminal. I'd not tell that Middleditch one breath. Give her a whisper and next morning it's in the* North-Eastern Gazette. 'What's that?'

'We were just saying, Miss Banks, that perhaps we shouldn't wait on this cold station for an hour. We think we'll take you for some breakfast at Lady Madeleine's club.'

Alice could think of very little to say to this.

'You must be so tired. We must find you somewhere nice to sit down.'

'I've been sat down all night.'

'But – a good cup of coffee?'

'I 'ave me sandwiches.'

'We feel it's not very pleasant here.'

'What I don't fathom,' said Alice to Madeleine, woman to woman, 'is what you're doing 'ere your age at all before eight

213

o'clock in the morning. You was to meet me t'other end. You must have got up bright and early to get 'ere in time to take me back down again. Are you taking me back? I'd say you ought to be careful of yourself.'

'Ah,' said Madeleine, looking up at the blank train-times indicator.

At once a message flickered up on it announcing Alice's destination. 'Arriving one minute,' it said. 'Front four coaches only.'

It arrived.

The general seized the luggage, The Missus clutched her parcels, and they ran. 'Don't *change*,' cried the general, sounding like a romantic film, and The Missus found herself in an almost empty compartment, bound for East Kent. 'You're to cross the footbridge when you get there and there'll be someone meeting you,' he cried.

'Who?' she shrieked back through the window – but Madeleine could not be asked. She could only just be seen far away up the platform under the indicator, her fur hat, her opened newspaper.

'Don't worry,' called the general guiltily, 'please don't worry.'

And The Missus's baleful face disappeared into the dark morning.

− 34 −

Jack awoke the morning after his conversation with Jocasta to find that he no longer loved her.

The knowledge astonished him. The experience of falling out of love was not new, he had done it often, seldom with women, of whom he had little experience, but he had lost other passions. Mathematics had left him early. Physics had deserted him at the university just before his final examinations and he had walked out of them. The passion for Oxford, where he had gone next, to learn some Architecture, had been intense and he had for a time walked in the Celestial City. Then one blustery dead day in the vacation it had withered and died.

The ensuing passion had been for God and that had led him to ordination and to his affair with Holy Church and its rituals, its ancient words, its magnificent music, but all this had weakened when he came upon the Muslims in Bangladesh, the Buddhists in India. God Himself he had never abandoned, quite sure by now of his need for the everlasting arms to comfort and hold him at the end of his every adventure.

There had been women, crowds of them, but only for gazing at and loving in a perfectly pastoral way. He had seen splinters of God in each and had enjoyed adoring all of them, but he could scarcely remember a name now, hardly a face. Some radiant moments only.

Jack's passions consumed him but vanished always, and it was this aspect of himself that saddened him and gave him his rueful, gentle face, the face that was his fortune and disarmed the world. But he wondered why God had deprived him of the talent for fidelity he would have so much enjoyed. In the end he had decided that his incapacity to concentrate on being faithful must be treated as his Pauline thorn in the flesh, the cross he had to bear.

And at last he had been rewarded. Jocasta had walked in and at once swept away the years of his fickleness. Lost, ill, looking for love, here was God's requested gift. She was the only one he had ever asked to marry him and he was in terror lest, should she accept him, he would at once go off her.

She had given him no answer for weeks, but kept out of his way, spent most of her time in her own room or the Art rooms, wandered the countryside by herself, gone sitting about in cafés in Whitby, begun to take an intense interest, at last, in her little boy. Jack had kept his distance and his regretful face, allowing himself to look increasingly unparsonic, rougher, to remind her of her hippie years. He had stopped washing for a while, and eating, worn threadbare clothes. He was a man who suited a hollow face and as it grew more so he thought this might attract Jocasta, remind her of hungry seductive India. In the fields those first months at The Priors she saw him standing with his cassock hooked up like a medieval French saint. At night over the stove he sat in contemplation, his face turned from her, trying to despise himself for such affectation.

She would sit apart drawing or sewing, sulky, almost ugly, he thought. Not entertaining. A bore. And he waited for these conclusions to bring the blessed release from his obsession. And then she would look up and smile wearily and he was wild for her again. 'Marry me, marry me,' he begged in a silence she could feel. She would gather up her stuff and leave the room.

At length she had said she would. It was directly after Andrew had visited with Holly Fox, after they had become engaged, and Holly Fox had looked at Jocasta and said – in front of her – 'Golly. Aren't you *wonderful*!' Holly Fox had said, laughing, to Jack, 'I've told Andrew I'm jealous. His patient, if you please! Shocking!' Holly Fox had tried to be friendly to Jocasta, who had seemed tongue-tied, quite overwhelmed, had tried to keep out of sight. Holly Fox had grown noisier and slightly embarrassing.

Jocasta had kept her thrilling distance from Jack until their wedding and straight after that she had caught some virus and they had still not slept together. Two nights later they had joined up with the ecumenical expedition to Nepal, where they had slept in sleeping sacks in community huts and he had scarcely been alone with her. He had been happy enough, though, seeing her so excited and grateful for being in the mountains.

On that expedition everyone as usual fell for Jack, which he as usual accepted. He did not notice, because he was so taken up with her himself, that nobody talked easily to Jocasta or seemed to want her company. He would of course have expected them to keep their distance. She was his wife. 'My wife,' he kept saying, watching for reactions. There seemed to be none. Neither Jack nor Jocasta mentioned to anyone that they were on their honeymoon.

Then home again. Sometimes Jack thought that his unprecedented continuing passion for her was only because she still would not sleep with him, and he half feared the moment she would change her mind. Thus the idea of possession was spiced with danger and he had to discipline himself not to think of it. It became in the end a superstition. He must not, must not, think of it or the worst would happen. All would be lost.

During the latter part of the honeymoon trip she had seemed to be growing nearer to him and would smile up at him from the seat beside him on the truck. Leaning from a parapet over a road one day high above two tremendous ice-green rivers that converged at a place called Marriage she suddenly took his bony hand, and he kissed her small brown one, the hand with his ring on it. That day he risked buying her – he was no great one for presents – a necklace made of chunks of red amber, which she stroked and put against her face and let him hang round her neck, though she didn't say thank you.

When they got back to England she put the necklace away. She seemed cold and dismal and not quite well. Philip, who had spent the honeymoon with The Missus eating chips and learning Bridge, seemed unmoved by their return.

In time they slept together, but it wasn't a success. She was passive and apart and he was unnerved. She made him feel inexperienced and feeble. There was always the suggestion in her that she was living somewhere else, listening for another voice, waiting for a different caress. This made him unable to think her frigid, which was troubling, too, but more troubling was his fear, very secret, that, should she change and grant him the passion he knew she possessed, he might as usual back off; run for God again.

And this he deplored. He loathed himself for it. Inactive. Timorous. Maybe masochistic. Perhaps he was that nastiest of monsters, the apologetic rapist?

And so the balance was kept, and on he suffered, and soon Jocasta had told him of her wish to be celibate, at least for the present, and would he understand?

But he was never unaware of her, wherever she was in The Priors or the studios or the fields. He prayed for her and for himself endlessly. Then was grateful. He was proud of having her, of the impact she made when people saw her first. 'That astonishingly beautiful woman.' He was always amazed that she was even supposedly his.

And for six years they had lived like this, his obsession holding fast until for some reason – it was about the time of Holly Fox's death – a cold wind began to blow from somewhere upon Jack. When he had heard of Holly's death he had put down the phone, turned to Jocasta and told her before going off up the moor. And he'd seen something shocking in Jocasta's eyes. He couldn't place it. 'Holly Fox is dead.' What had he seen? Delight and fury, both together. It was very bewildering. Very terrible.

Knowledge goes ahead of the expression of it as the blow strikes ahead of the pain and the axe drops ahead of the sound of the chop. When Jack had gone up to Jocasta's room last night, at once after Philip had told him she was barren, he still imagined himself in love with her. Tired and cold and hungry after the ghastly day – even Philip turning and screaming at him down in the caravan park – as he sat on her bed he was still adoring the long hair loose on the pillow, the neat fingers folded over the back of the unread book.

That night he had fallen into deep sleep and woken with the thought that some enormous trouble had come to an end, a huge stone tablet lifted off his chest just before it crushed him for ever. He felt dizzy. Not himself at all. He got up and walked over to the chapel but could not pray. He decided to prostrate himself full length before the altar as he had done at his ordination, offer himself utterly to God.

Yet there he stood, unmoving, not even thinking. Standing. In the church there was no sense of any presence, not even his own. No love here. No godliness. He might have been an empty body, a creature long dead and forgotten, like a ghost of the monks who had lived here in the past.

The air was icy. The wooden cross on the shabby altar very small. Meaningless. The dawn had not begun and though he stood for ages watching the east window, it scarcely lightened. He thought of summer mornings here after nights that scarcely happened, when the sky never really grew dark, one of the most beautiful things about the life of this place.

I shall never leave it, he thought. *I shall always need to be here. And the dark in the winter always shifts at last.*

He knelt to say the Office but it was evasive. He tried to say the Magnificat but it faded out. At length, instead, he said, 'I do not love her. I have stopped. It is simple.'

The window began to lighten above him and soon some sort of brightness struck through and fell across the stone floor. 'It was an inordinate love,' he said. 'It was wrong. "Nought shall separate us from the love of God." But she has separated me from it. She filled my being and my being should be filled only with God.'

She was in the kitchen ahead of him, wearing a hefty grey sweater and old trousers, her hair on top of her head untidy, in a rubber band. Without The Missus, the stove was still sulky and cold. The electric kettle had disappeared and Jocasta was filling the heavy iron one to take to the fire in the refectory. Her cold fingers poked through the ends of her mittens.

She said, 'Not much bread. I'll have to get some,' and he thought, *This is the woman. The woman who has tried to destroy me. I have been screaming for her and about her to God and now I'm screaming against her. But how ordinary she looks.*

'Sugar, Jack?'

She is so quiet. So ordinary. It is only Jocasta. My Jocasta. I've manufactured a demon out of her.

But as she made tea and came back and walked about the room, went over to the door and called across the courtyard to Philip to make him hurry, like any boy's mother, Jack knew that something had happened. It had happened last night as they talked and she had said that she and Andrew had betrayed him. And her eyes had hated him for saying it didn't matter. For being simple. 'You can carry forgiveness too far,' her look had said.

So. She had reached the same conclusion as he. Long ago maybe. And it had taken him six years to be out of danger. Out of love.

'Oh, Jocasta,' he said now, 'I'm out of danger.'

And she looked over at him with her usual lack of curiosity. She yawned. 'What?'

' "Not as if you and Andrew had been having an affair",' he said, and stood watching her. She brought him the mug of tea and he drank it. He said, looking out of the window, 'I'm in the clear, Jocasta. You're free of me. I don't love you any more,' and when she looked at him he saw her eyes become unclouded, wide and alive.

When she said, 'Oh Jack, whatever are you on about now?' he was silent. In the silence he saw her at length grow frightened and knew that he had come through to the unconcern that had so reliably ended his every passion every time.

He swam again towards God, allowing himself one fleeting moment of avenged delight.

And yet the day went on as usual. Not another word. 'I'll pick up the rest of the Christmas stuff after I've dropped Philip off,' she said. 'I can't do anything about lunch. Can you find yourself a tin of something? Or could you go over to the Tibs? They always have something even if it's marshmallows. Or get them to come over here. I'll bring something frozen for supper. I've some paint to get near the supermarket for the backdrop for Christmas Eve so I won't be early back.'

'Backdrop?'

'I've told you. I tell you every day. Nativity tableau. Abstract thing. It's going to look all right.'

'Don't be too late. It will snow today.'

'I'll stay in Whitby till it's time to fetch Philip home again.'

'Don't worry about here,' he said. 'It may well be today that Pammie Jeffreys arrives. Jefford? Jefferson? If she broke the journey last night she might even be here by lunchtime. She'll take over. I suppose there's a room ready?'

'Will she start in straight away, then? Are you paying her anything, Jack?'

'Paying her?'

'Well, why should she do it otherwise?'

'D'you know, I never thought about it. She's very well-off. I don't think she'd accept money.'

'But why should she come?'

'I didn't beg her. I scarcely asked. She jumped at it.'

He remembered the reassuring voice over the phone. He remembered her capable kindness. *Such a steady, sensible woman.* He saw her open face. *No hang-ups there at all. Pretty. Getting on a bit, but a delightful woman. Rather innocent. Deep Christian too, someone said. Surprising from that neck of the woods.*

(*And she was taken with me.*)

'I'm off,' said Jocasta.

On the top road sleet was falling. The three giant golf balls were dirty white shadows above the clean snow.

'Horrible drive,' said Philip to his mother. 'Jocasta, could I board next term?'

'Yes,' she said at once, 'you certainly *could*. I thought you hated the place.'

'Oh, it's OK. They do go on a bit, but I know them now. The Head's OK.'

'You'd miss going down to D & T's. Are you doing better?'

'No. But they're not bad.'

'Are you sick of The Priors?'

'Yep.'

'I see.'

She dropped him at the school gates and he went without glancing back or saying goodbye. *Boys do that*, she thought; *girls don't. Right up to being men they go without a backward glance. Until they're old and then you have to prise away their fingers. Philip has never kissed me or put his arms round me or given me one present. In London he just dreamed about. Sometimes looked me over. Hardly knew who I was. That's Communities for you. I thought they'd make us all stronger. His father the same. Beardless boy, saffron robe. Beads, pot, parents Maida Vale with chequebook to call him home. Mind-blown lazy lout now, I dare say. Maybe banker. Never heard*

221

of Philip. Never shall. Oh, I truly believed in all that, I truly did.

Philip's not like him, she thought. *Not like me either. Nor anybody. My lamb. Could Jack afford boarding fees?*

Then the new knowledge flooded in. Jack would not be finding any more money for Philip now, or for anything else to do with her. The minute Pammie whatshername arrived, she and Philip would have to go.

Last night's conversation and this morning's revelations had swept away the last six years. There had been a weight about Jack she had not felt before. She had seen him angry sometimes, but not sickened, almost poisoned with surprise. Could Andrew run to school fees? Would he if he could? Could Jack just order us to leave?

Jocasta realised all at once and quite certainly as she eased the car down off the moor towards the treacherous hill into the town, peering forward through the clotted windscreen, which the wipers were trying frenziedly to clear, that Andrew didn't want her either and that she had known it for some time. She had known it even when he packed her off up here six years ago, before he'd even met Holly Fox. He had found her a burden even then. A sexual delight, but a burden. He had enjoyed her as a serious temptation, the only thing in his life that had made him skid off course, the only unwise thing he'd ever done since he was born. He had needed it, his liberating rebellious act twenty years late, marking the moment when at last he stopped trying to please his Jack-crazed mother.

But the returned desire for her, Jocasta, after Holly's death had been self-pity. It was the reaction of any young man widowed, to take a woman as different as possible from the wife so that in bed there would be no comparisons and out of bed there need never be a loving thought.

It was because he couldn't bear to think of Holly he came back to me. So much for his scratching on the window the day he brought Faith. 'I want you in my bed'. In time, when her memory fades, he'll find another Holly and in the end he'll muddle which was which.

Everything alters,

And one by one we drop away.

I don't want either brother, thought Jocasta, *and of the two I need Andrew even less.* 'Right,' she said as the car slithered into the supermarket car park beyond the quay. *He took away my womb but I don't have to be grateful. Anyone could have done it. I wish it had been a woman surgeon – why are there no women surgeons? – a woman would not think of it as tissue and blood but my female gender, the source of life. Has Andrew ever considered the source of life? Poor Jack, of course, thinks of nothing else, and look where it's got him. Holy poverty on the Yorkshire moors and sycophantic ladies from Surrey.*

Well, 'We're all mad here, said the mad hatter'. The whole bloody wash-bag is mad. My trouble, I suppose, is I'm not mad enough. I brood and suffer but I've no mad passions. I never had. I was never born.

At the supermarket checkout, paying for the turkey, she saw Ernie Smike standing by the doors, presumably waiting for the weather. He looked forlorn in black. He was alone. She said, 'I thought you were working with sheep today,' and he said, 'Do us a favour,' and nodded at the storm. 'Anyway, it's me day off.'

'D'you want a lift home?'

'I got me bike.'

'You can't bike in this. I'll take you. Come and have some coffee.'

They sat in the coffee shop, a strange pair, Jocasta almost invisible, but precise inside a huge duffle coat she had picked off the back of the kitchen door, Ernie towering above her, beringed in ears and nose, his hair short to nakedness, his weighty leather jacket somehow suggesting more nakedness beneath. His head jerked to the music playing inside the black discs over his ears. Tinny reverberations enclosed him.

'Give it a rest, Ernie.'

'Sorry.' He switched himself off.

'What's the matter with you? You look more miserable every time I see you.'

'D'yer wonder at it?'

'You mean Nick going?'

'Oh, let 'im. 'E'll be back. That bitch won't keep 'im.'

'Something wrong somewhere with you, then?'

'You could say.'

'Love trouble?'

'Nar. Is Philip goin' down 'is gran's this week? I can tek 'im.'

'I don't want him to. I don't think he wants to, as a matter of fact. Something happened down there the last time he had a lift with you. He's not himself. He's forever washing his hands.'

'Yeah – well.'

'What happened? He went out with you and Nick, didn't he?'

' 'E just hung about. 'E got to 'is gran's.'

'Was he out with your lot first?'

' 'E went off to Dolly an' Toots.'

'There are things in your part of the forest, Ernie, I don't want Philip to know about. I'm not having Philip going the way you went. I mean it. I'm not enlightened about gays. See?'

'Thanks a bunch. So what about you, then?'

'You are being insolent.'

'You're to be the model for 'im, are you? You and Andrew?'

'You're being insufferable.'

' "In-siff-er-able". You was an unmarried mother, wan't yer? I'se no time for slags. Wan-parint families. An' what yer do fer yer keep now?'

'A great deal more than you do. And I teach.'

'Teach wogs 'ow to colour pitchers.'

'Ernie,' she said, 'don't. Don't say these awful things. It's not like you. I'm sorry for what I said about gays, but – I'm all Philip's got. It's not like you to be foul to me. What have I done? It's Nick going, isn't it?'

'It is not. Nick's life's 'is own. If you want to know, it's Jack. An' Toots an' Dolly.'

'Jack?'

'The way 'e's bein' used. Innocent, that's Jack. I 'ates seein' 'im made moonkey of and Dolly an' Toots too, widout a clue. We're not daft, you know. Nick an' I 'ates yer – you and that Andrew. That's why The Missus went.'

She said, looking away, 'I shall soon be going too. I shall be taking Philip. Andrew won't be coming back. He'll probably take Faith away.'

'Get on. Don' flatter thesen. What good does it do Jack everyone packin' off – and Nick goin' and wogs an' all – who's to look to Jack? That's what you don't give a fuck for.'

'Somebody's coming from Surrey.'

'From down there? That bossy posh dyke? Gi's a break, Jocasta, it'll last five minutes.'

'I'm going for Philip. Do you want a lift?'

'I tellt thee, no. I'd not take no lift from thee.'

She sat meekly as he lumbered off.

She saw nothing but sorrow and mess, a pool of unhappiness. She tried to find some spark of meaning in their lives, in any of their lives, one by one, and she couldn't. And yet she knew there was some central matter there if she could only catch hold of it. Sometimes, now and then, she had caught a breath of it. A sunlit day. A sigh of breeze. She nearly caught it now, here in the warm coffee place, people about, laughing and yattering on about Christmas. Happiness. Fading. Lost. She let it go.

I'll go for the paint, she thought, *finish the backcloth. That's all right anyway. It'll be good. I'll finish it whatever, before I go. I'll leave it for them, even if they throw it away afterwards. It will be my present to Jack. Forever. God knows if he'll have a clue what it means. But it is the best thing I've ever done in my life.*

She passed Ernie near the early warning system globes, head down over the bike, helmeted like Camelot. He raised a great black arm in greeting as she went by and she tooted back, surprised and pleased by the salute.

So pleased that she found tears in her eyes.

He's only a kid, she thought; *poor little soul, what is there for him? Nick gone, he'll be in trouble in five minutes. All Jack will do is pray for him and stand around helpless. Poor lad, he's never made a good decision in his life. It'll be drugs and Aids by the time he's thirty. Poor little rat.*

'Where's Philip?' asked Jack when she reached The Priors. She said, 'Oh God – I forgot him.'

– 35 –

'And so, my dear Madeleine, who's to meet her at the other end, if I may ask? I thought you were?'

'Goodness, no. I only got up to London last night. I have my Christmas shopping to do; one can't do it in *Deal*. Dear Henry's meeting her.'

'How can he know which train? And who's Henry?'

'I don't think anyone knows which train these days. I'll telephone him in a minute. They amalgamate them all, you know. If they don't get enough in one train they let it lie about and fill up with the ones aiming for the next one. I wonder what they do with the extra drivers. Oh, it's all so different, Robert—'

'Giles.'

'Giles. I often wonder if there *are* any drivers, as a matter of fact. You never see them. Each end looks exactly the same, like caterpillars. I expect it's all computers. Darling Giles, how we all take our lives in our hands. It was so much safer in the war.'

'We must telephone Henry whoever-he-is at once,' said Giles. 'I don't think that woman's been about much.'

'She seemed very much in control to me. Very *au fait*. Not at all overawed by anything. She's like these people you see in television plays or on the radio. You rarely meet any in real life. I don't think these creative people, writers and so on, go about very much outside their own sort. Much less than Alice Banks. Of course, you don't *have* to. Look at Balzac: far too busy to do any research. But then, he knew something to start with.'

'I hope she gets something to eat on the train,' said kind Giles. 'She must be eighty.'

Madeleine looked vain – and indifferent. 'They put a trolley on at Ashford. Henry's my *man*, Giles.'

'Your man?'

'Those trolleys are marvellous when they remember to put them on. Curry sandwiches. Beer. I do rather enjoy beer. Shall we go to the Academic Ladies?'

'Whoever are they?'

'My club, beloved Giles. Where I stayed, of course, last night.'

'Why "of course"? I thought you couldn't leave Puffy overnight. I thought that was why we had to find you Miss Banks?'

'And you did find me Miss Banks, you and dear Thomasina, and I can't tell you how grateful . . . And I did get up and come to the station this morning at a very early hour to look her over, didn't I? Whatever would we have found to talk about if we'd gone down together to the coast? No. I've seen her. She will be marvellous. So now, you and I shall set off for the Club. I'll give you breakfast and you shall give me lunch. Don't be silly, you've *plenty* of time. Then we'll do a little Christmas shopping and go to the cinema. We'll go to the Chelsea Classic in the King's Road.'

'It's been gone these twenty years, Madeleine.'

'Ah,' she said, 'they disappear before you can say you loved them. "What's become of Waring . . ." '

Giles paid off the taxi and they went into the Academic Ladies' Club, where various academic ladies were quietly eating toast.

'Breakfast's over,' said the severe academic lady on the desk.

Madeleine smiled at another one chomping bacon in a corner.

'We are only *obliging* Dr Crass.'

'Then do oblige us. We are ravenous after a journey.'

'You had breakfast at seven o'clock, Lady Madeleine, at some disturbance to the kitchen.'

But breakfast was brought. When the coffee had been returned and replaced for some that was hotter, Madeleine smiled around the shabby pastel dining room, lightening the colourless December day.

'Coffee's good.' Giles was warming up, too, beginning to accept the bizarre morning (and still scarcely after nine). 'What a surprise, you and I here together, Madeleine.'

'Not exactly. Such a chance. To meet alone. After so *very* long.'

The sunlight on her skin lit the pale freckles on her hands. A fawn blotch like the map of Northern Ireland shaded her left cheek. He felt love and sadness.

They lunched at the Royal Academy and proceeded on foot to the Sainsbury wing of the National Gallery ('Such a strange hobby for a grocer') and then on to the Courtauld exhibition in the Strand.

'We might have tea in a McDonald's. There's one by the Law Courts somewhere.'

'Can one sit down in them?'

'You're not *tired*, Miles?'

'Giles. No. Wonky leg.'

'Oh, men and their legs. Tea, my dear child. China, please.'

'I think you order from the counter, Madeleine.'

'Then you shall order for me. Child, excuse me. May we have a *smoking* table, please. A silly thing to have to say; it sounds as if we're on the slopes of Mount Etna. What? *None* of them? Oh how strong-minded you all are these days. What a curious menu – all kinds of fried things and sauces, and three o'clock in the afternoon. I shall have the chicken nuggets – no, the fish.'

'Fish?' Giles was having a cup of tea.

'Yes, it'll save us bothering with any dinner. I shall dine at the Club.'

'Madeleine,' he reached for her hand, 'you'll do nothing of the sort and you know it and you are lying. You'll ring up some old flame and get taken to Claridge's.'

'You're my only old flame, Richard.'

'Rubbish. Giles.'

'Giles – you are my one volcano. My conflagration.'

'Well, I'd never have guessed.' (*Why the hell couldn't she have been like this at twenty?*)

'Giles, how strange, they've put this fish in a paper bag.

Inside a bread roll. And where are the knives and forks?'

'I don't think they have them. Shall we order two milk shakes?'

'How lovely. I feel American – fish and milk shakes at tea time. Ralph, d'you see how they're looking at my fur hat? Am I overdressed? Ralph, it's years since I had such fun.'

'Giles. Yes. I suppose life's not very jolly for you with Puffy, poor old boy.'

But she said at once, 'Life is no fun at all *for* Puffy, that's what one has to remember. England has died for him. He probably suffers more than any of us. He looks the stupidest of us, but he is in fact the most intelligent. I'll never leave Puffy, Giles. Never. He is heroic and wonderful. Yes, please, delicious tartare sauce, and what a pretty little plastic thing it's in, just like an aeroplane. We can take it home, where there will be scissors, and spread it on something. No, Puffy is a wonderful man. That's why I have employed this excellent though expensive woman. Dear Thomasina – so clever to find her. Thomasina, Giles, will be in time a woman who can accomplish anything. Anything. She will become the strongest of us. At present she's only the most astringent. The most inarticulate and very much the loneliest. But she will become the strongest.'

He saw her into a taxi, *en route* for some Scarlatti and her granddaughter, whom she'd got him to telephone from the McDonald's wall phone. 'She's the fat one who got married the other day. A frightful wedding. They kept blowing hunting horns and all the people round the church gate were wanting to chop up foxes. I'll tell you all about it one day.'

'Anthony,' she said from the taxi, 'think whether you can cope with somebody so *serious* as Thomasina. She might kill you. Goodbye, my love.'

Crossing the bridge back to Waterloo for the train to Surrey, he remembered he was supposed to have been buying pasta for supper and reaching Thomasina well in time for tea.

– 36 –

The grey-faced Missus slept through most of Kent, missing the hop-poles and the oasts and the regiments of poplars protecting the bagatelle boards of the orchards. A refreshment trolley did appear at Ashford but it had run out of tea. She asked for a cup of water but was told that the urn was dry. There was Coke at a pound, orange fizz or alcohol, and she gave the fat teenager with the sad face a look.

'Can't you get another job?' she asked.

No, she was told, and: 'They've even stopped us using the lifts to get an urn fill-up at the depot. It's to save electricity.'

'I'd run up and down the stairs if I was you,' said The Missus, and the trolley wended its depressing way.

A station or so later, so did the only other passenger in the compartment. The train clattered on through the desolation round the entrance to the French tunnel. At Dover the sea arrived and then the white cliffs with long yellow-ochre stains running down them from the rain. *Like lavatory pans*, thought The Missus.

A castle stood on a green hill, looking like a toy. The Missus thought it not a patch on Whitby Abbey and probably a fake. The train groaned into a small tunnel of its own and stopped. In the dark silence The Missus listened to the whisper of the sea. The train ground out of the tunnel and for a time the sea seemed to be lapping its rails, slapping its flanks. Stony beaches lay below, like glittering whirlpools in the wet. The sea had a thick streak of blue-black horizon with bumps on it. France.

South, thought The Missus. *You won't get me over there. South does for you. I don't travel. Gracie Fields.*

The train stopped at her station and she flung out her suitcases one by one, and then the bundles, climbing down after them. There was a nicely painted footbridge over the line to a ticket office, where hanging flower baskets were waiting for summer. Posh. A couple of damp-looking youths were horsing about the platform shelter but when they saw The Missus they ran off. The Missus couldn't understand what they said. Maybe they were over from France.

She gathered her belongings about her in the shelter and sat on the cold bench. 'I'm not shifting till I'm fetched. That's the head and tail of it,' she said. Rain clattered on the roof and the wind blew. 'The long and the short of it,' said The Missus. She began to eat her sandwiches, which were damp and limp as wet handkerchiefs but very welcome. After half an hour she said, 'That's the top and bottom of it. Here I stay.'

A figure was crossing the bridge towards her. Dressed in a pillbox hat and a short cloak that swung as he walked. He stood before her in the shelter and looked her over.

'Miss Banks?'

'I am.' She crumpled her sandwich paper and stood up and held out her hand. It was ignored.

'I am Henry Jones. I am the Seton-Fairley manservant.'

'Oh, you are.'

'I am in charge of staff.'

'I see.'

'I'm very sorry to be late but I have only just received the time of your arrival.'

'It doesn't surprise me. I thought they'd forget. Where's the car?'

'I'm afraid the Seton-Fairleys are both too old to own a car.'

'Well, the taxi.'

'Taxis have to be ordered in advance and it is no great distance. You seem to have a lot of luggage.'

'Well, I'm supposed to be here for permanent. Get me a taxi.'

'I'm sure we shall manage.'

Again the cases were heaved up, the bundles clutched, and they set off, Henry Jones swinging his cloak ahead of her along the edge of the little town, up a steep wooden staircase to the ramparts, down into a cobbled street of medieval houses.

'They've got this in York,' said The Missus, 'but bigger.'

'This is one of only three perfect medieval towns in the

country, built on the old grid system. It attracts a particular class of person. We live to a great age here, what with the golf and the good medical attention. Like Frinton. We have standards here.'

'Didn't think there was anything perfect in this country any more.'

'Times have certainly changed,' said Henry Jones, inclining his head. (*Thinks he's a butler. He's seen that film. Can't be thirty. Nice boy, though.*) 'For example, staff is very short these days. Living-in staff, that's to say. I'm worked off my feet about the town. I look after half a dozen. Dying off now, of course, a great many of them, the India and Kenya expats. You used to be able to get eight different kinds of chutney in The Stores. I should prefer one place only but it's out of the question. I get calls from all and sundry. Often at night.'

I can imagine the sundry, she thought. 'Is everybody old here, then? Sort of sheltered accommodation place?'

'It is elderly.'

Godalmighty, thought The Missus.

'Here we are,' said he.

She was surprised to see that the Seton-Fairley establishment was far from large. It was also far from medieval, being a sensible bungalow on a 1950s estate protected from its neighbours by a wattle fence that waved a little in the rainy wind. A heavy roof was clamped down over low compressed-brick walls. The metal windows had rusty trickles of damp from the corners and were shrouded in thick net curtains. Inside, in the stingy sitting room, was a gleaming orthopaedic chair of giant proportions, a hoist with handle and bar hanging above it like a gallows. On the chair, reclining at a steep angle, lay colossal Puffy gazing upwards at a small chandelier.

'This is Miss Banks,' said Henry Jones. 'Colonel Seton-Fairley.'

Again The Missus held out her hand and again it was ignored. She regarded him.

'I shall make tea,' said Henry Jones. 'The colonel and I have had our lunch.'

When he had left the room The Missus with difficulty walked round the chair. Puffy blew air out of his lips and turned his head away. The Missus saw great legs, the fat paws of a bear, the head of a dying lion.

'Thank you, Mr Jones,' she said when he came in with the tea, 'I'll manage now. I'll cook myself something. I've come a long way. Off you go.'

He was halted by this. He had removed his pillbox hat and his pigtail lay over his shoulder.

'You remind me of our Ernie,' she said. 'A very nice boy, though you'd not think it to look at him. Quite my favourite except for Philip. I'll tell you about Philip later on. Now Ernie stays aloof. Feckless but good-hearted. Not like his friend Nick, oh dear me no. Nick's not your nancy-boy type, he's been a burglar. There's a lot of crime where I come from. Very rough place now.'

Henry Jones made to speak.

'A lot of good things, too, mind you. I'll enjoy telling you. From the telly, you see, you get the wrong picture. Different habits. Shaking hands for one. It's thought to be polite with us, shared with France, though I'd not go near the place myself. Well, it'd be us taught them, the Normans. We'd likely been shaking hands before the Normans, having natural good manners when you understand us. Maybe from the Romans. We still have history up there, you see. Not that Nick type, though. Mind you, if Romans is Italians I'd doubt it – they're all for kissing. No, where I come from we're formal. Surnames and titles. So you'll be Mr Jones to me and I'm Miss Banks. Now, if you've poured that tea for the colonel you can go.'

'I'm afraid that I am in charge here, Miss Banks—'

'Not now, you're not, Mr Jones.'

'I think your manners are not French at all. They are uncouth.'

'Now then, stop that. I'm old enough to be your granny and you don't talk to me like that. Leave your phone number in case there's disaster in the night. I'm not sure of this hoist. Well, I'm not sure of nursing at all and it wasn't mentioned, but we'll see how we get on.'

233

'I think that you and I should have a discussion . . .'

'Yes. Well. When her ladyship gets herself back's time enough. Just take me things to me bedroom, will you, and then get yourself away.'

He went.

He turned with a petulant flourish at the door but she waved him on. She looked her bedroom over and thought little of it after the hospitium, returned to the sitting room and again walked round the chair.

'Did you get any decent dinner?' she enquired.

A blue eye rolled in her direction and a surprisingly soft voice, high and courteous, said, 'Thank you, yes.'

'You've drunk that tea?'

'Just now.'

'No cakes or biscuits?'

'Alas – not allowed.'

She went to the kitchen and saw that salads had been put out for supper. She began to cook a pound of pork sausages she had brought with her in one of her bundles and when they were thoroughly blackened and shining she added onions and a lot of butter. In the speckled fat she made fried bread and carried it all on two plates along with a fresh pot of strong tea into the sitting room.

'How do you eat?'

'I fear,' he said, 'that you feed me.'

'It's sausages.'

'I'm not allowed sausages.'

'Oh, bugger that,' said The Missus.

She experimented with the chair and at length managed to manoeuvre it into a more upright position. She pumped at a lever to lower it and stuck a bit of sausage into the rather dizzy Puffy's mouth. He munched.

He finished two sausages in this manner, then some bread and butter as well as the fried bread. She held the teacup to his mouth. 'I can do that bit,' he said, and took the cup into his paws.

She left him to it and took her own plate on her knee.

'We'll have to see to a civilised table tomorrow,' she said.

234

'D'you play cards?' asked a gentle voice.

'I do.'

'There's cards in the sewing table.'

'Well – a sewing table. We had one in Rochdale in 1940. Is it for Mr Jones? He looks a sewing sort of man.'

'Now then!' said Puffy. 'He's just a bit of a romantic.'

'He has to be kept in his place. I'll deal.'

They played for an hour, and she brought him cocoa.

'He'll be back to put you to bed, will he, or do I do that?'

'No, no. That is for the nurse.'

'Whoever else have you got?'

'There is a gardener and an odd-job man and there's the woman. And someone called The Silver Lady for the forks. And Henry Jones. And the Social Services call, and once a month someone comes to take our blood pressure. And the barber. And the doctor once a fortnight. Madeleine often misses the blood-pressure nurse; she's away a great deal. They think I'm past doing anything.'

'You're not past taking two pounds off me in an hour's bezique.'

'I could take more off them. You're a very good player, Miss Banks. But where's the use? Where do I spend it?'

'On all these servants, sounds like to me. I'm a good player because I play a lot with a little lad where I live. Mind, we don't play for money there, it's religious. By, you do look better than when I walked in: you've a sparkle in the eye. We'll play again tomorrow.'

'Miss Banks,' he said as she got up to answer the door to the nurse, 'you'd better hide my sausage plate. It will put them in a frenzy. They tell me I haven't many more tomorrows.'

'Well, they may as well be good ones, then,' said The Missus.

- 37 -

The fearful weather and wind off the sea continued for a week after the departure of The Missus. Dolly and Toots thought of little but how she was getting on, and how the rest of them could possibly be managing up at The Priors.

The Priors filled their lives. They telephoned endlessly, sometimes getting a reply, more often not. For three days now they had not, and discussion raged about whether the lines were down or whether everyone was away with sheep or whether – this was Toots's view, strongly supported by Mrs Middleditch when she sat in on the matter – Jocasta somehow knew the tone of their telephone calls and did not lift up the receiver.

'And that baby,' said Mrs Middleditch – often – 'how is she getting along? You've not seen her yet, have you? What a shame. You'll be missing all her early little habits. They go so quickly. And the first smile. I must say if the weather was anything like, we'd take you up there ourselves. We'd drop everything. Very happy to. Bingham would be only too glad. He's very fond of old people, you know. It really hurts him to see them neglected. He often says to me, "Mother, you need never worry we'd put you in a Home. I'd never allow it." But then, Bingham's not just anyone. I'm very fortunate.'

'I'd put that Bingham in a Home,' said Toots when she'd gone. 'I'd out the whole bloody lot of them to a Home.'

'She means it kindly, though, Toots. You know, when the weather improves, if it does before Christmas, I'd like to take her up on it. I mean it. I'd like to go. I don't care about being beholden. I could make her a gingerbread. You never know with Christmas. What if it snows? We ought to take any chance we can, if it fairs up before.'

'We'll go our two selves alone,' he said.

236

'You're being ridiculous.'

'In a taxi. Just hang on. Hang on.'

Dolly woke, after several more days of sleet in the wind and the rattle of torn rose thorns against the glass, to darkness – no sign yet of dawn – and a strange silence. It was profound and she at once decided that it was the silence of death and went flopping downstairs without her slippers and not even stopping for the coat. Toots was lying with all the curtains drawn back on the dark. The church clock boomed out five.

'That's the clock,' he said.

'I know it's the clock.'

'The wind's dropped. That's why we hear it so loud. It's to be a grand day. You'll see. What's the matter with you?'

'I thought you were so quiet. The quiet brought me stark awake.'

Dolly never caressed Toots. For years she had not held his hand. But his days and nights were long and they both knew it. At some point they would be over for one of them. They both knew that that day would finish the one that was left.

Out of the window a low moon bowled along just above the trees, lighting the frost-crisp garden. 'Still as doom,' said Toots. 'We might get up there today.'

'Wherever?'

'Up yonder. Priors. We ought to get there. Right away. Get yourself ready.'

'It's five o'clock in the morning.'

'It'll take time to get straight. Taxi place opens eight o'clock. We order it right off. On the dot. Get ourselves dressed, breakfast done with, all left shipshape. We could start now.'

'We'll have to tell people we're going, else we'd cause a hue and cry. We can't just take off.'

'We're telling no one. We're off. We'll take the presents, then they'll be off our minds. You're all set with them? All done up? And that cake you've made. And there'll be keys to find and doors and drawers to lock and money for the man – did you get our pensions? And I'll need my suit.'

'You'll need your breakfast. If you don't calm down you'll

have a seizure. I never heard . . .' She went off and started breaking eggs.

'No call for eggs,' he shouted. 'Hot tea's all we want. And hot-water bottles.'

But he ate the eggs and wrote out some lists to be left lying on various stretches of the mantelpiece. While Dolly was upstairs dressing, he hauled himself along the passage to the bathroom and got himself into the warm combinations waiting over the radiator. Leaning on the zimmer he waited for her to bring him his clean shirt.

'You should by rights have had a bath,' she said. 'I don't like you going all that way without a bath.'

'There's none of them there spends time on baths from the look of them. That Jocasta's a dirty-looking—'

'Now then, stop that. She's got a dark pigmentation, that's all. Come here while I comb your hair, such as there is. Then I'll get the luggage together.' Up and down the stairs she tramped with Christmas presents. 'We could get the taxi man to carry down the chair.'

'What chair's this? What are you giving away now?'

'I'm giving her the chair that was her father's. Faith. The nursing chair. It's not big and it's a good chance. Mrs Middleditch'll just make a song and dance if we ask her. There's no room in that Bingham's car, it's all for show.'

'Don't start trying to get it down yourself, then. We've to get hold of the taxi yet. They're not the sort at that place I'd want going round the bedrooms. We'll see the whites of his eyes before we ask him.'

Toots was fast losing confidence. He fumbled for the taxi number. He wrote it down clearly on a page in an old exercise book and added: 'Taxi Ordered 8.10 a.m.' He closed the book and put it away.

'Get on, then, Toots, order it. Here's your frame. You can get down that passage again if you try. I want to put my hat on, it's nearly quarter past. They'll be open.'

'I'll give it five minutes. I'm a bit lame this morning. Can you not do it? I've the number here. I'll listen.' As she went off to dial he wrote in his financial diary the name and address of the taxi firm and then 'Maximum £5'.

'Thirty pounds, he says,' said Dolly. 'I've cancelled it. Out of hand. It's a try-on.'

'We'll see about that.' Toots sprang off the bed and humped off down the passage at speed. He seized the phone.

'See here, what's all this? My godfathers! Toots Braithwaite, lad, d'you know who you're talking to? We're off on a Christmas visit. Thirty pounds, you're highwaymen! I remember you. Red-haired. Five A. You were rubbish. Aye, well, I dare say it is a long way but it's a clear road this time in the morning and there's no snow falling. We'd have heard if it was blocked. Aye, we're ready. Been ready an hour. You can come when you like. Twenty pounds, then? Ridiculous. All right, since it's Christmas. I'd have thought you'd have done it for nothing, old people like ourselves, going to see their only grandchild. Have you a good taxi now? Last one stank of cigarettes and drink. And you've got to get a chair down.'

'We're going,' he said. He looked very nervous now. 'Don't forget your heart pills. We ought to take the hot-water bottles. I'm not joking. But we're not taking that plastic bed bottle, mind.'

Dolly had dropped into sad silence.

'What is it?'

'We might get stuck up there, Toots. We'd be a nuisance to them. We're old people. It's selfish putting the mountain rescue on alert. It's what we've always said ourselves: people are plain selfish going off this weather in ordinary shoes and no proper clothes.'

'We've good clothes and shoes and we're not leaving that taxi. So don't be so silly. "Climbing". It's not Everest and crampons. It's Sutton Bank in a station taxi.'

But as they waited he wrote several more notes. One he propped by the mantelpiece clock for those who would perhaps need information. 'TAXI 8.30,' he wrote. 'THE PRIORS. Return journey commences 2.30 latest. Estimated arrival home, five o'clock latest. Aim for 4.30 sharp. Tel. No. see hall table, lines possibly down. Documents bottom wardrobe.' He repeated the information in his notebook, adding, but not showing Dolly, the name of the funeral director he favoured and the telephone number of Andrew's London hospital. 'Milk,' he said, 'cancel', and began to write a note to be attached to the front door knob.

'That's just inviting burglars, you're going off your head. Here,' said Dolly, 'I've done up the thermos and I'll fill the hot bottles when I hear the taxi.'

'Eight thirty-five. Not here. The bugger's late. It's all off.'

'I'll ring again.'

'No. It's all off. Forget it. We're not right. We're wandering, Dolly. It's dotage. I don't know what we were thinking of, setting off this daft game. I'm not feeling very well. We'll have to call Middleditch.'

'It's here,' she said, from the front door. 'Here's your coat.'

At The Priors the low moon lit the ruined arches and the moors but left the dell where the new buildings stood in darkness. There were sheep clumped up together in the dipping place beside the chapel, keeping each other warm. Sometimes there was a cough or a rattling short bleat from them, but they stood as they had done all night, tense but quiet. Here and there the moon lit their eyes, green staring lanterns. They were to be Ernie's job today. These were the sick sheep brought away from the others. He was to anoint their green eyes with penicillin. Jack would hold them, Ernie squeeze the ointment over both top and bottom lid and let each sheep spring away. Ernie was good with sheep, better than Jack, whose hands were too slight to hold them steady. Nick was strongest of them all, but awkward. The two wide-shouldered Tibetan men had helped once but hadn't caught the knack. It had made Jocasta wonder if they were Tibetans at all. Jack had said perhaps they worked only with goats. The Missus had said for her money they weren't from any mountains, all they liked was rice and you don't grow rice in the Himalayas. Jocasta had said Yes, you do. The matter rested. The Tibetans went back to their sheds and ate chocolate.

'What happens if you just leave their eyes?' the A-level girl asked Ernie, and he had said, 'They go blind. They stoomble about.'

'Does it matter?'

'It does to them. And they break their legs and walk over edges. It's nasty. It's very infectious, this disease.'

'Maybe it's what Faith had.'

'You never know.'

Jack, listening, considered whether the maggots of sheep might serve for a sermon on seeing, but did not see Faith in the picture.

Jocasta was best of all of them with sheep, small as she was. She had hard hands. Ernie wanted her help today rather than Jack's and had suggested it and it had been agreed. The backcloth was nearly finished and Philip was now boarding at school. They were going to get on with the job at first light, for it would take most of the day.

It was now five days since The Missus had left, four since Jack had killed Jocasta: that's to say, killed the dark fairy who had haunted him since the minute he met her. The woman who moved about The Priors, now, he saw for the first time. She was deft, thoughtful, abstracted by her own thoughts, but efficiently getting on with each day, managing well the curiosities of Alice Banks's ménage, preparing rather nice food, helping all round. Maybe she had always been so. Neither of them spoke much. Neither mentioned either The Missus or Andrew.

And, to Jocasta, Jack now seemed sterner, more self-reliant, without a trace of homage for her. He gave sensible orders to the lads, did the accounts at the kitchen table at night undistracted by her presence or by anything. He made phone calls about orders of feed, subsidies, veterinary bills. He never consulted her. Maybe he never had. She watched his lean body out over the fields in all weathers, never tired, never considering the life hard. She liked this.

They were at once aloof from each other like people dazed after an earthquake and yet aware that they shared something cataclysmic known to no one else. It was not so much that each was sloughing the other off as that they were both becoming aware of what had been there all along, unshared under the skin.

So that the day when Jocasta had sat so quiet and lost in the Whitby supermarket and had forgotten Philip had been the day when she was not so much beginning to change as beginning to emerge under her own colours. When Jack had almost hit her when she came home without Philip she had been terrified and not tried to hide it. She had shielded her face and gasped. Jack had been horrified, both by himself and by the fact that the cowering had looked so experienced. Jocasta had been hit before.

He'd said, 'Oh Jocasta – oh, God! I'm sorry. You didn't really think I would . . . ?'

She'd said, in the controlled, old-world, educated voice that her hippie years hadn't touched, 'No, no. Of course not. I'll go for Philip. It's no distance. I'll go now. I'll ring him. He's mine.' She was shivering.

'I think Nick might go. Or Ernie. Wherever they are.'

'I'm afraid for Philip, in the sidecar.'

'Yes. Of course. Come and sit down.'

In a while he said, 'I'm going to phone the school and ask them to keep him for the night. No, don't argue. The Head's wife is a nice woman; she's suggested before.'

'Has she? Yes, Phil likes her. I expect they think we're not their sort.'

When he brought her a mug of tea he said rather distantly, 'All fixed. Quite all right. I'm so sorry, you've had a lot to bear lately, Jocasta.' And she thought, *He sounds like some counsellor.*

When she had drunk the tea she said, 'So have you, Jack.'

They both thought of Andrew. There had been no word. And no word of The Missus. Nor of Pammie, whose date of arrival was still vague though Jack had telephoned her affectionately several times, Jocasta in the same room.

'I've done all the big shopping now,' she said, 'all the stuff for the Tibs. And our turkey. It'll have to go in the freezer. It's a shame, but it's just too long a time to leave it out. It was too early, really, to do the Christmas stuff today, but if the weather goes really wrong . . .'

'Could you – do you know how to cook a turkey? That's if you stay, of course.'

'I could cook a turkey, I suppose. If I stay.'

They sat on, looking into their tea mugs.

'I hope it's big enough. I can't make out how many are coming.'

'A host of motley,' he said. 'There's Toots and Dolly, they're the essentials. They still haven't . . .'

She was looking at him and he held her stare. There was guilt in the air. She said, 'I know. They haven't seen her yet. It's dreadful. Andrew and I did try. We nearly made it, you know, when they decided to keep her in the hospital, but the weather . . .'

He said, 'And we have been otherwise engaged.'

He was disappointed when she got up then and began to unpack all the shopping. 'Must you do that?'

'A lot of it's for the freezer, it can't hang about. The Tibs need theirs right away, they're almost out. They're doing all their own cooking now.'

'Yes. Jocasta. It's Nick and Ernie's night off. We are on our own tonight. Is that going to be all right?'

'Yes. All right. I bought some smoked salmon. I had a cheque sent for Christmas.'

He thought, *Andrew. I won't eat Andrew's smoked salmon. Or maybe it's another man. The father of Philip, whoever he is. She's a dark woman.*

'It was from Thomasina. To buy you a present in case something stops her coming.'

'She'll make every excuse not to come, I'm afraid. She always does. Ever since poor Holly . . . I don't know why.'

'She's still very frightened of seeing Faith,' said Jocasta.

'Is she? I'd no idea.'

'I knew you hadn't,' said Jocasta. Had it not been the raw, exposed, adulterous Jocasta, he'd have said she was looking at him with simple kindness. Almost affection. 'She's afraid of hating her, Jack.'

They sat at supper together at each end of the table, both of them in sweaters and boots. Jocasta saw that Jack's fingers were purple with cold. 'We should wear mitts to eat,' she said. The wind howled outside through the broken stones. 'Poor sheep tonight,' she said. 'I hope Toots and Dolly are all right.' She looked at Jack. 'It's time I saw them again. I was taken up with . . . all that other business the last time.'

It occurred to them both that if they were to take Faith together to her grandparents it might seal this evening they were passing together so extraordinarily. So quietly.

'I don't get on with Toots,' she said. 'Your mother's all right.'

These were things she had never said.

'Nobody gets on with Toots, I'm afraid.'

'He has a right to see Faith,' she said, surprising herself. 'I'll drive you down there if you like.' She waited. There was a very great pause and she felt afraid.

'Oh, there's no need. Pammie Jefford will want to go down and they're keen to meet her. She's a jewel of a woman.'

'Very well.'

'Unless of course you particularly want to go?'

She thought of her last visit to the old creatures with Andrew, though Andrew hadn't reached the end of the journey. She thought of the delirious hour with him on the way home, the wonder of being alone with him as her lover again. The clinging together, the warmth of him, his skin, the certainty of him. She waited for the familiar surge of love and longing for Andrew to warm her to the heart. She concentrated on the first time she had seen him after Holly's death, here, in this room, at the window, the child on the table ignored. His head leaning on the glass, 'I want you in my bed. My tongue in your mouth.' She waited for the lurch of lust.

It took its time coming. It subsided feebly. She saw herself, this now older creature, shabby in every way, morose, looking down at empty hands in a cold kitchen with the man who was her uncaring husband.

Quickly she said, 'Jack, we must take Faith to them. Right away. Anything could happen. They're old. If they were ill, or if it snowed so they couldn't get here, they'd not see her even for Christmas and it would be scandalous. I don't mean it would be *thought* scandalous, though it would; it would *be* scandalous. Oh, you childless people – oh Lord! I'm so sorry.'

'It's all right,' he said, quite kindly. 'Yes, we'll go. If we can prise the child from Pema.'

'Let Pema come too. She'd get on with your mother and give Toots plenty to talk about for months.'

'I'm not sure that Toots—'

'Oh, never mind him. If you won't go down with her I'll take her myself. Or I'll go with Philip.'

He stared. 'Of course I'll go,' he said.

'With me? Are you sure? Alone?'

'I will. We'll go together, there is nothing against it. We won't tell them, just turn up. They're never out.'

'I have a chicken. I could cook it tonight. Oh yes, and I bought a chocolate-log thing.'

He thought, *This is Jocasta. We sound married. We never did sound married. This sounds like an accustomed marriage.*

Unable to go on with this, he jumped up and said he was going across to the chapel.

Steam rose from the huddle of sheep and also from the sheds of the Tibetan women as he crossed the cloister. The smell of spice from the sheds was so pungent he thought, *It'll make the sheep's eyes water*, and then: *Rather a good joke, that. I must tell Jocasta.* After his prayers he came back across the courtyard and thought that the wind had dropped a little and that it seemed warmer.

'It is warmer,' she said in the morning. She was dressed for out-of-doors, standing by the hot stove they'd all now mastered. 'It's definitely warmer. There's still frost and it'll be snowy on the top but we could drive there perfectly well if we're careful. I'll go over and ask Pema and they can get Faith's foods together and her stuff. They'll want to dress her up.'

'Oughtn't we to be doing all that?'

'Some hope. Pema won't let anyone near Faith. Jack . . . ?'

'Yes, I know.'

'Pema's going to be bereft. Do they really mean it, that they're going?'

'Don't ask me. I understand nothing,' he said, suddenly sounding like his father.

The low moon lit the sheep as Jocasta crossed to the sheds to tell of the visit. The A-level girl was there. Pema, she said, was not well. Yes, the others could get Faith ready but better not tell Pema she was being taken fifteen miles away. Let her think she was just going to spend the day over in the kitchens.

'If you're all going away for ever, Pema will have to get used to being without her.'

'I'll say,' said the girl, 'that's what we tell her, don't fret. You can't reason with her. She's very old. And look what she's been through. Ten years ago she walked out of China. Six hundred miles. You lot knows nowt.'

There was no sign in the sheds of Faith, who was in her hammock slung in the roof struts, subsumed into the place, into the smells of spices and cigarette smoke, dark cloths and the flickering row of lamps that the third woman – there seemed to be only three Tibetans to be seen now – was lighting. The lamps were arranged along a shelf. They had grown fewer, too, the last weeks.

The girl had told her there was a lamp for every human soul living at The Priors. Jocasta wondered for a moment about Faith wrapped tightly in the nest of these cocksure foreigners. She realised that she was putting her mind into the mind of the baby and felt obscure unease.

In the house she found Jack holding up an old flannelette blanket. The carrycot Faith had arrived in was standing on the table.

'I think it may be too small for her now,' he said, to her and his own surprise.

She said, 'My goodness. Yes. I suppose it is. Obviously. I don't notice these things. Phil always travelled on my back. I'd better have her on my lap in the car.'

'Won't Pema want to hold her?'

'Pema's ill,' she said. 'We're going alone. You'll have to drive. You can't hold her. You'll forget she's there.'

'I'm not exactly the best driver . . .'

'You are,' she said. 'You can. Oh, Jack . . .'

They packed up the old car with Christmas presents, in case Dolly and Toots didn't make it on Christmas Eve, and the carrycot full of Faith's belongings. They carried Faith out to the car. As usual she was passive and sleepy. Ernie appeared.

'These sheep's left to me, then?'

'Get Nick to help you.'

'He's useless.'

'Get the Tibs.'

'Where'd yer be widout me?'

'Lost,' said Jocasta, and smiled.

Ernie stood looking after the car, wondering if he'd seen aright. The two of them together with the baby.

When Nick came frowsting out of his room with the A-level girl, his arm round her neck, Ernie said, 'Yer to 'elp me, the pair on yer. They're away down to Toots an' Dolly. Jocasta's pleasant.'

The moon had set and the sun was reluctantly rising as the car made the ridge road. The white moors stretched pure. The sheep were all down in the pastures and there were no birds, the road silken, lavender-pink, as the low sun shone between miles of empty frozen heather.

'What time do we get there? Ten o'clock?'

'Maybe a bit later but it will be just about right,' he said. 'They'll be up and dressed. It takes them ages.'

'Take care, Jack. We slithered. You'll destroy the Saxon cross.'

But Jack was taken up with the glory of God arranging itself down the valleys, the sky turning to ice-blue above the early warning system of the golf balls.

– 38 –

Toots sat in noble silence for the first five miles. Dolly was keeping up a loving monologue addressed to the taxi driver, saying how good of him this was. So early. Such a wintry day. So hard on him to have to turn out at such an hour and then to be having to hang about through lunch, waiting to bring them home. She was absolutely sure there would be some lunch for him and anyway she had brought mince pies. Yes, it was a remote place but he'd find it very interesting and there was only one field gate to open now. When she and Mr Braithwaite had been younger and driven their own *very* nice little car, such a good little car, she'd been able to jump out at every gate for him to drive through. There had been seven gates. It was still a lovely drive of course.

After another few miles she asked him if he knew the way. Well, what a shame. But it didn't surprise her, there were very few Teesside people bothered with the moors, it was all Spain and Tenerife. Five miles more and she informed him that her son, who lived on the moors, was an unusual person. It was a priory they were going to. A ruined priory. Her son was a clergyman.

The driver lit up a fag.

Toots said, 'Put that out, boy. Mrs Braithwaite has a chest.'

The driver put it out. But spat.

'Oh dear,' said Dolly, 'it does seem a shame to ask you. People used to smoke all the time before the Tory government. It must be hard on you now, when nobody does.'

'Plenty do in this taxi,' said Toots. 'It stinks. Here, watch out. Where you going? Left here – left over the bridge. By gad, the river's full. Look at that snow up the top there. Rotten rattle-trap taxi, this. Filthy, too. Is it going to get there?'

'It's the recession,' said Dolly. 'Everything used to be so

different. Leather seats and little tassels and concertina stools. Lovely for weddings.'

The driver said nothing but took the next hill at speed. They climbed above an icy reservoir in its girdle of pines and the strange knoll that bulges out of the first stretch of moorland like a grassy abscess.

'A Roman lookout,' said Dolly. 'Now, when we were young people, Mr Braithwaite and I used to come up here spooning, and to watch the moon rise.'

The driver still preserved his silence but the taxi met the information with a heavy and threatening clanking.

'Whatever is that?'

'Exhaust,' said the driver. 'We'll look in at a garidge.'

'What garage?' asked Toots, surveying the horizon. He was beginning to enjoy himself now, with the excitement of the event heightened by the imbecility of the taxi driver. Empty snowy acres on every side were lit by a sudden torch of sunlight.

'Now that is wonderful,' said Dolly. 'Isn't that wonderful, Toots? Do you want a hot drink? Do you want – you know – *the bottle*?'

'Landsakes, we've not been going half an hour.' Toots was cheering up no end. He was in the thick again. 'They think we're daft, you know – women,' he told the man. 'Light up, laddie. We're up in the fresh air now; we can open the window.'

The driver spurned this suggestion, pressed hard on the accelerator and the loose exhaust pipe roused itself to a crescendo of drumming and fell off in the road. The driver got out and threw it away in the snow. When he reached the bottom of Ellen's Bank he took another confident left fork and roared up the corkscrew hill to Ellen Brow, where a garage of a sort stood to the side of the road near a shuttered and barred hotel, the hotel in which Thomasina and the general had debated the pros and cons of the Seton-Fairley wedding.

The driver slammed off. They heard him round the back of the garage beating on a door.

He returned and said, 'It's gonner tek time, it's morent

exhaust. Yer can get yersens a sarnie int pub,' and went off again.

Dolly said that she sometimes understood why North Country people were thought to be common. Toots said that the man was plain scum.

Dolly undid herself from the strap and managed in a moment to get out of the car. She put her feet down carefully in the sharp, crunchy snow and, holding the side of the taxi, sidestepped crabwise round to the boot, where, balancing herself, she toppled out the zimmer frame. 'I'm not having you sitting frozen here,' she said, opening Toots's door and presenting it to him.

'Hold on, now,' he said. 'Do nothing we'll regret. We could sit tight.'

'I'm going to get you in the warm. There'll be a door open to the hotel somewhere; they'd not leave it all winter empty.'

Toots grasped the handles of the frame. 'Take it easy, now,' he said. 'Stop getting hysterical.'

'I'm not uttering one word. Get your feet down.'

Toots did so, took his bearings, then gazed into the distance. He started with a few hiccuping steps very slowly towards the hotel and fell heavily on the flagstones outside its front door.

'It's all up,' he cried. 'We should never have come. Broken leg. Possibly pelvis. I'm finished.'

'I'll go and fetch someone. Don't move.'

'I can't move, you silly woman.'

'I'll get the blanket. There'll have to be an ambulance. It'll be hypothermia in no time. I never knew such a driver. This country, now . . .'

'Get yourself off inside the hotel and keep warm. Send someone out for me. Whatever's this now?'

It was the dogmatic waitress in her bulging turquoise jacket arriving in her car. The jacket she whipped off and had over Toots in thirty seconds. She fastened it round him, hauled him up to his feet and balanced him on his legs.

'What's this, then? Dead drunk at ten o'clock in the morning? Now then, arms round me neck, we'll see you right. Whatever you doin' 'ere?'

'Get Dolly some brandy – she's a sick woman,' said Toots in the bar. 'Look at my trousers. Best suit. Feller's gone round the back of the garage. He can stay there. He can rot. If you hadn't come we'd be finished.'

'Well, I did. So what were you on with? Skiing holiday? Sit down. We're closed, so you can have your breakfasts int bar. Are you right? I can ring t' doctor. He's very good; he'd come. Dear oh dear, 'ere's some buns with your tea. Where you off to?'

The driver came in.

'What the hell you mean leaving them out there, yer daft soggit! Fallen int snow and yer liable. *Oh*, yes – when they're in yer care, yer liable. I'll be witness if there's a leg broke.'

'There's a car broke. It'll tekt morning. I'm ringing in: where's telephone?'

'Station Taxis was always a disgrace. Get yerselluf away. I'll tek 'em on wherever.'

'It's Ellerby Priors. Our son is a clergyman there and we're visiting. Just for a very short spell.'

'A very short spell? You don't mean Jack's? Yer off for a spell wi' *Jack*?'

'Well, only an hour or so. We've come up to see our grandchild.'

'But would you ever get down that lane? Did they say it was clear?'

Toots said, looking out of the window, vaguely, 'Perfect day for the drive, we both thought.'

Dolly said, 'We didn't actually say we were coming. It was to be a surprise.'

'Git off, then, yer great lump,' said the waitress. 'I'll see to them. No distance. Get yerselluf together and be ready when we come back. You're a scandal.'

'I'm afraid there's quite a lot of things in the back of the cab,' said Dolly, 'and a chair.'

'Then he teks it all out and loads it up in my car,' she said, 'while you drink your teas and rests.'

'You are very good. I can't tell you how good.'

'Deserve a medal,' said Toots. 'Proper recognition. I'll write to *The Gazette*.'

'Write to nothing. Are you ready?'

'I'd like the cloakroom,' said Dolly, and while she was gone Toots had a go at catching hold of the waitress's hand and she had a go at slapping him off.

Outside, while the taxi driver blackly struggled with the chair on which once upon a time Jack had been held in Dolly's arms, Jack himself drove by unseen with Jocasta and Faith, heading in the direction of the estuary.

'It's all right,' Jocasta was saying. 'There's been a car up just now.'

'How is she?'

'Just lying here looking at me. She looks puzzled. Sometimes puzzled and then she screws her face up and looks amused. They've dressed her to kill. She's like a furry monkey. A mini-yeti.'

'I think we'll get something of a reception.' He smiled at Jocasta in the mirror.

Half an hour later the waitress's car nosed its way slowly and jerkily down the lane towards Ellerby Priors. Sheep stood about there, blinking their eyes, in the company of a languid girl and The Smikes, who were battling with more sheep in some pens. There was an air of emptiness, somehow.

'They've gone down to thee,' said Nick. 'They've tooken Faith to show yer. Did yer never pass them? The phone's gone down. We can't ring.'

'Is *nobody* here?' asked Dolly. 'Isn't even Philip here?'

'No, they've left him int school.'

Dolly began to cry.

- 39 -

It was a curious quartet that was proceeding up the A1 on the twenty-second of December. It was much later than Pammie had planned but she had decided that there were things that must be done about her private life if she was really contemplating leaving it behind her for good. Or even perhaps only for the spring. Jack had been having many humble conversations with her now for over a fortnight, almost every evening at first but now more intermittent. Neither of them fully addressed the matter in hand, what her duties were supposed to be, her terms of employment, her accommodation, how long she would stay. They talked of the weather, the Nativity tableau, the difficulties of bereavement, of Pammie's parish church and how it would be the first time in years she would be missing its Christmas services. Jack had said, 'Perhaps you should just hop on a train and come up right away? Don't think of luggage. I don't want to beg you – what right have I? But we do miss Alice Banks.'

He did not mention Jocasta and he didn't specify exactly what it was about Alice Banks that he missed. He had found to his guilty shame that it wasn't really all that much. He thought of her angry, rusty presence over the spluttering pans and then imagined Pammie in her bright clothes and manner, talkative in shiny Surrey lipstick, catering with ease for any batch of needy souls that might present itself. Carrying little Faith about against her tweedy shoulder.

But Pammie had needed time. Her house had to be in order, her Christmas telephoning complete. No Christmas cards to send this year – the widow's privilege – but many friends who'd offered to have her for Christmas had to be placated and told she was going away, and where, and to whom. The dog had to be dumped on the long-suffering gardener, water and central heating switched off, burglar alarms pepped up and the halogen lights to the drive and the recording of a pack of Rottweilers made ready for anyone who approached the wrought-iron gates – except, of course, the postman, who knew you have to slink round the side along the wall like any self-respecting thief would do. 'Also,' said Pammie, 'how very ridiculous if Giles and Thomasina are going up there that we shouldn't all travel together.'

'Alas,' said Giles, 'Pammie – I'm afraid we've undertaken Madeleine.'

'*Madeleine*? Madeleine Seton-*Fairley*. Never! And not Puffy? Left *behind*? And what does Thomasina think of *that*, I wonder?'

'Puffy's being looked after by some woman, a Miss Banks. She's already arrived.'

'So that's where the frightful little woman went. Poor Jack. He's been very badly let down.'

'Rather a crisis going on up there, I gather. One thing and another,' said Giles. 'And very good of you to sort it out, if I may say so, Pammie. Queer sort of Christmas break for you.'

'It's probably for much longer than Christmas,' she said, looking at her nails. 'Jack may want me there with him for some time.'

'In which case,' said Thomasina, 'you'll have a mass of stuff to take and we'll need more than one car. And, after all, we'll need our own car, to come home again.'

'Oh – back on the train,' said Pammie. 'Much faster. I'll drive you to a station from The Priors. Actually, I'd like your company on the way. If you would. It might be just a bit embarrassing for me, arriving alone.' She looked coy and Thomasina looked sickened. Thomasina also looked and sounded tired.

'There will be Madeleine to transport, too,' Giles warned Pammie. 'She's immovable.'

'Oh, there'll be plenty of room. I'm only taking tweeds and woollies and boots and a present or two. Is she large? I forget.'

'No,' said Giles.

'Yes,' said Thomasina. 'Big-boned.'

*

The main difficulty that the journey presented was getting everyone together at the same place at the same time.

Madeleine had elected to stay all the time in London since the arrival of The Missus in Kent. She said she travelled light and had her mink with her for the cold to come and Puffy sounded to be perfectly splendid, not thinking of Christmas at all. She had a wonderful woman for Puffy. Did Giles know? Had she told him? She was growing hazier about Puffy and told Thomasina on the telephone how she had always loved him so, rather as if Puffy had already left the stage. She told Pammie that she had phoned him from the Academic Ladies one night and there had been no reply, so she had had to ring the police, who were used to her and very kind and calming and had discovered Puffy's phone had been taken off the hook. 'Probably gambling,' she said. 'People don't altogether know, Pammie, what I have had to bear.'

Then there was the general. He had had to go back to his house to see to things: excuse himself from all the drinks parties, and tell the Chaplain he couldn't take the bag round at the midnight service, and leave a present for the milkman, and countermand the two turkey steaks that he had been thinking of taking over to Thomasina on Christmas Day.

Pammie and Thomasina planned to travel from their Surrey dwellings together, side by side in Pammie's car, and pick up Madeleine and Giles in central London.

Madeleine took charge. Not stirring from one of the chintz chairs of the Academic Ladies, she arranged for the party to gather outside it and at two toots on the horn from Pammie after breakfast on the twenty-second she and Giles would step out of the door and into the car and off. Giles would of course be staying the night before with her at the Club.

'But I have my own club,' said the general.

'Mine is much more convenient.'

('I do not believe in Madeleine,' said Thomasina to Pammie. 'I think Giles has invented her to hurt me.' 'Then get rid of him,' said Pammie. 'Drop him. Drop her. Let them both melt like morning dew.' But Thomasina didn't reply.)

'I am not *sure*,' said Giles, 'that it is possible for me to stay at a woman's club, Maddie. I'm neither an academic nor a lady.'

Madeleine said, 'My dear, I'm not at all sure that *I* am,' and that the place was full of old generals staying with their ex-girlfriends.

This alarmed him more than anything. 'Look here, Maddie. I suppose you do realise that Thomasina and I are, well, pretty close and so on?'

But she only smiled.

He was relieved to find that he was allotted a bedroom that was decidedly single. A very nice room, virginal clean and collegiate, but a section of it had been annexed as bathroom for the room next door. An academic lady could be heard singing there in her shower. When he tiptoed with his sponge bag along the corridor in the morning he found another one making herself tea. She had ranked metal bars across her head and was reading *Sonnets from the Portuguese*. It was a world he had not met.

Madeleine had drifted mysteriously away the evening before and he'd rather wondered if it had been round the corner to the Dorchester, but there she was in the Academic Ladies foyer at a quarter to eight, waiting for the car, watching from the window. She was wearing wellingtons. Her fur coat was over a chair; her skin luminous with money and French creams. She was surrounded by luggage, enough for a cruise to Bombay.

'Edward!'

'Giles.'

'*Giles*! Did you sleep? Did the bells wake you?'

'Bells? No. There was a bit of singing.'

'Oh, I do love London at Christmas. Bells. Singing. Fortnum & Mason pâté. You can often see the Queen there, you know. I've seen Charles buying his cheese at Paxton's. I do rather wonder why we're leaving it all.'

So did Giles. But then he thought how helpless and romantic and reminiscent Madeleine looked: every now and then a flicker, not exactly a smile, reminded him of what she had been. Well, still was. Somewhere. Very pretty woman. Diana

Cooper type. Bloody unkind really, this crumbly wrinkly stuff they all go on about. Not on.

He sat beside her. 'I'd much rather be staying in London, if you want to know, Maddie. Some coffee?'

'You shouldn't tangle with widows,' she said. 'There's great safety in a husband about, even if it's silly old Bertie.'

'Puffy.'

'Ah yes, Puffy.'

'Coffee only in the breakfast room,' the Desk said to Giles. 'And I don't believe you're a member here.'

Madeleine said, 'Do you know, it may be nice after all to be leaving London.'

He said, 'Now – Madeleine, I want you to think very hard indeed and tell me why it is you are coming with us to Yorkshire.'

'Oh, loneliness,' she said, 'curiosity. Trying to keep ahead of my wits, or lack of them. Being with you again, Giles.'

'And Puffy?'

'Oh darling, shut up, Puffy's *gone*. Marvellous man, but he's *gone*. I always wanted to marry you. You were an awful fool.'

Outside, Pammie could be seen marching round her small Peugeot and kicking its tyres thoughtfully, considering the hours ahead. Thomasina, in the front passenger seat, did not get out or turn her head. Giles went out, opened her door and kissed her cheek in a conjugal way and then began to arrange luggage in the boot. As well as the cases, Madeleine was transporting some large bowls of spring bulbs, bought at Harrods, that were to go in last. Giles himself was taking a gun.

'A gun, Giles?' asked Thomasina.

'Might get a bit,' he said, 'according to Maddie.'

'A gun at The Priors?' said Pammie. 'I'm afraid you're out of luck. It's a very religious place.'

'I know The Priors,' said Thomasina. 'You probably didn't notice that it's a farm. Naturally there are guns. They have sheep.'

Madeleine stood on the pavement. 'Oh, Giles won't have to shoot *sheep*, Thoms,' she said. 'We're staying with old, old friends of mine nearby with quantities of birds to shoot. Tony Faylesafe. Darling man.'

'I'm not,' said Pammie.

'No, *you're* not, of course, you're going to be cook to the parson. I hope he's paying you. They try and get away with that sort of thing, you know, parsons. Always did. I hope he isn't Catholic; they're the worst with willing women. But then I'm hopeless at religion. It all seems so unlikely. Tony Faylesafe's *very* nice. I simply rang him. "Faylesafe," I said, "I'm bringing a couple of friends with me to stay with you over Christmas," and he was absolutely thrilled.'

'Well, I hope so.'

'No doubt about it, Giles. I told him you couldn't possibly stay at that ghastly hotel where they put the lights out over the cheese – yes, you told me about it, however else could I know? Do you think my memory's gone? – and I said, "We aren't religious enough for this funny fellow," and *he* said, "Well, all right, come if you like, Maddie, but tell them I'm not a great one for Christmas." '

There was a short silence.

'Perhaps he's a Buddhist,' said Pammie. 'We have some at The Priors.'

'I don't think so, darling. I think he's a misanthropist.'

The silence deepened. Thomasina, who had been thinking that Thoms was the name only Giles had ever called her, and that he must also have told Madeleine about the fiasco of the moorland hotel, said slowly, 'I shan't be staying with the Faylesafes, Madeleine.'

They were on the move now, driving down South Audley Street, the flower shops, patisseries and jewellers all awakening for a lavish day. Early in the morning the Christmas trees were lit. The huge plane tree rooted in asphalt outside the Hilton Hotel was slung with its thousand electric bulbs like moonstone drops. Hyde Park was a green haze touched with frost.

'I think I'd better warn everybody,' said the general, 'that I have to be back quite soon. Committee meetings. Thirty-first at the latest.'

Thomasina had sunk to silence beside Pammie. Aromatic Madeleine reclined beside Giles in the back. Giles's long old legs were jacknifed almost under his chin. The gun lay at their feet.

He thought, *This is a blasted awful situation*, and remembered last Christmas drowsing and boozing in a chair in Wiltshire with an old cousin; and the one before with Hilda, at the golf club. No women allowed in the bar there even on Christmas Day, but she'd never minded. Glad of a gas with the other girls.

Girls, he thought. *Good girl, Hilda. Whiskers on the chin but reliable. Herself always. Full of fight. Off round the links with the dog in those terrible trousers after lunch. Cooked Christmas dinner in the evening. No fuss. No haute cuisine nonsense. Turkey and sprouts – all warmed up but very nice. Couple of old friends round for Bridge afterwards. Never got tired, Hilda. Always had my old blue smoking jacket cleaned for Christmas. Good pals. Boxing Day: walked the plantations round the garrison, feet in the sand under the Wellingtonias. Wonderful trees. Planted after Waterloo to commemorate the Iron Duke.*

Pammie was rounding the bottom of Park Lane with Apsley House afloat on its island. *Tables all laid up exactly as they were for the Waterloo Ball*, thought Giles. *The Great Reception. Battalions of crystal, cartloads of porcelain, half a ton of silver. Ivory placement cards. Cream of Europe.*

Who the hell knows a thing about Waterloo now? he wondered, watching a covey of Arab ladies with slits for their eyes rolling over a pedestrian crossing by Marble Arch. *Never even heard of it.*

Glancing down Oxford Street he saw the huge, unlighted metal banners – Donald Ducks, Father Christmases – waiting for the dark, like the shredded flags in churches that commemorate old triumphs. The laden car plunged northward into the Edgware Road.

— 40 —

'Braithwaite,' said the Head, 'I suppose your parents do know, do they, that the school broke up over a week ago and that you are here only for extra coaching? Out of choice?'

Philip looked amazed. 'I thought it had been arranged.'

'I suggested it to you. You said you would enquire. You came back in here, to my office, and said that it was on.'

'Yes. I like it here now.'

'You've been doing very well. Philip, I did just wonder. Friday is Christmas Eve. Are there any arrangements to collect you?'

'Oh, I'll ring.'

'We've tried. The line is out of order at The Priors. You don't want to miss Christmas at home, do you? Do you? *Now* where are you going?'

'Oh, just out. Along—'

'You're going to wash your hands, aren't you?'

'Yes. I might.'

'Philip, could you talk about it? Do you know why you're always washing your hands?'

'They're always dirty.'

'That used not to bother you.'

'No.' He looked innocent. 'No, actually it didn't. Emma was saying that.'

'Does my wife allow you to call her Emma?'

'Yes. She's not exactly mad about it, but she lets me.'

'I see. She says, Braithwaite, that you've been having nightmares. She's had to wake you up a couple of times. We wonder if you really do want to stay here? Or, can you tell me, is there some trouble at home?'

'I'm not exactly mad about telling private stuff.'

'Very well. But it seems such a shame when you're beginning

260

to get on so well otherwise. Do you want to stay on next term? Boarding?'

'Yeah, well—'

'Don't say "yeah, well". Will you answer my question. Is it the new sister? Have you had enough of her?'

'You can't get near her. She's always with Jack's Tibetans. But they're going.'

'So who will look after her then? Will your mother be in charge? Is that it, Braithwaite? Are you miserable about the baby – jealous? It's very normal if you are.'

'I don't know who's going to have her,' Philip said at last. 'There's nobody really. There's a woman coming but she's only a cook. Miss Banks left.'

'I heard something about that.'

'She doesn't write to any of us. We don't know why she went. Jack's hopeless.'

'Ah. Hopeless. Your father.'

'He's not my father. I don't know who my father is and I'm not mad about finding out. And Jocasta's not her mother. Faith's mother's dead. Jocasta has nothing to do with Faith. Well, I don't know what's going to happen.'

'Do you ask?'

'No. I don't go in for questions like that. My grandparents are great. I could really live with my grandparents and so could Faith, but they're so old and they live in a foul place on the estuary.'

'I know Toots and Dolly. Toots taught me. He must be getting on a bit now.'

'He's got more sense than Jack,' said Philip, and then shut up.

'Go off and have tea now. I'll join you all in a minute. Emma and I will drive you home for Christmas if no one turns up to fetch you, but I'll go across myself tomorrow and remind them.'

'Jocasta'll wake up all of a sudden and remember, I expect,' said Philip, 'but thanks.'

Making a Lego city on the floor with the Head's children after tea, he thought, *I wouldn't mind Jocasta forgetting, but it's supposed to be Faith's christening. I bet they've forgotten that, too.* The children crawled on him and he shook them off and they began a cheerful fight with him until he eased himself out and lay on the sofa. The family dog was on the sofa, and it rested its head on his stomach. A child tried to wheedle him back to the floor.

'It's cold ham for supper,' Emma called. 'Phil – yours with the little ones or later with us?'

'Later, please.'

'Well, well. Something new. You're growing up.'

'I'd better—'

'Where are you off to now?'

'Just washing my—'

'Phil,' she said, and stopped him. She led him into the kitchen. She took his hands and opened them up and kissed each palm. 'Clean and fresh as a newborn baby's. What's up, Phil?' She put his hair out of his eyes, but he flung away.

'Nothing.'

'Come on.'

'Oh well, just Jack.'

'But Jack is the kindest man in the history of the world.'

'He may be,' said Philip, 'but he gets taken in. He doesn't understand people. Jocasta does, when she thinks, and I do, but Jack's silly. It's the sort of people he thinks he can help. He takes in rubbish.'

'They're Indian, aren't they? Artists? They sound so interesting.'

'Those ones are going. It's the next lot. He wants some down-and-outs to look after; they're off the caravan site on the salt marsh. Except he can't look after a louse.'

'Well, that's quite a good-hearted wish, isn't it?'

'He can't distinguish good people from bad. He's all set on a sod coming—'

'Thank you. Not sod, please.'

'Yes, he is. I know him. He won't come, though, because when he saw me sitting in Jack's car he disappeared fast. But Jack just *believing* he's OK! Jack's useless not to see. *Anyone* could see he was a filthy pervert.'

'You know this, do you?'

'Oh yes.'

'Could you tell me?'

'I could tell you a bit,' he said, and did.

'Oh, poor Phil,' she said. 'You should have told Jocasta. Or anyone.'

'There was no one. They're either old or mad or foreign or disgusting. All of them. Everyone's disgusting.'

He began crying and she held him tight. He cried like a four-year-old, howling and gulping for some time. Her husband came in and Emma shook her head at him and waved him away.

When Philip was quieter she said, 'There's a Pink Panther video. D'you want to watch it after supper? Or I could bring you some supper to bed. You don't have to sit up with us.'

'It might be my last night here,' he said. 'I'd better sit up.'

'We could all eat now. Or d'you want your bath first?'

'No,' he said.

She scanned his face and thought how children's faces are never marred for long by tears, but other than their faces, very long. 'I hear your French is coming on,' she said. 'Maybe the school's going to France next year.'

'I mightn't be here.'

'You will,' she said. 'I promise you will. I'll not let anyone take you away – see? What's all this about? Is everyone leaving Ellerby Priors?'

'They don't know what they're doing. There's something wrong with everyone.'

'What about this baby?'

'Nobody's thinking about her. Nobody at all but me. I'm not mad about growing up, if you want to know.'

'Go and wash your hands,' she said, forgetting.

'What – now?' he said. 'I'm fine. I'll have supper.'

Jocasta and Jack stood on the doorstep. Faith was in Jocasta's arms, her eyes wide, her cheeks red, her face full of alert pleasure, her mouth a rose. There was no reply to knock or ring and the rain fell, with sleet in the wind.

'I'll look through Toots's window,' said Jocasta. Holding Faith against her shoulder, she tiptoed into the frost-painted wallflowers, to see Toots's bed inside tidily made up with its bedcover pulled smooth. The rug was turned back from the hearth although the electric fire was switched off. There was no sign of bed table, bottles, pills, zimmer frame. The daily paper lay neat and unread on a chair. The Christmas cards on the mantelpiece had been pushed back to make way for a good many white postcards and half pages of white memo paper.

'But they *never* go out,' said Jack. 'Something has happened.'

They knew that they must call on Mrs Middleditch and, putting another wrap round Faith, they walked slowly down the terrace and uneasily rang her bell.

'I'm sure I've no idea,' she said, looking over their heads, not asking them in. 'I've heard nothing at all. No, I haven't seen them this morning. I have my own life to see to. They know where I am if they want me.'

'Of course. We knew you would be the only one who might have—'

'Oh yes. That's what everyone says in this terrace. I've become known as the only one. When Miss Bean died, who found her? So thin you'd have thought I'd never taken her a crust. Sat up in bed at a right angle like she always was, and dead two days. I had to lay her down and she snapped. There was a crack. Like sticks under your feet. Oh yes. *And* Mr Ramshaw. *And* Mrs Scott, and her daughter never coming near in five years. They say I get left things in wills. I can tell you it's not my wish. I'd return it all if I could, half of it's rubbish, and I *don't* want your mother's tallboy, Jack. No. There's two things only I have to say to you this morning. One is that Toots was ruder to me last night than he's ever been and only because I mentioned – quite privately while Dolly was out of the room – about him fancying the woman who comes for his toenails. And also, I have to tell you, you've chosen a bad morning, my point of view. Why? Because my Bingham's left home. Just before Christmas. He's gone with an older woman in her car.'

'Oh, I am so sorry. What a troubled Christmas time for you. First Alice Banks and now—'

'If we could perhaps . . . ?' said Jocasta.

'What? Oh, step inside. Is that the baby? Well, they will be pleased, I'm sure. She's big, isn't she? Getting on now, of course. Dolly's fondest of tiny babies. New ones. Well, she won't have the pleasure of *that*, I'm afraid. I'll just get some newspaper for you to stand on. Have you rung the police?'

Emotions were at war in Mrs Middleditch. The disappearance of Toots and Dolly would have been rich meat for a year had it occurred only yesterday. The departure of Bingham infuriated her quite as much by its timing as by the fact that she had at last lost him. In her heart she had longed for a daughter-in-law for Bingham to bring home, a little fair thing who wouldn't meet your eyes. She could have been shown the perfection it is possible to achieve in a home and in a mother. Mrs Middleditch knew, as it happened, all about the absence of Toots and Dolly because she had seen the taxi go by and was furious that she hadn't been consulted, that they had hired transport of their own accord instead of letting her organise and drive them. She might naturally have had to refuse because of the trauma of Bingham, but she should have been given the opportunity for suffering and service.

The Lobster Inn, Saltburn, is where she thought they'd have gone. Turkey, stuffing, gravy, trimmings, sprouts, plum pudding, glass of red wine: three pounds twenty-five and daylight robbery. She'd offered them a Christmas dinner with her, knowing this lark to the moors was pie in the sky. That's where they'd be. Saltburn-by-the-Sea.

'D'you want to ring anybody?' she asked. 'Maybe you should contact the Social Services. I did see them going by in a taxi about half-past eight.'

'Ah!'

'To Saltburn, I'd think.'

'Saltburn at eight-thirty in the morning?'

'I'd not slept the night, what with Mr Middleditch not at all himself about Bingham. They're doing these special dinners. I'd think it was because poor Dolly has been very low lately when she thought she wouldn't be seeing the family, wouldn't you? They've had a long wait for this baby, you know. Well, isn't she pretty? I'll tell Dolly all about her. They have these bolshy fits, ordering taxis, you know, or Toots does anyway, poor Dolly. "Little gestures of independence", the doctor calls them, but I call them ugly rebellion. Ugly rebellion. It's not as if they've many friends left to go out with now, the two of them. If it's a meal, it has to be together. And wherever else have they to go to except . . . ?'

An incredulous dawning was taking place in Jocasta and Mrs Middleditch; rather more slowly in Jack.

'Unless . . .'

They eyed each other across the spotless hall.

'We must go back at once,' said Jocasta. 'It's been a very easy drive down and we'll go straight back again. We must get Faith home. At once. It was a sudden idea. We should have thought of it before. It's so easy, and she is such a very peaceful baby.'

'We used to take our Bingham everywhere,' she said. 'Up and down to Spain and once there was a typhoon.'

She shut the door on them.

On the way home, in silence, they passed the moorland hotel and the waitress's parked car. Toots and Dolly were invisible in the bar, waiting for the taxi repair, which was going on out of sight round the back of the garage. The waitress was frying bacon and eggs and supplying more hot drinks. Toots, who had refused a whisky, was sitting thoughtfully. *Half an hour, maybe three-quarters of an hour, home. We'll miss them. They'll be on their way back now unless Middleditch is in a good mood and keeps them down there. She didn't look to be in a good mood when we passed the house this morning.*

The failure of the mission drew Jack and Jocasta together a little and humbled them. The Priors seemed empty and dead when they returned and there was nobody to tell who would even begin to understand. Jocasta thought belatedly of Philip. She felt that somehow, if Philip had been there, if he'd come down with them to his grandparents, he would have known what to do. He'd have climbed in and they could have waited, made the place warm, got a meal going. Philip might have known where to find a key. Why ever hadn't they asked Middleditch for a key? Why hadn't Middleditch offered? She was sure to have one. If she'd been a normal woman she'd have seen them in, and everyone would have waited together for Dolly and Toots's return, and laughed.

Laughed. Not much laughter these days.

As Jocasta thought this Jack said, 'As time goes on I find I'm thinking such a lot about Holly Fox. You have to wonder sometimes if Faith, everyone, would be different, everything all right, if Faith still had her mother.' Then, seeing Jocasta's face, he said, 'You know what I mean. A real mother. You've been a real mother, I know.'

'No,' she said, 'I don't think I have. Phil runs me. I'm hopeless with children.'

'If he's so self-reliant, then you are a good mother.'

'I'm not sure he is. But he never notices me, Jack. He never turns to me. He never says goodbye or hello at school. I know I dragged him about the world at the start but I never, never, left him. I've never left him for a night except in hospital and our honeymoon and at that funeral. I could have dumped him. It was always going on in these Communities. The children were held in common. Back home I was so clueless it's a wonder he wasn't taken into care. But I'd not have dreamed of leaving him. Yet he doesn't love me. He never touches me. I'm useless, Jack.'

All he had to say was, 'Where is Philip now? Oughtn't he to have broken up?'

267

'He never said the date.'

'I'd have thought that by the twenty-second of December . . . ?'

'Yes. Oh heavens, yes. He *should* be home by now. They won't have been able to telephone us. Jack, I must go over. I'll go now.'

She had taken the uncomplaining Faith back to the sheds and was getting back into her car, when a Land-Rover drove under the hospitium gatehouse with Philip's headmaster in it. Phil didn't want to come home and they would be very happy to keep him till Christmas Eve. Would Jocasta agree? Phil was no trouble at all. Doing well with his reading; French oral outstanding. And they had to say that he was being an amazing help with the children. And Emma adored him.

'But I think I'd *like* him home,' said Jocasta. 'It's Christmas time.'

The schoolmaster pointedly did not look around the chaotic kitchen: the unlit fire, Jack and Jocasta dismally muffled in outdoor clothes, not a sign of festivity. 'I'd like to talk about Phil sometime,' he said. 'It's about time for another conference. He will, of course, be staying next term? There was some doubt, I seem to remember. He said something about some of you moving south?'

'He said what? We've never mentioned it to him.'

'Phil picks up news as he breathes. I'd like to keep him at least another year. Preferably three. To move him now would, to my mind, be a great pity. I'd like him to board.'

'I'm not sure . . .' Jocasta walked across the room to the teapot and stroked it, looking out of the window.

'If it's the fees . . .' the Head said.

'It's not the fees,' said Jack. 'We'd manage somehow. He's our only one.'

'Let me know, then. I'll be off.'

He was back in the Land-Rover before Jocasta could think of any message for her son, shaken as she was by Jack.

'Our only one'.

'*Our only one*'.

Turning to Jack, she found him gone.

268

– 42 –

At Peterborough Madeleine announced that there was only half an hour more.

She had been engaged upon genealogical exposition, *Billy* Faylesafe being the *nephew* not the son of Tony Faylesafe, who married, if you remember, Stephanie *Besant*, that frightful woman's daughter, not altogether someone you could know, but then the *second* wife was of course Loveday *Madden*, such a pretty girl but epileptic and not altogether reliable because of that awful business with the son. Who disappeared, you know. They don't talk about it but I expect he was in the Foreign Service – Puffy always says M.I.6. He was a radio ham. Now *Bridget* Faylesafe would be Emma's cousin. *Nice* girl, Emma – it's where we're staying. Very provincial, of course, and mad about children and rather a bore if you're not that sort. Very poor clothes, but pretty and frightfully OK. Born somewhere splendid and connections in Ireland – I mean real Ireland, Low-Church, not Catholic of course, somewhere near Dublin, decent country house. Hasn't an accent, naturally, neither an Irish nor a Yorkshire one, but otherwise a bit wild and woolly. And, *need* I say, left-wing. My dear, she's married a school-master, though not too bad at all – Winchester and related to the Bartram-Flites. I dare say we'll see her, unless it's the father we're staying with. I'm really not quite clear.'

'You surely know where you've invited us, Maddie.'

'Well, it's one or the other,' she said. 'Now here we are at Stamford and we can get them to carry in all the luggage. Excellent hotel.'

'We're not staying here, Madeleine,' said Pammie, 'we're stopping for lunch.'

'Of course we're staying here. I booked us all in. We can't do the journey in a day. We're far too old. Anyway, it's a chance for a fling.'

'I certainly hope you have *not* booked us all in,' said Giles. 'It's a hundred pounds a night.'

'And dinner on top,' she said. 'Wonderful dinner.'

'You live in a world of dreams,' he said.

But, as it turned out, not all the time, for three rooms had indeed been booked in the name of Seton-Fairley a week ago, and only just in time, for the hotel was very full.

'I can't possibly afford this,' said Thomasina.

'Neither can I,' said Pammie.

The general didn't like to say that neither could he, though it was true – which was more than it was for either of the other two – and it would be even truer if he had to pay for Thomasina.

'You'd be spending much more if you were in Cyprus, Thomasina,' said Madeleine, looking sharp for a moment, 'you and Pammie. And you, Giles, stodging away in the garrison. I don't know what you spend your money on. You always had stacks of it.'

Thomasina looked thoughtful. She had insisted on Egypt being a Dutch treat.

'We can't *all* stay,' said Pammie, who had been examining the details at the desk. 'There are only three rooms booked – two single and one double.'

Neither Thomasina nor Giles could find the right words. The reception clerk waited, pen in air. The porter stood among the masses of luggage and bulb bowls, all surmounted by the general's gun.

'Well, I shall have to have one of the single rooms, obviously,' said Madeleine, 'and so will Giles. Surely you two girls can share? We all did at school, now and then.'

Giles said nothing. (*And that is* it, thought Thomasina.)

'Well,' Thomasina said, 'if we really are staying – and I think it's totally unnecessary, *I'm* quite able to drive up even to the north of Scotland in a day, but I suppose I'm that much younger than any of you – *if* we must stay, and we all have our credit cards, I don't mind sharing with Pammie. Unless it's a double bed.'

'I'm afraid it is a double bed. It is all that is left, madam. They're not popular any more. It's always the double beds that go last now. It's a sign of the times. But it is a four-poster.'

Lying side by side that night Pammie and Thomasina stared unbelievingly at the ruched satin lining of the tester above them. It had, against all the rules, been a far from unpleasant afternoon. After lunch in a conservatory full of forced spring flowers and potted palms, all but Thomasina had gone for a siesta, arranging, as they left, to meet again at tea.

Thomasina had set off for a walk through the church-lined streets of Stamford and on to the great park. She had walked fast and far, on and on, until it grew dark and she had turned back and seen the spires and towers of Rutland and Lincolnshire fading in the night as the stars came out. Back in the town she walked slowly, looking in tinselled shop windows. All the bright fruit shops. The Sally Army was singing in a square. Office workers in some tall eighteenth-century houses were looking down at them. A young woman with her children waited to cross a road. She had a baby in a sling against her stomach, a child on either hand. One child looked up and said something and the mother looked first down at her, then up at the lights across the street, and the starry sky. She laughed, and it was Holly's laugh.

It was Holly. It was five years from now. It was Holly with Faith and her younger children. They were on their way home. Andrew had a job at Stamford Hospital – '*Marvellous* luck. *Wonderful* place. Burleigh *Horse* trials' – for Holly had started riding again – '*Such* nice people. You'd love it, Ma. You must come every year. Or come and live near. I shall have ten children: you'll always be wanted.'

Then the girl turned and she was plastered in make-up and chewing something. When she spoke it was broad Lincolnshire. The middle child, all of three years old, had a great dummy stuck in its mouth. Oh Holly, Holly, Holly, Holly, Holly.

They played a little Bridge after tea, until Madeleine fell asleep and Pammie disappeared to her room again.

Giles said, 'Thomasina, we must talk.'

'Not before Christmas,' she said. 'Let's let things be till then.'

'I'm sorry,' he said. 'That business about the room. Felt rather embarrassed, to tell you the truth. I've been thinking – were we quite ourselves, do you think, in the autumn?'

'I'm not sure. I thought you had been sent to save me.'

'I thought you were a splendid girl.'

'Yes. You kept saying so. But, you see, I began to love you, Giles.'

'Ah. Yes. I'm afraid I've treated you rather badly. Madeleine's a frightful bore. I can't get shot of her. Old times' sake, and Puffy and so on. I can't abandon her now. We should never have gone to that wedding, Thomasina. Everything was going so well before that.'

'I said not, if you remember.'

'No. *I* said not. I said you should go to see your – the baby.'

'I'm going up to change for dinner now.'

'Oh, I don't think you need to change. Very informal.'

'I think I need to change.'

After dinner she said, 'Sleep well, Giles,' and went up to the four-poster and Pammie. She heard Madeleine's voice after a time calling, 'Giles, *which* is the number of my room? Oh my dear, I'm so glad you're next door. I do miss Puffy in hotels. I think I shall telephone him now. I do every night, you know, though I don't believe he notices.'

'Oh Pammie,' said Thomasina in bed, 'oh Pammie. What a ghastly business.'

'Oh, I don't know. Makes me think of my days on the fringes of royalty, this great bed. I used to stay at Blenheim, you know. There's plenty of pillows to put down the bed between us. It used to be bolsters, but you can't get bolsters now except in France.'

'Have you ever slept with a bolster down the bed?' (*I'll bet*, Thomasina thought, *she was a friend of the housekeeper.*)

'Yes. I once slept with a queer. Art student. Sweet boy.'

'I'd not have thought you'd need a bolster if he was a queer.'
They laughed.

Thomasina thought how much she liked Pammie. 'I never thought I'd be sharing a bed with you, Pammie, and Giles along the corridor.'

'You must be a bit fed up, aren't you? *I'll* be no trouble anyway. I don't suppose he was either, was he? Was he any good?'

'Pammie! Shut up. You sound sixteen.' (*And*, she thought, *I don't know you well enough for this.*)

'Oh, we're all sixteen, Thomasina, now and then.'

'You didn't understand, did you? How I could have done it?' and she thought, as she had been doing in the car, of the gulf between women with children and those who have none.

Pammie said nothing.

'You thought I was fickle to Holly, didn't you? Going off with some old man?'

'Yes.'

'Debauched?'

'Well, no. Superficial. I couldn't have done it. When Hugo died – and, of course, a husband's death must be worse – I found myself starting to get excited about doing up the house, and I stopped. It wasn't on. Not appropriate. But I think that meeting Jack has helped me so very much.'

'So what about Jack, then?' Thomasina thought, *Poor Pammie. And maybe, you know, you wouldn't have had the chance with Giles. Or with anyone, the way you strut about. You can't call Jack exactly a chance.*

'Don't be silly, Thomasina. Jack's just a spiritual adviser, and I must say it was nice to be looked at affectionately after years of being thought just a jolly old thing. Death makes us self-indulgent. Mind you, men are worse. Widowers turn to *any* woman when their wives die. Searching for mother.'

'I can't remember my mother,' said Thomasina. 'Do widows go looking for father? I can't remember him either. Hardly.'

'That's probably why you got this thing about Holly. You and Holly.'

'Holly had no thing for me, Pammie, nor anyone – she never

knew anything about me. She never analysed. She was uncomplicated. She trusted and it always worked. Until Faith finished her.'

'Well, she'd you to thank for being so happy. You're the one who lost out. You were smashing. We all thought you were from the start a wonderful mother – so easy and nice. I was bloody jealous. Oh, I'm so glad you're talking about her at last.' Stretching her hand across the pillows she took Thomasina's hand and squeezed it. 'Is this Giles thing over?'

'Yes. Yes, it is.'

'Well, thank God for that.'

'Why?'

'You could find a better man. If you want one.'

'There was only one,' said Thomasina, so low Pammie wondered if she'd imagined it.

The two women in their face cream, glasses of water beside them on the bedside tables, Pammie's blood-pressure pills, Thomasina's rings, both their spectacles folded near, fell side by side asleep.

Along the corridor the general stretched to answer the bedside phone and got Madeleine in mid-sentence.

'. . . playing his old seventy-eights.'

'What's this? What? Whatever time is it, Madeleine?'

'Oh, not late. Half past eleven. I've just rung Puffy and I'm afraid there's something wrong.'

'What? Wrong?'

'There's such a noise going on down there and Henry sounded quite tiddly. I couldn't speak to Puffy at all. Henry said that he and Miss Banks and Henry's friend Jerry had been playing poker, but it's very far past the time when Puffy gets put to bed. In the end I *insisted* on speaking to Miss Banks and she sounded rather tiddly, too. They'd just been having a snack and some music, she said.'

'I shouldn't worry, Maddie. We'll ring in the morning.'

'But why wouldn't they let me speak to Puffy? I don't know what staff are coming to. Do you think he didn't want to speak to me?'

'In the morning. Don't worry.'
'I do worry. They are telling lies, Edward.'

– 43 –

Andrew was getting Christmas off, maybe, he thought, out of compassion, maybe to reflect his status. After the holiday he was being promoted to a new job, as Registrar, no longer sleeping in the hospital, no longer doing three doctors' work, no longer on duty twenty-four hours a day. Knowing he'd made it at last – it had been slow: they'd thought him smug, acting above his station, condescending from a height, until Holly died, and then they'd grown sympathetic – knowing he'd made it at last and would be leaving this hospital for another, he felt not revitalised but numb. Stuck in his tracks.

On the morning of the twenty-third, Andrew was sitting on the edge of the narrow bed of his cubicle with an empty suitcase on the floor, unable to get going, get dressed, do anything. Even think.

He had bought no Christmas presents. This was the crisis grown vast in his mind. Nothing for Thomasina, nothing for Pammie, nothing for Miss Banks, to all of whom he owed so much. Nothing for the baby – though she was too young for it really to matter. Nothing for Philip, which was bad. Nothing for Jack, nothing for Toots and Dolly. He'd planned to do the lot this morning before setting off. Nip down Piccadilly to a bookshop, get some bestsellers. Ought to get Pammie something big, like a piece of jewellery. Dolly a scarf or something. Liberty's. Toots his whisky. Jocasta. Here he stopped.

Jocasta. Something small enough not to cause comment, but large enough, significant enough, for her to know he remembered what had been between them. Couldn't give her a sweater. He could have given Holly a sweater. Often had. All Holly's stuff still in the flat. His mind swooped away.

Somehow he dressed and trudged out of the residential wing, but now that it was almost for the last time his feet had turned to lead. He was almost too tired to pass through the glass doors to the tired shops. Last shopping day. Oh God, he couldn't.

Last year he and Holly had packed off to Thailand, telephoned Toots and Dolly from a phone box under a coconut palm, listened to Dolly talking about Mrs Middleditch in the draughty passage with the coloured Victorian tiles, the line of coat hooks, the calendar of church services, as they watched some elephants swinging their trunks and people bathing in a dark pool afloat with lotus leaves. Holly in a white bikini, big and broad beside the Thai girls, and gorgeous. *Can't go buying diaries in Hatchards this morning. I cannot.*

A friend stopped him and said come for a drink.

'Presents,' said Andrew. 'Off north in a minute. No presents.'

'Forget them. We all know that everyone except you and me has bought their Christmas presents. Forget them. Come to lunch.'

He was having lunch with his anaesthetist wife, a tall, silent girl with coils of dark hair, who was also exhausted, also on leave for Christmas. They were going home to Oxfordshire right after lunch. 'Come with us,' she said.

'I'm going to Yorkshire.'

'Oh, to see the baby?'

'Yes.'

'You don't look right for that journey. Are you driving?'

'Sure. Done it all my life. Home for the hols.'

'Who's got the baby now?'

'Oh, my brother. And his wife. And Thomasina's going up and the woman who looked after her when she was born. And my parents are up there. I can't not turn up. After all, she's mine.'

'She seems to have plenty of people. Why don't you ring up and tell them you can't face it and you'll come in the New Year? The baby's too young ever to remember you didn't turn up. Come back with us.'

'Or just come and stay overnight,' said the husband. 'Leave

from us early in the morning.'

'These presents . . .'

'Take them later. They know you're busy.'

'That's what they don't. The only kind of work they think is work up there is slaving in the soil – they're farmers. Or creating Art.'

'Art?'

'Jack's wife's arty.' He felt huge shame. 'She's a wonderfully talented woman. Lives in a bit of another world, too. Professional. Like us.'

'I'd let her get on with it,' said William. 'Come on home with us for a goddamned sleep.'

He woke on the morning of Christmas Eve to William's wife opening his curtains, shutting his window, bringing him tea across. The room was full of light.

'Snow,' she said.

'Oh, God.'

'Nothing like so bad as up north, apparently. Andrew, I don't think you're going to make it.'

'I must.'

'Turn on the radio and listen. Don't hurry up. You'll have to leave it till tomorrow.'

'Christmas Day?'

'Why not? Leave at six in the morning. You'll walk in for dinner. They'll be thrilled.'

He stood moodily at the sitting-room window. Diamond-bright snow across the lawn. A dog prancing. Inside, a huge log fire; gold baubles hanging from oak beams; hyacinths in bowls. Laughter from the kitchen.

'I'll ring my parents.'

'Right.'

Dolly was adamant. 'Now, you're not to come, Andrew. Promise me. Freezing fog. Just think if anything should happen, we'd never forgive ourselves. We can't even get to them up there ourselves, not even on their telephone. Toots says they've forgotten to pay the bill but it's their wires down, Mrs Middleditch says. It's the worst for years. We don't mind,

277

though. We'll see them later. We're quite resigned.'

'Have you seen Faith lately?'

'Well, no. Not lately. But we shall. And we'll see you. Very soon. Have you somewhere to go? Oh good, dear. That sounds just right for you. A jolly time. Now, have a lovely Christmas.'

'Not coming,' she said to Toots, sitting down heavy on her chair.

'Thought not,' said he.

'He did sound tired. He's probably been up all night. He's with a nice couple near Didcot. Doctors, of course,' she said proudly.

'Won't be a lot of fun with a couple. I hope they haven't a baby.'

'I expect they mean well. Kindness to ask him. I expect it'll be a jolly party and I don't think there'll be anything much going on at The Priors. Holly's mother will never get there, for a start. She's far too delicate-looking. And Jack and Jocasta are not exactly . . . well, I shouldn't say it, especially of my Jack, but they're not all that light-hearted.'

Toots said nothing, but lay on, thinking of Didcot.

'We've Athene Price coming to dinner tonight,' said William. 'OK?'

'OK,' said Andrew, 'but she scares me stiff. Can't stand that imperious type.' (In the kitchen, out of sight, William and wife nudged each other and mouthed, 'Holly Fox!') 'OK, I'll behave. Will she be by herself?'

'With one or two more.'

It was a feast. There was a lot of wine. There was a goose. Afterwards various people lay about drowsing by the fire. Affectionately. William's wife went off to wrap presents. Other people went off home. William took the dog for a last walk in the snow. Athene Price, in her short grey velvet dress and the sexiest legs you ever saw (he thought), said to him, 'I miss Holly.'

'Oh. Yes. I didn't realise . . . ?'

'We were at baby-school together.'

'Holly seems to have been at school with everyone. She must have kept getting expelled, she was at so many. Or something.'

'Holly expelled? Andrew, she was perfect. Lovely friend. In a way, dying young like that and everybody thinking you wonderful, it's not bad.'

'Isn't it?'

'Andrew, what I must say is how terribly, terribly sorry I am about the baby.'

'What?'

'That you lost the baby.'

'We didn't. We didn't lose the baby, what d'you mean? She's with her grandparents. She's fine. Called Faith.'

Athene Price stared at him. 'I heard – I *did* hear. Someone said – oh God, how do things like that get around? Oh, thank goodness. Oh, I'm so sorry. They said you'd lost her. I've thought about her so often. I even dreamed about it. The other night. I dreamed about you losing the baby.' She looked so horrified by what she'd said that he went over to her and put his arms round her, thinking, *This is glacial Athene Price.*

He laid his head on her velvet dress. She was not glacial.

'I'm going up to see her crack of dawn tomorrow,' he said. 'I'll send you a lock of her hair.'

But he did neither.

Emma and Philip were making up beds. The children were screaming about. Things downstairs on oven hobs were boiling over. The headmaster was hoovering up needles around the Christmas tree. There was music blasting out from somewhere and someone calling from the kitchen. The postman, Jimmie, was sitting to his cup of tea. The dishwasher was broken, as was the tumble-drier, and in a minute Emma would have to start pegging things out on the line, where they would turn into art forms in cardboard in the frost. A dog lay chewing something precious and there were wrapping papers, ribbons and decorations afloat on every floor of the school-house.

'Oh, we're nearly there,' said Emma. 'Who's flapping? All I'd like to know is how many are coming. I suppose you don't happen to know, Phil? They're your lot.'

'Coming here?'

'They were going to my father's but he said no. Grump, grump. He's coming here for Christmas Day, though he always says he won't. Somebody rang him up, someone to do with your people at The Priors, and said she was bringing a party from London for Christmas. He said no. Then she wrote to say they'd all be arriving about four o'clock and how very kind of him and so he roared at us over the phone and we said we'd have them. But he didn't know how many.'

'Maybe about a hundred,' said Philip.

'Well, there's the dormitories.'

'There's only Andrew of ours lives in London,' Philip said, 'and he'll be staying with us in the gatehouse, like he does. There's Alice, but she's disappeared and she'd come back home too if she was coming back at all.'

'Someone called Pammie? No? Someone called Thomasina?'

'Thomasina's Holly's mother. Holly's dead. She's called Thomasina Fox.'

'Holly Fox's mother? I was at school with Holly Fox.'

'She's my sister's mother.'

Emma looked thoughtfully at him.

'I think there's some man, a general,' she said, 'and this old woman called Madeleine.'

'Don't know 'em.'

'Neither does my father, but that means nothing.'

'He sounds like mine. I mean Jack. I haven't got a father. Jocasta dumped him.'

'Come on, Phil,' said Emma, 'we've heard all that. You have half a dozen fathers. Jack. Andrew in London. Toots. Nick. Ernie Smike.'

'Nick an' Ernie would be terrible fathers.'

'You never know. Pass that blanket.'

'Is it a horse blanket?'

'Yes.'

'Hope Thomasina isn't allergic.'

They laughed.

I'm going to miss this one, she thought. *Funny boy. Where does it come from? Humourless Jocasta, solemn Jack? The Indian father, I guess. He must have been one of the Marx brothers. Thomasina Fox, well, well. Wonder if Pa knows.*

'Holly Fox was quite a friend of mine,' she said. 'Then she went off with a girl called Stephanie. Girls are like that at school. Everyone was mad about Holly. I thought she was a bit of a bore actually, sometimes. Don't tell anyone. What's the baby like?'

'She's wonderful,' he said, 'when I get to see her. She's over three months now. She's almost walking.'

'*Really*! Do you play with her?'

'She's up in a hammock most of the time. The Tibetans look after her. But I read to her.'

'It must be the blind leading the blind.'

'She's not blind at all. She had a messy eye once but it's better. They're all knitting eyes over there in the sheds, the Tibetans. On sort of panels.'

'Knitting eyes?'

'Yes.'

They looked at each other and started laughing again.

'Funny world,' said Emma. 'Come on down and talk while I get lunch.'

'Do I have to go home tonight, Emma? Can't I come back after Jocasta's play? Could I have Christmas here?'

'Nope. I'm not a kidnapper.'

'*Please*. I'll help you with Thomasina. She's my other granny. In a sense.'

'We'll see. We'll see if she turns up. Or anyone. The sky's heavy with snow. Look.'

At the foot of the hotel staircase the general was standing gravely. He strode a few paces forward, examined the pictures of stagecoaches and eighteenth-century travellers. He looked towards the staircase. He strode a few paces back. He examined the newspapers that were laid out upon a table. When Thomasina came down he leapt towards her, took her arm and led her into the empty dark coffee room.

'Good morning, Giles.'

'I have to speak to you.'

'There's nothing you need say. Nothing at all. Let's not get embarrassing.'

'Embarrassing?'

'About sleeping arrangements.'

He looked bewildered. 'Oh. Ha. Yes. Sleeping arrangements. No, it isn't that. That has nothing to do with anything.'

'I see.'

'No. You don't see. Well. Last night Madeleine was in a flap about a phone call she made home, and I straightened her out and sent her to bed. But I thought maybe I'd give old Puffy a ring myself, and I did. And he was dead.'

'But . . .'

'Bad business. Some sort of nonsense going on down there. I've just rung again. I asked to speak to Miss Banks, but she's left. The young man there is very upset. She's gone off on the London train, leaving her luggage. They've got Puffy away to a mortuary.'

'Madeleine?'

'I managed to stop her from telephoning. I haven't told her. I told her he'd been taken ill. I'll tell her he's dead on the train.'

'*Train*?'

'Yes. We'll go south on the Euston train from Lincoln if Pammie will drive us. Taxi to Waterloo, train down to Kent.'

'Giles, it's the day before Christmas Eve. It won't be easy. She's very old. I'm sure Pammie would lend you her car, and she and I could go on up north by train together.'

'No, no. All fixed. Here she comes.'

Breakfast in the dining room was delicious. Madeleine kept saying so. She talked of other breakfasts. Paris before the war. With Winston Churchill at Chequers. With little Jackie Bouverie in New York ('Sweet child and how she suffered'). She told the waitress that she was sure she knew her. Or her mother: Elsie Bacon who'd been parlour maid at Blackfriars Hall? No? So like her. She said goodbye at the desk with such an air of devotion to everyone that porters emerged and stood in a row for her to pass to the door ('Giles, see to it, won't you? Purse not about'). They were bowed into Pammie's car. Thomasina had passed Pammie a note on the back of the breakfast menu. 'Puffy's dead. They're off south again,' and met Pammie's outraged eyes.

On the platform Madeleine turned to Thomasina and kissed her.

'I'm so sorry, Madeleine,' said Thomasina. 'I do hope that Puffy will soon . . .'

They embraced.

'I'm sad too,' said Madeleine. 'No. Not that Puffy's dead, that's wonderful for him – yes, of course I know he's dead. Silly old Alfred's like a glass of water. I don't know how he was ever a general, you can read his face like a map. No, not sorry he's dead and he had that excellent Alice with him. No. I'm just so sorry it's Christmas. So inconvenient for the poor undertakers. And sorry – well, sorry (Yes, Miles, I'm coming), sorry, darling, for you.'

'For me?'

'For you. In a way. Though this is for the best. I do know that. You'll not miss him. He's so boring. Just right for me, though, because I can remember how sweet he was long ago. Such love untapped. The odd thing is that I didn't want him then. I thought I did, but not deep down. Now I'm landed with him.'

'Maddie, *please*.' Giles was holding the carriage door, waving the gun case. There were shouts. The train was crowded for Christmas.

'Goodbye, Giles,' said Thomasina. 'Glad you're able to go with her. And first class. You're having rather an expensive outing.'

'Yes. Thomasina, I shan't forget . . .'

'No.'

'The Mena House and the Texans. And that splendid place at Karnak.'

'The Nile,' she said, 'and the man in the pink nightshirt who wanted to clean our shoes.'

283

He seemed puzzled by this. 'Wasn't that—?' He looked towards Madeleine climbing aboard, smiling round the packed, carousing passengers. 'I thought that was . . . Oh yes. Of course. Goodbye, Thomasina,' and he heaved his lanky frame up the high step, turning to look back at her, stern and awkward.

He is ashamed and old, she thought. *Whatever was I doing? Poor old wooden general.*

'The party shrinks,' said Pammie. 'We'll be able to get a move on now. D'you want a tissue?'

'No. I told you last night. It's over.'

'Thank your stars you're not damaged in any way – or not more than you are. You can't see straight after a death, or you'd never have gone near him.'

'I don't agree. I won't say that.'

'You were clinging to youth.'

'For God's sake – he's seventy-two.'

'To the old order?'

'Well, maybe. Why not?'

'It's time you grew up.'

'*You* say this? For heaven's sake, what about the old man in the mountains?'

'It's what I'm telling you. One goes mad at these times. I'll recover. I think.'

'But maybe he won't recover. Dear Jack. He's very lovable.'

'What – unbridled passion for fat Mrs Jefford of Coombe? Come off it, Thomasina.'

'He's someone, Pammie. He's reckless. He's some sort of saint. I love Jack.'

'Well,' she said, 'I've never met anyone like him, I'll say that. But he's married, you know. To Madame Gloom.'

When they were well on, past Worksop, past the Doncaster bypass, boiling along towards Wetherby and the Wolds, Pammie said, 'There's something I should like to have seen and now I never shall. I'd like to have seen how Madeleine would have made out with Jack. What he'd have thought of her.'

Thomasina said, after several more miles, 'I think she would have tested his policy of universal love.'

'Where do I turn off?'

'Soon. Giles gave me directions. Oh good gracious!'

'What now?'

'His map says we're going right up the top again, near that hotel he and I went to. It's not the Faylesafe pile – it's a *school*. "The Moors School". It'll be dormitories. It's outrageous of that woman. We'll go to The Priors.'

'We might just look,' said Pammie. 'It's getting dark. They'll be expecting us. With any luck it'll be all right even if it's basic and it won't be far to turn out again for this concert thing tomorrow.'

'A Nativity play,' said Thomasina, 'and, let's hope, a christening.'

'Your granddaughter.'

'Yes. Hope she's thriving, I must say. So fearfully cold.'

'*Faith.*'

'Yes.'

'Say it.'

'Say what?'

'Faith.'

'Faith, then.'

'Wasn't there a girl called Faylesafe? Friend of Holly?'

'Was there?'

'At her school. Emma Faylesafe? Didn't you know the family?'

'Yes. I suppose there was. Madeleine told us so. For hours.'

'Say it, then. Who was she?'

'Holly's friend. At school. First term boarding. I think actually, Pammie, I'd quite like to go direct to The Priors, if you don't mind.'

'I do mind. I'm sick of people changing their mind about where they're going in this car. It's my car, I'm driving and I say where.'

'Which is here,' she said on the top of the moor. 'I say!

Wuthering Heights with school dinners. Gird up your loins, dear. What's this?'

The front door opened and light stained the snow. Emma Faylesafe-as-was came out with her husband and children and Philip.

'Quickly, quickly, in you come,' she called. 'You must be dead! Only two of you? Oh dear.' She took Thomasina's hands. 'Come in, Holly's ma.'

– 44 –

And it was not so dreadful after all up on the moors on Christmas Eve.

The snow was thick on the roads up from the coast and there was no hope of Dolly and Toots reaching The Priors on Christmas Day, but the freezing fog was nowhere to be seen and the wind had dropped. The heather stuck up through the snow like prickles through a blanket – a continent of midget forest trees. The lower fields lay on the hillsides like white handkerchiefs out to dry. After dawn the sky cleared and a great sun rose through queer dragging clouds. Their trailing tentacles stroked the horizon. It was going to be warmer.

Thomasina and Pammie awoke at the schoolhouse and wondered if they should ring Kent. Thomasina seemed not to care to. Emma said that she thought that surely the general would ring *them* up. Would he not?

Nobody knew.

So they sat over breakfast eating bacon in the dappled sunshine off the moor, Emma scrubbing potatoes and rolling them into the back of the stove for lunch, slashing up cabbages, stirring up stew. More coffee was produced. Someone was practising scales on a piano. The headmaster was in full voice, singing as he threw salt over the yard. Philip was busy somewhere with computers.

A wondrous lethargy settled upon Thomasina and Pammie. Emma talked, they listened. They watched her wading through a chaos of children about her feet, making a pudding at the far end of the kitchen table, taking tin measurefuls of flour from a sack in the corner, scattering it into the bowl from a height to get air into it. Flour hung in the sunlight. Some settled on Emma's hair and powdered her cheek.

'We're to be there by four,' she said. 'The concert thing's at five. Or so. I don't think they really know – they're like that. Phil wants to be early to find out what he's meant to be doing. There's some ceremony with the baby, isn't there? I wonder if it's Tibetan?'

'It's her christening,' said Pammie, 'and about time too.'

'I think there's to be some lovely Tibetan music. And then some carols. And then a supper. That Nick person's been over to borrow plates. I'm afraid plates are sometimes as far as they get. I'll take a big pie.'

'I don't suppose there'll be many of us,' said Thomasina. 'The snow will stop everyone. I haven't heard a word from Andrew. Are you all coming?'

'We are,' said Emma. 'Each and every one. Great honour. Never asked before. I'm dying to see the Tibetans. And the baby.'

'I should really be getting myself across there this morning,' said Pammie. 'I'm to try housekeeping for them, you know. I've been invited to be on the permanent staff.'

'Oh,' said Emma. 'Well, I wonder. It's pretty serious over there. But I'm not saying a word. I'm not very pious.'

'I *am* religious,' said Pammie, whose faith had returned during Jack's telephone calls. Thomasina looked out of the window. 'Jack and I hit it off rather well.' She turned pink.

'Yes. Everybody hits it off with Jack,' said Emma. 'He's a saint. But they're not the easiest. I suppose I shouldn't say this, but somehow, with Holly about, I feel I can. Thomasina . . . ?'

But Thomasina had left the room to find Philip.

They set off in the school Land-Rover, wrapped up warm in the near dark, at about half past three. 'I've a hip flask and some sleeping bags,' said the headmaster, but it was decidedly warmer. Big loose flakes were starting to fall. They left the Land-Rover up at the Saxon cross to be on the safe side. There was already a minibus there and the Smike motorbike covered with a tarpaulin.

'Afraid of not getting out again,' said the headmaster. 'They've brought them up. Well, nobody'll steal them tonight. Did someone say the Tibetans are leaving at Christmas?'

'Nobody can make them out,' said Philip.

'Are they nice people?'

'Pema's a bit weird. She's boring about Faith and she can't speak English. The rest are just normal, like us. The young ones. The men have gone away somewhere. Hi, Ernie.'

Ernie and Nick were walking out to the sheds.

'Gi's 'and, Philip.'

Philip ran across to them and into the studio.

Jocasta was sitting huddled small in a pew in the chapel. She wore a striking necklace of chunks of red amber, and when Thomasina and Pammie came in she turned, then crossed straight to them. She kissed Thomasina, smiled at Pammie and whispered, 'Do sit down, or do you want to go in and get warm? Are the school people all here?'

'Yes. I'll go over to the solar and start helping,' said Pammie.

'All done,' she said, 'but do go in. I have to stay and see to the tableau.' She smiled and said, 'It's wonderful that you've made it.'

'Whatever's happened?' wondered Thomasina, and Pammie said, 'She's quite changed. Utterly different woman. Oh, whoever's that?'

Out in the falling snow Pema, dressed in a great broadside of a coat that stood out around her like a hairy box filled the doorway of her shed and stood watching them pass. Her face was broad and dark beneath a hat like a headdress atop her scarfed head. In her arms was a bundle of heavy cloths, scarlet and orange on white. On the baby's head was a little woven cap with ear-flaps; on her hands, red mittens decorated with amber beads. Her face was almost covered by her wrappings. She did not stir. A woven icon of an eye hung round her neck.

Thomasina saw only a glimpse of Faith's own eyes, round and faraway, all that seemed alive in the doll-like swathe in the old woman's arms.

Pema began to shout suddenly, on and on, very angry. A girl came up behind her and tried to pull her away, away inside and out of sight.

'What's she saying? What have we done?'

'She's telling you about us,' said the girl.

'What is she saying?'

Pema's voice rose to a desolate wailing and she heaved herself backwards into the dark of the shed.

'What was all that?'

'She says about exile,' said the girl, 'about you knowing nothing here. She says about walking six hundred miles to Nepal below the Mother of Earth at sixteen thousand feet. She says the Chinese kill and beat and torture. She says eighty-seven thousand exiles left Tibet, two thousand seven hundred monasteries destroyed, a hundred thousand Chinese troops walked into our country. Her baby sisters died on the journey, her grandmother died. In India her little brother later died of sickness we did not have at home. She says you all have suffered nothing. She despises you and kisses the bone of her mother which she carries next to her heart.'

'Well, I hope she doesn't let it anywhere near the baby,' said Pammie.

'How extraordinary,' said Thomasina. 'I have absolutely nothing against Tibetans, I'm very sorry for them. I am very sorry. How could we know? But please, we should like to see Faith now. I suppose three hundred miles is nothing to travel, comparatively, but we've done it for our faith too, you know, in a sense. For Faith.'

But the Tibetans had shut their door.

'Why aren't the Tibetans joining us, and where's Faith?' Thomasina asked Jack. They were in the refectory now, where everyone was drinking tea out of mugs. Some rather oily, whitish mince pies were about on trays and some small squares of cheese with sticks in them. Emma had brought crackers, and her pie was warming in the stove.

'You must tell me what to do about supper,' Pammie said.

'Oh, supper,' said Jocasta. 'Are we all here?'

'So sad about Toots and Dolly,' said Thomasina, dredging up a normal remark. She felt all at once beyond hope, beyond care for anything, for anyone. That comatose bundle. That aged crone. Age and death. Deaths, deaths. Giles's stiff leg following him up into the railway carriage. That idiot Madeleine. Dead Puffy. Everyone dying. Nothing left. What about Andrew? No word. *I am the one should be dead*, she thought. *Why was it Holly? What use am I?*

'Has anyone heard from Andrew?'

Nobody had except Jocasta and she wasn't saying. The letter had been the letter she had been expecting for some time so that when she had read it she had felt it was old, dug out from some antique trunk. 'Dear Jocasta,' it had said in his tiny writing, so small that it seemed to be trying to hide its meaning; close, neat, no crossings-out. A fair copy.

Dear Jocasta,

I think that you and I have decided both together that what happened between us has been a monumental mistake. I expect that by the time you read this I shall have received a similar letter from you.

When we last saw each other after Alice Banks had gone I saw your face as it looked up at Jack. I couldn't decide what I'd seen at first. Something like utter despair of happiness in you ever again. Disillusion. And then I saw Jack, walking so trusting beside you. He touched your neck as you both went into the refectory. You looked up at him without happiness but with such familiarity. I saw you together as a woman with her husband.

The night before you had said, 'Don't leave me.' That

was when I realised that the only thing was for us to break off our life with each other.

I shall have to come at Christmas. Nothing will stop me. I know my duty to the child. But now it will be only as your brother-in-law.

I will of course always love you,
    Andrew

'I will of course always love you.' *They always end like that*, thought Jocasta. The letter had left her light and strange and she'd chucked it on the stove and gone over at once to the work sheds. There, with Ernie's help, she had spread the great canvas across the floor under the uncertain eye of the A-level girl. It had taken hours to straighten and line it with paper, and roll it right. Then they had polished the wooden crib that was to stand on the floor in front of the white space at its centre. It was lovely. Scarlet lacquered, shaped like the bowl of a lute on cross-over black legs, graced with scarlet seals.

The Smikes had come in, Nick carrying a bundle of hay. Ernie had said, 'Is Jack really wantin' live animals round the thing? They'll muct place up, sheep. And who's to go for them, as if I didn't know?'

Ernie, Nick and Jocasta had gone over to the chapel early on the morning of Christmas Eve to make space for the backcloth, fix the lights for it, and strew with hay the stone floor before it.

When all was done Jocasta said, 'Switch on.'

'Go live,' said Ernie.

The chapel fell into shadow. Through its windows the ancient buildings disappeared. The dazzle of the canvas was the only light. It seemed to drink down into itself all the colours of the world.

The life-sized painted figures of the holy family were vague. The model for the Madonna, the A-level girl, was gawky, smashed, without nationality, her arms spread towards the empty centre on the screen. Joseph, with Jack's brooding bent head, stood near her, looking down at the lighted space. On the other side were village people. One was the postman,

Jimmie. Somebody, a woman in a turquoise padded jacket, was holding out a cake and thermos flask. Entangled in the painted arch of the ruined apse was a languid angel with a gold earring and black leather armour. It had the face of Ernie, watching. In opposite profile near him sat Jocasta leaning against the parapet of a bridge with a frowning face, drawing. She was drawing the light in the centre of the backcloth, drawing space, drawing her life, drawing the timeless moment. Her dark face, not dismissive, not derisive, not discontented, was concentrated on one thing only, the holiness of vision.

' 'Sgreat, Jocasta,' said Nick. 'Why int Philip in it? Where's The Missus? An' me?'

'The Missus cleared off. I left her out. Philip will be in it for real when he carries Faith up in her cradle. He stands it here, see? Centre of the blank. Two bits of flesh and blood, Faith and Phil, OK?'

'And me?'

'I couldn't see where you fit in, Nick. I couldn't decide whether you'd want to be in it or not. You never tell us where you stand.'

'OK,' said Ernie. 'And Nick, OK, right? It's great, though. Hey, it's . . . well, OK, Jocasta.'

'Right. Take it back across there, then, till the evening.'

Nick and Ernie carried it on their shoulders, one behind the other.

So when everyone came walking down the lane from the Land-Rover and followed the rolled-up backcloth back into the chapel, Jocasta was sitting thinking only of the tableau.

'Turn all the lights out,' Jocasta called to Ernie. 'I want this to be a sudden blaze.'

'I can't leave hold of it.'

'OK. Lay it carefully down.'

'It gonna get damaged.'

'No.' She went over to Ernie and suddenly put her arms round him and kissed him.

Then everyone came in and then out again towards the tea, and Jack arrived with his hands full of mangolds, asking if

Jocasta wanted any for decorating the tableau of the stable, and he'd forgotten to get in some sheep. 'We'll manage,' said Jocasta. They went together to the solar.

'Here is Pammie, Jack,' Jocasta said.

They greeted each other with surprise and disappointment, for Jack had noticed her across at the stove already, a dumpy oldish woman bustling about in a kilt, and not recognised her. She saw a faded, tall, shabby-looking parson, far from charismatic, rather sour-looking and distant, nothing much at all. She couldn't help seeing the colour of the hands holding the mangelwurzels. He couldn't help noticing her hard grey permanent wave.

He said, 'Jocasta, could I . . . ?'

'Yes, what?'

'I'm just going to put my notes together. I'll preach first, then some prayers. Then we'll have Philip coming up with the child for the tableau, and then the christening. Is that all right? No Andrew, I'm afraid, yet.'

'Quite all right.'

'It's – who now – godparents? Mrs Jefford and Philip and, well, it was to have been Alice Banks but she's not to be seen. Two will have to do.'

'Of course. What about the Tibs?'

'They are a law unto themselves, Jocasta.' They smiled at each other. 'I don't expect them.'

'They'll watch from a distance through their third eye,' she said, and for the first time since The Missus left she touched his arm.

'Oh Jocasta,' he said, 'what horrible times we've had. What things I've said to you.'

'The horrible times are over,' she said.

Soon she began to move everybody into the chapel. Nick was sent to the sheds to say that Faith should be brought across now and to ask the others to come too.

The congregation, in boots and coats and mufflers, assembled itself on the hard pews in the dark, among the plopping noises of the paraffin stoves, and as Jack appeared from behind the altar in his vestments the door opened and not only the three Tibetan women filed in but, in a flurry, Mr and Mrs Middleditch and Alice Banks.

Jack, unperturbed, made the sign of the cross and waited while the newcomers settled themselves, the Middleditch party well to the front, the Tibetans on the back row. Then Pema got up again and went out. Nick seemed to be arguing about something with the A-level girl and then suddenly went out too. His feet could be heard clattering over the stones of the courtyard.

Jack stood in silence for so long that Mrs Middleditch began to purse her lips and look questioningly about her. Even Jocasta looked up questioningly at him in the end. The Missus glared ahead.

At last Jack said, 'In the name of the Father and the Son and of the Holy Ghost, and in the name of God in all religions and languages, we ask Thy mercy on all of us here gathered together to grant Thy blessing on the life of this child, and remember the life of the eternal Holy Child born this night. Let us pray.

'This year has had its sorrows for most of us here tonight. Its terrors, its difficulties, doubts and temptations. We ask it to be true, oh God, that we are at least nearer to Thee than we were when the year began, that we have learned a little of Thy mercy as well as of Thy might.

'Since the death of our dear Holly Fox, it has seemed that most of us here have been bewitched in some way by our own individual daemon. We have found ourselves awash in times we don't understand any better than the eastern visitors in our midst. Yet we live in the ruins of a place which should give us strength, that has inspired the worship of God for a thousand years. The sun and the moon above us, the snow, the wind and the rain are the same as those known to the people who built this holy place long ago. Why have we felt alone? Do we only now at Christmas realise that the reason is that we have forgotten the message of Christmas? It is the child. Faith came to us and we congratulated ourselves on having taken her in, but only Pema, and I think Philip, ever really considered the baby herself. Did any of us really care about *Faith*? Let us thank God that we have time to put this right. We will stand in silence now for a few moments to say our own personal prayers. Let us pray.'

As they stood, a beaky man came in and clattered forward to stand by Thomasina. Emma looked round, nudged her husband, leaned sideways and said, 'Thought you didn't keep Christmas, Pa!' The man stared ahead. Thomasina gripped the pew in front.

'Who is it? D'you know him?' asked Pammie in a loud voice. 'Is it Faylesafe?'

'Ssh.'

'Let us pray,' said Jack again.

The Thoughts of All

Thomasina thought, *Pray? Our Father which art— Dear God, have mercy on us all and hear us. I don't know where I am or what my future will be. Watch over me. Holly gone, Herbert gone, Giles gone. Garden left, must think of it. Pammie left and Les Girls and the golf club. Wish Dolly and Toots here. Tony Faylesafe. Unbelievable. Father of Hol's friend Emma. A man of long before. If he's here, why not Holly? Where is she? O Lord, I pray for beloved Holly and may she be in everlasting light, may light perpetual shine upon her. Tell me what I'm doing in this place and tell me, I beseech thee, O God, how I'm to fill up the rest of my life.*

Pammie prayed, *I thank Thee, O God, for sending me out into this place to see if it is Thy will for me to work to Thy glory here and serve Thee and Jack and Jocasta all my days. All the kitchen needs is a good lime-wash and the beams treated – say, five hundred pounds. New stove – say, two thousand. Take up flagstones, turn and scour, not polish. Very nice refectory table, needs treating oil and varnish. No sign of dishwasher, absolutely necessary, serious catering. Flowers in outer hall,* *visitors' book, spring clean office: make big difference. Modern bunk beds for groups. My bedroom, gatehouse, very romantic, probably. Ideal conference in big retreat centre. Billy Graham? Jack spiritual leader. I could pull strings for a Royal visit. The South only a concept, as is the North. Use me, O Lord, make me a channel for Thy peace. Thomasina often here and golf at Scarborough. Who is this man? Why isn't Andrew here? No sign of Alice the dragoness. Oh, good Lord, who's this – it's her? It can't be! Who's the couple she's with? Very pompous. Dreadful Dannimacs. And may it please thee, O Lord, to look graciously upon all of us here gathered to celebrate the birth of Thy dear Son that we may be purged of all our sins and selfishness. Bless my Hugo in heaven. Lighten our darkness we beseech Thee, O Lord – and whoever is this? A troupe of gypsies? And the queer and the hippie – well, tax-gatherers and sinners. What a long way from Coombe Hill. Forgive my unbelief. Yours sinc— I mean, in the name of the Father, etc.* 'Amen.'

Emma prayed, *Dear Lord, we thank Thee for Thy great mercy and for drawing us all together here today from different parts of the world to celebrate Christmas. Have mercy on this little motherless child that she may find some motherly arms.* 'Shut up, Vanessa, you can't hold Phil's hand. Now, leave him alone. No, Patsie, you can*not* go up with him and carry the baby. The baby's not even here yet. Shush!' *Oh well, yes, it looks as if she is. The crib's come in anyway. It's standing at the back. And that Smike's gone out again – I hope it's not too heavy for Phil.* 'The boy has rings in his nose because he likes to be like that, Lucy. No, you can't put a string through it like a bull. Darling, do sit still.' *I thank Thee, Lord, for our creation, preservation and for all the blessings of this life but chiefly for Thine inestimable love, for the gift of grace and the hope of glory – and for its continual surprises and variety. Father in church! Forgot he knew Holly's mum. Old friend. Always met on Sports Day. Holly always won the races . . . oh poor Holly, where are you? Wish you were here, you great philistine. Please bless my family and Philip. Let us be family to Philip* too. *Let us have the say in his education, let no harm befall him. Never let him believe again that he must be forever washing his hands.* 'Amen.'

Ernie thought, *I'm not getting on my knees this bloody floor, anyway I gotter 'old this end of t' backcloth straight some'ow, bloody 'ell. Wherst Nick for t'other end? Bringin' int baby, likely. Is 'e really off wi' yon lass? More fool 'im, 'e'll be back be Friday. They'se New Age travellers gone soft, bloody gypsies, not my type. Jack's conned. 'E'll be conned all 'is life. Jocasta's better. Much better. No chicken. Not a slag. Shouldn't 'ave said it. Bloody good poster she's made. Great. Pity no Toots an' Dolly. It a bin a great day out. Bike up the top, why not chance a visit? Down the arcades, miss this do 'ere afterwards wi' all the toffs. God, I wish Nick wunt go off. London trash place, everything loose shag, no fam'ly life. 'Ostels. Pavements. Cardboard boxes. Christ save 'im. This bloody post's 'eavy. When we gant unrollt bloody thing? I's not strong enough. Need a man 'ere, where's bloody Nick t' 'elp me?* 'Amen,' he added as the rest said it.

The waitress from Ellerby Moor Hotel prayed, *Our Father which art in 'eaven 'allowed be Thy name Thy kingdom come Thy will be done on earth as it is in 'eaven funny how most people still know it – mind, they say not everywhere now, the streets of London they won't. These foreigners all coming in just look at them not clean all them wrappers. Is one of them got that baby under there? It's not right it's a English baby why can't it be with its granny very nice old woman and that daft old man I took to them I really did I'd've brought them up 'ere today if it'd been fit. Terrible sad when she cried, nobody 'ere, but 'im marvellous: 'Don't upset yerself now Dorothy we've had a great ride out' wish I'd sent them a card for Christmas. No picnic getting 'ere this afternoon, nice that Jocasta woman asked me. They said I was in it somewhere – some play they're putting on don't know what they mean. Said I 'ad to come, that Jocasta apologising for this place all empty that morning. Comes to see me. Not 'er fault they say she's much better. Fits* *in more. Used to just sit and I never like that, folks sitting when there's work to do. That look. She's got a nice face when you catch sight of it looking over at old Jack, like. Said they never got on and she was off in the heather I'd not think so. There's that woman what was with that old army cove well I never. I didn't fancy her, stuck up. Sitting next 'is lordship old-fashioned type like 'im, nice suit she's got on. Fancy all them people knowing each other. Everyone knows Jack do anything for 'im. There's that Alice Banks agen they say she was off after twenty years I'll bet they wish she was miserable old lemon can't stand 'er. Hope she didn't do the tea we're to 'ave and the peace of God which passeth all understanding keep our hearts and minds in the knowledge of the power and the glory,* 'Amen.'

Mrs Middleditch said to God, *As you know Arnold and I are by birth Methodists, as so I always thought was Bingham, though Church we've come to. I'm thankful to you, God, for my Arnold seeing me through so many dangers and difficulties with Bingham – nobody knows the half but us. And Thee. And for help with Toots and Dolly. Nobody knows the trouble they are getting and who can tell the end? But Thee. I've never liked Toots. There, I'll say it, God forgive me. You can't not like Dolly, mind, but she's a very silly woman and she gives way to him every time. They think they're a cut above because of Toots being educated in London somewhere and she having something about her in her manner, though I don't see why they're any better than us, I'm sure. You should see their bathroom and the upstairs toilet – all brown stains. Well, it's her eyes. An overhead chain, fancy, these days! No upstairs carpets, only lino down since the war, and that linen basket in the corner with its lid off. It had its lid off when I started looking after them five years since and it only needs a twist of raffia. Bingham could've done it, only I didn't like to say I'd noticed, not having been asked upstairs. Officially. I don't know how they manage. He must drink all his pension. Not Dolly, mind. Very respectable woman. More than you can say for Bingham's painted thing nearly Dolly's age. God, please* *send Bingham home again without her. I hope they never saw us go past, Dolly and Toots. Well, they wouldn't in this snow. The cheek of this Banks. I ask you! Landing up in Station Taxis complaining and not tipping – Christmas Eve (not maybe that I blame her)! – and saying, 'Here's me auntie's gold watch and I want you to get me for Christmas to The Priors.' Well, Arnold's a good man. We didn't ask questions, didn't even speak. I can't bring myself to look in her direction here beside me. Sitting in the car back muttering, singing bits of songs. St Luke's for her, she'll not even need assessing. I'll have to complain to Dolly about it. She's their connection, not mine, and would she go to see them? Refused. Will we get back home tonight if it freezes up again? Have to sleep up here. If Bingham and that thing comes round they'll find an empty house. It's hoping they'll come round decided me on bringing this Alice. 'Arnold,' I said, 'let him come. We're never out. It'll bring him up short.' Never being out is our strength to people, but tonight we'll lock up and go. We'll miss the Midnight at St James's. They'll be lost without Arnold. Who'll carry the plate? Who's to count the money? Funny this is all the services we'll have and in a priory too, I always understood Henry VIII. In the name of thy Son our Saviour Jesus Christ, 'Amen. Arnold, you're wanted to hold the other end of the magic lantern screen.'*

Jimmie the postman prayed, *Our Father which art in heaven hallowed be Thy name etc., learned it at school they don't now it's all sex education and yoga I like Prayers meself puts a shape on things. Our Father – well, fancy me being here Christmas Eve they'll be wondering. Poor old Jack, though, you don't like to disappoint him. Dear God I pray for Jack Braithwaite remembering him sitting there in the heather back to the Cross and his bottom sopping from the wet grass. 'Good morning, Post.' Looking like a child. Tears running. Heard about his brother's wife. By, she were a smasher saw her once made that Jocasta look a shadder. Jack. Well. There's a gang here tonight all right. I'd not be here if I hadn't been stopping off all day here and there taking folkses bits of shopping and* *papers from t'shop let's hope they don't find out you're not supposed to take anything but post now int van and three-quarters of it junk. Time was old Heart-throb at Ellerby Hotel said you could ask Post to carry chickens live with their feet tied together, and a bag of manure. It's all changed now with the deep-freezes. But I like me job, finished eleven o'clock good days. You get your interests – lonely women on t'farms asking you in for all sorts. Great. They say yon Jocasta . . . but it's all talk. Can't have been easy with that Missus. Well, nobody knows what's going to happen do they God? They say I'm in this play somewhere, there's that Ernie not able to hold up the slide-screen affair, mebbe I better give 'im an 'and, no, there's that feller with the stomach going up. Where's that Nick? Now, why's all this black lot walking out? Funny places you can fetch up Christmas Eve. Well, deliver us from evil, 'Amen.'*

Jocasta closed her eyes and concentrated on the Good. She emptied her mind of images, sounds, scents, tastes, sensations. She lifted herself out of her body until she was out of the chapel. Not outside in the snow, nor above it in the icy air, but higher, higher, farther towards the moon, towards the moon, towards the sun, beyond the sun, approaching the dark that she knew would one day take her, envelop her, twist her and at last fling her out into everlasting knowledge, the presence of Truth. Beyond prayer, beyond words, Jocasta sat asking nothing, being nothing, wanting nothing, hoping nothing.

Philip, looking across at her from the pew where he sat with Emma, saw that she was no longer there with Jack, with Andrew, with him, with anyone. He didn't care. What's a mother? Faith hadn't got one. She was OK. All this was for her. All these people. Even Ernie. And Alice back again. Card games again. He wasn't mad about that. He was with Emma now. Boarding. *'I am Jocasta's son.' Oh great. Tell us another. Where's Nick? Happy Christmas, I don't think. Stupid old Jack, but Emma says it's just because he's so holy. He doesn't see what's under his nose. I love Emma. I love Emma. Who wants a mother?*

300

'Did you say Amen?' asked Emma of Susannah. 'Say Amen, Philip.'

'Oh, all right,' said Philip and under his breath: 'Ah bloody men.' *Alice looks awful. I wonder what's up.*

'Salley, Salleeeeee, Pride of our Alleeeee,' shouted the great and glorious voice of Gracie Fields in Alice's ears. **Alice** turned her collar up and shrank into it, her pointed face lined and drawn, her eyes tight shut, her knobbed hands clasped in prayer. Jack was strong on that. *You pray properly, not lolling about like that postman or that great tussock in the turquoise-blue bomber jacket from the pub, bossing them all about – wonder they get any customers at all. Now then, tired, yes, but let's get to grips. Dear God, thank you for all the experiences of these past days, particularly the opportunity of seeing Thy works in other places, and so that I can pray for all them stuck in London on the trains and in the streets, bundled in plastic bags, God help them. Also I pray for that gorilla feller and that fat lass with the trolley never able to get up and down in the lift for water owing to the wastage of electricity. God bless that fond Madeleine in her trouble she'll come through, being so good at acting. God bless the general. Very kind of him coming out so early to get me off that bus. Very good manners, poor old soul, with his little moustache. Paid the taxi and would have paid the fare down, I'm not a pauper. God bless Henry Jones and his friend Jerry. You meet some funny people, but we had some laughs. 'Come back,' says Henry. 'Plenty of work down here. They're in their dotage. It's an old folks home, this place, but they've plenty of money and they understand service. They're very nice, and many with titles.' I took to Henry Jones and I'll flatter myself he took to me. Dozy place, though, nothing going on, not like a farm or here or back in Lancashire. God bless Mother and Father and that cat. God rest their souls, all of them. Yes. And God bless our Philip and I didn't like not saying goodbye. He's looking peaky – we'll have a hand of cards on Boxing Day. Who's all these people he's in among? It's that Emma at the school. Like the Ovaltine girl. Reminds me of that Holly. Well, no Dolly and Toots. And no*

Andrew. No loss. No general. No loss either. That general's down with Madeleine, seeing to her. In her grief. They can't be together in the house with his chair still in the sitting room, it'll be a hotel. Expensive. Best of luck. Well, Puffy. He's out of his chains. Gone. God bless him. It wasn't the sausages. Last thing he said was, 'Don't blame yourself, Alice.' Perfect gentleman. I liked that man, God. I'd have stayed with him. Noticed me more than Jack ever did. Funny so damaged. So deep, deep sick, so pinned down hand and foot and neck – like that Gulliver. My Puffy. My Puffy. Made me put on that gramophone. Damn near forced me. Threatened me till I put it on. 'Salleeeee in our Alleeee'. 'A grand Lancashire lass,' he said. 'You remind me of her, Alice,' and he laughs, wheeze, wheeze, while I carries on and on. 'You love her really,' he says. 'All that sound coming out. All that life. You would have liked to be Gracie Fields, Alice Banks.' Then he'd call out, 'Where are you, Gracie?' He'd laugh till the tears came. Dear God, I'm missing the funeral, but no odds. He was mine for a while. I loved him. And he loved me, so there. Forgive me, dear God, for loving another woman's husband. I've nothing against her. She's South, that's all. South and posh and daft. God bless us all. 'Amen.'

'Amen,' said Jack. 'Will you all please sit. Philip, will you go now to the cradle and be ready. Nick? Where is he? Disappeared. Well, perhaps you, Ernie, then, would be ready with the lighting. Jimmie – how good to see you – could you hold the other end of the, er, backcloth, and be ready to unroll it?'

Mr Middleditch and Jimmie unrolled the backcloth. Philip, after a couple of nudges and 'Go on, you'll be fine,' from Emma, walked to the back of the chapel, towards the cradle in the semidark.

'All lights out, please,' said Jocasta. Now only the light of the snow shone blue at the windows. The tiny flames of the paraffin heaters spluttered. 'Right, switch on.'

The great, blazing, triumphant celebration of birth burst over the tatty chapel. Everyone gasped. In a moment, whispers. 'Look at that. It's Ernie.' 'Look, it's her – the woman up at the ridge hotel. Look, that's the postman. Isn't Jocasta terrific? She's a genius. Look at the background. Look at the moors spread behind.' 'No. It's not moors. It's real high mountains. It's the Himalayas. Look, that space in the middle, it's like a great eye.'

'Philip,' Jack called. 'Right? Bring her up, boy, come along.'

Philip was standing behind the crib at the back of the chapel aisle. He was looking down into the lute-shaped nest. He was rubbing one leg against the other, his arms hanging down, his hair over his eyes. Everyone was turning to watch him. Behind his glasses he was staring steadily, deeply, thoughtfully, into the cot. Then he ran back down the aisle and pushed himself along a pew and in beside Jocasta. He flung himself at her, held her tight with both arms and placed his head in her bosom. A sob, then a great yell of pain, came from him.

Emma quickly ran up from her pew to the cot-cradle and looked in, then looked desperately towards her husband. Alice Banks stood black-eyed, grim, beside the electrified Middleditches, facing Jack and the altar, not looking round. It was Thomasina who pushed Emma aside.

'Jack,' she called. 'Faith's not here. The crib is empty.'

Christmas Eve
– and –
Christmas Morning

On the late afternoon of Christmas Eve Toots and Dolly were watching television. They had not closed the curtains over the big Victorian windows of Toots's room and the night shone blackly in. If they switched off the main light – which they seldom did, Toots saying that he liked to see what he was doing even if it was nothing at all – the white patches on the grass could be seen outside and snowflakes still falling thickly all the time. Each had been thinking to draw the curtains but somehow had gone on watching the coloured square, the glitter of a leg-show, a comedian with the face of a horse, advertisements for cars, autumn leaves falling in Spain, Father Christmases dancing in line in Rome. Then the news at six, then the soap that they both enjoyed because there was no unpleasantness in it, not like *EastEnders*. The programmes for the rest of the evening went up.

'Christmas Eve. No better than any other night,' said Toots. 'Same stuff, only worse.'

'Now, we had the wireless carols at three o'clock. They never let you down, King's College Chapel.'

'It's because you can't see them. It puts you off, seeing them. I've seen a lot of boys. I can see through ruffs and cassocks.'

'They sing like angels.'

'I never saw an angel.'

'It's heavenly. There's nothing like it.'

'I can't get to grips with heavenly. Shut the curtains,

Dorothy.'

'Dorothy – well I never! What do you want for supper, *Tom?*'

They sat on, watching a newsflash about the weather.

'Well, there was no two ways about it in the end,' she said. 'Andrew couldn't possibly have come up in this today. I dare say nobody else will have come, either. If they're there, they'll be stuck. They'll be stuck for all the holiday. Thank goodness I was firm with him. It would have been sheer bravado.'

'Aye. We're fine our two selves.'

'I think, mind you, Toots, it'll be Mrs Middleditch's tomorrow. Be ready for it. Don't create. She'll cook a lovely dinner. You're not to complain.'

'I'll not complain. I never complain. She's a good woman. Just a bit close to home. I'll take them a bottle of sherry.'

'Yes. At least. All she does for us.'

'One bottle's about right. I thought I saw her today in that car going off with Arnold somewhere.'

'They'd never go out in this.'

'It was her. About four o'clock. Have you tried Jack again?'

'They're still out of order. Did you say eggs?'

'No, I'll not bother.'

'Now you must eat, Toots.'

'Well, a bit of bread and butter. I wonder if Holly's mother got north? Not very likely.'

'No. It'll be a bad time for her this year. Toots?'

'Yes.'

'I could do with Holly walking in.'

'It seems early for it, but I think I might just as well go to bed. There'll be nobody coming tonight. Not many at the Midnight; there'll be no calling in before or after.'

'No stockings to fill now,' said Dolly.

'Not for thirty years. They used to give us one.'

'Andrew did. Jack always forgot, bless him.' They thought of all the years with Jack in his wilderness, then of Andrew going, then Andrew's triumphant return with Holly.

'I always made up a stocking for Holly, even last year when she was away,' said Dolly. 'Sellotape and sticky labels and writing paper and a book of stamps. I posted it. A tube of Glymiel jelly for her hands. Hard to find. You'd have thought it was diamonds.'

'She'd have brought Faith up right,' said Toots. 'Thank-you letters and that. Like her own mother did her. By God, Dolly, it's a bloody awful condition, humanity. Everyone dying except the ones you'd never miss, and not a body coming in to see you.'

'There's someone coming now. I heard the gate.'

'Well, I hope the door's locked. It's a terrible night. One thing, there'll be no criminals out. By heaven, what a racket! They're going to break the door down. Don't open it, Dolly. Just ask through the vestibule.'

Dolly first drew a shawl round her and then all the curtains across, leaving no cracks. The beating on the door increased; the bell pealed. She opened Toots's door, unlocked the inner vestibule door, glazed red and blue and white, and stood in the icy space between it and the front door and called, 'Yes?'

'Let us in, Dolly, Chrissake, it's Nick.'

'Nick? Wait a minute.'

'Don't open it, now, unless you're sure,' Toots shouted. 'We're sitting ducks here.'

Dolly undid the bolts and then turned the key of the mortice lock and found it troublesome. 'We should have had this seen to. I don't know. I'm getting so woolly-minded, I forgot. Just a minute, the sneck's sticking.'

'*Dolly*! Will yer hoory oop!'

'I can't. I'm sorry, Nick. Could you go round the back? No – wait a minute. Yes, it's coming. Here we are. Oh, the snow. Whatever's all this you've got? Now, you needn't have bothered with presents, we didn't expect . . .'

Nick pushed past her, all snow and wet leather, carrying Faith's old carrycot by its two handles. He dumped it on the carpet.

'Whatever – Nick!'

'I brung 'er. They was all over t' place messing wi' magic lanterns and that Pema's gone barmy. The others is OK but they're scared of that one. I was goin' off wi' them tonight but I

didn't. They're away int van now. I was bringin' Faith ower t'
chapel and this Pema starts carryin' on, wanted her away wi'
them int van, so I took off and brung 'er down 'ere. Put her int
sidecar an' brung 'er. It was 'er christening but they left that
Pema to get 'er ready, never thought of 'er. Backcloths and tea.
They get yer down, oop there. S'long, I'm goin' to t' pub.'

'Nick. Nick. You can't go. Whatever – they don't know
where she is. Nick—'

The door slammed. In a moment they heard the bike start
up. The cot lay on the floor between Toots's bed and Dolly's
saggy chair. Toots was upright in the bed, wild-eyed.

'Get Mrs Middleditch. Get on that phone now. We can't
have this. What do we do? She may be dead.'

Dolly got slowly down on her knees and looked into the
carrycot, which seemed to be packed tight with a bale of coarse
coloured cloth. She removed the plastic cover off the cot.

'It's wet through,' she said, 'but this carpet stuff is dry. I'll
have to ease her out.'

'Now be careful. Use your senses. Don't do anything.
Maybe we should tell the police.'

'Here we are,' said Dolly. '*Here* we are.' She got her fingers
beneath the bundle and lifted it out and began to undo it.
'Whatever've they dressed her in? Whatever is this? She's in
somebody's old curtains and I sent up that robe of your
mother's a month ago. She's got something hung on her front.
It's a bit of knitting on a card. Looks like a big eye. *Here* we
are.'

Faith emerged from her wrappings. She was wearing a pale-
blue plastic spacesuit with a hood. Her round eyes were wide.
She stared at Dolly attentively.

'Toots, look at her. What eyes! Nothing wrong there. Let's
get her out of this common thing. She's a big baby. However'd
he squeeze her into this? She's that solid.'

'I tell you Dolly, get the police.'

'*Now* then. *Here* we are. Look at this hair – it's getting to
curl. Toots, d'you see? You can see the marks of the waves
coming. I think she's losing a bit round the back. They rub it off
first thing and then there's more comes, beautiful. Isn't she

307

good? There now! That's better, without all this clobber, far too hot. Look at those arms. And the hands. Toots, they're your hands, I'd know them anywhere. Hello! *Hello!* Aren't you lovely? Aren't you beautiful, Faith. *Faith.* Just look at that mouth, Toots.'

'Faith?' said Toots climbing off the bed, hanging his legs down the side of it, with some dignity. 'Faith? Faithy? Cock-a-doodle-doo.'

'I must get her a feed. She'll need a feed. I've got the milk powder and all the paraphernalia. I knew I should. Here, Toots, you'll have to take her. And I had some nappies.'

'You'll never do it, Dolly. I tell you, ring someone up. We're old people.'

'I said take her. Here, sit in your chair and for goodness' sake don't stir. Here's your frame in front of you. Now hold her.'

'Well,' he said. 'By Gad, what happens now? Yes, I've got her. Cock-a-doodle-doo.'

Faith beheld her grandfather and frowned. A deep line appeared between the eyes. She looked away in disdain. Then she swung an arm up at him and biffed his jaw. Then she opened her mouth. The top lip was the apex of an isosceles triangle. Up it went, the mouth, opening, opening. Faith yawned.

'She yawned, Dolly.'

'She's tired.'

'I think she's just waking up. By, she's got big eyes. What's happening now?'

Faith's mouth stayed open but she turned dark red, then purplish. Her eyes she shut tight. Her arms began to work up and down like creations on springs. From the mouth came a roar.

'Here, Dolly, she's crying. I can't manage.'

'You'll have to manage. Hold on to her and don't panic, I'm sterilising bottles. Rock her. She'll never have been held in a chair like a Christian.'

At nine o'clock Faith was still roaring and Dolly was pacing with her up and down. Toots was in torment. Though Dolly had shouted 'No!' he had rung Mrs Middleditch. To no avail. He had rung the vicar, who was about his Christmas duties and on an answer machine. Toots left a wild and incomprehensible message.

'There's nothing wrong with her.'

'How do you know there's nothing wrong with her?'

'I know,' said Dolly, the baby's frantic small face contorted beneath her grandmother's chin. 'I know. I know a cry when it's a pain and this is not a pain.'

'What is it, then? They said she never cried. They said she was a quiet baby, the quietest anyone had ever known. Always half asleep.'

Faith began to flail her fists. Dolly lifted her higher on her shoulder and Faith flung herself at Dolly's chin and began to suck it. Dolly shouted with joy.

'She's just hungry. It's the different sort of milk, I expect. They'll have her on cows' milk up there. I'll try her with another bottle, but I'll change her first.'

'I'm getting out of here,' said Toots. 'This noise going on. You'll never manage.'

'No, you're not. You can just help me. I'm lying her down on your bed while I go for some Harringtons I have somewhere and some talcum like they say they never use now – ridiculous! I've a baby-bath upstairs somewhere but I won't risk it tonight with my legs. Hush now. Hush now.'

'Great Scot, anyone passing will be thinking it's child abuse.'

'Don't be silly, nobody's passing. *Here* we are. *There* we are. Now then, she's taking the bottle. Look, she was ravenous again.'

Faith's furious rolling eyes fixed themselves on Toots as she sucked. She sucked and sucked and, as she sucked, one hand opened and closed, opened and closed, over Dolly's finger. But she kept her gaze on Toots. When Dolly rearranged herself more comfortably in her chair, Faith still sucked and sucked, her gaze swivelling again towards the rosy Toots with his tufts of fluffy hair. The milk in the antique bottle went down and down, to the last drop, and she detached herself milkily and belched. She lay replete, still staring, staring, at Toots. She blinked.

'She can't take her eyes off you, Tom.' Dolly was all composure, lifting the child to her shoulder, patting her back, rearranging a little blanket she'd made into a shawl. '*There* we are. Now I'll put her down.'

But as soon as Faith was in the cot she turned purple and began to bellow. As soon as Dolly lifted her out she stopped, and stared at Toots.

'We can't go on like this all night,' said Dolly. 'With my two I just put them down and let them cry and in five minutes they were asleep. Go to the phone, Toots, just see if we can get them. They'll be frantic; they'll be out all over the snow. They'll be wild. That Nick!'

But when Toots left the room Faith began to roar and he had to come back. Dolly laid Faith on the bed and went to phone them herself but there was still no reply. When she came back into the room again Toots was sitting with his chair drawn up near his bed where Faith lay, his eyes at Faith's level, his head leaning against the quilt, and Faith had turned her face towards him. But Faith had gone to sleep.

'There'll be no bed for us, Dolly, tonight. I'll just sit in this chair.'

'Don't be so silly. That's bad training. You'll go back in your bed and she in her cot.'

Dolly looked young. She hurried about the room, reorganising small blankets. Shaking them. She picked up the tapestry eye and set it on the mantelpiece among the Christmas cards and brass candlesticks and the photograph of Andrew and Holly at their wedding, Holly looking regal in a great white hat.

'It's watching us,' said Toots, 'that eye, whatever it is. We've to keep a watch on that thing. You won't see me sleeping tonight.'

He did sleep at last. Faith slept, too. But Dolly sat up all night beside the cot. She set the reading lamp on the floor with a screen of books round it and moved back the electric fire into the hearth so that if she slept everything would be safe. She watched over Faith, who now slept so deep that her eyes almost disappeared, far away back in her head. She lay with a remote air, confident, proud, unconquerable. Sometimes her lips chewed, as if she dreamed of milk. Sometimes her eyes moved beneath the veined, tight lids. She lay closely wrapped, still as a small yule log inside Dolly's old blankets, and when Dolly put a hand down inside the cot to see if she needed a hot-bottle or another cover she found her warm as an animal in straw, as fruit beneath a foreign sun.

'Dolly? Hello?'
   'Shush. She's just gone off again.'
   'We dreamed it.'
   'Be quiet. I'll get you your tea.'
   'Where is she?'
   'Well, she's here of course. Here in her bed on the floor.'
   'She cried all night?'
   'She did no such thing.'
   'You're worn out?'
   'I am not worn out, so be quiet. A happy Christmas. I'll pull back the curtains.'
   'I want to look at her again.'
   'All in good time.'
   'I couldn't stand many nights like last night. I don't know how we did it.'
   'Don't be so soft. We were only awake an hour. She's a wonderful baby.'
   'Why's she looking at me like that?'
   'She's not, she's sleeping. Oh – yes she is, she's awake. You've woken her.'
   'Goosie-goosie-gander.   Cock-a-doodle-doo.   Yacker-pusser. Tweet tweet. Here, Dolly, look at this.'
   Faith's arrogant stare was softening. Her head was rearing up off its blanket. Her mouth was opening in the triangle again and suddenly a hoot came out from it. Then a crow. Then a crazy noise like whooping cough.
   'She's laughing. I've made her laugh. By God, Dolly, it's half

past seven. We've not done badly.'

'They'll be down soon. It'll be over soon,' said Dolly, drinking tea.

Faith made a noise like a new lamb, lair-lair-lair, and began to squirm about.

'Just wait till I've finished my tea,' Dolly said. 'Which of them will it be, Toots? Which one will twig she mightn't have been kidnapped? Which of them'll think of us?'

'They'll be scouring after those foreigners. The one that comes down for her will be the one who knows. The one that understands her. The one to take her and keep her. You'll see.'

When the bell rang it was still dark. 'Want to bet?' said Toots.

'Oh, I hope it isn't Mrs Middleditch,' said Dolly.

'No. It'll be Thomasina.'

And he called to her, as Dolly opened the door and he heard Holly's mother's voice: 'Come on in, Apple Green. She's all yours.'